THE MAN IN THE IRON MASK

Alexandre Dumas

COLLINS

Harper Press
An imprint of HarperCollins*Publishers*
77–85 Fulham Palace Road
Hammersmith
London W6 8JB

This Harper Press paperback edition published 2012

Alexandre Dumas asserts the moral right to be identified as the author of this work

A catalogue record for this book is available from the British Library

ISBN: 978-0-00-744988-0

Printed and bound in Great Britain by Clays Ltd, St Ives plc

MIX
Paper from
responsible sources
FSC™ C007454

FSC™ is a non-profit international organisation established to promote
the responsible management of the world's forests. Products carrying the
FSC label are independently certified to assure consumers that they come
from forests that are managed to meet the social, economic and
ecological needs of present and future generations,
and other controlled sources.

Find out more about HarperCollins and the environment at
www.harpercollins.co.uk/green

Life & Times section © Gerard Cheshire
Classic Literature: Words and Phrases adapted from
Collins English Dictionary
Typesetting in Kalix by Palimpsest Book Production Limited,
Falkirk, Stirlingshire

10 9 8 7 6 5 4 3 2 1

History of Collins

In 1819, millworker William Collins from Glasgow, Scotland, set up a company for printing and publishing pamphlets, sermons, hymn books and prayer books. That company was Collins and was to mark the birth of HarperCollins Publishers as we know it today. The long tradition of Collins dictionary publishing can be traced back to the first dictionary William published in 1824, *Greek and English Lexicon*. Indeed, from 1840 onwards, he began to produce illustrated dictionaries and even obtained a licence to print and publish the Bible.

Soon after, William published the first Collins novel, *Ready Reckoner*, however it was the time of the Long Depression, where harvests were poor, prices were high, potato crops had failed and violence was erupting in Europe. As a result, many factories across the country were forced to close down and William chose to retire in 1846, partly due to the hardships he was facing.

Aged 30, William's son, William II took over the business. A keen humanitarian with a warm heart and a generous spirit, William II was truly 'Victorian' in his outlook. He introduced new, up-to-date steam presses and published affordable editions of Shakespeare's works and *Pilgrim's Progress*, making them available to the masses for the first time. A new demand for educational books meant that success came with the publication of travel books, scientific books, encyclopaedias and dictionaries. This demand to be educated led to the later publication of atlases and Collins also held the monopoly on scripture writing at the time.

In the 1860s Collins began to expand and diversify

and the idea of 'books for the millions' was developed. Affordable editions of classical literature were published and in 1903 Collins introduced 10 titles in their Collins Handy Illustrated Pocket Novels. These proved so popular that a few years later this had increased to an output of 50 volumes, selling nearly half a million in their year of publication. In the same year, The Everyman's Library was also instituted, with the idea of publishing an affordable library of the most important classical works, biographies, religious and philosophical treatments, plays, poems, travel and adventure. This series eclipsed all competition at the time and the introduction of paperback books in the 1950s helped to open that market and marked a high point in the industry.

HarperCollins is and has always been a champion of the classics and the current Collins Classics series follows in this tradition – publishing classical literature that is affordable and available to all. Beautifully packaged, highly collectible and intended to be reread and enjoyed at every opportunity.

Life & Times

About the Author

Alexandre Dumas (1802–70) was a contemporary of another great French novelist, Victor Hugo (1802–85). While Hugo's chosen genre was humanistic romanticism, Dumas' was adventurous romanticism. Among his works are his three novels about d'Artagnan, *The Count of Monte Cristo* and *The Corsican Brothers*. He is best known for the first d'Artagnan story *The Three Musketeers* (1844). D'Artagnan is not actually one of the musketeers of the title, although he does become a musketeer at the end of the story. Together with his musketeer friends Porthos, Athos and Aramis, they experience swashbuckling and rollicking adventures which captured the imagination of a wide readership not only in France, but worldwide. The three novels are set in seventeenth-century France and are often described as 'cloak and sword' in style.

Dumas was of mixed racial ancestry – his grandmother was Creole (of European and African descent) and he suffered racism all of his life. When he died the authorities delivered a final insult by only allowing him to be buried in his place of birth, Villers-Cotterêts, despite his great success and fame. In 2002, his remains were eventually interred in the Pantheon in Paris, alongside Hugo and other luminaries.

Inspiration and Influence

It is useful to consider the state of France at the time Dumas was writing to understand the mindset of society that the author was surrounded by. In post-revolutionary France Napoleon Bonaparte had left the nation in a state of disarray upon his abdication as emperor in 1814. Then there came an attempt to restore the monarchy, which led to the July

Revolution of 1830. The French were left unsure about how to still the waters and memories of the past became an attractive sanctuary.

This air of nostalgia and sentimentality made France a good setting for Dumas' novels, albeit largely clichéd and caricatured in his description of characters. For the reader it was all about escapism. They could enter a world of gung-ho adventure and excitement, where characters were injured or killed in an occasionally farcical way and as a result Dumas' novels became the blockbusters of their time and sold accordingly. As for inspiration, it seems that Dumas' father was key. A General in Bonaparte's army, Dumas' father experienced many genuine adventures, including fighting in many battles, being poisoned and being imprisoned. He died only four years after the birth of Dumas, but the anecdotes were retold by his mother, who was very protective of her son and schooled him at home. Consequently, Dumas was nurtured in a solitary environment where he learnt to absorb himself in his reading and writing.

By the time he moved to Paris as a young man he knew that writing was his forte and wished to earn his living in that way. He took a job as a clerk due to his precise and fast handwriting skills, and this set him on the road to success. In fact, he first made headway as a playwright and saw several of his dramas performed in the early 1830s. It wasn't until the 1840s though that he broke through as a novelist.

On the back of his success, Dumas was able to live a frivolous life. He had lavish tastes and spent his money as fast as it came in. Lacking any kind of fiscal wisdom he actually managed to find himself in considerable debt with creditors chasing him at every turn. A friend eventually regulated his accounts to save him from being arrested, but he was never able to amass the fortune that one might have expected because he had such a whimsical and capricious disposition. In many ways his nature was the personification of his writing style – he was popular and entertaining. People did not read Dumas for philosophical insight and gravitas, and he never wrote with that in mind either. For Dumas, it was not about the quality of the prose or allegory, it was simply about writing a good 'page turner'. If Dumas were alive and writing today his work might even be described as 'pulp fiction' such was its mass appeal. Needless to say, critics would not consider it to be high literature.

If one were to apply some amateur psychological analysis to Dumas' personality, one might come to the conclusion that he used his fiction to explore elements that were missing from his own life. The legend of his father was clearly at the forefront of his mind when he wrote his adventure novels, and in addition the sense of bonhomie and camaraderie between d'Artagnan and the musketeers was something that was notably absent from his own childhood, since he spent it largely in isolation. As a result he inadvertently tapped into the state of the human condition at the time. The kind of lifestyles that most people led were generally quite stayed and safe, so the idea of adventure was appealing.

Collaboration

Auguste Maquet (1813–88) collaborated with Dumas in the writing of the d'Artagnan novels, *The Count of Monte Cristo* – a more contemporary story – and more than a dozen others. Maquet was in fact responsible for the meticulous planning and plotting of the novels, while Dumas wrote the narrative, monologue and dialogue. He was a modest man, initially happy to have his name absent from the title pages of the novels and to accept considerable fees for his efforts. While Dumas died in virtual poverty from having squandered his fortune, Maquet remained very wealthy.

Maquet's involvement will always put a question mark over the true extent of Dumas' creative genius. Of course, this does not detract from Dumas' ability to write lively prose, but it seems that he was not the complete author that we suppose and many of his novels may not have been completed were it not for Maquet. Maquet eventually took Dumas to court in an attempt to secure his share of the royalties for all of the books he had co-written, but only succeeded in receiving unpaid fees. The erratic Dumas insisted that he was the only truly creative mind in the process and that Maquet played a lesser role in merely piloting each project to its conclusion. As a result, there has always been contention about Maquet's contribution. He may have just been a good organizer and a sounding board for Dumas' ideas. On the other hand, he may have devised some of the essential plot devices that hold the novels together. We will never know.

History records that following the dissolution of their partnership, Dumas was left unable to write anything to match their collaborations, while Maquet wrote a number of competent works in his own name. He may not have had Dumas' flair and spontaneity for the written word, but he was certainly not without literary talent and it was his to turn ideas into books.

Dumas also collaborated with Paul Meurice (1818–1905) on a number of projects. Meurice, like Maquet, is also known to have ghostwritten for Dumas on occasion. It seems that Dumas needed other people to organize his creative thoughts and that without this assistance he struggled to form a coherent whole. Perhaps Dumas thought of himself in a similar way to the great painters, who would typically use assistants to draught and block-in their ideas before adding the finishing touches themselves.

The Man in the Iron Mask

The Man in the Iron Mask (1850) was inspired by the true tale of a mysterious prisoner who was held captive during the reign of King Louis XIV of France – otherwise known as the Sun King. The man was incarcerated for 34 years and always wore a mask whenever visited or relocated. The general consensus is that the man was related to the king in such a way that he presented a threat to the monarchy, which is why he had to be kept under lock and key. In the novel Dumas has him as Philippe, the twin brother of the king, with equal right to the throne. The musketeer Aramis plots to substitute Philippe for Louis as part of a plan he has hatched to further his ambition to become a cardinal. Having made the substitution things become complicated and do not go the way Aramis had intended.

Some historians now think it more likely that the real man in the mask was Louis's biological father. King Louis XIII had been estranged from Louis XIV's mother for some 20 years when she fell pregnant, so it seems reasonable to conclude that she had been impregnated by a lover. The hypothesis is that the biological father had been sent abroad but decided to return, perhaps to extort money from his son, Louis XIV. As a result he was arrested and imprisoned to prevent anyone from finding out the truth as it would have meant that Louis XIV was not the rightful heir to the throne, but rather his uncle.

As the truth can never be known one can see why the story caught the public imagination and why Dumas chose to incorporate his own version into his novel. People love conspiracy theories, because they have endless possibility and turn the banal into something more mysterious and exciting. Dumas' version clearly influenced Mark Twain, who adapted the basic idea into his novel *The Prince and the Pauper* (1882). Twain imagined what events might unravel if an English prince and a London pauper accidentally swapped places because they happened to be identical in appearance. Dumas and Twain thus invented the 'mistaken identity' or 'substitution' genre of novel, which has seen various subsequent manifestations.

THE MAN IN THE IRON MASK

CONTENTS

Introduction   xvii

Chapter 1   The Prisoner.   1

Chapter 2   How Mouston Had Become Fatter
             without Giving Porthos Notice
             Thereof, and of the Troubles
             Which Consequently Befell that
             Worthy Gentleman.   32

Chapter 3   Who Messire Jean Percerin Was.   42

Chapter 4   The Patterns.   50

Chapter 5   Where, Probably, Moliere Obtained
             His First Idea of the Bourgeois
             Gentilhomme.   61

Chapter 6   The Bee-Hive, the Bees,
             and the Honey.   69

Chapter 7   Another Supper at the Bastille.   80

Chapter 8   The General of the Order.   89

Chapter 9   The Tempter.   99

Chapter 10   Crown and Tiara.   109

Chapter 11   The Chateau de Vaux-le-Vicomte.   119

Chapter 12   The Wine of Melun.   126

Chapter 13	Nectar and Ambrosia.	133
Chapter 14	A Gascon, and a Gascon and a Half.	139
Chapter 15	Colbert.	154
Chapter 16	Jealousy.	162
Chapter 17	High Treason.	170
Chapter 18	A Night at the Bastille.	181
Chapter 19	The Shadow of M. Fouquet.	189
Chapter 20	The Morning.	208
Chapter 21	The King's Friend.	218
Chapter 22	Showing How the Countersign Was Respected at the Bastille.	238
Chapter 23	The King's Gratitude.	248
Chapter 24	The False King.	258
Chapter 25	In Which Porthos Thinks He Is Pursuing a Duchy.	270
Chapter 26	The Last Adieux.	276
Chapter 27	Monsieur de Beaufort.	283
Chapter 28	Preparations for Departure.	293
Chapter 29	Planchet's Inventory.	303
Chapter 30	The Inventory of M. de Beaufort.	310
Chapter 31	The Silver Dish.	318
Chapter 32	Captive and Jailers.	327
Chapter 33	Promises.	339
Chapter 34	Among Women.	353
Chapter 35	The Last Supper.	363
Chapter 36	In M. Colbert's Carriage.	372
Chapter 37	The Two Lighters.	381

Chapter 38   Friendly Advice.   390
Chapter 39   How the King, Louis XIV.,
              Played His Little Part.   397
Chapter 40   The White Horse and the Black.   407
Chapter 41   In Which the Squirrel Falls,
              –the Adder Flies.   416
Chapter 42   Belle-Ile-en-Mer.   427
Chapter 43   Explanations by Aramis.   438
Chapter 44   Result of the Ideas of the King,
              and the Ideas of D'Artagnan.   451
Chapter 45   The Ancestors of Porthos.   455
Chapter 46   The Son of Biscarrat.   461
Chapter 47   The Grotto of Locmaria.   468
Chapter 48   The Grotto.   476
Chapter 49   An Homeric Song.   486
Chapter 50   The Death of a Titan.   493
Chapter 51   Porthos's Epitaph.   500
Chapter 52   M. de Gesvres's Round.   508
Chapter 53   King Louis XIV.   515
Chapter 54   M. Fouquet's Friends.   525
Chapter 55   Porthos's Will.   533
Chapter 56   The Old Age of Athos.   540
Chapter 57   Athos's Vision.   546
Chapter 58   The Angel of Death.   553
Chapter 59   The Bulletin.   559
Chapter 60   The Last Canto of the Poem.   566

Epilogue   573

INTRODUCTION

In the months of March–July in 1844, in the magazine *Le Siecle*, the first portion of a story appeared, penned by the celebrated playwright Alexandre Dumas. It was based, he claimed, on some manuscripts he had found a year earlier in the Bibliotheque Nationale while researching a history he planned to write on Louis XIV. They chronicled the adventures of a young man named D'Artagnan who, upon entering Paris, became almost immediately embroiled in court intrigues, international politics, and ill-fated affairs between royal lovers. Over the next six years, readers would enjoy the adventures of this youth and his three famous friends, Porthos, Athos, and Aramis, as their exploits unraveled behind the scenes of some of the most momentous events in French and even English history.

Eventually these serialized adventures were published in novel form, and became the three D'Artagnan Romances known today. Here is a brief summary of the first two novels:

The Three Musketeers (serialized March–July, 1844): The year is 1625. The young D'Artagnan arrives in Paris at the tender age of 18, and almost immediately offends three musketeers, Porthos, Aramis, and Athos. Instead of dueling, the four are attacked by five of the Cardinal's guards, and the courage of the youth is made apparent during the battle.

The four become fast friends, and, when asked by D'Artagnan's landlord to find his missing wife, embark upon an adventure that takes them across both France and England in order to thwart the plans of the Cardinal Richelieu. Along the way, they encounter a beautiful young spy, named simply Milady, who will stop at nothing to disgrace Queen Anne of Austria before her husband, Louis XIII, and take her revenge upon the four friends.

Twenty Years After (serialized January–August, 1845): The year is now 1648, twenty years since the close of the last story. Louis XIII has died, as has Cardinal Richelieu, and while the crown of France may sit upon the head of Anne of Austria as Regent for the young Louis XIV, the real power resides with the Cardinal Mazarin, her secret husband. D'Artagnan is now a lieutenant of musketeers, and his three friends have retired to private life. Athos turned out to be a nobleman, the Comte de la Fere, and has retired to his home with his son, Raoul de Bragelonne. Aramis, whose real name is D'Herblay, has followed his intention of shedding the musketeer's cassock for the priest's robes, and Porthos has married a wealthy woman, who left him her fortune upon her death. But trouble is stirring in both France and England. Cromwell menaces the institution of royalty itself while marching against Charles I, and at home the Fronde is threatening to tear France apart. D'Artagnan brings his friends out of retirement to save the threatened English monarch, but Mordaunt, the son of Milady, who seeks to avenge his mother's death at the musketeers' hands, thwarts their valiant efforts. Undaunted, our heroes return to France just in time to help save the young Louis XIV, quiet the Fronde, and tweak the nose of Cardinal Mazarin.

The third novel, *The Vicomte de Bragelonne* (serialized October, 1847–January, 1850), has enjoyed a strange history in its English translation. It has been split into three, four, or five volumes at various points in its history. The five-volume edition generally does not give titles to the smaller portions, but the others do.

The Vicomte de Bragelonne: It is the year 1660, and D'Artagnan, after thirty-five years of loyal service, has become disgusted with serving King Louis XIV while the real power resides with the Cardinal Mazarin, and has tendered his resignation. He embarks on his own project, that of restoring Charles II to the throne of England, and, with the help of Athos, succeeds, earning himself quite a fortune in the process. D'Artagnan returns to Paris to live the life of a rich citizen, and Athos, after negotiating the marriage of Philip, the king's brother, to Princess Henrietta of England, likewise retires to his own estate, La Fere. Meanwhile, Mazarin has finally died, and left Louis to assume the reigns of power, with the assistance of M. Colbert, formerly Mazarin's trusted clerk. Colbert has an intense hatred for M. Fouquet, the king's superintendent of finances, and has resolved to use any means necessary to bring about his fall. With the new rank of intendant bestowed on him by Louis, Colbert succeeds in having two of Fouquet's loyal friends tried and executed. He then brings to the king's attention that Fouquet is fortifying the island of Belle-Ile-en-Mer, and could possibly be planning to use it as a base for some military operation against the king. Louis calls D'Artagnan out of retirement and sends him to investigate the island, promising him a tremendous salary and his long-promised promotion to captain of the musketeers upon his return. At Belle-Isle, D'Artagnan discovers that the engineer of the fortifications is, in fact, Porthos, now the Baron du Vallon, and that's not all. The blueprints for the island, although in Porthos's handwriting, show evidence of another script that has been erased, that of Aramis. D'Artagnan later discovers that Aramis has become the bishop of Vannes, which is, coincidentally, a parish belonging to M. Fouquet. Suspecting that D'Artagnan has arrived on the king's behalf to investigate, Aramis tricks D'Artagnan into wandering around Vannes in search of Porthos, and sends Porthos on an heroic ride back to Paris to warn Fouquet of the danger. Fouquet rushes to the king, and gives him Belle-Isle as a present, thus allaying any suspicion, and at the same time humiliating Colbert, just minutes before the usher announces someone else seeking an audience with the king.

Ten Years Later: As 1661 approaches, Princess Henrietta of England arrives for her marriage, and throws the court of France into complete disorder. The jealousy of the Duke of Buckingham, who is in love with her, nearly occasions a war on the streets of Le Havre, thankfully prevented by Raoul's timely and tactful intervention. After the marriage, though, Monsieur Philip becomes horribly jealous of Buckingham, and has him exiled. Before leaving, however, the duke fights a duel with M. de Wardes at Calais. De Wardes is a malicious and spiteful man, the sworn enemy of D'Artagnan, and, by the same token, that of Athos, Aramis, Porthos, and Raoul as well. Both men are seriously wounded, and the duke is taken back to England to recover. Raoul's friend, the Comte de Guiche, is the next to succumb to Henrietta's charms, and Monsieur obtains his exile as well, though De Guiche soon effects a reconciliation. But then the king's eye falls on Madame Henrietta during the comte's absence, and this time Monsieur's jealousy has no recourse. Anne of Austria intervenes, and the king and his sister-in-law decide to pick a young lady with whom the king can pretend to be in love, the better to mask their own affair. They unfortunately select Louise de la Valliere, Raoul's fiancee. While the court is in residence at Fontainebleau, the king unwittingly overhears Louise confessing her love for him while chatting with her friends beneath the royal oak, and the king promptly forgets his affection for Madame. That same night, Henrietta over-hears, at the same oak, De Guiche confessing his love for her to Raoul. The two embark on their own affair. A few days later, during a rainstorm, Louis and Louise are trapped alone together, and the whole court begins to talk of the scandal while their love affair blossoms. Aware of Louise's attachment, the king arranges for Raoul to be sent to England for an indefinite period.

Meanwhile, the struggle for power continues between Fouquet and Colbert. Although the Belle-Isle plot backfired, Colbert prompts the king to ask Fouquet for more and more money, and without his two friends to raise it for him, Fouquet is sorely pressed. The situation gets so bad that his new mistress, Madame de Belliere, must resort to selling all her jewels and her gold and silver plate. Aramis, while this is going on, has grown friendly with the governor of the Bastille, M. de Baisemeaux, a fact that Baisemeaux unwittingly reveals to D'Artagnan while inquiring of him as to Aramis's where-abouts. This further arouses the suspicions of the musketeer, who was made to look ridiculous by Aramis. He had ridden overnight at an insane pace, but arrived a few minutes after Fouquet had already presented Belle-Isle to the king. Aramis learns from the governor the location of a mysterious prisoner, who bears a remarkable resemblance to Louis XIV—in fact, the two are identical. He uses the existence of this secret to persuade a dying Franciscan monk, the general of the society of the Jesuits, to name him, Aramis, the new general of the order. On Aramis's advice, hoping to use Louise's influence with the king to counteract Colbert's influence, Fouquet also writes a love letter to La Valliere, unfortunately undated. It never reaches its destination, however, as the servant ordered to deliver it turns out to be an agent of Colbert's.

Louise de la Valliere: Believing D'Artagnan occupied at Fontainebleau and Porthos safely tucked away at Paris, Aramis holds a funeral for the dead Franciscan—but in fact, Aramis is wrong in both suppositions. D'Artagnan has left Fontainebleau, bored to tears by the *fetes*, retrieved Porthos, and is visiting the country-house of Planchet, his old lackey. This house happens to be right next door to the graveyard, and upon observing Aramis at this funeral, and his subsequent meeting with a mysterious hooded lady, D'Artagnan, suspicions aroused, resolves to make a little trouble for the bishop. He presents Porthos to the king at the same time as Fouquet presents Aramis, thereby surprising the wily prelate. Aramis's professions of affection and innocence do only a little to allay D'Artagnan's concerns, and he continues to regard Aramis's actions with a curious and wary eye. Meanwhile, much to his delight, Porthos is invited to dine with the king as a result of his presentation, and with D'Artagnan's guidance, manages to behave in such a manner as to procure the king's marked favor.

The mysterious woman turns out to be the Duchesse de Chevreuse, a notorious schemer and former friend of Anne of Austria. She comes bearing more bad news for Fouquet, who is already in trouble, as the king has invited himself to a *fete* at Vaux, Fouquet's magnificent mansion, that will surely bankrupt the poor superintendent. The Duchesse has letters from Mazarin that prove that Fouquet has received thirteen million francs from the royal coffers, and she wishes to sell these letters to Aramis. Aramis refuses, and the letters are instead sold to Colbert. Fouquet, meanwhile, discovers that the receipt that proves his innocence in the affair has been stolen from him. Even worse, Fouquet, desperate for money, is forced to sell the parliamentary position that renders him untouchable by any court proceedings. As part of her deal with Colbert, though, Chevreuse also obtains a secret audience with the queen-mother, where the two discuss a shocking secret—Louis XIV has a twin brother, long believed, however, to be dead.

Meanwhile, in other quarters, De Wardes, Raoul's inveterate enemy, has returned from Calais, barely recovered from his wounds, and no sooner does he return than he begins again to insult people, particularly La Valliere, and this time the comte de Guiche is the one to challenge him. The duel leaves De Guiche horribly wounded, but enables Madame to use her influence to destroy De Wardes's standing at court. The *fetes*, however, come to an end, and the court returns to Paris. The king has been more than obvious about his affections for Louise, and Madame, the queen-mother, and the queen join forces to destroy her. She is dishonorably discharged from court, and in despair, she flees to the convent at Chaillot. Along the way, though, she runs into D'Artagnan, who manages to get word back to the king of what has taken place. By literally begging Madame in tears, Louis manages to secure Louise's return to court—but Madame still places every obstacle possible before the lovers. They have to resort to building a secret staircase and meeting in the apartments of M. de Saint-Aignan, where Louis has a painter create a portrait of Louise. But Madame recalls Raoul from London and shows him these proofs of Louise's infidelity. Raoul, crushed, challenges Saint-Aignan to a duel, which the king prevents, and Athos, furious, breaks his sword before the king. The king has D'Artagnan arrest Athos, and at the Bastille they encounter Aramis, who is paying Baisemeaux another visit. Raoul learns of Athos's arrest, and with Porthos in tow, they effect a daring rescue, surprising the carriage containing D'Artagnan and Athos as they leave the Bastille. Although quite impressive, the intrepid raid is in vain, as D'Artagnan has already secured Athos's pardon from the king. Instead, everybody switches modes of transport; D'Artagnan and Porthos take the horses back to Paris, and Athos and Raoul take the carriage back to La Fere, where they intend to reside permanently, as the king is now their sworn enemy, Raoul cannot bear to see Louise, and they have no more dealings in Paris.

Aramis, left alone with Baisemeaux, inquires the governor of the prison about his loyalties, in particular to the Jesuits. The bishop reveals that he is a confessor of the society, and invokes their regulations in order to obtain access to this mysterious prisoner who bears such a striking resemblance to Louis XIV . . .

   And so Baisemeaux is conducting Aramis to the prisoner
as the final section of *The Vicomte de Bragelonne* and this final
story of the D'Artagnan Romances opens.

John Bursey

CHAPTER 1

The Prisoner.

Since Aramis's singular transformation into a confessor of the order, Baisemeaux was no longer the same man. Up to that period, the place which Aramis had held in the worthy governor's estimation was that of a prelate whom he respected and a friend to whom he owed a debt of gratitude; but now he felt himself an inferior, and that Aramis was his master. He himself lighted a lantern, summoned a turnkey, and said, returning to Aramis, "I am at your orders, monseigneur." Aramis merely nodded his head, as much as to say, "Very good"; and signed to him with his hand to lead the way. Baisemeaux advanced, and Aramis followed him. It was a calm and lovely starlit night; the steps of three men resounded on the flags of the terraces, and the clinking of the keys hanging from the jailer's girdle made itself heard up to the stories of the towers, as if to remind the prisoners that the liberty of earth was a luxury beyond their reach. It might have been said that the alteration effected in Baisemeaux extended even to the prisoners. The turnkey, the same who, on Aramis's first arrival had shown himself so inquisitive and curious, was now not only silent, but impassible. He held his head down, and seemed afraid to keep his ears open. In this wise they reached the basement of the Bertaudiere, the two first stories of which were mounted silently and somewhat slowly; for Baisemeaux, though far from disobeying, was far from exhibiting any eagerness to obey. On arriving at the door, Baisemeaux showed a disposition to enter the prisoner's chamber; but Aramis, stopping him on the threshold, said, "The rules do not allow the governor to hear the prisoner's confession."

Baisemeaux bowed, and made way for Aramis, who took the lantern and entered; and then signed to them to close the door behind him. For an instant he remained standing, listening whether Baisemeaux and the turnkey had retired; but as soon as he was assured by the sound of their descending footsteps that they had left the tower, he put the lantern on the table and gazed around. On a bed of green serge, similar in all respect to the other beds in the Bastille, save that it was newer, and under curtains half-drawn, reposed a young man, to whom we have already once before introduced Aramis. According to custom, the prisoner was without a light. At the hour of curfew, he was bound to extinguish his lamp, and we perceive how much he was favored, in being allowed to keep it burning even till then. Near the bed a large leathern armchair, with twisted legs, sustained his clothes. A little table—without pens, books, paper, or ink—stood neglected in sadness near the window; while several plates, still unemptied, showed that the prisoner had scarcely touched his evening meal. Aramis saw that the young man was stretched upon his bed, his face half concealed by his arms. The arrival of a visitor did not caused any change of position; either he was waiting in expectation, or was asleep. Aramis lighted the candle from the lantern, pushed back the armchair, and approached the bed with an evident mixture of interest and respect. The young man raised his head. "What is it?" said he.

"You desired a confessor?" replied Aramis.

"Yes."

"Because you were ill?"

"Yes."

"Very ill?"

The young man gave Aramis a piercing glance, and answered, "I thank you." After a moment's silence, "I have seen you before," he continued. Aramis bowed.

Doubtless the scrutiny the prisoner had just made of the cold, crafty, and imperious character stamped upon the features of the bishop of Vannes was little reassuring to one in his situation, for he added, "I am better."

"And so?" said Aramis.

"Why, then—being better, I have no longer the same need of a confessor, I think."

"Not even of the hair-cloth, which the note you found in your bread informed you of?"

The young man started; but before he had either assented or denied, Aramis continued, "Not even of the ecclesiastic from whom you were to hear an important revelation?"

"If it be so," said the young man, sinking again on his pillow, "it is different; I am listening."

Aramis then looked at him more closely, and was struck with the easy majesty of his mien, one which can never be acquired unless Heaven has implanted it in the blood or heart. "Sit down, monsieur," said the prisoner.

Aramis bowed and obeyed. "How does the Bastille agree with you?" asked the bishop.

"Very well."

"You do not suffer?"

"No."

"You have nothing to regret?"

"Nothing."

"Not even your liberty?"

"What do you call liberty, monsieur?" asked the prisoner, with the tone of a man who is preparing for a struggle.

"I call liberty, the flowers, the air, light, the stars, the happiness of going whithersoever the sinewy limbs of one-and-twenty chance to wish to carry you."

The young man smiled, whether in resignation or contempt, it was difficult to tell. "Look," said he, "I have in that Japanese vase two roses gathered yesterday evening in the bud from the governor's garden; this morning they have blown and spread their vermilion chalice beneath my gaze; with every opening petal they unfold the treasures of their perfumes, filling my chamber with a fragrance that embalms it. Look now on these two roses; even among roses these are beautiful, and the rose is the most beautiful of flowers. Why, then, do you bid me desire other flowers when I possess the loveliest of all?"

Aramis gazed at the young man in surprise.

"If *flowers* constitute liberty," sadly resumed the captive, "I am free, for I possess them."

"But the air!" cried Aramis; "air is so necessary to life!"

"Well, monsieur," returned the prisoner; "draw near to the window; it is open. Between high heaven and earth the wind whirls on its waftages of hail and lightning, exhales its torrid mist or breathes in gentle breezes. It caresses my face. When mounted on the back of this armchair, with my arm around the bars of the window to sustain myself, I fancy I am swimming the wide expanse before me." The countenance of Aramis darkened as the young man continued: "Light I have! what is better than light? I have the sun, a friend who comes to visit me every day without the permission of the governor or the jailer's company. He comes in at the window, and traces in my room a square the shape of the window, which lights up the hangings of my bed and floods the very floor. This luminous square increases from ten o'clock till midday, and decreases from one till three slowly, as if, having hastened to my presence, it sorrowed at bidding me farewell. When its last ray disappears I have enjoyed its presence for five hours. Is not that sufficient? I have been told that there are unhappy beings who dig in quarries, and laborers who toil in mines, who never behold it at all." Aramis wiped the drops from his brow. "As to the stars which are so delightful to view," continued the young man, "they all resemble each other save in size and brilliancy. I am a favored mortal, for if you had not lighted that candle you would have been able to see the beautiful stars which I was gazing at from my couch before your arrival, whose silvery rays were stealing through my brain."

Aramis lowered his head; he felt himself overwhelmed with the bitter flow of that sinister philosophy which is the religion of the captive.

"So much, then, for the flowers, the air, the daylight, and the stars," tranquilly continued the young man; "there remains but exercise. Do I not walk all day in the governor's garden if it is fine—here if it rains? in the fresh air if it is warm; in perfect warmth, thanks to my winter stove, if it be cold? Ah! monsieur, do you fancy," continued the prisoner, not without bitterness, "that men have not done everything for me that a man can hope for or desire?"

"Men!" said Aramis; "be it so; but it seems to me you are forgetting Heaven."

"Indeed I have forgotten Heaven," murmured the prisoner, with emotion; "but why do you mention it? Of what use is it to talk to a prisoner of Heaven?"

Aramis looked steadily at this singular youth, who possessed the resignation of a martyr with the smile of an atheist. "Is not Heaven in everything?" he murmured in a reproachful tone.

"Say rather, at the end of everything," answered the prisoner, firmly.

"Be it so," said Aramis; "but let us return to our starting-point."

"I ask nothing better," returned the young man.

"I am your confessor."

"Yes."

"Well, then, you ought, as a penitent, to tell me the truth."

"My whole desire is to tell it you."

"Every prisoner has committed some crime for which he has been imprisoned. What crime, then, have you committed?"

"You asked me the same question the first time you saw me," returned the prisoner.

"And then, as now you evaded giving me an answer."

"And what reason have you for thinking that I shall now reply to you?"

"Because this time I am your confessor."

"Then if you wish me to tell what crime I have committed, explain to me in what a crime consists. For as my conscience does not accuse me, I aver that I am not a criminal."

"We are often criminals in the sight of the great of the earth, not alone for having ourselves committed crimes, but because we know that crimes have been committed."

The prisoner manifested the deepest attention.

"Yes, I understand you," he said, after a pause; "yes, you are right, monsieur; it is very possible that, in such a light, I am a criminal in the eyes of the great of the earth."

"Ah! then you know something," said Aramis, who thought he had pierced not merely through a defect in the harness, but through the joints of it.

"No, I am not aware of anything," replied the young man; "but sometimes I think—and I say to myself—"

"What do you say to yourself?"

"That if I were to think but a little more deeply I should either go mad or I should divine a great deal."

"And then—and then?" said Aramis, impatiently.

"Then I leave off."

"You leave off?"

"Yes; my head becomes confused and my ideas melancholy; I feel *ennui* overtaking me; I wish—"

"What?"

"I don't know; but I do not like to give myself up to

longing for things which I do not possess, when I am so happy with what I have."

"You are afraid of death?" said Aramis, with a slight uneasiness.

"Yes," said the young man, smiling.

Aramis felt the chill of that smile, and shuddered. "Oh, as you fear death, you know more about matters than you say," he cried.

"And you," returned the prisoner, "who bade me to ask to see you; you, who, when I did ask to see you, came here promising a world of confidence; how is it that, nevertheless, it is you who are silent, leaving it for me to speak? Since, then, we both wear masks, either let us both retain them or put them aside together."

Aramis felt the force and justice of the remark, saying to himself, "This is no ordinary man; I must be cautious.—Are you ambitious?" said he suddenly to the prisoner, aloud, without preparing him for the alteration.

"What do you mean by ambitious?" replied the youth.

"Ambition," replied Aramis, "is the feeling which prompts a man to desire more—much more—than he possesses."

"I said that I was contented, monsieur; but, perhaps, I deceive myself. I am ignorant of the nature of ambition; but it is not impossible I may have some. Tell me your mind; that is all I ask."

"An ambitious man," said Aramis, "is one who covets that which is beyond his station."

"I covet nothing beyond my station," said the young man, with an assurance of manner which for the second time made the bishop of Vannes tremble.

He was silent. But to look at the kindling eye, the knitted brow, and the reflective attitude of the captive, it was evident that he expected something more than silence,—a silence which Aramis now broke. "You lied the first time I saw you," said he.

"Lied!" cried the young man, starting up on his couch, with such a tone in his voice, and such a lightning in his eyes, that Aramis recoiled, in spite of himself.

"I *should* say," returned Aramis, bowing, "you concealed from me what you knew of your infancy."

"A man's secrets are his own, monsieur," retorted the prisoner, "and not at the mercy of the first chance-comer."

"True," said Aramis, bowing still lower than before, "'tis true; pardon me, but to-day do I still occupy the place of a chance-comer? I beseech you to reply, monseigneur."

This title slightly disturbed the prisoner; but nevertheless he did not appear astonished that it was given him. "I do not know you, monsieur," said he.

"Oh, but if I dared, I would take your hand and kiss it!"

The young man seemed as if he were going to give Aramis his hand; but the light which beamed in his eyes faded away, and he coldly and distrustfully withdrew his hand again. "Kiss the hand of a prisoner," he said, shaking his head, "to what purpose?"

"Why did you tell me," said Aramis, "that you were happy here? Why, that you aspired to nothing? Why, in a word, by thus speaking, do you prevent me from being frank in my turn?"

The same light shone a third time in the young man's eyes, but died ineffectually away as before.

"You distrust me," said Aramis.

"And why say you so, monsieur?"

"Oh, for a very simple reason; if you know what you ought to know, you ought to mistrust everybody."

"Then do not be astonished that I am mistrustful, since you suspect me of knowing what I do not know."

Aramis was struck with admiration at this energetic resistance. "Oh, monseigneur! you drive me to despair," said he, striking the armchair with his fist.

"And, on my part, I do not comprehend you, monsieur."

"Well, then, try to understand me." The prisoner looked fixedly at Aramis.

"Sometimes it seems to me," said the latter, "that I have before me the man whom I seek, and then—"

"And then your man disappears,—is it not so?" said the prisoner, smiling. "So much the better."

Aramis rose. "Certainly," said he; "I have nothing further to say to a man who mistrusts me as you do."

"And I, monsieur," said the prisoner, in the same tone, "have nothing to say to a man who will not understand that a prisoner ought to be mistrustful of everybody."

"Even of his old friends," said Aramis. "Oh, monseigneur, you are *too* prudent!"

"Of my old friends?—you one of my old friends, —you?"

"Do you no longer remember," said Aramis, "that you once saw, in the village where your early years were spent—"

"Do you know the name of the village?" asked the prisoner.

"Noisy-le-Sec, monseigneur," answered Aramis, firmly.

"Go on," said the young man, with an immovable aspect.

"Stay, monseigneur," said Aramis; "if you are positively resolved to carry on this game, let us break off. I am here to tell you many things, 'tis true; but you must allow me to see that, on your side, you have a desire to know them. Before revealing the important matters I still withhold, be assured I am in need of some encouragement, if not candor; a little sympathy, if not confidence. But you keep yourself intrenched in a pretended which paralyzes me. Oh, not for the reason you think; for, ignorant as you may be, or indifferent as you feign to be, you are none the less what you are, monseigneur, and there is nothing—nothing, mark me! which can cause you not to be so."

"I promise you," replied the prisoner, "to hear you without impatience. Only it appears to me that I have a right to repeat the question I have already asked, 'Who *are* you?'"

"Do you remember, fifteen or eighteen years ago, seeing at Noisy-le-Sec a cavalier, accompanied by a lady in black silk, with flame-colored ribbons in her hair?"

"Yes," said the young man; "I once asked the name of this cavalier, and they told me that he called himself the Abbe d'Herblay. I was astonished that the abbe had so warlike an air, and they replied that there was nothing singular in that, seeing that he was one of Louis XIII.'s musketeers."

"Well," said Aramis, "that musketeer and abbe, afterwards bishop of Vannes, is your confessor now."

"I know it; I recognized you."

"Then, monseigneur, if you know that, I must further add a fact of which you are ignorant—that if the king were to know this evening of the presence of this musketeer, this abbe, this bishop, this confessor, *here*—he, who has risked everything to visit you, to-morrow would behold the steely glitter of the executioner's axe in a dungeon more gloomy, more obscure than yours."

While listening to these words, delivered with emphasis, the young man had raised himself on his couch, and was now gazing more and more eagerly at Aramis.

The result of his scrutiny was that he appeared to derive some confidence from it. "Yes," he murmured, "I remember perfectly. The woman of whom you speak came once with you, and twice afterwards with another." He hesitated.

"With another, who came to see you every month—is it not so, monseigneur?"

"Yes."

"Do you know who this lady was?"

The light seemed ready to flash from the prisoner's eyes. "I am aware that she was one of the ladies of the court," he said.

"You remember that lady well, do you not?"

"Oh, my recollection can hardly be very confused on this head," said the young prisoner. "I saw that lady once with a gentleman about forty-five years old. I saw her once with you, and with the lady dressed in black. I have seen her twice since then with the same person. These four people, with my master, and old Perronnette, my jailer, and the governor of the prison, are the only persons with whom I have ever spoken, and, indeed, almost the only persons I have ever seen."

"Then you were in prison?"

"If I am a prisoner here, then I was comparatively free, although in a very narrow sense—a house I never quitted, a garden surrounded with walls I could not climb, these constituted my residence, but you know it, as you have been there. In a word, being accustomed to live within these bounds, I never cared to leave them. And so you will understand, monsieur, that having never seen anything of the world, I have nothing left to care for; and therefore, if you relate anything, you will be obliged to explain each item to me as you go along."

"And I will do so," said Aramis, bowing; "for it is my duty, monseigneur."

"Well, then, begin by telling me who was my tutor."

"A worthy and, above all, an honorable gentleman, monseigneur; fit guide for both body and soul. Had you ever any reason to complain of him?"

"Oh, no; quite the contrary. But this gentleman of yours often used to tell me that my father and mother were dead. Did he deceive me, or did he speak the truth?"

"He was compelled to comply with the orders given him."

"Then he lied?"

"In one respect. Your father is dead."

"And my mother?"

"She is dead *for you.*"

"But then she lives for others, does she not?"

"Yes."

"And I—and I, then" (the young man looked sharply at Aramis) "am compelled to live in the obscurity of a prison?"

"Alas! I fear so."

"And that because my presence in the world would lead to the revelation of a great secret?"

"Certainly, a very great secret."

"My enemy must indeed be powerful, to be able to shut up in the Bastille a child such as I then was."

"He is."

"More powerful than my mother, then?"

"And why do you ask that?"

Because my mother would have taken my part."

Aramis hesitated. "Yes, monseigneur; more powerful than your mother."

"Seeing, then, that my nurse and preceptor were carried off, and that I, also, was separated from them—either they were, or I am, very dangerous to my enemy?"

"Yes; but you are alluding to a peril from which he freed himself, by causing the nurse and preceptor to disappear," answered Aramis, quietly.

"Disappear!" cried the prisoner, "how did they disappear?"

"In a very sure way," answered Aramis—"they are dead."

The young man turned pale, and passed his hand tremblingly over his face. "Poison?" he asked.

"Poison."

The prisoner reflected a moment. "My enemy must indeed have been very cruel, or hard beset by necessity, to assassinate those two innocent people, my sole support; for the worthy gentleman and the poor nurse had never harmed a living being."

"In your family, monseigneur, necessity is stern. And so it is necessity which compels me, to my great regret, to tell you that this gentleman and the unhappy lady have been assassinated."

"Oh, you tell me nothing I am not aware of," said the prisoner, knitting his brows.

"How?"

"I suspected it."

"Why?"

"I will tell you."

At this moment the young man, supporting himself on his two elbows, drew close to Aramis's face, with such an expression of dignity, of self-command and of defiance even, that the bishop felt the electricity of enthusiasm strike in devouring flashes from that great heart of his, into his brain of adamant.

"Speak, monseigneur. I have already told you that by conversing with you I endanger my life. Little value as it has, I implore you to accept it as the ransom of your own."

"Well," resumed the young man, "this is why I suspected they had killed my nurse and my preceptor—"

"Whom you used to call your father?"

"Yes; whom I called my father, but whose son I well knew I was not."

"Who caused you to suppose so?"

"Just as you, monsieur, are too respectful for a friend, he was also too respectful for a father."

"I, however," said Aramis, "have no intention to disguise myself."

The young man nodded assent and continued: "Undoubtedly, I was not destined to perpetual seclusion," said the prisoner; "and that which makes me believe so, above all, now, is the care that was taken to render me as accomplished a cavalier as possible. The gentleman attached to my person taught me everything he knew himself—mathematics, a little geometry, astronomy, fencing and riding. Every morning I went through military exercises, and practiced on horseback. Well, one morning during the summer, it being very hot, I went to sleep in the hall. Nothing, up to that period, except the respect paid me, had enlightened me, or even roused my suspicions. I lived as children, as birds, as plants, as the air and the sun do. I had just turned my fifteenth year—"

"This, then, is eight years ago?"

"Yes, nearly; but I have ceased to reckon time."

"Excuse me; but what did your tutor tell you, to encourage you to work?"

"He used to say that a man was bound to make for himself, in the world, that fortune which Heaven had refused him at his birth. He added that, being a poor, obscure orphan, I had no one but myself to look to; and that nobody either did, or ever would, take any interest in me. I was, then, in the hall I have spoken of, asleep from fatigue with long fencing. My preceptor was in his room on the first floor, just over me. Suddenly I heard him exclaim, and then he called: 'Perronnette! Perronnette!' It was my nurse whom he called."

"Yes, I know it," said Aramis. "Continue, monseigneur."

"Very likely she was in the garden; for my preceptor came hastily downstairs. I rose, anxious at seeing him anxious. He opened the garden-door, still crying out, 'Perronnette! Perronnette!' The windows of the hall looked into the court; the shutters were closed; but through a chink in them I saw my tutor draw near a large well, which was almost directly under the windows of his study. He stooped over the brim, looked into the well, and again cried out, and made wild and affrighted gestures. Where I was, I could not only see, but hear—and see and hear I did."

"Go on, I pray you," said Aramis.

"Dame Perronnette came running up, hearing the governor's cries. He went to meet her, took her by the arm, and drew her quickly towards the edge; after which, as they both bent over it together, 'Look, look,' cried he, 'what a misfortune!'

"'Calm yourself, calm yourself,' said Perronnette; 'what is the matter?'

"'The letter!' he exclaimed; 'do you see that letter?' pointing to the bottom of the well.

"'What letter?' she cried.

"'The letter you see down there; the last letter from the queen.'

"At this word I trembled. My tutor—he who passed for my father, he who was continually recommending me modesty and humility—in correspondence with the queen!

"'The queen's last letter!' cried Perronnette, without showing more astonishment than at seeing this letter at the bottom of the well; 'but how came it there?'

"'A chance, Dame Perronnette—a singular chance. I was entering my room, and on opening the door, the window, too, being open, a puff of air came suddenly and carried off this paper—this letter of her majesty's; I darted after it, and gained the window just in time to see it flutter a moment in the breeze and disappear down the well.'

"'Well,' said Dame Perronnette; 'and if the letter has fallen into the well, 'tis all the same as if it was burnt; and as the queen burns all her letters every time she comes—'

"And so you see this lady who came every month was the queen," said the prisoner.

"'Doubtless, doubtless,' continued the old gentleman; 'but this letter contained instructions—how can I follow them?'

"'Write immediately to her; give her a plain account of the accident, and the queen will no doubt write you another letter in place of this.'

"'Oh! the queen would never believe the story,' said the good gentleman, shaking his head; 'she will imagine that I want to keep this letter instead of giving it up like the rest, so as to have a hold over her. She is so distrustful, and M. de Mazarin so—Yon devil of an Italian is capable of having us poisoned at the first breath of suspicion.'"

Aramis almost imperceptibly smiled.

"'You know, Dame Perronnette, they are both so suspicious in all that concerns Philippe.'

"Philippe was the name they gave me," said the prisoner.

"'Well, 'tis no use hesitating,' said Dame Perronnette, 'somebody must go down the well.'

"'Of course; so that the person who goes down may read the paper as he is coming up.'

"'But let us choose some villager who cannot read, and then you will be at ease.'

"'Granted; but will not any one who descends guess that a paper must be important for which we risk a man's life? However, you have given me an idea, Dame Perronnette; somebody shall go down the well, but that somebody shall be myself.'

"But at this notion Dame Perronnette lamented and cried in such a manner, and so implored the old nobleman, with tears in her eyes, that he promised her to obtain a ladder long enough to reach down, while she went in search of some stout-hearted youth, whom she was to persuade that a jewel had fallen into the well, and that this jewel was wrapped in a paper. 'And as paper,' remarked my preceptor, 'naturally unfolds in water, the young man would not be surprised at finding nothing, after all, but the letter wide open.'

"'But perhaps the writing will be already effaced by that time,' said Dame Perronnette.

"'No consequence, provided we secure the letter. On returning it to the queen, she will see at once that we have not betrayed her; and consequently, as we shall not rouse the distrust of Mazarin, we shall have nothing to fear from him.'

"Having come to this resolution, they parted. I pushed

back the shutter, and, seeing that my tutor was about to re-enter, I threw myself on my couch, in a confusion of brain caused by all I had just heard. My governor opened the door a few moments after, and thinking I was asleep gently closed it again. As soon as ever it was shut, I rose, and, listening, heard the sound of retiring footsteps. Then I returned to the shutters, and saw my tutor and Dame Perronnette go out together. I was alone in the house. They had hardly closed the gate before I sprang from the window and ran to the well. Then, just as my governor had leaned over, so leaned I. Something white and luminous glistened in the green and quivering silence of the water. The brilliant disk fascinated and allured me; my eyes became fixed, and I could hardly breathe. The well seemed to draw me downwards with its slimy mouth and icy breath; and I thought I read, at the bottom of the water, characters of fire traced upon the letter the queen had touched. Then, scarcely knowing what I was about, and urged on by one of those instinctive impulses which drive men to destruction, I lowered the cord from the windlass of the well to within about three feet of the water, leaving the bucket dangling, at the same time taking infinite pains not to disturb that coveted letter, which was beginning to change its white tint for the hue of chrysoprase,—proof enough that it was sinking,—and then, with the rope weltering in my hands, slid down into the abyss. When I saw myself hanging over the dark pool, when I saw the sky lessening above my head, a cold shudder came over me, a chill fear got the better of me, I was seized with giddiness, and the hair rose on my head; but my strong will still reigned supreme over all the terror and disquietude. I gained the water, and at once plunged into it, holding on by one hand, while I immersed the other and seized the dear letter, which, alas! came in two in my grasp. I concealed the two fragments in my body-coat, and, helping myself with my feet against the sides of the pit, and clinging on with my hands, agile and vigorous as I was, and, above all, pressed for time, I regained the brink, drenching it as I touched it with the water that streamed off me. I was no sooner out of the well with my prize, than I rushed into the sunlight, and took refuge in a kind of shrubbery at the bottom of the garden. As I entered my hiding-place, the bell which resounded when the great gate was opened, rang. It was my preceptor come back again. I had but just time. I calculated that it would take ten minutes before he would gain my place of concealment, even if, guessing where I was, he came straight to it; and twenty if he were obliged to look for me. But this was time enough to allow me to read the cherished letter, whose fragments I hastened to unite again. The writing was already fading, but I managed to decipher it all.

"And will you tell me what you read therein, monseigneur?" asked Aramis, deeply interested.

"Quite enough, monsieur, to see that my tutor was a man of noble rank, and that Perronnette, without being a lady of quality, was far better than a servant; and also to perceived that I must myself be high-born, since the queen, Anne of Austria, and Mazarin, the prime minister, commended me so earnestly to their care." Here the young man paused, quite overcome.

"And what happened?" asked Aramis.

"It happened, monsieur," answered he, "that the workmen they had summoned found nothing in the well, after the closest search; that my governor perceived that the brink was all watery; that I was not so dried by the sun as to prevent Dame Perronnette spying that my garments were moist; and, lastly, that I was seized with a violent fever, owing to the chill and the excitement of my discovery, an attack of delirium supervening, during which I related the whole adventure; so that, guided by my avowal, my governor found the pieces of the queen's letter inside the bolster where I had concealed them."

"Ah!" said Aramis, "now I understand."

"Beyond this, all is conjecture. Doubtless the unfortunate lady and gentleman, not daring to keep the occurrence secret, wrote of all this to the queen and sent back the torn letter."

"After which," said Aramis, "you were arrested and removed to the Bastille."

"As you see."

"Your two attendants disappeared?"

"Alas!"

"Let us not take up our time with the dead, but see what can be done with the living. You told me you were resigned."

"I repeat it."

"Without any desire for freedom?"

"As I told you."

"Without ambition, sorrow, or thought?"

The young man made no answer.

"Well," asked Aramis, "why are you silent?"

"I think I have spoken enough," answered the prisoner, "and that now it is your turn. I am weary."

Aramis gathered himself up, and a shade of deep solemnity spread itself over his countenance. It was evident that he had reached the crisis in the part he had come to the prison to play. "One question," said Aramis.

"What is it? speak."

"In the house you inhabited there were neither looking-glasses nor mirrors?"

"What are those two words, and what is their meaning?" asked the young man; "I have no sort of knowledge of them."

"They designate two pieces of furniture which reflect objects; so that, for instance, you may see in them your own lineaments, as you see mine now, with the naked eye."

"No; there was neither a glass nor a mirror in the house," answered the young man.

Aramis looked round him. "Nor is there anything of the kind here, either," he said; "they have again taken the same precaution."

"To what end?"

"You will know directly. Now, you have told me that you were instructed in mathematics, astronomy, fencing, and riding; but you have not said a word about history."

"My tutor sometimes related to me the principal deeds of the king, St. Louis, King Francis I., and King Henry IV."

"Is that all?"

"Very nearly."

"This also was done by design, then; just as they deprived you of mirrors, which reflect the present, so they left you in ignorance of history, which reflects the past. Since your imprisonment, books have been forbidden you; so that you are unacquainted with a number of facts, by means of which you would be able to reconstruct the shattered mansion of your recollections and your hopes."

"It is true," said the young man.

"Listen, then; I will in a few words tell you what has passed in France during the last twenty-three or twenty-four years; that is, from the probable date of your birth; in a word, from the time that interests you."

"Say on." And the young man resumed his serious and attentive attitude.

"Do you know who was the son of Henry IV.?"

"At least I know who his successor was."

"How?"

"By means of a coin dated 1610, which bears the effigy of Henry IV.; and another of 1612, bearing that of Louis XIII. So I presumed that, there being only two years between the two dates, Louis was Henry's successor."

"Then," said Aramis, "you know that the last reigning monarch was Louis XIII.?"

"I do," answered the youth, slightly reddening.

"Well, he was a prince full of noble ideas and great projects, always, alas! deferred by the trouble of the times and the dread struggle that his minister Richelieu had to maintain against the great nobles of France. The king himself was of a feeble character, and died young and unhappy."

"I know it."

"He had been long anxious about having a heir; a care which weighs heavily on princes, who desire to leave behind them more than one pledge that their best thoughts and works will be continued."

"Did the king, then, die childless?" asked the prisoner, smiling.

"No, but he was long without one, and for a long while thought he should be the last of his race. This idea had reduced him to the depths of despair, when suddenly, his wife, Anne of Austria—"

The prisoner trembled.

"Did you know," said Aramis, "that Louis XIII.'s wife was called Anne of Austria?"

"Continue," said the young man, without replying to the question.

"When suddenly," resumed Aramis, "the queen announced an interesting event. There was great joy at the intelligence, and all prayed for her happy delivery. On the 5th of September, 1638, she gave birth to a son."

Here Aramis looked at his companion, and thought he observed him turning pale. "You are about to hear," said Aramis, "an account which few indeed could now avouch; for it refers to a secret which they imagined buried with the dead, entombed in the abyss of the confessional."

"And you will tell me this secret?" broke in the youth.

"Oh!" said Aramis, with unmistakable emphasis, "I do not know that I ought to risk this secret by intrusting it to one who has no desire to quit the Bastille."

"I hear you, monsieur."

"The queen, then, gave birth to a son. But while the court was rejoicing over the event, when the king had show the new-born child to the nobility and people, and was sitting gayly down to table, to celebrate the event, the queen, who was alone in her room, was again taken ill and gave birth to a second son."

"Oh!" said the prisoner, betraying a bitter acquaintance with affairs than he had owned to, "I thought that Monsieur was only born in—"

Aramis raised his finger; "Permit me to continue," he said.

The prisoner sighed impatiently, and paused.

"Yes," said Aramis, "the queen had a second son, whom Dame Perronnette, the midwife, received in her arms."

"Dame Perronnette!" murmured the young man.

"They ran at once to the banqueting-room, and whispered to the king what had happened; he rose and quitted the table. But this time it was no longer happiness that his face expressed, but something akin to terror. The birth of twins changed into bitterness the joy to which that of an only son had given rise, seeing that in France (a fact you are assuredly ignorant of) it is the oldest of the king's sons who succeeds his father."

"I know it."

"And that the doctors and jurists assert that there is ground for doubting whether the son that first makes his appearance is the elder by the law of heaven and of nature."

The prisoner uttered a smothered cry, and became whiter than the coverlet under which he hid himself.

"Now you understand," pursued Aramis, "that the king, who with so much pleasure saw himself repeated in one, was in despair about two; fearing that the second might dispute the first's claim to seniority, which had been recognized only two hours before; and so this second son, relying on party interests and caprices, might one day sow discord and engender civil war throughout the kingdom; by these means destroying the very dynasty he should have strengthened."

"Oh, I understand!—I understand!" murmured the young man.

"Well," continued Aramis; "this is what they relate, what they declare; this is why one of the queen's two sons, shamefully parted from his brother, shamefully sequestered, is buried in profound obscurity; this is why that second son has disappeared, and so completely, that not a soul in France, save his mother, is aware of his existence."

"Yes! his mother, who has cast him off," cried the prisoner in a tone of despair.

"Except, also," Aramis went on, "the lady in the black dress; and, finally, excepting—"

"Excepting yourself—is it not? You who come and relate all this; you, who rouse in my soul curiosity, hatred, ambition, and, perhaps, even the thirst of vengeance; except you, monsieur, who, if you are the man to whom I expect, whom the note I have received applies to, whom, in short, Heaven ought to send me, must possess about you—"

"What?" asked Aramis.

"A portrait of the king, Louis XIV., who at this moment reigns upon the throne of France."

"Here is the portrait," replied the bishop, handing the prisoner a miniature in enamel, on which Louis was depicted life-like, with a handsome, lofty mien. The prisoner eagerly seized the portrait, and gazed at it with devouring eyes.

"And now, monseigneur," said Aramis, "here is a mirror." Aramis left the prisoner time to recover his ideas.

"So high!—so high!" murmured the young man, eagerly comparing the likeness of Louis with his own countenance reflected in the glass.

"What do you think of it?" at length said Aramis.

"I think that I am lost," replied the captive; "the king will never set me free."

"And I—I demand to know," added the bishop, fixing his piercing eyes significantly upon the prisoner, "I demand to know which of these two is king; the one this miniature portrays, or whom the glass reflects?"

"The king, monsieur," sadly replied the young man, "is he who is on the throne, who is not in prison; and who, on the other hand, can cause others to be entombed there. Royalty means power; and you behold how powerless I am."

"Monseigneur," answered Aramis, with a respect he had not yet manifested, "the king, mark me, will, if you desire it, be the one that, quitting his dungeon, shall maintain himself upon the throne, on which his friends will place him."

"Tempt me not, monsieur," broke in the prisoner bitterly.

"Be not weak, monseigneur," persisted Aramis; "I have brought you all the proofs of your birth; consult them; satisfy yourself that you are a king's son; it is for *us* to act."

"No, no; it is impossible."

"Unless, indeed," resumed the bishop ironically, "it be the destiny of your race, that the brothers excluded from the throne should be always princes void of courage and honesty, as was your uncle, M. Gaston d'Orleans, who ten times conspired against his brother Louis XIII."

"What!" cried the prince, astonished; "my uncle Gaston 'conspired against his brother'; conspired to dethrone him?"

"Exactly, monseigneur; for no other reason. I tell you the truth."

"And he had friends—devoted friends?"

"As much so as I am to you."

"And, after all, what did he do?—Failed!"

"He failed, I admit; but always through his own fault; and, for the sake of purchasing—not his life—for the life of the king's brother is sacred and inviolable—but his liberty, he sacrificed the lives of all his friends, one after another. And so, at this day, he is a very blot on history, the detestation of a hundred noble families in this kingdom."

"I understand, monsieur; either by weakness or treachery, my uncle slew his friends."

"By weakness; which, in princes, is always treachery."

"And cannot a man fail, then, from incapacity and ignorance? Do you really believe it possible that a poor captive such as I, brought up, not only at a distance from the court, but even from the world—do you believe it possible that such a one could assist those of his friends who should attempt to serve him?" And as Aramis was about to reply, the young man suddenly cried out, with a violence which betrayed the temper of his blood, "We are speaking of friends; but how can I have any friends—I, whom no one knows; and have neither liberty, money, nor influence, to gain any?"

"I fancy I had the honor to offer myself to your royal highness."

"Oh, do not style me so, monsieur; 'tis either treachery or cruelty. Bid me not think of aught beyond these prison-walls, which so grimly confine me; let me again love, or, at least, submit to my slavery and my obscurity."

"Monseigneur, monseigneur; if you again utter these desperate words—if, after having received proof of your high birth, you still remain poor-spirited in body and soul, I will comply with your desire, I will depart, and renounce forever the service of a master, to whom so eagerly I came to devote my assistance and my life!"

"Monsieur," cried the prince, "would it not have been better for you to have reflected, before telling me all that you have done, that you have broken my heart forever?"

"And so I desire to do, monseigneur."

"To talk to me about power, grandeur, eye, and to prate of thrones! Is a prison the fit place? You wish to make me believe in splendor, and we are lying lost in night; you boast of glory, and we are smothering our words in the curtains of this miserable bed; you give me glimpses of power absolute whilst I hear the footsteps of the every-watchful jailer in the corridor—that step which, after all, makes you tremble more than it does me. To render me somewhat less incredulous, free me from the Bastille; let me breathe the fresh air; give me my spurs and trusty sword, then we shall begin to understand each other."

"It is precisely my intention to give you all this, monseigneur, and more; only, do you desire it?"

"A word more," said the prince. "I know there are guards in every gallery, bolts to every door, cannon and soldiery at every barrier. How will you overcome the sentries—spike the guns? How will you break through the bolts and bars?"

"Monseigneur,—how did you get the note which announced my arrival to you?"

"You can bribe a jailer for such a thing as a note."

"If we can corrupt one turnkey, we can corrupt ten."

"Well; I admit that it may be possible to release a poor captive from the Bastille; possible so to conceal him that the king's people shall not again ensnare him; possible, in some unknown retreat, to sustain the unhappy wretch in some suitable manner."

"Monseigneur!" said Aramis, smiling.

"I admit that, whoever would do this much for me, would seem more than mortal in my eyes; but as you tell me I am a prince, brother of the king, how can you restore me the rank and power which my mother and my brother have deprived me of? And as, to effect this, I must pass a life of war and hatred, how can you cause me to prevail in those combats—render me invulnerable by my enemies? Ah! monsieur, reflect on all this; place me, to-morrow, in some dark cavern at a mountain's base; yield me the delight of hearing in freedom sounds of the river, plain and valley, of beholding in freedom the sun of the blue heavens, or the stormy sky, and it is enough. Promise me no more than this, for, indeed, more you cannot give, and it would be a crime to deceive me, since you call yourself my friend."

Aramis waited in silence. "Monseigneur," he resumed, after a moment's reflection, "I admire the firm, sound sense which dictates your words; I am happy to have discovered my monarch's mind."

"Again, again! oh, God! for mercy's sake," cried the prince, pressing his icy hands upon his clammy brow, "do not play with me! I have no need to be a king to be the happiest of men."

"But I, monseigneur, wish you to be a king for the good of humanity."

"Ah!" said the prince, with fresh distrust inspired by the word; "ah! with what, then, has humanity to reproach my brother?"

"I forgot to say, monseigneur, that if you would allow me to guide you, and if you consent to become the most powerful monarch in Christendom, you will have promoted the interests of all the friends whom I devote to the success of your cause, and these friends are numerous."

"Numerous?"

"Less numerous than powerful, monseigneur."

"Explain yourself."

"It is impossible; I will explain, I swear before Heaven, on that day that I see you sitting on the throne of France."

"But my brother?"

"You shall decree his fate. Do you pity him?"

"Him, who leaves me to perish in a dungeon? No, no. For him I have no pity!"

"So much the better."

"He might have himself come to this prison, have taken me by the hand, and have said, 'My brother, Heaven created us to love, not to contend with one another. I come to you. A barbarous prejudice has condemned you to pass your days in obscurity, far from mankind, deprived of every joy. I will make you sit down beside me; I will buckle round your waist our father's sword. Will you take advantage of this reconciliation to put down or restrain me? Will you employ that sword to spill my blood?' 'Oh! never,' I would have replied to him,

'I look on you as my preserver, I will respect you as my master. You give me far more than Heaven bestowed; for through you I possess liberty and the privilege of loving and being loved in this world.'"

"And you would have kept your word, monseigneur?"

"On my life! While now—now that I have guilty ones to punish—"

"In what manner, monseigneur?"

"What do you say as to the resemblance that Heaven has given me to my brother?"

"I say that there was in that likeness a providential instruction which the king ought to have heeded; I say that your mother committed a crime in rendering those different in happiness and fortune whom nature created so startlingly alike, of her own flesh, and I conclude that the object of punishment should be only to restore the equilibrium."

"By which you mean—"

"That if I restore you to your place on your brother's throne, he shall take yours in prison."

"Alas! there's such infinity of suffering in prison, especially it would be so for one who has drunk so deeply of the cup of enjoyment."

"Your royal highness will always be free to act as you may desire; and if it seems good to you, after punishment, you will have it in your power to pardon."

"Good. And now, are you aware of one thing, monsieur?"

"Tell me, my prince."

"It is that I will hear nothing further from you till I am clear of the Bastille."

"I was going to say to your highness that I should only have the pleasure of seeing you once again."

"And when?"

"The day when my prince leaves these gloomy walls."

"Heavens! how will you give me notice of it?"

"By myself coming to fetch you."

"Yourself?"

"My prince, do not leave this chamber save with me, or if in my absence you are compelled to do so, remember that I am not concerned in it."

"And so I am not to speak a word of this to any one whatever, save to you?"

"Save only to me." Aramis bowed very low. The prince offered his hand.

"Monsieur," he said, in a tone that issued from his heart, "one word more, my last. If you have sought me for my destruction; if you are only a tool in the hands of my enemies; if from our conference, in which you have sounded the depths of my mind, anything worse than captivity result, that is to say, if death befall me, still receive my blessing, for you will have ended my troubles and given me repose from the tormenting fever that has preyed on me for eight long, weary years."

"Monseigneur, wait the results ere you judge me," said Aramis.

"I say that, in such a case, I bless and forgive you. If, on the other hand, you are come to restore me to that position in the sunshine of fortune and glory to which I was destined by Heaven; if by your means I am enabled to live in the memory of man, and confer luster on my race by deeds of valor, or by solid benefits bestowed upon my people; if, from my present depths of sorrow, aided by your generous hand, I raise myself to the very height of honor, then to you, whom I thank with blessings, to you will I offer half my power and my glory: though you would still be but partly recompensed, and your share must always remain incomplete, since I could not divide with you the happiness received at your hands."

"Monseigneur," replied Aramis, moved by the pallor and excitement of the young man, "the nobleness of your heart fills me with joy and admiration. It is not you who will have to thank me, but rather the nation whom you will render happy, the posterity whose name you will make glorious. Yes; I shall indeed have bestowed upon you more than life, I shall have given you immortality."

The prince offered his hand to Aramis, who sank upon his knee and kissed it.

"It is the first act of homage paid to our future king," said he. "When I see you again, I shall say, 'Good day, sire.'"

"Till then," said the young man, pressing his wan and wasted fingers over his heart,—"till then, no more dreams, no more strain on my life—my heart would break! Oh, monsieur, how small is my prison—how low the window—how narrow are the doors! To think that so much pride, splendor, and happiness, should be able to enter in and to remain here!"

"Your royal highness makes me proud," said Aramis, "since you infer it is I who brought all this." And he rapped immediately on the door. The jailer came to open it with Baisemeaux, who, devoured by fear and uneasiness, was beginning, in spite of himself, to listen at the door. Happily, neither of the speakers had forgotten to smother his voice, even in the most passionate outbreaks.

"What a confessor!" said the governor, forcing a laugh; "who would believe that a compulsory recluse, a man as though in the very jaws of death, could have committed crimes so numerous, and so long to tell of?"

Aramis made no reply. He was eager to leave the Bastille, where the secret which overwhelmed him seemed to double the weight of the walls. As soon as they reached Baisemeaux's quarters, "Let us proceed to business, my dear governor," said Aramis.

"Alas!" replied Baisemeaux.

"You have to ask me for my receipt for one hundred and fifty thousand livres," said the bishop.

"And to pay over the first third of the sum," added the poor governor, with a sigh, taking three steps towards his iron strong-box.

"Here is the receipt," said Aramis.

"And here is the money," returned Baisemeaux, with a threefold sigh.

"The order instructed me only to give a receipt; it said nothing about receiving the money," rejoined Aramis. "Adieu, monsieur le governeur!"

And he departed, leaving Baisemeaux almost more than stifled with joy and surprise at this regal present so liberally bestowed by the confessor extraordinary to the Bastille.

CHAPTER 2

How Mouston Had Become Fatter without Giving Porthos Notice Thereof, and of the Troubles Which Consequently Befell that Worthy Gentleman.

Since the departure of Athos for Blois, Porthos and D'Artagnan were seldom together. One was occupied with harassing duties for the king, the other had been making many purchases of furniture which he intended to forward to his estate, and by aid of which he hoped to establish in his various residences something of the courtly luxury he had witnessed in all its dazzling brightness in his majesty's society. D'Artagnan, ever faithful, one morning during an interval of service thought about Porthos, and being uneasy at not having heard anything of him for a fortnight, directed his steps towards his hotel, and pounced upon him just as he was getting up. The worthy baron had a pensive—nay, more than pensive—melancholy air. He was sitting on his bed, only half-dressed, and with legs dangling over the edge, contemplating a host of garments, which with their fringes, lace, embroidery, and slashes of ill-assorted hues, were strewed all over the floor. Porthos, sad and reflective as La Fontaine's hare, did not observe D'Artagnan's entrance, which was, moreover, screened at this moment by M. Mouston, whose personal corpulency, quite enough at any time to hide one man from another, was effectually doubled by a scarlet coat which the intendant was holding up for his master's inspection, by the sleeves, that he might the better see it all over. D'Artagnan stopped at the threshold and looked in at the pensive Porthos and then, as the sight of the innumerable garments strewing the floor caused mighty sighs to heave the bosom of that excellent gentleman, D'Artagnan thought it time to put an end to these dismal reflections, and coughed by way of announcing himself.

"Ah!" exclaimed Porthos, whose countenance brightened with joy; "ah! ah! Here is D'Artagnan. I shall then get hold of an idea!"

At these words Mouston, doubting what was going on behind him, got out of the way, smiling kindly at the friend of his master, who thus found himself freed from the material obstacle which had prevented his reaching D'Artagnan. Porthos made his sturdy knees crack again in rising, and crossing the room in two strides, found himself face to face with his friend, whom he folded to his breast with a force of affection that seemed to increase with every day. "Ah!" he repeated, "you are always welcome, dear friend; but just now you are more welcome than ever."

"But you seem to have the megrims here!" exclaimed D'Artagnan.

Porthos replied by a look expressive of dejection. "Well, then, tell me all about it, Porthos, my friend, unless it is a secret."

"In the first place," returned Porthos, "you know I have no secrets from you. This, then, is what saddens me."

"Wait a minute, Porthos; let me first get rid of all this litter of satin and velvet!"

"Oh, never mind," said Porthos, contemptuously; "it is all trash."

"Trash, Porthos! Cloth at twenty-five livres an ell! gorgeous satin! regal velvet!"

"Then you think these clothes are—"

"Splendid, Porthos, splendid! I'll wager that you alone in France have so many; and suppose you never had any more made, and were to live to be a hundred years of age, which wouldn't astonish me in the very least, you could still wear a new dress the day of your death, without being obliged to see the nose of a single tailor from now till then."

Porthos shook his head.

"Come, my friend," said D'Artagnan, "this unnatural melancholy in you frightens me. My dear Porthos, pray get it out, then. And the sooner the better."

"Yes, my friend, so I will: if, indeed, it is possible."

"Perhaps you have received bad news from Bracieux?"

"No: they have felled the wood, and it has yielded a third more than the estimate."

"Then there has been a falling-off in the pools of Pierrefonds?"

"No, my friend: they have been fished, and there is enough left to stock all the pools in the neighborhood."

"Perhaps your estate at Vallon has been destroyed by an earthquake?"

"No, my friend; on the contrary, the ground was struck with lightning a hundred paces from the chateau, and a fountain sprung up in a place entirely destitute of water."

"What in the world *is* the matter, then?"

"The fact is, I have received an invitation for the *fete* at Vaux," said Porthos, with a lugubrious expression.

"Well! do you complain of that? The king has caused a hundred mortal heart-burnings among the courtiers by refusing invitations. And so, my dear friend, you are really going to Vaux?"

"Indeed I am!"

"You will see a magnificent sight."

"Alas! I doubt it, though."

"Everything that is grand in France will be brought together there!"

"Ah!" cried Porthos, tearing out a lock of hair in his despair.

"Eh! good heavens, are you ill?" cried D'Artagnan.

"I am as firm as the Pont-Neuf! It isn't that."

"But what is it, then?"

"'Tis that I have no clothes!"

D'Artagnan stood petrified. "No clothes! Porthos, no clothes!" he cried, "when I see at least fifty suits on the floor."

"Fifty, truly; but not one which fits me!"

"What? not one that fits you? But are you not measured, then, when you give an order?"

"To be sure he is," answered Mouston; "but unfortunately *I* have gotten stouter!"

"What! *you* stouter!"

"So much so that I am now bigger than the baron. Would you believe it, monsieur?"

"*Parbleu!* it seems to me that is quite evident."

"Do you see, stupid?" said Porthos, "that is quite evident!"

"Be still, my dear Porthos," resumed D'Artagnan, becoming slightly impatient, "I don't understand why your clothes should not fit you, because Mouston has grown stouter."

"I am going to explain it," said Porthos. "You remember having related to me the story of the Roman general Antony, who had always seven wild boars kept roasting, each cooked up to a different point; so that he might be able to have his dinner at any time of the day he chose to ask for it. Well, then, I resolved, as at any time I might be invited to court to spend a week, I resolved to have always seven suits ready for the occasion."

"Capitally reasoned, Porthos—only a man must have a fortune like yours to gratify such whims. Without counting the time lost in being measured, the fashions are always changing."

"That is exactly the point," said Porthos, "in regard to which I flattered myself I had hit on a very ingenious device."

"Tell me what it is; for I don't doubt your genius."

"You remember what Mouston once was, then?"

"Yes; when he used to call himself Mousqueton."

"And you remember, too, the period when he began to grow fatter?"

"No, not exactly. I beg your pardon, my good Mouston."

"Oh! you are not in fault, monsieur," said Mouston, graciously. "You were in Paris, and as for us, we were at Pierrefonds."

"Well, well, my dear Porthos; there was a time when Mouston began to grow fat. Is that what you wished to say?"

"Yes, my friend; and I greatly rejoice over the period."

"Indeed, I believe you do," exclaimed D'Artagnan.

"You understand," continued Porthos, "what a world of trouble it spared for me."

"No, I don't—by any means."

"Look here, my friend. In the first place, as you have said, to be measured is a loss of time, even though it occur only once a fortnight. And then, one may be travelling; and then you wish to have seven suits always with you. In short, I have a horror of letting any one take my measure. Confound it! either one is a nobleman or not. To be scrutinized and scanned by a fellow who completely analyzes you, by inch and line—'tis degrading! Here, they find you too hollow; there, too prominent. They recognize your strong and weak points. See, now, when we leave the measurer's hands, we are like those strongholds whose angles and different thicknesses have been ascertained by a spy."

"In truth, my dear Porthos, you possess ideas entirely original."

"Ah! you see when a man is an engineer—"

"And has fortified Belle-Isle—'tis natural, my friend."

"Well, I had an idea, which would doubtless have proved a good one, but for Mouston's carelessness."

D'Artagnan glanced at Mouston, who replied by a slight movement of his body, as if to say, "You will see whether I am at all to blame in all this."

"I congratulated myself, then," resumed Porthos, "at seeing Mouston get fat; and I did all I could, by means of substantial feeding, to make him stout—always in the hope that he would come to equal myself in girth, and could then be measured in my stead."

"Ah!" cried D'Artagnan. "I see—that spared you both time and humiliation."

"Consider my joy when, after a year and a half's judicious feeding—for I used to feed him up myself—the fellow—"

"Oh! I lent a good hand myself, monsieur," said Mouston, humbly.

"That's true. Consider my joy when, one morning, I perceived Mouston was obliged to squeeze in, as I once did myself, to get through the little secret door that those fools of architects had made in the chamber of the late Madame du Vallon, in the chateau of Pierrefonds. And, by the way, about that door, my friend, I should like to ask you, who know everything, why these wretches of architects, who ought to have the compasses run into them, just to remind them, came to make doorways through which nobody but thin people can pass?"

"Oh, those doors," answered D'Artagnan, "were meant for gallants, and they have generally slight and slender figures."

"Madame du Vallon had no gallant!" answered Porthos, majestically.

"Perfectly true, my friend," resumed D'Artagnan; "but the architects were probably making their calculations on a basis of the probability of your marrying again."

"Ah! that is possible," said Porthos. "And now I have received an explanation of how it is that doorways are made too narrow, let us return to the subject of Mouston's fatness. But see how the two things apply to each other. I have always noticed that people's ideas run parallel. And so, observe this phenomenon, D'Artagnan. I was talking to you of Mouston, who is fat, and it led us on to Madame du Vallon—"

"Who was thin?"

"Hum! Is it not marvelous?"

"My dear friend, a *savant* of my acquaintance, M. Costar, has made the same observation as you have, and he calls the process by some Greek name which I forget."

"What! my remark is not then original?" cried Porthos, astounded. "I thought I was the discoverer."

"My friend, the fact was known before Aristotle's days— that is to say, nearly two thousand years ago."

"Well, well, 'tis no less true," said Porthos, delighted at the idea of having jumped to a conclusion so closely in agreement with the greatest sages of antiquity.

"Wonderfully—but suppose we return to Mouston. It seems to me, we have left him fattening under our very eyes."

"Yes, monsieur," said Mouston.

"Well," said Porthos, "Mouston fattened so well, that he gratified all my hopes, by reaching my standard; a fact of which I was well able to convince myself, by seeing the rascal, one day, in a waistcoat of mine, which he had turned into a coat—a waistcoat, the mere embroidery of which was worth a hundred pistoles."

"'Twas only to try it on, monsieur," said Mouston.

"From that moment I determined to put Mouston in communication with my tailors, and to have him measured instead of myself."

"A capital idea, Porthos; but Mouston is a foot and a half shorter than you."

"Exactly! They measured him down to the ground, and the end of the skirt came just below my knee."

"What a marvelous man you are, Porthos! Such a thing could happen only to you."

"Ah! yes; pay your compliments; you have ample grounds to go upon. It was exactly at that time—that is to say, nearly two years and a half ago—that I set out for Belle-Isle, instructing Mouston (so as always to have, in every event, a pattern of every fashion) to have a coat made for himself every month."

"And did Mouston neglect complying with your instructions? Ah! that was anything but right, Mouston."

"No, monsieur, quite the contrary; quite the contrary!"

"No, he never forgot to have his coats made; but he forgot to inform me that he had got stouter!"

"But it was not my fault, monsieur! your tailor never told me."

"And this to such an extent, monsieur," continued Porthos, "that the fellow in two years has gained eighteen inches in girth, and so my last dozen coats are all too large, from a foot to a foot and a half."

"But the rest; those which were made when you were of the same size?"

"They are no longer the fashion, my dear friend. Were I to put them on, I should look like a fresh arrival from Siam; and as though I had been two years away from court."

"I understand your difficulty. You have how many new suits? nine? thirty-six? and yet not one to wear. Well, you must have a thirty-seventh made, and give the thirty-six to Mouston."

"Ah! monsieur!" said Mouston, with a gratified air. "The truth is, that monsieur has always been very generous to me."

"Do you mean to insinuate that I hadn't that idea, or that I was deterred by the expense? But it wants only two days to the *fete*; I received the invitation yesterday; made

Mouston post hither with my wardrobe, and only this morning discovered my misfortune; and from now till the day after to-morrow, there isn't a single fashionable tailor who will undertake to make me a suit."

"That is to say, one covered all over with gold, isn't it?"

"I wish it so! undoubtedly, all over."

"Oh, we shall manage it. You won't leave for three days. The invitations are for Wednesday, and this is only Sunday morning."

"'Tis true; but Aramis has strongly advised me to be at Vaux twenty-four hours beforehand."

"How, Aramis?"

"Yes, it was Aramis who brought me the invitation."

"Ah! to be sure, I see. You are invited on the part of M. Fouquet?"

"By no means! by the king, dear friend. The letter bears the following as large as life: 'M. le Baron du Vallon is informed that the king has condescended to place him on the invitation list—'"

"Very good; but you leave with M. Fouquet?"

"And when I think," cried Porthos, stamping on the floor, "when I think I shall have no clothes, I am ready to burst with rage! I should like to strangle somebody or smash something!"

"Neither strangle anybody nor smash anything, Porthos; I will manage it all; put on one of your thirty-six suits, and come with me to a tailor."

"Pooh! my agent has seen them all this morning."

"Even M. Percerin?"

"Who is M. Percerin?"

"Oh! only the king's tailor!"

"Oh, ah, yes," said Porthos, who wished to appear to know the king's tailor, but now heard his name mentioned for the first time; "to M. Percerin's, by Jove! I was afraid he would be too busy."

"Doubtless he will be; but be at ease, Porthos; he will do for me what he wouldn't do for another. Only you must allow yourself to be measured!"

"Ah!" said Porthos, with a sigh, "'tis vexatious, but what would you have me do?"

"Do? As others do; as the king does."

"What! do they measure the king, too? does he put up with it?"

"The king is a beau, my good friend, and so are you, too, whatever you may say about it."

Porthos smiled triumphantly. "Let us go to the king's tailor," he said; "and since he measures the king, I think, by my faith, I may do worse than allow him to measure *me!*"

CHAPTER 3

Who Messire Jean Percerin Was.

The king's tailor, Messire Jean Percerin, occupied a rather large house in the Rue St. Honore, near the Rue de l'Arbre Sec. He was a man of great taste in elegant stuffs, embroideries, and velvets, being hereditary tailor to the king. The preferment of his house reached as far back as the time of Charles IX.; from whose reign dated, as we know, fancy in *bravery* difficult enough to gratify. The Percerin of that period was a Huguenot, like Ambrose Pare, and had been spared by the Queen of Navarre, the beautiful Margot, as they used to write and say, too, in those days; because, in sooth, he was the only one who could make for her those wonderful riding-habits which she so loved to wear, seeing that they were marvelously well suited to hide certain anatomical defects, which the Queen of Navarre used very studiously to conceal. Percerin being saved, made, out of gratitude, some beautiful black bodices, very inexpensively indeed, for Queen Catherine, who ended by being pleased at the preservation of a Huguenot people, on whom she had long looked with detestation. But Percerin was a very prudent man; and having heard it said that there was no more dangerous sign for a Protestant than to be smiled upon by Catherine, and having observed that her smiles were more frequent than usual, he speedily turned

Catholic with all his family; and having thus become irreproachable, attained the lofty position of master tailor to the Crown of France. Under Henry III., gay king as he was, this position was a grand as the height of one of the loftiest peaks of the Cordilleras. Now Percerin had been a clever man all his life, and by way of keeping up his reputation beyond the grave, took very good care not to make a bad death of it, and so contrived to die very skillfully; and that at the very moment he felt his powers of invention declining. He left a son and a daughter, both worthy of the name they were called upon to bear; the son, a cutter as unerring and exact as the square rule; the daughter, apt at embroidery, and at designing ornaments. The marriage of Henry IV. and Marie de Medici, and the exquisite court-mourning for the afore-mentioned queen, together with a few words let fall by M. de Bassompiere, king of the *beaux* of the period, made the fortune of the second generation of Percerins. M. Concino Concini, and his wife Galligai, who subsequently shone at the French court, sought to Italianize the fashion, and introduced some Florentine tailors; but Percerin, touched to the quick in his patriotism and his self-esteem, entirely defeated these foreigners, and that so well that Concino was the first to give up his compatriots, and held the French tailor in such esteem that he would never employ any other, and thus wore a doublet of his on the very day that Vitry blew out his brains with a pistol at the Pont du Louvre.

And so it was a doublet issuing from M. Percerin's workshop, which the Parisians rejoiced in hacking into so many pieces with the living human body it contained. Notwithstanding the favor Concino Concini had shown Percerin, the king, Louis XIII., had the generosity to bear no malice to his tailor, and to retain him in his service. At the time that Louis the Just afforded this great example of equity, Percerin had brought up two sons, one of whom made his *debut* at the marriage of Anne of Austria, invented that

43

admirable Spanish costume, in which Richelieu danced a saraband, made the costumes for the tragedy of "Mirame," and stitched on to Buckingham's mantle those famous pearls which were destined to be scattered about the pavements of the Louvre. A man becomes easily notable who has made the dresses of a Duke of Buckingham, a M. de Cinq-Mars, a Mademoiselle Ninon, a M. de Beaufort, and a Marion de Lorme. And thus Percerin the third had attained the summit of his glory when his father died. This same Percerin III., old, famous and wealthy, yet further dressed Louis XIV.; and having no son, which was a great cause of sorrow to him, seeing that with himself his dynasty would end, he had brought up several hopeful pupils. He possessed a carriage, a country house, men-servants the tallest in Paris; and by special authority from Louis XIV., a pack of hounds. He worked for MM. de Lyonne and Letellier, under a sort of patronage; but politic man as he was, and versed in state secrets, he never succeeded in fitting M. Colbert. This is beyond explanation; it is a matter for guessing or for intuition. Great geniuses of every kind live on unseen, intangible ideas; they act without themselves knowing why. The great Percerin (for, contrary to the rule of dynasties, it was, above all, the last of the Percerins who deserved the name of Great), the great Percerin was inspired when he cut a robe for the queen, or a coat for the king; he could mount a mantle for Monsieur, the clock of a stocking for Madame; but, in spite of his supreme talent, he could never hit off anything approaching a creditable fit for M. Colbert. "That man," he used often to say, "is beyond my art; my needle can never dot him down." We need scarcely say that Percerin was M. Fouquet's tailor, and that the super-intendent highly esteemed him. M. Percerin was nearly eighty years old, nevertheless still fresh, and at the same time so dry, the courtiers used to say, that he was positively brittle. His renown and his fortune were great enough for M. le Prince, that king of fops, to take his arm when talking over the fashions; and for those least eager to pay never to dare to leave their accounts in arrear with him; for Master Percerin would for the first time make clothes upon credit, but the second never, unless paid for the former order.

It is easy to see at once that a tailor of such renown, instead of running after customers, made difficulties about obliging any fresh ones. And so Percerin declined to fit *bourgeois*, or those who had but recently obtained patents of nobility. A story used to circulate that even M. de Mazarin, in exchange for Percerin supplying him with a full suit of ceremonial vestments as cardinal, one fine day slipped letters of nobility into his pocket.

It was to the house of this grand llama of tailors that D'Artagnan took the despairing Porthos; who, as they were going along, said to his friend, "Take care, my good D'Artagnan, not to compromise the dignity of a man such as I am with the arrogance of this Percerin, who will, I expect, be very impertinent; for I give you notice, my friend, that if he is wanting in respect I will infallibly chastise him."

"Presented by me," replied D'Artagnan, "you have nothing to fear, even though you were what you are not."

"Ah! 'tis because—"

"What? Have you anything against Percerin, Porthos?"

"I think that I once sent Mouston to a fellow of that name."

"And then?"

"The fellow refused to supply me."

"Oh, a misunderstanding, no doubt, which it will be now exceedingly easy to set right. Mouston must have made a mistake."

"Perhaps."

"He has confused the names."

"Possibly. That rascal Mouston never can remember names."

"I will take it all upon myself."

"Very good."

"Stop the carriage, Porthos; here we are."

"Here! how here? We are at the Halles; and you told me the house was at the corner of the Rue de l'Arbre Sec."

"'Tis true, but look."

"Well, I do look, and I see—"

"What?"

"*Pardieu!* that we are at the Halles!"

"You do not, I suppose, want our horses to clamber up on the roof of the carriage in front of us?"

"No."

"Nor the carriage in front of us to mount on top of the one in front of it. Nor that the second should be driven over the roofs of the thirty or forty others which have arrived before us."

"No, you are right, indeed. What a number of people! And what are they all about?"

"'Tis very simple. They are waiting their turn."

"Bah! Have the comedians of the Hotel de Bourgogne shifted their quarters?"

"No; their turn to obtain an entrance to M. Percerin's house."

"And we are going to wait too?"

"Oh, we shall show ourselves prompter and not so proud."

"What are we to do, then?"

"Get down, pass through the footmen and lackeys, and enter the tailor's house, which I will answer for our doing, if you go first."

"Come along, then," said Porthos.

They accordingly alighted and made their way on foot towards the establishment. The cause of the confusion was that M. Percerin's doors were closed, while a servant, standing before them, was explaining to the illustrious customers of the illustrious tailor that just then M. Percerin could not receive anybody. It was bruited about outside still, on the authority of what the great lackey had told some great noble whom he favored, in confidence, that M. Percerin was engaged on five costumes for the king, and that, owing to the urgency of the case, he was meditating in his office on the ornaments, colors, and cut of these five suits. Some, contented with this reason, went away again, contented to repeat the tale to others, but others, more tenacious, insisted on having the doors opened, and among these last three Blue Ribbons, intended to take parts in a ballet, which would inevitably fail unless the said three had their costumes shaped by the very hand of the great Percerin himself. D'Artagnan, pushing on Porthos, who scattered the groups of people right and left, succeeded in gaining the counter, behind which the journeyman tailors were doing their best to answer queries. (We forgot to mention that at the door they wanted to put off Porthos like the rest, but D'Artagnan, showing himself, pronounced merely these words, "The king's order," and was let in with his friend.) The poor fellows had enough to do, and did their best, to reply to the demands of the customers in the absence of their master, leaving off drawing a stitch to knit a sentence; and when wounded pride, or disappointed expectation, brought down upon them too cutting a rebuke, he who was attacked made a dive and disappeared under the counter. The line of discontented lords formed a truly remarkable picture. Our captain of musketeers, a man of sure and rapid observation, took it all in at a glance; and having run over the groups, his eye rested on a man in front of him. This man, seated upon a stool, scarcely showed his head above the counter that sheltered him. He was about forty years of age, with a melancholy aspect, pale face, and soft luminous eyes. He was looking at D'Artagnan and the rest, with his chin resting upon his hand, like a calm and inquiring amateur. Only on perceiving, and doubtless recognizing, our captain, he pulled his hat down over his eyes. It was this action, perhaps, that attracted

D'Artagnan's attention. If so, the gentleman who had pulled down his hat produced an effect entirely different from what he had desired. In other respects his costume was plain, and his hair evenly cut enough for customers, who were not close observers, to take him for a mere tailor's apprentice, perched behind the board, and carefully stitching cloth or velvet. Nevertheless, this man held up his head too often to be very productively employed with his fingers. D'Artagnan was not deceived,—not he; and he saw at once that if this man was working at anything, it certainly was not at velvet.

"Eh!" said he, addressing this man, "and so you have become a tailor's boy, Monsieur Moliere!"

"Hush, M. d'Artagnan!" replied the man, softly, "you will make them recognize me."

"Well, and what harm?"

"The fact is, there is no harm, but—"

"You were going to say there is no good in doing it either, is it not so?"

"Alas! no; for I was occupied in examining some excellent figures."

"Go on—go on, Monsieur Moliere. I quite understand the interest you take in the plates—I will not disturb your studies."

"Thank you."

"But on one condition; that you tell me where M. Percerin really is."

"Oh! willingly; in his own room. Only—"

"Only that one can't enter it?"

"Unapproachable."

"For everybody?"

"Everybody. He brought me here so that I might be at my ease to make my observations, and then he went away."

"Well, my dear Monsieur Moliere, but you will go and tell him I am here."

"I!" exclaimed Moliere, in the tone of a courageous dog,

from which you snatch the bone it has legitimately gained; "I disturb myself! Ah! Monsieur d'Artagnan, how hard you are upon me!"

"If you don't go directly and tell M. Percerin that I am here, my dear Moliere," said D'Artagnan, in a low tone, "I warn you of one thing: that I won't exhibit to you the friend I have brought with me."

Moliere indicated Porthos by an imperceptible gesture, "This gentleman, is it not?"

"Yes."

Moliere fixed upon Porthos one of those looks which penetrate the minds and hearts of men. The subject doubtless appeared a very promising one, for he immediately rose and led the way into the adjoining chamber.

CHAPTER 4

The Patterns.

During all this time the noble mob was slowly heaving away, leaving at every angle of the counter either a murmur or a menace, as the waves leave foam or scattered seaweed on the sands, when they retire with the ebbing tide. In about ten minutes Moliere reappeared, making another sign to D'Artagnan from under the hangings. The latter hurried after him, with Porthos in the rear, and after threading a labyrinth of corridors, introduced him to M. Percerin's room. The old man, with his sleeves turned up, was gathering up in folds a piece of gold-flowered brocade, so as the better to exhibit its luster. Perceiving D'Artagnan, he put the silk aside, and came to meet him, by no means radiant with joy, and by no means courteous, but, take it altogether, in a tolerably civil manner.

"The captain of the king's musketeers will excuse me, I am sure, for I am engaged."

"Eh! yes, on the king's costumes; I know that, my dear Monsieur Percerin. You are making three, they tell me."

"Five, my dear sir, five."

"Three or five, 'tis all the same to me, my dear monsieur; and I know that you will make them most exquisitely."

"Yes, I know. Once made they will be the most beautiful in the world, I do not deny it; but that they may be the most beautiful in the world, they must first be made; and to do this, captain, I am pressed for time."

"Oh, bah! there are two days yet; 'tis much more than you require, Monsieur Percerin," said D'Artagnan, in the coolest possible manner.

Percerin raised his head with the air of a man little accustomed to be contradicted, even in his whims; but D'Artagnan did not pay the least attention to the airs which the illustrious tailor began to assume.

"My dear M. Percerin," he continued, "I bring you a customer."

"Ah! ah!" exclaimed Percerin, crossly.

"M. le Baron du Vallon de Bracieux de Pierrefonds," continued D'Artagnan. Percerin attempted a bow, which found no favor in the eyes of the terrible Porthos, who, from his first entry into the room, had been regarding the tailor askance.

"A very good friend of mine," concluded D'Artagnan.

"I will attend to monsieur," said Percerin, "but later."

"Later? but when?"

"When I have time."

"You have already told my valet as much," broke in Porthos, discontentedly.

"Very likely," said Percerin; "I am nearly always pushed for time."

"My friend," returned Porthos, sententiously, "there is always time to be found when one chooses to seek it."

Percerin turned crimson; an ominous sign indeed in old men blanched by age.

"Monsieur is quite at liberty to confer his custom elsewhere."

"Come, come, Percerin," interposed D'Artagnan, "you are not in a good temper to-day. Well, I will say one more word to you, which will bring you on your knees; monsieur is not only a friend of mine, but more, a friend of M. Fouquet's."

"Ah! ah!" exclaimed the tailor, "that is another thing." Then turning to Porthos, "Monsieur le baron is attached to the superintendent?" he inquired.

"I am attached to myself," shouted Porthos, at the very moment that the tapestry was raised to introduce a new speaker in the dialogue. Moliere was all observation, D'Artagnan laughed, Porthos swore.

"My dear Percerin," said D'Artagnan, "you will make a dress for the baron. 'Tis I who ask you."

"To you I will not say nay, captain."

"But that is not all; you will make it for him at once."

"'Tis impossible within eight days."

"That, then, is as much as to refuse, because the dress is wanted for the *fete* at Vaux."

"I repeat that it is impossible," returned the obstinate old man.

"By no means, dear Monsieur Percerin, above all if *I* ask you," said a mild voice at the door, a silvery voice which made D'Artagnan prick up his ears. It was the voice of Aramis.

"Monsieur d'Herblay!" cried the tailor.

"Aramis," murmured D'Artagnan.

"Ah! our bishop!" said Porthos.

"Good morning, D'Artagnan; good morning, Porthos; good-morning, my dear friends," said Aramis. "Come, come, M. Percerin, make the baron's dress; and I will answer for it you will gratify M. Fouquet." And he accompanied the words with a sign, which seemed to say, "Agree, and dismiss them."

It appeared that Aramis had over Master Percerin an influence superior even to D'Artagnan's, for the tailor bowed in assent, and turning round upon Porthos, said, "Go and get measured on the other side."

Porthos colored in a formidable manner. D'Artagnan saw the storm coming, and addressing Moliere, said to him, in an undertone, "You see before you, my dear monsieur, a man who considers himself disgraced, if you measure the flesh and bones that Heaven has given him; study this type for me, Master Aristophanes, and profit by it."

Moliere had no need of encouragement, and his gaze dwelt long and keenly on the Baron Porthos. "Monsieur," he said, "if you will come with me, I will make them take your measure without touching you."

"Oh!" said Porthos, "how do you make that out, my friend?"

"I say that they shall apply neither line nor rule to the seams of your dress. It is a new method we have invented for measuring people of quality, who are too sensitive to allow low-born fellows to touch them. We know some susceptible persons who will not put up with being measured, a process which, as I think, wounds the natural dignity of a man; and if perchance monsieur should be one of these—"

"*Corboeuf!* I believe I am too!"

"Well, that is a capital and most consolatory coincidence, and you shall have the benefit of our invention."

"But how in the world can it be done?" asked Porthos, delighted.

"Monsieur," said Moliere, bowing, "if you will deign to follow me, you will see."

Aramis observed this scene with all his eyes. Perhaps he fancied from D'Artagnan's liveliness that he would leave with Porthos, so as not to lose the conclusion of a scene well begun. But, clear-sighted as he was, Aramis deceived himself. Porthos and Moliere left together: D'Artagnan remained with Percerin. Why? From curiosity, doubtless; probably to enjoy a little longer the society of his good friend Aramis. As Moliere and Porthos disappeared, D'Artagnan drew near the bishop of Vannes, a proceeding which appeared particularly to disconcert him.

"A dress for you, also, is it not, my friend?"

Aramis smiled. "No," said he.

"You will go to Vaux, however?"

"I shall go, but without a new dress. You forget, dear D'Artagnan, that a poor bishop of Vannes is not rich enough to have new dresses for every *fete*."

"Bah!" said the musketeer, laughing, "and do we write no more poems now, either?"

"Oh! D'Artagnan," exclaimed Aramis, "I have long ago given up all such tomfoolery."

"True," repeated D'Artagnan, only half convinced. As for Percerin, he was once more absorbed in contemplation of the brocades.

"Don't you perceive," said Aramis, smiling, "that we are greatly boring this good gentleman, my dear D'Artagnan?"

"Ah! ah!" murmured the musketeer, aside; "that is, I am boring you, my friend." Then aloud, "Well, then, let us leave; I have no further business here, and if you are as disengaged as I, Aramis—"

"No, not I—I wished—"

"Ah! you had something particular to say to M. Percerin? Why did you not tell me so at once?"

"Something particular, certainly," repeated Aramis, "but not for you, D'Artagnan. But, at the same time, I hope you will believe that I can never have anything so particular to say that a friend like you may not hear it."

"Oh, no, no! I am going," said D'Artagnan, imparting to his voice an evident tone of curiosity; for Aramis's annoyance, well dissembled as it was, had not a whit escaped him; and he knew that, in that impenetrable mind, every thing, even the most apparently trivial, was designed to some end; an unknown one, but an end that, from the knowledge he had of his friend's character, the musketeer felt must be important.

On his part, Aramis saw that D'Artagnan was not without suspicion, and pressed him. "Stay, by all means," he said, "this is what it is." Then turning towards the tailor, "My dear

Percerin," said he,—"I am even very happy that you are here, D'Artagnan."

"Oh, indeed," exclaimed the Gascon, for the third time, even less deceived this time than before.

Percerin never moved. Aramis roused him violently, by snatching from his hands the stuff upon which he was engaged. "My dear Percerin," said he, "I have, near hand, M. Lebrun, one of M. Fouquet's painters."

"Ah, very good," thought D'Artagnan; "but why Lebrun?"

Aramis looked at D'Artagnan, who seemed to be occupied with an engraving of Mark Antony. "And you wish that I should make him a dress, similar to those of the Epicureans?" answered Percerin. And while saying this, in an absent manner, the worthy tailor endeavored to recapture his piece of brocade.

"An Epicurean's dress?" asked D'Artagnan, in a tone of inquiry.

"I see," said Aramis, with a most engaging smile, "it is written that our dear D'Artagnan shall know all our secrets this evening. Yes, friend, you have surely heard speak of M. Fouquet's Epicureans, have you not?"

"Undoubtedly. Is it not a kind of poetical society, of which La Fontaine, Loret, Pelisson, and Moliere are members, and which holds its sittings at Saint-Mande?"

"Exactly so. Well, we are going to put our poets in uniform, and enroll them in a regiment for the king."

"Oh, very well, I understand; a surprise M. Fouquet is getting up for the king. Be at ease; if that is the secret about M. Lebrun, I will not mention it."

"Always agreeable, my friend. No, Monsieur Lebrun has nothing to do with this part of it; the secret which concerns him is far more important than the other."

"Then, if it is so important as all that, I prefer not to know it," said D'Artagnan, making a show of departure.

"Come in, M. Lebrun, come in," said Aramis, opening

a side-door with his right hand, and holding back D'Artagnan with his left.

"I'faith, I too, am quite in the dark," quoth Percerin.

Aramis took an "opportunity," as is said in theatrical matters.

"My dear M. de Percerin," Aramis continued, "you are making five dresses for the king, are you not? One in brocade; one in hunting-cloth; one in velvet; one in satin; and one in Florentine stuffs."

"Yes; but how—do you know all that, monseigneur?" said Percerin, astounded.

"It is all very simple, my dear monsieur; there will be a hunt, a banquet, concert, promenade and reception; these five kinds of dress are required by etiquette."

"You know everything, monseigneur!"

"And a thing or two in addition," muttered D'Artagnan.

"But," cried the tailor, in triumph, "what you do not know, monseigneur—prince of the church though you are— what nobody will know—what only the king, Mademoiselle de la Valliere, and myself do know, is the color of the materials and nature of the ornaments, and the cut, the *ensemble*, the finish of it all!"

"Well," said Aramis, "that is precisely what I have come to ask you, dear Percerin."

"Ah, bah!" exclaimed the tailor, terrified, though Aramis had pronounced these words in his softest and most honeyed tones. The request appeared, on reflection, so exaggerated, so ridiculous, so monstrous to M. Percerin that first he laughed to himself, then aloud, and finished with a shout. D'Artagnan followed his example, not because he found the matter so "very funny," but in order not to allow Aramis to cool.

"At the outset, I appear to be hazarding an absurd question, do I not?" said Aramis. "But D'Artagnan, who is incarnate wisdom itself, will tell you that I could not do otherwise than ask you this."

"Let us see," said the attentive musketeer, perceiving with his wonderful instinct that they had only been skirmishing till now, and that the hour of battle was approaching.

"Let us see," said Percerin, incredulously.

"Why, now," continued Aramis, "does M. Fouquet give the king a *fete?*—Is it not to please him?"

"Assuredly," said Percerin. D'Artagnan nodded assent.

"By delicate attentions? by some happy device? by a succession of surprises, like that of which we were talking?—the enrolment of our Epicureans."

"Admirable."

"Well, then; this is the surprise we intend. M. Lebrun here is a man who draws most excellently."

"Yes," said Percerin; "I have seen his pictures, and observed that his dresses were highly elaborated. That is why I at once agreed to make him a costume—whether to agree with those of the Epicureans, or an original one."

"My dear monsieur, we accept your offer, and shall presently avail ourselves of it; but just now, M. Lebrun is not in want of the dresses you will make for himself, but of those you are making for the king."

Percerin made a bound backwards, which D'Artagnan—calmest and most appreciative of men, did not consider overdone, so many strange and startling aspects wore the proposal which Aramis had just hazarded. "The king's dresses! Give the king's dresses to any mortal whatever! Oh! for once, monseigneur, your grace is mad!" cried the poor tailor in extremity.

"Help me now, D'Artagnan," said Aramis, more and more calm and smiling. "Help me now to persuade monsieur, for *you* understand; do you not?"

"Eh! eh!—not exactly, I declare."

"What! you do not understand that M. Fouquet wishes to afford the king the surprise of finding his portrait on his arrival at Vaux; and that the portrait, which be a striking resemblance, ought to be dressed exactly as the king will be on the day it is shown?"

"Oh! yes, yes," said the musketeer, nearly convinced, so plausible was this reasoning. "Yes, my dear Aramis, you are right; it is a happy idea. I will wager it is one of your own, Aramis."

"Well, I don't know," replied the bishop; "either mine or M. Fouquet's." Then scanning Percerin, after noticing D'Artagnan's hesitation, "Well, Monsieur Percerin," he asked, "what do you say to this?"

"I say, that—"

"That you are, doubtless, free to refuse. I know well—and I by no means count upon compelling you, my dear monsieur. I will say more, I even understand all the delicacy you feel in taking up with M. Fouquet's idea; you dread appearing to flatter the king. A noble spirit, M. Percerin, a noble spirit!" The tailor stammered. "It would, indeed, be a very pretty compliment to pay the young prince," continued Aramis; "but as the surintendant told me, 'if Percerin refuse, tell him that it will not at all lower him in my opinion, and I shall always esteem him, only—'"

"'Only?'" repeated Percerin, rather troubled.

"'Only,'" continued Aramis, "'I shall be compelled to say to the king,'—you understand, my dear Monsieur Percerin, that these are M. Fouquet's words,—'I shall be constrained to say to the king, "Sire, I had intended to present your majesty with your portrait, but owing to a feeling of delicacy, slightly exaggerated perhaps, although creditable, M. Percerin opposed the project."'"

"Opposed!" cried the tailor, terrified at the responsibility which would weigh upon him; "I to oppose the desire, the will of M. Fouquet when he is seeking to please the king! Oh, what a hateful word you have uttered, monseigneur. Oppose! Oh, 'tis not I who said it, Heaven have mercy on me. I call the captain of the musketeers to witness it! Is it not true, Monsieur d'Artagnan, that I have opposed nothing?"

D'Artagnan made a sign indicating that he wished to remain neutral. He felt that there was an intrigue at the bottom of it, whether comedy or tragedy; he was at his wit's end at not being able to fathom it, but in the meanwhile wished to keep clear.

But already Percerin, goaded by the idea that the king was to be told he stood in the way of a pleasant surprise, had offered Lebrun a chair, and proceeded to bring from a wardrobe four magnificent dresses, the fifth being still in the workmen's hands; and these masterpieces he successively fitted upon four lay figures, which, imported into France in the time of Concini, had been given to Percerin II. by Marshal d'Onore, after the discomfiture of the Italian tailors ruined in their competition. The painter set to work to draw and then to paint the dresses. But Aramis, who was closely watching all the phases of his toil, suddenly stopped him.

"I think you have not quite got it, my dear Lebrun," he said; "your colors will deceive you, and on canvas we shall lack that exact resemblance which is absolutely requisite. Time is necessary for attentively observing the finer shades."

"Quite true," said Percerin, "but time is wanting, and on that head, you will agree with me, monseigneur, I can do nothing."

"Then the affair will fail," said Aramis, quietly, "and that because of a want of precision in the colors."

Nevertheless Lebrun went on copying the materials and ornaments with the closest fidelity—a process which Aramis watched with ill-concealed impatience.

"What in the world, now, is the meaning of this imbroglio?" the musketeer kept saying to himself.

"That will never do," said Aramis: "M. Lebrun, close your box, and roll up your canvas."

"But, monsieur," cried the vexed painter, "the light is abominable here."

"An idea, M. Lebrun, an idea! If we had a pattern of the materials, for example, and with time, and a better light—"

"Oh, then," cried Lebrun, "I would answer for the effect."

"Good!" said D'Artagnan, "this ought to be the knotty point of the whole thing; they want a pattern of each of the materials. *Mordioux!* Will this Percerin give in now?"

Percerin, beaten from his last retreat, and duped, moreover, by the feigned good-nature of Aramis, cut out five patterns and handed them to the bishop of Vannes.

"I like this better. That is your opinion, is it not?" said Aramis to D'Artagnan.

"My dear Aramis," said D'Artagnan, "my opinion is that you are always the same."

"And, consequently, always your friend," said the bishop in a charming tone.

"Yes, yes," said D'Artagnan, aloud; then, in a low voice, "If I am your dupe, double Jesuit that you are, I will not be your accomplice; and to prevent it, 'tis time I left this place.— Adieu, Aramis," he added aloud, "adieu; I am going to rejoin Porthos."

"Then wait for me," said Aramis, pocketing the patterns, "for I have done, and shall be glad to say a parting word to our dear old friend."

Lebrun packed up his paints and brushes, Percerin put back the dresses into the closet, Aramis put his hand on his pocket to assure himself the patterns were secure,—and they all left the study.

CHAPTER 5

Where, Probably, Moliere Obtained His
First Idea of the Bourgeois Gentilhomme.

D'Artagnan found Porthos in the adjoining chamber; but
no longer an irritated Porthos, or a disappointed Porthos,
but Porthos radiant, blooming, fascinating, and chattering
with Moliere, who was looking upon him with a species of
idolatry, and as a man would who had not only never seen
anything greater, but not even ever anything so great.
Aramis went straight up to Porthos and offered him his
white hand, which lost itself in the gigantic clasp of his old
friend,—an operation which Aramis never hazarded without
a certain uneasiness. But the friendly pressure having been
performed not too painfully for him, the bishop of Vannes
passed over to Moliere.

"Well, monsieur," said he, "will you come with me to
Saint-Mande?"

"I will go anywhere you like, monseigneur," answered
Moliere.

"To Saint-Mande!" cried Porthos, surprised at seeing the
proud bishop of Vannes fraternizing with a journeyman tailor.
"What, Aramis, are you going to take this gentleman to
Saint-Mande?"

"Yes," said Aramis, smiling, "our work is pressing."

"And besides, my dear Porthos," continued D'Artagnan, "M. Moliere is not altogether what he seems."

"In what way?" asked Porthos.

"Why, this gentleman is one of M. Percerin's chief clerks, and is expected at Saint-Mande to try on the dresses which M. Fouquet has ordered for the Epicureans."

"'Tis precisely so," said Moliere.

"Yes, monsieur."

"Come, then, my dear M. Moliere," said Aramis, "that is, if you have done with M. du Vallon."

"We have finished," replied Porthos.

"And you are satisfied?" asked D'Artagnan.

"Completely so," replied Porthos.

Moliere took his leave of Porthos with much ceremony, and grasped the hand which the captain of the musketeers furtively offered him.

"Pray, monsieur," concluded Porthos, mincingly, "above all, be exact."

"You will have your dress the day after to-morrow, monsieur le baron," answered Moliere. And he left with Aramis.

Then D'Artagnan, taking Porthos's arm, "What has this tailor done for you, my dear Porthos," he asked, "that you are so pleased with him?"

"What has he done for me, my friend! done for me!" cried Porthos, enthusiastically.

"Yes, I ask you, what has he done for you?"

"My friend, he has done that which no tailor ever yet accomplished: he has taken my measure without touching me!"

"Ah, bah! tell me how he did it."

"First, then, they went, I don't know where, for a number of lay figures, of all heights and sizes, hoping there would be one to suit mine, but the largest—that of the drum-major of the Swiss guard—was two inches too short, and a half foot too narrow in the chest."

"Indeed!"

"It is exactly as I tell you, D'Artagnan; but he is a great man, or at the very least a great tailor, is this M. Moliere. He was not at all put at fault by the circumstance."

"What did he do, then?"

"Oh! it is a very simple matter. I'faith, 'tis an unheard-of thing that people should have been so stupid as not to have discovered this method from the first. What annoyance and humiliation they would have spared me!"

"Not to mention of the costumes, my dear Porthos."

"Yes, thirty dresses."

"Well, my dear Porthos, come, tell me M. Moliere's plan."

"Moliere? You call him so, do you? I shall make a point of recollecting his name."

"Yes; or Poquelin, if you prefer that."

"No; I like Moliere best. When I wish to recollect his name, I shall think of *voliere* [an aviary]; and as I have one at Pierrefonds—"

"Capital!" returned D'Artagnan. "And M. Moliere's plan?"

"'Tis this: instead of pulling me to pieces, as all these rascals do—of making me bend my back, and double my joints— all of them low and dishonorable practices—" D'Artagnan made a sign of approbation with his head. "'Monsieur,' he said to me," continued Porthos, "'a gentleman ought to measure himself. Do me the pleasure to draw near this glass;' and I drew near the glass. I must own I did not exactly understand what this good M. Voliere wanted with me."

"Moliere!"

"Ah! yes, Moliere—Moliere. And as the fear of being measured still possessed me, 'Take care,' said I to him, 'what you are going to do with me; I am very ticklish, I warn you.' But he, with his soft voice (for he is a courteous fellow, we must admit, my friend), he with his soft voice, 'Monsieur,' said he, 'that your dress may fit you well, it must be made according to your figure. Your figure is exactly reflected in this mirror. We shall take the measure of this reflection.'"

"In fact," said D'Artagnan, "you saw yourself in the glass; but where did they find one in which you could see your whole figure?"

"My good friend, it is the very glass in which the king is used to look to see himself."

"Yes; but the king is a foot and a half shorter than you are."

"Ah! well, I know not how that may be; it is, no doubt, a cunning way of flattering the king; but the looking-glass was too large for me. 'Tis true that its height was made up of three Venetian plates of glass, placed one above another, and its breadth of three similar parallelograms in juxtaposition."

"Oh, Porthos! what excellent words you have command of. Where in the word did you acquire such a voluminous vocabulary?"

"At Belle-Isle. Aramis and I had to use such words in our strategic studies and castramentative experiments."

D'Artagnan recoiled, as though the sesquipedalian syllables had knocked the breath out of his body.

"Ah! very good. Let us return to the looking-glass, my friend."

"Then, this good M. Voliere—"

"Moliere."

"Yes—Moliere—you are right. You will see now, my dear friend, that I shall recollect his name quite well. This excellent M. Moliere set to work tracing out lines on the mirror, with a piece of Spanish chalk, following in all the make of my arms and my shoulders, all the while expounding this maxim, which I thought admirable: 'It is advisable that a dress should not incommode its wearer.'"

"In reality," said D'Artagnan, "that is an excellent maxim, which is, unfortunately, seldom carried out in practice."

"That is why I found it all the more astonishing, when he expatiated upon it."

"Ah! he expatiated?"

"*Parbleu!*"

"Let me hear his theory."

"'Seeing that,' he continued, 'one may, in awkward circumstances, or in a troublesome position, have one's doublet on one's shoulder, and not desire to take one's doublet off—'"

"True," said D'Artagnan.

"'And so,' continued M. Voliere—"

"Moliere."

"Moliere, yes. 'And so,' went on M. Moliere, 'you want to draw your sword, monsieur, and you have your doublet on your back. What do you do?'

"'I take it off,' I answered.

"'Well, no,' he replied.

"'How no?'

"'I say that the dress should be so well made, that it will in no way encumber you, even in drawing your sword.'

"'Ah, ah!'

"'Throw yourself on guard,' pursued he.

"I did it with such wondrous firmness, that two panes of glass burst out of the window.

"''Tis nothing, nothing,' said he. 'Keep your position.'

"I raised my left arm in the air, the forearm gracefully bent, the ruffle drooping, and my wrist curved, while my right arm, half extended, securely covered my wrist with the elbow, and my breast with the wrist."

"Yes," said D'Artagnan, "'tis the true guard—the academic guard."

"You have said the very word, dear friend. In the meanwhile, Voliere—"

"Moliere."

"Hold! I should certainly, after all, prefer to call him—what did you say his other name was?"

"Poquelin."

"I prefer to call him Poquelin."

"And how will you remember this name better than the other?"

"You understand, he calls himself Poquelin, does he not?"

"Yes."

"If I were to call to mind Madame Coquenard."

"Good."

"And change *Coc* into *Poc*, *nard* into *lin*; and instead of Coquenard I shall have Poquelin."

"'Tis wonderful," cried D'Artagnan, astounded. "Go on, my friend, I am listening to you with admiration."

"This Coquelin sketched my arm on the glass."

"I beg your pardon—Poquelin."

"What did I say, then?"

"You said Coquelin."

"Ah! true. This Poquelin, then, sketched my arm on the glass; but he took his time over it; he kept looking at me a good deal. The fact is, that I must have been looking particularly handsome."

"'Does it weary you?' he asked.

"'A little,' I replied, bending a little in my hands, 'but I could hold out for an hour or so longer.'

"'No, no, I will not allow it; the willing fellows will make it a duty to support your arms, as of old, men supported those of the prophet.'

"'Very good,' I answered.

"'That will not be humiliating to you?'

"'My friend,' said I, 'there is, I think, a great difference between being supported and being measured.'"

"The distinction is full of the soundest sense," interrupted D'Artagnan.

"Then," continued Porthos, "he made a sign: two lads approached; one supported my left arm, while the other, with infinite address, supported my right."

"'Another, my man,' cried he. A third approached. 'Support monsieur by the waist,' said he. The *garcon* complied."

"So that you were at rest?" asked D'Artagnan.

"Perfectly; and Pocquenard drew me on the glass."

"Poquelin, my friend."

"Poquelin—you are right. Stay, decidedly I prefer calling him Voliere."

"Yes; and then it was over, wasn't it?"

"During that time Voliere drew me as I appeared in the mirror."

"'Twas delicate in him."

"I much like the plan; it is respectful, and keeps every one in his place."

"And there it ended?"

"Without a soul having touched me, my friend."

"Except the three *garcons* who supported you."

"Doubtless; but I have, I think, already explained to you the difference there is between supporting and measuring."

"'Tis true," answered D'Artagnan; who said afterwards to himself, "I'faith, I greatly deceive myself, or I have been the means of a good windfall to that rascal Moliere, and we shall assuredly see the scene hit off to the life in some comedy or other." Porthos smiled.

"What are you laughing at?" asked D'Artagnan.

"Must I confess? Well, I was laughing over my good fortune."

"Oh, that is true; I don't know a happier man than you. But what is this last piece of luck that has befallen you?'

"Well, my dear fellow, congratulate me."

"I desire nothing better."

"It seems that I am the first who has had his measure taken in that manner."

"Are you so sure of it?"

"Nearly so. Certain signs of intelligence which passed between Voliere and the other *garcons* showed me the fact."

"Well, my friend, that does not surprise me from Moliere," said D'Artagnan.

"Voliere, my friend."

"Oh, no, no, indeed! I am very willing to leave you to go on saying Voliere; but, as for me, I shall continued to say Moliere. Well, this, I was saying, does not surprise me, coming from Moliere, who is a very ingenious fellow, and inspired you with this grand idea."

"It will be of great use to him by and by, I am sure."

"Won't it be of use to him, indeed? I believe you, it will, and that in the highest degree;—for you see my friend Moliere is of all known tailors the man who best clothes our barons, comtes, and marquises—according to their measure."

On this observation, neither the application nor depth of which we shall discuss, D'Artagnan and Porthos quitted M. de Percerin's house and rejoined their carriages, wherein we will leave them, in order to look after Moliere and Aramis at Saint-Mande.

CHAPTER 6

The Bee-Hive, the Bees, and the Honey.

The bishop of Vannes, much annoyed at having met D'Artagnan at M. Percerin's, returned to Saint-Mande in no very good humor. Moliere, on the other hand, quite delighted at having made such a capital rough sketch, and at knowing where to find his original again, whenever he should desire to convert his sketch into a picture, Moliere arrived in the merriest of moods. All the first story of the left wing was occupied by the most celebrated Epicureans in Paris, and those on the freest footing in the house—every one in his compartment, like the bees in their cells, employed in producing the honey intended for that royal cake which M. Fouquet proposed to offer his majesty Louis XIV. during the *fete* at Vaux. Pelisson, his head leaning on his hand, was engaged in drawing out the plan of the prologue to the "Facheux," a comedy in three acts, which was to be put on the stage by Poquelin de Moliere, as D'Artagnan called him, or Coquelin de Voliere, as Porthos styled him. Loret, with all the charming innocence of a gazetteer,—the gazetteers of all ages have always been so artless!— Loret was composing an account of the *fetes* at Vaux, before those *fetes* had taken place. La Fontaine sauntered about from one to the other, a peripatetic, absent-minded, boring, unbearable dreamer, who kept buzzing and humming at everybody's elbow a thousand poetic abstractions. He so often disturbed Pelisson, that the latter, raising his head, crossly said, "At least, La Fontaine, supply me with a rhyme, since you have the run of the gardens at Parnassus."

"What rhyme do you want?" asked the *Fabler* as Madame de Sevigne used to call him.

"I want a rhyme to *lumiere.*"

"*Orniere,*" answered La Fontaine.

"Ah, but, my good friend, one cannot talk of *wheel-ruts* when celebrating the delights of Vaux," said Loret.

"Besides, it doesn't rhyme," answered Pelisson.

"What! doesn't rhyme!" cried La Fontaine, in surprise.

"Yes; you have an abominable habit, my friend,—a habit which will ever prevent your becoming a poet of the first order. You rhyme in a slovenly manner."

"Oh, oh, you think so, do you, Pelisson?"

"Yes, I do, indeed. Remember that a rhyme is never good so long as one can find a better."

"Then I will never write anything again save in prose," said La Fontaine, who had taken up Pelisson's reproach in earnest. "Ah! I often suspected I was nothing but a rascally poet! Yes, 'tis the very truth."

"Do not say so; your remark is too sweeping, and there is much that is good in your 'Fables.'"

"And to begin," continued La Fontaine, following up his idea, "I will go and burn a hundred verses I have just made."

"Where are your verses?"

"In my head."

"Well, if they are in your head you cannot burn them."

"True," said La Fontaine; "but if I do not burn them—"

"Well, what will happen if you do not burn them?"

"They will remain in my mind, and I shall never forget them!"

"The deuce!" cried Loret; "what a dangerous thing! One would go mad with it!"

"The deuce! the deuce!" repeated La Fontaine; "what can I do?"

"I have discovered the way," said Moliere, who had entered just at this point of the conversation.

"What way?"

"Write them first and burn them afterwards."

"How simple! Well, I should never have discovered that. What a mind that devil of a Moliere has!" said La Fontaine. Then, striking his forehead, "Oh, thou wilt never be aught but an ass, Jean La Fontaine!" he added.

"*What* are you saying there, my friend?" broke in Moliere, approaching the poet, whose aside he had heard.

"I say I shall never be aught but an ass," answered La Fontaine, with a heavy sigh and swimming eyes. "Yes, my friend," he added, with increasing grief, "it seems that I rhyme in a slovenly manner."

"Oh, 'tis wrong to say so."

"Nay, I am a poor creature!"

"Who said so?"

"*Parbleu!* 'twas Pelisson; did you not, Pelisson?"

Pelisson, again absorbed in his work, took good care not to answer.

"But if Pelisson said you were so," cried Moliere, "Pelisson has seriously offended you."

"Do you think so?"

"Ah! I advise you, as you are a gentleman, not to leave an insult like that unpunished."

"*What!*" exclaimed La Fontaine.

"Did you ever fight?"

"Once only, with a lieutenant in the light horse."

"What wrong had he done you?"

"It seems he ran away with my wife."

"Ah, ah!" said Moliere, becoming slightly pale; but as, at La Fontaine's declaration, the others had turned round, Moliere kept upon his lips the rallying smile which had so nearly died away, and continuing to make La Fontaine speak—

"And what was the result of the duel?"

"The result was, that on the ground my opponent disarmed me, and then made an apology, promising never again to set foot in my house."

"And you considered yourself satisfied?" said Moliere.

"Not at all! on the contrary, I picked up my sword. 'I beg your pardon, monsieur,' I said, 'I have not fought you because you were my wife's friend, but because I was told I ought to fight. So, as I have never known any peace save since you made her acquaintance, do me the pleasure to continue your visits as heretofore, or *morbleu!* let us set to again.' And so," continued La Fontaine, "he was compelled to resume his friendship with madame, and I continue to be the happiest of husbands."

All burst out laughing. Moliere alone passed his hand across his eyes. Why? Perhaps to wipe away a tear, perhaps to smother a sigh. Alas! we know that Moliere was a moralist, but he was not a philosopher. "'Tis all one," he said, returning to the topic of the conversation, "Pelisson has insulted you."

"Ah, truly! I had already forgotten it."

"And I am going to challenge him on your behalf."

"Well, you can do so, if you think it indispensable."

"I do think it indispensable, and I am going to—"

"Stay," exclaimed La Fontaine, "I want your advice."

"Upon what? this insult?"

"No; tell me really now whether *lumiere* does not rhyme with *orniere.*"

"I should make them rhyme."

"Ah! I knew you would."

"And I have made a hundred thousand such rhymes in my time."

"A hundred thousand!" cried La Fontaine. "Four times as many as 'La Pucelle,' which M. Chaplain is meditating. Is it also on this subject, too, that you have composed a hundred thousand verses?"

"Listen to me, you eternally absent-minded creature," said Moliere.

"It is certain," continued La Fontaine, "that *legume*, for instance, rhymes with *posthume*."

"In the plural, above all."

"Yes, above all in the plural, seeing that then it rhymes not with three letters, but with four; as *orniere* does with *lumiere*."

"But give me *ornieres* and *lumieres* in the plural, my dear Pelisson," said La Fontaine, clapping his hand on the shoulder of his friend, whose insult he had quite forgotten, "and they will rhyme."

"Hem!" coughed Pelisson.

"Moliere says so, and Moliere is a judge of such things; he declares he has himself made a hundred thousand verses."

"Come," said Moliere, laughing, "he is off now."

"It is like *rivage*, which rhymes admirably with *herbage*. I would take my oath of it."

"But—" said Moliere.

"I tell you all this," continued La Fontaine, "because you are preparing a *divertissement* for Vaux, are you not?"

"Yes, the 'Facheux.'"

"Ah, yes, the 'Facheux;' yes, I recollect. Well, I was thinking a prologue would admirably suit your *divertissement*."

"Doubtless it would suit capitally."

"Ah! you are of my opinion?"

"So much so, that I have asked you to write this very prologue."

"You asked *me* to write it?"

"Yes, you, and on your refusal begged you to ask Pelisson, who is engaged upon it at this moment."

"Ah! that is what Pelisson is doing, then? I'faith, my dear Moliere, you are indeed often right."

"When?"

"When you call me absent-minded. It is a monstrous defect; I will cure myself of it, and do your prologue for you."

"But inasmuch as Pelisson is about it!—"

"Ah, true, miserable rascal that I am! Loret was indeed right in saying I was a poor creature."

"It was not Loret who said so, my friend."

"Well, then, whoever said so, 'tis the same to me! And so your *divertissement* is called the 'Facheux?' Well, can you make *heureux* rhyme with *facheux?*"

"If obliged, yes."

"And even with *capriceux.*"

"Oh, no, no."

"It would be hazardous, and yet why so?"

"There is too great a difference in the cadences."

"I was fancying," said La Fontaine, leaving Moliere for Loret—"I was fancying—"

"What were you fancying?" said Loret, in the middle of a sentence. "Make haste."

"You are writing the prologue to the 'Facheux,' are you not?"

"No! *mordieu!* it is Pelisson."

"Ah, Pelisson," cried La Fontaine, going over to him, "I was fancying," he continued, "that the nymph of Vaux—"

"Ah, beautiful!" cried Loret. "The nymph of Vaux! thank you, La Fontaine; you have just given me the two concluding verses of my paper."

"Well, if you can rhyme so well, La Fontaine," said Pelisson, "tell me now in what way you would begin my prologue?"

"I should say, for instance, 'Oh! nymph, who—' After 'who' I should place a verb in the second person singular of the present indicative; and should go on thus: 'this grot profound.'"

"But the verb, the verb?" asked Pelisson.

"To admire the greatest king of all kings round," continued La Fontaine.

"But the verb, the verb," obstinately insisted Pelisson. "This second person singular of the present indicative?"

"Well, then; quittest: Oh, nymph, who quittest now this grot profound, To admire the greatest king of all kings round."

"You would not put 'who quittest,' would you?"

"Why not?"

"'Quittest,' after 'you who'?"

"Ah! my dear fellow," exclaimed La Fontaine, "you are a shocking pedant!"

"Without counting," said Moliere, "that the second verse, 'king of all kings round,' is very weak, my dear La Fontaine."

"Then you see clearly I am nothing but a poor creature,—a shuffler, as you said."

"I never said so."

"Then, as Loret said."

"And it was not Loret either; it was Pelisson."

"Well, Pelisson was right a hundred times over. But what annoys me more than anything, my dear Moliere, is, that I fear we shall not have our Epicurean dresses."

"You expected yours, then, for the *fete?*"

"Yes, for the *fete*, and then for after the *fete*. My housekeeper told me that my own is rather faded."

"*Diable!* your housekeeper is right; rather more than faded."

"Ah, you see," resumed La Fontaine, "the fact is, I left it on the floor in my room, and my cat—"

"Well, your cat—"

"She made her nest upon it, which has rather changed its color."

Moliere burst out laughing; Pelisson and Loret followed his example. At this juncture, the bishop of Vannes appeared, with a roll of plans and parchments under his arm. As if the angel of death had chilled all gay and sprightly fancies—as if that wan form had scared away the Graces to whom Xenocrates sacrificed—silence immediately reigned through the study, and every one resumed his self-possession and his pen. Aramis distributed the notes of invitation, and thanked them in the name of M. Fouquet. "The superintendent," he said, "being kept to his room by business, could not come and see them, but begged them to send him some of the fruits of their day's work, to enable him to forget the fatigue of his labor in the night."

At these words, all settled down to work. La Fontaine placed himself at a table, and set his rapid pen an endless dance across the smooth white vellum; Pelisson made a fair copy of his prologue; Moliere contributed fifty fresh verses, with which his visit to Percerin had inspired him; Loret, an article on the marvelous *fetes* he predicted; and Aramis, laden with his booty like the king of the bees, that great black drone, decked with purple and gold, re-entered his apartment, silent and busy. But before departing, "Remember, gentlemen," said he, "we leave to-morrow evening."

"In that case, I must give notice at home," said Moliere.

"Yes; poor Moliere!" said Loret, smiling; "he loves his home."

"'*He* loves,' yes," replied Moliere, with his sad, sweet smile. "'He loves,' that does not mean, they love *him*."

"As for me," said La Fontaine, "they love me at Chateau Thierry, I am very sure."

Aramis here re-entered after a brief disappearance.

"Will any one go with me?" he asked. "I am going by Paris, after having passed a quarter of an hour with M. Fouquet. I offer my carriage."

"Good," said Moliere, "I accept it. I am in a hurry."

"I shall dine here," said Loret. "M. de Gourville has promised me some craw-fish."

"He has promised me some whitings. Find a rhyme for that, La Fontaine."

Aramis went out laughing, as only he could laugh, and Moliere followed him. They were at the bottom of the stairs, when La Fontaine opened the door, and shouted out:

"He has promised us some whitings, In return for these our writings."

The shouts of laughter reached the ears of Fouquet at the moment Aramis opened the door of the study. As to Moliere, he had undertaken to order the horses, while Aramis went to exchange a parting word with the superintendent. "Oh, how they are laughing there!" said Fouquet, with a sigh.

"Do you not laugh, monseigneur?"

"I laugh no longer now, M. d'Herblay. The *fete* is approaching; money is departing."

"Have I not told you that was my business?"

"Yes, you promised me millions."

"You shall have them the day after the king's *entree* into Vaux."

Fouquet looked closely at Aramis, and passed the back of his icy hand across his moistened brow. Aramis perceived that the superintendent either doubted him, or felt he was powerless to obtain the money. How could Fouquet suppose that a poor bishop, ex-abbe, ex-musketeer, could find any?

"Why doubt me?" said Aramis. Fouquet smiled and shook his head.

"Man of little faith!" added the bishop.

"My dear M. d'Herblay," answered Fouquet, "if I fall—"

"Well; if you 'fall'?"

"I shall, at least, fall from such a height, that I shall shatter myself in falling." Then giving himself a shake, as though to escape from himself, "Whence came you," said he, "my friend?"

"From Paris—from Percerin."

"And what have you been doing at Percerin's, for I suppose you attach no great importance to our poets' dresses?"

"No; I went to prepare a surprise."

"Surprise?"

"Yes; which you are going to give to the king."

"And will it cost much?"

"Oh! a hundred pistoles you will give Lebrun."

"A painting?—Ah! all the better! And what is this painting to represent?"

"I will tell you; then at the same time, whatever you may say or think of it, I went to see the dresses for our poets."

"Bah! and they will be rich and elegant?"

"Splendid! There will be few great monseigneurs with so good. People will see the difference there is between the courtiers of wealth and those of friendship."

"Ever generous and grateful, dear prelate."

"In your school."

Fouquet grasped his hand. "And where are you going?" he said.

"I am off to Paris, when you shall have given a certain letter."

"For whom?"

"M. de Lyonne."

"And what do you want with Lyonne?"

"I wish to make him sign a *lettre de cachet.*"

"'*Lettre de cachet!*' Do you desire to put somebody in the Bastille?"

"On the contrary—to let somebody out."

"And who?"

"A poor devil—a youth, a lad who has been Bastilled these ten years, for two Latin verses he made against the Jesuits."

"'Two Latin verses!' and, for 'two Latin verses,' the miserable being has been in prison for ten years!"

"Yes!"

"And has committed no other crime?"

"Beyond this, he is as innocent as you or I."

"On your word?"

"On my honor!"

"And his name is—"

"Seldon."

"Yes.—But it is too bad. You knew this, and you never told me!"

"'Twas only yesterday his mother applied to me, monseigneur."

"And the woman is poor!"

"In the deepest misery."

"Heaven," said Fouquet, "sometimes bears with such injustice on earth, that I hardly wonder there are wretches who doubt of its existence. Stay, M. d'Herblay." And Fouquet, taking a pen, wrote a few rapid lines to his colleague Lyonne. Aramis took the letter and made ready to go.

"Wait," said Fouquet. He opened his drawer, and took out ten government notes which were there, each for a thousand francs. "Stay," he said; "set the son at liberty, and give this to the mother; but, above all, do not tell her—"

"What, monseigneur?"

"That she is ten thousand livres richer than I. She would say I am but a poor superintendent! Go! and I pray that God will bless those who are mindful of his poor!"

"So also do I pray," replied Aramis, kissing Fouquet's hand.

And he went out quickly, carrying off the letter for Lyonne and the notes for Seldon's mother, and taking up Moliere, who was beginning to lose patience.

CHAPTER 7

Another Supper at the Bastille.

Seven o'clock sounded from the great clock of the Bastille, that famous clock, which, like all the accessories of the state prison, the very use of which is a torture, recalled to the prisoners' minds the destination of every hour of their punishment. The time-piece of the Bastille, adorned with figures, like most of the clocks of the period, represented St. Peter in bonds. It was the supper hour of the unfortunate captives. The doors, grating on their enormous hinges, opened for the passage of the baskets and trays of provisions, the abundance and the delicacy of which, as M. de Baisemeaux has himself taught us, was regulated by the condition in life of the prisoner. We understand on this head the theories of M. de Baisemeaux, sovereign dispenser of gastronomic delicacies, head cook of the royal fortress, whose trays, full-laden, were ascending the steep staircases, carrying some consolation to the prisoners in the shape of honestly filled bottles of good vintages. This same hour was that of M. le gouverneur's supper also. He had a guest to-day, and the spit turned more heavily than usual. Roast partridges, flanked with quails and flanking a larded leveret; boiled fowls; hams, fried and sprinkled with white wine, *cardons* of Guipuzcoa and *la bisque ecrevisses*: these, together with soups and *hors d'oeuvres*, constituted the governor's bill of fare. Baisemeaux, seated at table, was rubbing his hands and looking at the bishop of Vannes, who, booted like a cavalier, dressed in gray and sword at side, kept talking of his hunger and testifying the liveliest impatience. M. de Baisemeaux de Montlezun was not accustomed to the unbending movements of his greatness my lord of Vannes, and this evening Aramis, becoming sprightly, volunteered confidence on confidence. The prelate had again a little touch of the musketeer about him. The bishop just trenched on the borders only of license in his style of conversation. As for M. de Baisemeaux, with the facility of vulgar people, he gave himself up entirely upon this point of his guest's freedom. "Monsieur," said he, "for indeed to-night I dare not call you monseigneur."

"By no means," said Aramis; "call me monsieur; I am booted."

"Do you know, monsieur, of whom you remind me this evening?"

"No! faith," said Aramis, taking up his glass; "but I hope I remind you of a capital guest."

"You remind me of two, monsieur. Francois, shut the window; the wind may annoy his greatness."

"And let him go," added Aramis. "The supper is completely served, and we shall eat it very well without waiters. I like exceedingly to be *tete-a-tete* when I am with a friend." Baisemeaux bowed respectfully.

"I like exceedingly," continued Aramis, "to help myself."

"Retire, Francois," cried Baisemeaux. "I was saying that your greatness puts me in mind of two persons; one very illustrious, the late cardinal, the great Cardinal de la Rochelle, who wore boots like you."

"Indeed," said Aramis; "and the other?"

"The other was a certain musketeer, very handsome, very brave, very adventurous, very fortunate, who, from being abbe, turned musketeer, and from musketeer turned abbe." Aramis condescended to smile. "From abbe," continued Baisemeaux, encouraged by Aramis's smile—"from abbe, bishop—and from bishop—"

"Ah! stay there, I beg," exclaimed Aramis.

"I have just said, monsieur, that you gave me the idea of a cardinal."

"Enough, dear M. Baisemeaux. As you said, I have on the boots of a cavalier, but I do not intend, for all that, to embroil myself with the church this evening."

"But you have wicked intentions, nevertheless, monseigneur."

"Oh, yes, wicked, I own, as everything mundane is."

"You traverse the town and the streets in disguise?"

"In disguise, as you say."

"And you still make use of your sword?"

"Yes, I should think so; but only when I am compelled. Do me the pleasure to summon Francois."

"Have you no wine there?"

"'Tis not for wine, but because it is hot here, and the window is shut."

"I shut the windows at supper-time so as not to hear the sounds or the arrival of couriers."

"Ah, yes. You hear them when the window is open?"

"But too well, and that disturbs me. You understand?"

"Nevertheless I am suffocated. Francois." Francois entered. "Open the windows, I pray you, Master Francois," said Aramis. "You will allow him, dear M. Baisemeaux?"

"You are at home here," answered the governor. The window was opened. "Do you not think," said M. de Baisemeaux, "that you will find yourself very lonely, now M. de la Fere has returned to his household gods at Blois? He is a very old friend, is he not?"

"You know it as I do, Baisemeaux, seeing that you were in the musketeers with us."

"Bah! with my friends I reckon neither bottles of wine nor years."

"And you are right. But I do more than love M. de la Fere, dear Baisemeaux; I venerate him."

"Well, for my part, though 'tis singular," said the governor, "I prefer M. d'Artagnan to him. There is a man for you, who drinks long and well! That kind of people allow you at least to penetrate their thoughts."

"Baisemeaux, make me tipsy to-night; let us have a merry time of it as of old, and if I have a trouble at the bottom of my heart, I promise you, you shall see it as you would a diamond at the bottom of your glass."

"Bravo!" said Baisemeaux, and he poured out a great glass of wine and drank it off at a draught, trembling with joy at the idea of being, by hook or by crook, in the secret of some high archiepiscopal misdemeanor. While he was drinking he did not see with what attention Aramis was noting the sounds in the great court. A courier came in about eight o'clock as Francois brought in the fifth bottle, and, although the courier made a great noise, Baisemeaux heard nothing.

"The devil take him," said Aramis.

"What! who?" asked Baisemeaux. "I hope 'tis neither the wine you drank nor he who is the cause of your drinking it."

"No; it is a horse, who is making noise enough in the court for a whole squadron."

"Pooh! some courier or other," replied the governor, redoubling his attention to the passing bottle. "Yes; and may the devil take him, and so quickly that we shall never hear him speak more. Hurrah! hurrah!"

"You forget me, Baisemeaux! my glass is empty," said Aramis, lifting his dazzling Venetian goblet.

"Upon my honor, you delight me. Francois, wine!" Francois entered. "Wine, fellow! and better."

"Yes, monsieur, yes; but a courier has just arrived."

"Let him go to the devil, I say."

"Yes, monsieur, but—"

"Let him leave his news at the office; we will see to it to-morrow. To-morrow, there will be time to-morrow; there will be daylight," said Baisemeaux, chanting the words.

"Ah, monsieur," grumbled the soldier Francois, in spite of himself, "monsieur."

"Take care," said Aramis, "take care!"

"Of what? dear M. d'Herblay," said Baisemeaux, half intoxicated.

"The letter which the courier brings to the governor of a fortress is sometimes an order."

"Nearly always."

"Do not orders issue from the ministers?"

"Yes, undoubtedly; but—"

"And what to these ministers do but countersign the signature of the king?"

"Perhaps you are right. Nevertheless, 'tis very tiresome when you are sitting before a good table, *tete-a-tete* with a friend—Ah! I beg your pardon, monsieur; I forgot it is I who engage you at supper, and that I speak to a future cardinal."

"Let us pass over that, dear Baisemeaux, and return to our soldier, to Francois."

"Well, and what has Francois done?"

"He has demurred!"

"He was wrong, then?"

"However, he *has* demurred, you see; 'tis because there is something extraordinary in this matter. It is very possible that it was not Francois who was wrong in demurring, but you, who are in the wrong in not listening to him."

"Wrong? I to be wrong before Francois? that seems rather hard."

"Pardon me, merely an irregularity. But I thought it my duty to make an observation which I deem important."

"Oh! perhaps you are right," stammered Baisemeaux. "The king's order is sacred; but as to orders that arrive when one is at supper, I repeat that the devil—"

"If you had said as much to the great cardinal—hem! my dear Baisemeaux, and if his order had any importance."

"I do it that I may not disturb a bishop. *Mordioux!* am I not, then, excusable?"

"Do not forget, Baisemeaux, that I have worn the soldier's coat, and I am accustomed to obedience everywhere."

"You wish, then—"

"I wish that you would do your duty, my friend; yes, at least before this soldier."

"'Tis mathematically true," exclaimed Baisemeaux. Francois still waited: "Let them send this order of the king's up to me," he repeated, recovering himself. And he added in a low tone, "Do you know what it is? I will tell you something about as interesting as this. 'Beware of fire near the powder magazine;' or, 'Look close after such and such a one, who is clever at escaping,' Ah! if you only knew, monseigneur, how many times I have been suddenly awakened from the very sweetest, deepest slumber, by messengers arriving at full gallop to tell me, or rather, bring me a slip of paper containing these words: 'Monsieur de Baisemeaux, what news?' 'Tis clear enough that those who waste their time writing such orders have never slept in the Bastille. They would know better; they have never considered the thickness of my walls, the vigilance of my officers, the number of rounds we go. But, indeed, what can you expect, monseigneur? It is their business to write and torment me when I am at rest, and to trouble me when I am happy," added Baisemeaux, bowing to Aramis. "Then let them do their business."

"And do you do yours," added the bishop, smiling.

Francois re-entered; Baisemeaux took from his hands the minister's order. He slowly undid it, and as slowly read it.

Aramis pretended to be drinking, so as to be able to watch his host through the glass. Then, Baisemeaux, having read it: "What was I just saying?" he exclaimed.

"What is it?" asked the bishop.

"An order of release! There, now; excellent news indeed to disturb us!"

"Excellent news for him whom it concerns, you will at least agree, my dear governor!"

"And at eight o'clock in the evening!"

"It is charitable!"

"Oh! charity is all very well, but it is for that fellow who says he is so weary and tired, but not for me who am amusing myself," said Baisemeaux, exasperated.

"Will you lose by him, then? And is the prisoner who is to be set at liberty a good payer?"

"Oh, yes, indeed! a miserable, five-franc rat!"

"Let me see it," asked M. d'Herblay. "It is no indiscretion?"

"By no means; read it."

"There is 'Urgent,' on the paper; you have seen that, I suppose?"

"Oh, admirable! 'Urgent!'—a man who has been there ten years! It is *urgent* to set him free to-day, this very evening, at eight o'clock!— *urgent!*" And Baisemeaux, shrugging his shoulders with an air of supreme disdain, flung the order on the table and began eating again.

"They are fond of these tricks!" he said, with his mouth full; "they seize a man, some fine day, keep him under lock and key for ten years, and write to you, 'Watch this fellow well,' or 'Keep him very strictly.' And then, as soon as you are accustomed to look upon the prisoner as a dangerous man, all of a sudden, without rhyme or reason they write—'Set him at liberty,' and actually add to their missive—'urgent.' You will own, my lord, 'tis enough to make a man at dinner shrug his shoulders!"

"What do you expect? It is for them to write," said Aramis, "for you to execute the order."

"Good! good! execute it! Oh, patience! You must not imagine that I am a slave."

"Gracious Heaven! my very good M. Baisemeaux, who ever said so? Your independence is well known."

"Thank Heaven!"

"But your goodness of heart is also known."

"Ah! don't speak of it!"

"And your obedience to your superiors. Once a soldier, you see, Baisemeaux, always a soldier."

"And I shall directly obey; and to-morrow morning, at daybreak, the prisoner referred to shall be set free."

"To-morrow?"

"At dawn."

"Why not this evening, seeing that the *lettre de cachet* bears, both on the direction and inside, '*urgent*'?"

"Because this evening we are at supper, and our affairs are urgent, too!"

"Dear Baisemeaux, booted though I be, I feel myself a priest, and charity has higher claims upon me than hunger and thirst. This unfortunate man has suffered long enough, since you have just told me that he has been your prisoner these ten years. Abridge his suffering. His good time has come; give him the benefit quickly. God will repay you in Paradise with years of felicity."

"You wish it?"

"I entreat you."

"What! in the very middle of our repast?"

"I implore you; such an action is worth ten Benedicites."

"It shall be as you desire, only our supper will get cold."

"Oh! never heed that."

Baisemeaux leaned back to ring for Francois, and by a very natural motion turned round towards the door. The order had remained on the table; Aramis seized the opportunity when Baisemeaux was not looking to change the paper for another, folded in the same manner, which he drew swiftly from his pocket. "Francois," said the governor, "let the major come up here with the turnkeys of the Bertaudiere." Francois bowed and quitted the room, leaving the two companions alone.

CHAPTER 8

The General of the Order.

There was now a brief silence, during which Aramis never removed his eyes from Baisemeaux for a moment. The latter seemed only half decided to disturb himself thus in the middle of supper, and it was clear he was trying to invent some pretext, whether good or bad, for delay, at any rate till after dessert. And it appeared also that he had hit upon an excuse at last.

"Eh! but it is impossible!" he cried.

"How impossible?" said Aramis. "Give me a glimpse of this impossibility."

"'Tis impossible to set a prisoner at liberty at such an hour. Where can he go to, a man so unacquainted with Paris?"

"He will find a place wherever he can."

"You see, now, one might as well set a blind man free!"

"I have a carriage, and will take him wherever he wishes."

"You have an answer for everything. Francois, tell monsieur le major to go and open the cell of M. Seldon, No. 3, Bertaudiere."

"Seldon!" exclaimed Aramis, very naturally. "You said Seldon, I think?"

"I said Seldon, of course. 'Tis the name of the man they set free."

"Oh! you mean to say Marchiali?" said Aramis.

"Marchiali? oh! yes, indeed. No, no, Seldon."

"I think you are making a mistake, Monsieur Baisemeaux."

"I have read the order."

"And I also."

"And I saw 'Seldon' in letters as large as that," and Baisemeaux held up his finger.

"And I read 'Marchiali' in characters as large as this," said Aramis, also holding up two fingers.

"To the proof; let us throw a light on the matter," said Baisemeaux, confident he was right. "There is the paper, you have only to read it."

"I read 'Marchiali,'" returned Aramis, spreading out the paper. "Look."

Baisemeaux looked, and his arms dropped suddenly. "Yes, yes," he said, quite overwhelmed; "yes, Marchiali. 'Tis plainly written Marchiali! Quite true!"

"Ah!—"

"How? the man of whom we have talked so much? The man whom they are every day telling me to take such care of?"

"There is 'Marchiali,'" repeated the inflexible Aramis.

"I must own it, monseigneur. But I understand nothing about it."

"You believe your eyes, at any rate."

"To tell me very plainly there is 'Marchiali.'"

"And in a good handwriting, too."

"'Tis a wonder! I still see this order and the name of Seldon, Irishman. I see it. Ah! I even recollect that under this name there was a blot of ink."

"No, there is no ink; no, there is no blot."

"Oh! but there was, though; I know it, because I rubbed my finger—this very one—in the powder that was over the blot."

"In a word, be it how it may, dear M. Baisemeaux," said

Aramis, "and whatever you may have seen, the order is signed to release Marchiali, blot or no blot."

"The order is signed to release Marchiali," replied Baisemeaux, mechanically, endeavoring to regain his courage.

"And you are going to release this prisoner. If your heart dictates you to deliver Seldon also, I declare to you I will not oppose it the least in the world." Aramis accompanied this remark with a smile, the irony of which effectually dispelled Baisemeaux's confusion of mind, and restored his courage.

"Monseigneur," he said, "this Marchiali is the very same prisoner whom the other day a priest confessor of *our order* came to visit in so imperious and so secret a manner."

"I don't know that, monsieur," replied the bishop.

"'Tis no such long time ago, dear Monsieur d'Herblay."

"It is true. But *with us*, monsieur, it is good that the man of to-day should no longer know what the man of yesterday did."

"In any case," said Baisemeaux, "the visit of the Jesuit confessor must have given happiness to this man."

Aramis made no reply, but recommended eating and drinking. As for Baisemeaux, no longer touching anything that was on the table, he again took up the order and examined it every way. This investigation, under ordinary circumstances, would have made the ears of the impatient Aramis burn with anger; but the bishop of Vannes did not become incensed for so little, above all, when he had murmured to himself that to do so was dangerous. "Are you going to release Marchiali?" he said. "What mellow, fragrant and delicious sherry this is, my dear governor."

"Monseigneur," replied Baisemeaux, "I shall release the prisoner Marchiali when I have summoned the courier who brought the order, and above all, when, by interrogating him, I have satisfied myself."

"The order is sealed, and the courier is ignorant of the contents. What do you want to satisfy yourself about?"

"Be it so, monseigneur; but I shall send to the ministry, and M. de Lyonne will either confirm or withdraw the order."

"What is the good of all that?" asked Aramis, coldly.

"What good?"

"Yes; what is your object, I ask?"

"The object of never deceiving oneself, monseigneur, nor being wanting in the respect which a subaltern owes to his superior officers, nor infringing the duties of a service one has accepted of one's own free will."

"Very good; you have just spoken so eloquently, that I cannot but admire you. It is true that a subaltern owes respect to his superiors; he is guilty when he deceives himself, and he should be punished if he infringed either the duties or laws of his office."

Baisemeaux looked at the bishop with astonishment.

"It follows," pursued Aramis, "that you are going to ask advice, to put your conscience at ease in the matter?"

"Yes, monseigneur."

"And if a superior officer gives you orders, you will obey?"

"Never doubt it, monseigneur."

"You know the king's signature well, M. de Baisemeaux?"

"Yes, monseigneur."

"Is it not on this order of release?"

"It is true, but it may—"

"Be forged, you mean?"

"That is evident, monseigneur."

"You are right. And that of M. de Lyonne?"

"I see it plain enough on the order; but for the same reason that the king's signature may have been forged, so also, and with even greater probability, may M. de Lyonne's."

"Your logic has the stride of a giant, M. de Baisemeaux," said Aramis; "and your reasoning is irresistible. But on what special grounds do you base your idea that these signatures are false?"

"On this: the absence of counter-signatures. Nothing

checks his majesty's signature; and M. de Lyonne is not there to tell me he has signed."

"Well, Monsieur de Baisemeaux," said Aramis, bending an eagle glance on the governor, "I adopt so frankly your doubts, and your mode of clearing them up, that I will take a pen, if you will give me one."

Baisemeaux gave him a pen.

"And a sheet of white paper," added Aramis.

Baisemeaux handed him some paper.

"Now, I—I, also—I, here present—incontestably, I—am going to write an order to which I am certain you will give credence, incredulous as you are!"

Baisemeaux turned pale at this icy assurance of manner. It seemed to him that the voice of the bishop's, but just now so playful and gay, had become funereal and sad; that the wax lights changed into the tapers of a mortuary chapel, the very glasses of wine into chalices of blood.

Aramis took a pen and wrote. Baisemeaux, in terror, read over his shoulder.

"A. M. D. G.," wrote the bishop; and he drew a cross under these four letters, which signify *ad majorem Dei gloriam*, "to the greater glory of God;" and thus he continued: "It is our pleasure that the order brought to M. de Baisemeaux de Montlezun, governor, for the king, of the castle of the Bastille, be held by him good and effectual, and be immediately carried into operation."

(Signed) D'HERBLAY

"General of the Order, by the grace of God."

Baisemeaux was so profoundly astonished, that his features remained contracted, his lips parted, and his eyes fixed. He did not move an inch, nor articulate a sound. Nothing could be heard in that large chamber but the wing-whisper of a little moth, which was fluttering to its death about the candles. Aramis, without even deigning to look at the man whom he had reduced to so miserable a condition, drew from his pocket a small case of black wax; he sealed the letter, and stamped it with a seal suspended at his breast, beneath his doublet, and when the operation was concluded, presented—still in silence—the missive to M. de Baisemeaux. The latter, whose hands trembled in a manner to excite pity, turned a dull and meaningless gaze upon the letter. A last gleam of feeling played over his features, and he fell, as if thunder-struck, on a chair.

"Come, come," said Aramis, after a long silence, during which the governor of the Bastille had slowly recovered his senses, "do not lead me to believe, dear Baisemeaux, that the presence of the general of the order is as terrible as His, and that men die merely from having seen Him. Take courage, rouse yourself; give me your hand—obey."

Baisemeaux, reassured, if not satisfied, obeyed, kissed Aramis's hand, and rose. "Immediately?" he murmured.

"Oh, there is no pressing haste, my host; take your place again, and do the honors over this beautiful dessert."

"Monseigneur, I shall never recover such a shock as this; I who have laughed, who have jested with you! I who have dared to treat you on a footing of equality!"

"Say nothing about it, old comrade," replied the bishop, who perceived how strained the cord was and how dangerous it would have been to break it; "say nothing about it. Let us each live in our own way; to you, my protection and my friendship; to me, your obedience. Having exactly fulfilled these two requirements, let us live happily."

Baisemeaux reflected; he perceived, at a glance, the consequence of this withdrawal of a prisoner by means of a forged order; and, putting in the scale the guarantee offered him by the official order of the general, did not consider it of any value.

Aramis divined this. "My dear Baisemeaux," said he, "you are a simpleton. Lose this habit of reflection when I give myself the trouble to think for you."

And at another gesture he made, Baisemeaux bowed again. "How shall I set about it?" he said.

"What is the process for releasing a prisoner?"

"I have the regulations."

"Well, then, follow the regulations, my friend."

"I go with my major to the prisoner's room, and conduct him, if he is a personage of importance."

"But this Marchiali is not an important personage," said Aramis carelessly.

"I don't know," answered the governor, as if he would have said, "It is for you to instruct me."

"Then if you don't know it, I am right; so act towards Marchiali as you act towards one of obscure station."

"Good; the regulations so provide. They are to the effect that the turnkey, or one of the lower officials, shall bring the prisoner before the governor, in the office."

"Well, 'tis very wise, that; and then?"

"Then we return to the prisoner the valuables he wore at the time of his imprisonment, his clothes and papers, if the minister's orders have not otherwise dictated."

"What was the minister's order as to this Marchiali?"

"Nothing; for the unhappy man arrived here without jewels, without papers, and almost without clothes."

"See how simple, then, all is. Indeed, Baisemeaux, you make a mountain of everything. Remain here, and make them bring the prisoner to the governor's house."

Baisemeaux obeyed. He summoned his lieutenant, and gave him an order, which the latter passed on, without disturbing himself about it, to the next whom it concerned.

Half an hour afterwards they heard a gate shut in the court; it was the door to the dungeon, which had just rendered up its prey to the free air. Aramis blew out all the candles which lighted the room but one, which he left burning behind the door. This flickering glare prevented the sight from resting steadily on any object. It multiplied tenfold the changing forms and shadows of the place, by its wavering uncertainty. Steps drew near.

"Go and meet your men," said Aramis to Baisemeaux.

The governor obeyed. The sergeant and turnkeys disappeared. Baisemeaux re-entered, followed by a prisoner. Aramis had placed himself in the shade; he saw without being seen. Baisemeaux, in an agitated tone of voice, made the young man acquainted with the order which set him at liberty. The prisoner listened, without making a single gesture or saying a word.

"You will swear ('tis the regulation that requires it)," added the governor, "never to reveal anything that you have seen or heard in the Bastille."

The prisoner perceived a crucifix; he stretched out his hands and swore with his lips. "And now, monsieur, you are free. Whither do you intend going?"

The prisoner turned his head, as if looking behind him for some protection, on which he ought to rely. Then was it that Aramis came out of the shade: "I am here," he said, "to render the gentleman whatever service he may please to ask."

The prisoner slightly reddened, and, without hesitation, passed his arm through that of Aramis. "God have you in his holy keeping," he said, in a voice the firmness of which made the governor tremble as much as the form of the blessing astonished him.

Aramis, on shaking hands with Baisemeaux, said to him; "Does my order trouble you? Do you fear their finding it here, should they come to search?"

"I desire to keep it, monseigneur," said Baisemeaux. "If they found it here, it would be a certain indication I should be lost, and in that case you would be a powerful and a last auxiliary for me."

"Being your accomplice, you mean?" answered Aramis, shrugging his shoulders. "Adieu, Baisemeaux," said he.

The horses were in waiting, making each rusty spring reverberate the carriage again with their impatience. Baisemeaux accompanied the bishop to the bottom of the steps. Aramis caused his companion to mount before him, then followed, and without giving the driver any further order, "Go on," said he. The carriage rattled over the pavement of the courtyard. An officer with a torch went before the horses, and gave orders at every post to let them pass. During the time taken in opening all the barriers, Aramis barely breathed, and you might have heard his "sealed heart knock against his ribs." The prisoner, buried in a corner of the carriage, made no more sign of life than his companion. At length, a jolt more sever than the others announced to them that they had cleared the last watercourse. Behind the carriage closed the last gate, that in the Rue St. Antoine. No more walls either on the right or the left; heaven everywhere, liberty everywhere, and life everywhere. The horses, kept in check by a vigorous hand, went quietly as far as the middle of the faubourg. There they began to trot. Little by little, whether they were warming to their work, or whether they were urged, they gained in swiftness, and once past Bercy, the carriage seemed to fly, so great was the ardor of the coursers. The horses galloped thus as far as Villeneuve St. George's, where relays were waiting. Then four instead of two whirled the carriage away in the direction of Melun, and pulled up for a moment in the middle of the forest of Senart. No doubt the order had been given the postilion beforehand, for Aramis had no occasion even to make a sign.

"What is the matter?" asked the prisoner, as if waking from a long dream.

"The matter is, monseigneur," said Aramis, "that before going further, it is necessary your royal highness and I should converse."

"I will await an opportunity, monsieur," answered the young prince.

"We could not have a better, monseigneur. We are in the middle of a forest, and no one can hear us."

"The postilion?"

"The postilion of this relay is deaf and dumb, monseigneur."

"I am at your service, M. d'Herblay."

"Is it your pleasure to remain in the carriage?"

"Yes; we are comfortably seated, and I like this carriage, for it has restored me to liberty."

"Wait, monseigneur; there is yet a precaution to be taken."

"What?"

"We are here on the highway; cavaliers or carriages traveling like ourselves might pass, and seeing us stopping, deem us in some difficulty. Let us avoid offers of assistance, which would embarrass us."

"Give the postilion orders to conceal the carriage in one of the side avenues."

"'Tis exactly what I wished to do, monseigneur."

Aramis made a sign to the deaf and dumb driver of the carriage, whom he touched on the arm. The latter dismounted, took the leaders by the bridle, and led them over the velvet sward and the mossy grass of a winding alley, at the bottom of which, on this moonless night, the deep shades formed a curtain blacker than ink. This done, the man lay down on a slope near his horses, who, on either side, kept nibbling the young oak shoots.

"I am listening," said the young prince to Aramis; "but what are you doing there?"

"I am disarming myself of my pistols, of which we have no further need, monseigneur."

CHAPTER 9

The Tempter.

"My prince," said Aramis, turning in the carriage towards his companion, "weak creature as I am, so unpretending in genius, so low in the scale of intelligent beings, it has never yet happened to me to converse with a man without penetrating his thoughts through that living mask which has been thrown over our mind, in order to retain its expression. But to-night, in this darkness, in the reserve which you maintain, I can read nothing on your features, and something tells me that I shall have great difficulty in wresting from you a sincere declaration. I beseech you, then, not for love of me, for subjects should never weigh as anything in the balance which princes hold, but for love of yourself, to retain every syllable, every inflexion which, under the present most grave circumstances, will all have a sense and value as important as any every uttered in the world."

"I listen," replied the young prince, "decidedly, without either eagerly seeking or fearing anything you are about to say to me." And he buried himself still deeper in the thick cushions of the carriage, trying to deprive his companion not only of the sight of him, but even of the very idea of his presence.

Black was the darkness which fell wide and dense from

the summits of the intertwining trees. The carriage, covered in by this prodigious roof, would not have received a particle of light, not even if a ray could have struggled through the wreaths of mist that were already rising in the avenue.

"Monseigneur," resumed Aramis, "you know the history of the government which to-day controls France. The king issued from an infancy imprisoned like yours, obscure as yours, and confined as yours; only, instead of ending, like yourself, this slavery in a prison, this obscurity in solitude, these straightened circumstances in concealment, he was fain to bear all these miseries, humiliations, and distresses, in full daylight, under the pitiless sun of royalty; on an elevation flooded with light, where every stain appears a blemish, every glory a stain. The king has suffered; it rankles in his mind; and he will avenge himself. He will be a bad king. I say not that he will pour out his people's blood, like Louis XI., or Charles IX.; for he has no mortal injuries to avenge; but he will devour the means and substance of his people; for he has himself undergone wrongs in his own interest and money. In the first place, then, I acquit my conscience, when I consider openly the merits and the faults of this great prince; and if I condemn him, my conscience absolves me."

Aramis paused. It was not to listen if the silence of the forest remained undisturbed, but it was to gather up his thoughts from the very bottom of his soul—to leave the thoughts he had uttered sufficient time to eat deeply into the mind of his companion.

"All that Heaven does, Heaven does well," continued the bishop of Vannes; "and I am so persuaded of it that I have long been thankful to have been chosen depositary of the secret which I have aided you to discover. To a just Providence was necessary an instrument, at once penetrating, persevering, and convinced, to accomplish a great work. I am this instrument. I possess penetration, perseverance, conviction; I govern a mysterious people, who has taken for its motto, the motto of God, '*Patiens quia oeternus.*'" The prince moved. "I divine, monseigneur, why you are raising your head, and are surprised at the people I have under my command. You did not know you were dealing with a king— oh! monseigneur, king of a people very humble, much disinherited; humble because they have no force save when creeping; disinherited, because never, almost never in this world, do my people reap the harvest they sow, nor eat the fruit they cultivate. They labor for an abstract idea; they heap together all the atoms of their power, to from a single man; and round this man, with the sweat of their labor, they create a misty halo, which his genius shall, in turn, render a glory gilded with the rays of all the crowns in Christendom. Such is the man you have beside you, monseigneur. It is to tell you that he has drawn you from the abyss for a great purpose, to raise you above the powers of the earth—above himself."[1]

The prince lightly touched Aramis's arm. "You speak to me," he said, "of that religious order whose chief you are. For me, the result of your words is, that the day you desire to hurl down the man you shall have raised, the event will be accomplished; and that you will keep under your hand your creation of yesterday."

"Undeceive yourself, monseigneur," replied the bishop. "I should not take the trouble to play this terrible game with your royal highness, if I had not a double interest in gaining it. The day you are elevated, you are elevated forever; you will overturn the footstool, as you rise, and will send it rolling so far, that not even the sight of it will ever again recall to you its right to simple gratitude."

"Oh, monsieur!"

[1] "He is patient because he is eternal." is how the Latin translates. It is from St. Augustine. This motto was sometimes applied to the Papacy, but not to the Jesuits.

"Your movement, monseigneur, arises from an excellent disposition. I thank you. Be well assured, I aspire to more than gratitude! I am convinced that, when arrived at the summit, you will judge me still more worthy to be your friend; and then, monseigneur, we two will do such great deeds, that ages hereafter shall long speak of them."

"Tell me plainly, monsieur—tell me without disguise— what I am to-day, and what you aim at my being to-morrow."

"You are the son of King Louis XIII., brother of Louis XIV., natural and legitimate heir to the throne of France. In keeping you near him, as Monsieur has been kept—Monsieur, your younger brother—the king reserved to himself the right of being legitimate sovereign. The doctors only could dispute his legitimacy. But the doctors always prefer the king who is to the king who is not. Providence has willed that you should be persecuted; this persecution to-day consecrates you king of France. You had, then, a right to reign, seeing that it is disputed; you had a right to be proclaimed seeing that you have been concealed; and you possess royal blood, since no one has dared to shed yours, as that of your servants has been shed. Now see, then, what this Providence, which you have so often accused of having in every way thwarted you, has done for you. It has given you the features, figure, age, and voice of your brother; and the very causes of your persecution are about to become those of your triumphant restoration. To-morrow, after to-morrow—from the very first, regal phantom, living shade of Louis XIV., you will sit upon his throne, whence the will of Heaven, confided in execution to the arm of man, will have hurled him, without hope of return."

"I understand," said the prince, "my brother's blood will not be shed, then."

"You will be sole arbiter of his fate."

"The secret of which they made an evil use against me?"

"You will employ it against him. What did he do to conceal it? He concealed you. Living image of himself, you will defeat the conspiracy of Mazarin and Anne of Austria. You, my prince, will have the same interest in concealing him, who will, as a prisoner, resemble you, as you will resemble him as a king."

"I fall back on what I was saying to you. Who will guard him?"

"Who guarded *you?*"

"You know this secret—you have made use of it with regard to myself. Who else knows it?"

"The queen-mother and Madame de Chevreuse."

"What will they do?"

"Nothing, if you choose."

"How is that?"

"How can they recognize you, if you act in such a manner that no one can recognize you?"

"'Tis true; but there are grave difficulties."

"State them, prince."

"My brother is married; I cannot take my brother's wife."

"I will cause Spain to consent to a divorce; it is in the interest of your new policy; it is human morality. All that is really noble and really useful in this world will find its account therein."

"The imprisoned king will speak."

"To whom do you think he will speak—to the walls?"

"You mean, by walls, the men in whom you put confidence."

"If need be, yes. And besides, your royal highness—"

"Besides?"

"I was going to say, that the designs of Providence do not stop on such a fair road. Every scheme of this caliber is completed by its results, like a geometrical calculation. The king, in prison, will not be for you the cause of embarrassment that you have been for the king enthroned. His soul is naturally proud and impatient; it is, moreover, disarmed and enfeebled, by being accustomed to honors, and by the license of supreme power. The same Providence which has willed that the concluding step in the geometrical calculation I have had the honor of describing to your royal highness should be your ascension to the throne, and the destruction of him who is hurtful to you, has also determined that the conquered one shall soon end both his own and your sufferings. Therefore, his soul and body have been adapted for but a brief agony. Put into prison as a private individual, left alone with your doubts, deprived of everything, you have exhibited the most sublime, enduring principle of life in withstanding all this. But your brother, a captive, forgotten, and in bonds, will not long endure the calamity; and Heaven will resume his soul at the appointed time—that is to say, soon."

At this point in Aramis's gloomy analysis, a bird of night uttered from the depths of the forest that prolonged and plaintive cry which makes every creature tremble.

"I will exile the deposed king," said Philippe, shuddering; "'twill be more human."

"The king's good pleasure will decide the point," said Aramis. "But has the problem been well put? Have I brought out of the solution according to the wishes or the foresight of your royal highness?"

"Yes, monsieur, yes; you have forgotten nothing—except, indeed, two things."

"The first?"

"Let us speak of it at once, with the same frankness we have already conversed in. Let us speak of the causes which may bring about the ruin of all the hopes we have conceived. Let us speak of the risks we are running."

"They would be immense, infinite, terrific, insurmountable, if, as I have said, all things did not concur to render them of absolutely no account. There is no danger either for you or for me, if the constancy and intrepidity of your royal highness are equal to that perfection of resemblance to your brother which nature has bestowed upon you. I repeat it, there are no dangers, only obstacles; a word, indeed, which I find in all languages, but have always ill-understood, and, were I king, would have obliterated as useless and absurd."

"Yes, indeed, monsieur; there is a very serious obstacle, an insurmountable danger, which you are forgetting."

"Ah!" said Aramis.

"There is conscience, which cries aloud; remorse, that never dies."

"True, true," said the bishop; "there is a weakness of heart of which you remind me. You are right, too, for that, indeed, is an immense obstacle. The horse afraid of the ditch, leaps into the middle of it, and is killed! The man who trembling crosses his sword with that of another leaves loopholes whereby his enemy has him in his power."

"Have you a brother?" said the young man to Aramis.

"I am alone in the world," said the latter, with a hard, dry voice.

"But, surely, there is some one in the world whom you love?" added Philippe.

"No one!—Yes, I love you."

The young man sank into so profound a silence, that the mere sound of his respiration seemed like a roaring tumult for Aramis. "Monseigneur," he resumed, "I have not said all I had to say to your royal highness; I have not offered you all the salutary counsels and useful resources which I have at my disposal. It is useless to flash bright visions before the eyes of one who seeks and loves darkness: useless, too, is it to let the magnificence of the cannon's roar make itself heard in the ears of one who loves repose and the quiet of the country. Monseigneur, I have your happiness spread out before me in my thoughts; listen to my words; precious they indeed are, in their import and their sense, for you who look with such tender regard upon the bright heavens, the verdant meadows, the pure air. I know a country instinct with delights of every kind, an unknown paradise, a secluded corner of the world—where alone, unfettered and unknown, in the thick covert of the woods, amidst flowers, and streams of rippling water, you will forget all the misery that human folly has so recently allotted you. Oh! listen to me, my prince. I do not jest. I have a heart, and mind, and soul, and can read your own,—aye, even to its depths. I will not take you unready for your task, in order to cast you into the crucible of my own desires, of my caprice, or my ambition. Let it be all or nothing. You are chilled and galled, sick at heart, overcome by excess of the emotions which but one hour's liberty has produced in you. For me, that is a certain and unmistakable sign that you do not wish to continue at liberty. Would you prefer a more humble life, a life more suited to your strength? Heaven is my witness, that I wish your happiness to be the result of the trial to which I have exposed you."

"Speak, speak," said the prince, with a vivacity which did not escape Aramis.

"I know," resumed the prelate, "in the Bas-Poitou, a canton, of which no one in France suspects the existence. Twenty leagues of country is immense, is it not? Twenty leagues, monseigneur, all covered with water and herbage, and reeds of the most luxuriant nature; the whole studded with islands covered with woods of the densest foliage. These large marshes, covered with reeds as with a thick mantle, sleep silently and calmly beneath the sun's soft and genial rays. A few fishermen with their families indolently pass their lives away there, with their great living-rafts of poplar and alder, the flooring formed of reeds, and the roof woven out of thick rushes. These barks, these floating-houses, are wafted to and fro by the changing winds. Whenever they touch a bank, it is but by chance; and so gently, too, that the sleeping fisherman is not awakened by the shock. Should he wish to land, it is merely because he has seen a large flight of landrails or plovers, of wild ducks, teal, widgeon, or woodchucks, which fall an easy pray to net or gun. Silver shad, eels, greedy pike, red and gray mullet, swim in shoals into his nets; he has but to choose the finest and largest, and return the others to the waters. Never yet has the food of the stranger, be he soldier or simple citizen, never has any one, indeed, penetrated into that district. The sun's rays there are soft and tempered: in plots of solid earth, whose soil is swart and fertile, grows the vine, nourishing with generous juice its purple, white, and golden grapes. Once a week, a boat is sent to deliver the bread which has been baked at an oven—the common property of all. There—like the seigneurs of early days—powerful in virtue of your dogs, your fishing-lines, your guns, and your beautiful reed-built house, would you live, rich in the produce of the chase, in plentitude of absolute secrecy. There would years of your life roll away, at the end of which, no longer recognizable, for you would have been perfectly transformed, you would have succeeded in acquiring a destiny accorded to you by Heaven. There are a thousand pistoles in this bag, monseigneur—more, far more, than sufficient to purchase the whole marsh of which I have spoken; more than enough to live there as many years as you have days to live; more than enough to constitute you the richest, the freest, and the happiest man in the country. Accept it, as I offer it you—sincerely, cheerfully. Forthwith, without a moment's pause, I will unharness two of my horses, which are attached to the carriage yonder, and they, accompanied by my servant—my deaf and dumb attendant—shall conduct you—traveling throughout the night, sleeping during the day—to the locality I have described; and I shall, at least, have the satisfaction of knowing that I have rendered to my prince the major service he himself preferred. I shall have made one human being happy; and Heaven for that will hold me in better account than if I had made one man powerful; the former task is far more difficult. And now, monseigneur, your answer to this proposition? Here is the money. Nay, do not hesitate. At Poitou, you can risk nothing, except the chance of catching the fevers prevalent there; and even of them, the so-called wizards of the country will cure you, for the sake of your pistoles. If you play the other game, you run the chance of being assassinated on a throne, strangled in a prison-cell. Upon my soul, I assure you, now I begin to compare them together, I myself should hesitate which lot I should accept."

"Monsieur," replied the young prince, "before I determine, let me alight from this carriage, walk on the ground, and consult that still voice within me, which Heaven bids us all to hearken to. Ten minutes is all I ask, and then you shall have your answer."

"As you please, monseigneur," said Aramis, bending before him with respect, so solemn and august in tone and address had sounded these strange words.

CHAPTER 10

Crown and Tiara.

Aramis was the first to descend from the carriage; he held the door open for the young man. He saw him place his foot on the mossy ground with a trembling of the whole body, and walk round the carriage with an unsteady and almost tottering step. It seemed as if the poor prisoner was unaccustomed to walk on God's earth. It was the 15th of August, about eleven o'clock at night; thick clouds, portending a tempest, overspread the heavens, and shrouded every light and prospect underneath their heavy folds. The extremities of the avenues were imperceptibly detached from the copse, by a lighter shadow of opaque gray, which, upon closer examination, became visible in the midst of the obscurity. But the fragrance which ascended from the grass, fresher and more penetrating than that which exhaled from the trees around him; the warm and balmy air which enveloped him for the first time for many years past; the ineffable enjoyment of liberty in an open country, spoke to the prince in so seductive a language, that notwithstanding the preternatural caution, we would almost say dissimulation of his character, of which we have tried to give an idea, he could not restrain his emotion, and breathed a sigh of ecstasy. Then, by degrees, he raised his aching head and inhaled the softly scented air, as it was wafted in gentle gusts to his uplifted face. Crossing his arms on his chest, as if to control this new sensation of delight, he drank in delicious draughts of that mysterious air which interpenetrates at night the loftiest forests. The sky he was contemplating, the murmuring waters, the universal freshness—was not all this reality? Was not Aramis a madman to suppose that he had aught else to dream of in this world? Those exciting pictures of country life, so free from fears and troubles, the ocean of happy days that glitters incessantly before all young imaginations, are real allurements wherewith to fascinate a poor, unhappy prisoner, worn out by prison cares, emaciated by the stifling air of the Bastille. It was the picture, it will be remembered, drawn by Aramis, when he offered the thousand pistoles he had with him in the carriage to the prince, and the enchanted Eden which the deserts of Bas-Poitou hid from the eyes of the world. Such were the reflections of Aramis as he watched, with an anxiety impossible to describe, the silent progress of the emotions of Philippe, whom he perceived gradually becoming more and more absorbed in his meditations. The young prince was offering up an inward prayer to Heaven, to be divinely guided in this trying moment, upon which his life or death depended. It was an anxious time for the bishop of Vannes, who had never before been so perplexed. His iron will, accustomed to overcome all obstacles, never finding itself inferior or vanquished on any occasion, to be foiled in so vast a project from not having foreseen the influence which a view of nature in all its luxuriance would have on the human mind! Aramis, overwhelmed by anxiety, contemplated with emotion the painful struggle that was taking place in Philippe's mind. This suspense lasted the whole ten minutes which the young man had requested. During this space of time, which appeared an eternity, Philippe continued gazing with an imploring and sorrowful look towards the heavens; Aramis did not remove the piercing glance he had fixed on Philippe. Suddenly the young man bowed his head. His thought returned to the earth, his looks perceptibly hardened, his brow contracted, his mouth assuming an expression of undaunted courage; again his looks became fixed, but this time they wore a worldly expression, hardened by covetousness, pride, and strong desire. Aramis's look immediately became as soft as it had before been gloomy. Philippe, seizing his hand in a quick, agitated manner, exclaimed:

"Lead me to where the crown of France is to be found."

"Is this your decision, monseigneur?" asked Aramis.

"It is."

"Irrevocably so?"

Philippe did not even deign to reply. He gazed earnestly at the bishop, as if to ask him if it were possible for a man to waver after having once made up his mind.

"Such looks are flashes of the hidden fire that betrays men's character," said Aramis, bowing over Philippe's hand; "you will be great, monseigneur, I will answer for that."

"Let us resume our conversation. I wished to discuss two points with you; in the first place the dangers, or the obstacles we may meet with. That point is decided. The other is the conditions you intend imposing on me. It is your turn to speak, M. d'Herblay."

"The conditions, monseigneur?"

"Doubtless. You will not allow so mere a trifle to stop me, and you will not do me the injustice to suppose that I think you have no interest in this affair. Therefore, without subterfuge or hesitation, tell me the truth—"

"I will do so, monseigneur. Once a king—"

"When will that be?"

"To-morrow evening—I mean in the night."

"Explain yourself."

"When I shall have asked your highness a question."

"Do so."

"I sent to your highness a man in my confidence with instructions to deliver some closely written notes, carefully drawn up, which will thoroughly acquaint your highness with the different persons who compose and will compose your court."

"I perused those notes."

"Attentively?"

"I know them by heart."

"And understand them? Pardon me, but I may venture to ask that question of a poor, abandoned captive of the Bastille? In a week's time it will not be requisite to further question a mind like yours. You will then be in full possession of liberty and power."

"Interrogate me, then, and I will be a scholar representing his lesson to his master."

"We will begin with your family, monseigneur."

"My mother, Anne of Austria! all her sorrows, her painful malady. Oh! I know her—I know her."

"Your second brother?" asked Aramis, bowing.

"To these notes," replied the prince, "you have added portraits so faithfully painted, that I am able to recognize the persons whose characters, manners, and history you have so carefully portrayed. Monsieur, my brother, is a fine, dark young man, with a pale face; he does not love his wife, Henrietta, whom I, Louis XIV., loved a little, and still flirt with, even although she made me weep on the day she wished to dismiss Mademoiselle de la Valliere from her service in disgrace."

"You will have to be careful with regard to the watchfulness of the latter," said Aramis; "she is sincerely attached to the actual king. The eyes of a woman who loves are not easily deceived."

"She is fair, has blue eyes, whose affectionate gaze reveals her identity. She halts slightly in her gait; she writes a letter every day, to which I have to send an answer by M. de Saint-Aignan."

"Do you know the latter?"

"As if I saw him, and I know the last verses he composed for me, as well as those I composed in answer to his."

"Very good. Do you know your ministers?"

"Colbert, an ugly, dark-browed man, but intelligent enough, his hair covering his forehead, a large, heavy, full head; the mortal enemy of M. Fouquet."

"As for the latter, we need not disturb ourselves about him."

"No; because necessarily you will not require me to exile him, I suppose?"

Aramis, struck with admiration at the remark, said, "You will become very great, monseigneur."

"You see," added the prince, "that I know my lesson by heart, and with Heaven's assistance, and yours afterwards, I shall seldom go wrong."

"You have still an awkward pair of eyes to deal with, monseigneur."

"Yes, the captain of the musketeers, M. d'Artagnan, your friend."

"Yes; I can well say 'my friend.'"

"He who escorted La Valliere to Le Chaillot; he who delivered up Monk, cooped in an iron box, to Charles II.; he who so faithfully served my mother; he to whom the crown of France owes so much that it owes everything. Do you intend to ask me to exile him also?"

"Never, sire. D'Artagnan is a man to whom, at a certain given time, I will undertake to reveal everything; but be on your guard with him, for if he discovers our plot before it is revealed to him, you or I will certainly be killed or taken. He is a bold and enterprising man."

"I will think it over. Now tell me about M. Fouquet; what do you wish to be done with regard to him?"

"One moment more, I entreat you, monseigneur; and forgive me, if I seem to fail in respect to questioning you further."

"It is your duty to do so, nay, more than that, your right."

"Before we pass to M. Fouquet, I should very much regret forgetting another friend of mine."

"M. du Vallon, the Hercules of France, you mean; oh! as far as he is concerned, his interests are more than safe."

"No; it is not he whom I intended to refer to."

"The Comte de la Fere, then?"

"And his son, the son of all four of us."

"That poor boy who is dying of love for La Valliere, whom my brother so disloyally bereft him of? Be easy on that score. I shall know how to rehabilitate his happiness. Tell me only one thing, Monsieur d'Herblay; do men, when they love, forget the treachery that has been shown them? Can a man ever forgive the woman who has betrayed him? Is that a French custom, or is it one of the laws of the human heart?"

"A man who loves deeply, as deeply as Raoul loves Mademoiselle de la Valliere, finishes by forgetting the fault or crime of the woman he loves; but I do not yet know whether Raoul will be able to forget."

"I will see after that. Have you anything further to say about your friend?"

"No; that is all."

"Well, then, now for M. Fouquet. What do you wish me to do for him?"

"To keep him on as surintendant, in the capacity in which he has hitherto acted, I entreat you."

"Be it so; but he is the first minister at present."

"Not quite so."

"A king, ignorant and embarrassed as I shall be, will, as a matter of course, require a first minister of state."

"Your majesty will require a friend."

"I have only one, and that is yourself."

"You will have many others by and by, but none so devoted, none so zealous for your glory."

"You shall be my first minister of state."

"Not immediately, monseigneur, for that would give rise to too much suspicion and astonishment."

"M. de Richelieu, the first minister of my grandmother, Marie de Medici, was simply bishop of Lucon, as you are bishop of Vannes."

"I perceive that your royal highness has studied my notes to great advantage; your amazing perspicacity overpowers me with delight."

"I am perfectly aware that M. de Richelieu, by means of the queen's protection, soon became cardinal."

"It would be better," said Aramis, bowing, "that I should not be appointed first minister until your royal highness has procured my nomination as cardinal."

"You shall be nominated before two months are past, Monsieur d'Herblay. But that is a matter of very trifling moment; you would not offend me if you were to ask more than that, and you would cause me serious regret if you were to limit yourself to that."

"In that case, I have something still further to hope for, monseigneur."

"Speak! speak!"

"M. Fouquet will not keep long at the head of affairs, he will soon get old. He is fond of pleasure, consistently, I mean, with all his labors, thanks to the youthfulness he still retains; but this protracted youth will disappear at the approach of the first serious annoyance, or at the first illness he may experience. We will spare him the annoyance, because he is an agreeable and noble-hearted man; but we cannot save him from ill-health. So it is determined. When you shall have paid all M. Fouquet's debts, and restored the finances to a sound condition, M. Fouquet will be able to remain the sovereign ruler in his little court of poets and painters,—we shall have

115

made him rich. When that has been done, and I have become your royal highness's prime minister, I shall be able to think of my own interests and yours."

The young man looked at his interrogator.

"M. de Richelieu, of whom we were speaking just now, was very much to blame in the fixed idea he had of governing France alone, unaided. He allowed two kings, King Louis XIII. and himself, to be seated on the self-same throne, whilst he might have installed them more conveniently upon two separate and distinct thrones."

"Upon two thrones?" said the young man, thoughtfully.

"In fact," pursued Aramis, quietly, "a cardinal, prime minister of France, assisted by the favor and by the countenance of his Most Christian Majesty the King of France, a cardinal to whom the king his master lends the treasures of the state, his army, his counsel, such a man would be acting with twofold injustice in applying these mighty resources to France alone. Besides," added Aramis, "you will not be a king such as your father was, delicate in health, slow in judgment, whom all things wearied; you will be a king governing by your brain and by your sword; you will have in the government of the state no more than you will be able to manage unaided; I should only interfere with you. Besides, our friendship ought never to be, I do not say impaired, but in any degree affected, by a secret thought. I shall have given you the throne of France, you will confer on me the throne of St. Peter. Whenever your loyal, firm, and mailed hand should joined in ties of intimate association the hand of a pope such as I shall be, neither Charles V., who owned two-thirds of the habitable globe, nor Charlemagne, who possessed it entirely, will be able to reach to half your stature. I have no alliances, I have no predilections; I will not throw you into persecutions of heretics, nor will I cast you into the troubled waters of family dissension; I will simply say to you: The whole universe is our own; for me the minds of men, for you their bodies. And as I shall be the first to die, you will have my inheritance. What do you say of my plan, monseigneur?"

"I say that you render me happy and proud, for no other reason than that of having comprehended you thoroughly. Monsieur d'Herblay, you shall be cardinal, and when cardinal, my prime minister; and then you will point out to me the necessary steps to be taken to secure your election as pope, and I will take them. You can ask what guarantees from me you please."

"It is useless. Never shall I act except in such a manner that you will be the gainer; I shall never ascend the ladder of fortune, fame, or position, until I have first seen you placed upon the round of the ladder immediately above me; I shall always hold myself sufficiently aloof from you to escape incurring your jealousy, sufficiently near to sustain your personal advantage and to watch over your friendship. All the contracts in the world are easily violated because the interests included in them incline more to one side than to another. With us, however, this will never be the case; I have no need of any guarantees."

"And so—my dear brother—will disappear?"

"Simply. We will remove him from his bed by means of a plank which yields to the pressure of the finger. Having retired to rest a crowned sovereign, he will awake a captive. Alone you will rule from that moment, and you will have no interest dearer and better than that of keeping me near you."

"I believe it. There is my hand on it, Monsieur d'Herblay."

"Allow me to kneel before you, sire, most respectfully. We will embrace each other on the day we shall have upon our temples, you the crown, I the tiara."

"Still embrace me this very day also, and be, for and towards me, more than great, more than skillful, more than sublime in genius; be kind and indulgent—be my father!"

Aramis was almost overcome as he listened to his voice;

he fancied he detected in his own heart an emotion hitherto unknown; but this impression was speedily removed. "His father!" he thought; "yes, his Holy Father."

And they resumed their places in the carriage, which sped rapidly along the road leading to Vaux-le-Vicomte.

CHAPTER 11

The Chateau de Vaux-le-Vicomte.

The chateau of Vaux-le-Vicomte, situated about a league from Melun, had been built by Fouquet in 1655, at a time when there was a scarcity of money in France; Mazarin had taken all that there was, and Fouquet expended the remainder. However, as certain men have fertile, false, and useful vices, Fouquet, in scattering broadcast millions of money in the construction of this palace, had found a means of gathering, as the result of his generous profusion, three illustrious men together: Levau, the architect of the building; Lenotre, the designer of the gardens; and Lebrun, the decorator of the apartments. If the Chateau de Vaux possessed a single fault with which it could be reproached, it was its grand, pretentious character. It is even at the present day proverbial to calculate the number of acres of roofing, the restoration of which would, in our age, be the ruin of fortunes cramped and narrowed as the epoch itself. Vaux-le-Vicomte, when its magnificent gates, supported by caryatides, have been passed through, has the principal front of the main building opening upon a vast, so-called, court of honor, inclosed by deep ditches, bordered by a magnificent stone balustrade. Nothing could be more noble in appearance than the central forecourt raised upon the flight of steps, like a king upon his throne, having around it four pavilions at the angles, the immense Ionic columns of which rose majestically to the whole height of the building. The friezes ornamented with arabesques, and the pediments which crowned the pilasters, conferred richness and grace on every part of the building, while the domes which surmounted the whole added proportion and majesty. This mansion, built by a subject, bore a far greater resemblance to those royal residences which Wolsey fancied he was called upon to construct, in order to present them to his master form the fear of rendering him jealous. But if magnificence and splendor were displayed in any one particular part of this palace more than another,—if anything could be preferred to the wonderful arrangement of the interior, to the sumptuousness of the gilding, and to the profusion of the paintings and statues, it would be the park and gardens of Vaux. The *jets d'eau*, which were regarded as wonderful in 1653, are still so, even at the present time; the cascades awakened the admiration of kings and princes; and as for the famous grotto, the theme of so many poetical effusions, the residence of that illustrious nymph of Vaux, whom Pelisson made converse with La Fontaine, we must be spared the description of all its beauties. We will do as Despreaux did,—we will enter the park, the trees of which are of eight years' growth only—that is to say, in their present position—and whose summits even yet, as they proudly tower aloft, blushingly unfold their leaves to the earliest rays of the rising sun. Lenotre had hastened the pleasure of the Maecenas of his period; all the nursery-grounds had furnished trees whose growth had been accelerated by careful culture and the richest plant-food. Every tree in the neighborhood which presented a fair appearance of beauty or stature had been taken up by its roots and transplanted to the park. Fouquet could well afford to purchase trees to ornament his park, since he had bought up three villages and their appurtenances (to use a legal word) to increase its extent. M. de Scudery said of this palace, that, for the purpose of keeping the grounds and gardens well watered, M. Fouquet had divided a river into a thousand fountains, and gathered the waters of a thousand fountains into torrents. This same Monsieur de Scudery said a great many other things in his "Clelie," about this palace of Valterre, the charms of which he describes most minutely. We should be far wiser to send our curious readers to Vaux to judge for themselves, than to refer them to "Clelie;" and yet there are as many leagues from Paris to Vaux, as there are volumes of the "Clelie."

This magnificent palace had been got ready for the reception of the greatest reigning sovereign of the time. M. Fouquet's friends had transported thither, some their actors and their dresses, others their troops of sculptors and artists; not forgetting others with their ready-mended pens,—floods of impromptus were contemplated. The cascades, somewhat rebellious nymphs though they were, poured forth their waters brighter and clearer than crystal: they scattered over the bronze triton and nereids their waves of foam, which glistened like fire in the rays of the sun. An army of servants were hurrying to and fro in squadrons in the courtyard and corridors; while Fouquet, who had only that morning arrived, walked all through the palace with a calm, observant glance, in order to give his last orders, after his intendants had inspected everything.

It was, as we have said, the 15th of August. The sun poured down its burning rays upon the heathen deities of marble and bronze: it raised the temperature of the water in the conch shells, and ripened, on the walls, those magnificent peaches, of which the king, fifty years later, spoke so regretfully, when, at Marly, on an occasion of a scarcity of the finer sorts of peaches being complained of, in the beautiful gardens there—gardens which had cost

France double the amount that had been expended on Vaux—the *great king* observed to some one: "You are far too young to have eaten any of M. Fouquet's peaches."

Oh, fame! Oh, blazon of renown! Oh, glory of this earth! That very man whose judgment was so sound and accurate where merit was concerned—he who had swept into his coffers the inheritance of Nicholas Fouquet, who had robbed him of Lenotre and Lebrun, and had sent him to rot for the remainder of his life in one of the state prisons—merely remembered the peaches of that vanquished, crushed, forgotten enemy! It was to little purpose that Fouquet had squandered thirty millions of francs in the fountains of his gardens, in the crucibles of his sculptors, in the writing-desks of his literary friends, in the portfolios of his painters; vainly had he fancied that thereby he might be remembered. A peach—a blushing, rich-flavored fruit, nestling in the trellis work on the garden-wall, hidden beneath its long, green leaves,—this little vegetable production, that a dormouse would nibble up without a thought, was sufficient to recall to the memory of this great monarch the mournful shade of the last surintendant of France.

With a perfect reliance that Aramis had made arrangements fairly to distribute the vast number of guests throughout the palace, and that he had not omitted to attend to any of the internal regulations for their comfort, Fouquet devoted his entire attention to the *ensemble* alone. In one direction Gourville showed him the preparations which had been made for the fireworks; in another, Moliere led him over the theater; at last, after he had visited the chapel, the *salons*, and the galleries, and was again going downstairs, exhausted with fatigue, Fouquet saw Aramis on the staircase. The prelate beckoned to him. The surintendant joined his friend, and, with him, paused before a large picture scarcely finished. Applying himself, heart and soul, to his work, the painter Lebrun, covered with perspiration, stained with paint, pale from fatigue and the inspiration of genius, was putting the last finishing touches with his rapid brush. It was the portrait of the king, whom they were expecting, dressed in the court suit which Percerin had condescended to show beforehand to the bishop of Vannes. Fouquet placed himself before this portrait, which seemed to live, as one might say, in the cool freshness of its flesh, and in its warmth of color. He gazed upon it long and fixedly, estimated the prodigious labor that had been bestowed upon it, and, not being able to find any recompense sufficiently great for this Herculean effort, he passed his arm round the painter's neck and embraced him. The surintendant, by this action, had utterly ruined a suit of clothes worth a thousand pistoles, but he had satisfied, more than satisfied, Lebrun. It was a happy moment for the artist; it was an unhappy moment for M. Percerin, who was walking behind Fouquet, and was engaged in admiring, in Lebrun's painting, the suit that he had made for his majesty, a perfect *objet d'art*, as he called it, which was not to be matched except in the wardrobe of the surintendant. His distress and his exclamations were interrupted by a signal which had been given from the summit of the mansion. In the direction of Melun, in the still empty, open plain, the sentinels of Vaux had just perceived the advancing procession of the king and the queens. His majesty was entering Melun with his long train of carriages and cavaliers.

"In an hour—" said Aramis to Fouquet.

"In an hour!" replied the latter, sighing.

"And the people who ask one another what is the good of these royal *fetes*!" continued the bishop of Vannes, laughing, with his false smile.

"Alas! I, too, who am not the people, ask myself the same thing."

"I will answer you in four and twenty hours, monseigneur. Assume a cheerful countenance, for it should be a day of true rejoicing."

"Well, believe me or not, as you like, D'Herblay," said the surintendant, with a swelling heart, pointing at the *cortege* of Louis, visible in the horizon, "he certainly loves me but very little, and I do not care much more for him; but I cannot tell you how it is, that since he is approaching my house—"

"Well, what?"

"Well, since I know he is on his way here, as my guest, he is more sacred than ever for me; he is my acknowledged sovereign, and as such is very dear to me."

"Dear? yes," said Aramis, playing upon the word, as the Abbe Terray did, at a later period, with Louis XV.

"Do not laugh, D'Herblay; I feel that, if he really seemed to wish it, I could love that young man."

"You should not say that to me," returned Aramis, "but rather to M. Colbert."

"To M. Colbert!" exclaimed Fouquet. "Why so?"

"Because he would allow you a pension out of the king's privy purse, as soon as he becomes surintendant," said Aramis, preparing to leave as soon as he had dealt this last blow.

"Where are you going?" returned Fouquet, with a gloomy look.

"To my own apartment, in order to change my costume, monseigneur."

"Whereabouts are you lodging, D'Herblay?"

"In the blue room on the second story."

"The room immediately over the king's room?"

"Precisely."

"You will be subject to very great restraint there. What an idea to condemn yourself to a room where you cannot stir or move about!"

"During the night, monseigneur, I sleep or read in my bed."

"And your servants?"

"I have but one attendant with me. I find my reader

quite sufficient. Adieu, monseigneur; do not overfatigue your-self; keep yourself fresh for the arrival of the king."

"We shall see you by and by, I suppose, and shall see your friend Du Vallon also?"

"He is lodging next to me, and is at this moment dressing."

And Fouquet, bowing, with a smile, passed on like a commander-in-chief who pays the different outposts a visit after the enemy has been signaled in sight.[2]

[2] In the five-volume edition, Volume 4 ends here.

CHAPTER 12

The Wine of Melun.

The king had, in point of fact, entered Melun with the intention of merely passing through the city. The youthful monarch was most eagerly anxious for amusements; only twice during the journey had he been able to catch a glimpse of La Valliere, and, suspecting that his only opportunity of speaking to her would be after nightfall, in the gardens, and after the ceremonial of reception had been gone through, he had been very desirous to arrive at Vaux as early as possible. But he reckoned without his captain of the musketeers, and without M. Colbert. Like Calypso, who could not be consoled at the departure of Ulysses, our Gascon could not console himself for not having guessed why Aramis had asked Percerin to show him the king's new costumes. "There is not a doubt," he said to himself, "that my friend the bishop of Vannes had some motive in that;" and then he began to rack his brains most uselessly. D'Artagnan, so intimately acquainted with all the court intrigues, who knew the position of Fouquet better than even Fouquet himself did, had conceived the strangest fancies and suspicions at the announcement of the *fete*, which would have ruined a wealthy man, and which became impossible, utter madness even, for a man so poor as he was. And then, the presence of Aramis, who had returned from

Belle-Isle, and been nominated by Monsieur Fouquet inspector-general of all the arrangements; his perseverance in mixing himself up with all the surintendant's affairs; his visits to Baisemeaux; all this suspicious singularity of conduct had excessively troubled and tormented D'Artagnan during the last two weeks.

"With men of Aramis's stamp," he said, "one is never the stronger except sword in hand. So long as Aramis continued a soldier, there was hope of getting the better of him; but since he has covered his cuirass with a stole, we are lost. But what can Aramis's object possibly be?" And D'Artagnan plunged again into deep thought. "What does it matter to me, after all," he continued, "if his only object is to overthrow M. Colbert? And what else can he be after?" And D'Artagnan rubbed his forehead—that fertile land, whence the plowshare of his nails had turned up so many and such admirable ideas in his time. He, at first, thought of talking the matter over with Colbert, but his friendship for Aramis, the oath of earlier days, bound him too strictly. He revolted at the bare idea of such a thing, and, besides, he hated the financier too cordially. Then, again, he wished to unburden his mind to the king; but yet the king would not be able to understand the suspicions which had not even a shadow of reality at their base. He resolved to address himself to Aramis, direct, the first time he met him. "I will get him," said the musketeer, "between a couple of candles, suddenly, and when he least expects it, I will place my hand upon his heart, and he will tell me—What will he tell me? Yes, he will tell me something, for *mordioux!* there is something in it, I know."

Somewhat calmer, D'Artagnan made every preparation for the journey, and took the greatest care that the military household of the king, as yet very inconsiderable in numbers, should be well officered and well disciplined in its meager and limited proportions. The result was that, through the captain's arrangements, the king, on arriving at Melun, saw himself at the head of both the musketeers and Swiss guards, as well as a picket of the French guards. It might almost have been called a small army. M. Colbert looked at the troops with great delight: he even wished they had been a third more in number.

"But why?" said the king.

"In order to show greater honor to M. Fouquet," replied Colbert.

"In order to ruin him the sooner," thought D'Artagnan.

When this little army appeared before Melun, the chief magistrates came out to meet the king, and to present him with the keys of the city, and invited him to enter the Hotel de Ville, in order to partake of the wine of honor. The king, who expected to pass through the city and to proceed to Vaux without delay, became quite red in the face from vexation.

"Who was fool enough to occasion this delay?" muttered the king, between his teeth, as the chief magistrate was in the middle of a long address.

"Not I, certainly," replied D'Artagnan, "but I believe it was M. Colbert."

Colbert, having heard his name pronounced, said, "What was M. d'Artagnan good enough to say?"

"I was good enough to remark that it was you who stopped the king's progress, so that he might taste the *vin de Brie*. Was I right?"

"Quite so, monsieur."

"In that case, then, it was you whom the king called some name or other."

"What name?"

"I hardly know; but wait a moment—idiot, I think it was—no, no, it was fool or dolt. Yes; his majesty said that the man who had thought of the *vin de Melun* was something of the sort."

D'Artagnan, after this broadside, quietly caressed his

mustache; M. Colbert's large head seemed to become larger and larger than ever. D'Artagnan, seeing how ugly anger made him, did not stop half-way. The orator still went on with his speech, while the king's color was visibly increasing.

"*Mordioux!*" said the musketeer, coolly, "the king is going to have an attack of determination of blood to the head. Where the deuce did you get hold of that idea, Monsieur Colbert? You have no luck."

"Monsieur," said the financier, drawing himself up, "my zeal for the king's service inspired me with the idea."

"Bah!"

"Monsieur, Melun is a city, an excellent city, which pays well, and which it would be imprudent to displease."

"There, now! I, who do not pretend to be a financier, saw only one idea in your idea."

"What was that, monsieur?"

"That of causing a little annoyance to M. Fouquet, who is making himself quite giddy on his donjons yonder, in waiting for us."

This was a home-stroke, hard enough in all conscience. Colbert was completely thrown out of the saddle by it, and retired, thoroughly discomfited. Fortunately, the speech was now at an end; the king drank the wine which was presented to him, and then every one resumed the progress through the city. The king bit his lips in anger, for the evening was closing in, and all hope of a walk with La Valliere was at an end. In order that the whole of the king's household should enter Vaux, four hours at least were necessary, owing to the different arrangements. The king, therefore, who was boiling with impatience, hurried forward as much as possible, in order to reach it before nightfall. But, at the moment he was setting off again, other and fresh difficulties arose.

"Is not the king going to sleep at Melun?" said Colbert, in a low tone of voice, to D'Artagnan.

M. Colbert must have been badly inspired that day, to

address himself in that manner to the chief of the musketeers; for the latter guessed that the king's intention was very far from that of remaining where he was. D'Artagnan would not allow him to enter Vaux except he were well and strongly accompanied; and desired that his majesty would not enter except with all the escort. On the other hand, he felt that these delays would irritate that impatient monarch beyond measure. In what way could he possibly reconcile these difficulties? D'Artagnan took up Colbert's remark, and determined to repeated it to the king.

"Sire," he said, "M. Colbert has been asking me if your majesty does not intend to sleep at Melun."

"Sleep at Melun! What for?" exclaimed Louis XIV. "Sleep at Melun! Who, in Heaven's name, can have thought of such a thing, when M. Fouquet is expecting us this evening?"

"It was simply," replied Colbert, quickly, "the fear of causing your majesty the least delay; for, according to established etiquette, you cannot enter any place, with the exception of your own royal residences, until the soldiers' quarters have been marked out by the quartermaster, and the garrison properly distributed."

D'Artagnan listened with the greatest attention, biting his mustache to conceal his vexation; and the queens were not less interested. They were fatigued, and would have preferred to go to rest without proceeding any farther; more especially, in order to prevent the king walking about in the evening with M. de Saint-Aignan and the ladies of the court, for, if etiquette required the princesses to remain within their own rooms, the ladies of honor, as soon as they had performed the services required of them, had no restrictions placed upon them, but were at liberty to walk about as they pleased. It will easily be conjectured that all these rival interests, gathering together in vapors, necessarily produced clouds, and that the clouds were likely to be followed by a tempest. The king had no mustache to gnaw,

and therefore kept biting the handle of his whip instead,
with ill-concealed impatience. How could he get out of it?
D'Artagnan looked as agreeable as possible, and Colbert as
sulky as he could. Who was there he could get in a passion
with?

"We will consult the queen," said Louis XIV., bowing to
the royal ladies. And this kindness of consideration softened
Maria Theresa's heart, who, being of a kind and generous
disposition, when left to her own free-will, replied:

"I shall be delighted to do whatever your majesty wishes."

"How long will it take us to get to Vaux?" inquired Anne
of Austria, in slow and measured accents, placing her hand
upon her bosom, where the seat of her pain lay.

"An hour for your majesty's carriages," said D'Artagnan;
"the roads are tolerably good."

The king looked at him. "And a quarter of an hour for
the king," he hastened to add.

"We should arrive by daylight?" said Louis XIV.

"But the billeting of the king's military escort," objected
Colbert, softly, "will make his majesty lose all the advantage
of his speed, however quick he may be."

"Double ass that you are!" thought D'Artagnan; "if I
had any interest or motive in demolishing your credit with
the king, I could do it in ten minutes. If I were in the king's
place," he added aloud, "I should, in going to M. Fouquet,
leave my escort behind me; I should go to him as a friend; I
should enter accompanied only by my captain of the guards;
I should consider that I was acting more nobly, and should
be invested with a still more sacred character by doing so."

Delight sparkled in the king's eyes. "That is indeed a
very sensible suggestion. We will go to see a friend as friends;
the gentlemen who are with the carriages can go slowly: but
we who are mounted will ride on." And he rode off, accompanied by all those who were mounted. Colbert hid his ugly
head behind his horse's neck.

"I shall be quits," said D'Artagnan, as he galloped along, "by getting a little talk with Aramis this evening. And then, M. Fouquet is a man of honor. *Mordioux!* I have said so, and it must be so."

And this was the way how, towards seven o'clock in the evening, without announcing his arrival by the din of trumpets, and without even his advanced guard, without out-riders or musketeers, the king presented himself before the gate of Vaux, where Fouquet, who had been informed of his royal guest's approach, had been waiting for the last half-hour, with his head uncovered, surrounded by his household and his friends.

CHAPTER 13

Nectar and Ambrosia.

M. Fouquet held the stirrup of the king, who, having dismounted, bowed most graciously, and more graciously still held out his hand to him, which Fouquet, in spite of a slight resistance on the king's part, carried respectfully to his lips. The king wished to wait in the first courtyard for the arrival of the carriages, nor had he long to wait, for the roads had been put into excellent order by the superintendent, and a stone would hardly have been found of the size of an egg the whole way from Melun to Vaux; so that the carriages, rolling along as though on a carpet, brought the ladies to Vaux, without jolting or fatigue, by eight o'clock. They were received by Madame Fouquet, and at the moment they made their appearance, a light as bright as day burst forth from every quarter, trees, vases, and marble statues. This species of enchantment lasted until their majesties had retired into the palace. All these wonders and magical effects which the chronicler has heaped up, or rather embalmed, in his recital, at the risk of rivaling the brain-born scenes of romancers; these splendors whereby night seemed vanquished and nature corrected, together with every delight and luxury combined for the satisfaction of all the senses, as well as the imagination, Fouquet did in real truth offer to his sovereign in that enchanting retreat of which no monarch could at that time boast of possessing an equal. We do not intend to describe the grand banquet, at which the royal guests were present, nor the concerts, nor the fairy-like and more than magic transformations and metamorphoses; it will be enough for our purpose to depict the countenance the king assumed, which, from being gay, soon wore a very gloomy, constrained, and irritated expression. He remembered his own residence, royal though it was, and the mean and indifferent style of luxury that prevailed there, which comprised but little more than what was merely useful for the royal wants, without being his own personal property. The large vases of the Louvre, the older furniture and plate of Henry II., of Francis I., and of Louis XI., were but historic monuments of earlier days; nothing but specimens of art, the relics of his predecessors; while with Fouquet, the value of the article was as much in the workmanship as in the article itself. Fouquet ate from a gold service, which artists in his own employ had modeled and cast for him alone. Fouquet drank wines of which the king of France did not even know the name, and drank them out of goblets each more valuable than the entire royal cellar.

What, too, was to be said of the apartments, the hangings, the pictures, the servants and officers, of every description, of his household? What of the mode of service in which etiquette was replaced by order; stiff formality by personal, unrestrained comfort; the happiness and contentment of the guest became the supreme law of all who obeyed the host? The perfect swarm of busily engaged persons moving about noiselessly; the multitude of guests,—who were, however, even less numerous than the servants who waited on them,— the myriad of exquisitely prepared dishes, of gold and silver vases; the floods of dazzling light, the masses of unknown flowers of which the hot-houses had been despoiled, redundant with luxuriance of unequaled scent and beauty; the perfect harmony of the surroundings, which, indeed, was no more than the prelude of the promised *fete*, charmed all who were there; and they testified their admiration over and over again, not by voice or gesture, but by deep silence and rapt attention, those two languages of the courtier which acknowledge the hand of no master powerful enough to restrain them.

As for the king, his eyes filled with tears; he dared not look at the queen. Anne of Austria, whose pride was superior to that of any creature breathing, overwhelmed her host by the contempt with which she treated everything handed to her. The young queen, kind-hearted by nature and curious by disposition, praised Fouquet, ate with an exceedingly good appetite, and asked the names of the strange fruits as they were placed upon the table. Fouquet replied that he was not aware of their names. The fruits came from his own stores; he had often cultivated them himself, having an intimate acquaintance with the cultivation of exotic fruits and plants. The king felt and appreciated the delicacy of the replies, but was only the more humiliated; he thought the queen a little too familiar in her manners, and that Anne of Austria resembled Juno a little too much, in being too proud and haughty; his chief anxiety, however, was himself, that he might remain cold and distant in his behavior, bordering lightly the limits of supreme disdain or simple admiration.

But Fouquet had foreseen all this; he was, in fact, one of those men who foresee everything. The king had expressly declared that, so long as he remained under Fouquet's roof, he did not wish his own different repasts to be served in accordance with the usual etiquette, and that he would, consequently, dine with the rest of society; but by the thoughtful attention of the surintendant, the king's dinner was served up separately, if one may so express it, in the middle of the general table; the dinner, wonderful in every respect, from the dishes of which was composed, comprised everything the king liked and generally preferred to anything else. Louis had no excuse—he, indeed, who had the keenest appetite in his kingdom—for saying that he was not hungry. Nay, M. Fouquet did even better still; he certainly, in obedience to the king's expressed desire, seated himself at the table, but as soon as the soups were served, he arose and personally waited on the king, while Madame Fouquet stood behind the queen-mother's armchair. The disdain of Juno and the sulky fits of temper of Jupiter could not resist this excess of kindly feeling and polite attention. The queen ate a biscuit dipped in a glass of San-Lucar wine; and the king ate of everything, saying to M. Fouquet: "It is impossible, monsieur le surintendant, to dine better anywhere." Whereupon the whole court began, on all sides, to devour the dishes spread before them with such enthusiasm that it looked as though a cloud of Egyptian locusts was settling down on green and growing crops.

As soon, however, as his hunger was appeased, the king became morose and overgloomed again; the more so in proportion to the satisfaction he fancied he had previously manifested, and particularly on account of the deferential manner which his courtiers had shown towards Fouquet. D'Artagnan, who ate a good deal and drank but little, without allowing it to be noticed, did not lose a single opportunity, but made a great number of observations which he turned to good profit.

When the supper was finished, the king expressed a wish not to lose the promenade. The park was illuminated; the moon, too, as if she had placed herself at the orders of the lord of Vaux, silvered the trees and lake with her own bright and quasi-phosphorescent light. The air was strangely soft and balmy; the daintily shell-gravelled walks through the thickly set avenues yielded luxuriously to the feet. The *fete* was complete in every respect, for the king, having met La Valliere in one of the winding paths of the wood, was able to press her hand and say, "I love you," without any one overhearing him except M. d'Artagnan, who followed, and M. Fouquet, who preceded him.

The dreamy night of magical enchantments stole smoothly on. The king having requested to be shown to his room, there was immediately a movement in every direction. The queens passed to their own apartments, accompanied by them music of theorbos and lutes; the king found his musketeers awaiting him on the grand flight of steps, for M. Fouquet had brought them on from Melun and had invited them to supper. D'Artagnan's suspicions at once disappeared. He was weary, he had supped well, and wished, for once in his life, thoroughly to enjoy a *fete* given by a man who was in every sense of the word a king. "M. Fouquet," he said, "is the man for me."

The king was conducted with the greatest ceremony to the chamber of Morpheus, of which we owe some cursory description to our readers. It was the handsomest and largest in the palace. Lebrun had painted on the vaulted ceiling the happy as well as the unhappy dreams which Morpheus inflicts on kings as well on other men. Everything that sleep gives birth to that is lovely, its fairy scenes, its flowers and nectar, the wild voluptuousness or profound repose of the senses, had the painter elaborated on his frescoes. It was a composition as soft and pleasing in one part as dark and gloomy and terrible in another. The poisoned chalice, the glittering dagger suspended over the head of the sleeper; wizards and phantoms with terrific masks, those half-dim shadows more alarming than the approach of fire or the somber face of midnight, these, and such as these, he had made the companions of his more pleasing pictures. No sooner had the king entered his room than a cold shiver seemed to pass through him, and on

Fouquet asking him the cause of it, the king replied, as pale as death:

"I am sleepy, that is all."

"Does your majesty wish for your attendants at once?"

"No; I have to talk with a few persons first," said the king. "Will you have the goodness to tell M. Colbert I wish to see him."

Fouquet bowed and left the room.

CHAPTER 14

A Gascon, and a Gascon and a Half.

D'Artagnan had determined to lose no time, and in fact he
never was in the habit of doing so. After having inquired for
Aramis, he had looked for him in every direction until he had
succeeded in finding him. Besides, no sooner had the king
entered Vaux, than Aramis had retired to his own room,
meditating, doubtless, some new piece of gallant attention for
his majesty's amusement. D'Artagnan desired the servants to
announce him, and found on the second story (in a beautiful
room called the Blue Chamber, on account of the color of its
hangings) the bishop of Vannes in company with Porthos and
several of the modern Epicureans. Aramis came forward to
embrace his friend, and offered him the best seat. As it was
after awhile generally remarked among those present that the
musketeer was reserved, and wished for an opportunity for
conversing secretly with Aramis, the Epicureans took their
leave. Porthos, however, did not stir; for true it is that, having
dined exceedingly well, he was fast asleep in his armchair;
and the freedom of conversation therefore was not interrupted
by a third person. Porthos had a deep, harmonious snore, and
people might talk in the midst of its loud bass without fear
of disturbing him. D'Artagnan felt that he was called upon
to open the conversation.

"Well, and so we have come to Vaux," he said.

"Why, yes, D'Artagnan. And how do you like the place?"

"Very much, and I like M. Fouquet, also."

"Is he not a charming host?"

"No one could be more so."

"I am told that the king began by showing great distance of manner towards M. Fouquet, but that his majesty grew much more cordial afterwards."

"You did not notice it, then, since you say you have been told so?"

"No; I was engaged with the gentlemen who have just left the room about the theatrical performances and the tournaments which are to take place to-morrow."

"Ah, indeed! you are the comptroller-general of the *fetes* here, then?"

"You know I am a friend of all kinds of amusement where the exercise of the imagination is called into activity; I have always been a poet in one way or another."

"Yes, I remember the verses you used to write, they were charming."

"I have forgotten them, but I am delighted to read the verses of others, when those others are known by the names of Moliere, Pelisson, La Fontaine, etc."

"Do you know what idea occurred to me this evening, Aramis?"

"No; tell me what it was, for I should never be able to guess it, you have so many."

"Well, the idea occurred to me, that the true king of France is not Louis XIV."

"*What!*" said Aramis, involuntarily, looking the musketeer full in the eyes.

"No, it is Monsieur Fouquet."

Aramis breathed again, and smiled. "Ah! you are like all the rest, jealous," he said. "I would wager that it was M. Colbert who turned that pretty phrase." D'Artagnan, in order to throw Aramis off his guard, related Colbert's misadventures with regard to the *vin de Melun.*

"He comes of a mean race, does Colbert," said Aramis.

"Quite true."

"When I think, too," added the bishop, "that that fellow will be your minister within four months, and that you will serve him as blindly as you did Richelieu or Mazarin—"

"And as you serve M. Fouquet," said D'Artagnan.

"With this difference, though, that M. Fouquet is not M. Colbert."

"True, true," said D'Artagnan, as he pretended to become sad and full of reflection; and then, a moment after, he added, "Why do you tell me that M. Colbert will be minister in four months?"

"Because M. Fouquet will have ceased to be so," replied Aramis.

"He will be ruined, you mean?" said D'Artagnan.

"Completely so."

"Why does he give these *fetes*, then?" said the musketeer, in a tone so full of thoughtful consideration, and so well assumed, that the bishop was for the moment deceived by it. "Why did you not dissuade him from it?"

The latter part of the phrase was just a little too much, and Aramis's former suspicions were again aroused. "It is done with the object of humoring the king."

"By ruining himself?"

"Yes, by ruining himself for the king."

"A most eccentric, one might say, sinister calculation, that."

"Necessity, necessity, my friend."

"I don't see that, dear Aramis."

"Do you not? Have you not remarked M. Colbert's daily increasing antagonism, and that he is doing his utmost to drive the king to get rid of the superintendent?"

"One must be blind not to see it."

"And that a cabal is already armed against M. Fouquet?"

"That is well known."

"What likelihood is there that the king would join a party formed against a man who will have spent everything he had to please him?"

"True, true," said D'Artagnan, slowly, hardly convinced, yet curious to broach another phase of the conversation. "There are follies, and follies," he resumed, "and I do not like those you are committing."

"What do you allude to?"

"As for the banquet, the ball, the concert, the theatricals, the tournaments, the cascades, the fireworks, the illuminations, and the presents—these are well and good, I grant; but why were not these expenses sufficient? Why was it necessary to have new liveries and costumes for your whole household?"

"You are quite right. I told M. Fouquet that myself; he replied, that if he were rich enough he would offer the king a newly erected chateau, from the vanes at the houses to the very sub-cellars; completely new inside and out; and that, as soon as the king had left, he would burn the whole building and its contents, in order that it might not be made use of by any one else."

"How completely Spanish!"

"I told him so, and he then added this: 'Whoever advises me to spare expense, I shall look upon as my enemy.'"

"It is positive madness; and that portrait, too!"

"What portrait?" said Aramis.

"That of the king, and the surprise as well."

"What surprise?"

"The surprise you seem to have in view, and on account of which you took some specimens away, when I met you at Percerin's." D'Artagnan paused. The shaft was discharged, and all he had to do was to wait and watch its effect.

"That is merely an act of graceful attention," replied Aramis.

D'Artagnan went up to his friend, took hold of both his hands, and looking him full in the eyes, said, "Aramis, do you still care for me a very little?"

"What a question to ask!"

"Very good. One favor, then. Why did you take some patterns of the king's costumes at Percerin's?"

"Come with me and ask poor Lebrun, who has been working upon them for the last two days and nights."

"Aramis, that may be truth for everybody else, but for me—"

"Upon my word, D'Artagnan, you astonish me."

"Be a little considerate. Tell me the exact truth; you would not like anything disagreeable to happen to me, would you?"

"My dear friend, you are becoming quite incomprehensible. What suspicion can you have possibly got hold of?"

"Do you believe in my instinctive feelings? Formerly you used to have faith in them. Well, then, an instinct tells me that you have some concealed project on foot."

"I—a project?"

"I am convinced of it."

"What nonsense!"

"I am not only sure of it, but I would even swear it."

"Indeed, D'Artagnan, you cause me the greatest pain. Is it likely, if I have any project in hand that I ought to keep secret from you, I should tell you about it? If I had one that I could and ought to have revealed, should I not have long ago divulged it?"

"No, Aramis, no. There are certain projects which are never revealed until the favorable opportunity arrives."

"In that case, my dear fellow," returned the bishop, laughing, "the only thing now is, that the 'opportunity' has not yet arrived."

D'Artagnan shook his head with a sorrowful expression. "Oh, friendship, friendship!" he said, "what an idle word you are! Here is a man who, if I were but to ask it, would suffer himself to be cut in pieces for my sake."

"You are right," said Aramis, nobly.

"And this man, who would shed every drop of blood in his veins for me, will not open up before me the least corner in his heart. Friendship, I repeat, is nothing but an unsubstantial shadow—a lure, like everything else in this bright, dazzling world."

"It is not thus you should speak of *our* friendship," replied the bishop, in a firm, assured voice; "for ours is not of the same nature as those of which you have been speaking."

"Look at us, Aramis; three out of the old 'four.' You are deceiving me; I suspect you; and Porthos is fast asleep. An admirable trio of friends, don't you think so? What an affecting relic of the former dear old times!"

"I can only tell you one thing, D'Artagnan, and I swear it on the Bible: I love you just as I used to do. If I ever suspect you, it is on account of others, and not on account of either of us. In everything I may do, and should happen to succeed in, you will find your fourth. Will you promise me the same favor?"

"If I am not mistaken, Aramis, your words—at the moment you pronounce them—are full of generous feeling."

"Such a thing is very possible."

"You are conspiring against M. Colbert. If that be all, *mordioux*, tell me so at once. I have the instrument in my own hand, and will pull out the tooth easily enough."

Aramis could not conceal a smile of disdain that flitted over his haughty features. "And supposing that I were conspiring against Colbert, what harm would there be in *that?*"

"No, no; that would be too trifling a matter for you to take in hand, and it was not on that account you asked Percerin for those patterns of the king's costumes. Oh! Aramis, we are not enemies, remember—we are brothers. Tell me what you wish to undertake, and, upon the word of a D'Artagnan, if I cannot help you, I will swear to remain neuter."

"I am undertaking nothing," said Aramis.

"Aramis, a voice within me speaks and seems to trickle forth a rill of light within my darkness: it is a voice that has never yet deceived me. It is the king you are conspiring against."

"The king?" exclaimed the bishop, pretending to be annoyed.

"Your face will not convince me; the king, I repeat."

"Will you help me?" said Aramis, smiling ironically.

"Aramis, I will do more than help you—I will do more than remain neuter—I will save you."

"You are mad, D'Artagnan."

"I am the wiser of the two, in this matter."

"You to suspect me of wishing to assassinate the king!"

"Who spoke of such a thing?" smiled the musketeer.

"Well, let us understand one another. I do not see what any one can do to a legitimate king as ours is, if he does not assassinate him." D'Artagnan did not say a word. "Besides, you have your guards and your musketeers here," said the bishop.

"True."

"You are not in M. Fouquet's house, but in your own."

"True; but in spite of that, Aramis, grant me, for pity's sake, one single word of a true friend."

"A true friend's word is ever truth itself. If I think of touching, even with my finger, the son of Anne of Austria, the true king of this realm of France—if I have not the firm intention of prostrating myself before his throne—if in every idea I may entertain to-morrow, here at Vaux, will not be the most glorious day my king ever enjoyed—may Heaven's light-ning blast me where I stand!" Aramis had pronounced these words with his face turned towards the alcove of his own bedroom, where D'Artagnan, seated with his back towards the alcove, could not suspect that any one was lying concealed. The earnestness of his words, the studied slowness with which he pronounced them, the solemnity of his oath, gave the musketeer the most complete satisfaction. He took hold of both Aramis's hands, and shook them cordially. Aramis had endured reproaches without turning pale, and had blushed as he listened to words of praise. D'Artagnan, deceived, did him honor; but D'Artagnan, trustful and reliant, made him feel ashamed. "Are you going away?" he said, as he embraced him, in order to conceal the flush on his face.

"Yes. Duty summons me. I have to get the watch-word. It seems I am to be lodged in the king's ante-room. Where does Porthos sleep?"

"Take him away with you, if you like, for he rumbles through his sleepy nose like a park of artillery."

"Ah! he does not stay with you, then?" said D'Artagnan.

"Not the least in the world. He has a chamber to himself, but I don't know where."

"Very good!" said the musketeer; from whom this separation of the two associates removed his last suspicion, and he touched Porthos lightly on the shoulder; the latter replied by a loud yawn. "Come," said D'Artagnan.

"What, D'Artagnan, my dear fellow, is that you? What a lucky chance! Oh, yes—true; I have forgotten; I am at the *fete* at Vaux."

"Yes; and your beautiful dress, too."

"Yes, it was very attentive on the part of Monsieur Coquelin de Voliere, was it not?"

"Hush!" said Aramis. "You are walking so heavily you will make the flooring give way."

"True," said the musketeer; "this room is above the dome, I think."

"And I did not choose it for a fencing-room, I assure

you," added the bishop. "The ceiling of the king's room has all the lightness and calm of wholesome sleep. Do not forget, therefore, that my flooring is merely the covering of his ceiling. Good night, my friends, and in ten minutes I shall be asleep myself." And Aramis accompanied them to the door, laughing quietly all the while. As soon as they were outside, he bolted the door, hurriedly; closed up the chinks of the windows, and then called out, "Monseigneur!—monseigneur!" Philippe made his appearance from the alcove, as he pushed aside a sliding panel placed behind the bed.

"M. d'Artagnan entertains a great many suspicions, it seems," he said.

"Ah!—you recognized M. d'Artagnan, then?"

"Before you called him by his name, even."

"He is your captain of musketeers."

"He is very devoted to *me*," replied Philippe, laying a stress upon the personal pronoun.

"As faithful as a dog; but he bites sometimes. If D'Artagnan does not recognize you before *the other* has disappeared, rely upon D'Artagnan to the end of the world; for in that case, if he has seen nothing, he will keep his fidelity. If he sees, when it is too late, he is a Gascon, and will never admit that he has been deceived."

"I thought so. What are we to do, now?"

"Sit in this folding-chair. I am going to push aside a portion of the flooring; you will look through the opening, which answers to one of the false windows made in the dome of the king's apartment. Can you see?"

"Yes," said Philippe, starting as at the sight of an enemy; "I see the king!"

"What is he doing?"

"He seems to wish some man to sit down close to him."

"M. Fouquet?"

"No, no; wait a moment—"

147

"Look at the notes and the portraits, my prince."

"The man whom the king wishes to sit down in his presence is M. Colbert."

"Colbert sit down in the king's presence!" exclaimed Aramis. "It is impossible."

"Look."

Aramis looked through the opening in the flooring. "Yes," he said. "Colbert himself. Oh, monseigneur! what can we be going to hear—and what can result from this intimacy?"

"Nothing good for M. Fouquet, at all events."

The prince did not deceive himself.

We have seen that Louis XIV. had sent for Colbert, and Colbert had arrived. The conversation began between them by the king according to him one of the highest favors that he had ever done; it was true the king was alone with his subject. "Colbert," said he, "sit down."

The intendant, overcome with delight, for he feared he was about to be dismissed, refused this unprecedented honor.

"Does he accept?" said Aramis.

"No, he remains standing."

"Let us listen, then." And the future king and the future pope listened eagerly to the simple mortals they held under their feet, ready to crush them when they liked.

"Colbert," said the king, "you have annoyed me exceedingly to-day."

"I know it, sire."

"Very good; I like that answer. Yes, you knew it, and there was courage in the doing of it."

"I ran the risk of displeasing your majesty, but I risked, also, the concealment of your best interests."

"What! you were afraid of something on *my* account?"

"I was, sire, even if it were nothing more than an indigestion," said Colbert; "for people do not give their sovereigns such banquets as the one of to-day, unless it be to stifle them beneath the burden of good living." Colbert awaited the effect this coarse jest would produce upon the king; and Louis XIV., who was the vainest and the most fastidiously delicate man in his kingdom, forgave Colbert the joke.

"The truth is," he said, "that M. Fouquet has given me too good a meal. Tell me, Colbert, where does he get all the money required for this enormous expenditure,—can you tell?"

"Yes, I do know, sire."

"Will you be able to prove it with tolerable certainty?"

"Easily; and to the utmost farthing."

"I know you are very exact."

"Exactitude is the principal qualification required in an intendant of finances."

"But all are not so."

"I thank you majesty for so flattering a compliment from your own lips."

"M. Fouquet, therefore, is rich—very rich, and I suppose every man knows he is so."

"Every one, sire; the living as well as the dead."

"What does that mean, Monsieur Colbert?"

"The living are witnesses of M. Fouquet's wealth,—they admire and applaud the result produced; but the dead, wiser and better informed than we are, know how that wealth was obtained—and they rise up in accusation."

"So that M. Fouquet owes his wealth to some cause or other."

"The occupation of an intendant very often favors those who practice it."

"You have something to say to me more confidentially, I perceive; do not be afraid, we are quite alone."

"I am never afraid of anything under the shelter of my own conscience, and under the protection of your majesty," said Colbert, bowing.

"If the dead, therefore, were to speak—"

"They do speak sometimes, sire,—read."

"Ah!" murmured Aramis, in the prince's ear, who, close beside him, listened without losing a syllable, "since you are placed here, monseigneur, in order to learn your vocation of a king, listen to a piece of infamy—of a nature truly royal. You are about to be a witness of one of those scenes which the foul fiend alone conceives and executes. Listen attentively,—you will find your advantage in it."

The prince redoubled his attention, and saw Louis XIV. take from Colbert's hands a letter the latter held out to him.

"The late cardinal's handwriting," said the king.

"Your majesty has an excellent memory," replied Colbert, bowing; "it is an immense advantage for a king who is destined for hard work to recognize handwritings at the first glance."

The king read Mazarin's letter, and, as its contents are already known to the reader, in consequence of the misunderstanding between Madame de Chevreuse and Aramis, nothing further would be learned if we stated them here again.

"I do not quite understand," said the king, greatly interested.

"Your majesty has not acquired the utilitarian habit of checking the public accounts."

"I see that it refers to money that had been given to M. Fouquet."

"Thirteen millions. A tolerably good sum."

"Yes. Well, these thirteen millions are wanting to balance the total of the account. That is what I do not very well understand. How was this deficit possible?"

"Possible I do not say; but there is no doubt about fact that it is really so."

"You say that these thirteen millions are found to be wanting in the accounts?"

"I do not say so, but the registry does."

"And this letter of M. Mazarin indicates the employment

of that sum and the name of the person with whom it was deposited?"

"As your majesty can judge for yourself."

"Yes; and the result is, then, that M. Fouquet has not yet restored the thirteen millions."

"That results from the accounts, certainly, sire."

"Well, and, consequently—"

"Well, sire, in that case, inasmuch as M. Fouquet has not yet given back the thirteen millions, he must have appropriated them to his own purpose; and with those thirteen millions one could incur four times and a little more as much expense, and make four times as great a display, as your majesty was able to do at Fontainebleau, where we only spent three millions altogether, if you remember."

For a blunderer, the *souvenir* he had evoked was a rather skillfully contrived piece of baseness; for by the remembrance of his own *fete* he, for the first time, perceived its inferiority compared with that of Fouquet. Colbert received back again at Vaux what Fouquet had given him at Fontainebleau, and, as a good financier, returned it with the best possible interest. Having once disposed the king's mind in this artful way, Colbert had nothing of much importance to detain him. He felt that such was the case, for the king, too, had again sunk into a dull and gloomy state. Colbert awaited the first words from the king's lips with as much impatience as Philippe and Aramis did from their place of observation.

"Are you aware what is the usual and natural consequence of all this, Monsieur Colbert?" said the king, after a few moments' reflection.

"No, sire, I do not know."

"Well, then, the fact of the appropriation of the thirteen millions, if it can be proved—"

"But it is so already."

"I mean if it were to be declared and certified, M. Colbert."

"I think it will be to-morrow, if your majesty—"

"Were we not under M. Fouquet's roof, you were going to say, perhaps," replied the king, with something of nobility in his demeanor.

"The king is in his own palace wherever he may be—especially in houses which the royal money has constructed."

"I think," said Philippe in a low tone to Aramis, "that the architect who planned this dome ought, anticipating the use it could be put to at a future opportunity, so to have contrived that it might be made to fall upon the heads of scoundrels such as M. Colbert."

"I think so too," replied Aramis; "but M. Colbert is so very *near the king* at this moment."

"That is true, and that would open the succession."

"Of which your younger brother would reap all the advantage, monseigneur. But stay, let us keep quiet, and go on listening."

"We shall not have long to listen," said the young prince.

"Why not, monseigneur?"

"Because, if I were king, I should make no further reply."

"And what would you do?"

"I should wait until to-morrow morning to give myself time for reflection."

Louis XIV. at last raised his eyes, and finding Colbert attentively waiting for his next remarks, said, hastily, changing the conversation, "M. Colbert, I perceive it is getting very late, and I shall now retire to bed. By to-morrow morning I shall have made up my mind."

"Very good, sire," returned Colbert, greatly incensed, although he restrained himself in the presence of the king.

The king made a gesture of adieu, and Colbert withdrew with a respectful bow. "My attendants!" cried the king; and, as they entered the apartment, Philippe was about to quit his post of observation.

"A moment longer," said Aramis to him, with his

accustomed gentleness of manner; "what has just now taken place is only a detail, and to-morrow we shall have no occasion to think anything more about it; but the ceremony of the king's retiring to rest, the etiquette observed in addressing the king, that indeed is of the greatest importance. Learn, sire, and study well how you ought to go to bed of a night. Look! look!"

CHAPTER 15

Colbert.

History will tell us, or rather history has told us, of the various events of the following day, of the splendid *fetes* given by the surintendant to his sovereign. Nothing but amusement and delight was allowed to prevail throughout the whole of the following day; there was a promenade, a banquet, a comedy to be acted, and a comedy, too, in which, to his great amazement, Porthos recognized "M. Coquelin de Voliere" as one of the actors, in the piece called "Les Facheux." Full of preoccupation, however, from the scene of the previous evening, and hardly recovered from the effects of the poison which Colbert had then administered to him, the king, during the whole of the day, so brilliant in its effects, so full of unexpected and startling novelties, in which all the wonders of the "Arabian Night's Entertainments" seemed to be reproduced for his especial amusement—the king, we say, showed himself cold, reserved, and taciturn. Nothing could smooth the frowns upon his face; every one who observed him noticed that a deep feeling of resentment, of remote origin, increased by slow degrees, as the source becomes a river, thanks to the thousand threads of water that increase its body, was keenly alive in the depths of the king's heart. Towards the middle of the day only did he begin to resume a little serenity of manner, and by that time he had, in all probability, made up his mind. Aramis, who followed him step by step in his thoughts, as in his walk, concluded that the event he was expecting would not be long before it was announced. This time Colbert seemed to walk in concert with the bishop of Vannes, and had he received for every annoyance which he inflicted on the king a word of direction from Aramis, he could not have done better. During the whole of the day the king, who, in all probability, wished to free himself from some of the thoughts which disturbed his mind, seemed to seek La Valliere's society as actively as he seemed to show his anxiety to flee that of M. Colbert or M. Fouquet. The evening came. The king had expressed a wish not to walk in the park until after cards in the evening. In the interval between supper and the promenade, cards and dice were introduced. The king won a thousand pistoles, and, having won them, put them in his pocket, and then rose, saying, "And now, gentlemen, to the park." He found the ladies of the court were already there. The king, we have before observed, had won a thousand pistoles, and had put them in his pocket; but M. Fouquet had somehow contrived to lose ten thousand, so that among the courtiers there was still left a hundred and ninety thousand francs' profit to divide, a circumstance which made the countenances of the courtiers and the officers of the king's household the most joyous countenances in the world. It was not the same, however, with the king's face; for, notwithstanding his success at play, to which he was by no means insensible, there still remained a slight shade of dissatisfaction. Colbert was waiting for or upon him at the corner of one of the avenues; he was most probably waiting there in consequence of a rendezvous which had been given him by the king, as Louis XIV., who had avoided him, or who had seemed to avoid him, suddenly made him a sign, and they then struck into the depths of the park together. But La Valliere, too, had observed the king's gloomy aspect and kindling glances; she had remarked this—and as nothing which lay hidden or smoldering in his heart was hidden from the gaze of her affection, she understood that this repressed wrath menaced some one; she prepared to withstand the current of his vengeance, and intercede like an angel of mercy. Overcome by sadness, nervously agitated, deeply distressed at having been so long separated from her lover, disturbed at the sight of the emotion she had divined, she accordingly presented herself to the king with an embarrassed aspect, which in his then disposition of mind the king interpreted unfavorably. Then, as they were alone—nearly alone, inasmuch as Colbert, as soon as he perceived the young girl approaching, had stopped and drawn back a dozen paces—the king advanced towards La Valliere and took her by the hand. "Mademoiselle," he said to her, "should I be guilty of an indiscretion if I were to inquire if you were indisposed? for you seem to breathe as if you were oppressed by some secret cause of uneasiness, and your eyes are filled with tears."

"Oh! sire, if I be indeed so, and if my eyes are indeed full of tears, I am sorrowful only at the sadness which seems to oppress your majesty."

"My sadness? You are mistaken, mademoiselle; no, it is not sadness I experience."

"What is it, then, sire?"

"Humiliation."

"Humiliation? oh! sire, what a word for you to use!"

"I mean, mademoiselle, that wherever I may happen to be, no one else ought to be the master. Well, then, look round you on every side, and judge whether I am not eclipsed—I, the king of France—before the monarch of these wide domains. Oh!" he continued, clenching his hands and teeth, "when I think that this king—"

"Well, sire?" said Louise, terrified.

"—That this king is a faithless, unworthy servant, who grows proud and self-sufficient upon the strength of property that belongs to me, and which he has stolen. And therefore I am about to change this impudent minister's *fete* into sorrow and mourning, of which the nymph of Vaux, as the poets say, shall not soon lose the remembrance."

"Oh! your majesty—"

"Well, mademoiselle, are you about to take M. Fouquet's part?" said Louis, impatiently.

"No, sire; I will only ask whether you are well informed. Your majesty has more than once learned the value of accusations made at court."

Louis XIV. made a sign for Colbert to approach. "Speak, Monsieur Colbert," said the young prince, "for I almost believe that Mademoiselle de la Valliere has need of your assistance before she can put any faith in the king's word. Tell mademoiselle what M. Fouquet has done; and you, mademoiselle, will perhaps have the kindness to listen. It will not be long."

Why did Louis XIV. insist upon it in such a manner? A very simple reason—his heart was not at rest, his mind was not thoroughly convinced; he imagined there lay some dark, hidden, tortuous intrigue behind these thirteen millions of francs; and he wished that the pure heart of La Valliere, which had revolted at the idea of theft or robbery, should approve—even were it only by a single word—the resolution he had taken, and which, nevertheless, he hesitated before carrying into execution.

"Speak, monsieur," said La Valliere to Colbert, who had advanced; "speak, since the king wishes me to listen to you. Tell me, what is the crime with which M. Fouquet is charged?"

"Oh! not very heinous, mademoiselle," he returned, "a mere abuse of confidence."

"Speak, speak, Colbert; and when you have related it, leave us, and go and inform M. d'Artagnan that I have certain orders to give him."

"M. d'Artagnan, sire!" exclaimed La Valliere; "but why send for M. d'Artagnan? I entreat you to tell me."

"*Pardieu!* in order to arrest this haughty, arrogant Titan who, true to his menace, threatens to scale my heaven."

"Arrest M. Fouquet, do you say?"

"Ah! does that surprise you?"

"In his own house!"

"Why not? If he be guilty, he is as guilty in his own house as anywhere else."

"M. Fouquet, who at this moment is ruining himself for his sovereign."

"In plain truth, mademoiselle, it seems as if you were defending this traitor."

Colbert began to chuckle silently. The king turned round at the sound of this suppressed mirth.

"Sire," said La Valliere, "it is not M. Fouquet I am defending; it is yourself."

"Me! you are defending me?"

"Sire, you would dishonor yourself if you were to give such an order."

"Dishonor myself!" murmured the king, turning pale with anger. "In plain truth, mademoiselle, you show a strange persistence in what you say."

"If I do, sire, my only motive is that of serving your majesty," replied the noble-hearted girl: "for that I would risk, I would sacrifice my very life, without the least reserve."

Colbert seemed inclined to grumble and complain. La Valliere, that timid, gentle lamb, turned round upon him, and with a glance like lightning imposed silence upon him. "Monsieur," she said, "when the king acts well, whether, in doing so, he does either myself or those who belong to me an injury, I have nothing to say; but were the king to confer a benefit either upon me or mine, and if he acted badly, I should tell him so."

"But it appears to me, mademoiselle," Colbert ventured to say, "that I too love the king."

"Yes, monseigneur, we both love him, but each in a different manner," replied La Valliere, with such an accent that the heart of the young king was powerfully affected by it. "I love him so deeply, that the whole world is aware of it; so purely, that the king himself does not doubt my affection. He is my king and my master; I am the least of all his servants. But whoso touches his honor assails my life. Therefore, I repeat, that they dishonor the king who advise him to arrest M. Fouquet under his own roof."

Colbert hung down his head, for he felt that the king had abandoned him. However, as he bent his head, he murmured, "Mademoiselle, I have only one word to say."

"Do not say it, then, monsieur; for I would not listen to it. Besides, what could you have to tell me? That M. Fouquet has been guilty of certain crimes? I believe he has, because the king has said so; and, from the moment the king said, 'I think so,' I have no occasion for other lips to say, 'I affirm it.' But, were M. Fouquet the vilest of men, I should say aloud, 'M. Fouquet's person is sacred to the king because he is the guest of M. Fouquet. Were his house a den of thieves, were Vaux a cave of coiners or robbers, his home is sacred, his palace is inviolable, since his wife is living in it; and that is an asylum which even executioners would not dare to violate.'"

La Valliere paused, and was silent. In spite of himself the king could not but admire her; he was overpowered by the passionate energy of her voice; by the nobleness of the cause she advocated. Colbert yielded, overcome by the inequality of the struggle. At last the king breathed again more freely, shook his head, and held out his hand to La Valliere.

"Mademoiselle," he said, gently, "why do you decide against me? Do you know what this wretched fellow will do, if I give him time to breathe again?"

"Is he not a prey which will always be within your grasp?"

"Should he escape, and take to flight?" exclaimed Colbert.

"Well, monsieur, it will always remain on record, to the king's eternal honor, that he allowed M. Fouquet to flee; and the more guilty he may have been, the greater will the king's honor and glory appear, compared with such unnecessary misery and shame."

Louis kissed La Valliere's hand, as he knelt before her.

"I am lost," thought Colbert; then suddenly his face brightened up again. "Oh! no, no, aha, old fox!—not yet," he said to himself.

And while the king, protected from observation by the thick covert of an enormous lime, pressed La Valliere to his breast, with all the ardor of ineffable affection, Colbert tranquilly fumbled among the papers in his pocket-book and drew out of it a paper folded in the form of a letter, somewhat yellow, perhaps, but one that must have been most precious, since the intendant smiled as he looked at it; he then bent a look, full of hatred, upon the charming group which the young girl and the king formed together—a group revealed but for a moment, as the light of the approaching torches shone upon it. Louis noticed the light reflected upon La Valliere's white dress. "Leave me, Louise," he said, "for some one is coming."

"Mademoiselle, mademoiselle, some one is coming," cried Colbert, to expedite the young girl's departure.

Louise disappeared rapidly among the trees; and then, as the king, who had been on his knees before the young girl, was rising from his humble posture, Colbert exclaimed, "Ah! Mademoiselle de la Valliere has let something fall."

"What is it?" inquired the king.

"A paper—a letter—something white; look there, sire."

The king stooped down immediately and picked up the letter, crumpling it in his hand, as he did so; and at the same moment the torches arrived, inundating the blackness of the scene with a flood of light as bright as day.

CHAPTER 16

Jealousy.

The torches we have just referred to, the eager attention every one displayed, and the new ovation paid to the king by Fouquet, arrived in time to suspend the effect of a resolution which La Valliere had already considerably shaken in Louis XIV.'s heart. He looked at Fouquet with a feeling almost of gratitude for having given La Valliere an opportunity of showing herself so generously disposed, so powerful in the influence she exercised over his heart. The moment of the last and greatest display had arrived. Hardly had Fouquet conducted the king towards the chateau, when a mass of fire burst from the dome of Vaux, with a prodigious uproar, pouring a flood of dazzling cataracts of rays on every side, and illumining the remotest corners of the gardens. The fire-works began. Colbert, at twenty paces from the king, who was surrounded and *feted* by the owner of Vaux, seemed, by the obstinate persistence of his gloomy thoughts, to do his utmost to recall Louis's attention, which the magnificence of the spectacle was already, in his opinion, too easily diverting. Suddenly, just as Louis was on the point of holding it out to Fouquet, he perceived in his hand the paper which, as he believed, La Valliere had dropped at his feet as she hurried away. The still stronger magnet of love drew the young prince's attention towards the *souvenir* of his idol; and, by the brilliant light, which increased momentarily in beauty, and drew from the neighboring villages loud cheers of admiration, the king read the letter, which he supposed was a loving and tender epistle La Valliere had destined for him. But as he read it, a death-like pallor stole over his face, and an expression of deep-seated wrath, illumined by the many-colored fire which gleamed so brightly, soaringly around the scene, produced a terrible spectacle, which every one would have shuddered at, could they only have read into his heart, now torn by the most stormy and most bitter passions. There was no truce for him now, influenced as he was by jealousy and mad passion. From the very moment when the dark truth was revealed to him, every gentler feeling seemed to disappear; pity, kindness of consideration, the religion of hospitality, all were forgotten. In the bitter pang which wrung his heart, he, still too weak to hide his sufferings, was almost on the point of uttering a cry of alarm, and calling his guards to gather round him. This letter which Colbert had thrown down at the king's feet, the reader has doubtlessly guessed, was the same that had disappeared with the porter Toby at Fontainebleau, after the attempt which Fouquet had made upon La Valliere's heart. Fouquet saw the king's pallor, and was far from guessing the evil; Colbert saw the king's anger, and rejoiced inwardly at the approach of the storm. Fouquet's voice drew the young prince from his wrathful reverie.

"What is the matter, sire?" inquired the superintendent, with an expression of graceful interest.

Louis made a violent effort over himself, as he replied, "Nothing."

"I am afraid your majesty is suffering?"

"I am suffering, and have already told you so, monsieur; but it is nothing."

And the king, without waiting for the termination of the fireworks, turned towards the chateau. Fouquet accompanied him, and the whole court followed, leaving the remains of the fireworks consuming for their own amusement. The superintendent endeavored again to question Louis XIV., but did not succeed in obtaining a reply. He imagined there had been some misunderstanding between Louis and La Valliere in the park, which had resulted in a slight quarrel; and that the king, who was not ordinarily sulky by disposition, but completely absorbed by his passion for La Valliere, had taken a dislike to every one because his mistress had shown herself offended with him. This idea was sufficient to console him; he had even a friendly and kindly smile for the young king, when the latter wished him good night. This, however, was not all the king had to submit to; he was obliged to undergo the usual ceremony, which on that evening was marked by close adherence to the strictest etiquette. The next day was the one fixed for the departure; it was but proper that the guests should thank their host, and show him a little attention in return for the expenditure of his twelve millions. The only remark, approaching to amiability, which the king could find to say to M. Fouquet, as he took leave of him, were in these words, "M. Fouquet, you shall hear from me. Be good enough to desire M. d'Artagnan to come here."

But the blood of Louis XIV., who had so profoundly dissimulated his feelings, boiled in his veins; and he was perfectly willing to order M. Fouquet to be put an end to with the same readiness, indeed, as his predecessor had caused the assassination of le Marechal d'Ancre; and so he disguised the terrible resolution he had formed beneath one of those royal smiles which, like lightning-flashes, indicated *coups d'etat.* Fouquet took the king's hand and kissed it; Louis shuddered throughout his whole frame, but allowed M. Fouquet to touch his hand with his lips. Five minutes afterwards, D'Artagnan, to whom the royal order had been communicated, entered Louis XIV.'s apartment. Aramis and Philippe were in theirs, still eagerly attentive, and still listening with all their ears.

The king did not even give the captain of the musketeers time to approach his armchair, but ran forward to meet him. "Take care," he exclaimed, "that no one enters here."

"Very good, sire," replied the captain, whose glance had for a long time past analyzed the stormy indications on the royal countenance. He gave the necessary order at the door; but, returning to the king, he said, "Is there something fresh the matter, your majesty?"

"How many men have you here?" inquired the king, without making any other reply to the question addressed to him.

"What for, sire?"

"How many men have you, I say?" repeated the king, stamping upon the ground with his foot.

"I have the musketeers."

"Well; and what others?"

"Twenty guards and thirteen Swiss."

"How many men will be required to—"

"To do what, sire?" replied the musketeer, opening his large, calm eyes.

"To arrest M. Fouquet."

D'Artagnan fell back a step.

"To arrest M. Fouquet!" he burst forth.

"Are you going to tell me that it is impossible?" exclaimed the king, in tones of cold, vindictive passion.

"I never say that anything is impossible," replied D'Artagnan, wounded to the quick.

"Very well; do it, then."

D'Artagnan turned on his heel, and made his way towards the door; it was but a short distance, and he cleared it in half a dozen paces; when he reached it he suddenly paused, and said, "Your majesty will forgive me, but, in order to effect this arrest, I should like written directions."

"For what purpose—and since when has the king's word been insufficient for you?"

"Because the word of a king, when it springs from a feeling of anger, may possibly change when the feeling changes."

"A truce to set phrases, monsieur; you have another thought besides that?"

"Oh, I, at least, have certain thoughts and ideas, which, unfortunately, others have not," D'Artagnan replied, impertinently.

The king, in the tempest of his wrath, hesitated, and drew back in the face of D'Artagnan's frank courage, just as a horse crouches on his haunches under the strong hand of a bold and experienced rider. "What is your thought?" he exclaimed.

"This, sire," replied D'Artagnan: "you cause a man to be arrested when you are still under his roof; and passion is alone the cause of that. When your anger shall have passed, you will regret what you have done; and then I wish to be in a position to show you your signature. If that, however, should fail to be a reparation, it will at least show us that the king was wrong to lose his temper."

"Wrong to lose his temper!" cried the king, in a loud, passionate voice. "Did not my father, my grandfathers, too, before me, lose their temper at times, in Heaven's name?"

"The king your father and the king your grandfather never lost their temper except when under the protection of their own palace."

"The king is master wherever he may be."

"That is a flattering, complimentary phrase which cannot proceed from any one but M. Colbert; but it happens not to be the truth. The king is at home in every man's house when he has driven its owner out of it."

The king bit his lips, but said nothing.

"Can it be possible?" said D'Artagnan; "here is a man who is positively ruining himself in order to please you, and you wish to have him arrested! *Mordioux!* Sire, if my name was Fouquet, and people treated me in that manner, I would swallow at a single gulp all sorts of fireworks and other things, and I would set fire to them, and send myself and everybody else in blown-up atoms to the sky. But it is all the same; it is your wish, and it shall be done."

"Go," said the king; "but have you men enough?"

"Do you suppose I am going to take a whole host to help me? Arrest M. Fouquet! why, that is so easy that a very child might do it! It is like drinking a glass of wormwood; one makes an ugly face, and that is all."

"If he defends himself?"

"He! it is not at all likely. Defend himself when such extreme harshness as you are going to practice makes the man a very martyr! Nay, I am sure that if he has a million of francs left, which I very much doubt, he would be willing enough to give it in order to have such a termination as this. But what does that matter? it shall be done at once."

"Stay," said the king; "do not make his arrest a public affair."

"That will be more difficult."

"Why so?"

"Because nothing is easier than to go up to M. Fouquet in the midst of a thousand enthusiastic guests who surround him, and say, 'In the king's name, I arrest you.' But to go up to him, to turn him first one way and then another, to drive him up into one of the corners of the chess-board, in such a way that he cannot escape; to take him away from his guests, and keep him a prisoner for you, without one of them, alas! having heard anything about it; that, indeed, is a genuine difficulty, the greatest of all, in truth; and I hardly see how it is to be done."

"You had better say it is impossible, and you will have finished much sooner. Heaven help me, but I seem to be surrounded by people who prevent me doing what I wish."

"I do not prevent your doing anything. Have you indeed decided?"

"Take care of M. Fouquet, until I shall have made up my mind by to-morrow morning."

"That shall be done, sire."

"And return, when I rise in the morning, for further orders; and now leave me to myself."

"You do not even want M. Colbert, then?" said the musketeer, firing his last shot as he was leaving the room. The king started. With his whole mind fixed on the thought of revenge, he had forgotten the cause and substance of the offense.

"No, no one," he said; "no one here! Leave me."

D'Artagnan quitted the room. The king closed the door with his own hands, and began to walk up and down his apartment at a furious pace, like a wounded bull in an arena, trailing from his horn the colored streamers and the iron darts. At last he began to take comfort in the expression of his violent feelings.

"Miserable wretch that he is! not only does he squander my finances, but with his ill-gotten plunder he corrupts secretaries, friends, generals, artists, and all, and tries to rob me of the one to whom I am most attached. This is the reason that perfidious girl so boldly took his part! Gratitude! and who can tell whether it was not a stronger feeling—love itself?" He gave himself up for a moment to the bitterest reflections. "A satyr!" he thought, with that abhorrent hate with which young men regard those more advanced in life, who still think of love. "A man who has never found opposition or resistance in any one, who lavishes his gold and jewels in every direction, and who retains his staff of painters in order to take the portraits of his mistresses in the costume of goddesses." The king trembled with passion as he continued, "He pollutes and profanes everything that belongs to me! He destroys everything that is mine. He will be my death at last, I know. That man is too much for me; he is my mortal enemy, but he shall forthwith fall! I hate him—I hate him—I hate him!" and as he pronounced these words, he struck the arm of the chair in which he was sitting violently, over and over again, and then rose like one in an epileptic fit. "To-morrow! to-morrow! oh, happy day!" he murmured, "when the sun rises, no other rival shall that brilliant king of space possess but me. That man shall fall so low that when people look at the abject ruin my anger shall have wrought, they will be forced to confess at last and at least that I am indeed greater than he." The king, who was incapable of mastering his emotions any longer, knocked over with a blow of his fist a small table placed close to his bedside, and in the very bitterness of anger, almost weeping, and half-suffocated, he threw himself on his bed, dressed as he was, and bit the sheets in his extremity of passion, trying to find repose of body at least there. The bed creaked beneath his weight, and with the exception of a few broken sounds, emerging, or, one might say, exploding, from his overburdened chest, absolute silence soon reigned in the chamber of Morpheus.

CHAPTER 17

High Treason.

The ungovernable fury which took possession of the king at the sight and at the perusal of Fouquet's letter to La Valliere by degrees subsided into a feeling of pain and extreme weariness. Youth, invigorated by health and lightness of spirits, requiring soon that what it loses should be immediately restored—youth knows not those endless, sleepless nights which enable us to realize the fable of the vulture unceasingly feeding on Prometheus. In cases where the man of middle life, in his acquired strength of will and purpose, and the old, in their state of natural exhaustion, find incessant augmentation of their bitter sorrow, a young man, surprised by the sudden appearance of misfortune, weakens himself in sighs, and groans, and tears, directly struggling with his grief, and is thereby far sooner overthrown by the inflexible enemy with whom he is engaged. Once overthrown, his struggles cease. Louis could not hold out more than a few minutes, at the end of which he had ceased to clench his hands, and scorch in fancy with his looks the invisible objects of his hatred; he soon ceased to attack with his violent imprecations not M. Fouquet alone, but even La Valliere herself; from fury he subsided into despair, and from despair to prostration. After he had thrown himself for a few minutes to and fro convulsively on his bed, his nerveless arms fell quietly down; his head lay languidly on his pillow; his limbs, exhausted with excessive emotion, still trembled occasionally, agitated by muscular contractions; while from his breast faint and infrequent sighs still issued. Morpheus, the tutelary deity of the apartment, towards whom Louis raised his eyes, wearied by his anger and reconciled by his tears, showered down upon him the sleep-inducing poppies with which his hands are ever filled; so presently the monarch closed his eyes and fell asleep. Then it seemed to him, as it often happens in that first sleep, so light and gentle, which raises the body above the couch, and the soul above the earth—it seemed to him, we say, as if the god Morpheus, painted on the ceiling, looked at him with eyes resembling human eyes; that something shone brightly, and moved to and fro in the dome above the sleeper; that the crowd of terrible dreams which thronged together in his brain, and which were interrupted for a moment, half revealed a human face, with a hand resting against the mouth, and in an attitude of deep and absorbed meditation. And strange enough, too, this man bore so wonderful a resemblance to the king himself, that Louis fancied he was looking at his own face reflected in a mirror; with the exception, however, that the face was saddened by a feeling of the profoundest pity. Then it seemed to him as if the dome gradually retired, escaping from his gaze, and that the figures and attributes painted by Lebrun became darker and darker as the distance became more and more remote. A gentle, easy movement, as regular as that by which a vessel plunges beneath the waves, had succeeded to the immovableness of the bed. Doubtless the king was dreaming, and in this dream the crown of gold, which fastened the curtains together, seemed to recede from his vision, just as the dome, to which it remained suspended, had done, so that the winged genius which, with both its hand, supported the crown, seemed, though vainly so, to call upon the king, who was fast disappearing from it. The bed still sunk. Louis, with his eyes open, could not resist the deception of this cruel hallucination. At last, as the light of the royal chamber faded away into darkness and gloom, something cold, gloomy, and inexplicable in its nature seemed to infect the air. No paintings, nor gold, nor velvet hangings, were visible any longer, nothing but walls of a dull gray color, which the increasing gloom made darker every moment. And yet the bed still continued to descend, and after a minute, which seemed in its duration almost an age to the king, it reached a stratum of air, black and chill as death, and then it stopped. The king could no longer see the light in his room, except as from the bottom of a well we can see the light of day. "I am under the influence of some atrocious dream," he thought. "It is time to awaken from it. Come! let me wake."

Every one has experienced the sensation the above remark conveys; there is hardly a person who, in the midst of a nightmare whose influence is suffocating, has not said to himself, by the help of that light which still burns in the brain when every human light is extinguished, "It is nothing but a dream, after all." This was precisely what Louis XIV. said to himself; but when he said, "Come, come! wake up," he perceived that not only was he already awake, but still more, that he had his eyes open also. And then he looked all round him. On his right hand and on his left two armed men stood in stolid silence, each wrapped in a huge cloak, and the face covered with a mask; one of them held a small lamp in his hand, whose glimmering light revealed the saddest picture a king could look upon. Louis could not help saying to himself that his dream still lasted, and that all he had to do to cause it to disappear was to move his arms or to say something aloud; he darted from his bed, and found himself upon the damp, moist ground. Then, addressing himself to the man who held the lamp in his hand, he said:

"What is this, monsieur, and what is the meaning of this jest?"

"It is no jest," replied in a deep voice the masked figure that held the lantern.

"Do you belong to M. Fouquet?" inquired the king, greatly astonished at his situation.

"It matters very little to whom we belong," said the phantom; "we are your masters now, that is sufficient."

The king, more impatient than intimidated, turned to the other masked figure. "If this is a comedy," he said, "you will tell M. Fouquet that I find it unseemly and improper, and that I command it should cease."

The second masked person to whom the king had addressed himself was a man of huge stature and vast circumference. He held himself erect and motionless as any block of marble. "Well!" added the king, stamping his foot, "you do not answer!"

"We do not answer you, my good monsieur," said the giant, in a stentorian voice, "because there is nothing to say."

"At least, tell me what you want," exclaimed Louis, folding his arms with a passionate gesture.

"You will know by and by," replied the man who held the lamp.

"In the meantime tell me where I am."

"Look."

Louis looked all round him; but by the light of the lamp which the masked figure raised for the purpose, he could perceive nothing but the damp walls which glistened here and there with the slimy traces of the snail. "Oh—oh!—a dungeon," cried the king.

"No, a subterranean passage."

"Which leads—?"

"Will you be good enough to follow us?"

"I shall not stir from hence!" cried the king.

"If you are obstinate, my dear young friend," replied the

taller of the two, "I will lift you up in my arms, and roll you up in your own cloak, and if you should happen to be stifled, why—so much the worse for you."

As he said this, he disengaged from beneath his cloak a hand of which Milo of Crotona would have envied him the possession, on the day when he had that unhappy idea of rending his last oak. The king dreaded violence, for he could well believe that the two men into whose power he had fallen had not gone so far with any idea of drawing back, and that they would consequently be ready to proceed to extremities, if necessary. He shook his head and said: "It seems I have fallen into the hands of a couple of assassins. Move on, then."

Neither of the men answered a word to this remark. The one who carried the lantern walked first, the king followed him, while the second masked figure closed the procession. In this manner they passed along a winding gallery of some length, with as many staircases leading out of it as are to be found in the mysterious and gloomy palaces of Ann Radcliffe's creation. All these windings and turnings, during which the king heard the sound of running water *over his head*, ended at last in a long corridor closed by an iron door. The figure with the lamp opened the door with one of the keys he wore suspended at his girdle, where, during the whole of the brief journey, the king had heard them rattle. As soon as the door was opened and admitted the air, Louis recognized the balmy odors that trees exhale in hot summer nights. He paused, hesitatingly, for a moment or two; but the huge sentinel who followed him thrust him out of the subterranean passage.

"Another blow," said the king, turning towards the one who had just had the audacity to touch his sovereign; "what do you intend to do with the king of France?"

"Try to forget that word," replied the man with the lamp, in a tone which as little admitted of a reply as one of the famous decrees of Minos.

"You deserve to be broken on the wheel for the words

that you have just made use of," said the giant, as he extinguished the lamp his companion handed to him; "but the king is too kind-hearted."

Louis, at that threat, made so sudden a movement that it seemed as if he meditated flight; but the giant's hand was in a moment placed on his shoulder, and fixed him motionless where he stood. "But tell me, at least, where we are going," said the king.

"Come," replied the former of the two men, with a kind of respect in his manner, and leading his prisoner towards a carriage which seemed to be in waiting.

The carriage was completely concealed amid the trees. Two horses, with their feet fettered, were fastened by a halter to the lower branches of a large oak.

"Get in," said the same man, opening the carriage-door and letting down the step. The king obeyed, seated himself at the back of the carriage, the padded door of which was shut and locked immediately upon him and his guide. As for the giant, he cut the fastenings by which the horses were bound, harnessed them himself, and mounted on the box of the carriage, which was unoccupied. The carriage set off immediately at a quick trot, turned into the road to Paris, and in the forest of Senart found a relay of horses fastened to the trees in the same manner the first horses had been, and without a postilion. The man on the box changed the horses, and continued to follow the road towards Paris with the same rapidity, so that they entered the city about three o'clock in the morning. They carriage proceeded along the Faubourg Saint-Antoine, and, after having called out to the sentinel, "By the king's order," the driver conducted the horses into the circular inclosure of the Bastille, looking out upon the courtyard, called La Cour du Gouvernement. There the horses drew up, reeking with sweat, at the flight of steps, and a sergeant of the guard ran forward. "Go and wake the governor," said the coachman in a voice of thunder.

With the exception of this voice, which might have been heard at the entrance of the Faubourg Saint-Antoine, everything remained as calm in the carriage as in the prison. Ten minutes afterwards, M. de Baisemeaux appeared in his dressing-gown on the threshold of the door. "What is the matter now?" he asked; "and whom have you brought me there?"

The man with the lantern opened the carriage-door, and said two or three words to the one who acted as driver, who immediately got down from his seat, took up a short musket which he kept under his feet, and placed its muzzle on his prisoner's chest.

"And fire at once if he speaks!" added aloud the man who alighted from the carriage.

"Very good," replied his companion, without another remark.

With this recommendation, the person who had accompanied the king in the carriage ascended the flight of steps, at the top of which the governor was awaiting him. "Monsieur d'Herblay!" said the latter.

"Hush!" said Aramis. "Let us go into your room."

"Good heavens! what brings you here at this hour?"

"A mistake, my dear Monsieur de Baisemeaux," Aramis replied, quietly. "It appears that you were quite right the other day."

"What about?" inquired the governor.

"About the order of release, my dear friend."

"Tell me what you mean, monsieur—no, monseigneur," said the governor, almost suffocated by surprise and terror.

"It is a very simple affair: you remember, dear M. de Baisemeaux, that an order of release was sent to you."

"Yes, for Marchiali."

"Very good! we both thought that it was for Marchiali?"

"Certainly; you will recollect, however, that I would not credit it, but that you compelled me to believe it."

"Oh! Baisemeaux, my good fellow, what a word to make use of!—strongly recommended, that was all."

"Strongly recommended, yes; strongly recommended to give him up to you; and that you carried him off with you in your carriage."

"Well, my dear Monsieur de Baisemeaux, it was a mistake; it was discovered at the ministry, so that I now bring you an order from the king to set at liberty Seldon,—that poor Seldon fellow, you know."

"Seldon! are you sure this time?"

"Well, read it yourself," added Aramis, handing him the order.

"Why," said Baisemeaux, "this order is the very same that has already passed through my hands."

"Indeed?"

"It is the very one I assured you I saw the other evening. *Parbleu!* I recognize it by the blot of ink."

"I do not know whether it is that; but all I know is, that I bring it for you."

"But then, what about the other?"

"What other?"

"Marchiali."

"I have got him here with me."

"But that is not enough for me. I require a new order to take him back again."

"Don't talk such nonsense, my dear Baisemeaux; you talk like a child! Where is the order you received respecting Marchiali?"

Baisemeaux ran to his iron chest and took it out. Aramis seized hold of it, coolly tore it in four pieces, held them to the lamp, and burnt them. "Good heavens! what are you doing?" exclaimed Baisemeaux, in an extremity of terror.

"Look at your position quietly, my good governor," said Aramis, with imperturbable self-possession, "and you will see how very simple the whole affair is. You no longer possess any order justifying Marchiali's release."

"I am a lost man!"

"Far from it, my good fellow, since I have brought Marchiali back to you, and all accordingly is just the same as if he had never left."

"Ah!" said the governor, completely overcome by terror.

"Plain enough, you see; and you will go and shut him up immediately."

"I should think so, indeed."

"And you will hand over this Seldon to me, whose liberation is authorized by this order. Do you understand?" "I—I—"

"You do understand, I see," said Aramis. "Very good." Baisemeaux clapped his hands together.

"But why, at all events, after having taken Marchiali away from me, do you bring him back again?" cried the unhappy governor, in a paroxysm of terror, and completely dumbfounded.

"For a friend such as you are," said Aramis—"for so devoted a servant, I have no secrets;" and he put his mouth close to Baisemeaux's ear, as he said, in a low tone of voice, "you know the resemblance between that unfortunate fellow, and—"

"And the king?—yes!"

"Very good; the first use that Marchiali made of his liberty was to persist—Can you guess what?"

"How is it likely I should guess?"

"To persist in saying that he was king of France; to dress himself up in clothes like those of the king; and then pretend to assume that he was the king himself."

"Gracious heavens!"

"That is the reason why I have brought him back again, my dear friend. He is mad and lets every one see how mad he is."

"What is to be done, then?"

"That is very simple; let no one hold any communication with him. You understand that when his peculiar style of madness came to the king's ears, the king, who had pitied his terrible affliction, and saw that all his kindness had been repaid by black ingratitude, became perfectly furious; so that, now—and remember this very distinctly, dear Monsieur de Baisemeaux, for it concerns you most closely—so that there is now, I repeat, sentence of death pronounced against all those who may allow him to communicate with any one else but me or the king himself. You understand, Baisemeaux, sentence of death!"

"You need not ask me whether I understand."

"And now, let us go down, and conduct this poor devil back to his dungeon again, unless you prefer he should come up here."

"What would be the good of that?"

"It would be better, perhaps, to enter his name in the prison-book at once!"

"Of course, certainly; not a doubt of it."

"In that case, have him up."

Baisemeaux ordered the drums to be beaten and the bell to be rung, as a warning to every one to retire, in order to avoid meeting a prisoner, about whom it was desired to observe a certain mystery. Then, when the passages were free, he went to take the prisoner from the carriage, at whose breast Porthos, faithful to the directions which had been given him, still kept his musket leveled. "Ah! is that you, miserable wretch?" cried the governor, as soon as he perceived the king. "Very good, very good." And immediately, making the king get out of the carriage, he led him, still accompanied by Porthos, who had not taken off his mask, and Aramis, who again resumed his, up the stairs, to the second Bertaudiere, and opened the door of the room in which Philippe for six long years had bemoaned his existence. The king entered the cell without pronouncing a single word:

he faltered in as limp and haggard as a rain-struck lily. Baisemeaux shut the door upon him, turned the key twice in the lock, and then returned to Aramis. "It is quite true," he said, in a low tone, "that he bears a striking resemblance to the king; but less so than you said."

"So that," said Aramis, "you would not have been deceived by the substitution of the one for the other?"

"What a question!"

"You are a most valuable fellow, Baisemeaux," said Aramis; "and now, set Seldon free."

"Oh, yes. I was going to forget that. I will go and give orders at once."

"Bah! to-morrow will be time enough."

"To-morrow!—oh, no. This very minute."

"Well; go off to your affairs, I will go away to mine. But it is quite understood, is it not?"

"What 'is quite understood'?"

"That no one is to enter the prisoner's cell, expect with an order from the king; an order which I will myself bring."

"Quite so. Adieu, monseigneur."

Aramis returned to his companion. "Now, Porthos, my good fellow, back again to Vaux, and as fast as possible."

"A man is light and easy enough, when he has faithfully served his king; and, in serving him, saved his country," said Porthos. "The horses will be as light as if our tissues were constructed of the wind of heaven. So let us be off." And the carriage, lightened of a prisoner, who might well be—as he in fact was—very heavy in the sight of Aramis, passed across the drawbridge of the Bastille, which was raised again immediately behind it.

CHAPTER 18

A Night at the Bastille.

Pain, anguish, and suffering in human life are always in proportion to the strength with which a man is endowed. We will not pretend to say that Heaven always apportions to a man's capability of endurance the anguish with which he afflicts him; for that, indeed, would not be true, since Heaven permits the existence of death, which is, sometimes, the only refuge open to those who are too closely pressed—too bitterly afflicted, as far as the body is concerned. Suffering is in proportion to the strength which has been accorded; in other words, the weak suffer more, where the trial is the same, than the strong. And what are the elementary principles, we may ask, that compose human strength? Is it not—more than anything else—exercise, habit, experience? We shall not even take the trouble to demonstrate this, for it is an axiom in morals, as in physics. When the young king, stupefied and crushed in every sense and feeling, found himself led to a cell in the Bastille, he fancied death itself is but a sleep; that it, too, has its dreams as well; that the bed had broken through the flooring of his room at Vaux; that death had resulted from the occurrence; and that, still carrying out his dream, the king, Louis XIV., now no longer living, was dreaming one of those horrors, impossible to realize in life, which is termed dethronement, imprisonment, and insult towards a sovereign who formerly wielded unlimited power. To be present at—an actual witness, too—of this bitterness of death; to float, indecisively, in an incomprehensible mystery, between resemblance and reality; to hear everything, to see everything, without interfering in a single detail of agonizing suffering, was—so the king thought within himself—a torture far more terrible, since it might last forever. "Is this what is termed eternity—hell?" he murmured, at the moment the door was closed upon him, which we remember Baisemeaux had shut with his own hands. He did not even look round him; and in the room, leaning with his back against the wall, he allowed himself to be carried away by the terrible supposition that he was already dead, as he closed his eyes, in order to avoid looking upon something even worse still. "How can I have died?" he said to himself, sick with terror. "The bed might have been let down by some artificial means? But no! I do not remember to have felt a bruise, nor any shock either. Would they not rather have poisoned me at my meals, or with the fumes of wax, as they did my ancestress, Jeanne d'Albret?" Suddenly, the chill of the dungeons seemed to fall like a wet cloak upon Louis's shoulders. "I have seen," he said, "my father lying dead upon his funeral couch, in his regal robes. That pale face, so calm and worn; those hands, once so skillful, lying nerveless by his side; those limbs stiffened by the icy grasp of death; nothing there betokened a sleep that was disturbed by dreams. And yet, how numerous were the dreams which Heaven might have sent that royal corpse—him whom so many others had preceded, hurried away by him into eternal death! No, that king was still the king: he was enthroned still upon that funeral couch, as upon a velvet armchair; he had not abdicated one title of his majesty. God, who had not punished him, cannot, will not punish me, who have done nothing." A strange sound attracted the young man's attention. He looked round him, and saw on the mantel-shelf, just below an enormous crucifix, coarsely painted in fresco on the wall, a rat of enormous size engaged in nibbling a piece of dry bread, but fixing all the time, an intelligent and inquiring look upon the new occupant of the cell. The king could not resist a sudden impulse of fear and disgust: he moved back towards the door, uttering a loud cry; and as if he but needed this cry, which escaped from his breast almost unconsciously, to recognize himself, Louis knew that he was alive and in full possession of his natural senses. "A prisoner!" he cried. "I—I, a prisoner!" He looked round him for a bell to summon some one to him. "There are no bells in the Bastille," he said, "and it is in the Bastille I am imprisoned. In what way can I have been made a prisoner? It must have been owing to a conspiracy of M. Fouquet. I have been drawn to Vaux, as to a snare. M. Fouquet cannot be acting alone in this affair. His agent—That voice that I but just now heard was M. d'Herblay's; I recognized it. Colbert was right, then. But what is Fouquet's object? To reign in my place and stead?—Impossible. Yet who knows!" thought the king, relapsing into gloom again. "Perhaps my brother, the Duc d'Orleans, is doing that which my uncle wished to do during the whole of his life against my father. But the queen?—My mother, too? And La Valliere? Oh! La Valliere, she will have been abandoned to Madame. Dear, dear girl! Yes, it is—it must be so. They have shut her up as they have me. We are separated forever!" And at this idea of separation the poor lover burst into a flood of tears and sobs and groans.

"There is a governor in this place," the king continued, in a fury of passion; "I will speak to him, I will summon him to me."

He called—no voice replied to his. He seized hold of his chair, and hurled it against the massive oaken door. The wood resounded against the door, and awakened many a mournful echo in the profound depths of the staircase; but from a human creature, none.

This was a fresh proof for the king of the slight regard in which he was held at the Bastille. Therefore, when his first fit of anger had passed away, having remarked a barred window through which there passed a stream of light, lozenge-shaped, which must be, he knew, the bright orb of approaching day, Louis began to call out, at first gently enough, then louder and louder still; but no one replied. Twenty other attempts which he made, one after another, obtained no other or better success. His blood began to boil within him, and mount to his head. His nature was such, that, accustomed to command, he trembled at the idea of disobedience. The prisoner broke the chair, which was too heavy for him to lift, and made use of it as a battering ram to strike against the door. He struck so loudly, and so repeatedly, that the perspiration soon began to pour down his face. The sound became tremendous and continuous; certain stifled, smothered cries replied in different directions. This sound produced a strange effect upon the king. He paused to listen; it was the voice of the prisoners, formerly his victims, now his companions. The voices ascended like vapors through the thick ceilings and the massive walls, and rose in accusations against the author of this noise, as doubtless their sighs and tears accused, in whispered tones, the author of their captivity. After having deprived so many people of their liberty, the king came among them to rob them of their rest. This idea almost drove him mad; it redoubled his strength, or rather his well, bent upon obtaining some information, or a conclusion to the affair. With a portion of the broken chair he recommenced the noise. At the end of an hour, Louis heard something in the corridor, behind the door of his cell, and a violent blow, which was returned upon the door itself, made him cease his own.

"Are you mad?" said a rude, brutal voice. "What is the matter with you this morning?"

"This morning!" thought the king; but he said aloud, politely, "Monsieur, are you the governor of the Bastille?"

"My good fellow, your head is out of sorts," replied the voice; "but that is no reason why you should make such a terrible disturbance. Be quiet; *mordioux!*"

"Are you the governor?" the king inquired again.

He heard a door on the corridor close; the jailer had just left, not condescending to reply a single word. When the king had assured himself of his departure, his fury knew no longer any bounds. As agile as a tiger, he leaped from the table to the window, and struck the iron bars with all his might. He broke a pane of glass, the pieces of which fell clanking into the courtyard below. He shouted with increasing hoarseness, "The governor, the governor!" This excess lasted fully an hour, during which time he was in a burning fever. With his hair in disorder and matted on his forehead, his dress torn and covered with dust and plaster, his linen in shreds, the king never rested until his strength was utterly exhausted, and it was not until then that he clearly understood the pitiless thickness of the walls, the impenetrable nature of the cement, invincible to every influence but that of time, and that he possessed no other weapon but despair. He leaned his forehead against the door, and let the feverish throbbings of his heart calm by degrees; it had seemed as if one single additional pulsation would have made it burst.

"A moment will come when the food which is given to the prisoners will be brought to me. I shall then see some one, I shall speak to him, and get an answer."

And the king tried to remember at what hour the first repast of the prisoners was served at the Bastille; he was ignorant even of this detail. The feeling of remorse at this remembrance smote him like the thrust of a dagger, that he should have lived for five and twenty years a king, and in the enjoyment of every happiness, without having bestowed a moment's thought on the misery of those who had been unjustly deprived of their liberty. The king blushed for very shame. He felt that Heaven, in permitting this fearful humiliation, did no more than render to the man the same torture as had been inflicted by that man upon so many others. Nothing could be more efficacious for reawakening his mind to religious influences than the prostration of his heart and mind and soul beneath the feeling of such acute wretchedness. But Louis dared not even kneel in prayer to God to entreat him to terminate his bitter trial.

"Heaven is right," he said; "Heaven acts wisely. It would be cowardly to pray to Heaven for that which I have so often refused my own fellow-creatures."

He had reached this stage of his reflections, that is, of his agony of mind, when a similar noise was again heard behind his door, followed this time by the sound of the key in the lock, and of the bolts being withdrawn from their staples. The king bounded forward to be nearer to the person who was about to enter, but, suddenly reflecting that it was a movement unworthy of a sovereign, he paused, assumed a noble and calm expression, which for him was easy enough, and waited with his back turned towards the window, in order, to some extent, to conceal his agitation from the eyes of the person who was about to enter. It was only a jailer with a basket of provisions. The king looked at the man with restless anxiety, and waited until he spoke.

"Ah!" said the latter, "you have broken your chair. I said you had done so! Why, you have gone quite mad."

"Monsieur," said the king, "be careful what you say; it will be a very serious affair for you."

The jailer placed the basket on the table, and looked at his prisoner steadily. "What do you say?" he said.

"Desire the governor to come to me," added the king, in accents full of calm and dignity.

"Come, my boy," said the turnkey, "you have always been very quiet and reasonable, but you are getting vicious, it seems, and I wish you to know it in time. You have broken your chair, and made a great disturbance; that is an offense punishable by imprisonment in one of the lower dungeons. Promise me not to begin over again, and I will not say a word about it to the governor."

"I wish to see the governor," replied the king, still governing his passions.

"He will send you off to one of the dungeons, I tell you; so take care."

"I insist upon it, do you hear?"

"Ah! ah! your eyes are becoming wild again. Very good! I shall take away your knife."

And the jailer did what he said, quitted the prisoner, and closed the door, leaving the king more astounded, more wretched, more isolated than ever. It was useless, though he tried it, to make the same noise again on his door, and equally useless that he threw the plates and dishes out of the window; not a single sound was heard in recognition. Two hours afterwards he could not be recognized as a king, a gentleman, a man, a human being; he might rather be called a madman, tearing the door with his nails, trying to tear up the flooring of his cell, and uttering such wild and fearful cries that the old Bastille seemed to tremble to its very foundations for having revolted against its master. As for the governor, the jailer did not even think of disturbing him; the turnkeys and the sentinels had reported the occurrence to him, but what was the good of it? Were not these madmen common enough in such a prison? and were not the walls still stronger? M. de Baisemeaux, thoroughly impressed with what Aramis had told him, and in perfect conformity with the king's order, hoped only that one thing might happen; namely, that the madman Marchiali might be mad enough to hang himself to the canopy of his bed, or to one of the bars of the window. In fact, the prisoner was anything but a profitable investment for M. Baisemeaux, and became more annoying than agreeable to him. These complications of Seldon and Marchiali—the complications first of setting at liberty and then imprisoning again, the complications arising from the strong likeness in question—had at last found a very proper *denouement*. Baisemeaux even thought he had remarked that D'Herblay himself was not altogether dissatisfied with the result.

"And then, really," said Baisemeaux to his next in command, "an ordinary prisoner is already unhappy enough in being a prisoner; he suffers quite enough, indeed, to induce one to hope, charitably enough, that his death may not be far distant. With still greater reason, accordingly, when the prisoner has gone mad, and might bite and make a terrible disturbance in the Bastille; why, in such a case, it is not simply an act of mere charity to wish him dead; it would be almost a good and even commendable action, quietly to have him put out of his misery."

And the good-natured governor thereupon sat down to his late breakfast.

CHAPTER 19

The Shadow of M. Fouquet.

D'Artagnan, still confused and oppressed by the conversation he had just had with the king, could not resist asking himself if he were really in possession of his senses, if he were really and truly at Vaux; if he, D'Artagnan, were really the captain of the musketeers, and M. Fouquet the owner of the chateau in which Louis XIV. was at that moment partaking of his hospitality. These reflections were not those of a drunken man, although everything was in prodigal profusion at Vaux, and the surintendant's wines had met with a distinguished reception at the *fete*. The Gascon, however, was a man of calm self-possession; and no sooner did he touch his bright steel blade, than he knew how to adopt morally the cold, keen weapon as his guide of action.

"Well," he said, as he quitted the royal apartment, "I seem now to be mixed up historically with the destinies of the king and of the minister; it will be written, that M. d'Artagnan, a younger son of a Gascon family, placed his hand on the shoulder of M. Nicolas Fouquet, the surintendant of the finances of France. My descendants, if I have any, will flatter themselves with the distinction which this arrest will confer, just as the members of the De Luynes family have done with regard to the estates of the poor

Marechal d'Ancre. But the thing is, how best to execute the king's directions in a proper manner. Any man would know how to say to M. Fouquet, 'Your sword, monsieur.' But it is not every one who would be able to take care of M. Fouquet without others knowing anything about it. How am I to manage, then, so that M. le surintendant pass from the height of favor to the direst disgrace; that Vaux be turned into a dungeon for him; that after having been steeped to his lips, as it were, in all the perfumes and incense of Ahasuerus, he is transferred to the gallows of Haman; in other words, of Enguerrand de Marigny?" And at this reflection, D'Artagnan's brow became clouded with perplexity. The musketeer had certain scruples on the matter, it must be admitted. To deliver up to death (for not a doubt existed that Louis hated Fouquet mortally) the man who had just shown himself so delightful and charming a host in every way, was a real insult to one's conscience. "It almost seems," said D'Artagnan to himself, "that if I am not a poor, mean, miserable fellow, I should let M. Fouquet know the opinion the king has about him. Yet, if I betray my master's secret, I shall be a false-hearted, treacherous knave, a traitor, too, a crime provided for and punishable by military laws—so much so, indeed, that twenty times, in former days when wars were rife, I have seen many a miserable fellow strung up to a tree for doing, in but a small degree, what my scruples counsel me to undertake upon a great scale now. No, I think that a man of true readiness of wit ought to get out of this difficulty with more skill than that. And now, let us admit that I do possess a little readiness of invention; it is not at all certain, though, for, after having for forty years absorbed so large a quantity, I shall be lucky if there were to be a pistole's-worth left." D'Artagnan buried his head in his hands, tore at his mustache in sheer vexation, and added, "What can be the reason of M. Fouquet's disgrace? There seem to be three good ones: the first, because M. Colbert doesn't like him; the second, because he wished to fall in love with Mademoiselle de la Valliere; and lastly, because the king likes M. Colbert and loves Mademoiselle de la Valliere. Oh! he is lost! But shall I put my foot on his neck, I, of all men, when he is falling a prey to the intrigues of a pack of women and clerks? For shame! If he be dangerous, I will lay him low enough; if, however, he be only persecuted, I will look on. I have come to such a decisive determination, that neither king nor living man shall change my mind. If Athos were here, he would do as I have done. Therefore, instead of going, in cold blood, up to M. Fouquet, and arresting him off-hand and shutting him up altogether, I will try and conduct myself like a man who understands what good manners are. People will talk about it, of course; but they shall talk well of it, I am determined." And D'Artagnan, drawing by a gesture peculiar to himself his shoulder-belt over his shoulder, went straight off to M. Fouquet, who, after he had taken leave of his guests, was preparing to retire for the night and to sleep tranquilly after the triumphs of the day. The air was still perfumed, or infected, whichever way it may be considered, with the odors of the torches and the fireworks. The wax-lights were dying away in their sockets, the flowers fell unfastened from the garlands, the groups of dancers and courtiers were separating in the salons. Surrounded by his friends, who complimented him and received his flattering remarks in return, the surintendant half-closed his wearied eyes. He longed for rest and quiet; he sank upon the bed of laurels which had been heaped up for him for so many days past; it might almost have been said that he seemed bowed beneath the weight of the new debts which he had incurred for the purpose of giving the greatest possible honor to this *fete*. Fouquet had just retired to his room, still smiling, but more than half-asleep. He could listen to nothing more, he could hardly keep his eyes open; his bed seemed to possess a fascinating and irresistible attraction for him. The god Morpheus, the presiding deity of the dome painted by Lebrun, had extended his influence over the adjoining rooms, and showered down his most sleep-inducing poppies upon the master of the house. Fouquet, almost entirely alone, was being assisted by his *valet de chambre* to undress, when M. d'Artagnan appeared at the entrance of the room. D'Artagnan had never been able to succeed in making himself common at the court; and notwithstanding he was seen everywhere and on all occasions, he never failed to produce an effect wherever and whenever he made his appearance. Such is the happy privilege of certain natures, which in that respect resemble either thunder or lightning; every one recognizes them; but their appearance never fails to arouse surprise and astonishment, and whenever they occur, the impression is always left that the last was the most conspicuous or most important.

"What! M. d'Artagnan?" said Fouquet, who had already taken his right arm out of the sleeve of his doublet.

"At your service," replied the musketeer.

"Come in, my dear M. d'Artagnan."

"Thank you."

"Have you come to criticise the *fete?* You are ingenious enough in your criticisms, I know."

"By no means."

"Are not your men looked after properly?"

"In every way."

"You are not comfortably lodged, perhaps?"

"Nothing could be better."

"In that case, I have to thank you for being so amiably disposed, and I must not fail to express my obligations to you for all your flattering kindness."

These words were as much as to say, "My dear D'Artagnan, pray go to bed, since you have a bed to lie down on, and let me do the same."

D'Artagnan did not seem to understand it.

"Are you going to bed already?" he said to the superintendent.

"Yes; have you anything to say to me?"

"Nothing, monsieur, nothing at all. You sleep in this room, then?"

"Yes; as you see."

"You have given a most charming *fete* to the king."

"Do you think so?"

"Oh! beautiful!"

"Is the king pleased?"

"Enchanted."

"Did he desire you to say as much to me?"

"He would not choose so unworthy a messenger, monseigneur."

"You do not do yourself justice, Monsieur d'Artagnan."

"Is that your bed, there?"

"Yes; but why do you ask? Are you not satisfied with your own?"

"My I speak frankly to you?"

"Most assuredly."

"Well, then, I am not."

Fouquet started; and then replied, "Will you take my room, Monsieur d'Artagnan?"

"What! deprive you of it, monseigneur? never!"

"What am I to do, then?"

"Allow me to share yours with you."

Fouquet looked at the musketeer fixedly. "Ah! ah!" he said, "you have just left the king."

"I have, monseigneur."

"And the king wishes you to pass the night in my room?"

"Monseigneur—"

"Very well, Monsieur d'Artagnan, very well. You are the master here."

"I assure you, monseigneur, that I do not wish to abuse—"

Fouquet turned to his valet, and said, "Leave us." When the man had left, he said to D'Artagnan, "You have something to say to me?"

"I?"

"A man of your superior intelligence cannot have come to talk with a man like myself, at such an hour as the present, without grave motives."

"Do not interrogate me."

"On the contrary. What do you want with me?"

"Nothing more than the pleasure of your society."

"Come into the garden, then," said the superintendent suddenly, "or into the park."

"No," replied the musketeer, hastily, "no."

"Why?"

"The fresh air—"

"Come, admit at once that you arrest me," said the superintendent to the captain.

"Never!" said the latter.

"You intend to look after me, then?"

"Yes, monseigneur, I do, upon my honor."

"Upon your honor—ah! that is quite another thing! So I am to be arrested in my own house."

"Do not say such a thing."

"On the contrary, I will proclaim it aloud."

"If you do so, I shall be compelled to request you to be silent."

"Very good! Violence towards me, and in my own house, too."

"We do not seem to understand one another at all. Stay a moment; there is a chess-board there; we will have a game, if you have no objections."

"Monsieur d'Artagnan, I am in disgrace, then?"

"Not at all; but—"

"I am prohibited, I suppose, from withdrawing from your sight."

"I do not understand a word you are saying, monseigneur; and if you wish me to withdraw, tell me so."

"My dear Monsieur d'Artagnan, your mode of action is enough to drive me mad; I was almost sinking for want of sleep, but you have completely awakened me."

"I shall never forgive myself, I am sure; and if you wish to reconcile me with myself, why, go to sleep in your bed in my presence; and I shall be delighted."

"I am under surveillance, I see."

"I will leave the room if you say any such thing."

"You are beyond my comprehension."

"Good night, monseigneur," said D'Artagnan, as he pretended to withdraw.

Fouquet ran after him. "I will not lie down," he said. "Seriously, and since you refuse to treat me as a man, and since you finesse with me, I will try and set you at bay, as a hunter does a wild boar."

"Bah!" cried D'Artagnan, pretending to smile.

"I shall order my horses, and set off for Paris," said Fouquet, sounding the captain of the musketeers.

"If that be the case, monseigneur, it is very difficult."

"You will arrest me, then?"

"No, but I shall go along with you."

"That is quite sufficient, Monsieur d'Artagnan," returned Fouquet, coldly. "It was not for nothing you acquired your reputation as a man of intelligence and resource; but with me all this is quite superfluous. Let us come to the point. Do me a service. Why do you arrest me? What have I done?"

"Oh! I know nothing about what you may have done; but I do not arrest you—this evening, at least!"

"This evening!" said Fouquet, turning pale, "but to-morrow?"

"It is not to-morrow just yet, monseigneur. Who can ever answer for the morrow?"

"Quick, quick, captain! let me speak to M. d'Herblay."

"Alas! that is quite impossible, monseigneur. I have strict orders to see that you hold no communication with any one."

"With M. d'Herblay, captain—with your friend!"

"Monseigneur, is M. d'Herblay the only person with whom you ought to be prevented holding any communication?"

Fouquet colored, and then assuming an air of resignation, he said: "You are right, monsieur; you have taught me a lesson I ought not to have evoked. A fallen man cannot assert his right to anything, even from those whose fortunes he may have made; for a still stronger reason, he cannot claim anything from those to whom he may never have had the happiness of doing a service."

"Monseigneur!"

"It is perfectly true, Monsieur d'Artagnan; you have always acted in the most admirable manner towards me—in such a manner, indeed, as most becomes the man who is destined to arrest me. You, at least, have never asked me anything."

"Monsieur," replied the Gascon, touched by his eloquent and noble tone of grief, "will you—I ask it as a favor—pledge me your word as a man of honor that you will not leave this room?"

"What is the use of it, dear Monsieur d'Artagnan, since you keep watch and ward over me? Do you suppose I should contend against the most valiant sword in the kingdom?"

"It is not that, at all, monseigneur; but that I am going to look for M. d'Herblay, and, consequently, to leave you alone."

Fouquet uttered a cry of delight and surprise.

"To look for M. d'Herblay! to leave me alone!" he exclaimed, clasping his hands together.

"Which is M. d'Herblay's room? The blue room is it not?"

"Yes, my friend, yes."

"Your friend! thank you for that word, monseigneur; you confer it upon me to-day, at least, if you have never done so before."

"Ah! you have saved me."

"It will take a good ten minutes to go from hence to the blue room, and to return?" said D'Artagnan.

"Nearly so."

"And then to wake Aramis, who sleeps very soundly, when he is asleep, I put that down at another five minutes; making a total of fifteen minutes' absence. And now, monseigneur, give me your word that you will not in any way attempt to make your escape, and that when I return I shall find you here again."

"I give it, monsieur," replied Fouquet, with an expression of the warmest and deepest gratitude.

D'Artagnan disappeared. Fouquet looked at him as he quitted the room, waited with a feverish impatience until the door was closed behind him, and as soon as it was shut, flew to his keys, opened two or three secret doors concealed in various articles of furniture in the room, looked vainly for certain papers, which doubtless he had left at Saint-Mande, and which he seemed to regret not having found in them; then hurriedly seizing hold of letters, contracts, papers, writings, he heaped them up into a pile, which he burnt in the extremest haste upon the marble hearth of the fireplace, not even taking time to draw from the interior of it the vases and pots of flowers with which it was filled. As soon as he had finished, like a man who has just escaped an imminent danger, and whose strength abandons him as soon as the danger is past, he sank down, completely overcome, on a couch. When D'Artagnan returned, he found Fouquet in the same position; the worthy musketeer had not the slightest doubt that Fouquet, having given his word, would not even think of failing to keep it, but he had thought it most likely that

Fouquet would turn his (D'Artagnan's) absence to the best advantage in getting rid of all the papers, memorandums, and contracts, which might possibly render his position, which was even now serious enough, more dangerous than ever. And so, lifting up his head like a dog who has regained the scent, he perceived an odor resembling smoke he had relied on finding in the atmosphere, and having found it, made a movement of his head in token of satisfaction. As D'Artagnan entered, Fouquet, on his side, raised his head, and not one of D'Artagnan's movements escaped him. And then the looks of the two men met, and they both saw that they had understood each other without exchanging a syllable.

"Well!" asked Fouquet, the first to speak, "and M. d'Herblay?"

"Upon my word, monseigneur," replied D'Artagnan, "M. d'Herblay must be desperately fond of walking out at night, and composing verses by moonlight in the park of Vaux, with some of your poets, in all probability, for he is not in his own room."

"What! not in his own room?" cried Fouquet, whose last hope thus escaped him; for unless he could ascertain in what way the bishop of Vannes could assist him, he perfectly well knew that he could expect assistance from no other quarter.

"Or, indeed," continued D'Artagnan, "if he is in his own room, he has very good reasons for not answering."

"But surely you did not call him in such a manner that he could have heard you?"

"You can hardly suppose, monseigneur, that having already exceeded my orders, which forbade me leaving you a single moment—you can hardly suppose, I say, that I should have been mad enough to rouse the whole house and allow myself to be seen in the corridor of the bishop of Vannes, in order that M. Colbert might state with positive certainty that I gave you time to burn your papers."

"My papers?"

"Of course; at least that is what I should have done in your place. When any one opens a door for me I always avail myself of it."

"Yes, yes, and I thank you, for I have availed myself of it."

"And you have done perfectly right. Every man has his own peculiar secrets with which others have nothing to do. But let us return to Aramis, monseigneur."

"Well, then, I tell you, you could not have called loud enough, or Aramis would have heard you."

"However softly any one may call Aramis, monseigneur, Aramis always hears when he has an interest in hearing. I repeat what I said before—Aramis was not in his own room, or Aramis had certain reasons for not recognizing my voice, of which I am ignorant, and of which you may be even ignorant yourself, notwithstanding your liege-man is His Greatness the Lord Bishop of Vannes."

Fouquet drew a deep sigh, rose from his seat, took three or four turns in his room, and finished by seating himself, with an expression of extreme dejection, upon his magnificent bed with velvet hangings, and costliest lace. D'Artagnan looked at Fouquet with feelings of the deepest and sincerest pity.

"I have seen a good many men arrested in my life," said the musketeer, sadly; "I have seen both M. de Cinq-Mars and M. de Chalais arrested, though I was very young then. I have seen M. de Conde arrested with the princes; I have seen M. de Retz arrested; I have seen M. Broussel arrested. Stay a moment, monseigneur, it is disagreeable to have to say, but the very one of all those whom you most resemble at this moment was that poor fellow Broussel. You were very near doing as he did, putting your dinner napkin in your portfolio, and wiping your mouth with your papers. *Mordioux!* Monseigneur Fouquet, a man like you ought not to be dejected in this manner. Suppose your friends saw you?"

"Monsieur d'Artagnan," returned the surintendant, with a smile full of gentleness, "you do not understand me; it is precisely because my friends are not looking on, that I am as you see me now. I do not live, exist even, isolated from others; I am nothing when left to myself. Understand that throughout my whole life I have passed every moment of my time in making friends, whom I hoped to render my stay and support. In times of prosperity, all these cheerful, happy voices—rendered so through and by my means—formed in my honor a concert of praise and kindly actions. In the least disfavor, these humbler voices accompanied in harmonious accents the murmur of my own heart. Isolation I have never yet known. Poverty (a phantom I have sometimes beheld, clad in rags, awaiting me at the end of my journey through life)—poverty has been the specter with which many of my own friends have trifled for years past, which they poetize and caress, and which has attracted me towards them. Poverty! I accept it, acknowledge it, receive it, as a disinherited sister; for poverty is neither solitude, nor exile, nor imprisonment. Is it likely I shall ever be poor, with such friends as Pelisson, as La Fontaine, as Moliere? with such a mistress as—Oh! if you knew how utterly lonely and desolate I feel at this moment, and how you, who separate me from all I love, seem to resemble the image of solitude, of annihilation—death itself."

"But I have already told you, Monsieur Fouquet," replied D'Artagnan, moved to the depths of his soul, "that you are woefully exaggerating. The king likes you."

"No, no," said Fouquet, shaking his head.

"M. Colbert hates you."

"M. Colbert! What does that matter to me?"

"He will ruin you."

"Ah! I defy him to do that, for I am ruined already."

At this singular confession of the superintendent, D'Artagnan cast his glance all round the room; and although he did not open his lips, Fouquet understood him so thoroughly, that he added: "What can be done with such wealth of substance as surrounds us, when a man can no longer cultivate his taste for the magnificent? Do you know what good the greater part of the wealth and the possessions which we rich enjoy, confer upon us? merely to disgust us, by their very splendor even, with everything which does not equal it! Vaux! you will say, and the wonders of Vaux! What of it? What boot these wonders? If I am ruined, how shall I fill with water the urns which my Naiads bear in their arms, or force the air into the lungs of my Tritons? To be rich enough, Monsieur d'Artagnan, a man must be too rich."

D'Artagnan shook his head.

"Oh! I know very well what you think," replied Fouquet, quickly. "If Vaux were yours, you would sell it, and would purchase an estate in the country; an estate which should have woods, orchards, and land attached, so that the estate should be made to support its master. With forty millions you might—"

"Ten millions," interrupted D'Artagnan.

"Not a million, my dear captain. No one in France is rich enough to give two millions for Vaux, and to continue to maintain it as I have done; no one could do it, no one would know how."

"Well," said D'Artagnan, "in any case, a million is not abject misery."

"It is not far from it, my dear monsieur. But you do not understand me. No; I will not sell my residence at Vaux; I will give it to you, if you like;" and Fouquet accompanied these words with a movement of the shoulders to which it would be impossible to do justice.

"Give it to the king; you will make a better bargain."

"The king does not require me to give it to him," said

Fouquet; "he will take it away from me with the most absolute ease and grace, if it pleases him to do so; and that is the very reason I should prefer to see it perish. Do you know, Monsieur d'Artagnan, that if the king did not happen to be under my roof, I would take this candle, go straight to the dome, and set fire to a couple of huge chests of fusees and fireworks which are in reserve there, and would reduce my palace to ashes."

"Bah!" said the musketeer, negligently. "At all events, you would not be able to burn the gardens, and that is the finest feature of the place."

"And yet," resumed Fouquet, thoughtfully, "what was I saying? Great heavens! burn Vaux! destroy my palace! But Vaux is not mine; these wonderful creations are, it is true, the property, as far as sense of enjoyment goes, of the man who has paid for them; but as far as duration is concerned, they belong to those who created them. Vaux belongs to Lebrun, to Lenotre, to Pelisson, to Levau, to La Fontaine, to Moliere; Vaux belongs to posterity, in fact. You see, Monsieur d'Artagnan, that my very house has ceased to be my own."

"That is all well and good," said D'Artagnan; "the idea is agreeable enough, and I recognize M. Fouquet himself in it. That idea, indeed, makes me forget that poor fellow Broussel altogether; and I now fail to recognize in you the whining complaints of that old Frondeur. If you are ruined, monsieur, look at the affair manfully, for you too, *mordioux!* belong to posterity, and have no right to lessen yourself in any way. Stay a moment; look at me, I who seem to exercise in some degree a kind of superiority over you, because I am arresting you; fate, which distributes their different parts to the comedians of this world, accorded me a less agreeable and less advantageous part to fill than yours has been. I am one of those who think that the parts which kings and powerful nobles are called upon to act are infinitely of more worth than the parts of beggars or lackeys. It is far better on the stage—on the stage, I mean, of another theater than the theater of this world—it is far better to wear a fine coat and to talk a fine language, than to walk the boards shod with a pair of old shoes, or to get one's backbone gently polished by a hearty dressing with a stick. In one word, you have been a prodigal with money, you have ordered and been obeyed—have been steeped to the lips in enjoyment; while I have dragged my tether after me, have been commanded and have obeyed, and have drudged my life away. Well, although I may seem of such trifling importance beside you, monseigneur, I do declare to you, that the recollection of what I have done serves me as a spur, and prevents me from bowing my old head too soon. I shall remain unto the very end a trooper; and when my turn comes, I shall fall perfectly straight, all in a heap, still alive, after having selected my place beforehand. Do as I do, Monsieur Fouquet, you will not find yourself the worse for it; a fall happens only once in a lifetime to men like yourself, and the chief thing is, to take it gracefully when the chance presents itself. There is a Latin proverb—the words have escaped me, but I remember the sense of it very well, for I have thought over it more than once—which says, 'The end crowns the work!'"

Fouquet rose from his seat, passed his arm round D'Artagnan's neck, and clasped him in a close embrace, whilst with the other hand he pressed his hand. "An excellent homily," he said, after a moment's pause.

"A soldier's, monseigneur."

"You have a regard for me, in telling me all that."

"Perhaps."

Fouquet resumed his pensive attitude once more, and then, a moment after, he said: "Where can M. d'Herblay be? I dare not ask you to send for him."

"You would not ask me, because I would not do it,

Monsieur Fouquet. People would learn it, and Aramis, who is not mixed up with the affair, might possibly be compromised and included in your disgrace."

"I will wait here till daylight," said Fouquet.

"Yes; that is best."

"What shall we do when daylight comes?"

"I know nothing at all about it, monseigneur."

"Monsieur d'Artagnan, will you do me a favor?"

"Most willingly."

"You guard me, I remain; you are acting in the full discharge of your duty, I suppose?"

"Certainly."

"Very good, then; remain as close to me as my shadow if you like; and I infinitely prefer such a shadow to any one else."

D'Artagnan bowed to the compliment.

"But, forget that you are Monsieur d'Artagnan, captain of the musketeers; forget that I am Monsieur Fouquet, surintendant of the finances; and let us talk about my affairs."

"That is rather a delicate subject."

"Indeed?"

"Yes; but, for your sake, Monsieur Fouquet, I will do what may almost be regarded as an impossibility."

"Thank you. What did the king say to you?"

"Nothing."

"Ah! is that the way you talk?"

"The deuce!"

"What do you think of my situation?"

"I do not know."

"However, unless you have some ill feeling against me—"

"Your position is a difficult one."

"In what respect?"

"Because you are under your own roof."

"However difficult it may be, I understand it very well."

"Do you suppose that, with any one else but yourself, I should have shown so much frankness?"

"What! so much frankness, do you say? you, who refuse to tell me the slightest thing?"

"At all events, then, so much ceremony and consideration."

"Ah! I have nothing to say in that respect."

"One moment, monseigneur: let me tell you how I should have behaved towards any one but yourself. It might be that I happened to arrive at your door just as your guests or your friends had left you—or, if they had not gone yet, I should wait until they were leaving, and should then catch them one after the other, like rabbits; I should lock them up quietly enough, I should steal softly along the carpet of your corridor, and with one hand upon you, before you suspected the slightest thing amiss, I should keep you safely until my master's breakfast in the morning. In this way, I should just the same have avoided all publicity, all disturbance, all opposition; but there would also have been no warning for M. Fouquet, no consideration for his feelings, none of those delicate concessions which are shown by persons who are essentially courteous in their natures, whenever the decisive moment may arrive. Are you satisfied with the plan?"

"It makes me shudder."

"I thought you would not like it. It would have been very disagreeable to have made my appearance to-morrow, without any preparation, and to have asked you to deliver up your sword."

"Oh! monsieur, I should have died of shame and anger."

"Your gratitude is too eloquently expressed. I have not done enough to deserve it, I assure you."

"Most certainly, monsieur, you will never get me to believe that."

"Well, then, monseigneur, if you are satisfied with what I have done, and have somewhat recovered from the shock which I prepared you for as much as I possibly could, let us allow the few hours that remain to pass away undisturbed. You are harassed, and should arrange your thoughts; I beg you, therefore, go to sleep, or pretend to go to sleep, either on your bed, or in your bed; I will sleep in this armchair; and when I fall asleep, my rest is so sound that a cannon would not wake me."

Fouquet smiled. "I expect, however," continued the musketeer, "the case of a door being opened, whether a secret door, or any other; or the case of any one going out of, or coming into, the room—for anything like that my ear is as quick and sensitive as the ear of a mouse. Creaking noises make me start. It arises, I suppose, from a natural antipathy to anything of the kind. Move about as much as you like; walk up and down in any part of the room, write, efface, destroy, burn,—nothing like that will prevent me from going to sleep or even prevent me from snoring, but do not touch either the key or the handle of the door, for I should start up in a moment, and that would shake my nerves and make me ill."

"Monsieur d'Artagnan," said Fouquet, "you are certainly the most witty and the most courteous man I ever met with; and you will leave me only one regret, that of having made your acquaintance so late."

D'Artagnan drew a deep sigh, which seemed to say, "Alas! you have perhaps made it too soon." He then settled himself in his armchair, while Fouquet, half lying on his bed and leaning on his arm, was meditating on his misadventures. In this way, both of them, leaving the candles burning, awaited the first dawn of the day; and when Fouquet happened to sigh too loudly, D'Artagnan only snored the louder. Not a single visit, not even from Aramis, disturbed their quietude: not a sound even was heard throughout the whole vast palace. Outside, however, the guards of honor on duty, and the patrol of musketeers, paced up and down; and the sound of their feet could be heard on the gravel walks. It seemed to act as an additional soporific for the sleepers, while the murmuring of the wind through the trees, and the unceasing music of the fountains whose waters tumbled in the basin, still went on uninterruptedly, without being disturbed at the slight noises and items of little moment that constitute the life and death of human nature.

CHAPTER 20

The Morning.

In vivid contrast to the sad and terrible destiny of the king imprisoned in the Bastille, and tearing, in sheer despair, the bolts and bars of his dungeon, the rhetoric of the chroniclers of old would not fail to present, as a complete antithesis, the picture of Philippe lying asleep beneath the royal canopy. We do not pretend to say that such rhetoric is always bad, and always scatters, in places where they have no right to grow, the flowers with which it embellishes and enlivens history. But we shall, on the present occasion, carefully avoid polishing the antithesis in question, but shall proceed to draw another picture as minutely as possible, to serve as foil and counterfoil to the one in the preceding chapter. The young prince alighted from Aramis's room, in the same way the king had descended from the apartment dedicated to Morpheus. The dome gradually and slowly sank down under Aramis's pressure, and Philippe stood beside the royal bed, which had ascended again after having deposited its prisoner in the secret depths of the subterranean passage. Alone, in the presence of all the luxury which surrounded him; alone, in the presence of his power; alone, with the part he was about to be forced to act, Philippe for the first time felt his heart, and mind, and soul expand beneath the influence of a thousand mutable emotions, which are the vital throbs of a king's heart. He could not help changing color when he looked upon the empty bed, still tumbled by his brother's body. This mute accomplice had returned, after having completed the work it had been destined to perform; it returned with the traces of the crime; it spoke to the guilty author of that crime, with the frank and unreserved language which an accomplice never fears to use in the company of his companion in guilt; for it spoke the truth. Philippe bent over the bed, and perceived a pocket-handkerchief lying on it, which was still damp from the cold sweat which had poured from Louis XIV.'s face. This sweat-bestained handkerchief terrified Philippe, as the gore of Abel frightened Cain.

"I am face to face with my destiny," said Philippe, his eyes on fire, and his face a livid white. "Is it likely to be more terrifying than my captivity has been sad and gloomy? Though I am compelled to follow out, at every moment, the sovereign power and authority I have usurped, shall I cease to listen to the scruples of my heart? Yes! the king has lain on this bed; it is indeed his head that has left its impression on this pillow; his bitter tears that have stained this handkerchief: and yet, I hesitate to throw myself on the bed, or to press in my hand the handkerchief which is embroidered with my brother's arms. Away with such weakness; let me imitate M. d'Herblay, who asserts that a man's action should be always one degree above his thoughts; let me imitate M. d'Herblay, whose thoughts are of and for himself alone, who regards himself as a man of honor, so long as he injures or betrays his enemies only. I, I alone, should have occupied this bed, if Louis XIV. had not, owing to my mother's criminal abandonment, stood in my way; and this handkerchief, embroidered with the arms of France, would in right and justice belong to me alone, if, as M. d'Herblay observes, I had been left my royal cradle. Philippe, son of France, take your place on that bed; Philippe, sole king of France, resume the blazonry that is yours!

Philippe, sole heir presumptive to Louis XIII., your father, show yourself without pity or mercy for the usurper who, at this moment, has not even to suffer the agony of the remorse of all that you have had to submit to."

With these words, Philippe, notwithstanding an instinctive repugnance of feeling, and in spite of the shudder of terror which mastered his will, threw himself on the royal bed, and forced his muscles to press the still warm place where Louis XIV. had lain, while he buried his burning face in the handkerchief still moistened by his brother's tears. With his head thrown back and buried in the soft down of his pillow, Philippe perceived above him the crown of France, suspended, as we have stated, by angels with outspread golden wings.

A man may be ambitious of lying in a lion's den, but can hardly hope to sleep there quietly. Philippe listened attentively to every sound; his heart panted and throbbed at the very suspicion of approaching terror and misfortune; but confident in his own strength, which was confirmed by the force of an overpoweringly resolute determination, he waited until some decisive circumstance should permit him to judge for himself. He hoped that imminent danger might be revealed to him, like those phosphoric lights of the tempest which show the sailors the altitude of the waves against which they have to struggle. But nothing approached. Silence, that mortal enemy of restless hearts, and of ambitious minds, shrouded in the thickness of its gloom during the remainder of the night the future king of France, who lay there sheltered beneath his stolen crown. Towards the morning a shadow, rather than a body, glided into the royal chamber; Philippe expected his approach and neither expressed nor exhibited any surprise.

"Well, M. d'Herblay?"

"Well, sire, all is accomplished."

"How?"

"Exactly as we expected."

"Did he resist?"

"Terribly! tears and entreaties."

"And then?"

"A perfect stupor."

"But at last?"

"Oh! at last, a complete victory, and absolute silence."

"Did the governor of the Bastille suspect anything?"

"Nothing."

"The resemblance, however—"

"Was the cause of the success."

"But the prisoner cannot fail to explain himself. Think well of that. I have myself been able to do as much as that, on former occasion."

"I have already provided for every chance. In a few days, sooner if necessary, we will take the captive out of his prison, and will send him out of the country, to a place of exile so remote—"

"People can return from their exile, Monsieur d'Herblay."

"To a place of exile so distant, I was going to say, that human strength and the duration of human life would not be enough for his return."

Once more a cold look of intelligence passed between Aramis and the young king.

"And M. du Vallon?" asked Philippe in order to change the conversation.

"He will be presented to you to-day, and confidentially will congratulate you on the danger which that conspirator has made you run."

"What is to be done with him?"

"With M. du Vallon?"

"Yes; confer a dukedom on him, I suppose."

"A dukedom," replied Aramis, smiling in a significant manner.

"Why do you laugh, Monsieur d'Herblay?"

"I laugh at the extreme caution of your idea."

"Cautious, why so?"

"Your majesty is doubtless afraid that poor Porthos may possible become a troublesome witness, and you wish to get rid of him."

"What! in making him a duke?"

"Certainly; you would assuredly kill him, for he would die from joy, and the secret would die with him."

"Good heavens!"

"Yes," said Aramis, phlegmatically; "I should lose a very good friend."

At this moment, and in the middle of this idle conversation, under the light tone of which the two conspirators concealed their joy and pride at their mutual success, Aramis heard something which made him prick up his ears.

"What is that?" said Philippe.

"The dawn, sire."

"Well?"

"Well, before you retired to bed last night, you probably decided to do something this morning at break of day."

"Yes, I told my captain of the musketeers," replied the young man hurriedly, "that I should expect him."

"If you told him that, he will certainly be here, for he is a most punctual man."

"I hear a step in the vestibule."

"It must be he."

"Come, let us begin the attack," said the young king resolutely.

"Be cautious for Heaven's sake. To begin the attack, and with D'Artagnan, would be madness. D'Artagnan knows nothing, he has seen nothing; he is a hundred miles from suspecting our mystery in the slightest degree, but if he comes into this room the first this morning, he will be sure to detect something of what has taken place, and which he would imagine it his business to occupy himself about. Before we allow D'Artagnan to penetrate into this room, we must air the room thoroughly, or introduce so many people into it, that the keenest scent in the whole kingdom may be deceived by the traces of twenty different persons."

"But how can I send him away, since I have given him a rendezvous?" observed the prince, impatient to measure swords with so redoubtable an antagonist.

"I will take care of that," replied the bishop, "and in order to begin, I am going to strike a blow which will completely stupefy our man."

"He, too, is striking a blow, for I hear him at the door," added the prince, hurriedly.

And, in fact, a knock at the door was heard at that moment. Aramis was not mistaken; for it was indeed D'Artagnan who adopted that mode of announcing himself.

We have seen how he passed the night in philosophizing with M. Fouquet, but the musketeer was very weary even of feigning to fall asleep, and as soon as earliest dawn illumined with its gloomy gleams of light the sumptuous cornices of the superintendent's room, D'Artagnan rose from his armchair, arranged his sword, brushed his coat and hat with his sleeve, like a private soldier getting ready for inspection.

"Are you going out?" said Fouquet.

"Yes, monseigneur. And you?"

"I shall remain."

"You pledge your word?"

"Certainly."

"Very good. Besides, my only reason for going out is to try and get that reply,—you know what I mean?"

"That sentence, you mean—"

"Stay, I have something of the old Roman in me. This morning, when I got up, I remarked that my sword had got caught in one of the *aiguillettes*, and that my shoulder-belt had slipped quite off. That is an infallible sign."

"Of prosperity?"

"Yes, be sure of it; for every time that that confounded belt of mine stuck fast to my back, it always signified a punishment from M. de Treville, or a refusal of money by M. de Mazarin. Every time my sword hung fast to my shoulder-belt, it always predicted some disagreeable commission or another for me to execute, and I have had showers of them all my life through. Every time, too, my sword danced about in its sheath, a duel, fortunate in its result, was sure to follow: whenever it dangled about the calves of my legs, it signified a slight wound; every time it fell completely out of the scabbard, I was booked, and made up my mind that I should have to remain on the field of battle, with two or three months under surgical bandages into the bargain."

"I did not know your sword kept you so well informed," said Fouquet, with a faint smile, which showed how he was struggling against his own weakness. "Is your sword bewitched, or under the influence of some imperial charm?"

"Why, you must know that my sword may almost be regarded as part of my own body. I have heard that certain men seem to have warnings given them by feeling something the matter with their legs, or a throbbing of their temples. With me, it is my sword that warns me. Well, it told me of nothing this morning. But, stay a moment—look here, it has just fallen of its own accord into the last hole of the belt. Do you know what that is a warning of?"

"No."

"Well, that tells me of an arrest that will have to be made this very day."

"Well," said the surintendant, more astonished than annoyed by this frankness, "if there is nothing disagreeable predicted to you by your sword, I am to conclude that it is not disagreeable for you to arrest me."

"You! arrest *you!*"

"Of course. The warning—"

"Does not concern you, since you have been arrested ever since yesterday. It is not you I shall have to arrest, be assured of that. That is the reason why I am delighted, and also the reason why I said that my day will be a happy one."

And with these words, pronounced with the most affectionate graciousness of manner, the captain took leave of Fouquet in order to wait upon the king. He was on the point of leaving the room, when Fouquet said to him, "One last mark of kindness."

"What is it, monseigneur?"

"M. d'Herblay; let me see Monsieur d'Herblay."

"I am going to try and get him to come to you."

D'Artagnan did not think himself so good a prophet. It was written that the day would pass away and realize all the predictions that had been made in the morning. He had accordingly knocked, as we have seen, at the king's door. The door opened. The captain thought that it was the king who had just opened it himself; and this supposition was not altogether inadmissible, considering the state of agitation in which he had left Louis XIV. the previous evening; but instead of his royal master, whom he was on the point of saluting with the greatest respect, he perceived the long, calm features of Aramis. So extreme was his surprise that he could hardly refrain from uttering a loud exclamation. "Aramis!" he said.

"Good morning, dear D'Artagnan," replied the prelate, coldly.

"You here!" stammered out the musketeer.

"His majesty desires you to report that he is still sleeping, after having been greatly fatigued during the whole night."

"Ah!" said D'Artagnan, who could not understand how the bishop of Vannes, who had been so indifferent a favorite the previous evening, had become in half a dozen hours the most magnificent mushroom of fortune that had ever sprung up in a sovereign's bedroom. In fact, to transmit the orders of the king even to the mere threshold of that monarch's room, to serve as an intermediary of Louis XIV. so as to be able to give a single order in his name at a couple paces from him, he must have become more than Richelieu had ever been to Louis XIII. D'Artagnan's expressive eye, half-opened lips, his curling mustache, said as much indeed in the plainest language to the chief favorite, who remained calm and perfectly unmoved.

"Moreover," continued the bishop, "you will be good enough, monsieur le capitaine des mousquetaires, to allow those only to pass into the king's room this morning who have special permission. His majesty does not wish to be disturbed just yet."

"But," objected D'Artagnan, almost on the point of refusing to obey this order, and particularly of giving unrestrained passage to the suspicions which the king's silence had aroused—"but, monsieur l'eveque, his majesty gave me a rendezvous for this morning."

"Later, later," said the king's voice, from the bottom of the alcove; a voice which made a cold shudder pass through the musketeer's veins. He bowed, amazed, confused, and stupefied by the smile with which Aramis seemed to overwhelm him, as soon as these words had been pronounced.

"And then," continued the bishop, "as an answer to what you were coming to ask the king, my dear D'Artagnan, here is an order of his majesty, which you will be good enough to attend to forthwith, for it concerns M. Fouquet."

D'Artagnan took the order which was held out to him. "To be set at liberty!" he murmured. "Ah!" and he uttered a second "ah!" still more full of intelligence than the former; for this order explained Aramis's presence with the king, and that Aramis, in order to have obtained Fouquet's pardon, must have made considerable progress in the royal favor, and that this favor explained, in its tenor, the hardly conceivable assurance with which M. d'Herblay issued the order in the king's name. For D'Artagnan it was quite sufficient to have understood something of the matter in hand to order to understand the rest. He bowed and withdrew a couple of paces, as though he were about to leave.

"I am going with you," said the bishop.

"Where to?"

"To M. Fouquet; I wish to be a witness of his delight."

"Ah! Aramis, how you puzzled me just now!" said D'Artagnan again.

"But you understand *now*, I suppose?"

"Of course I understand," he said aloud; but added in a low tone to himself, almost hissing the words between his teeth, "No, no, I do not understand yet. But it is all the same, for here is the order for it." And then he added, "I will lead the way, monseigneur," and he conducted Aramis to Fouquet's apartments.

CHAPTER 21

The King's Friend.

Fouquet was waiting with anxiety; he had already sent away many of his servants and friends, who, anticipating the usual hour of his ordinary receptions, had called at his door to inquire after him. Preserving the utmost silence respecting the danger which hung suspended by a hair above his head, he only asked them, as he did every one, indeed, who came to the door, where Aramis was. When he saw D'Artagnan return, and when he perceived the bishop of Vannes behind him, he could hardly restrain his delight; it was fully equal to his previous uneasiness. The mere sight of Aramis was a complete compensation to the surintendant for the unhappiness he had undergone in his arrest. The prelate was silent and grave; D'Artagnan completely bewildered by such an accumulation of events.

"Well, captain, so you have brought M. d'Herblay to me."

"And something better still, monseigneur."

"What is that?"

"Liberty."

"I am free!"

"Yes; by the king's order."

Fouquet resumed his usual serenity, that he might interrogate Aramis with a look.

"Oh! yes, you can thank M. l'eveque de Vannes," pursued D'Artagnan, "for it is indeed to him that you owe the change that has taken place in the king."

"Oh!" said Fouquet, more humiliated at the service than grateful at its success.

"But you," continued D'Artagnan, addressing Aramis—"you, who have become M. Fouquet's protector and patron, can you not do something for me?"

"Anything in the wide world you like, my friend," replied the bishop, in his calmest tones.

"One thing only, then, and I shall be perfectly satisfied. How on earth did you manage to become the favorite of the king, you who have never spoken to him more than twice in your life?"

"From a friend such as you are," said Aramis, "I cannot conceal anything."

"Ah! very good, tell me, then."

"Very well. You think that I have seen the king only twice, whilst the fact is I have seen him more than a hundred times; only we have kept it very secret, that is all." And without trying to remove the color which at this revelation made D'Artagnan's face flush scarlet, Aramis turned towards M. Fouquet, who was as much surprised as the musketeer. "Monseigneur," he resumed, "the king desires me to inform you that he is more than ever your friend, and that your beautiful *fete*, so generously offered by you on his behalf, has touched him to the very heart."

And thereupon he saluted M. Fouquet with so much reverence of manner, that the latter, incapable of understanding a man whose diplomacy was of so prodigious a character, remained incapable of uttering a single syllable, and equally incapable of thought or movement. D'Artagnan fancied he perceived that these two men had something to say to each other, and he was about to yield to that feeling of instinctive politeness which in such a case hurries a man towards the door, when he feels his presence is an inconvenience for others; but his eager curiosity, spurred on by so many mysteries, counseled him to remain.

Aramis thereupon turned towards him, and said, in a quiet tone, "You will not forget, my friend, the king's order respecting those whom he intends to receive this morning on rising." These words were clear enough, and the musketeer understood them; he therefore bowed to Fouquet, and then to Aramis,—to the latter with a slight admixture of ironical respect,—and disappeared.

No sooner had he left, than Fouquet, whose impatience had hardly been able to wait for that moment, darted towards the door to close it, and then returning to the bishop, he said, "My dear D'Herblay, I think it now high time you should explain all that has passed, for, in plain and honest truth, I do not understand anything."

"We will explain all that to you," said Aramis, sitting down, and making Fouquet sit down also. "Where shall I begin?"

"With this first of all. Why does the king set me at liberty?"

"You ought rather to ask me what his reason was for having you arrested."

"Since my arrest, I have had time to think over it, and my idea is that it arises out of some slight feeling of jealousy. My *fete* put M. Colbert out of temper, and M. Colbert discovered some cause of complaint against me; Belle-Isle, for instance."

"No; there is no question at all just now of Belle-Isle."

"What is it, then?"

"Do you remember those receipts for thirteen millions which M. de Mazarin contrived to steal from you?"

"Yes, of course!"

"Well, you are pronounced a public robber."

"Good heavens!"

"Oh! that is not all. Do you also remember that letter you wrote to La Valliere?"

"Alas! yes."

"And that proclaims you a traitor and a suborner."

"Why should he have pardoned me, then?"

"We have not yet arrived at that part of our argument. I wish you to be quite convinced of the fact itself. Observe this well: the king knows you to be guilty of an appropriation of public funds. Oh! of course *I* know that you have done nothing of the kind; but, at all events, the king has seen the receipts, and he can do no other than believe you are incriminated."

"I beg your pardon, I do not see—"

"You will see presently, though. The king, moreover, having read your love-letter to La Valliere, and the offers you there made her, cannot retain any doubt of your intentions with regard to that young lady; you will admit that, I suppose?"

"Certainly. Pray conclude."

"In the fewest words. The king, we may henceforth assume, is your powerful, implacable, and eternal enemy."

"Agreed. But am I, then, so powerful, that he has not dared to sacrifice me, notwithstanding his hatred, with all the means which my weakness, or my misfortunes, may have given him as a hold upon me?"

"It is clear, beyond all doubt," pursued Aramis, coldly, "that the king has quarreled with you—irreconcilably."

"But, since he has absolved me—"

"Do you believe it likely?" asked the bishop, with a searching look.

"Without believing in his sincerity, I believe it in the accomplished fact."

Aramis slightly shrugged his shoulders.

"But why, then, should Louis XIV. have commissioned you to tell me what you have just stated?"

"The king charged me with no message for you."

"With nothing!" said the superintendent, stupefied. "But, that order—"

"Oh! yes. You are quite right. There *is* an order, certainly;" and these words were pronounced by Aramis in so strange a tone, that Fouquet could not resist starting.

"You are concealing something from me, I see. What is it?"

Aramis softly rubbed his white fingers over his chin, but said nothing.

"Does the king exile me?"

"Do not act as if you were playing at the game children play at when they have to try and guess where a thing has been hidden, and are informed, by a bell being rung, when they are approaching near to it, or going away from it."

"Speak, then."

"Guess."

"You alarm me."

"Bah! that is because you have not guessed, then."

"What did the king say to you? In the name of our friendship, do not deceive me."

"The king has not said one word to me."

"You are killing me with impatience, D'Herblay. Am I still superintendent?"

"As long as you like."

"But what extraordinary empire have you so suddenly acquired over his majesty's mind?"

"Ah! that's the point."

"He does your bidding?"

"I believe so."

"It is hardly credible."

"So any one would say."

"D'Herblay, by our alliance, by our friendship, by everything you hold dearest in the world, speak openly, I implore you. By what means have you succeeded in overcoming Louis XIV.'s prejudices, for he did not like you, I am certain."

"The king will like me *now*," said Aramis, laying stress upon the last word.

"You have something particular, then, between you?"

"Yes."

"A secret, perhaps?"

"A secret."

"A secret of such a nature as to change his majesty's interests?"

"You are, indeed, a man of superior intelligence, monseigneur, and have made a particularly accurate guess. I have, in fact, discovered a secret, of a nature to change the interests of the king of France."

"Ah!" said Fouquet, with the reserve of a man who does not wish to ask any more questions.

"And you shall judge of it yourself," pursued Aramis; "and you shall tell me if I am mistaken with regard to the importance of this secret."

"I am listening, since you are good enough to unbosom yourself to me; only do not forget that I have asked you about nothing which it may be indiscreet in you to communicate."

Aramis seemed, for a moment, as if he were collecting himself.

"Do not speak!" said Fouquet: "there is still time enough."

"Do you remember," said the bishop, casting down his eyes, "the birth of Louis XIV.?"

"As if it were yesterday."

"Have you ever heard anything particular respecting his birth?"

"Nothing; except that the king was not really the son of Louis XIII."

"That does not matter to us, or the kingdom either; he is the son of his father, says the French law, whose father is recognized by law."

"True; but it is a grave matter, when the quality of races is called into question."

"A merely secondary question, after all. So that, in fact, you have never learned or heard anything in particular?"

"Nothing."

"That is where my secret begins. The queen, you must know, instead of being delivered of a son, was delivered of twins."

Fouquet looked up suddenly as he replied:

"And the second is dead?"

"You will see. These twins seemed likely to be regarded as the pride of their mother, and the hope of France; but the weak nature of the king, his superstitious feelings, made him apprehend a series of conflicts between two children whose rights were equal; so he put out of the way—he suppressed—one of the twins."

"Suppressed, do you say?"

"Have patience. Both the children grew up; the one on the throne, whose minister you are—the other, who is my friend, in gloom and isolation."

"Good heavens! What are you saying, Monsieur d'Herblay? And what is this poor prince doing?"

"Ask me, rather, what has he done."

"Yes, yes."

"He was brought up in the country, and then thrown into a fortress which goes by the name of the Bastille."

"Is it possible?" cried the surintendant, clasping his hands.

"The one was the most fortunate of men: the other the most unhappy and miserable of all living beings."

"Does his mother not know this?"

"Anne of Austria knows it all."

"And the king?"

"Knows absolutely nothing."

"So much the better," said Fouquet.

This remark seemed to make a great impression on Aramis; he looked at Fouquet with the most anxious expression of countenance.

"I beg your pardon; I interrupted you," said Fouquet.

"I was saying," resumed Aramis, "that this poor prince was the unhappiest of human beings, when Heaven, whose thoughts are over all His creatures, undertook to come to his assistance."

"Oh! in what way? Tell me."

"You will see. The reigning king—I say the reigning king—you can guess very well why?"

"No. Why?"

"Because *both* of them, being legitimate princes, ought to have been kings. Is not that your opinion?"

"It is, certainly."

"Unreservedly?"

"Most unreservedly; twins are one person in two bodies."

"I am pleased that a legist of your learning and authority should have pronounced such an opinion. It is agreed, then, that each of them possessed equal rights, is it not?"

"Incontestably! but, gracious heavens, what an extraordinary circumstance!"

"We are not at the end of it yet.—Patience."

"Oh! I shall find 'patience' enough."

"Heaven wished to raise up for that oppressed child an avenger, or a supporter, or vindicator, if you prefer it. It happened that the reigning king, the usurper—you are quite of my opinion, I believe, that it is an act of usurpation quietly to enjoy, and selfishly to assume the right over, an inheritance to which a man has only half a right?"

"Yes, usurpation is the word."

"In that case, I continue. It was Heaven's will that the

usurper should possess, in the person of his first minister, a man of great talent, of large and generous nature."

"Well, well," said Fouquet, "I understand you; you have relied upon me to repair the wrong which has been done to this unhappy brother of Louis XIV. You have thought well; I will help you. I thank you, D'Herblay, I thank you."

"Oh, no, it is not that at all; you have not allowed me to finish," said Aramis, perfectly unmoved.

"I will not say another word, then."

"M. Fouquet, I was observing, the minister of the reigning sovereign, was suddenly taken into the greatest aversion, and menaced with the ruin of his fortune, loss of liberty, loss of life even, by intrigue and personal hatred, to which the king gave too readily an attentive ear. But Heaven permits (still, however, out of consideration for the unhappy prince who had been sacrificed) that M. Fouquet should in his turn have a devoted friend who knew this state secret, and felt that he possessed strength and courage enough to divulge this secret, after having had the strength to carry it locked up in his own heart for twenty years.

"Go no farther," said Fouquet, full of generous feelings. "I understand you, and can guess everything now. You went to see the king when the intelligence of my arrest reached you; you implored him, he refused to listen to you; then you threatened him with that secret, threatened to reveal it, and Louis XIV., alarmed at the risk of its betrayal, granted to the terror of your indiscretion what he refused to your generous intercession. I understand, I understand; you have the king in your power; I understand."

"You understand *nothing*—as yet," replied Aramis, "and again you interrupt me. Then, too, allow me to observe that you pay no attention to logical reasoning, and seem to forget what you ought most to remember."

"What do you mean?"

"You know upon what I laid the greatest stress at the beginning of our conversation?"

"Yes, his majesty's hate, invincible hate for me; yes, but what feeling of hate could resist the threat of such a revelation?"

"Such a revelation, do you say? that is the very point where your logic fails you. What! do you suppose that if I had made such a revelation to the king, I should have been alive now?"

"It is not ten minutes ago that you were with the king."

"That may be. He might not have had the time to get me killed outright, but he would have had the time to get me gagged and thrown in a dungeon. Come, come, show a little consistency in your reasoning, *mordieu!*"

And by the mere use of this word, which was so thoroughly his old musketeer's expression, forgotten by one who never seemed to forget anything, Fouquet could not but understand to what a pitch of exaltation the calm, impenetrable bishop of Vannes had wrought himself. He shuddered.

"And then," replied the latter, after having mastered his feelings, "should I be the man I really am, should I be the true friend you believe me, if I were to expose you, whom the king already hates so bitterly, to a feeling more than ever to be dreaded in that young man? To have robbed him, is nothing; to have addressed the woman he loves, is not much; but to hold in your keeping both his crown and his honor, why, he would pluck out your heart with his own hands."

"You have not allowed him to penetrate your secret, then?"

"I would sooner, far sooner, have swallowed at one draught all the poisons that Mithridates drank in twenty years, in order to try and avoid death, than have betrayed my secret to the king."

"What have you done, then?"

"Ah! now we are coming to the point, monseigneur. I

think I shall not fail to excite in you a little interest. You are listening, I hope."

"How can you ask me if I am listening? Go on."

Aramis walked softly all round the room, satisfied himself that they were alone, and that all was silent, and then returned and placed himself close to the armchair in which Fouquet was seated, awaiting with the deepest anxiety the revelation he had to make.

"I forgot to tell you," resumed Aramis, addressing himself to Fouquet, who listened to him with the most absorbed attention—"I forgot to mention a most remarkable circumstance respecting these twins, namely, that God had formed them so startlingly, so miraculously, like each other, that it would be utterly impossible to distinguish the one from the other. Their own mother would not be able to distinguish them."

"Is it possible?" exclaimed Fouquet.

"The same noble character in their features, the same carriage, the same stature, the same voice."

"But their thoughts? degree of intelligence? their knowledge of human life?"

"There is inequality there, I admit, monseigneur. Yes; for the prisoner of the Bastille is, most incontestably, superior in every way to his brother; and if, from his prison, this unhappy victim were to pass to the throne, France would not, from the earliest period of its history, perhaps, have had a master more powerful in genius and nobility of character."

Fouquet buried his face in his hands, as if he were overwhelmed by the weight of this immense secret. Aramis approached him.

"There is a further inequality," he said, continuing his work of temptation, "an inequality which concerns yourself, monseigneur, between the twins, both sons of Louis XIII., namely, the last comer does not know M. Colbert."

Fouquet raised his head immediately—his features were

pale and distorted. The bolt had hit its mark—not his heart, but his mind and comprehension.

"I understand you," he said to Aramis; "you are proposing a conspiracy to me?"

"Something like it."

"One of those attempts which, as you said at the beginning of this conversation, alters the fate of empires?"

"And of superintendents, too; yes, monseigneur."

"In a word, you propose that I should agree to the substitution of the son of Louis XIII., who is now a prisoner in the Bastille, for the son of Louis XIII., who is at this moment asleep in the Chamber of Morpheus?"

Aramis smiled with the sinister expression of the sinister thought which was passing through his brain. "Exactly," he said.

"Have you thought," continued Fouquet, becoming animated with that strength of talent which in a few seconds originates, and matures the conception of a plan, and with that largeness of view which foresees all consequences, and embraces every result at a glance—"have you thought that we must assemble the nobility, the clergy, and the third estate of the realm; that we shall have to depose the reigning sovereign, to disturb by so frightful a scandal the tomb of their dead father, to sacrifice the life, the honor of a woman, Anne of Austria, the life and peace of mind and heart of another woman, Maria Theresa; and suppose that it were all done, if we were to succeed in doing it—"

"I do not understand you," continued Aramis, coldly. "There is not a single syllable of sense in all you have just said."

"What!" said the superintendent, surprised, "a man like you refuse to view the practical bearing of the case! Do you confine yourself to the childish delight of a political illusion, and neglect the chances of its being carried into execution; in other words, the reality itself, is it possible?"

"My friend," said Aramis, emphasizing the word with a kind of disdainful familiarity, "what does Heaven do in order to substitute one king for another?"

"Heaven!" exclaimed Fouquet—"Heaven gives directions to its agent, who seizes upon the doomed victim, hurries him away, and seats the triumphant rival on the empty throne. But you forget that this agent is called death. Oh! Monsieur d'Herblay, in Heaven's name, tell me if you have had the idea—"

"There is no question of that, monseigneur; you are going beyond the object in view. Who spoke of Louis XIV.'s death? who spoke of adopting the example which Heaven sets in following out the strict execution of its decrees? No, I wish you to understand that Heaven effects its purposes without confusion or disturbance, without exciting comment or remark, without difficulty or exertion; and that men, inspired by Heaven, succeed like Heaven itself, in all their undertakings, in all they attempt, in all they do."

"What do you mean?"

"I mean, my *friend*," returned Aramis, with the same intonation on the word friend that he had applied to it the first time—"I mean that if there has been any confusion, scandal, and even effort in the substitution of the prisoner for the king, I defy you to prove it."

"What!" cried Fouquet, whiter than the handkerchief with which he wiped his temples, "what do you say?"

"Go to the king's apartment," continued Aramis, tranquilly, "and you who know the mystery, I defy even you to perceive that the prisoner of the Bastille is lying in his brother's bed."

"But the king," stammered Fouquet, seized with horror at the intelligence.

"What king?" said Aramis, in his gentlest tone; "the one who hates you, or the one who likes you?"

"The king—of—*yesterday*."

"The king of yesterday! be quite easy on that score; he has gone to take the place in the Bastille which his victim occupied for so many years."

"Great God! And who took him there?"

"I."

"You?"

"Yes, and in the simplest way. I carried him away last night. While he was descending into midnight, the other was ascending into day. I do not think there has been any disturbance whatever. A flash of lightning without thunder awakens nobody."

Fouquet uttered a thick, smothered cry, as if he had been struck by some invisible blow, and clasping his head between his clenched hands, he murmured: "You did that?"

"Cleverly enough, too; what do you think of it?"

"You dethroned the king? imprisoned him, too?"

"Yes, that has been done."

"And such an action was committed *here*, at Vaux?"

"Yes, here, at Vaux, in the Chamber of Morpheus. It would almost seem that it had been built in anticipation of such an act."

"And at what time did it occur?"

"Last night, between twelve and one o'clock."

Fouquet made a movement as if he were on the point of springing upon Aramis; he restrained himself. "At Vaux; under my roof!" he said, in a half-strangled voice.

"I believe so! for it is still your house, and it is likely to continue so, since M. Colbert cannot rob you of it now."

"It was under my roof, then, monsieur, that you committed this crime?"

"This crime?" said Aramis, stupefied.

"This abominable crime!" pursued Fouquet, becoming more and more excited; "this crime more execrable than an assassination! this crime which dishonors my name forever, and entails upon me the horror of posterity."

"You are not in your senses, monsieur," replied Aramis, in an irresolute tone of voice; "you are speaking too loudly; take care!"

"I will call out so loudly, that the whole world shall hear me."

"Monsieur Fouquet, take care!"

Fouquet turned round towards the prelate, whom he looked at full in the face. "You have dishonored me," he said, "in committing so foul an act of treason, so heinous a crime upon my guest, upon one who was peacefully reposing beneath my roof. Oh! woe, woe is me!"

"Woe to the man, rather, who beneath your roof meditated the ruin of your fortune, your life. Do you forget that?"

"He was my guest, my sovereign."

Aramis rose, his eyes literally bloodshot, his mouth trembling convulsively. "Have I a man out of his senses to deal with?" he said.

"You have an honorable man to deal with."

"You are mad."

"A man who will prevent you consummating your crime."

"You are mad, I say."

"A man who would sooner, oh! far sooner, die; who would kill you even, rather than allow you to complete his dishonor."

And Fouquet snatched up his sword, which D'Artagnan had placed at the head of his bed, and clenched it resolutely in his hand. Aramis frowned, and thrust his hand into his breast as if in search of a weapon. This movement did not escape Fouquet, who, full of nobleness and pride in his magnanimity, threw his sword to a distance from him, and approached Aramis so close as to touch his shoulder with his disarmed hand. "Monsieur," he said, "I would sooner die here on the spot than survive this terrible disgrace; and if you have any pity left for me, I entreat you to take my life."

Aramis remained silent and motionless.

"You do not reply?" said Fouquet.

Aramis raised his head gently, and a glimmer of hope might be seen once more to animate his eyes. "Reflect, monseigneur," he said, "upon everything we have to expect. As the matter now stands, the king is still alive, and his imprisonment saves your life."

"Yes," replied Fouquet, "you may have been acting on my behalf, but I will not, do not, accept your services. But, first of all, I do not wish your ruin. You will leave this house."

Aramis stifled the exclamation which almost escaped his broken heart.

"I am hospitable towards all who are dwellers beneath my roof," continued Fouquet, with an air of inexpressible majesty; "you will not be more fatally lost than he whose ruin you have consummated."

"You will be so," said Aramis, in a hoarse, prophetic voice, "you will be so, believe me."

"I accept the augury, Monsieur d'Herblay; but nothing shall prevent me, nothing shall stop me. You will leave Vaux—you must leave France; I give you four hours to place yourself out of the king's reach."

"Four hours?" said Aramis, scornfully and incredulously.

"Upon the word of Fouquet, no one shall follow you before the expiration of that time. You will therefore have four hours' advance of those whom the king may wish to dispatch after you."

"Four hours!" repeated Aramis, in a thick, smothered voice.

"It is more than you will need to get on board a vessel and flee to Belle-Isle, which I give you as a place of refuge."

"Ah!" murmured Aramis.

"Belle-Isle is as much mine for you, as Vaux is mine for the king. Go, D'Herblay, go! as long as I live, not a hair of your head shall be injured."

"Thank you," said Aramis, with a cold irony of manner.

"Go at once, then, and give me your hand, before we both hasten away; you to save your life, I to save my honor."

Aramis withdrew from his breast the hand he had concealed there; it was stained with his blood. He had dug his nails into his flesh, as if in punishment for having nursed so many projects, more vain, insensate, and fleeting than the life of the man himself. Fouquet was horror-stricken, and then his heart smote him with pity. He threw open his arms as if to embrace him.

"I had no arms," murmured Aramis, as wild and terrible in his wrath as the shade of Dido. And then, without touching Fouquet's hand, he turned his head aside, and stepped back a pace or two. His last word was an imprecation, his last gesture a curse, which his blood-stained hand seemed to invoke, as it sprinkled on Fouquet's face a few drops of blood which flowed from his breast. And both of them darted out of the room by the secret staircase which led down to the inner courtyard. Fouquet ordered his best horses, while Aramis paused at the foot of the staircase which led to Porthos's apartment. He reflected profoundly and for some time, while Fouquet's carriage left the courtyard at full gallop.

"Shall I go alone?" said Aramis to himself, "or warn the prince? Oh! fury! Warn the prince, and then—do what? Take him with me? To carry this accusing witness about with me everywhere? War, too, would follow—civil war, implacable in its nature! And without any resource save myself—it is impossible! What could he do without me? Oh! without me he will be utterly destroyed. Yet who knows—let destiny be fulfilled—condemned he was, let him remain so then! Good or evil Spirit—gloomy and scornful Power, whom men call the genius of humanity, thou art a power more restlessly uncertain, more baselessly useless, than wild mountain wind! Chance, thou term'st thyself, but thou art nothing; thou inflamest everything with thy breath, crumblest mountains at thy approach, and suddenly art thyself destroyed at the presence of the Cross of dead wood behind which stand another Power invisible like thyself— whom thou deniest, perhaps, but whose avenging hand is on thee, and hurls thee in the dust dishonored and unnamed! Lost!—I am lost! What can be done? Flee to Belle-Isle? Yes, and leave Porthos behind me, to talk and relate the whole affair to every one! Porthos, too, who will have to suffer for what he has done. I will not let poor Porthos suffer. He seems like one of the members of my own frame; and his grief or misfortune would be mine as well. Porthos shall leave with me, and shall follow my destiny. It must be so."

And Aramis, apprehensive of meeting any one to whom his hurried movements might appear suspicious, ascended the staircase without being perceived. Porthos, so recently returned from Paris, was already in a profound sleep; his huge body forgot its fatigue, as his mind forgot its thoughts. Aramis entered, light as a shadow, and placed his nervous grasp on the giant's shoulder. "Come, Porthos," he cried, "come."

Porthos obeyed, rose from his bed, opened his eyes, even before his intelligence seemed to be aroused.

"We leave immediately," said Aramis.

"Ah!" returned Porthos.

"We shall go mounted, and faster than we have ever gone in our lives."

"Ah!" repeated Porthos.

"Dress yourself, my friend."

And he helped the giant to dress himself, and thrust his gold and diamonds into his pocket. Whilst he was thus engaged, a slight noise attracted his attention, and on looking up, he saw D'Artagnan watching them through the half-opened door. Aramis started.

"What the devil are you doing there in such an agitated manner?" said the musketeer.

"Hush!" said Porthos.

"We are going off on a mission of great importance," added the bishop.

"You are very fortunate," said the musketeer.

"Oh, dear me!" said Porthos, "I feel so wearied; I would far sooner have been fast asleep. But the service of the king. . . ."

"Have you seen M. Fouquet?" said Aramis to D'Artagnan.

"Yes, this very minute, in a carriage."

"What did he say to you?"

"'Adieu;' nothing more."

"Was that all?"

"What else do you think he could say? Am I worth anything now, since you have got into such high favor?"

"Listen," said Aramis, embracing the musketeer; "your good times are returning again. You will have no occasion to be jealous of any one."

"Ah! bah!"

"I predict that something will happen to you to-day which will increase your importance more than ever."

"Really?"

"You know that I know all the news?"

"Oh, yes!"

"Come, Porthos, are you ready? Let us go."

"I am quite ready, Aramis."

"Let us embrace D'Artagnan first."

"Most certainly."

"But the horses?"

"Oh! there is no want of them here. Will you have mine?"

"No; Porthos has his own stud. So adieu! adieu!"

The fugitives mounted their horses beneath the very eyes of the captain of the musketeers, who held Porthos's stirrup for him, and gazed after them until they were out of sight.

"On any other occasion," thought the Gascon, "I should say that those gentlemen were making their escape; but in these days politics seem so changed that such an exit is termed going on a mission. I have no objection; let me attend to my own affairs, that is more than enough for *me*,"—and he philosophically entered his apartments.

CHAPTER 22

Showing How the Countersign Was
Respected at the Bastille.

Fouquet tore along as fast as his horses could drag him. On
his way he trembled with horror at the idea of what had just
been revealed to him.

"What must have been," he thought, "the youth of those
extraordinary men, who, even as age is stealing fast upon
them, are still able to conceive such gigantic plans, and carry
them through without a tremor?"

At one moment he could not resist the idea that all
Aramis had just been recounting to him was nothing more
than a dream, and whether the fable itself was not the snare;
so that when Fouquet arrived at the Bastille, he might possibly
find an order of arrest, which would send him to join the
dethroned king. Strongly impressed with this idea, he gave
certain sealed orders on his route, while fresh horses were
being harnessed to his carriage. These orders were addressed
to M. d'Artagnan and to certain others whose fidelity to the
king was far above suspicion.

"In this way," said Fouquet to himself, "prisoner or not,
I shall have performed the duty that I owe my honor. The
orders will not reach them until after my return, if I should
return free, and consequently they will not have been

unsealed. I shall take them back again. If I am delayed; it will be because some misfortune will have befallen me; and in that case assistance will be sent for me as well as for the king."

Prepared in this manner, the superintendent arrived at the Bastille; he had traveled at the rate of five leagues and a half the hour. Every circumstance of delay which Aramis had escaped in his visit to the Bastille befell Fouquet. It was useless giving his name, equally useless his being recognized; he could not succeed in obtaining an entrance. By dint of entreaties, threats, commands, he succeeded in inducing a sentinel to speak to one of the subalterns, who went and told the major. As for the governor they did not even dare disturb him. Fouquet sat in his carriage, at the outer gate of the fortress, chafing with rage and impatience, awaiting the return of the officers, who at last re-appeared with a sufficiently sulky air.

"Well," said Fouquet, impatiently, "what did the major say?"

"Well, monsieur," replied the soldier, "the major laughed in my face. He told me that M. Fouquet was at Vaux, and that even were he at Paris, M. Fouquet would not get up at so early an hour as the present."

"*Mordieu!* you are an absolute set of fools," cried the minister, darting out of the carriage; and before the subaltern had time to shut the gate, Fouquet sprang through it, and ran forward in spite of the soldier, who cried out for assistance. Fouquet gained ground, regardless of the cries of the man, who, however, having at last come up with Fouquet, called out to the sentinel of the second gate, "Look out, look out, sentinel!" The man crossed his pike before the minister; but the latter, robust and active, and hurried away, too, by his passion, wrested the pike from the soldier and struck him a violent blow on the shoulder with it. The subaltern, who approached too closely, received a share of the blows as well. Both of them uttered loud and furious cries, at the sound of which the whole of the first body of the advanced guard poured out of the guardhouse. Among them there was one, however, who recognized the superintendent, and who called, "Monseigneur, ah! monseigneur. Stop, stop, you fellows!" And he effectually checked the soldiers, who were on the point of revenging their companions. Fouquet desired them to open the gate, but they refused to do so without the countersign; he desired them to inform the governor of his presence; but the latter had already heard the disturbance at the gate. He ran forward, followed by his major, and accompanied by a picket of twenty men, persuaded that an attack was being made on the Bastille. Baisemeaux also recognized Fouquet immediately, and dropped the sword he bravely had been brandishing.

"Ah! monseigneur," he stammered, "how can I excuse—"

"Monsieur," said the superintendent, flushed with anger, and heated by his exertions, "I congratulate you. Your watch and ward are admirably kept."

Baisemeaux turned pale, thinking that this remark was made ironically, and portended a furious burst of anger. But Fouquet had recovered his breath, and, beckoning the sentinel and the subaltern, who were rubbing their shoulders, towards him, he said, "There are twenty pistoles for the sentinel, and fifty for the officer. Pray receive my compliments, gentlemen. I will not fail to speak to his majesty about you. And now, M. Baisemeaux, a word with you."

And he followed the governor to his official residence, accompanied by a murmur of general satisfaction. Baisemeaux was already trembling with shame and uneasiness. Aramis's early visit, from that moment, seemed to possess consequences, which a functionary such as he (Baisemeaux) was, was perfectly justified in apprehending. It was quite another thing, however, when Fouquet in a sharp tone of voice, and with an imperious look, said, "You have seen M. d'Herblay this morning?"

"Yes, monseigneur."

"And are you not horrified at the crime of which you have made yourself an accomplice?"

"Well," thought Baisemeaux, "good so far;" and then he added, aloud, "But what crime, monseigneur, do you allude to?"

"That for which you can be quartered alive, monsieur—do not forget that! But this is not a time to show anger. Conduct me immediately to the prisoner."

"To what prisoner?" said Baisemeaux, trembling.

"You pretend to be ignorant? Very good—it is the best plan for you, perhaps; for if, in fact, you were to admit your participation in such a crime, it would be all over with you. I wish, therefore, to seem to believe in your assumption of ignorance."

"I entreat you, monseigneur—"

"That will do. Lead me to the prisoner."

"To Marchiali?"

"Who is Marchiali?"

"The prisoner who was brought back this morning by M. d'Herblay."

"He is called Marchiali?" said the superintendent, his conviction somewhat shaken by Baisemeaux's cool manner.

"Yes, monseigneur; that is the name under which he was inscribed here."

Fouquet looked steadily at Baisemeaux, as if he would read his very heart; and perceived, with that clear-sightedness most men possess who are accustomed to the exercise of power, that the man was speaking with perfect sincerity. Besides, in observing his face for a few moments, he could not believe that Aramis would have chosen such a confidant.

"It is the prisoner," said the superintendent to him, "whom M. d'Herblay carried away the day before yesterday?"

"Yes, monseigneur."

"And whom he brought back this morning?" added

Fouquet, quickly: for he understood immediately the mechanism of Aramis's plan.

"Precisely, monseigneur."

"And his name is Marchiali, you say?"

"Yes, Marchiali. If monseigneur has come here to remove him, so much the better, for I was going to write about him."

"What has he done, then?"

"Ever since this morning he has annoyed me extremely. He has had such terrible fits of passion, as almost to make me believe that he would bring the Bastille itself down about our ears."

"I will soon relieve you of his possession," said Fouquet.

"Ah! so much the better."

"Conduct me to his prison."

"Will monseigneur give me the order?"

"What order?"

"An order from the king."

"Wait until I sign you one."

"That will not be sufficient, monseigneur. I must have an order from the king."

Fouquet assumed an irritated expression. "As you are so scrupulous," he said, "with regard to allowing prisoners to leave, show me the order by which this one was set at liberty."

Baisemeaux showed him the order to release Seldon.

"Very good," said Fouquet; "but Seldon is not Marchiali."

"But Marchiali is not at liberty, monseigneur; he is here."

"But you said that M. d'Herblay carried him away and brought him back again."

"I did not say so."

"So surely did you say it, that I almost seem to hear it now."

"It was a slip of my tongue, then, monseigneur."

"Take care, M. Baisemeaux, take care."

"I have nothing to fear, monseigneur; I am acting according to the very strictest regulation."

"Do you dare to say so?"

"I would say so in the presence of one of the apostles. M. d'Herblay brought me an order to set Seldon at liberty. Seldon is free."

"I tell you that Marchiali has left the Bastille."

"You must prove that, monseigneur."

"Let me see him."

"You, monseigneur, who govern this kingdom, know very well that no one can see any of the prisoners without an express order from the king."

"M. d'Herblay has entered, however."

"That remains to be proved, monseigneur."

"M. de Baisemeaux, once more I warn you to pay particular attention to what you are saying."

"All the documents are there, monseigneur."

"M. d'Herblay is overthrown."

"Overthrown?—M. d'Herblay! Impossible!"

"You see that he has undoubtedly influenced you."

"No, monseigneur; what does, in fact, influence me, is the king's service. I am doing my duty. Give me an order from him, and you shall enter."

"Stay, M. le gouverneur, I give you my word that if you allow me to see the prisoner, I will give you an order from the king at once."

"Give it to me now, monseigneur."

"And that, if you refuse me, I will have you and all your officers arrested on the spot."

"Before you commit such an act of violence, monseigneur, you will reflect," said Baisemeaux, who had turned very pale, "that we will only obey an order signed by the king; and that it will be just as easy for you to obtain one to see Marchiali as to obtain one to do me so much injury; me, too, who am perfectly innocent."

"True. True!" cried Fouquet, furiously; "perfectly true. M. de Baisemeaux," he added, in a sonorous voice, drawing the unhappy governor towards him, "do you know why I am so anxious to speak to the prisoner?"

"No, monseigneur; and allow me to observe that you are terrifying me out of my senses; I am trembling all over—in fact, I feel as though I were about to faint."

"You will stand a better chance of fainting outright, Monsieur Baisemeaux, when I return here at the head of ten thousand men and thirty pieces of cannon."

"Good heavens, monseigneur, you are losing your senses."

"When I have roused the whole population of Paris against you and your accursed towers, and have battered open the gates of this place, and hanged you to the topmost tree of yonder pinnacle!"

"Monseigneur! monseigneur! for pity's sake!"

"I give you ten minutes to make up your mind," added Fouquet, in a calm voice. "I will sit down here, in this armchair, and wait for you; if, in ten minutes' time, you still persist, I leave this place, and you may think me as mad as you like. Then—you shall *see!*"

Baisemeaux stamped his foot on the ground like a man in a state of despair, but he did not reply a single syllable; whereupon Fouquet seized a pen and ink, and wrote:

"Order for M. le Prevot des Marchands to assemble the municipal guard and to march upon the Bastille on the king's immediate service."

Baisemeaux shrugged his shoulders. Fouquet wrote:

"Order for the Duc de Bouillon and M. le Prince de Conde to assume the command of the Swiss guards, of the king's guards, and to march upon the Bastille on the king's immediate service."

Baisemeaux reflected. Fouquet still wrote:

"Order for every soldier, citizen, or gentleman to seize

and apprehend, wherever he may be found, le Chevalier d'Herblay, Eveque de Vannes, and his accomplices, who are: first, M. de Baisemeaux, governor of the Bastille, suspected of the crimes of high treason and rebellion—"

"Stop, monseigneur!" cried Baisemeaux; "I do not understand a single jot of the whole matter; but so many misfortunes, even were it madness itself that had set them at their awful work, might happen here in a couple of hours, that the king, by whom I must be judged, will see whether I have been wrong in withdrawing the countersign before this flood of imminent catastrophes. Come with me to the keep, monseigneur, you shall see Marchiali."

Fouquet darted out of the room, followed by Baisemeaux as he wiped the perspiration from his face. "What a terrible morning!" he said; "what a disgrace for *me!*"

"Walk faster," replied Fouquet.

Baisemeaux made a sign to the jailer to precede them. He was afraid of his companion, which the latter could not fail to perceive.

"A truce to this child's play," he said, roughly. "Let the man remain here; take the keys yourself, and show me the way. Not a single person, do you understand, must hear what is going to take place here."

"Ah!" said Baisemeaux, undecided.

"Again!" cried M. Fouquet. "Ah! say 'no' at once, and I will leave the Bastille and will myself carry my own dispatches."

Baisemeaux bowed his head, took the keys, and unaccompanied, except by the minister, ascended the staircase. The higher they advanced up the spiral staircase, the more clearly did certain muffled murmurs become distinct appeals and fearful imprecations.

"What is that?" asked Fouquet.

"That is your Marchiali," said the governor; "this is the way these madmen scream."

And he accompanied that reply with a glance more pregnant with injurious allusion, as far as Fouquet was concerned, than politeness. The latter trembled; he had just recognized in one cry more terrible than any that had preceded it, the king's voice. He paused on the staircase, snatching the bunch of keys from Baisemeaux, who thought this new madman was going to dash out his brains with one of them. "Ah!" he cried, "M. d'Herblay did not say a word about that."

"Give me the keys at once!" cried Fouquet, tearing them from his hand. "Which is the key of the door I am to open?"

"That one."

A fearful cry, followed by a violent blow against the door, made the whole staircase resound with the echo.

"Leave this place," said Fouquet to Baisemeaux, in a threatening tone.

"I ask nothing better," murmured the latter, to himself. "There will be a couple of madmen face to face, and the one will kill the other, I am sure."

"Go!" repeated Fouquet. "If you place your foot on this staircase before I call you, remember that you shall take the place of the meanest prisoner in the Bastille."

"This job will kill me, I am sure it will," muttered Baisemeaux, as he withdrew with tottering steps.

The prisoner's cries became more and more terrible. When Fouquet had satisfied himself that Baisemeaux had reached the bottom of the staircase, he inserted the key in the first lock. It was then that he heard the hoarse, choking voice of the king, crying out, in a frenzy of rage, "Help, help! I am the king." The key of the second door was not the same as the first, and Fouquet was obliged to look for it on the bunch. The king, however, furious and almost mad with rage and passion, shouted at the top of his voice, "It was M. Fouquet who brought me here. Help me against M. Fouquet! I am the king! Help the king against

M. Fouquet!" These cries filled the minister's heart with terrible emotions. They were followed by a shower of blows leveled against the door with a part of the broken chair with which the king had armed himself. Fouquet at last succeeded in finding the key. The king was almost exhausted; he could hardly articulate distinctly as he shouted, "Death to Fouquet! death to the traitor Fouquet!" The door flew open.

CHAPTER 23

The King's Gratitude.

The two men were on the point of darting towards each other when they suddenly and abruptly stopped, as a mutual recognition took place, and each uttered a cry of horror.

"Have you come to assassinate me, monsieur?" said the king, when he recognized Fouquet.

"The king in this state!" murmured the minister.

Nothing could be more terrible indeed than the appearance of the young prince at the moment Fouquet had surprised him; his clothes were in tatters; his shirt, open and torn to rags, was stained with sweat and with the blood which streamed from his lacerated breast and arms. Haggard, ghastly pale, his hair in disheveled masses, Louis XIV. presented the most perfect picture of despair, distress, anger and fear combined that could possibly be united in one figure. Fouquet was so touched, so affected and disturbed by it, that he ran towards him with his arms stretched out and his eyes filled with tears. Louis held up the massive piece of wood of which he had made such a furious use.

"Sire," said Fouquet, in a voice trembling with emotion, "do you not recognize the most faithful of your friends?"

"A friend—you!" repeated Louis, gnashing his teeth in a

manner which betrayed his hate and desire for speedy vengeance.

"The most respectful of your servants," added Fouquet, throwing himself on his knees. The king let the rude weapon fall from his grasp. Fouquet approached him, kissed his knees, and took him in his arms with inconceivable tenderness.

"My king, my child," he said, "how you must have suffered!"

Louis, recalled to himself by the change of situation, looked at himself, and ashamed of the disordered state of his apparel, ashamed of his conduct, and ashamed of the air of pity and protection that was shown towards him, drew back. Fouquet did not understand this movement; he did not perceive that the king's feeling of pride would never forgive him for having been a witness of such an exhibition of weakness.

"Come, sire," he said, "you are free."

"Free?" repeated the king. "Oh! you set me at liberty, then, after having dared to lift up your hand against me."

"You do not believe that!" exclaimed Fouquet, indignantly; "you cannot believe me to be guilty of such an act."

And rapidly, warmly even, he related the whole particulars of the intrigue, the details of which are already known to the reader. While the recital continued, Louis suffered the most horrible anguish of mind; and when it was finished, the magnitude of the danger he had run struck him far more than the importance of the secret relative to his twin brother.

"Monsieur," he said, suddenly to Fouquet, "this double birth is a falsehood; it is impossible—you cannot have been the dupe of it."

"Sire!"

"It is impossible, I tell you, that the honor, the virtue of my mother can be suspected, and my first minister has not yet done justice on the criminals!"

"Reflect, sire, before you are hurried away by anger," replied Fouquet. "The birth of your brother—"

"I have only one brother—and that is Monsieur. You know it as well as myself. There is a plot, I tell you, beginning with the governor of the Bastille."

"Be careful, sire, for this man has been deceived as every one else has by the prince's likeness to yourself."

"Likeness? Absurd!"

"This Marchiali must be singularly like your majesty, to be able to deceive every one's eye," Fouquet persisted.

"Ridiculous!"

"Do not say so, sire; those who had prepared everything in order to face and deceive your ministers, your mother, your officers of state, the members of your family, must be quite confident of the resemblance between you."

"But where are these persons, then?" murmured the king.

"At Vaux."

"At Vaux! and you suffer them to remain there!"

"My most instant duty appeared to me to be your majesty's release. I have accomplished that duty; and now, whatever your majesty may command, shall be done. I await your orders."

Louis reflected for a few moments.

"Muster all the troops in Paris," he said.

"All the necessary orders are given for that purpose," replied Fouquet.

"You have given orders!" exclaimed the king.

"For that purpose, yes, sire; your majesty will be at the head of ten thousand men in less than an hour."

The only reply the king made was to take hold of Fouquet's hand with such an expression of feeling, that it was very easy to perceive how strongly he had, until that remark, maintained his suspicions of the minister, notwithstanding the latter's intervention.

"And with these troops," he said, "we shall go at once and besiege in your house the rebels who by this time will have established and intrenched themselves therein."

"I should be surprised if that were the case," replied Fouquet.

"Why?"

"Because their chief—the very soul of the enterprise—having been unmasked by me, the whole plan seems to me to have miscarried."

"You have unmasked this false prince also?"

"No, I have not seen him."

"Whom have you seen, then?"

"The leader of the enterprise, not that unhappy young man; the latter is merely an instrument, destined through his whole life to wretchedness, I plainly perceive."

"Most certainly."

"It is M. l'Abbe d'Herblay, Eveque de Vannes."

"Your friend?"

"He was my friend, sire," replied Fouquet, nobly.

"An unfortunate circumstance for you," said the king, in a less generous tone of voice.

"Such friendships, sire, had nothing dishonorable in them so long as I was ignorant of the crime."

"You should have foreseen it."

"If I am guilty, I place myself in your majesty's hands."

"Ah! Monsieur Fouquet, it was not that I meant," returned the king, sorry to have shown the bitterness of his thought in such a manner. "Well! I assure you that, notwithstanding the mask with which the villain covered his face, I had something like a vague suspicion that he was the very man. But with this chief of the enterprise there was a man of prodigious strength, the one who menaced me with a force almost herculean; what is he?"

"It must be his friend the Baron du Vallon, formerly one of the musketeers."

"The friend of D'Artagnan? the friend of the Comte de la Fere? Ah!" exclaimed the king, as he paused at the name of the latter, "we must not forget the connection that existed between the conspirators and M. de Bragelonne."

"Sire, sire, do not go too far. M. de la Fere is the most honorable man in France. Be satisfied with those whom I deliver up to you."

"With those whom you deliver up to me, you say? Very good, for you will deliver up those who are guilty to me."

"What does your majesty understand by that?" inquired Fouquet.

"I understand," replied the king, "that we shall soon arrive at Vaux with a large body of troops, that we will lay violent hands upon that nest of vipers, and that not a soul shall escape."

"Your majesty will put these men to death!" cried Fouquet.

"To the very meanest of them."

"Oh! sire."

"Let us understand one another, Monsieur Fouquet," said the king, haughtily. "We no longer live in times when assassination was the only and the last resource kings held in reservation at extremity. No, Heaven be praised! I have parliaments who sit and judge in my name, and I have scaffolds on which supreme authority is carried out."

Fouquet turned pale. "I will take the liberty of observing to your majesty, that any proceedings instituted respecting these matters would bring down the greatest scandal upon the dignity of the throne. The august name of Anne of Austria must never be allowed to pass the lips of the people accompanied by a smile."

"Justice must be done, however, monsieur."

"Good, sire; but royal blood must not be shed upon a scaffold."

"The royal blood! you believe that!" cried the king with

fury in his voice, stamping his foot on the ground. "This double birth is an invention; and in that invention, particularly, do I see M. d'Herblay's crime. It is the crime I wish to punish rather than the violence, or the insult."

"And punish it with death, sire?"

"With death; yes, monsieur, I have said it."

"Sire," said the surintendant, with firmness, as he raised his head proudly, "your majesty will take the life, if you please, of your brother Philippe of France; that concerns you alone, and you will doubtless consult the queen-mother upon the subject. Whatever she may command will be perfectly correct. I do not wish to mix myself up in it, not even for the honor of your crown, but I have a favor to ask of you, and I beg to submit it to you."

"Speak," said the king, in no little degree agitated by his minister's last words. "What do you require?"

"The pardon of M. d'Herblay and of M. du Vallon."

"My assassins?"

"Two rebels, sire, that is all."

"Oh! I understand, then, you ask me to forgive your friends."

"My friends!" said Fouquet, deeply wounded.

"Your friends, certainly; but the safety of the state requires that an exemplary punishment should be inflicted on the guilty."

"I will not permit myself to remind your majesty that I have just restored you to liberty, and have saved your life."

"Monsieur!"

"I will not allow myself to remind your majesty that had M. d'Herblay wished to carry out his character of an assassin, he could very easily have assassinated your majesty this morning in the forest of Senart, and all would have been over." The king started.

"A pistol-bullet through the head," pursued Fouquet, "and the disfigured features of Louis XIV., which no one could have recognized, would be M. d'Herblay's complete and entire justification."

The king turned pale and giddy at the bare idea of the danger he had escaped.

"If M. d'Herblay," continued Fouquet, "had been an assassin, he had no occasion to inform me of his plan in order to succeed. Freed from the real king, it would have been impossible in all futurity to guess the false. And if the usurper had been recognized by Anne of Austria, he would still have been—her son. The usurper, as far as Monsieur d'Herblay's conscience was concerned, was still a king of the blood of Louis XIII. Moreover, the conspirator, in that course, would have had security, secrecy, impunity. A pistol-bullet would have procured him all that. For the sake of Heaven, sire, grant me his forgiveness."

The king, instead of being touched by the picture, so faithfully drawn in all details, of Aramis's generosity, felt himself most painfully and cruelly humiliated. His unconquerable pride revolted at the idea that a man had held suspended at the end of his finger the thread of his royal life. Every word that fell from Fouquet's lips, and which he thought most efficacious in procuring his friend's pardon, seemed to pour another drop of poison into the already ulcerated heart of Louis XIV. Nothing could bend or soften him. Addressing himself to Fouquet, he said, "I really don't know, monsieur, why you should solicit the pardon of these men. What good is there in asking that which can be obtained without solicitation?"

"I do not understand you, sire."

"It is not difficult, either. Where am I now?"

"In the Bastille, sire."

"Yes; in a dungeon. I am looked upon as a madman, am I not?"

"Yes, sire."

"And no one is known here but Marchiali?"

"Certainly."

"Well; change nothing in the position of affairs. Let the poor madman rot between the slimy walls of the Bastille, and M. d'Herblay and M. du Vallon will stand in no need of my forgiveness. Their new king will absolve them."

"Your majesty does me a great injustice, sire; and you are wrong," replied Fouquet, dryly; "I am not child enough, nor is M. d'Herblay silly enough, to have omitted to make all these reflections; and if I had wished to make a new king, as you say, I had no occasion to have come here to force open the gates and doors of the Bastille, to free you from this place. That would show a want of even common sense. Your majesty's mind is disturbed by anger; otherwise you would be far from offending, groundlessly, the very one of your servants who has rendered you the most important service of all."

Louis perceived that he had gone too far; that the gates of the Bastille were still closed upon him, whilst, by degrees, the floodgates were gradually being opened, behind which the generous-hearted Fouquet had restrained his anger. "I did not say that to humiliate you, Heaven knows, monsieur," he replied. "Only you are addressing yourself to me in order to obtain a pardon, and I answer according to my conscience. And so, judging by my conscience, the criminals we speak of are not worthy of consideration or forgiveness."

Fouquet was silent.

"What I do is as generous," added the king, "as what you have done, for I am in your power. I will even say it is more generous, inasmuch as you place before me certain conditions upon which my liberty, my life, may depend; and to reject which is to make a sacrifice of both."

"I was wrong, certainly," replied Fouquet. "Yes,—I had the appearance of extorting a favor; I regret it, and entreat your majesty's forgiveness."

"And you are forgiven, my dear Monsieur Fouquet,"

said the king, with a smile, which restored the serene expression of his features, which so many circumstances had altered since the preceding evening.

"I have my own forgiveness," replied the minister, with some degree of persistence; "but M. d'Herblay, and M. du Vallon?"

"They will never obtain theirs, as long as I live," replied the inflexible king. "Do me the kindness not to speak of it again."

"Your majesty shall be obeyed."

"And you will bear me no ill-will for it?"

"Oh! no, sire; for I anticipated the event."

"You had 'anticipated' that I should refuse to forgive those gentlemen?"

"Certainly; and all my measures were taken in consequence."

"What do you mean to say?" cried the king, surprised.

"M. d'Herblay came, as may be said, to deliver himself into my hands. M. d'Herblay left to me the happiness of saving my king and my country. I could not condemn M. d'Herblay to death; nor could I, on the other hand, expose him to your majesty's justifiable wrath; it would have been just the same as if I had killed him myself."

"Well! and what have you done?"

"Sire, I gave M. d'Herblay the best horses in my stables and four hours' start over all those your majesty might, probably, dispatch after him."

"Be it so!" murmured the king. "But still, the world is wide enough and large enough for those whom I may send to overtake your horses, notwithstanding the 'four hours' start' which you have given to M. d'Herblay."

"In giving him these four hours, sire, I knew I was giving him his life, and he will save his life."

"In what way?"

"After having galloped as hard as possible, with the four

hours' start, before your musketeers, he will reach my chateau of Belle-Isle, where I have given him a safe asylum."

"That may be! But you forget that you have made me a present of Belle-Isle."

"But not for you to arrest my friends."

"You take it back again, then?"

"As far as that goes—yes, sire."

"My musketeers shall capture it, and the affair will be at an end."

"Neither your musketeers, nor your whole army could take Belle-Isle," said Fouquet, coldly. "Belle-Isle is impregnable."

The king became perfectly livid; a lightning flash seemed to dart from his eyes. Fouquet felt that he was lost, but he as not one to shrink when the voice of honor spoke loudly within him. He bore the king's wrathful gaze; the latter swallowed his rage, and after a few moments' silence, said, "Are we going to return to Vaux?"

"I am at your majesty's orders," replied Fouquet, with a low bow; "but I think that your majesty can hardly dispense with changing your clothes previous to appearing before your court."

"We shall pass by the Louvre," said the king. "Come." And they left the prison, passing before Baisemeaux, who looked completely bewildered as he saw Marchiali once more leave; and, in his helplessness, tore out the major portion of his few remaining hairs. It was perfectly true, however, that Fouquet wrote and gave him an authority for the prisoner's release, and that the king wrote beneath it, "Seen and approved, Louis"; a piece of madness that Baisemeaux, incapable of putting two ideas together, acknowledged by giving himself a terrible blow on the forehead with his own fist.

CHAPTER 24

The False King.

In the meantime, usurped royalty was playing out its part bravely at Vaux. Philippe gave orders that for his *petit lever* the *grandes entrees*, already prepared to appear before the king, should be introduced. He determined to give this order notwithstanding the absence of M. d'Herblay, who did not return—our readers know the reason. But the prince, not believing that absence could be prolonged, wished, as all rash spirits do, to try his valor and his fortune far from all protection and instruction. Another reason urged him to this—Anne of Austria was about to appear; the guilty mother was about to stand in the presence of her sacrificed son. Philippe was not willing, if he had a weakness, to render the man a witness of it before whom he was bound thenceforth to display so much strength. Philippe opened his folding doors, and several persons entered silently. Philippe did not stir whilst his *valets de chambre* dressed him. He had watched, the evening before, all the habits of his brother, and played the king in such a manner as to awaken no suspicion. He was thus completely dressed in hunting costume when he received his visitors. His own memory and the notes of Aramis announced everybody to him, first of all Anne of Austria, to whom Monsieur gave his hand, and then Madame with M. de Saint-Aignan. He smiled at seeing these countenances, but trembled on recognizing his mother. That still so noble and imposing figure, ravaged by pain, pleaded in his heart the cause of the famous queen who had immolated a child to reasons of state. He found his mother still handsome. He knew that Louis XIV. loved her, and he promised himself to love her likewise, and not to prove a scourge to her old age. He contemplated his brother with a tenderness easily to be understood. The latter had usurped nothing, had cast no shades athwart his life. A separate tree, he allowed the stem to rise without heeding its elevation or majestic life. Philippe promised himself to be a kind brother to this prince, who required nothing but gold to minister to his pleasures. He bowed with a friendly air to Saint-Aignan, who was all reverences and smiles, and trembling held out his hand to Henrietta, his sister-in-law, whose beauty struck him; but he saw in the eyes of that princess an expression of coldness which would facilitate, as he thought, their future relations.

"How much more easy," thought he, "it will be to be the brother of that woman than her gallant, if she evinces towards me a coldness that my brother could not have for her, but which is imposed upon me as a duty." The only visit he dreaded at this moment was that of the queen; his heart—his mind—had just been shaken by so violent a trial, that, in spite of their firm temperament, they would not, perhaps, support another shock. Happily the queen did not come. Then commenced, on the part of Anne of Austria, a political dissertation upon the welcome M. Fouquet had given to the house of France. She mixed up hostilities with compliments addressed to the king, and questions as to his health, with little maternal flatteries and diplomatic artifices.

"Well, my son," said she, "are you convinced with regard to M. Fouquet?"

"Saint-Aignan," said Philippe, "have the goodness to go and inquire after the queen."

At these words, the first Philippe had pronounced aloud, the slight difference that there was between his voice and that of the king was sensible to maternal ears, and Anne of Austria looked earnestly at her son. Saint-Aignan left the room, and Philippe continued:

"Madame, I do not like to hear M. Fouquet ill-spoken of, you know I do not—and you have even spoken well of him yourself."

"That is true; therefore I only question you on the state of your sentiments with respect to him."

"Sire," said Henrietta, "I, on my part, have always liked M. Fouquet. He is a man of good taste,—a superior man."

"A superintendent who is never sordid or niggardly," added Monsieur; "and who pays in gold all the orders I have on him."

"Every one in this thinks too much of himself, and nobody for the state," said the old queen. "M. Fouquet, it is a fact, M. Fouquet is ruining the state."

"Well, mother!" replied Philippe, in rather a lower key, "do you likewise constitute yourself the buckler of M. Colbert?"

"How is that?" replied the old queen, rather surprised.

"Why, in truth," replied Philippe, "you speak that just as your old friend Madame de Chevreuse would speak."

"Why do you mention Madame de Chevreuse to me?" said she, "and what sort of humor are you in to-day towards me?"

Philippe continued: "Is not Madame de Chevreuse always in league against somebody? Has not Madame de Chevreuse been to pay you a visit, mother?"

"Monsieur, you speak to me now in such a manner that I can almost fancy I am listening to your father."

"My father did not like Madame de Chevreuse, and had good reason for not liking her," said the prince. "For my part, I like her no better than *he* did, and if she thinks proper to come here as she formerly did, to sow divisions and hatreds under the pretext of begging money—why—"

"Well! what?" said Anne of Austria, proudly, herself provoking the storm.

"Well!" replied the young man firmly, "I will drive Madame de Chevreuse out of my kingdom—and with her all who meddle with its secrets and mysteries."

He had not calculated the effect of this terrible speech, or perhaps he wished to judge the effect of it, like those who, suffering from a chronic pain, and seeking to break the monotony of that suffering, touch their wound to procure a sharper pang. Anne of Austria was nearly fainting; her eyes, open but meaningless, ceased to see for several seconds; she stretched out her arms towards her other son, who supported and embraced her without fear of irritating the king.

"Sire," murmured she, "you are treating your mother very cruelly."

"In what respect, madame?" replied he. "I am only speaking of Madame de Chevreuse; does my mother prefer Madame de Chevreuse to the security of the state and of my person? Well, then, madame, I tell you Madame de Chevreuse has returned to France to borrow money, and that she addressed herself to M. Fouquet to sell him a certain secret."

"A certain secret!" cried Anne of Austria.

"Concerning pretended robberies that monsieur le surintendant had committed, which is false," added Philippe. "M. Fouquet rejected her offers with indignation, preferring the esteem of the king to complicity with such intriguers. Then Madame de Chevreuse sold the secret to M. Colbert, and as she is insatiable, and was not satisfied with having extorted a hundred thousand crowns from a servant of the state, she has taken a still bolder flight, in search of surer sources of supply. Is that true, madame?"

"You know all, sire," said the queen, more uneasy than irritated.

"Now," continued Philippe, "I have good reason to dislike this fury, who comes to my court to plan the shame of some and the ruin of others. If Heaven has suffered certain crimes to be committed, and has concealed them in the shadow of its clemency, I will not permit Madame de Chevreuse to counteract the just designs of fate."

The latter part of this speech had so agitated the queen-mother, that her son had pity on her. He took her hand and kissed it tenderly; she did not feel that in that kiss, given in spite of repulsion and bitterness of the heart, there was a pardon for eight years of suffering. Philippe allowed the silence of a moment to swallow the emotions that had just developed themselves. Then, with a cheerful smile:

"We will not go to-day," said he, "I have a plan." And, turning towards the door, he hoped to see Aramis, whose absence began to alarm him. The queen-mother wished to leave the room.

"Remain where you are, mother," said he, "I wish you to make your peace with M. Fouquet."

"I bear M. Fouquet no ill-will; I only dreaded his prodigalities."

"We will put that to rights, and will take nothing of the superintendent but his good qualities."

"What is your majesty looking for?" said Henrietta, seeing the king's eyes constantly turned towards the door, and wishing to let fly a little poisoned arrow at his heart, supposing he was so anxiously expecting either La Valliere or a letter from her.

"My sister," said the young man, who had divined her thought, thanks to that marvelous perspicuity of which fortune was from that time about to allow him the exercise, "my sister, I am expecting a most distinguished man, a most able counselor, whom I wish to present to you all, recommending him to your good graces. Ah! come in, then, D'Artagnan."

"What does your majesty wish?" said D'Artagnan, appearing.

"Where is monsieur the bishop of Vannes, your friend?"

"Why, sire—"

"I am waiting for him, and he does not come. Let him be sought for."

D'Artagnan remained for an instant stupefied; but soon, reflecting that Aramis had left Vaux privately on a mission from the king, he concluded that the king wished to preserve the secret. "Sire," replied he, "does your majesty absolutely require M. d'Herblay to be brought to you?"

"Absolutely is not the word," said Philippe; "I do not want him so particularly as that; but if he can be found—"

"I thought so," said D'Artagnan to himself.

"Is this M. d'Herblay the bishop of Vannes?"

"Yes, madame."

"A friend of M. Fouquet?"

"Yes, madame; an old musketeer."

Anne of Austria blushed.

"One of the four braves who formerly performed such prodigies."

The old queen repented of having wished to bite; she broke off the conversation, in order to preserve the rest of her teeth. "Whatever may be your choice, sire," said she, "I have no doubt it will be excellent."

All bowed in support of that sentiment.

"You will find in him," continued Philippe, "the depth and penetration of M. de Richelieu, without the avarice of M. de Mazarin!"

"A prime minister, sire?" said Monsieur, in a fright.

"I will tell you all about that, brother; but it is strange that M. d'Herblay is not here!"

He called out:

"Let M. Fouquet be informed that I wish to speak to him—oh! before you, before you; do not retire!"

M. de Saint-Aignan returned, bringing satisfactory news of the queen, who only kept her bed from precaution, and to have strength to carry out the king's wishes. Whilst everybody was seeking M. Fouquet and Aramis, the new king quietly continued his experiments, and everybody, family, officers, servants, had not the least suspicion of his identity, his air, his voice, and manners were so like the king's. On his side, Philippe, applying to all countenances the accurate descriptions and key-notes of character supplied by his accomplice Aramis, conducted himself so as not to give birth to a doubt in the minds of those who surrounded him. Nothing from that time could disturb the usurper. With what strange facility had Providence just reversed the loftiest fortune of the world to substitute the lowliest in its stead! Philippe admired the goodness of God with regard to himself, and seconded it with all the resources of his admirable nature. But he felt, at times, something like a specter gliding between him and the rays of his new glory. Aramis did not appear. The conversation had languished in the royal family; Philippe, preoccupied, forgot to dismiss his brother and Madame Henrietta. The latter were astonished, and began, by degrees, to lose all patience. Anne of Austria stooped towards her son's ear and addressed some words to him in Spanish. Philippe was completely ignorant of that language, and grew pale at this unexpected obstacle. But, as if the spirit of the imperturbable Aramis had covered him with his infallibility, instead of appearing disconcerted, Philippe rose. "Well! what?" said Anne of Austria.

"What is all that noise?" said Philippe, turning round towards the door of the second staircase.

And a voice was heard saying, "This way, this way! A few steps more, sire!"

"The voice of M. Fouquet," said D'Artagnan, who was standing close to the queen-mother.

"Then M. d'Herblay cannot be far off," added Philippe.

But he then saw what he little thought to have beheld

so near to him. All eyes were turned towards the door at which M. Fouquet was expected to enter; but it was not M. Fouquet who entered. A terrible cry resounded from all corners of the chamber, a painful cry uttered by the king and all present. It is given to but few men, even those whose destiny contains the strangest elements, and accidents the most wonderful, to contemplate such a spectacle similar to that which presented itself in the royal chamber at that moment. The half-closed shutters only admitted the entrance of an uncertain light passing through thick violet velvet curtains lined with silk. In this soft shade, the eyes were by degrees dilated, and every one present saw others rather with imagination than with actual sight. There could not, however, escape, in these circumstances, one of the surrounding details; and the new object which presented itself appeared as luminous as though it shone out in full sunlight. So it happened with Louis XIV., when he showed himself, pale and frowning, in the doorway of the secret stairs. The face of Fouquet appeared behind him, stamped with sorrow and determination. The queen-mother, who perceived Louis XIV., and who held the hand of Philippe, uttered a cry of which we have spoken, as if she beheld a phantom. Monsieur was bewildered, and kept turning his head in astonishment from one to the other. Madame made a step forward, thinking she was looking at the form of her brother-in-law reflected in a mirror. And, in fact, the illusion was possible. The two princes, both pale as death—for we renounce the hope of being able to describe the fearful state of Philippe—trembling, clenching their hands convulsively, measured each other with looks, and darted their glances, sharp as poniards, at each other. Silent, panting, bending forward, they appeared as if about to spring upon an enemy. The unheard-of resemblance of countenance, gesture, shape, height, even to the resemblance of costume, produced by chance—for Louis XIV. had been to the Louvre and put on a violet-colored dress—the perfect analogy of the two princes, completed the consternation of Anne of Austria. And yet she did not at once guess the truth. There are misfortunes in life so truly dreadful that no one will at first accept them; people rather believe in the supernatural and the impossible. Louis had not reckoned on these obstacles. He expected that he had only to appear to be acknowledged. A living sun, he could not endure the suspicion of equality with any one. He did not admit that every torch should not become darkness at the instant he shone out with his conquering ray. At the aspect of Philippe, then, he was perhaps more terrified than any one round him, and his silence, his immobility were, this time, a concentration and a calm which precede the violent explosions of concentrated passion.

But Fouquet! who shall paint his emotion and stupor in presence of this living portrait of his master! Fouquet thought Aramis was right, that this newly-arrived was a king as pure in his race as the other, and that, for having repudiated all participation in this *coup d'etat*, so skillfully got up by the General of the Jesuits, he must be a mad enthusiast, unworthy of ever dipping his hands in political grand strategy work. And then it was the blood of Louis XIII. which Fouquet was sacrificing to the blood of Louis XIII.; it was to a selfish ambition he was sacrificing a noble ambition; to the right of keeping he sacrificed the right of having. The whole extent of his fault was revealed to him at simple sight of the pretender. All that passed in the mind of Fouquet was lost upon the persons present. He had five minutes to focus meditation on this point of conscience; five minutes, that is to say five ages, during which the two kings and their family scarcely found energy to breathe after so terrible a shock. D'Artagnan, leaning against the wall, in front of Fouquet, with his hand to his brow, asked himself the cause of such a wonderful prodigy. He could not have said at once why he doubted, but he knew assuredly that he had reason to doubt, and that in this meeting of the two Louis XIV.s lay all the doubt and difficulty that during late days had rendered the conduct of Aramis so suspicious to the musketeer. These ideas were, however, enveloped in a haze, a veil of mystery. The actors in this assembly seemed to swim in the vapors of a confused waking. Suddenly Louis XIV., more impatient and more accustomed to command, ran to one of the shutters, which he opened, tearing the curtains in his eagerness. A flood of living light entered the chamber, and made Philippe draw back to the alcove. Louis seized upon this movement with eagerness, and addressing himself to the queen:

"My mother," said he, "do you not acknowledge your son, since every one here has forgotten his king!" Anne of Austria started, and raised her arms towards Heaven, without being able to articulate a single word.

"My mother," said Philippe, with a calm voice, "do you not acknowledge your son?" And this time, in his turn, Louis drew back.

As to Anne of Austria, struck suddenly in head and heart with fell remorse, she lost her equilibrium. No one aiding her, for all were petrified, she sank back in her fauteuil, breathing a weak, trembling sigh. Louis could not endure the spectacle and the affront. He bounded towards D'Artagnan, over whose brain a vertigo was stealing and who staggered as he caught at the door for support.

"*A moi! mousquetaire!*" said he. "Look us in the face and say which is the paler, he or I!"

This cry roused D'Artagnan, and stirred in his heart the fibers of obedience. He shook his head, and, without more hesitation, he walked straight up to Philippe, on whose shoulder he laid his hand, saying, "Monsieur, you are my prisoner!"

Philippe did not raise his eyes towards Heaven, nor stir from the spot, where he seemed nailed to the floor, his eye intently fixed upon the king his brother. He reproached him with a sublime silence for all misfortunes past, all tortures to come. Against this language of the soul the king felt he had no power; he cast down his eyes, dragging away precipitately his brother and sister, forgetting his mother, sitting motionless within three paces of the son whom she left a second time to be condemned to death. Philippe approached Anne of Austria, and said to her, in a soft and nobly agitated voice:

"If I were not your son, I should curse you, my mother, for having rendered me so unhappy."

D'Artagnan felt a shudder pass through the marrow of his bones. He bowed respectfully to the young prince, and said as he bent, "Excuse me, monseigneur, I am but a soldier, and my oaths are his who has just left the chamber."

"Thank you, M. d'Artagnan. . . . What has become of M. d'Herblay?"

"M. d'Herblay is in safety, monseigneur," said a voice behind them; "and no one, while I live and am free, shall cause a hair to fall from his head."

"Monsieur Fouquet!" said the prince, smiling sadly.

"Pardon me, monseigneur," said Fouquet, kneeling, "but he who is just gone out from hence was my guest."

"Here are," murmured Philippe, with a sigh, "brave friends and good hearts. They make me regret the world. On, M. d'Artagnan, I follow you."

At the moment the captain of the musketeers was about to leave the room with his prisoner, Colbert appeared, and, after remitting an order from the king to D'Artagnan, retired. D'Artagnan read the paper, and then crushed it in his hand with rage.

"What is it?" asked the prince.

"Read, monseigneur," replied the musketeer.

Philippe read the following words, hastily traced by the hand of the king:

"M. d'Artagnan will conduct the prisoner to the Ile

Sainte-Marguerite. He will cover his face with an iron vizor, which the prisoner shall never raise except at peril of his life."

"That is just," said Philippe, with resignation; "I am ready."

"Aramis was right," said Fouquet, in a low voice, to the musketeer, "this one is every whit as much a king as the other."

"More so!" replied D'Artagnan. "He wanted only you and me."

CHAPTER 25

In Which Porthos Thinks He Is Pursuing
a Duchy.

Aramis and Porthos, having profited by the time granted them by Fouquet, did honor to the French cavalry by their speed. Porthos did not clearly understand on what kind of mission he was forced to display so much velocity; but as he saw Aramis spurring on furiously, he, Porthos, spurred on in the same way. They had soon, in this manner, placed twelve leagues between them and Vaux; they were then obliged to change horses, and organize a sort of post arrangement. It was during a relay that Porthos ventured to interrogate Aramis discreetly.

"Hush!" replied the latter, "know only that our fortune depends on our speed."

As if Porthos had still been the musketeer, without a sou or a *maille* of 1626, he pushed forward. That magic word "fortune" always means something in the human ear. It means *enough* for those who have nothing; it means *too much* for those who have enough.

"I shall be made a duke!" said Porthos, aloud. He was speaking to himself.

"That is possible," replied Aramis, smiling after his own fashion, as Porthos's horse passed him. Aramis felt, notwithstanding, as though his brain were on fire; the activity of the body had not yet succeeded in subduing that of the mind. All there is of raging passion, mental toothache or mortal threat, raged, gnawed and grumbled in the thoughts of the unhappy prelate. His countenance exhibited visible traces of this rude combat. Free on the highway to abandon himself to every impression of the moment, Aramis did not fail to swear at every start of his horse, at every inequality in the road. Pale, at times inundated with boiling sweats, then again dry and icy, he flogged his horses till the blood streamed from their sides. Porthos, whose dominant fault was not sensibility, groaned at this. Thus traveled they on for eight long hours, and then arrived at Orleans. It was four o'clock in the afternoon. Aramis, on observing this, judged that nothing showed pursuit to be a possibility. It would be without example that a troop capable of taking him and Porthos should be furnished with relays sufficient to perform forty leagues in eight hours. Thus, admitting pursuit, which was not at all manifest, the fugitives were five hours in advance of their pursuers.

Aramis thought that there might be no imprudence in taking a little rest, but that to continue would make the matter more certain. Twenty leagues more, performed with the same rapidity, twenty more leagues devoured, and no one, not even D'Artagnan, could overtake the enemies of the king. Aramis felt obliged, therefore, to inflict upon Porthos the pain of mounting on horseback again. They rode on till seven o'clock in the evening, and had only one post more between them and Blois. But here a diabolical accident alarmed Aramis greatly. There were no horses at the post. The prelate asked himself by what infernal machination his enemies had succeeded in depriving him of the means of going further,—he who never recognized chance as a deity, who found a cause for every accident, preferred believing that the refusal of the postmaster, at such an hour, in such a country, was the consequence of an order emanating from above: an order given with a view of stopping short the king-maker in the midst of his flight. But at the moment he was about to fly into a passion, so as to procure either a horse or an explanation, he was struck with the recollection that the Comte de la Fere lived in the neighborhood.

"I am not traveling," said he; "I do not want horses for a whole stage. Find me two horses to go and pay a visit to a nobleman of my acquaintance who resides near this place."

"What nobleman?" asked the postmaster.

"M. le Comte de la Fere."

"Oh!" replied the postmaster, uncovering with respect, "a very worthy nobleman. But, whatever may be my desire to make myself agreeable to him, I cannot furnish you with horses, for all mine are engaged by M. le Duc de Beaufort."

"Indeed!" said Aramis, much disappointed.

"Only," continued the postmaster, "if you will put up with a little carriage I have, I will harness an old blind horse who has still his legs left, and peradventure will draw you to the house of M. le Comte de la Fere."

"It is worth a louis," said Aramis.

"No, monsieur, such a ride is worth no more than a crown; that is what M. Grimaud, the comte's intendant, always pays me when he makes use of that carriage; and I should not wish the Comte de la Fere to have to reproach me with having imposed on one of his friends."

"As you please," said Aramis, "particularly as regards disobliging the Comte de la Fere; only I think I have a right to give you a louis for your idea."

"Oh! doubtless," replied the postmaster with delight. And he himself harnessed the ancient horse to the creaking carriage. In the meantime Porthos was curious to behold. He imagined he had discovered a clew to the secret, and he felt pleased, because a visit to Athos, in the first place, promised him much satisfaction, and, in the next, gave him the hope of finding at the same time a good bed and good supper. The master, having got the carriage ready, ordered one of his men to drive the strangers to La Fere. Porthos took his seat by the side of Aramis, whispering in his ear, "I understand."

"Aha!" said Aramis, "and what do you understand, my friend?"

"We are going, on the part of the king, to make some great proposal to Athos."

"Pooh!" said Aramis.

"You need tell me nothing about it," added the worthy Porthos, endeavoring to reseat himself so as to avoid the jolting, "you need tell me nothing, I shall guess."

"Well! do, my friend; guess away."

They arrived at Athos's dwelling about nine o'clock in the evening, favored by a splendid moon. This cheerful light rejoiced Porthos beyond expression; but Aramis appeared annoyed by it in an equal degree. He could not help showing something of this to Porthos, who replied—"Ay! ay! I guess how it is! the mission is a secret one."

These were his last words in the carriage. The driver interrupted him by saying, "Gentlemen, we have arrived."

Porthos and his companion alighted before the gate of the little chateau, where we are about to meet again our old acquaintances Athos and Bragelonne, the latter of whom had disappeared since the discovery of the infidelity of La Valliere. If there be one saying truer than another, it is this: great griefs contain within themselves the germ of consolation. This painful wound, inflicted upon Raoul, had drawn him nearer to his father again; and God knows how sweet were the consolations which flowed from the eloquent mouth and generous heart of Athos. The wound was not cicatrized, but Athos, by dint of conversing with his son and mixing a little more of his life with that of the young man, had brought him to understand that this pang of a first infidelity is necessary to every human existence; and that no one has loved without encountering it. Raoul listened, again and again, but never understood. Nothing replaces in the deeply afflicted heart the remembrance and thought of the beloved object. Raoul then replied to the reasoning of his father:

"Monsieur, all that you tell me is true; I believe that no one has suffered in the affections of the heart so much as you have; but you are a man too great by reason of intelligence, and too severely tried by adverse fortune not to allow for the weakness of the soldier who suffers for the first time. I am paying a tribute that will not be paid a second time; permit me to plunge myself so deeply in my grief that I may forget myself in it, that I may drown even my reason in it."

"Raoul! Raoul!"

"Listen, monsieur. Never shall I accustom myself to the idea that Louise, the chastest and most innocent of women, has been able to so basely deceive a man so honest and so true a lover as myself. Never can I persuade myself that I see that sweet and noble mask change into a hypocritical lascivious face. Louise lost! Louise infamous! Ah! monseigneur, that idea is much more cruel to me than Raoul abandoned—Raoul unhappy!"

Athos then employed the heroic remedy. He defended Louise against Raoul, and justified her perfidy by her love. "A woman who would have yielded to a king because he is a king," said he, "would deserve to be styled infamous; but Louise loves Louis. Young, both, they have forgotten, he his rank, she her vows. Love absolves everything, Raoul. The two young people love each other with sincerity."

And when he had dealt this severe poniard-thrust, Athos, with a sigh, saw Raoul bound away beneath the rankling wound, and fly to the thickest recesses of the wood, or the solitude of his chamber, whence, an hour after, he would return, pale, trembling, but subdued. Then, coming up to Athos with a smile, he would kiss his hand, like the dog who, having been beaten, caresses a respected master, to redeem his fault. Raoul redeemed nothing but his weakness, and only confessed his grief. Thus passed away the days that followed that scene in which Athos had so violently shaken the indomitable pride of the king. Never, when conversing with his son, did he make any allusion to that scene; never did he give him the details of that vigorous lecture, which might, perhaps, have consoled the young man, by showing him his rival humbled. Athos did not wish that the offended lover should forget the respect due to his king. And when Bragelonne, ardent, angry, and melancholy, spoke with contempt of royal words, of the equivocal faith which certain madmen draw from promises that emanate from thrones, when, passing over two centuries, with that rapidity of a bird that traverses a narrow strait to go from one continent to the other, Raoul ventured to predict the time in which kings would be esteemed as less than other men, Athos said to him, in his serene, persuasive voice, "You are right, Raoul; all that you say will happen; kings will lose their privileges, as stars which have survived their aeons lose their splendor. But when that moment comes, Raoul, we shall be dead. And remember well what I say to you. In this world, all, men, women, and kings, must live for the present. We can only live for the future for God."

This was the manner in which Athos and Raoul were, as usual, conversing, and walking backwards and forwards in the long alley of limes in the park, when the bell which served to announce to the comte either the hour of dinner or the arrival of a visitor, was rung; and, without attaching any importance to it, he turned towards the house with his son; and at the end of the alley they found themselves in the presence of Aramis and Porthos.

CHAPTER 26

The Last Adieux.

Raoul uttered a cry, and affectionately embraced Porthos. Aramis and Athos embraced like old men; and this embrace itself being a question for Aramis, he immediately said, "My friend, we have not long to remain with you."

"Ah!" said the comte.

"Only time to tell you of my good fortune," interrupted Porthos.

"Ah!" said Raoul.

Athos looked silently at Aramis, whose somber air had already appeared to him very little in harmony with the good news Porthos hinted.

"What is the good fortune that has happened to you? Let us hear it," said Raoul, with a smile.

"The king has made me a duke," said the worthy Porthos, with an air of mystery, in the ear of the young man, "a duke by *brevet*."

But the *asides* of Porthos were always loud enough to be heard by everybody. His murmurs were in the diapason of ordinary roaring. Athos heard him, and uttered an exclamation which made Aramis start. The latter took Athos by the arm, and, after having asked Porthos's permission to say a word to his friend in private, "My dear Athos," he began, "you see me overwhelmed with grief and trouble."

"With grief and trouble, my dear friend?" cried the comte; "oh, what?"

"In two words. I have conspired against the king; that conspiracy has failed, and, at this moment, I am doubtless pursued."

"You are pursued!—a conspiracy! Eh! my friend, what do you tell me?"

"The saddest truth. I am entirely ruined."

"Well, but Porthos—this title of duke—what does all that mean?"

"That is the subject of my severest pain; that is the deepest of my wounds. I have, believing in infallible success, drawn Porthos into my conspiracy. He threw himself into it, as you know he would do, with all his strength, without knowing what he was about; and now he is as much compromised as myself—as completely ruined as I am."

"Good God!" And Athos turned towards Porthos, who was smiling complacently.

"I must make you acquainted with the whole. Listen to me," continued Aramis; and he related the history as we know it. Athos, during the recital, several times felt the sweat break from his forehead. "It was a great idea," said he, "but a great error."

"For which I am punished, Athos."

"Therefore, I will not tell you my entire thought."

"Tell it, nevertheless."

"It is a crime."

"A capital crime; I know it is. *Lese majeste*."

"Porthos! poor Porthos!"

"What would you advise me to do? Success, as I have told you, was certain."

"M. Fouquet is an honest man."

"And I a fool for having so ill-judged him," said Aramis.

"Oh, the wisdom of man! Oh, millstone that grinds the world! and which is one day stopped by a grain of sand which has fallen, no one knows how, between its wheels."

"Say by a diamond, Aramis. But the thing is done. How do you think of acting?"

"I am taking away Porthos. The king will never believe that that worthy man has acted innocently. He never can believe that Porthos has thought he was serving the king, whilst acting as he has done. His head would pay my fault. It shall not, must not, be so."

"You are taking him away, whither?"

"To Belle-Isle, at first. That is an impregnable place of refuge. Then, I have the sea, and a vessel to pass over into England, where I have many relations."

"You? in England?"

"Yes, or else in Spain, where I have still more."

"But, our excellent Porthos! you ruin him, for the king will confiscate all his property."

"All is provided for. I know how, when once in Spain, to reconcile myself with Louis XIV., and restore Porthos to favor."

"You have credit, seemingly, Aramis!" said Athos, with a discreet air.

"Much; and at the service of my friends."

These words were accompanied by a warm pressure of the hand.

"Thank you," replied the comte.

"And while we are on this head," said Aramis, "you also are a malcontent; you also, Raoul, have griefs to lay to the king. Follow our example; pass over into Belle-Isle. Then we shall see, I guarantee upon my honor, that in a month there will be war between France and Spain on the subject of this son of Louis XIII., who is an Infante likewise, and whom France detains inhumanly. Now, as Louis XIV. would have no inclination for a war on that subject,

I will answer for an arrangement, the result of which must bring greatness to Porthos and to me, and a duchy in France to you, who are already a grandee of Spain. Will you join us?"

"No; for my part I prefer having something to reproach the king with; it is a pride natural to my race to pretend to a superiority over royal races. Doing what you propose, I should become the obliged of the king; I should certainly be the gainer on that ground, but I should be a loser in my conscience.—No, thank you!"

"Then give me two things, Athos,—your absolution."

"Oh! I give it you if you really wished to avenge the weak and oppressed against the oppressor."

"That is sufficient for me," said Aramis, with a blush which was lost in the obscurity of the night. "And now, give me your two best horses to gain the second post, as I have been refused any under the pretext of the Duc de Beaufort being traveling in this country."

"You shall have the two best horses, Aramis; and again I recommend poor Porthos strongly to your care."

"Oh! I have no fear on that score. One word more: do you think I am maneuvering for him as I ought?"

"The evil being committed, yes; for the king would not pardon him, and you have, whatever may be said, always a supporter in M. Fouquet, who will not abandon you, he being himself compromised, notwithstanding his heroic action."

"You are right. And that is why, instead of gaining the sea at once, which would proclaim my fear and guilt, that is why I remain upon French ground. But Belle-Isle will be for me whatever ground I wish it to be, English, Spanish, or Roman; all will depend, with me, on the standard I shall think proper to unfurl."

"How so?"

"It was I who fortified Belle-Isle; and, so long as I defend it, nobody can take Belle-Isle from me. And then, as you have said just now, M. Fouquet is there. Belle-Isle will not be attacked without the signature of M. Fouquet."

"That is true. Nevertheless, be prudent. The king is both cunning and strong." Aramis smiled.

"I again recommend Porthos to you," repeated the count, with a sort of cold persistence.

"Whatever becomes of me, count," replied Aramis, in the same tone, "our brother Porthos will fare as I do—or *better*."

Athos bowed whilst pressing the hand of Aramis, and turned to embrace Porthos with emotion.

"I was born lucky, was I not?" murmured the latter, transported with happiness, as he folded his cloak round him.

"Come, my dear friend," said Aramis.

Raoul had gone out to give orders for the saddling of the horses. The group was already divided. Athos saw his two friends on the point of departure, and something like a mist passed before his eyes and weighed upon his heart.

"It is strange," thought he, "whence comes the inclination I feel to embrace Porthos once more?" At that moment Porthos turned round, and he came towards his old friend with open arms. This last endearment was tender as in youth, as in times when hearts were warm—life happy. And then Porthos mounted his horse. Aramis came back once more to throw his arms round the neck of Athos. The latter watched them along the high-road, elongated by the shade, in their white cloaks. Like phantoms they seemed to enlarge on their departure from the earth, and it was not in the mist, but in the declivity of the ground that they disappeared. At the end of the perspective, both seemed to have given a spring with their feet, which made them vanish as if evaporated into cloud-land.

Then Athos, with a very heavy heart, returned towards the house, saying to Bragelonne, "Raoul, I don't know what it is that has just told me that I have seen those two for the last time."

"It does not astonish me, monsieur, that you should have such a thought," replied the young man, "for I have at this moment the same, and think also that I shall never see Messieurs du Vallon and d'Herblay again."

"Oh! you," replied the count, "you speak like a man rendered sad by a different cause; you see everything in black; you are young, and if you chance never to see those old friends again, it will because they no longer exist in the world in which you have yet many years to pass. But I—"

Raoul shook his head sadly, and leaned upon the shoulder of the count, without either of them finding another word in their hearts, which were ready to overflow.

All at once a noise of horses and voices, from the extremity of the road to Blois, attracted their attention that way. Flambeaux-bearers shook their torches merrily among the trees of their route, and turned round, from time to time, to avoid distancing the horsemen who followed them. These flames, this noise, this dust of a dozen richly caparisoned horses, formed a strange contrast in the middle of the night with the melancholy and almost funereal disappearance of the two shadows of Aramis and Porthos. Athos went towards the house; but he had hardly reached the parterre, when the entrance gate appeared in a blaze; all the flambeaux stopped and appeared to enflame the road. A cry was heard of "M. le Duc de Beaufort"—and Athos sprang towards the door of his house. But the duke had already alighted from his horse, and was looking around him.

"I am here, monseigneur," said Athos.

"Ah! good evening, dear count," said the prince, with that frank cordiality which won him so many hearts. "Is it too late for a friend?"

"Ah! my dear prince, come in!" said the count.

And, M. de Beaufort leaning on the arm of Athos, they entered the house, followed by Raoul, who walked respectfully and modestly among the officers of the prince, with several of whom he was acquainted.

CHAPTER 27

Monsieur de Beaufort.

The prince turned round at the moment when Raoul, in order to leave him alone with Athos, was shutting the door, and preparing to go with the other officers into an adjoining apartment.

"Is that the young man I have heard M. le Prince speak so highly of?" asked M. de Beaufort.

"It is, monseigneur."

"He is quite the soldier; let him stay, count, we cannot spare him."

"Remain, Raoul, since monseigneur permits it," said Athos.

"*Ma foi!* he is tall and handsome!" continued the duke. "Will you give him to me, monseigneur, if I ask him of you?"

"How am I to understand you, monseigneur?" said Athos.

"Why, I call upon you to bid you farewell."

"Farewell!"

"Yes, in good truth. Have you no idea of what I am about to become?"

"Why, I suppose, what you have always been, monseigneur,—a valiant prince, and an excellent gentleman."

"I am going to become an African prince,—a Bedouin

283

gentleman. The king is sending me to make conquests among the Arabs."

"What is this you tell me, monseigneur?"

"Strange, is it not? I, the Parisian *par essence*, I who have reigned in the faubourgs, and have been called King of the Halles,—I am going to pass from the Place Maubert to the minarets of Gigelli; from a Frondeur I am becoming an adventurer!"

"Oh, monseigneur, if you did not yourself tell me that—"

"It would not be credible, would it? Believe me, nevertheless, and we have but to bid each other farewell. This is what comes of getting into favor again."

"Into favor?"

"Yes. You smile. Ah, my dear count, do you know why I have accepted this enterprise, can you guess?"

"Because your highness loves glory above—everything."

"Oh! no; there is no glory in firing muskets at savages. I see no glory in that, for my part, and it is more probable that I shall there meet with something else. But I have wished, and still wish earnestly, my dear count, that my life should have that last *facet*, after all the whimsical exhibitions I have seen myself make during fifty years. For, in short, you must admit that it is sufficiently strange to be born the grandson of a king, to have made war against kings, to have been reckoned among the powers of the age, to have maintained my rank, to feel Henry IV. within me, to be great admiral of France—and then to go and get killed at Gigelli, among all those Turks, Saracens, and Moors."

"Monseigneur, you harp with strange persistence on that theme," said Athos, in an agitated voice. "How can you suppose that so brilliant a destiny will be extinguished in that remote and miserable scene?"

"And can you believe, upright and simple as you are, that if I go into Africa for this ridiculous motive, I will not endeavor to come out of it without ridicule? Shall I not give the world cause to speak of me? And to be spoken of, nowadays, when there are Monsieur le Prince, M. de Turenne, and many others, my contemporaries, I, admiral of France, grandson of Henry IV., king of Paris, have I anything left but to get myself killed? *Cordieu!* I will be talked of, I tell you; I shall be killed whether or not; if no there, somewhere else."

"Why, monseigneur, this is mere exaggeration; and hitherto you have shown nothing exaggerated save in bravery."

"*Peste!* my dear friend, there is bravery in facing scurvy, dysentery, locusts, poisoned arrows, as my ancestor St. Louis did. Do you know those fellows still use poisoned arrows? And then, you know me of old, I fancy, and you know that when I once make up my mind to a thing, I perform it in grim earnest."

"Yes, you made up your mind to escape from Vincennes."

"Ay, but you aided me in that, my master; and, *a propos*, I turn this way and that, without seeing my old friend, M. Vaugrimaud. How is he?"

"M. Vaugrimaud is still your highness's most respectful servant," said Athos, smiling.

"I have a hundred pistoles here for him, which I bring as a legacy. My will is made, count."

"Ah! monseigneur! monseigneur!"

"And you may understand that if Grimaud's name were to appear in my will—" The duke began to laugh; then addressing Raoul, who, from the commencement of this conversation, had sunk into a profound reverie, "Young man," said he, "I know there is to be found here a certain De Vouvray wine, and I believe—" Raoul left the room precipitately to order the wine. In the meantime M. de Beaufort took the hand of Athos.

"What do you mean to do with him?" asked he.

"Nothing at present, monseigneur."

"Ah! yes, I know; since the passion of the king for La Valliere."

"Yes, monseigneur."

"That is all true, then, is it? I think I know her, that little La Valliere. She is not particularly handsome, if I remember right?"

"No, monseigneur," said Athos.

"Do you know whom she reminds me of?"

"Does she remind your highness of any one?"

"She reminds me of a very agreeable girl, whose mother lived in the Halles."

"Ah! ah!" said Athos, smiling.

"Oh! the good old times," added M. de Beaufort. "Yes, La Valliere reminds me of that girl."

"Who had a son, had she not?"[3]

"I believe she had," replied the duke, with careless *naivete* and a complaisant forgetfulness, of which no words could translate the tone and the vocal expression. "Now, here is poor Raoul, who is your son, I believe."

"Yes, he is my son, monseigneur."

"And the poor lad has been cut out by the king, and he frets."

"Still better, monseigneur, he abstains."

"You are going to let the boy rust in idleness; it is a mistake. Come, give him to me."

"My wish is to keep him at home, monseigneur. I have no longer anything in the world but him, and as long as he likes to remain—"

"Well, well," replied the duke. "I could, nevertheless, have soon put matters to rights again. I assure you, I think he has in him the stuff of which marechals of France are

---

[3] It is possible that the preceding conversation is an obscure allegorical allusion to the Fronde, or perhaps an intimation that the Duc was the father of Mordaunt, from *Twenty Years After,* but a definite interpretation still eludes modern scholars.

made; I have seen more than one produced from less likely rough material."

"That is very possible, monseigneur; but it is the king who makes marechals of France, and Raoul will never accept anything of the king."

Raoul interrupted this conversation by his return. He preceded Grimaud, whose still steady hands carried the plateau with one glass and a bottle of the duke's favorite wine. On seeing his old *protege*, the duke uttered an exclamation of pleasure.

"Grimaud! Good evening, Grimaud!" said he; "how goes it?"

The servant bowed profoundly, as much gratified as his noble interlocutor.

"Two old friends!" said the duke, shaking honest Grimaud's shoulder after a vigorous fashion; which was followed by another still more profound and delighted bow from Grimaud.

"But what is this, count, only one glass?"

"I should not think of drinking with your highness, unless your highness permitted me," replied Athos, with noble humility.

"*Cordieu!* you were right to bring only one glass, we will both drink out of it, like two brothers in arms. Begin, count."

"Do me the honor," said Athos, gently putting back the glass.

"You are a charming friend," replied the Duc de Beaufort, who drank, and passed the goblet to his companion. "But that is not all," continued he, "I am still thirsty, and I wish to do honor to this handsome young man who stands here. I carry good luck with me, vicomte," said he to Raoul; "wish for something while drinking out of my glass, and may the black plague grab me if what you wish does not come to pass!" He held the goblet to Raoul, who hastily moistened his lips, and replied with the same promptitude:

"I have wished for something, monseigneur." His eyes sparkled with a gloomy fire, and the blood mounted to his cheeks; he terrified Athos, if only with his smile.

"And what have you wished for?" replied the duke, sinking back into his fauteuil, whilst with one hand he returned the bottle to Grimaud, and with the other gave him a purse.

"Will you promise me, monseigneur, to grant me what I wish for?"

"*Pardieu!* That is agreed upon."

"I wished, monsieur le duc, to go with you to Gigelli."

Athos became pale, and was unable to conceal his agitation. The duke looked at his friend, as if desirous to assist him to parry this unexpected blow.

"That is difficult, my dear vicomte, very difficult," added he, in a lower tone of voice.

"Pardon me, monseigneur, I have been indiscreet," replied Raoul, in a firm voice; "but as you yourself invited me to wish—"

"To wish to leave me?" said Athos.

"Oh! monsieur—can you imagine—"

"Well, *mordieu!*" cried the duke, "the young vicomte is right! What can he do here? He will go moldy with grief."

Raoul blushed, and the excitable prince continued: "War is a distraction: we gain everything by it; we can only lose one thing by it—life—then so much the worse!"

"That is to say, memory," said Raoul, eagerly; "and that is to say, so much the better!"

He repented of having spoken so warmly when he saw Athos rise and open the window; which was, doubtless, to conceal his emotion. Raoul sprang towards the comte, but the latter had already overcome his emotion, and turned to the lights with a serene and impassible countenance. "Well, come," said the duke, "let us see! Shall he go, or shall he not? If he goes, comte, he shall be my aide-de-camp, my son."

"Monseigneur!" cried Raoul, bending his knee.

"Monseigneur!" cried Athos, taking the hand of the duke; "Raoul shall do just as he likes."

"Oh! no, monsieur, just as you like," interrupted the young man.

"*Par la corbleu!*" said the prince in his turn, "it is neither the comte nor the vicomte that shall have his way, it is I. I will take him away. The marine offers a superb fortune, my friend."

Raoul smiled again so sadly, that this time Athos felt his heart penetrated by it, and replied to him by a severe look. Raoul comprehended it all; he recovered his calmness, and was so guarded, that not another word escaped him. The duke at length rose, on observing the advanced hour, and said, with animation, "I am in great haste, but if I am told I have lost time in talking with a friend, I will reply I have gained—on the balance—a most excellent recruit."

"Pardon me, monsieur le duc," interrupted Raoul, "do not tell the king so, for it is not the king I wish to serve."

"Eh! my friend, whom, then, will you serve? The times are past when you might have said, 'I belong to M. de Beaufort.' No, nowadays, we all belong to the king, great or small. Therefore, if you serve on board my vessels, there can be nothing equivocal about it, my dear vicomte; it will be the king you will serve."

Athos waited with a kind of impatient joy for the reply about to be made to this embarrassing question by Raoul, the intractable enemy of the king, his rival. The father hoped that the obstacle would overcome the desire. He was thankful to M. de Beaufort, whose lightness or generous reflection had thrown an impediment in the way of the departure of a son, now his only joy. But Raoul, still firm and tranquil, replied: "Monsieur le duc, the objection you make I have already considered in my mind. I will serve on board your vessels, because you do me the honor to take me with you; but I shall there serve a more powerful master than the king: I shall serve God!"

"God! how so?" said the duke and Athos together.

"My intention is to make profession, and become a knight of Malta," added Bragelonne, letting fall, one by one, words more icy than the drops which fall from the bare trees after the tempests of winter.[4]

Under this blow Athos staggered and the prince himself was moved. Grimaud uttered a heavy groan, and let fall the bottle, which was broken without anybody paying attention. M. de Beaufort looked the young man in the face, and read plainly, though his eyes were cast down, the fire of resolution before which everything must give way. As to Athos, he was too well acquainted with that tender, but inflexible soul; he could not hope to make it deviate from the fatal road it had just chosen. He could only press the hand the duke held out to him. "Comte, I shall set off in two days for Toulon," said M. de Beaufort. "Will you meet me at Paris, in order that I may know your determination?"

"I will have the honor of thanking you there, *mon prince*, for all your kindness," replied the comte.

"And be sure to bring the vicomte with you, whether he follows me or does not follow me," added the duke; "he has my word, and I only ask yours."

Having thrown a little balm upon the wound of the paternal heart, he pulled the ear of Grimaud, whose eyes sparkled more than usual, and regained his escort in the parterre. The horses, rested and refreshed, set off with spirit through the lovely night, and soon placed a considerable distance between their master and the chateau.

Athos and Bragelonne were again face to face. Eleven o'clock was striking. The father and son preserved a profound

---

[4] The dictates of such a service would require Raoul to spend the rest of his life outside of France, hence Athos's and Grimaud's extreme reactions.

silence towards each other, where an intelligent observer would have expected cries and tears. But these two men were of such a nature that all emotion following their final resolutions plunged itself so deep into their hearts that it was lost forever. They passed, then, silently and almost breathlessly, the hour that preceded midnight. The clock, by striking, alone pointed out to them how many minutes had lasted the painful journey made by their souls in the immensity of their remembrances of the past and fear of the future. Athos rose first, saying, "it is late, then. . . . Till to-morrow."

Raoul rose, and in his turn embraced his father. The latter held him clasped to his breast, and said, in a tremulous voice, "In two days, you will have left me, my son—left me forever, Raoul!"

"Monsieur," replied the young man, "I had formed a determination, that of piercing my heart with my sword; but you would have thought that cowardly. I have renounced that determination, and *therefore* we must part."

"You leave me desolate by going, Raoul."

"Listen to me again, monsieur, I implore you. If I do not go, I shall die here of grief and love. I know how long a time I have to live thus. Send me away quickly, monsieur, or you will see me basely die before your eyes—in your house—this is stronger than my will—stronger than my strength—you may plainly see that within one month I have lived thirty years, and that I approach the end of my life."

"Then," said Athos, coldly, "you go with the intention of getting killed in Africa? Oh, tell me! do not lie!"

Raoul grew deadly pale, and remained silent for two seconds, which were to his father two hours of agony. Then, all at once: "Monsieur," said he, "I have promised to devote myself to God. In exchange for the sacrifice I make of my youth and liberty, I will only ask of Him one thing, and that is, to preserve me for you, because you are the only tie which attaches me to this world. God alone can give me the strength not to forget that I owe you everything, and that nothing ought to stand in my esteem before you."

Athos embraced his son tenderly, and said:

"You have just replied to me on the word of honor of an honest man; in two days we shall be with M. de Beaufort at Paris, and you will then do what will be proper for you to do. You are free, Raoul; adieu."

And he slowly gained his bedroom. Raoul went down into the garden, and passed the night in the alley of limes.

CHAPTER 28

Preparations for Departure.

Athos lost no more time in combating this immutable resolution. He gave all his attention to preparing, during the two days the duke had granted him, the proper appointments for Raoul. This labor chiefly concerned Grimaud, who immediately applied himself to it with the good-will and intelligence we know he possessed. Athos gave this worthy servant orders to take the route to Paris when the equipments should be ready; and, not to expose himself to the danger of keeping the duke waiting, or delaying Raoul, so that the duke should perceive his absence, he himself, the day after the visit of M. de Beaufort, set off for Paris with his son.

For the poor young man it was an emotion easily to be understood, thus to return to Paris amongst all the people who had known and loved him. Every face recalled a pang to him who had suffered so much; to him who had loved so much, some circumstance of his unhappy love. Raoul, on approaching Paris, felt as if he were dying. Once in Paris, he really existed no longer. When he reached Guiche's residence, he was informed that Guiche was with Monsieur. Raoul took the road to the Luxembourg, and when arrived, without suspecting that he was going to the place where La Valliere had lived, he heard so much music and respired so many perfumes, he heard so much joyous laughter, and saw so many dancing shadows, that if it had not been for a charitable woman, who perceived him so dejected and pale beneath a doorway, he would have remained there a few minutes, and then would have gone away, never to return. But, as we have said, in the first ante-chamber he had stopped, solely for the sake of not mixing himself with all those happy beings he felt were moving around him in the adjacent salons. And as one of Monsieur's servants, recognizing him, had asked him if he wished to see Monsieur or Madame, Raoul had scarcely answered him, but had sunk down upon a bench near the velvet doorway, looking at a clock, which had stopped for nearly an hour. The servant had passed on, and another, better acquainted with him, had come up, and interrogated Raoul whether he should inform M. de Guiche of his being there. This name did not even arouse the recollections of Raoul. The persistent servant went on to relate that De Guiche had just invented a new game of lottery, and was teaching it to the ladies. Raoul, opening his large eyes, like the absent man in Theophrastus, made no answer, but his sadness increased two shades. With his head hanging down, his limbs relaxed, his mouth half open for the escape of his sighs, Raoul remained, thus forgotten, in the ante-chamber, when all at once a lady's robe passed, rubbing against the doors of a side salon, which opened on the gallery. A lady, young, pretty, and gay, scolding an officer of the household, entered by that way, and expressed herself with much vivacity. The officer replied in calm but firm sentences; it was rather a little love pet than a quarrel of courtiers, and was terminated by a kiss on the fingers of the lady. Suddenly, on perceiving Raoul, the lady became silent, and pushing away the officer:

"Make your escape, Malicorne," said she; "I did not think

there was any one here. I shall curse you, if they have either heard or seen us!"

Malicorne hastened away. The young lady advanced behind Raoul, and stretching her joyous face over him as he lay:

"Monsieur is a gallant man," said she, "and no doubt—"

She here interrupted herself by uttering a cry. "Raoul!" said she, blushing.

"Mademoiselle de Montalais!" said Raoul, paler than death.

He rose unsteadily, and tried to make his way across the slippery mosaic of the floor; but she had comprehended that savage and cruel grief; she felt that in the flight of Raoul there was an accusation of herself. A woman, ever vigilant, she did not think she ought to let the opportunity slip of making good her justification; but Raoul, though stopped by her in the middle of the gallery, did not seem disposed to surrender without a combat. He took it up in a tone so cold and embarrassed, that if they had been thus surprised, the whole court would have no doubt about the proceedings of Mademoiselle de Montalais.

"Ah! monsieur," said she with disdain, "what you are doing is very unworthy of a gentleman. My heart inclines me to speak to you; you compromise me by a reception almost uncivil; you are wrong, monsieur; and you confound your friends with enemies. Farewell!"

Raoul had sworn never to speak of Louise, never even to look at those who might have seen Louise; he was going into another world, that he might never meet with anything Louise had seen, or even touched. But after the first shock of his pride, after having had a glimpse of Montalais, the companion of Louise—Montalais, who reminded him of the turret of Blois and the joys of youth—all his reason faded away.

"Pardon me, mademoiselle; it enters not, it cannot enter into my thoughts to be uncivil."

"Do you wish to speak to me?" said she, with the smile of former days. "Well! come somewhere else; for we may be surprised."

"Oh!" said he.

She looked at the clock, doubtingly, then, having reflected:

"In my apartment," said she, "we shall have an hour to ourselves." And taking her course, lighter than a fairy, she ran up to her chamber, followed by Raoul. Shutting the door, and placing in the hands of her *cameriste* the mantle she had held upon her arm:

"You were seeking M. de Guiche, were you not?" said she to Raoul.

"Yes, mademoiselle."

"I will go and ask him to come up here, presently, after I have spoken to you."

"Do so, mademoiselle."

"Are you angry with me?"

Raoul looked at her for a moment, then, casting down his eyes, "Yes," said he.

"You think I was concerned in the plot which brought about the rupture, do you not?"

"Rupture!" said he, with bitterness. "Oh! mademoiselle, there can be no rupture where there has been no love."

"You are in error," replied Montalais; "Louise did love you."

Raoul started.

"Not with love, I know; but she liked you, and you ought to have married her before you set out for London."

Raoul broke into a sinister laugh, which made Montalais shudder.

"You tell me that very much at your ease, mademoiselle. Do people marry whom they like? You forget that the king then kept for himself as his mistress her of whom we are speaking."

"Listen," said the young woman, pressing the hands of

Raoul in her own, "you were wrong in every way; a man of your age ought never to leave a woman of hers alone."

"There is no longer any faith in the world, then," said Raoul.

"No, vicomte," said Montalais, quietly. "Nevertheless, let me tell you that, if, instead of loving Louise coldly and philosophically, you had endeavored to awaken her to love—"

"Enough, I pray you, mademoiselle," said Raoul. "I feel as though you are all, of both sexes, of a different age from me. You can laugh, and you can banter agreeably. I, mademoiselle, I loved Mademoiselle de—" Raoul could not pronounce her name,—"I loved her well! I put my faith in her—now I am quits by loving her no longer."

"Oh, vicomte!" said Montalais, pointing to his reflection in a looking-glass.

"I know what you mean, mademoiselle; I am much altered, am I not? Well! Do you know why? Because my face is the mirror of my heart, the outer surface changed to match the mind within."

"You are consoled, then?" said Montalais, sharply.

"No, I shall never be consoled."

"I don't understand you, M. de Bragelonne."

"I care but little for that. I do not quite understand myself."

"You have not even tried to speak to Louise?"

"Who! I?" exclaimed the young man, with eyes flashing fire; "I!—Why do you not advise me to marry her? Perhaps the king would consent now." And he rose from his chair full of anger.

"I see," said Montalais, "that you are not cured, and that Louise has one enemy the more."

"One enemy the more!"

"Yes; favorites are but little beloved at the court of France."

"Oh! while she has her lover to protect her, is not that

enough? She has chosen him of such a quality that her enemies cannot prevail against her." But, stopping all at once, "And then she has you for a friend, mademoiselle," added he, with a shade of irony which did not glide off the cuirass.

"Who! I?—Oh, no! I am no longer one of those whom Mademoiselle de la Valliere condescends to look upon; but—"

This *but*, so big with menace and with storm; this *but*, which made the heart of Raoul beat, such griefs did it presage for her whom lately he loved so dearly; this terrible *but*, so significant in a woman like Montalais, was interrupted by a moderately loud noise heard by the speakers proceeding from the alcove behind the wainscoting. Montalais turned to listen, and Raoul was already rising, when a lady entered the room quietly by the secret door, which she closed after her.

"Madame!" exclaimed Raoul, on recognizing the sister-in-law of the king.

"Stupid wretch!" murmured Montalais, throwing herself, but too late, before the princess, "I have been mistaken in an hour!" She had, however, time to warn the princess, who was walking towards Raoul.

"M. de Bragelonne, Madame," and at these words the princess drew back, uttering a cry in her turn.

"Your royal highness," said Montalais, with volubility, "is kind enough to think of this lottery, and—"

The princess began to lose countenance. Raoul hastened his departure, without divining all, but he felt that he was in the way. Madame was preparing a word of transition to recover herself, when a closet opened in front of the alcove, and M. de Guiche issued, all radiant, also from that closet. The palest of the four, we must admit, was still Raoul. The princess, however, was near fainting, and was obliged to lean upon the foot of the bed for support. No one ventured to support her. This scene occupied several minutes of terrible suspense. But Raoul broke it. He went up to the count, whose inexpressible emotion made his knees tremble, and taking his hand, "Dear count," said he, "tell Madame I am too unhappy not to merit pardon; tell her also that I have loved in the course of my life, and that the horror of the treachery that has been practiced on me renders me inexorable towards all other treachery that may be committed around me. This is why, mademoiselle," said he, smiling to Montalais, "I never would divulge the secret of the visits of my friend to your apartment. Obtain from Madame—from Madame, who is so clement and so generous,—obtain her pardon for you whom she has just surprised also. You are both free, love each other, be happy!"

The princess felt for a moment a despair that cannot be described; it was repugnant to her, notwithstanding the exquisite delicacy which Raoul had exhibited, to feel herself at the mercy of one who had discovered such an indiscretion. It was equally repugnant to her to accept the evasion offered by this delicate deception. Agitated, nervous, she struggled against the double stings of these two troubles. Raoul comprehended her position, and came once more to her aid. Bending his knee before her: "Madame!" said he, in a low voice, "in two days I shall be far from Paris; in a fortnight I shall be far from France, where I shall never be seen again."

"Are you going away, then?" said she, with great delight.

"With M. de Beaufort."

"Into Africa!" cried De Guiche, in his turn. "You, Raoul— oh! my friend—into Africa, where everybody dies!"

And forgetting everything, forgetting that that forgetfulness itself compromised the princess more eloquently than his presence, "Ingrate!" said he, "and you have not even consulted me!" And he embraced him; during which time Montalais had led away Madame, and disappeared herself.

Raoul passed his hand over his brow, and said, with a smile, "I have been dreaming!" Then warmly to Guiche, who by degrees absorbed him, "My friend," said he, "I conceal nothing from you, who are the elected of my heart. I am going to seek death in yonder country; your secret will not remain in my breast more than a year."

"Oh, Raoul! a man!"

"Do you know what is my thought, count? This is it—I shall live more vividly, being buried beneath the earth, than I have lived for this month past. We are Christians, my friend, and if such sufferings were to continue, I would not be answerable for the safety of my soul."

De Guiche was anxious to raise objections.

"Not one word more on my account," said Raoul; "but advice to you, dear friend; what I am going to say to you is of much greater importance."

"What is that?"

"Without doubt you risk much more than I do, because you love."

"Oh!"

"It is a joy so sweet to me to be able to speak to you thus! Well, then, De Guiche, beware of Montalais."

"What! of that kind friend?"

"She was the friend of—her you know of. She ruined her by pride."

"You are mistaken."

"And now, when she has ruined her, she would ravish from her the only thing that renders that woman excusable in my eyes."

"What is that?"

"Her love."

"What do you mean by that?"

"I mean that there is a plot formed against her who is the mistress of the king—a plot formed in the very house of Madame."

"Can you think so?"

"I am certain of it."

"By Montalais?"

"Take her as the least dangerous of the enemies I dread for—the other!"

"Explain yourself clearly, my friend; and if I can understand you—"

"In two words. Madame has been long jealous of the king."

"I know she has—"

"Oh! fear nothing—you are beloved—you are beloved, count; do you feel the value of these three words? They signify that you can raise your head, that you can sleep tranquilly, that you can thank God every minute of you life. You are beloved; that signifies that you may hear everything, even the counsel of a friend who wishes to preserve your happiness. You are beloved, De Guiche, you are beloved! You do not endure those atrocious nights, those nights without end, which, with arid eye and fainting heart, others pass through who are destined to die. You will live long, if you act like the miser who, bit by bit, crumb by crumb, collects and heaps up diamonds and gold. You are beloved!— allow me to tell you what you must do that you may be beloved forever."

De Guiche contemplated for some time this unfortunate young man, half mad with despair, till there passed through his heart something like remorse at his own happiness. Raoul suppressed his feverish excitement, to assume the voice and countenance of an impassible man.

"They will make her, whose name I should wish still to be able to pronounce—they will make her suffer. Swear to me that you will not second them in anything—but that you will defend her when possible, as I would have done myself."

"I swear I will," replied De Guiche.

"And," continued Raoul, "some day, when you shall have rendered her a great service—some day when she shall thank you, promise me to say these words to her—'I have done you this kindness, madame, at the warm request of M. de Bragelonne, whom you so deeply injured.'"

"I swear I will," murmured De Guiche.

"That is all. Adieu! I set out to-morrow, or the day after, for Toulon. If you have a few hours to spare, give them to me."

"All! all!" cried the young man.

"Thank you!"

"And what are you going to do now?"

"I am going to meet M. le comte at Planchet's residence, where we hope to find M. d'Artagnan."

"M. d'Artagnan?"

"Yes, I wish to embrace him before my departure. He is a brave man, who loves me dearly. Farewell, my friend; you are expected, no doubt; you will find me, when you wish, at the lodgings of the comte. Farewell!"

The two young men embraced. Those who chanced to see them both thus, would not have hesitated to say, pointing to Raoul, "That is the happy man!"

CHAPTER 29

Planchet's Inventory.

Athos, during the visit made to the Luxembourg by Raoul, had gone to Planchet's residence to inquire after D'Artagnan. The comte, on arriving at the Rue des Lombards, found the shop of the grocer in great confusion; but it was not the encumberment of a lucky sale, or that of an arrival of goods. Planchet was not enthroned, as usual, on sacks and barrels. No. A young man with a pen behind his ear, and another with an account-book in his hand, were setting down a number of figures, whilst a third counted and weighed. An inventory was being taken. Athos, who had no knowledge of commercial matters, felt himself a little embarrassed by material obstacles and the majesty of those who were thus employed. He saw several customers sent away, and asked himself whether he, who came to buy nothing, would not be more properly deemed importunate. He therefore asked very politely if he could see M. Planchet. The reply, quite carelessly given, was that M. Planchet was packing his trunks. These words surprised Athos. "What! his trunks?" said he; "is M. Planchet going away?"

"Yes, monsieur, directly."

"Then, if you please, inform him that M. le Comte de la Fere desires to speak to him for a moment."

At the mention of the comte's name, one of the young

men, no doubt accustomed to hear it pronounced with respect, immediately went to inform Planchet. It was at this moment that Raoul, after his painful scene with Montalais and De Guiche, arrived at the grocer's house. Planchet left his job directly he received the comte's message.

"Ah! monsieur le comte!" exclaimed he, "how glad I am to see you! What good star brings you here?"

"My dear Planchet," said Athos, pressing the hand of his son, whose sad look he silently observed,—"we are come to learn of you—But in what confusion do I find you! You are as white as a miller; where have you been rummaging?"

"Ah, *diable!* take care, monsieur; don't come near me till I have well shaken myself."

"What for? Flour or dust only whiten."

"No, no; what you see on my arms is arsenic."

"Arsenic?"

"Yes; I am taking my precautions against rats."

"Ay, I suppose in an establishment like this, rats play a conspicuous part."

"It is not with this establishment I concern myself, monsieur le comte. The rats have robbed me of more here than they will ever rob me of again."

"What do you mean?"

"Why, you may have observed, monsieur, my inventory is being taken."

"Are you leaving trade, then?"

"Eh! *mon Dieu!* yes. I have disposed of my business to one of my young men."

"Bah! you are rich, then, I suppose?"

"Monsieur, I have taken a dislike to the city; I don't know whether it is because I am growing old, and as M. d'Artagnan one day said, when we grow old we more often think of the adventures of our youth; but for some time past I have felt myself attracted towards the country and gardening. I was a countryman formerly." And Planchet marked this confession with a rather pretentious laugh for a man making profession of humility.

Athos made a gesture of approval, and then added: "You are going to buy an estate, then?"

"I have bought one, monsieur."

"Ah! that is still better."

"A little house at Fontainebleau, with something like twenty acres of land round it."

"Very well, Planchet! Accept my compliments on your acquisition."

"But, monsieur, we are not comfortable here; the cursed dust makes you cough. *Corbleu!* I do not wish to poison the most worthy gentleman in the kingdom."

Athos did not smile at this little pleasantry which Planchet had aimed at him, in order to try his strength in mundane facetiousness.

"Yes," said Athos, "let us have a little talk by ourselves—in your own room, for example. You have a room, have you not?"

"Certainly, monsieur le comte."

"Upstairs, perhaps?" And Athos, seeing Planchet a little embarrassed, wished to relieve him by going first.

"It is—but—" said Planchet, hesitating.

Athos was mistaken in the cause of this hesitation, and, attributing it to a fear the grocer might have of offering humble hospitality, "Never mind, never mind," said he, still going up, "the dwelling of a tradesman in this quarter is not expected to be a palace. Come on."

Raoul nimbly preceded him, and entered first. Two cries were heard simultaneously—we may say three. One of these cries dominated the others; it emanated from a woman. Another proceeded from the mouth of Raoul; it was an exclamation of surprise. He had no sooner uttered it than he shut the door sharply. The third was from fright; it came from Planchet.

"I ask your pardon!" added he; "madame is dressing."

Raoul had, no doubt, seen that what Planchet said was true, for he turned round to go downstairs again.

"Madame—" said Athos. "Oh! pardon me, Planchet, I did not know that you had upstairs—"

"It is Truchen," added Planchet, blushing a little.

"It is whoever you please, my good Planchet; but pardon my rudeness."

"No, no; go up now, gentlemen."

"We will do no such thing," said Athos.

"Oh! madame, having notice, has had time—"

"No, Planchet; farewell!"

"Eh, gentlemen! you would not disoblige me by thus standing on the staircase, or by going away without having sat down."

"If we had known you had a lady upstairs," replied Athos, with his customary coolness, "we would have asked permission to pay our respects to her."

Planchet was so disconcerted by this little extravagance, that he forced the passage, and himself opened the door to admit the comte and his son. Truchen was quite dressed: in the costume of the shopkeeper's wife, rich yet coquettish; German eyes attacking French eyes. She left the apartment after two courtesies, and went down into the shop—but not without having listened at the door, to know what Planchet's gentlemen visitors would say of her. Athos suspected that, and therefore turned the conversation accordingly. Planchet, on his part, was burning to give explanations, which Athos avoided. But, as certain tenacities are stronger than others, Athos was forced to hear Planchet recite his idyls of felicity, translated into a language more chaste than that of Longus. So Planchet related how Truchen had charmed the years of his advancing age, and brought good luck to his business, as Ruth did to Boaz.

"You want nothing now, then, but heirs to your property."

"If I had one he would have three hundred thousand livres," said Planchet.

"Humph! you must have one, then," said Athos, phlegmatically, "if only to prevent your little fortune being lost."

This word *little fortune* placed Planchet in his rank, like the voice of the sergeant when Planchet was but a *piqueur* in the regiment of Piedmont, in which Rochefort had placed him. Athos perceived that the grocer would marry Truchen, and, in spite of fate, establish a family. This appeared the more evident to him when he learned that the young man to whom Planchet was selling the business was her cousin. Having heard all that was necessary of the happy prospects of the retiring grocer, "What is M. d'Artagnan about?" said he; "he is not at the Louvre."

"Ah! monsieur le comte, Monsieur d'Artagnan has disappeared."

"Disappeared!" said Athos, in surprise.

"Oh! monsieur, we know what that means."

"But *I* do not know."

"Whenever M. d'Artagnan disappears it is always for some mission or some great affair."

"Has he said anything to you about it?"

"Never."

"You were acquainted with his departure for England formerly, were you not?"

"On account of the speculation," said Planchet, heedlessly.

"The speculation!"

"I mean—" interrupted Planchet, quite confused.

"Well, well; neither your affairs nor those of your master are in question; the interest we take in him alone has induced me to apply to you. Since the captain of the musketeers is not here, and as we cannot learn from you where we are likely to find M. d'Artagnan, we will take our leave of you. *Au revoir*, Planchet, *au revoir*. Let us be gone, Raoul."

"Monsieur le comte, I wish I were able to tell you—"

"Oh, not at all; I am not the man to reproach a servant with discretion."

This word "servant" struck rudely on the ears of the *demi-millionnaire* Planchet, but natural respect and *bonhomie* prevailed over pride. "There is nothing indiscreet in telling you, monsieur le comte, M. d'Artagnan came here the other day—"

"Aha?"

"And remained several hours consulting a geographical chart."

"You are right, then, my friend; say no more about it."

"And the chart is there as a proof," added Planchet, who went to fetch from the neighboring wall, where it was suspended by a twist, forming a triangle with the bar of the window to which it was fastened, the plan consulted by the captain on his last visit to Planchet. This plan, which he brought to the comte, was a map of France, upon which the practiced eye of that gentleman discovered an itinerary, marked out with small pins; wherever a pin was missing, a hole denoted its having been there. Athos, by following with his eye the pins and holes, saw that D'Artagnan had taken the direction of the south, and gone as far as the Mediterranean, towards Toulon. It was near Cannes that the marks and the punctured places ceased. The Comte de la Fere puzzled his brains for some time, to divine what the musketeer could be going to do at Cannes, and what motive could have led him to examine the banks of the Var. The reflections of Athos suggested nothing. His accustomed perspicacity was at fault. Raoul's researches were not more successful than his father's.

"Never mind," said the young man to the comte, who silently, and with his finger, had made him understand the route of D'Artagnan; "we must confess that there is a Providence always occupied in connecting our destiny with that of M. d'Artagnan. There he is on the coast of Cannes, and you, monsieur, will, at least, conduct me as far as Toulon. Be assured that we shall meet with him more easily upon our route than on this map."

Then, taking leave of Planchet, who was scolding his shopmen, even the cousin of Truchen, his successor, the gentlemen set out to pay a visit to M. de Beaufort. On leaving the grocer's shop, they saw a coach, the future depository of the charms of Mademoiselle Truchen and Planchet's bags of crowns.

"Every one journeys towards happiness by the route he chooses," said Raoul, in a melancholy tone.

"Road to Fontainebleau!" cried Planchet to his coachman.

CHAPTER 30

The Inventory of M. de Beaufort.

To have talked of D'Artagnan with Planchet, to have seen Planchet quit Paris to bury himself in his country retreat, had been for Athos and his son like a last farewell to the noise of the capital—to their life of former days. What, in fact, did these men leave behind them—one of whom had exhausted the past age in glory, and the other, the present age in misfortune? Evidently neither of them had anything to ask of his contemporaries. They had only to pay a visit to M. de Beaufort, and arrange with him the particulars of departure. The duke was lodged magnificently in Paris. He had one of those superb establishments pertaining to great fortunes, the like of which certain old men remembered to have seen in all their glory in the times of wasteful liberality of Henry III.'s reign. Then, really, several great nobles were richer than the king. They knew it, used it, and never deprived themselves of the pleasure of humiliating his royal majesty when they had an opportunity. It was this egotistical aristocracy Richelieu had constrained to contribute, with its blood, its purse, and its duties, to what was from his time styled the king's service. From Louis XI.—that terrible mower-down of the great—to Richelieu, how many families had raised their heads! How many, from Richelieu to Louis

XIV., had bowed their heads, never to raise them again! But M. de Beaufort was born a prince, and of a blood which is not shed upon scaffolds, unless by the decree of peoples,—a prince who had kept up a grand style of living. How did he maintain his horses, his people, and his table? Nobody knew; himself less than others. Only there were then privileges for the sons of kings, to whom nobody refused to become a creditor, whether from respect or the persuasion that they would some day be paid.

Athos and Raoul found the mansion of the duke in as much confusion as that of Planchet. The duke, likewise, was making his inventory; that is to say, he was distributing to his friends everything of value he had in his house. Owing nearly two millions—an enormous amount in those days—M. de Beaufort had calculated that he could not set out for Africa without a good round sum, and, in order to find that sum, he was distributing to his old creditors plate, arms, jewels, and furniture, which was more magnificent in selling it, and brought him back double. In fact, how could a man to whom ten thousand livres were owing, refuse to carry away a present worth six thousand, enhanced in estimation from having belonged to a descendant of Henry IV.? And how, after having carried away that present, could he refuse ten thousand livres more to this generous noble? This, then, was what had happened. The duke had no longer a dwelling-house—that had become useless to an admiral whose place of residence is his ship; he had no longer need of superfluous arms, when he was placed amidst his cannons; no more jewels, which the sea might rob him of; but he had three or four hundred thousand crowns fresh in his coffers. And throughout the house there was a joyous movement of people who believed they were plundering monseigneur. The prince had, in a supreme degree, the art of making happy the creditors most to be pitied. Every distressed man, every empty purse, found in him patience and sympathy for his position. To some he said, "I wish I had what *you* have; I would give it you." And to others, "I have but this silver ewer; it is worth at least five hundred livres,—take it." The effect of which was—so truly is courtesy a current payment—that the prince constantly found means to renew his creditors. This time he used no ceremony; it might be called a general pillage. He gave up everything. The Oriental fable of the poor Arab who carried away from the pillage of palace a kettle at the bottom of which was concealed a bag of gold, and whom everybody allowed to pass without jealousy,—this fable had become a truth in the prince's mansion. Many contractors paid themselves upon the offices of the duke. Thus, the provision department, who plundered the clothes-presses and the harness-rooms, attached very little value to things which tailors and saddlers set great store by. Anxious to carry home to their wives presents given them by monseigneur, many were seen bounding joyously along, under the weight of earthen jars and bottles, gloriously stamped with the arms of the prince. M. de Beaufort finished by giving away his horses and the hay from his lofts. He made more than thirty happy with kitchen utensils; and thirty more with the contents of his cellar. Still further; all these people went away with the conviction that M. de Beaufort only acted in this manner to prepare for a new fortune concealed beneath the Arabs' tents. They repeated to each other, while pillaging his hotel, that he was sent to Gigelli by the king to reconstruct his lost fortunes; that the treasures of Africa would be equally divided between the admiral and the king of France; that these treasures consisted in mines of diamonds, or other fabulous stones; the gold and silver mines of Mount Atlas did not even obtain the honor of being named. In addition to the mines to be worked—which could not be begun till after the campaign—there would be the booty made by the army. M. de Beaufort would lay his hands on all the riches pirates had robbed Christendom of since the battle of Lepanto. The number of millions from these sources defied calculation. Why, then, should he, who was going in quest of such treasure, set any store by the poor utensils of his past life? And reciprocally, why should they spare the property of him who spared it so little himself?

Such was the position of affairs. Athos, with his piercing practiced glance, saw what was going on at once. He found the admiral of France a little exalted, for he was rising from a table of fifty covers, at which the guests had drunk long and deeply to the prosperity of the expedition; at the conclusion of which repast, the remains, with the dessert, had been given to the servants, and the empty dishes and plates to the curious. The prince was intoxicated with his ruin and his popularity at one and the same time. He had drunk his old wine to the health of his wine of the future. When he saw Athos and Raoul:

"There is my aide-de-camp being brought to me!" he cried. "Come hither, comte; come hither, vicomte."

Athos tried to find a passage through the heaps of linen and plate.

"Ah! step over, step over!" said the duke, offering a full glass to Athos. The latter drank it; Raoul scarcely moistened his lips.

"Here is your commission," said the prince to Raoul. "I had prepared it, reckoning upon you. You will go before me as far as Antibes."

"Yes, monseigneur."

"Here is the order." And De Beaufort gave Raoul the order. "Do you know anything of the sea?"

"Yes, monseigneur; I have traveled with M. le Prince."

"That is well. All these barges and lighters must be in attendance to form an escort and carry my provisions. The army must be prepared to embark in a fortnight at the very latest."

"That shall be done, monseigneur."

"The present order gives you the right to visit and search all the isles along the coast; you will there make the enrolments and levies you may want for me."

"Yes, monsieur le duc."

"And you are an active man, and will work freely, you will spend much money."

"I hope not, monseigneur."

"But I am sure you will. My intendant has prepared the orders of a thousand livres, drawn upon the cities of the south; he will give you a hundred of them. Now, dear vicomte, be gone."

Athos interrupted the prince. "Keep your money, monseigneur; war is to be waged among the Arabs with gold as well as lead."

"I wish to try the contrary," replied the duke; "and then you are acquainted with my ideas upon the expedition—plenty of noise, plenty of fire, and, if so it must be, I shall disappear in the smoke." Having spoken thus, M. de Beaufort began to laugh; but his mirth was not reciprocated by Athos and Raoul. He perceived this at once. "Ah," said he, with the courteous egotism of his rank and age, "you are such people as a man should not see after dinner; you are cold, stiff, and dry when I am all fire, suppleness, and wine. No, devil take me! I should always see you fasting, vicomte, and you, comte, if you wear such a face as that, you shall see me no more."

He said this, pressing the hand of Athos, who replied with a smile, "Monseigneur, do not talk so grandly because you happen to have plenty of money. I predict that within a month you will be dry, stiff, and cold, in presence of your strong-box, and that then, having Raoul at your elbow, fasting, you will be surprised to see him gay, animated, and generous, because he will have some new crowns to offer you."

"God grant it may be so!" cried the delighted duke. "Comte, stay with me!"

"No, I shall go with Raoul; the mission with which you charge him is a troublesome and difficult one. Alone it would be too much for him to execute. You do not observe, monseigneur, you have given him command of the first order."

"Bah!"

"And in your naval arrangements, too."

"That may be true. But one finds that such fine young fellows as your son generally do all that is required of them."

"Monseigneur, I believe you will find nowhere so much zeal and intelligence, so much real bravery, as in Raoul; but if he failed to arrange your embarkation, you would only meet the fate that you deserve."

"Humph! you are scolding me, then."

"Monseigneur, to provision a fleet, to assemble a flotilla, to enroll your maritime force, would take an admiral a year. Raoul is a cavalry officer, and you allow him a fortnight!"

"I tell you he will do it."

"He may; but I will go and help him."

"To be sure you will; I reckoned upon you, and still further believe that when we are once at Toulon you will not let him depart alone."

"Oh!" said Athos, shaking his head.

"Patience! patience!"

"Monseigneur, permit us to take our leave."

"Begone, then, and may my good luck attend you."

"Adieu! monseigneur; and may your own good luck attend you likewise."

"Here is an expedition admirably commenced!" said Athos to his son. "No provisions—no store flotilla! What can be done, thus?"

"Humph!" murmured Raoul; "if all are going to do as I am, provisions will not be wanted."

"Monsieur," replied Athos, sternly, "do not be unjust and senseless in your egotism, or your grief, whichever you please to call it. If you set out for this war solely with the intention of getting killed therein, you stand in need of nobody, and it was scarcely worth while to recommend you to M. de Beaufort. But when you have been introduced to the prime commandant—when you have accepted the responsibility of a post in his army, the question is no longer about *you*, but about all those poor soldiers, who, as well as you, have hearts and bodies, who will weep for their country and endure all the necessities of their condition. Remember, Raoul, that officers are ministers as useful to the world as priests, and that they ought to have more charity."

"Monsieur, I know it and have practiced it; I would have continued to do so still, but—"

"You forget also that you are of a country that is proud of its military glory; go and die if you like, but do not die without honor and without advantage to France. Cheer up, Raoul! do not let my words grieve you; I love you, and wish to see you perfect."

"I love your reproaches, monsieur," said the young man, mildly; "they alone may cure me, because they prove to me that some one loves me still."

"And now, Raoul, let us be off; the weather is so fine, the heavens so clear, those heavens which we always find above our heads, which you will see more clear still at Gigelli, and which will speak to you of me there, as they speak to me here of God."

The two gentlemen, after having agreed on this point, talked over the wild freaks of the duke, convinced that France would be served in a very incomplete manner, as regarded both spirit and practice, in the ensuing expedition; and having summed up the ducal policy under the one word vanity, they set forward, in obedience rather to their will than destiny. The sacrifice was half accomplished.

CHAPTER 31

The Silver Dish.

The journey passed off pretty well. Athos and his son traversed France at the rate of fifteen leagues per day; sometimes more, sometimes less, according to the intensity of Raoul's grief. It took them a fortnight to reach Toulón, and they lost all traces of D'Artagnan at Antibes. They were forced to believe that the captain of the musketeers was desirous of preserving an incognito on his route, for Athos derived from his inquiries an assurance that such a cavalier as he described had exchanged his horse for a well-closed carriage on quitting Avignon. Raoul was much affected at not meeting with D'Artagnan. His affectionate heart longed to take a farewell and received consolation from that heart of steel. Athos knew from experience that D'Artagnan became impenetrable when engaged in any serious affair, whether on his own account or on the service of the king. He even feared to offend his friend, or thwart him by too pressing inquiries. And yet when Raoul commenced his labor of classing the flotilla, and got together the *chalands* and lighters to send them to Toulon, one of the fishermen told the comte that his boat had been laid up to refit since a trip he had made on account of a gentleman who was in great haste to embark. Athos, believing that this man was telling a falsehood in order to be left at liberty to fish, and so gain more money when all his companions were gone, insisted upon having the details. The fisherman informed him that six days previously, a man had come in the night to hire his boat, for the purpose of visiting the island of St. Honnorat. The price was agreed upon, but the gentleman had arrived with an immense carriage case, which he insisted upon embarking, in spite of the many difficulties that opposed the operation. The fisherman wished to retract. He had even threatened, but his threats had procured him nothing but a shower of blows from the gentleman's cane, which fell upon his shoulders sharp and long. Swearing and grumbling, he had recourse to the syndic of his brotherhood at Antibes, who administer justice among themselves and protect each other; but the gentleman had exhibited a certain paper, at sight of which the syndic, bowing to the very ground, enjoined obedience from the fisherman, and abused him for having been refractory. They then departed with the freight.

"But all this does not tell us," said Athos, "how you injured your boat."

"This is the way. I was steering towards St. Honnorat as the gentleman desired me; but he changed his mind, and pretended that I could not pass to the south of the abbey."

"And why not?"

"Because, monsieur, there is in front of the square tower of the Benedictines, towards the southern point, the bank of the *Moines*."

"A rock?" asked Athos.

"Level with the water, but below water; a dangerous passage, yet one I have cleared a thousand times; the gentleman required me to land him at Sainte-Marguerite's."

"Well?"

"Well, monsieur!" cried the fisherman, with his *Provencal* accent, "a man is a sailor, or he is not; he knows his course, or he is nothing but a fresh-water lubber. I was obstinate, and wished to try the channel. The gentleman took me by the collar, and told me quietly he would strangle me. My mate armed himself with a hatchet, and so did I. We had the affront of the night before to pay him out for. But the gentleman drew his sword, and used it in such an astonishingly rapid manner, that we neither of us could get near him. I was about to hurl my hatchet at his head, and I had a right to do so, hadn't I, monsieur? for a sailor aboard is master, as a citizen is in his chamber; I was going, then, in self-defense, to cut the gentleman in two, when, all at once—believe me or not, monsieur—the great carriage case opened of itself, I don't know how, and there came out of it a sort of a phantom, his head covered with a black helmet and a black mask, something terrible to look upon, which came towards me threatening with its fist."

"And that was—" said Athos.

"That was the devil, monsieur; for the gentleman, with great glee, cried out, on seeing him: 'Ah! thank you, monseigneur!'"

"A most strange story!" murmured the comte, looking at Raoul.

"And what did you do?" asked the latter of the fisherman.

"You must know, monsieur, that two poor men, such as we are, could be no match for two gentlemen; but when one of them turned out to be the devil, we had no earthly chance! My companion and I did not stop to consult one another; we made but one jump into the sea, for we were within seven or eight hundred feet of the shore."

"Well, and then?"

"Why, and then, monseigneur, as there was a little wind from the southwest, the boat drifted into the sands of Sainte-Marguerite's."

"Oh!—but the travelers?"

"Bah! you need not be uneasy about them! It was pretty plain that one was the devil, and protected the other; for when we recovered the boat, after she got afloat again, instead of finding these two creatures injured by the shock, we found nothing, not even the carriage or the case."

"Very strange! very strange!" repeated the comte. "But after that, what did you do, my friend?"

"I made my complaint to the governor of Sainte-Marguerite's, who brought my finger under my nose by telling me if I plagued him with such silly stories he would have me flogged."

"What! did the governor himself say so?"

"Yes, monsieur; and yet my boat was injured, seriously injured, for the prow is left upon the point of Sainte-Marguerite's, and the carpenter asks a hundred and twenty livres to repair it."

"Very well," replied Raoul; "you will be exempted from the service. Go."

"We will go to Sainte-Marguerite's, shall we?" said the comte to Bragelonne, as the man walked away.

"Yes, monsieur, for there is something to be cleared up; that man does not seem to me to have told the truth."

"Nor to me either, Raoul. The story of the masked man and the carriage having disappeared, may be told to conceal some violence these fellows have committed upon their passengers in the open sea, to punish him for his persistence in embarking."

"I formed the same suspicion; the carriage was more likely to contain property than a man."

"We shall see to that, Raoul. The gentleman very much resembles D'Artagnan; I recognize his methods of proceeding. Alas! we are no longer the young invincibles of former days. Who knows whether the hatchet or the iron bar of this miserable coaster has not succeeded in doing that which the best blades of Europe, balls, and bullets have not been able to do in forty years?"

That same day they set out for Sainte-Marguerite's, on

board a *chasse-maree* come from Toulon under orders. The impression they experienced on landing was a singularly pleasing one. The island seemed loaded with flowers and fruits. In its cultivated part it served as a garden for the governor. Orange, pomegranate, and fig trees bent beneath the weight of their golden or purple fruits. All round this garden, in the uncultivated parts, red partridges ran about in conveys among the brambles and tufts of junipers, and at every step of the comte and Raoul a terrified rabbit quitted his thyme and heath to scuttle away to the burrow. In fact, this fortunate isle was uninhabited. Flat, offering nothing but a tiny bay for the convenience of embarkation, and under the protection of the governor, who went shares with them, smugglers made use of it as a provisional *entrepot*, at the expense of not killing the game or devastating the garden. With this compromise, the governor was in a situation to be satisfied with a garrison of eight men to guard his fortress, in which twelve cannons accumulated coats of moldy green. The governor was a sort of happy farmer, harvesting wines, figs, oil, and oranges, preserving his citrons and *cedrates* in the sun of his casemates. The fortress, encircled by a deep ditch, its only guardian, arose like three heads upon turrets connected with each other by terraces covered with moss.

Athos and Raoul wandered for some time round the fences of the garden without finding any one to introduce them to the governor. They ended by making their own way into the garden. It was at the hottest time of the day. Each living thing sought its shelter under grass or stone. The heavens spread their fiery veils as if to stifle all noises, to envelop all existences; the rabbit under the broom, the fly under the leaf, slept as the wave did beneath the heavens. Athos saw nothing living but a soldier, upon the terrace beneath the second and third court, who was carrying a basket of provisions on his head. This man returned almost immediately without his basket, and disappeared in the shade of his sentry-box. Athos supposed he must have been carrying dinner to some one, and, after having done so, returned to dine himself. All at once they heard some one call out, and raising their heads, perceived in the frame of the bars of the window something of a white color, like a hand that was waved backwards and forwards—something shining, like a polished weapon struck by the rays of the sun. And before they were able to ascertain what it was, a luminous train, accompanied by a hissing sound in the air, called their attention from the donjon to the ground. A second dull noise was heard from the ditch, and Raoul ran to pick up a silver plate which was rolling along the dry sand. The hand that had thrown this plate made a sign to the two gentlemen, and then disappeared. Athos and Raoul, approaching each other, commenced an attentive examination of the dusty plate, and they discovered, in characters traced upon the bottom of it with the point of a knife, this inscription:

"*I am the brother of the king of France—a prisoner to-day— a madman to-morrow. French gentlemen and Christians, pray to God for the soul and the reason of the son of your old rulers.*"

The plate fell from the hands of Athos whilst Raoul was endeavoring to make out the meaning of these dismal words. At the same moment they heard a cry from the top of the donjon. Quick as lightning Raoul bent down his head, and forced down that of his father likewise. A musket-barrel glittered from the crest of the wall. A white smoke floated like a plume from the mouth of the musket, and a ball was flattened against a stone within six inches of the two gentlemen.

"*Cordieu!*" cried Athos. "What, are people assassinated here? Come down, cowards as you are!"

"Yes, come down!" cried Raoul, furiously shaking his fist at the castle.

One of the assailants—he who was about to fire—replied to these cries by an exclamation of surprise; and, as his companion, who wished to continue the attack, had re-seized his loaded musket, he who had cried out threw up the weapon, and the ball flew into the air. Athos and Raoul, seeing them disappear from the platform, expected they would come down to them, and waited with a firm demeanor. Five minutes had not elapsed, when a stroke upon a drum called the eight soldiers of the garrison to arms, and they showed themselves on the other side of the ditch with their muskets in hand. At the head of these men was an officer, whom Athos and Raoul recognized as the one who had fired the first musket. The man ordered the soldiers to "make ready."

"We are going to be shot!" cried Raoul; "but, sword in hand, at least, let us leap the ditch! We shall kill at least two of these scoundrels, when their muskets are empty." And, suiting the action to the word, Raoul was springing forward, followed by Athos, when a well-known voice resounded behind them, "Athos! Raoul!"

"D'Artagnan!" replied the two gentlemen.

"Recover arms! *Mordioux!*" cried the captain to the soldiers. "I was sure I could not be mistaken!"

"What is the meaning of this?" asked Athos. "What! were we to be shot without warning?"

"It was I who was going to shoot you, and if the governor missed you, I should not have missed you, my dear friends. How fortunate it is that I am accustomed to take a long aim, instead of firing at the instant I raise my weapon! I thought I recognized you. Ah! my dear friends, how fortunate!" And D'Artagnan wiped his brow, for he had run fast, and emotion with him was not feigned.

"How!" said Athos. "And is the gentleman who fired at us the governor of the fortress?"

"In person."

"And why did he fire at us? What have we done to him?"

"*Pardieu!* You received what the prisoner threw to you?"

"That is true."

"That plate—the prisoner has written something on it, has he not?"

"Yes."

"Good heavens! I was afraid he had."

And D'Artagnan, with all the marks of mortal disquietude, seized the plate, to read the inscription. When he had read it, a fearful pallor spread across his countenance. "Oh! good heavens!" repeated he. "Silence!—Here is the governor."

"And what will he do to us? Is it our fault?"

"It is true, then?" said Athos, in a subdued voice. "It is true?"

"Silence! I tell you—silence! If he only believes you can read; if he only suspects you have understood; I love you, my dear friends, I would willingly be killed for you, but—"

"But—" said Athos and Raoul.

"But I could not save you from perpetual imprisonment if I saved you from death. Silence, then! Silence again!"

The governor came up, having crossed the ditch upon a plank bridge.

"Well!" said he to D'Artagnan, "what stops us?"

"You are Spaniards—you do not understand a word of French," said the captain, eagerly, to his friends in a low voice.

"Well!" replied he, addressing the governor, "I was right; these gentlemen are two Spanish captains with whom I was acquainted at Ypres, last year; they don't know a word of French."

"Ah!" said the governor, sharply. "And yet they were trying to read the inscription on the plate."

D'Artagnan took it out of his hands, effacing the characters with the point of his sword.

"How!" cried the governor, "what are you doing? I cannot read them now!"

"It is a state secret," replied D'Artagnan, bluntly; "and as you know that, according to the king's orders, it is under the penalty of death any one should penetrate it, I will, if you like, allow you to read it, and have you shot immediately afterwards."

During this apostrophe—half serious, half ironical—Athos and Raoul preserved the coolest, most unconcerned silence.

"But, is it possible," said the governor, "that these gentlemen do not comprehend at least some words?"

"Suppose they do! If they do understand a few spoken words, it does not follow that they should understand what is written. They cannot even read Spanish. A noble Spaniard, remember, ought never to know how to read."

The governor was obliged to be satisfied with these explanations, but he was still tenacious. "Invite these gentlemen to come to the fortress," said he.

"That I will willingly do. I was about to propose it to you." The fact is, the captain had quite another idea, and would have wished his friends a hundred leagues off. But he was obliged to make the best of it. He addressed the two gentlemen in Spanish, giving them a polite invitation, which they accepted. They all turned towards the entrance of the fort, and, the incident being at an end, the eight soldiers returned to their delightful leisure, for a moment disturbed by this unexpected adventure.

CHAPTER 32

Captive and Jailers.

When they had entered the fort, and whilst the governor was making some preparations for the reception of his guests, "Come," said Athos, "let us have a word of explanation whilst we are alone."

"It is simply this," replied the musketeer. "I have conducted hither a prisoner, who the king commands shall not be seen. You came here, he has thrown something to you through the lattice of his window; I was at dinner with the governor, I saw the object thrown, and I saw Raoul pick it up. It does not take long to understand this. I understood it, and I thought you in intelligence with my prisoner. And then—"

"And then—you commanded us to be shot."

"*Ma foi!* I admit it; but, if I was the first to seize a musket, fortunately, I was the last to take aim at you."

"If you had killed me, D'Artagnan, I should have had the good fortune to die for the royal house of France, and it would be an honor to die by your hand—you, its noblest and most loyal defender."

"What the devil, Athos, do you mean by the royal house?" stammered D'Artagnan. "You don't mean that you, a well-informed and sensible man, can place any faith in the nonsense written by an idiot?"

"I do believe in it."

"With so much the more reason, my dear chevalier, from your having orders to kill all those who do believe in it," said Raoul.

"That is because," replied the captain of the musketeers—"because every calumny, however absurd it may be, has the almost certain chance of becoming popular."

"No, D'Artagnan," replied Athos, promptly; "but because the king is not willing that the secret of his family should transpire among the people, and cover with shame the executioners of the son of Louis XIII."

"Do not talk in such a childish manner, Athos, or I shall begin to think you have lost your senses. Besides, explain to me how it is possible Louis XIII. should have a son in the Isle of Sainte-Marguerite."

"A son whom you have brought hither masked, in a fishing-boat," said Athos. "Why not?"

D'Artagnan was brought to a pause.

"Oh!" said he; "whence do you know that a fishing-boat—?"

"Brought you to Sainte-Marguerite's with the carriage containing the prisoner—with a prisoner whom you styled monseigneur. Oh! I am acquainted with all that," resumed the comte. D'Artagnan bit his mustache.

"If it were true," said he, "that I had brought hither in a boat and with a carriage a masked prisoner, nothing proves that this prisoner must be a prince—a prince of the house of France."

"Ask Aramis such riddles," replied Athos, coolly.

"Aramis," cried the musketeer, quite at a stand. "Have you seen Aramis?"

"After his discomfiture at Vaux, yes; I have seen Aramis, a fugitive, pursued, bewildered, ruined; and Aramis has told me enough to make me believe in the complaints this unfortunate young prince cut upon the bottom of the plate."

D'Artagnan's head sunk on his breast in some confusion. "This is the way," said he, "in which God turns to nothing that which men call wisdom! A fine secret must that be of which twelve or fifteen persons hold the tattered fragments! Athos, cursed be the chance which has brought you face to face with me in this affair! for now—"

"Well," said Athos, with his customary mild severity, "is your secret lost because I know it? Consult your memory, my friend. Have I not borne secrets heavier than this?"

"You have never borne one so dangerous," replied D'Artagnan, in a tone of sadness. "I have something like a sinister idea that all who are concerned with this secret will die, and die unhappily."

"The will of God be done!" said Athos, "but here is your governor."

D'Artagnan and his friends immediately resumed their parts. The governor, suspicious and hard, behaved towards D'Artagnan with a politeness almost amounting to obsequiousness. With respect to the travelers, he contented himself with offering good cheer, and never taking his eye from them. Athos and Raoul observed that he often tried to embarrass them by sudden attacks, or to catch them off their guard; but neither the one nor the other gave him the least advantage. What D'Artagnan had said was probable, if the governor did not believe it to be quite true. They rose from the table to repose awhile.

"What is this man's name? I don't like the looks of him," said Athos to D'Artagnan in Spanish.

"De Saint-Mars," replied the captain.

"He is, then, I suppose, the prince's jailer?"

"Eh! how can I tell? I may be kept at Sainte-Marguerite forever."

"Oh! no, not you!"

"My friend, I am in the situation of a man who finds a

treasure in the midst of a desert. He would like to carry it away, but he cannot; he would like to leave it, but he dares not. The king will not dare to recall me, for no one else would serve him as faithfully as I do; he regrets not having me near him, from being aware that no one would be of so much service near his person as myself. But it will happen as it may please God."

"But," observed Raoul, "your not being certain proves that your situation here is provisional, and you will return to Paris?"

"Ask these gentlemen," interrupted the governor, "what was their purpose in coming to Saint-Marguerite?"

"They came from learning there was a convent of Benedictines at Sainte-Honnorat which is considered curious; and from being told there was excellent shooting in the island."

"That is quite at their service, as well as yours," replied Saint-Mars.

D'Artagnan politely thanked him.

"When will they depart?" added the governor.

"To-morrow," replied D'Artagnan.

M. de Saint-Mars went to make his rounds, and left D'Artagnan alone with the pretended Spaniards.

"Oh!" exclaimed the musketeer, "here is a life and a society that suits me very little. I command this man, and he bores me, *mordioux!* Come, let us have a shot or two at the rabbits; the walk will be beautiful, and not fatiguing. The whole island is but a league and a half in length, with the breadth of a league; a real park. Let us try to amuse ourselves."

"As you please, D'Artagnan; not for the sake of amusing ourselves, but to gain an opportunity for talking freely."

D'Artagnan made a sign to a soldier, who brought the gentlemen some guns, and then returned to the fort.

"And now," said the musketeer, "answer me the question

put to you by that black-looking Saint-Mars: what did you come to do at the Lerin Isles?"

"To bid you farewell."

"Bid me farewell! What do you mean by that? Is Raoul going anywhere?"

"Yes."

"Then I will lay a wager it is with M. de Beaufort."

"With M. de Beaufort it is, my dear friend. You always guess correctly."

"From habit."

Whilst the two friends were commencing their conversation, Raoul, with his head hanging down and his heart oppressed, seated himself on a mossy rock, his gun across his knees, looking at the sea—looking at the heavens, and listening to the voice of his soul; he allowed the sportsmen to attain a considerable distance from him. D'Artagnan remarked his absence.

"He has not recovered the blow?" said he to Athos.

"He is struck to death."

"Oh! your fears exaggerate, I hope. Raoul is of a tempered nature. Around all hearts as noble as his, there is a second envelope that forms a cuirass. The first bleeds, the second resists."

"No," replied Athos, "Raoul will die of it."

"*Mordioux!*" said D'Artagnan, in a melancholy tone. And he did not add a word to this exclamation. Then, a minute after, "Why do you let him go?"

"Because he insists on going."

"And why do you not go with him?"

"Because I could not bear to see him die."

D'Artagnan looked his friend earnestly in the face. "You know one thing," continued the comte, leaning upon the arm of the captain; "you know that in the course of my life I have been afraid of but few things. Well! I have an incessant gnawing, insurmountable fear that an hour will come in which I shall hold the dead body of that boy in my arms."

"Oh!" murmured D'Artagnan; "oh!"

"He will die, I know, I have a perfect conviction of that; but I would not see him die."

"How is this, Athos? you come and place yourself in the presence of the bravest man, you say you have ever seen, of your own D'Artagnan, of that man without an equal, as you formerly called him, and you come and tell him, with your arms folded, that you are afraid of witnessing the death of your son, you who have seen all that can be seen in this world! Why have you this fear, Athos? Man upon this earth must expect everything, and ought to face everything."

"Listen to me, my friend. After having worn myself out upon this earth of which you speak, I have preserved but two religions: that of life, friendship, my duty as a father—that of eternity, love, and respect for God. Now, I have within me the revelation that if God should decree that my friend or my son should render up his last sigh in my presence—oh! no, I cannot even tell you, D'Artagnan!"

"Speak, speak, tell me!"

"I am strong against everything, except against the death of those I love. For that only there is no remedy. He who dies, gains; he who sees others die, loses. No, this is it—to know that I should no more meet on earth him whom I now behold with joy; to know that there would nowhere be a D'Artagnan any more, nowhere again be a Raoul, oh! I am old, look you, I have no longer courage; I pray God to spare me in my weakness; but if he struck me so plainly and in that fashion, I should curse him. A Christian gentleman ought not to curse his God, D'Artagnan; it is enough to once have cursed a king!"

"Humph!" sighed D'Artagnan, a little confused by this violent tempest of grief.

"Let me speak to him, Athos. Who knows?"

"Try, if you please, but I am convinced you will not succeed."

"I will not attempt to console him. I will serve him."

"You will?"

"Doubtless, I will. Do you think this would be the first time a woman had repented of an infidelity? I will go to him, I tell you."

Athos shook his head, and continued his walk alone, D'Artagnan, cutting across the brambles, rejoined Raoul and held out his hand to him. "Well, Raoul! You have something to say to me?"

"I have a kindness to ask of you," replied Bragelonne.

"Ask it, then."

"You will some day return to France?"

"I hope so."

"Ought I to write to Mademoiselle de la Valliere?"

"No, you must not."

"But I have many things to say to her."

"Go and say them to her, then."

"Never!"

"Pray, what virtue do you attribute to a letter, which your speech might not possess?"

"Perhaps you are right."

"She loves the king," said D'Artagnan, bluntly; "and she is an honest girl." Raoul started. "And you, you whom she abandons, she, perhaps, loves better than she does the king, but after another fashion."

"D'Artagnan, do you believe she loves the king?"

"To idolatry. Her heart is inaccessible to any other feeling. You might continue to live near her, and would be her best friend."

"Ah!" exclaimed Raoul, with a passionate burst of repugnance at such a hideous hope.

"Will you do so?"

"It would be base."

"That is a very absurd word, which would lead me to think slightly of your understanding. Please to understand, Raoul, that it is never base to do that which is imposed upon us by a superior force. If your heart says to you, 'Go there, or die,' why go, Raoul. Was she base or brave, she whom you loved, in preferring the king to you, the king whom her heart commanded her imperiously to prefer to you? No, she was the bravest of women. Do, then, as she has done. Oblige yourself. Do you know one thing of which I am sure, Raoul?"

"What is that?"

"Why, that by seeing her closely with the eyes of a jealous man—"

"Well?"

"Well! you would cease to love her."

"Then I am decided, my dear D'Artagnan."

"To set off to see her again?"

"No; to set off that I may *never* see her again. I wish to love her forever."

"Ha! I must confess," replied the musketeer, "that is a conclusion which I was far from expecting."

"This is what I wish, my friend. You will see her again, and you will give her a letter which, if you think proper, will explain to her, as to yourself, what is passing in my heart. Read it; I drew it up last night. Something told me I should see you to-day." He held the letter out, and D'Artagnan read:

"MADEMOISELLE,—You are not wrong in my
eyes in not loving me. You have only been guilty of
one fault towards me, that of having left me to
believe you loved me. This error will cost me my
life. I pardon you, but I cannot pardon myself. It is

said that happy lovers are deaf to the sorrows of rejected lovers. It will not be so with you, who did not love me, save with anxiety. I am sure that if I had persisted in endeavoring to change that friendship into love, you would have yielded out of a fear of bringing about my death, or lessening the esteem I had for you. It is much more delightful to me to die, knowing that *you* are free and satisfied. How much, then, will you love me, when you will no longer fear either my presence or reproaches? You will love me, because, however charming a new love may appear to you, God has not made me in anything inferior to him you have chosen, and because my devotedness, my sacrifice, and my painful end will assure me, in your eyes, a certain superiority over him. I have allowed to escape, in the candid credulity of my heart, the treasure I possessed. Many people tell me that you loved me enough to lead me to hope you would have loved me much. That idea takes from my mind all bitterness, and leads me only to blame myself. You will accept this last farewell, and you will bless me for having taken refuge in the inviolable asylum where hatred is extinguished, and where all love endures forever. Adieu, mademoiselle. If your happiness could be purchased by the last drop of my blood, I would shed that drop. I willingly make the sacrifice of it to my misery!

"RAOUL, VICOTME DE BRAGELONNE."

"The letter reads very well," said the captain. "I have only one fault to find with it."

"Tell me what that is!" said Raoul.

"Why, it is that it tells everything, except the thing which exhales, like a mortal poison from your eyes and from your

heart; except the senseless love which still consumes you."
Raoul grew paler, but remained silent.

"Why did you not write simply these words:

"'MADEMOISELLE,—Instead of cursing you, I love
you and I die.'"

"That is true," exclaimed Raoul, with a sinister kind of joy.

And tearing the letter he had just taken back, he wrote
the following words upon a leaf of his tablets:

"To procure the happiness of once more telling
you I love you, I commit the baseness of writing to you;
and to punish myself for that baseness, I die." And he
signed it.

"You will give her these tablets, captain, will you
not?"

"When?" asked the latter.

"On the day," said Bragelonne, pointing to the last
sentence, "on the day when you can place a date under these
words." And he sprang away quickly to join Athos, who was
returning with slow steps.

As they re-entered the fort, the sea rose with that rapid,
gusty vehemence which characterizes the Mediterranean;
the ill-humor of the element became a tempest. Something
shapeless, and tossed about violently by the waves, appeared
just off the coast.

"What is that?" said Athos,—"a wrecked boat?"

"No, it is not a boat," said D'Artagnan.

"Pardon me," said Raoul, "there is a bark gaining the
port rapidly."

"Yes, there is a bark in the creek, which is prudently
seeking shelter here; but that which Athos points to in the
sand is not a boat at all—it has run aground."

"Yes, yes, I see it."

"It is the carriage, which I threw into the sea after landing the prisoner."

"Well!" said Athos, "if you take my advice, D'Artagnan, you will burn that carriage, in order that no vestige of it may remain, without which the fishermen of Antibes, who have believed they had to do with the devil, will endeavor to prove that your prisoner was but a man."

"Your advice is good, Athos, and I will this night have it carried out, or rather, I will carry it out myself; but let us go in, for the rain falls heavily, and the lightning is terrific."

As they were passing over the ramparts to a gallery of which D'Artagnan had the key, they saw M. de Saint-Mars directing his steps towards the chamber inhabited by the prisoner. Upon a sign from D'Artagnan, they concealed themselves in an angle of the staircase.

"What is it?" said Athos.

"You will see. Look. The prisoner is returning from chapel."

And they saw, by the red flashes of lightning against the violet fog which the wind stamped upon the bank-ward sky, they saw pass gravely, at six paces behind the governor, a man clothed in black and masked by a vizor of polished steel, soldered to a helmet of the same nature, which altogether enveloped the whole of his head. The fire of the heavens cast red reflections on the polished surface, and these reflections, flying off capriciously, seemed to be angry looks launched by the unfortunate, instead of imprecations. In the middle of the gallery, the prisoner stopped for a moment, to contemplate the infinite horizon, to respire the sulphurous perfumes of the tempest, to drink in thirstily the hot rain, and to breathe a sigh resembling a smothered groan.

"Come on, monsieur," said Saint-Mars, sharply, to the prisoner, for he already became uneasy at seeing him look so long beyond the walls. "Monsieur, come on!"

"Say monseigneur!" cried Athos, from his corner, with

a voice so solemn and terrible, that the governor trembled from head to foot. Athos insisted upon respect being paid to fallen majesty. The prisoner turned round.

"Who spoke?" asked Saint-Mars.

"It was I," replied D'Artagnan, showing himself promptly. "You know that is the order."

"Call me neither monsieur nor monseigneur," said the prisoner in his turn, in a voice that penetrated to the very soul of Raoul; "call me ACCURSED!" He passed on, and the iron door croaked after him.

"There goes a truly unfortunate man!" murmured the musketeer in a hollow whisper, pointing out to Raoul the chamber inhabited by the prince.

CHAPTER 33

Promises.

Scarcely had D'Artagnan re-entered his apartment with his two friends, when one of the soldiers of the fort came to inform him that the governor was seeking him. The bark which Raoul had perceived at sea, and which appeared so eager to gain the port, came to Sainte-Marguerite with an important dispatch for the captain of the musketeers. On opening it, D'Artagnan recognized the writing of the king: "I should think," said Louis XIV., "you will have completed the execution of my orders, Monsieur d'Artagnan; return, then, immediately to Paris, and join me at the Louvre."

"There is the end of my exile!" cried the musketeer with joy; "God be praised, I am no longer a jailer!" And he showed the letter to Athos.

"So, then, you must leave us?" replied the latter, in a melancholy tone.

"Yes, but to meet again, dear friend, seeing that Raoul is old enough now to go alone with M. de Beaufort, and will prefer his father going back in company with M. d'Artagnan, to forcing him to travel two hundred leagues solitarily to reach home at La Fere; will you not, Raoul?"

"Certainly," stammered the latter, with an expression of tender regret.

"No, no, my friend," interrupted Athos, "I will never quit Raoul till the day his vessel disappears on the horizon. As long as he remains in France he shall not be separated from me."

"As you please, dear friend; but we will, at least, leave Sainte-Marguerite together; take advantage of the bark that will convey me back to Antibes."

"With all my heart; we cannot too soon be at a distance from this fort, and from the spectacle that shocked us so just now."

The three friends quitted the little isle, after paying their respects to the governor, and by the last flashes of the departing tempest they took their farewell of the white walls of the fort. D'Artagnan parted from his friend that same night, after having seen fire set to the carriage upon the shore by the orders of Saint-Mars, according to the advice the captain had given him. Before getting on horseback, and after leaving the arms of Athos: "My friends," said he, "you bear too much resemblance to two soldiers who are abandoning their post. Something warns me that Raoul will require being supported by you in his rank. Will you allow me to ask permission to go over into Africa with a hundred good muskets? The king will not refuse me, and I will take you with me."

"Monsieur d'Artagnan," replied Raoul, pressing his hand with emotion, "thanks for that offer, which would give us more than we wish, either monsieur le comte or I. I, who am young, stand in need of labor of mind and fatigue of body; monsieur le comte wants the profoundest repose. You are his best friend. I recommend him to your care. In watching over him, you are holding both our souls in your hands."

"I must go; my horse is all in a fret," said D'Artagnan, with whom the most manifest sign of a lively emotion was the change of ideas in conversation. "Come, comte, how many days longer has Raoul to stay here?"

"Three days at most."

"And how long will it take you to reach home?"

"Oh! a considerable time," replied Athos. "I shall not like the idea of being separated too quickly from Raoul. Time will travel too fast of itself to require me to aid it by distance. I shall only make half-stages."

"And why so, my friend? Nothing is more dull than traveling slowly; and hostelry life does not become a man like you."

"My friend, I came hither on post-horses; but I wish to purchase two animals of a superior kind. Now, to take them home fresh, it would not be prudent to make them travel more than seven or eight leagues a day."

"Where is Grimaud?"

"He arrived yesterday morning with Raoul's appointments; and I have left him to sleep."

"That is, never to come back again," D'Artagnan suffered to escape him. "Till we meet again, then, dear Athos—and if you are diligent, I shall embrace you the sooner." So saying, he put his foot in the stirrup, which Raoul held.

"Farewell!" said the young man, embracing him.

"Farewell!" said D'Artagnan, as he got into his saddle.

His horse made a movement which divided the cavalier from his friends. This scene had taken place in front of the house chosen by Athos, near the gates of Antibes, whither D'Artagnan, after his supper, had ordered his horses to be brought. The road began to branch off there, white and undulating in the vapors of the night. The horse eagerly respired the salt, sharp perfume of the marshes. D'Artagnan put him to a trot; and Athos and Raoul sadly turned towards the house. All at once they heard the rapid approach of a horse's steps, and first believed it to be one of those singular repercussions which deceive the ear at every turn in a road. But it was really the return of the horseman. They uttered a cry of joyous surprise; and the captain, springing to the ground like a young man, seized within his arms the two beloved heads of Athos and Raoul. He held them long embraced thus, without speaking a word, or suffering the sigh which was bursting his breast to escape him. Then, as rapidly as he had come back, he set off again, with a sharp application of his spurs to the sides of his fiery horse.

"Alas!" said the comte, in a low voice, "alas! alas!"

"An evil omen!" on his side, said D'Artagnan to himself, making up for lost time. "I could not smile upon them. An evil omen!"

The next day Grimaud was on foot again. The service commanded by M. de Beaufort was happily accomplished. The flotilla, sent to Toulon by the exertions of Raoul, had set out, dragging after it in little nutshells, almost invisible, the wives and friends of the fishermen and smugglers put in requisition for the service of the fleet. The time, so short, which remained for father and son to live together, appeared to go by with double rapidity, like some swift stream that flows towards eternity. Athos and Raoul returned to Toulon, which began to be filled with the noise of carriages, with the noise of arms, the noise of neighing horses. The trumpeters sounded their spirited marches; the drummers signalized their strength; the streets were overflowing with soldiers, servants, and tradespeople. The Duc de Beaufort was everywhere, superintending the embarkation with the zeal and interest of a good captain. He encouraged the humblest of his companions; he scolded his lieutenants, even those of the highest rank. Artillery, provisions, baggage, he insisted upon seeing all himself. He examined the equipment of every soldier; assured himself of the health and soundness of every horse. It was plain that, light, boastful, egotistical, in his hotel, the gentleman became the soldier again—the high noble, a captain—in face of the responsibility he had accepted. And yet, it must be admitted that, whatever was the care with which he presided over the preparations for departure, it was easy to perceive careless precipitation, and the absence of all the precaution that make the French soldier the first soldier in the world, because, in that world, he is the one most abandoned to his own physical and moral resources. All things having satisfied, or appearing to have satisfied, the admiral, he paid his compliments to Raoul, and gave the last orders for sailing, which was ordered the next morning at daybreak. He invited the comte had his son to dine with him; but they, under a pretext of service, kept themselves apart. Gaining their hostelry, situated under the trees of the great Place, they took their repast in haste, and Athos led Raoul to the rocks which dominate the city, vast gray mountains, whence the view is infinite and embraces a liquid horizon which appears, so remote is it, on a level with the rocks themselves. The night was fine, as it always is in these happy climes. The moon, rising behind the rocks, unrolled a silver sheet on the cerulean carpet of the sea. In the roadsteads maneuvered silently the vessels which had just taken their rank to facilitate the embarkation. The sea, loaded with phosphoric light, opened beneath the hulls of the barks that transported the baggage and munitions; every dip of the prow plowed up this gulf of white flames; from every oar dropped liquid diamonds. The sailors, rejoicing in the largesses of the admiral, were heard murmuring their slow and artless songs. Sometimes the grinding of the chains was mixed with the dull noise of shot falling into the holds. Such harmonies, such a spectacle, oppress the heart like fear, and dilate it like hope. All this life speaks of death. Athos had seated himself with his son, upon the moss, among the brambles of the promontory. Around their heads passed and repassed large bats, carried along by the fearful whirl of their blind chase. The feet of Raoul were over the edge of the cliff, bathed in that void which is peopled by vertigo, and provokes to self-annihilation. When the moon had risen to its fullest height, caressing with light the neighboring peaks, when the watery mirror was illumined in its full extent, and the little red fires had made their openings in the black masses of every ship, Athos, collecting all his ideas and all his courage, said:

"God has made all these things that we see, Raoul; He has made us also,—poor atoms mixed up with this monstrous universe. We shine like those fires and those stars; we sigh like those waves; we suffer like those great ships, which are worn out in plowing the waves, in obeying the wind that urges them towards an end, as the breath of God blows us towards a port. Everything likes to live, Raoul; and everything seems beautiful to living things."

"Monsieur," said Raoul, "we have before us a beautiful spectacle!"

"How good D'Artagnan is!" interrupted Athos, suddenly, "and what a rare good fortune it is to be supported during a whole life by such a friend as he is! That is what you have missed, Raoul."

"A friend!" cried Raoul, "I have wanted a friend!"

"M. de Guiche is an agreeable companion," resumed the comte, coldly, "but I believe, in the times in which you live, men are more engaged in their own interests and their own pleasures than they were in ours. You have sought a secluded life; that is a great happiness, but you have lost your strength thereby. We four, more weaned from those delicate abstractions that constitute your joy, furnished much more resistance when misfortune presented itself."

"I have not interrupted you, monsieur, to tell you that I had a friend, and that that friend is M. de Guiche. *Certes*, he is good and generous, and moreover he loves me. But I have lived under the guardianship of another friendship, monsieur, as precious and as strong as that of which you speak, since it is yours."

"I have not been a friend for you, Raoul," said Athos.

"Eh! monsieur, and in what respect not?"

"Because I have given you reason to think that life has but one face, because, sad and severe, alas! I have always cut off for you, without, God knows, wishing to do so, the joyous buds that spring incessantly from the fair tree of youth; so that at this moment I repent of not having made of you a more expansive, dissipated, animated man."

"I know why you say that, monsieur. No, it is not you who have made me what I am; it was love, which took me at the time when children only have inclinations; it is the constancy natural to my character, which with other creatures is but habit. I believed that I should always be as I was; I thought God had cast me in a path quite clear, quite straight, bordered with fruits and flowers. I had ever watching over me your vigilance and strength. I believed myself to be vigilant and strong. Nothing prepared me; I fell once, and that once deprived me of courage for the whole of my life. It is quite true that I wrecked myself. Oh, no, monsieur! you are nothing in my past but happiness—in my future but hope! No, I have no reproach to make against life such as you made it for me; I bless you, and I love you ardently."

"My dear Raoul, your words do me good. They prove to me that you will act a little for me in the time to come."

"I shall only act for you, monsieur."

"Raoul, what I have never hitherto done with respect to you, I will henceforward do. I will be your friend, not your father. We will live in expanding ourselves, instead of living and holding ourselves prisoners, when you come back. And that will be soon, will it not?"

"Certainly, monsieur, for such an expedition cannot last long."

"Soon, then, Raoul, soon, instead of living moderately on my income, I will give you the capital of my estates. It will suffice for launching you into the world till my death;

and you will give me, I hope, before that time, the consolation of not seeing my race extinct."

"I will do all you may command," said Raoul, much agitated.

"It is not necessary, Raoul, that your duty as aide-de-camp should lead you into too hazardous enterprises. You have gone through your ordeal; you are known to be a true man under fire. Remember that war with Arabs is a war of snares, ambuscades, and assassinations."

"So it is said, monsieur."

"There is never much glory in falling in an ambuscade. It is a death which always implies a little rashness or want of foresight. Often, indeed, he who falls in one meets with but little pity. Those who are not pitied, Raoul, have died to little purpose. Still further, the conqueror laughs, and we Frenchmen ought not to allow stupid infidels to triumph over our faults. Do you clearly understand what I am saying to you, Raoul? God forbid I should encourage you to avoid encounters."

"I am naturally prudent, monsieur, and I have very good fortune," said Raoul, with a smile which chilled the heart of his poor father; "for," the young man hastened to add, "in twenty combats through which I have been, I have only received one scratch."

"There is in addition," said Athos, "the climate to be dreaded: that is an ugly end, to die of fever! King Saint-Louis prayed God to send him an arrow or the plague, rather than the fever."

"Oh, monsieur! with sobriety, with reasonable exercise—"

"I have already obtained from M. de Beaufort a promise that his dispatches shall be sent off every fortnight to France. You, as his aide-de-camp, will be charged with expediting them, and will be sure not to forget me."

"No, monsieur," said Raoul, almost choked with emotion.

"Besides, Raoul, as you are a good Christian, and I am one also, we ought to reckon upon a more special protection of God and His guardian angels. Promise me that if anything evil should happen to you, on any occasion, you will think of me at once."

"First and at once! Oh! yes, monsieur."

"And will call upon me?"

"Instantly."

"You dream of me sometimes, do you not, Raoul?"

"Every night, monsieur. During my early youth I saw you in my dreams, calm and mild, with one hand stretched out over my head, and that it was which made me sleep so soundly—formerly."

"We love each other too dearly," said the comte, "that from this moment, in which we separate, a portion of both our souls should not travel with one and the other of us, and should not dwell wherever we may dwell. Whenever you may be sad, Raoul, I feel that my heart will be dissolved in sadness; and when you smile on thinking of me, be assured you will send me, from however remote a distance, a vital scintillation of your joy."

"I will not promise you to be joyous," replied the young man; "but you may be certain that I will never pass an hour without thinking of you, not one hour, I swear, unless I shall be dead."

Athos could contain himself no longer; he threw his arm round the neck of his son, and held him embraced with all the power of his heart. The moon began to be now eclipsed by twilight; a golden band surrounded the horizon, announcing the approach of the day. Athos threw his cloak over the shoulders of Raoul, and led him back to the city, where burdens and porters were already in motion, like a vast ant-hill. At the extremity of the plateau which Athos and Bragelonne were quitting, they saw a dark shadow moving uneasily backwards and forwards, as if in indecision or ashamed to be seen.

It was Grimaud, who in his anxiety had tracked his master, and was there awaiting him.

"Oh! my good Grimaud," cried Raoul, "what do you want? You are come to tell us it is time to be gone, have you not?"

"Alone?" said Grimaud, addressing Athos and pointing to Raoul in a tone of reproach, which showed to what an extent the old man was troubled.

"Oh! you are right!" cried the comte. "No, Raoul shall not go alone; no, he shall not be left alone in a strange land without some friendly hand to support him, some friendly heart to recall to him all he loved!"

"I?" said Grimaud.

"You, yes, you!" cried Raoul, touched to the inmost heart.

"Alas!" said Athos, "you are very old, my good Grimaud."

"So much the better," replied the latter, with an inexpressible depth of feeling and intelligence.

"But the embarkation is begun," said Raoul, "and you are not prepared."

"Yes," said Grimaud, showing the keys of his trunks, mixed with those of his young master.

"But," again objected Raoul, "you cannot leave monsieur le comte thus alone; monsieur le comte, whom you have never quitted?"

Grimaud turned his diamond eyes upon Athos and Raoul, as if to measure the strength of both. The comte uttered not a word.

"Monsieur le comte prefers my going," said Grimaud.

"I do," said Athos, by an inclination of the head.

At that moment the drums suddenly rolled, and the clarions filled the air with their inspiring notes. The regiments destined for the expedition began to debouch from the city. They advanced to the number of five, each composed of forty companies. Royals marched first, distinguished by their white uniform, faced with blue. The *ordonnance* colors, quartered cross-wise, violet and dead leaf, with a sprinkling of golden *fleurs-de-lis*, left the white-colored flag, with its *fleur-de-lised* cross, to dominate the whole. Musketeers at the wings, with their forked sticks and their muskets on their shoulders; pikemen in the center, with their lances, fourteen feet in length, marched gayly towards the transports, which carried them in detail to the ships. The regiments of Picardy, Navarre, Normandy, and Royal Vaisseau, followed after. M. de Beaufort had known well how to select his troops. He himself was seen closing the march with his staff—it would take a full hour before he could reach the sea. Raoul with Athos turned his steps slowly towards the beach, in order to take his place when the prince embarked. Grimaud, boiling with the ardor of a young man, superintended the embarkation of Raoul's baggage in the admiral's vessel. Athos, with his arm passed through that of the son he was about to lose, absorbed in melancholy meditation, was deaf to every noise around him. An officer came quickly towards them to inform Raoul that M. de Beaufort was anxious to have him by his side.

"Have the kindness to tell the prince," said Raoul, "that I request he will allow me this hour to enjoy the company of my father."

"No, no," said Athos, "an aide-de-camp ought not thus to quit his general. Please to tell the prince, monsieur, that the vicomte will join him immediately." The officer set off at a gallop.

"Whether we part here or part there," added the comte, "it is no less a separation." He carefully brushed the dust from his son's coat, and passed his hand over his hair as they walked along. "But, Raoul," said he, "you want money. M. de Beaufort's train will be splendid, and I am certain it will be agreeable to you to purchase horses and arms, which are very dear things in Africa. Now, as you are not actually in the service of the king or M. de Beaufort, and are simply a volunteer, you must not reckon upon either pay or largesse. But I should not like you to want for anything at Gigelli. Here are two hundred pistoles; if you would please me, Raoul, spend them."

Raoul pressed the hand of his father, and, at the turning of a street, they saw M. de Beaufort, mounted on a magnificent white *genet*, which responded by graceful curvets to the applause of the women of the city. The duke called Raoul, and held out his hand to the comte. He spoke to him for some time, with such a kindly expression that the heart of the poor father even felt a little comforted. It was, however, evident to both father and son that their walk amounted to nothing less than a punishment. There was a terrible moment—that at which, on quitting the sands of the shore, the soldiers and sailors exchanged the last kisses with their families and friends; a supreme moment, in which, notwithstanding the clearness of the heavens, the warmth of the sun, of the perfumes of the air, and the rich life that was circulating in their veins, everything appeared black, everything bitter, everything created doubts of Providence, nay, at the most, of God. It was customary for the admiral and his suite to embark last; the cannon waited to announce, with its formidable voice, that the leader had placed his foot on board his vessel. Athos, forgetful of both the admiral and the fleet, and of his own dignity as a strong man, opened his arms to his son, and pressed him convulsively to his heart.

"Accompany us on board," said the duke, very much affected; "you will gain a good half-hour."

"No," said Athos, "my farewell has been spoken, I do not wish to voice a second."

"Then, vicomte, embark—embark quickly!" added the prince, wishing to spare the tears of these two men, whose hearts were bursting. And paternally, tenderly, very much as

Porthos might have done, he took Raoul in his arms and placed him in the boat, the oars of which, at a signal, immediately were dipped in the waves. He himself, forgetful of ceremony, jumped into his boat, and pushed it off with a vigorous foot. "Adieu!" cried Raoul.

Athos replied only by a sign, but he felt something burning on his hand: it was the respectful kiss of Grimaud—the last farewell of the faithful dog. This kiss given, Grimaud jumped from the step of the mole upon the stem of a two-oared yawl, which had just been taken in tow by a *chaland* served by twelve galley-oars. Athos seated himself on the mole, stunned, deaf, abandoned. Every instant took from him one of the features, one of the shades of the pale face of his son. With his arms hanging down, his eyes fixed, his mouth open, he remained confounded with Raoul—in one same look, in one same thought, in one same stupor. The sea, by degrees, carried away boats and faces to that distance at which men become nothing but points,—loves, nothing but remembrances. Athos saw his son ascend the ladder of the admiral's ship, he saw him lean upon the rail of the deck, and place himself in such a manner as to be always an object in the eye of his father. In vain the cannon thundered, in vain from the ship sounded the long and lordly tumult, responded to by immense acclamations from the shore; in vain did the noise deafen the ear of the father, the smoke obscured the cherished object of his aspirations. Raoul appeared to him to the last moment; and the imperceptible atom, passing from black to pale, from pale to white, from white to nothing, disappeared for Athos—disappeared very long after, to all the eyes of the spectators, had disappeared both gallant ships and swelling sails. Towards midday, when the sun devoured space, and scarcely the tops of the masts dominated the incandescent limit of the sea, Athos perceived a soft aerial shadow rise, and vanish as soon as seen. This was the smoke of a cannon, which M. de

Beaufort ordered to be fired as a last salute to the coast of France. The point was buried in its turn beneath the sky, and Athos returned with slow and painful step to his deserted hostelry.

CHAPTER 34

Among Women.

D'Artagnan had not been able to hide his feelings from his friends so much as he would have wished. The stoical soldier, the impassive man-at-arms, overcome by fear and sad presentiments, had yielded, for a few moments, to human weakness. When, therefore, he had silenced his heart and calmed the agitation of his nerves, turning towards his lackey, a silent servant, always listening, in order to obey the more promptly:

"Rabaud," said he, "mind, we must travel thirty leagues a day."

"At your pleasure, captain," replied Rabaud.

And from that moment, D'Artagnan, accommodating his action to the pace of the horse, like a true centaur, gave up his thoughts to nothing—that is to say, to everything. He asked himself why the king had sent for him back; why the Iron Mask had thrown the silver plate at the feet of Raoul. As to the first subject, the reply was negative; he knew right well that the king's calling him was from necessity. He still further knew that Louis XIV. must experience an imperious desire for a private conversation with one whom the possession of such a secret placed on a level with the highest powers of the kingdom. But as to saying exactly what the king's wish was, D'Artagnan found himself completely at a loss. The musketeer had no doubts, either, upon the reason which had urged the unfortunate Philippe to reveal his character and birth. Philippe, buried forever beneath a mask of steel, exiled to a country where the men seemed little more than slaves of the elements; Philippe, deprived even of the society of D'Artagnan, who had loaded him with honors and delicate attentions, had nothing more to see than odious specters in this world, and, despair beginning to devour him, he poured himself forth in complaints, in the belief that his revelations would raise up some avenger for him. The manner in which the musketeer had been near killing his two best friends, the destiny which had so strangely brought Athos to participate in the great state secret, the farewell of Raoul, the obscurity of the future which threatened to end in a melancholy death; all this threw D'Artagnan incessantly back on lamentable predictions and forebodings, which the rapidity of his pace did not dissipate, as it used formerly to do. D'Artagnan passed from these considerations to the remembrance of the proscribed Porthos and Aramis. He saw them both, fugitives, tracked, ruined—laborious architects of fortunes they had lost; and as the king called for his man of execution in hours of vengeance and malice, D'Artagnan trembled at the very idea of receiving some commission that would make his very soul bleed. Sometimes, ascending hills, when the winded horse breathed hard from his red nostrils, and heaved his flanks, the captain, left to more freedom of thought, reflected on the prodigious genius of Aramis, a genius of acumen and intrigue, a match to which the Fronde and the civil war had produced but twice. Soldier, priest, diplomatist; gallant, avaricious, cunning; Aramis had never taken the good things of this life except as stepping-stones to rise to giddier ends. Generous in spirit, if not lofty in heart, he never did ill but for the sake of shining even yet more brilliantly. Towards the end of his career, at the moment of reaching the goal, like the patrician Fuscus, he had made a false step upon a plank, and had fallen into the sea. But Porthos, good, harmless Porthos! To see Porthos hungry, to see Mousqueton without gold lace, imprisoned, perhaps; to see Pierrefonds, Bracieux, razed to the very stones, dishonored even to the timber,—these were so many poignant griefs for D'Artagnan, and every time that one of these griefs struck him, he bounded like a horse at the sting of a gadfly beneath the vaults of foliage where he has sought shady shelter from the burning sun. Never was the man of spirit subjected to *ennui*, if his body was exposed to fatigue; never did the man of healthy body fail to find life light, if he had something to engage his mind. D'Artagnan, riding fast, thinking as constantly, alighted from his horse in Pairs, fresh and tender in his muscles as the athlete preparing for the gymnasium. The king did not expect him so soon, and had just departed for the chase towards Meudon. D'Artagnan, instead of riding after the king, as he would formerly have done, took off his boots, had a bath, and waited till his majesty should return dusty and tired. He occupied the interval of five hours in taking, as people say, the air of the house, and in arming himself against all ill chances. He learned that the king, during the last fortnight, had been gloomy; that the queen-mother was ill and much depressed; that Monsieur, the king's brother, was exhibiting a devotional turn; that Madame had the vapors; and that M. de Guiche was gone to one of his estates. He learned that M. Colbert was radiant; that M. Fouquet consulted a fresh physician every day, who still did not cure him, and that his principal complaint was one which physicians do not usually cure, unless they are political physicians. The king, D'Artagnan was told, behaved in the kindest manner to M. Fouquet, and did not allow him to be ever out of his sight; but the surintendant, touched to the heart, like one of those fine trees a worm has punctured, was declining daily, in spite of the royal smile, that sun of court trees. D'Artagnan learned that Mademoiselle de la Valliere had become indispensable to the king; that the king, during his sporting excursions, if he did not take her with him, wrote to her frequently, no longer verses, but, which was much worse, prose, and that whole pages at a time. Thus, as the political Pleiad of the day said, the *first king in the world* was seen descending from his horse *with an ardor beyond compare*, and on the crown of his hat scrawling bombastic phrases, which M. de Saint-Aignan, aide-de-camp in perpetuity, carried to La Valliere at the risk of foundering his horses. During this time, deer and pheasants were left to the free enjoyment of their nature, hunted so lazily that, it was said, the art of venery ran great risk of degenerating at the court of France. D'Artagnan then thought of the wishes of poor Raoul, of that desponding letter destined for a woman who passed her life in hoping, and as D'Artagnan loved to philosophize a little occasionally, he resolved to profit by the absence of the king to have a minute's talk with Mademoiselle de la Valliere. This was a very easy affair; while the king was hunting, Louise was walking with some other ladies in one of the galleries of the Palais Royal, exactly where the captain of the musketeers had some guards to inspect. D'Artagnan did not doubt that, if he could but open the conversation on Raoul, Louise might give him grounds for writing a consolatory letter to the poor exile; and hope, or at least consolation for Raoul, in the state of heart in which he had left him, was the sun, was life to two men, who were very dear to our captain. He directed his course, therefore, to the spot where he knew he should find Mademoiselle de la Valliere. D'Artagnan found La Valliere the center of the circle. In her apparent solitude, the king's favorite received, like a queen, more, perhaps, than the queen, a homage of which Madame had been so proud, when all the king's looks were directed to her and commanded the looks of the courtiers. D'Artagnan, although no squire of dames, received, nevertheless, civilities and attentions from the ladies; he was polite, as a brave man always is, and his terrible reputation had conciliated as much friendship among the men as admiration among the women. On seeing him enter, therefore, they immediately accosted him; and, as is not unfrequently the case with fair ladies, opened the attack by questions. "Where *had* he been? What *had* become of him so long? Why had they not seen him as usual make his fine horse curvet in such beautiful style, to the delight and astonishment of the curious from the king's balcony?"

He replied that he had just come from the land of oranges. This set all the ladies laughing. Those were times in which everybody traveled, but in which, notwithstanding, a journey of a hundred leagues was a problem often solved by death.

"From the land of oranges?" cried Mademoiselle de Tonnay-Charente. "From Spain?"

"Eh! eh!" said the musketeer.

"From Malta?" echoed Montalais.

"*Ma foi!* You are coming very near, ladies."

"Is it an island?" asked La Valliere.

"Mademoiselle," said D'Artagnan; "I will not give you the trouble of seeking any further; I come from the country where M. de Beaufort is, at this moment, embarking for Algiers."

"Have you seen the army?" asked several warlike fair ones.

"As plainly as I see you," replied D'Artagnan.

"And the fleet?"

"Yes, I saw everything."

"Have we any of us any friends there?" said Mademoiselle de Tonnay-Charente, coldly, but in a manner to attract attention to a question that was not without its calculated aim.

"Why," replied D'Artagnan, "yes; there were M. de la Guillotiere, M. de Manchy, M. de Bragelonne—"

La Valliere became pale. "M. de Bragelonne!" cried the perfidious Athenais. "Eh, what!—is he gone to the wars?—he!"

Montalais trod on her toe, but all in vain.

"Do you know what my opinion is?" continued she, addressing D'Artagnan.

"No, mademoiselle; but I should like very much to know it."

"My opinion is, then, that all the men who go to this war are desperate, desponding men, whom love has treated ill; and who go to try if they cannot find jet-complexioned women more kind than fair ones have been."

Some of the ladies laughed; La Valliere was evidently confused; Montalais coughed loud enough to waken the dead.

"Mademoiselle," interrupted D'Artagnan, "you are in error when you speak of black women at Gigelli; the women there have not jet faces; it is true they are not white—they are yellow."

"Yellow!" exclaimed the bevy of fair beauties.

"Eh! do not disparage it. I have never seen a finer color to match with black eyes and a coral mouth."

"So much the better for M. de Bragelonne," said Mademoiselle de Tonnay-Charente, with persistent malice. "He will make amends for his loss. Poor fellow!"

A profound silence followed these words; and D'Artagnan had time to observe and reflect that women—mild doves—treat each other more cruelly than tigers. But making La Valliere pale did not satisfy Athenais; she determined to make her blush likewise. Resuming the conversation without pause, "Do you know, Louise," said she, "that there is a great sin on your conscience?"

"What sin, mademoiselle?" stammered the unfortunate girl, looking round her for support, without finding it.

"Eh!—why," continued Athenais, "the poor young man was affianced to you; he loved you; you cast him off."

"Well, that is a right which every honest woman has," said Montalais, in an affected tone. "When we know we cannot constitute the happiness of a man, it is much better to cast him off."

"Cast him off! or refuse him!—that's all very well," said Athenais, "but that is not the sin Mademoiselle de la Valliere has to reproach herself with. The actual sin is sending poor Bragelonne to the wars; and to wars in which death is so very likely to be met with." Louise pressed her hand over her icy brow. "And if he dies," continued her pitiless tormentor, "you will have killed him. That is the sin."

Louise, half-dead, caught at the arm of the captain of the musketeers, whose face betrayed unusual emotion. "You wished to speak with me, Monsieur d'Artagnan," said she, in a voice broken by anger and pain. "What had you to say to me?"

D'Artagnan made several steps along the gallery, holding Louise on his arm; then, when they were far enough removed from the others—"What I had to say to you, mademoiselle," replied he, "Mademoiselle de Tonnay-Charente has just expressed; roughly and unkindly, it is true but still in its entirety."

She uttered a faint cry; pierced to the heart by this new wound, she went her way, like one of those poor birds which, struck unto death, seek the shade of the thicket in which to die. She disappeared at one door, at the moment the king was entering by another. The first glance of the king was directed towards the empty seat of his mistress. Not perceiving La Valliere, a frown came over his brow; but as soon as he saw D'Artagnan, who bowed to him—"Ah! monsieur!" cried he, "you *have* been diligent! I am much pleased with you." This was the superlative expression of royal satisfaction. Many men would have been ready to lay down their lives for such a speech from the king. The maids of honor and the courtiers, who had formed a respectful circle round the king on his entrance, drew back, on observing he wished to speak privately with his captain of the musketeers. The king led the way out of the gallery, after having again, with his eyes, sought everywhere for La Valliere, whose absence he could not account for. The moment they were out of the reach of curious ears, "Well! Monsieur d'Artagnan," said he, "the prisoner?"

"Is in his prison, sire."

"What did he say on the road?"

"Nothing, sire."

"What did he do?"

"There was a moment at which the fisherman—who took me in his boat to Sainte-Marguerite—revolted, and did his best to kill me. The—the prisoner defended me instead of attempting to fly."

The king became pale. "Enough!" said he; and D'Artagnan bowed. Louis walked about his cabinet with hasty steps. "Were you at Antibes," said he, "when Monsieur de Beaufort came there?"

"No, sire; I was setting off when monsieur le duc arrived."

"Ah!" which was followed by a fresh silence. "Whom did you see there?"

"A great many persons," said D'Artagnan, coolly.

The king perceived he was unwilling to speak. "I have sent for you, monsieur le capitaine, to desire you to go and prepare my lodgings at Nantes."

"At Nantes!" cried D'Artagnan.

"In Bretagne."

"Yes, sire, it is in Bretagne. Will you majesty make so long a journey as to Nantes?"

"The States are assembled there," replied the king. "I have two demands to make of them: I wish to be there."

"When shall I set out?" said the captain.

"This evening—to-morrow—to-morrow evening; for you must stand in need of rest."

"I have rested, sire."

"That is well. Then between this and to-morrow evening, when you please."

D'Artagnan bowed as if to take his leave; but, perceiving the king very much embarrassed, "Will you majesty," said he, stepping two paces forward, "take the court with you?"

"Certainly I shall."

"Then you majesty will, doubtless, want the musketeers?" And the eye of the king sank beneath the penetrating glance of the captain.

"Take a brigade of them," replied Louis.

"Is that all? Has your majesty no other orders to give me?"

"No—ah—yes."

"I am all attention, sire."

"At the castle of Nantes, which I hear is very ill arranged, you will adopt the practice of placing musketeers at the door of each of the principal dignitaries I shall take with me."

"Of the principal?"

"Yes."

"For instance, at the door of M. de Lyonne?"

"Yes."

"And that of M. Letellier?"

"Yes."

"Of M. de Brienne?"

"Yes."

"And of monsieur le surintendant?"

"Without doubt."

"Very well, sire. By to-morrow I shall have set out."

"Oh, yes; but one more word, Monsieur d'Artagnan. At Nantes you will meet with M. le Duc de Gesvres, captain of the guards. Be sure that your musketeers are placed before his guards arrive. Precedence always belongs to the first comer."

"Yes, sire."

"And if M. de Gesvres should question you?"

"Question me, sire! Is it likely that M. de Gesvres should question me?" And the musketeer, turning cavalierly on his heel, disappeared. "To Nantes!" said he to himself, as he descended from the stairs. "Why did he not dare to say, from thence to Belle-Isle?"

As he reached the great gates, one of M. Brienne's clerks came running after him, exclaiming, "Monsieur d'Artagnan! I beg your pardon—"

"What is the matter, Monsieur Ariste?"

"The king has desired me to give you this order."

"Upon your cash-box?" asked the musketeer.

"No, monsieur; on that of M. Fouquet."

D'Artagnan was surprised, but he took the order, which was in the king's own writing, and was for two hundred pistoles. "What!" thought he, after having politely thanked M. Brienne's clerk, "M. Fouquet is to pay for the journey, then! *Mordioux!* that is a bit of pure Louis XI. Why was not this order on the chest of M. Colbert? He would have paid it with such joy." And D'Artagnan, faithful to his principle of never letting an order at sight get cold, went straight to the house of M. Fouquet, to receive his two hundred pistoles.

CHAPTER 35

The Last Supper.

The superintendent had no doubt received advice of the approaching departure, for he was giving a farewell dinner to his friends. From the bottom to the top of the house, the hurry of the servants bearing dishes, and the diligence of the *registres*, denoted an approaching change in offices and kitchen. D'Artagnan, with his order in his hand, presented himself at the offices, when he was told it was too late to pay cash, the chest was closed. He only replied: "On the king's service."

The clerk, a little put out by the serious air of the captain, replied, that "that was a very respectable reason, but that the customs of the house were respectable likewise; and that, in consequence, he begged the bearer to call again next day." D'Artagnan asked if he could not see M. Fouquet. The clerk replied that M. le surintendant did not interfere with such details, and rudely closed the outer door in the captain's face. But the latter had foreseen this stroke, and placed his boot between the door and the door-case, so that the lock did not catch, and the clerk was still nose to nose with his interlocutor. This made him change his tone, and say, with terrified politeness, "If monsieur wishes to speak to M. le surintendant, he must go to the ante-chambers; these are the offices, where monseigneur never comes."

"Oh! very well! Where are they?" replied D'Artagnan.

"On the other side of the court," said the clerk, delighted to be free. D'Artagnan crossed the court, and fell in with a crowd of servants.

"Monseigneur sees nobody at this hour," he was answered by a fellow carrying a vermeil dish, in which were three pheasants and twelve quails.

"Tell him," said the captain, laying hold of the servant by the end of his dish, "that I am M. d'Artagnan, captain of his majesty's musketeers."

The fellow uttered a cry of surprise, and disappeared; D'Artagnan following him slowly. He arrived just in time to meet M. Pelisson in the ante-chamber: the latter, a little pale, came hastily out of the dining-room to learn what was the matter. D'Artagnan smiled.

"There is nothing unpleasant, Monsieur Pelisson; only a little order to receive the money for."

"Ah!" said Fouquet's friend, breathing more freely; and he took the captain by the hand, and, dragging him behind him, led him into the dining-room, where a number of friends surrounded the surintendant, placed in the center, and buried in the cushions of a *fauteuil*. There were assembled all the Epicureans who so lately at Vaux had done the honors of the mansion of wit and money in aid of M. Fouquet. Joyous friends, for the most part faithful, they had not fled their protector at the approach of the storm, and, in spite of the threatening heavens, in spite of the trembling earth, they remained there, smiling, cheerful, as devoted in misfortune as they had been in prosperity. On the left of the surintendant sat Madame de Belliere; on his right was Madame Fouquet; as if braving the laws of the world, and putting all vulgar reasons of propriety to silence, the two protecting angels of this man united to offer, at the moment of the crisis, the support of their twined arms. Madame de Belliere was pale, trembling, and full of respectful attentions for madame la surintendante, who, with one hand on her husband's, was looking anxiously towards the door by which Pelisson had gone out to bring D'Artagnan. The captain entered at first full of courtesy, and afterwards of admiration, when, with his infallible glance, he had divined as well as taken in the expression of every face. Fouquet raised himself up in his chair.

"Pardon me, Monsieur d'Artagnan," said he, "if I did not myself receive you when coming in the king's name." And he pronounced the last words with a sort of melancholy firmness, which filled the hearts of all his friends with terror.

"Monseigneur," replied D'Artagnan, "I only come to you in the king's name to demand payment of an order for two hundred pistoles."

The clouds passed from every brow but that of Fouquet, which still remained overcast.

"Ah! then," said he, "perhaps you also are setting out for Nantes?"

"I do not know whither I am setting out, monseigneur."

"But," said Madame Fouquet, recovered from her fright, "you are not going so soon, monsieur le capitaine, as not to do us the honor to take a seat with us?"

"Madame, I should esteem that a great honor done me, but I am so pressed for time, that, you see, I have been obliged to permit myself to interrupt your repast to procure payment of my note."

"The reply to which shall be gold," said Fouquet, making a sign to his intendant, who went out with the order D'Artagnan handed him.

"Oh!" said the latter, "I was not uneasy about the payment; the house is good."

A painful smile passed over the pale features of Fouquet.

"Are you in pain?" asked Madame de Belliere.

"Do you feel your attack coming on?" asked Madame Fouquet.

"Neither, thank you both," said Fouquet.

"Your attack?" said D'Artagnan, in his turn; "are you unwell, monseigneur?"

"I have a tertian fever, which seized me after the *fete* at Vaux."

"Caught cold in the grottos, at night, perhaps?"

"No, no; nothing but agitation, that was all."

"The too much heart you displayed in your reception of the king," said La Fontaine, quietly, without suspicion that he was uttering a sacrilege.

"We cannot devote too much heart to the reception of our king," said Fouquet, mildly, to his poet.

"Monsieur meant to say the too great ardor," interrupted D'Artagnan, with perfect frankness and much amenity. "The fact is, monseigneur, that hospitality was never practiced as at Vaux."

Madame Fouquet permitted her countenance to show clearly that if Fouquet had conducted himself well towards the king, the king had hardly done the like to the minister. But D'Artagnan knew the terrible secret. He alone with Fouquet knew it; those two men had not, the one the courage to complain, the other the right to accuse. The captain, to whom the two hundred pistoles were brought, was about to take his leave, when Fouquet, rising, took a glass of wine, and ordered one to be given to D'Artagnan.

"Monsieur," said he, "to the health of the king, *whatever may happen.*"

"And to your health, monseigneur, *whatever may happen,*" said D'Artagnan.

He bowed, with these words of evil omen, to all the company, who rose as soon as they heard the sound of his spurs and boots at the bottom of the stairs.

"I, for a moment, thought it was I and not my money he wanted," said Fouquet, endeavoring to laugh.

"You!" cried his friends; "and what for, in the name of Heaven!"

"Oh! do not deceive yourselves, my dear brothers in Epicurus," said the superintendent; "I do not wish to make a comparison between the most humble sinner on the earth, and the God we adore, but remember, he gave one day to his friends a repast which is called the Last Supper, and which was nothing but a farewell dinner, like that which we are making at this moment."

A painful cry of denial arose from all parts of the table. "Shut the doors," said Fouquet, and the servants disappeared. "My friends," continued Fouquet, lowering his voice, "what was I formerly? What am I now? Consult among yourselves and reply. A man like me sinks when he does not continue to rise. What shall we say, then, when he really sinks? I have no more money, no more credit; I have no longer anything but powerful enemies, and powerless friends."

"Quick!" cried Pelisson. "Since you explain yourself with such frankness, it is our duty to be frank, likewise. Yes, you are ruined—yes, you are hastening to your ruin—stop. And, in the first place, what money have we left?"

"Seven hundred thousand livres," said the intendant.

"Bread," murmured Madame Fouquet.

"Relays," said Pelisson, "relays, and fly!"

"Whither?"

"To Switzerland—to Savoy—but fly!"

"If monseigneur flies," said Madame Belliere, "it will be said that he was guilty—was afraid."

"More than that, it will be said that I have carried away twenty millions with me."

"We will draw up memoirs to justify you," said La Fontaine. "Fly!"

"I will remain," said Fouquet. "And, besides, does not everything serve me?"

"You have Belle-Isle," cried the Abbe Fouquet.

"And I am naturally going there, when going to Nantes," replied the superintendent. "Patience, then, patience!"

"Before arriving at Nantes, what a distance!" said Madame Fouquet.

"Yes, I know that well," replied Fouquet. "But what is to be done there? The king summons me to the States. I know well it is for the purpose of ruining me; but to refuse to go would be to evince uneasiness."

"Well, I have discovered the means of reconciling everything," cried Pelisson. "You are going to set out for Nantes."

Fouquet looked at him with an air of surprise.

"But with friends; but in your own carriage as far as Orleans; in your own barge as far as Nantes; always ready to defend yourself, if you are attacked; to escape, if you are threatened. In fact, you will carry your money against all chances; and, whilst flying, you will only have obeyed the king; then, reaching the sea, when you like, you will embark for Belle-Isle, and from Belle-Isle you will shoot out wherever it may please you, like the eagle that leaps into space when it has been driven from its eyrie."

A general assent followed Pelisson's words. "Yes, do so," said Madame Fouquet to her husband.

"Do so," said Madame de Belliere.

"Do it! do it!" cried all his friends.

"I will do so," replied Fouquet.

"This very evening?"

"In an hour?"

"Instantly."

"With seven hundred thousand livres you can lay the foundation of another fortune," said the Abbe Fouquet.

"What is there to prevent our arming corsairs at Belle-Isle?"

"And, if necessary, we will go and discover a new world," added La Fontaine, intoxicated with fresh projects and enthusiasm.

A knock at the door interrupted this concert of joy and hope. "A courier from the king," said the master of the ceremonies.

A profound silence immediately ensued, as if the message brought by this courier was nothing but a reply to all the projects given birth to a moment before. Every one waited to see what the master would do. His brow was streaming with perspiration, and he was really suffering from his fever at that instant. He passed into his cabinet, to receive the king's message. There prevailed, as we have said, such a silence in the chambers, and throughout the attendance, that from the dining-room could be heard the voice of Fouquet, saying, "That is well, monsieur." This voice was, however, broken by fatigue, and trembled with emotion. An instant after, Fouquet called Gourville, who crossed the gallery amidst the universal expectation. At length, he himself re-appeared among his guests; but it was no longer the same pale, spiritless countenance they had beheld when he left them; from pale he had become livid; and from spiritless, annihilated. A breathing, living specter, he advanced with his arms stretched out, his mouth parched, like a shade that comes to salute the friends of former days. On seeing him thus, every one cried out, and every one rushed towards Fouquet. The latter, looking at Pelisson, leaned upon his wife, and pressed the icy hand of the Marquise de Belliere.

"Well," said he, in a voice which had nothing human in it.

"What has happened, my God!" said some one to him.

Fouquet opened his right hand, which was clenched, but glistening with perspiration, and displayed a paper, upon which Pelisson cast a terrified glance. He read the following lines, written by the king's hand:

"'Dear and Well-Beloved Monsieur Fouquet, —
Give us, upon that which you have left of ours, the
sum of seven hundred thousand livres, of which
we stand in need to prepare for our departure.

"'And, as we know your health is not good,
we pray God to restore you, and to have you in
His holy keeping.

"'LOUIS.

"'The present letter is to serve as a receipt.'"

A murmur of terror circulated through the apartment.

"Well," cried Pelisson, in his turn, "you have received
that letter?"

"Received it, yes!"

"What will you do, then?"

"Nothing, since I have received it."

"But—"

"If I have received it, Pelisson, I have paid it," said the
surintendant, with a simplicity that went to the heart of all
present.

"You have paid it!" cried Madame Fouquet. "Then we
are ruined!"

"Come, no useless words," interrupted Pelisson. "Next
to money, life. Monseigneur, to horse! to horse!"

"What, leave us!" at once cried both the women, wild
with grief.

"Eh! monseigneur, in saving yourself, you save us all. To
horse!"

"But he cannot hold himself on. Look at him."

"Oh! if he takes time to reflect—" said the intrepid Pelisson.

"He is right," murmured Fouquet.

"Monseigneur! Monseigneur!" cried Gourville, rushing
up the stairs, four steps at once. "Monseigneur!"

"Well! what?"

"I escorted, as you desired, the king's courier with the money."

"Yes."

"Well! when I arrived at the Palais Royal, I saw—"

"Take breath, my poor friend, take breath; you are suffocating."

"What did you see?" cried the impatient friends.

"I saw the musketeers mounting on horseback," said Gourville.

"There, then!" cried every voice at once; "there, then! is there an instant to be lost?"

Madame Fouquet rushed downstairs, calling for her horses; Madame de Belliere flew after her, catching her in her arms, and saying: "Madame, in the name of his safety, do not betray anything, do not manifest alarm."

Pelisson ran to have the horses put to the carriages. And, in the meantime, Gourville gathered in his hat all that the weeping friends were able to throw into it of gold and silver— the last offering, the pious alms made to misery by poverty. The surintendant, dragged along by some, carried by others, was shut up in his carriage. Gourville took the reins, and mounted the box. Pelisson supported Madame Fouquet, who had fainted. Madame de Belliere had more strength, and was well paid for it; she received Fouquet's last kiss. Pelisson easily explained this precipitate departure by saying that an order from the king had summoned the minister to Nantes.

CHAPTER 36

In M. Colbert's Carriage.

As Gourville had seen, the king's musketeers were mounting
and following their captain. The latter, who did not like to
be confined in his proceedings, left his brigade under the
orders of a lieutenant, and set off on post horses, recommending his men to use all diligence. However rapidly they
might travel, they could not arrive before him. He had time,
in passing along the Rue des Petits-Champs, to see something
which afforded him plenty of food for thought and conjecture.
He saw M. Colbert coming out from his house to get into his
carriage, which was stationed before the door. In this carriage
D'Artagnan perceived the hoods of two women, and being
rather curious, he wished to know the names of the ladies
hid beneath these hoods. To get a glimpse at them, for they
kept themselves closely covered up, he urged his horse so near
the carriage, that he drove him against the step with such
force as to shake everything containing and contained. The
terrified women uttered, the one a faint cry, by which
D'Artagnan recognized a young woman, the other an imprecation, in which he recognized the vigor and *aplomb* that half
a century bestows. The hoods were thrown back: one of the
women was Madame Vanel, the other the Duchesse de
Chevreuse. D'Artagnan's eyes were quicker than those of

the ladies; he had seen and known them, whilst they did not recognize him; and as they laughed at their fright, pressing each other's hands,—

"Humph!" said D'Artagnan, "the old duchesse is no more inaccessible to friendship than formerly. *She* paying her court to the mistress of M. Colbert! Poor M. Fouquet! that presages you nothing good!"

He rode on. M. Colbert got into his carriage and the distinguished trio commenced a sufficiently slow pilgrimage toward the wood of Vincennes. Madame de Chevreuse set down Madame Vanel at her husband's house, and, left alone with M. Colbert, chatted upon affairs whilst continuing her ride. She had an inexhaustible fund of conversation, that dear duchesse, and as she always talked for the ill of others, though ever with a view to her own good, her conversation amused her interlocutor, and did not fail to leave a favorable impression.

She taught Colbert, who, poor man! was ignorant of the fact, how great a minister he was, and how Fouquet would soon become a cipher. She promised to rally around him, when he should become surintendant, all the old nobility of the kingdom, and questioned him as to the preponderance it would be proper to allow La Valliere. She praised him, she blamed him, she bewildered him. She showed him the secret of so many secrets that, for a moment, Colbert thought he was doing business with the devil. She proved to him that she held in her hand the Colbert of to-day, as she had held the Fouquet of yesterday; and as he asked her very simply the reason of her hatred for the surintendant: "Why do you yourself hate him?" said she.

"Madame, in politics," replied he, "the differences of system oft bring about dissentions between men. M. Fouquet always appeared to me to practice a system opposed to the true interests of the king."

She interrupted him.—"I will say no more to you about

M. Fouquet. The journey the king is about to take to Nantes will give a good account of him. M. Fouquet, for me, is a man gone by—and for you also."

Colbert made no reply. "On his return from Nantes," continued the duchesse, "the king, who is only anxious for a pretext, will find that the States have not behaved well—that they have made too few sacrifices. The States will say that the imposts are too heavy, and that the surintendant has ruined them. The king will lay all the blame on M. Fouquet, and then—"

"And then?" said Colbert.

"Oh! he will be disgraced. Is not that your opinion?"

Colbert darted a glance at the duchesse, which plainly said: "If M. Fouquet be only disgraced, you will not be the cause of it."

"Your place, M. Colbert," the duchesse hastened to say, "must be a high place. Do you perceive any one between the king and yourself, after the fall of M. Fouquet?"

"I do not understand," said he.

"You *will* understand. To what does your ambition aspire?"

"I have none."

"It was useless, then, to overthrow the superintendent, Monsieur Colbert. It was idle."

"I had the honor to tell you, madame—"

"Oh! yes, I know, all about the interest of the king—but, if you please, we will speak of your own."

"Mine! that is to say, the affairs of his majesty."

"In short, are you, or are you not endeavoring to ruin M. Fouquet? Answer without evasion."

"Madame, I ruin nobody."

"I am endeavoring to comprehend, then, why you purchased from me the letters of M. Mazarin concerning M. Fouquet. Neither can I conceive why you have laid those letters before the king."

Colbert, half stupefied, looked at the duchesse with an air of constraint.

"Madame," said he, "I can less easily conceive how you, who received the money, can reproach me on that head—"

"That is," said the old duchesse, "because we must will that which we wish for, unless we are not able to obtain what we wish."

"*Will!*" said Colbert, quite confounded by such coarse logic.

"You are not able, *hein!* Speak."

"I am not able, I allow, to destroy certain influences near the king."

"That fight in favor of M. Fouquet? What are they? Stop, let me help you."

"Do, madame."

"La Valliere?"

"Oh! very little influence; no knowledge of business, and small means. M. Fouquet has paid his court to her."

"To defend him would be to accuse herself, would it not?"

"I think it would."

"There is still another influence, what do you say to that?"

"Is it considerable?"

"The queen-mother, perhaps?"

"Her majesty, the queen-mother, has a weakness for M. Fouquet very prejudicial to her son."

"Never believe that," said the old duchesse, smiling.

"Oh!" said Colbert, with incredulity, "I have often experienced it."

"Formerly?"

"Very recently, madame, at Vaux. It was she who prevented the king from having M. Fouquet arrested."

"People do not forever entertain the same opinions, my dear monsieur. That which the queen may have wished recently, she would not wish, perhaps, to-day."

"And why not?" said Colbert, astonished.

"Oh! the reason is of very little consequence."

"On the contrary, I think it is of great consequence; for, if I were certain of not displeasing her majesty, the queen-mother, my scruples would be all removed."

"Well! have you never heard talk of a certain secret?"

"A secret?"

"Call it what you like. In short, the queen-mother has conceived a bitter hatred for all those who have participated, in one fashion or another, in the discovery of this secret, and M. Fouquet I believe is one of these."

"Then," said Colbert, "we may be sure of the assent of the queen-mother?"

"I have just left her majesty, and she assures me so."

"So be it, then, madame."

"But there is something further; do you happen to know a man who was the intimate friend of M. Fouquet, M. d'Herblay, a bishop, I believe?"

"Bishop of Vannes."

"Well! this M. d'Herblay, who also knew the secret, the queen-mother is pursuing with the utmost rancor."

"Indeed!"

"So hotly pursued, that if he were dead, she would not be satisfied with anything less than his head, to satisfy her he would never speak again."

"And is that the desire of the queen-mother?"

"An order is given for it."

"This Monsieur d'Herblay shall be sought for, madame."

"Oh! it is well known where he is."

Colbert looked at the duchesse.

"Say where, madame."

"He is at Belle-Ile-en-Mer."

"At the residence of M. Fouquet?"

"At the residence of M. Fouquet."

"He shall be taken."

It was now the duchesse's turn to smile. "Do not

fancy the capture so easy," said she; "do not promise it so lightly."

"Why not, madame?"

"Because M. d'Herblay is not one of those people who can be taken when and where you please."

"He is a rebel, then?"

"Oh! Monsieur Colbert, we have passed all our lives in making rebels, and yet you see plainly, that so far from being taken, we take others."

Colbert fixed upon the old duchesse one of those fierce looks of which no words can convey the expression, accompanied by a firmness not altogether wanting in grandeur. "The times are gone," said he, "in which subjects gained duchies by making war against the king of France. If M. d'Herblay conspires, he will perish on the scaffold. That will give, or will not give, pleasure to his enemies,—a matter, by the way, of little importance to *us*."

And this *us*, a strange word in the mouth of Colbert, made the duchesse thoughtful for a moment. She caught herself reckoning inwardly with this man—Colbert had regained his superiority in the conversation, and he meant to keep it.

"You ask me, madame," he said, "to have this M. d'Herblay arrested?"

"I?—I ask you nothing of the kind!"

"I thought you did, madame. But as I have been mistaken, we will leave him alone; the king has said nothing about him."

The duchesse bit her nails.

"Besides," continued Colbert, "what a poor capture would this bishop be! A bishop game for a king! Oh! no, no; I will not even take the slightest notice of him."

The hatred of the duchesse now discovered itself.

"Game for a woman!" said she. "Is not the queen a woman? If she wishes M. d'Herblay arrested, she has her reasons. Besides, is not M. d'Herblay the friend of him who is doomed to fall?"

"Oh! never mind that," said Colbert. "This man shall be spared, if he is not the enemy of the king. Is that displeasing to you?"

"I say nothing."

"Yes—you wish to see him in prison, in the Bastille, for instance."

"I believe a secret better concealed behind the walls of the Bastille than behind those of Belle-Isle."

"I will speak to the king about it; he will clear up the point."

"And whilst waiting for that enlightenment, Monsieur l'Eveque de Vannes will have escaped. I would do so."

"Escaped! he! and whither should he escape? Europe is ours, in will, if not in fact."

"He will always find an asylum, monsieur. It is evident you know nothing of the man you have to do with. You do not know D'Herblay; you do not know Aramis. He was one of those four musketeers who, under the late king, made Cardinal de Richelieu tremble, and who, during the regency, gave so much trouble to Monseigneur Mazarin."

"But, madame, what can he do, unless he has a kingdom to back him?"

"He has one, monsieur."

"A kingdom, he! what, Monsieur d'Herblay?"

"I repeat to you, monsieur, that if he wants a kingdom, he either has it or will have it."

"Well, as you are so earnest that this rebel should not escape, madame, I promise you he shall not escape."

"Belle-Isle is fortified, M. Colbert, and fortified by him."

"If Belle-Isle were also defended by him, Belle-Isle is not impregnable; and if Monsieur l'Eveque de Vannes is shut up in Belle-Isle, well, madame, the place shall be besieged, and he will be taken."

"You may be very certain, monsieur, that the zeal you display in the interest of the queen-mother will please her majesty mightily, and you will be magnificently rewarded; but what shall I tell her of your projects respecting this man?"

"That when once taken, he shall be shut up in a fortress from which her secret shall never escape."

"Very well, Monsieur Colbert, and we may say, that, dating from this instant, we have formed a solid alliance, that is, you and I, and that I am absolutely at your service."

"It is I, madame, who place myself at yours. This Chevalier d'Herblay is a kind of Spanish spy, is he not?"

"Much more."

"A secret ambassador?"

"Higher still."

"Stop—King Phillip III. of Spain is a bigot. He is, perhaps, the confessor of Phillip III."

"You must go higher even than that."

"*Mordieu!*" cried Colbert, who forgot himself so far as to swear in the presence of this great lady, of this old friend of the queen-mother. "He must then be the general of the Jesuits."

"I believe you have guessed it at last," replied the duchesse.

"Ah! then, madame, this man will ruin us all if we do not ruin him; and we must make haste, too."

"Such was my opinion, monsieur, but I did not dare to give it you."

"And it was lucky for us he has attacked the throne, and not us."

"But, mark this well, M. Colbert. M. d'Herblay is never discouraged; if he has missed one blow, he will be sure to make another; he will begin again. If he has allowed an opportunity to escape of making a king for himself, sooner or later, he will make another, of whom, to a certainty, you will not be prime minister."

Colbert knitted his brow with a menacing expression. "I

feel assured that a prison will settle this affair for us, madame, in a manner satisfactory for both."

The duchesse smiled again.

"Oh! if you knew," said she, "how many times Aramis has got out of prison!"

"Oh!" replied Colbert, "we will take care that he shall not get out *this* time."

"But you were not attending to what I said to you just now. Do you remember that Aramis was one of the four invincibles whom Richelieu so dreaded? And at that period the four musketeers were not in possession of that which they have now—money and experience."

Colbert bit his lips.

"We will renounce the idea of the prison," said he, in a lower tone: "we will find a little retreat from which the invincible cannot possibly escape."

"That was well spoken, our ally!" replied the duchesse. "But it is getting late; had we not better return?"

"The more willingly, madame, from my having my preparations to make for setting out with the king."

"To Paris!" cried the duchesse to the coachman.

And the carriage returned towards the Faubourg Saint Antoine, after the conclusion of the treaty that gave to death the last friend of Fouquet, the last defender of Belle-Isle, the former friend of Marie Michon, the new foe of the old duchesse.

CHAPTER 37

The Two Lighters.

D'Artagnan had set off; Fouquet likewise was gone, and with a rapidity which doubled the tender interest of his friends. The first moments of this journey, or better say, this flight, were troubled by a ceaseless dread of every horse and carriage to be seen behind the fugitive. It was not natural, in fact, if Louis XIV. was determined to seize this prey, that he should allow it to escape; the young lion was already accustomed to the chase, and he had bloodhounds sufficiently clever to be trusted. But insensibly all fears were dispersed; the surintendant, by hard traveling, placed such a distance between himself and his persecutors, that no one of them could reasonably be expected to overtake him. As to his position, his friends had made it excellent for him. Was he not traveling to join the king at Nantes, and what did the rapidity prove but his zeal to obey? He arrived, fatigued, but reassured, at Orleans, where he found, thanks to the care of a courier who had preceded him, a handsome lighter of eight oars. These lighters, in the shape of gondolas, somewhat wide and heavy, containing a small chamber, covered by the deck, and a chamber in the poop, formed by a tent, then acted as passage-boats from Orleans to Nantes, by the Loire, and this passage, a long one in our days, appeared then more easy and convenient than the high-road, with its post-hacks and its ill-hung carriages. Fouquet went on board this lighter, which set out immediately. The rowers, knowing they had the honor of conveying the surintendant of the finances, pulled with all their strength, and that magic word, the *finances*, promised them a liberal gratification, of which they wished to prove themselves worthy. The lighter seemed to leap the mimic waves of the Loire. Magnificent weather, a sunrise that empurpled all the landscape, displayed the river in all its limpid serenity. The current and the rowers carried Fouquet along as wings carry a bird, and he arrived before Beaugency without the slightest accident having signalized the voyage. Fouquet hoped to be the first to arrive at Nantes; there he would see the notables and gain support among the principal members of the States; he would make himself a necessity, a thing very easy for a man of his merit, and would delay the catastrophe, if he did not succeed in avoiding it entirely. "Besides," said Gourville to him, "at Nantes, you will make out, or we will make out, the intentions of your enemies; we will have horses always ready to convey you to Poitou, a bark in which to gain the sea, and when once upon the open sea, Belle-Isle is your inviolable port. You see, besides, that no one is watching you, no one is following." He had scarcely finished when they discovered at a distance, behind an elbow formed by the river, the masts of a huge lighter coming down. The rowers of Fouquet's boat uttered a cry of surprise on seeing this galley.

"What is the matter?" asked Fouquet.

"The matter is, monseigneur," replied the patron of the bark, "that it is a truly remarkable thing—that lighter comes along like a hurricane."

Gourville started, and mounted to the deck, in order to obtain a better view.

Fouquet did not go up with him, but said to Gourville, with restrained mistrust: "See what it is, dear friend."

The lighter had just passed the elbow. It came on so fast,

that behind it might be plainly seen the white wake illumined with the fires of the day.

"How they go," repeated the skipper, "how they go! They must be well paid! I did not think," he added, "that oars of wood could behave better than ours, but yonder oarsmen prove the contrary."

"Well they may," said one of the rowers, "they are twelve, and we but eight."

"Twelve rowers!" replied Gourville, "twelve! impossible."

The number of eight rowers for a lighter had never been exceeded, even for the king. This honor had been paid to monsieur le surintendant, more for the sake of haste than of respect.

"What does it mean?" said Gourville, endeavoring to distinguish beneath the tent, which was already apparent, travelers which the most piercing eye could not yet have succeeded in discovering.

"They must be in a hurry, for it is not the king," said the patron.

Fouquet shuddered.

"By what sign do you know that it is not the king?" said Gourville.

"In the first place, because there is no white flag with fleurs-de-lis, which the royal lighter always carries."

"And then," said Fouquet, "because it is impossible it should be the king, Gourville, as the king was still in Paris yesterday."

Gourville replied to the surintendant by a look which said: "You were there yourself yesterday."

"And by what sign do you make out they are in such haste?" added he, for the sake of gaining time.

"By this, monsieur," said the patron; "these people must have set out a long while after us, and they have already nearly overtaken us."

"Bah!" said Gourville, "who told you that they do not come from Beaugency or from Moit even?"

"We have seen no lighter of that shape, except at Orleans. It comes from Orleans, monsieur, and makes great haste."

Fouquet and Gourville exchanged a glance. The captain remarked their uneasiness, and, to mislead him, Gourville immediately said:

"Some friend, who has laid a wager he would catch us; let us win the wager, and not allow him to come up with us."

The patron opened his mouth to say that it was quite impossible, but Fouquet said with much *hauteur*,—"If it is any one who wishes to overtake us, let him come."

"We can try, monseigneur," said the man, timidly. "Come, you fellows, put out your strength; row, row!"

"No," said Fouquet, "on the contrary; stop short."

"Monseigneur! what folly!" interrupted Gourville, stooping towards his ear.

"Pull up!" repeated Fouquet. The eight oars stopped, and resisting the water, created a retrograde motion. It stopped. The twelve rowers in the other did not, at first, perceive this maneuver, for they continued to urge on their boat so vigorously that it arrived quickly within musket-shot. Fouquet was short-sighted, Gourville was annoyed by the sun, now full in his eyes; the skipper alone, with that habit and clearness which are acquired by a constant struggle with the elements, perceived distinctly the travelers in the neighboring lighter.

"I can see them!" cried he; "there are two."

"I can see nothing," said Gourville.

"You will not be long before you distinguish them; in twenty strokes of their oars they will be within ten paces of us."

But what the patron announced was not realized; the lighter imitated the movement commanded by Fouquet, and instead of coming to join its pretended friends, it stopped short in the middle of the river.

"I cannot comprehend this," said the captain.

"Nor I," cried Gourville.

"You who can see so plainly the people in that lighter," resumed Fouquet, "try to describe them to us, before we are too far off."

"I thought I saw two," replied the boatman. "I can only see one now, under the tent."

"What sort of man is he?"

"He is a dark man, broad-shouldered, bull-necked."

A little cloud at that moment passed across the azure, darkening the sun. Gourville, who was still looking, with one hand over his eyes, became able to see what he sought, and all at once, jumping from the deck into the chamber where Fouquet awaited him: "Colbert!" said he, in a voice broken by emotion.

"Colbert!" repeated Fouquet. "Too strange! but no, it is impossible!"

"I tell you I recognized him, and he, at the same time, so plainly recognized me, that he is just gone into the chamber on the poop. Perhaps the king has sent him on our track."

"In that case he would join us, instead of lying by. What is he doing there?"

"He is watching us, without a doubt."

"I do not like uncertainty," said Fouquet; "let us go straight up to him."

"Oh! monseigneur, do not do that, the lighter is full of armed men."

"He wishes to arrest me, then, Gourville? Why does he not come on?"

"Monseigneur, it is not consistent with your dignity to go to meet even your ruin."

"But to allow them to watch me like a malefactor!"

"Nothing yet proves that they are watching you, monseigneur; be patient!"

"What is to be done, then?"

"Do not stop; you were only going so fast to appear to obey the king's order with zeal. Redouble the speed. He who lives will see!"

"That is better. Come!" cried Fouquet; "since they remain stock-still yonder, let us go on."

The captain gave the signal, and Fouquet's rowers resumed their task with all the success that could be looked for from men who had rested. Scarcely had the lighter made a hundred fathoms, than the other, that with the twelve rowers, resumed its rapid course. This position lasted all day, without any increase or diminution of distance between the two vessels. Towards evening Fouquet wished to try the intentions of his persecutor. He ordered his rowers to pull towards the shore, as if to effect a landing. Colbert's lighter imitated this maneuver, and steered towards the shore in a slanting direction. By the merest chance, at the spot where Fouquet pretended to wish to land, a stableman, from the chateau of Langeais, was following the flowery banks leading three horses in halters. Without doubt the people of the twelve-oared lighter fancied that Fouquet was directing his course to these horses ready for flight, for four or five men, armed with muskets, jumped from the lighter on to the shore, and marched along the banks, as if to gain ground on the horseman. Fouquet, satisfied of having forced the enemy to a demonstration, considered his intention evident, and put his boat in motion again. Colbert's people returned likewise to theirs, and the course of the two vessels was resumed with fresh perseverance. Upon seeing this, Fouquet felt himself threatened closely, and in a prophetic voice—"Well, Gourville," said he, whisperingly, "what did I say at our last repast, at my house? Am I going, or not, to my ruin?"

"Oh! monseigneur!"

"These two boats, which follow each other with so much emulation, as if we were disputing, M. Colbert and I, a prize for swiftness on the Loire, do they not aptly represent our fortunes; and do you not believe, Gourville, that one of the two will be wrecked at Nantes?"

"At least," objected Gourville, "there is still uncertainty; you are about to appear at the States; you are about to show what sort of man you are; your eloquence and genius for business are the buckler and sword that will serve to defend you, if not to conquer with. The Bretons do not know you; and when they become acquainted with you your cause is won! Oh! let M. Colbert look to it well, for his lighter is as much exposed as yours to being upset. Both go quickly, his faster than yours, it is true; we shall see which will be wrecked first."

Fouquet, taking Gourville's hand—"My friend," said he, "everything considered, remember the proverb, 'First come, first served!' Well! M. Colbert takes care not to pass me. He is a prudent man is M. Colbert."

He was right; the two lighters held their course as far as Nantes, watching each other. When the surintendant landed, Gourville hoped he should be able to seek refuge at once, and have the relays prepared. But, at the landing, the second lighter joined the first, and Colbert, approaching Fouquet, saluted him on the quay with marks of the profoundest respect—marks so significant, so public, that their result was the bringing of the whole population upon La Fosse. Fouquet was completely self-possessed; he felt that in his last moments of greatness he had obligations towards himself. He wished to fall from such a height that his fall should crush some of his enemies. Colbert was there—so much the worse for Colbert. The surintendant, therefore, coming up to him, replied, with that arrogant semi-closure of the eyes peculiar to him—"What! is that you, M. Colbert?"

"To offer you my respects, monseigneur," said the latter.

"Were you in that lighter?"—pointing to the one with twelve rowers.

"Yes, monseigneur."

"Of twelve rowers?" said Fouquet; "what luxury, M. Colbert. For a moment I thought it was the queen-mother."

"Monseigneur!"—and Colbert blushed.

"This is a voyage that will cost those who have to pay for it dear, Monsieur l'Intendant!" said Fouquet. "But you have, happily, arrived!—You see, however," added he, a moment after, "that I, who had but eight rowers, arrived before you." And he turned his back towards him, leaving him uncertain whether the maneuvers of the second lighter had escaped the notice of the first. At least he did not give him the satisfaction of showing that he had been frightened. Colbert, so annoyingly attacked, did not give way.

"I have not been quick, monseigneur," he replied, "because I followed your example whenever you stopped."

"And why did you do that, Monsieur Colbert?" cried Fouquet, irritated by the base audacity; "as you had a superior crew to mine, why did you not either join me or pass me?"

"Out of respect," said the intendant, bowing to the ground.

Fouquet got into a carriage which the city had sent to him, we know not why or how, and he repaired to *la Maison de Nantes*, escorted by a vast crowd of people, who for several days had been agog with expectation of a convocation of the States. Scarcely was he installed when Gourville went out to order horses on the route to Poitiers and Vannes, and a boat at Paimboef. He performed these various operations with so much mystery, activity, and generosity, that never was Fouquet, then laboring under an attack of fever, more nearly saved, except for the counteraction of that immense disturber of human projects,—chance. A report was spread during the night, that the king was coming in great haste on post horses, and would arrive in ten or twelve hours at the latest. The people, while waiting for the king, were greatly rejoiced to see the musketeers, newly arrived, with Monsieur d'Artagnan, their captain, and quartered in the castle, of which they occupied all the posts, in quality of guard of honor. M. d'Artagnan, who was very polite, presented himself, about ten o'clock, at the lodgings of the surintendant to pay his respectful compliments; and although the minister suffered from fever, although he was in such pain as to be bathed in sweat, he would receive M. d'Artagnan, who was delighted with that honor, as will be seen by the conversation they had together.

CHAPTER 38

Friendly Advice.

Fouquet had gone to bed, like a man who clings to life, and wishes to economize, as much as possible, that slender tissue of existence, of which the shocks and frictions of this world so quickly wear out the tenuity. D'Artagnan appeared at the door of this chamber, and was saluted by the superintendent with a very affable "Good day."

"*Bon jour!* monseigneur," replied the musketeer; "how did you get through the journey?"

"Tolerably well, thank you."

"And the fever?"

"But poorly. I drink, as you perceive. I am scarcely arrived, and I have already levied a contribution of *tisane* upon Nantes."

"You should sleep first, monseigneur."

"Eh! *corbleu!* my dear Monsieur d'Artagnan, I should be very glad to sleep."

"Who hinders you?"

"Why, *you* in the first place."

"I? Oh, monseigneur!"

"No doubt you do. Is it at Nantes as at Paris? Do you not come in the king's name?"

"For Heaven's sake, monseigneur," replied the captain,

"leave the king alone! The day on which I shall come on the part of the king, for the purpose you mean, take my word for it, I will not leave you long in doubt. You will see me place my hand on my sword, according to the *ordonnance*, and you will hear my say at once, in ceremonial voice, 'Monseigneur, in the name of the king, I arrest you!'"

"You promise me that frankness?" said the superintendent.

"Upon my honor! But we have not come to that, believe me."

"What makes you think that, M. d'Artagnan? For my part, I think quite the contrary."

"I have heard speak of nothing of the kind," replied D'Artagnan.

"Eh! eh!" said Fouquet.

"Indeed, no. You are an agreeable man, in spite of your fever. The king should not, cannot help loving you, at the bottom of his heart."

Fouquet's expression implied doubt. "But M. Colbert?" said he; "does M. Colbert love me as much as you say?"

"I am not speaking of M. Colbert," replied D'Artagnan. "He is an exceptional man. He does not love you; so much is very possible; but, *mordioux!* the squirrel can guard himself against the adder with very little trouble."

"Do you know that you are speaking to me quite as a friend?" replied Fouquet; "and that, upon my life! I have never met with a man of your intelligence, and heart?"

"You are pleased to say so," replied D'Artagnan. "Why did you wait till to-day to pay me such a compliment?"

"Blind that we are!" murmured Fouquet.

"Your voice is getting hoarse," said D'Artagnan; "drink, monseigneur, drink!" And he offered him a cup of *tisane*, with the most friendly cordiality; Fouquet took it, and thanked him by a gentle smile. "Such things only happen to me," said the musketeer. "I have passed ten years under your very beard, while you were rolling about tons of gold. You were clearing an annual pension of four millions; you never observed me; and you find out there is such a person in the world, just at the moment you—"

"Just at the moment I am about to fall," interrupted Fouquet. "That is true, my dear Monsieur d'Artagnan."

"I did not say so."

"But you thought so; and that is the same thing. Well! if I fall, take my word as truth, I shall not pass a single day without saying to myself, as I strike my brow, 'Fool! fool!— stupid mortal! You had a Monsieur d'Artagnan under your eye and hand, and you did not employ him, you did not enrich him!'"

"You overwhelm me," said the captain. "I esteem you greatly."

"There exists another man, then, who does not think as M. Colbert thinks," said the surintendant.

"How this M. Colbert looms up in your imagination! He is worse than fever!"

"Oh! I have good cause," said Fouquet. "Judge for yourself." And he related the details of the course of the lighters, and the hypocritical persecution of Colbert. "Is not this a clear sign of my ruin?"

D'Artagnan became very serious. "That is true," he said. "Yes; it has an unsavory odor, as M. de Treville used to say." And he fixed on M. Fouquet his intelligent and significant look.

"Am I not clearly designated in that, captain? Is not the king bringing me to Nantes to get me away from Paris, where I have so many creatures, and to possess himself of Belle-Isle?"

"Where M. d'Herblay is," added D'Artagnan. Fouquet raised his head. "As for me, monseigneur," continued D'Artagnan, "I can assure you the king has said nothing to me against you."

"Indeed!"

"The king commanded me to set out for Nantes, it is true; and to say nothing about it to M. de Gesvres."

"My friend."

"To M. de Gesvres, yes, monseigneur," continued the musketeer, whose eyes did not cease to speak a language different from the language of his lips. "The king, moreover, commanded me to take a brigade of musketeers, which is apparently superfluous, as the country is quite quiet."

"A brigade!" said Fouquet, raising himself upon his elbow.

"Ninety-six horsemen, yes, monseigneur. The same number as were employed in arresting MM. de Chalais, de Cinq-Mars, and Montmorency."

Fouquet pricked up his ears at these words, pronounced without apparent value. "And what else?" said he.

"Oh! nothing but insignificant orders; such as guarding the castle, guarding every lodging, allowing none of M. de Gesvres's guards to occupy a single post."

"And as to myself," cried Fouquet, "what orders had you?"

"As to you, monseigneur?—not the smallest word."

"Monsieur d'Artagnan, my safety, my honor, perhaps my life are at stake. You would not deceive me?"

"I?—to what end? Are you threatened? Only there really is an order with respect to carriages and boats—"

"An order?"

"Yes; but it cannot concern you—a simple measure of police."

"What is it, captain?—what is it?"

"To forbid all horses or boats to leave Nantes, without a pass, signed by the king."

"Great God! but—"

D'Artagnan began to laugh. "All that is not to be put into execution before the arrival of the king at Nantes. So that you see plainly, monseigneur, the order in nowise concerns you."

Fouquet became thoughtful, and D'Artagnan feigned not to observe his preoccupation. "It is evident, by my thus confiding to you the orders which have been given to me, that I am friendly towards you, and that I am trying to prove to you that none of them are directed against you."

"Without doubt!—without doubt!" said Fouquet, still absent.

"Let us recapitulate," said the captain, his glance beaming with earnestness. "A special guard about the castle, in which your lodging is to be, is it not?"

"Do you know the castle?"

"Ah! monseigneur, a regular prison! The absence of M. de Gesvres, who has the honor of being one of your friends. The closing of the gates of the city, and of the river without a pass; but, only when the king shall have arrived. Please to observe, Monsieur Fouquet, that if, instead of speaking to man like you, who are one of the first in the kingdom, I were speaking to a troubled, uneasy conscience—I should compromise myself forever. What a fine opportunity for any one who wished to be free! No police, no guards, no orders; the water free, the roads free, Monsieur d'Artagnan obliged to lend his horses, if required. All this ought to reassure you, Monsieur Fouquet, for the king would not have left me thus independent, if he had any sinister designs. In truth, Monsieur Fouquet, ask me whatever you like, I am at your service; and, in return, if you will consent to do it, do me a service, that of giving my compliments to Aramis and Porthos, in case you embark for Belle-Isle, as you have a right to do without changing your dress, immediately, in your *robe de chambre*—just as you are." Saying these words, and with a profound bow, the musketeer, whose looks had lost none of their intelligent kindness, left the apartment. He had not reached the steps of the vestibule, when Fouquet, quite beside himself, hung to the bell-rope, and shouted, "My horses!—my lighter!" But nobody answered. The surintendant dressed himself with everything that came to hand.

"Gourville!—Gourville!" cried he, while slipping his watch into his pocket. And the bell sounded again, whilst Fouquet repeated, "Gourville!—Gourville!"

Gourville at length appeared, breathless and pale.

"Let us be gone! Let us be gone!" cried Fouquet, as soon as he saw him.

"It is too late!" said the surintendant's poor friend.

"Too late!—why?"

"Listen!" And they heard the sounds of trumpets and drums in front of the castle.

"What does that mean, Gourville?"

"It means the king is come, monseigneur."

"The king!"

"The king, who has ridden double stages, who has killed horses, and who is eight hours in advance of all our calculations."

"We are lost!" murmured Fouquet. "Brave D'Artagnan, all is over, thou has spoken to me too late!"

The king, in fact, was entering the city, which soon resounded with the cannon from the ramparts, and from a vessel which replied from the lower parts of the river. Fouquet's brow darkened; he called his *valets de chambre* and dressed in ceremonial costume. From his window, behind the curtains, he could see the eagerness of the people, and the movement of a large troop, which had followed the prince. The king was conducted to the castle with great pomp, and Fouquet saw him dismount under the portcullis, and say something in the ear of D'Artagnan, who held his stirrup. D'Artagnan, when the king had passed under the arch, directed his steps towards the house Fouquet was in; but so slowly, and stopping so frequently to speak to his musketeers, drawn up like a hedge, that it might be said he was counting the seconds, or the steps, before accomplishing his object. Fouquet opened the window to speak to him in the court.

"Ah!" cried D'Artagnan, on perceiving him, "are you still there, monseigneur?"

And that word *still* completed the proof to Fouquet of how much information and how many useful counsels were contained in the first visit the musketeer had paid him. The surintendant sighed deeply. "Good heavens! yes, monsieur," replied he. "The arrival of the king has interrupted me in the projects I had formed."

"Oh, then you know that the king has arrived?"

"Yes, monsieur, I have seen him; and this time you come from him—"

"To inquire after you, monseigneur; and, if your health is not too bad, to beg you to have the kindness to repair to the castle."

"Directly, Monsieur d'Artagnan, directly!"

"Ah, *mordioux!*" said the captain, "now the king is come, there is no more walking for anybody—no more free will; the password governs all now, you as much as me, me as much as you."

Fouquet heaved a last sigh, climbed with difficulty into his carriage, so great was his weakness, and went to the castle, escorted by D'Artagnan, whose politeness was not less terrifying this time than it had just before been consoling and cheerful.

CHAPTER 39

How the King, Louis XIV., Played His
Little Part.

As Fouquet was alighting from his carriage, to enter the castle
of Nantes, a man of mean appearance went up to him with
marks of the greatest respect, and gave him a letter. D'Artagnan
endeavored to prevent this man from speaking to Fouquet,
and pushed him away, but the message had been given to the
surintendant. Fouquet opened the letter and read it, and
instantly a vague terror, which D'Artagnan did not fail to
penetrate, was painted on the countenance of the first
minister. Fouquet put the paper into the portfolio which he
had under his arm, and passed on towards the king's apartments. D'Artagnan, through the small windows made at every
landing of the donjon stairs, saw, as he went up behind
Fouquet, the man who had delivered the note, looking round
him on the place and making signs to several persons, who
disappeared in the adjacent streets, after having themselves
repeated the signals. Fouquet was made to wait for a moment
on the terrace of which we have spoken,—a terrace which
abutted on the little corridor, at the end of which the cabinet
of the king was located. Here D'Artagnan passed on before
the surintendant, whom, till that time, he had respectfully
accompanied, and entered the royal cabinet.

"Well?" asked Louis XIV., who, on perceiving him, threw on to the table covered with papers a large green cloth.

"The order is executed, sire."

"And Fouquet?"

"Monsieur le surintendant follows me," said D'Artagnan.

"In ten minutes let him be introduced," said the king, dismissing D'Artagnan again with a gesture. The latter retired; but had scarcely reached the corridor at the extremity of which Fouquet was waiting for him, when he was recalled by the king's bell.

"Did he not appear astonished?" asked the king.

"Who, sire?"

"*Fouquet,*" replied the king, without saying monsieur, a peculiarity which confirmed the captain of the musketeers in his suspicions.

"No, sire," replied he.

"That's well!" And a second time Louis dismissed D'Artagnan.

Fouquet had not quitted the terrace where he had been left by his guide. He reperused his note, conceived thus:

"Something is being contrived against you. Perhaps they will not dare to carry it out at the castle; it will be on your return home. The house is already surrounded by musketeers. Do not enter. A white horse is in waiting for you behind the esplanade!"

Fouquet recognized the writing and zeal of Gourville. Not being willing that, if any evil happened to himself, this paper should compromise a faithful friend, the surintendant was busy tearing it into a thousand morsels, spread about by the wind from the balustrade of the terrace. D'Artagnan found him watching the snowflake fluttering of the last scraps in space.

"Monsieur," said he, "the king awaits you."

Fouquet walked with a deliberate step along the little corridor, where MM. de Brienne and Rose were at work, whilst the Duc de Saint-Aignan, seated on a chair, likewise in the corridor, appeared to be waiting for orders, with feverish impatience, his sword between his legs. It appeared strange to Fouquet that MM. Brienne, Rose, and de Saint-Aignan, in general so attentive and obsequious, should scarcely take the least notice, as he, the surintendant, passed. But how could he expect to find it otherwise among courtiers, he whom the king no longer called anything but *Fouquet?* He raised his head, determined to look every one and everything bravely in the face, and entered the king's apartment, where a little bell, which we already know, had already announced him to his majesty.

The king, without rising, nodded to him, and with interest: "Well! how are you, Monsieur Fouquet?" said he.

"I am in a high fever," replied the surintendant; "but I am at the king's service."

"That is well; the States assemble to-morrow; have you a speech ready?"

Fouquet looked at the king with astonishment. "I have not, sire," replied he; "but I will improvise one. I am too well acquainted with affairs to feel any embarrassment. I have only one question to ask; will your majesty permit me?"

"Certainly. Ask it."

"Why did not your majesty do his first minister the honor of giving him notice of this in Paris?"

"You were ill; I was not willing to fatigue you."

"Never did a labor—never did an explanation fatigue me, sire; and since the moment is come for me to demand an explanation of my king—"

"Oh, Monsieur Fouquet! an explanation? An explanation, pray, of what?"

"Of your majesty's intentions with respect to myself."

The king blushed. "I have been calumniated," continued Fouquet, warmly, "and I feel called upon to adjure the justice of the king to make inquiries."

"You say all this to me very uselessly, Monsieur Fouquet; I know what I know."

"Your majesty can only know the things that have been told to you; and I, on my part, have said nothing to you, whilst others have spoken many, many times—"

"What do you wish to say?" said the king, impatient to put an end to this embarrassing conversation.

"I will go straight to the facts, sire; and I accuse a certain man of having injured me in your majesty's opinion."

"Nobody has injured you, Monsieur Fouquet."

"That reply proves to me, sire, that I am right."

"Monsieur Fouquet, I do not like people to be accused."

"Not when one is accused?"

"We have already spoken too much about this affair."

"Your majesty will not allow me to justify myself?"

"I repeat that I do not accuse you."

Fouquet, with a half-bow, made a step backward. "It is certain," thought he, "that he has made up his mind. He alone who cannot go back can show such obstinacy. Not to see the danger now would be to be blind indeed; not to shun it would be stupid." He resumed aloud, "Did your majesty send for me on business?"

"No, Monsieur Fouquet, but for some advice I wish to give you."

"I respectfully await it, sire."

"Rest yourself, Monsieur Fouquet, do not throw away your strength; the session of the States will be short, and when my secretaries shall have closed it, I do not wish business to be talked of in France for a fortnight."

"Has the king nothing to say to me on the subject of this assembly of the States?"

"No, Monsieur Fouquet."

"Not to me, the surintendant of the finances?"

"Rest yourself, I beg you; that is all I have to say to you."

Fouquet bit his lips and hung his head. He was evidently

busy with some uneasy thought. This uneasiness struck the king. "Are you angry at having to rest yourself, M. Fouquet?" said he.

"Yes, sire, I am not accustomed to take rest."

"But you are ill; you must take care of yourself."

"Your majesty spoke just now of a speech to be pronounced to-morrow."

His majesty made no reply; this unexpected stroke embarrassed him. Fouquet felt the weight of this hesitation. He thought he could read danger in the eyes of the young prince, which fear would but precipitate. "If I appear frightened, I am lost," thought he.

The king, on his part, was only uneasy at the alarm of Fouquet. "Has he a suspicion of anything?" murmured he.

"If his first word is severe," again thought Fouquet; "if he becomes angry, or feigns to be angry for the sake of a pretext, how shall I extricate myself? Let us smooth the declivity a little. Gourville was right."

"Sire," said he, suddenly, "since the goodness of the king watches over my health to the point of dispensing with my labor, may I not be allowed to be absent from the council of to-morrow? I could pass the day in bed, and will entreat the king to grant me his physician, that we may endeavor to find a remedy against this fearful fever."

"So be it, Monsieur Fouquet, it shall be as you desire; you shall have a holiday to-morrow, you shall have the physician, and shall be restored to health."

"Thanks!" said Fouquet, bowing. Then, opening his game: "Shall I not have the happiness of conducting your majesty to my residence of Belle-Isle?"

And he looked Louis full in the face, to judge of the effect of such a proposal. The king blushed again.

"Do you know," replied he, endeavoring to smile, "that you have just said, 'My residence of Belle-Isle'?"

"Yes, sire."

"Well! do you not remember," continued the king in the same cheerful tone, "that you gave me Belle-Isle?"

"That is true again, sire. Only, as you have not taken it, you will doubtless come with me and take possession of it."

"I mean to do so."

"That was, besides, your majesty's intention as well as mine; and I cannot express to your majesty how happy and proud I have been to see all the king's regiments from Paris to help take possession."

The king stammered out that he did not bring the musketeers for that alone.

"Oh, I am convinced of that," said Fouquet, warmly; "your majesty knows very well that you have nothing to do but to come alone with a cane in your hand, to bring to the ground all the fortifications of Belle-Isle."

"*Peste!*" cried the king; "I do not wish those fine fortifications, which cost so much to build, to fall at all. No, let them stand against the Dutch and English. You would not guess what I want to see at Belle-Isle, Monsieur Fouquet; it is the pretty peasants and women of the lands on the sea-shore, who dance so well, and are so seducing with their scarlet petticoats! I have heard great boast of your pretty tenants, monsieur le surintendant; well, let me have a sight of them."

"Whenever your majesty pleases."

"Have you any means of transport? It shall be to-morrow, if you like."

The surintendant felt this stroke, which was not adroit, and replied, "No, sire; I was ignorant of your majesty's wish; above all, I was ignorant of your haste to see Belle-Isle, and I am prepared with nothing."

"You have a boat of your own, nevertheless?"

"I have five; but they are all in port, or at Paimboeuf; and to join them, or bring them hither, would require at least twenty-four hours. Have I any occasion to send a courier? Must I do so?"

"Wait a little, put an end to the fever,—wait till to-morrow."

"That is true. Who knows but that by to-morrow we may not have a hundred other ideas?" replied Fouquet, now perfectly convinced and very pale.

The king started, and stretched his hand out towards his little bell, but Fouquet prevented his ringing.

"Sire," said he, "I have an ague—I am trembling with cold. If I remain a moment longer, I shall most likely faint. I request your majesty's permission to go and fling myself beneath the bedclothes."

"Indeed, you are in a shiver; it is painful to behold! Come, Monsieur Fouquet, begone! I will send to inquire after you."

"Your majesty overwhelms me with kindness. In an hour I shall be better."

"I will call some one to reconduct you," said the king.

"As you please, sire; I would gladly take the arm of any one."

"Monsieur d'Artagnan!" cried the king, ringing his little bell.

"Oh, sire," interrupted Fouquet, laughing in such a manner as made the prince feel cold, "would you give me the captain of your musketeers to take me to my lodgings? An equivocal honor that, sire! A simple footman, I beg."

"And why, M. Fouquet? M. d'Artagnan conducts me often, and extremely well!"

"Yes, but when he conducts you, sire, it is to obey you; whilst me—"

"Go on!"

"If I am obliged to return home supported by the leader of the musketeers, it would be everywhere said you had had me arrested."

"Arrested!" replied the king, who became paler than Fouquet himself,—"arrested! oh!"

"And why should they not say so?" continued Fouquet, still laughing; "and I would lay a wager there would be people found wicked enough to laugh at it." This sally disconcerted the monarch. Fouquet was skillful enough, or fortunate enough, to make Louis XIV. recoil before the appearance of the deed he meditated. M. d'Artagnan, when he appeared, received an order to desire a musketeer to accompany the surintendant.

"Quite unnecessary," said the latter; "sword for sword; I prefer Gourville, who is waiting for me below. But that will not prevent me enjoying the society of M. d'Artagnan. I am glad he will see Belle-Isle, he is so good a judge of fortifications."

D'Artagnan bowed, without at all comprehending what was going on. Fouquet bowed again and left the apartment, affecting all the slowness of a man who walks with difficulty. When once out of the castle, "I am saved!" said he. "Oh! yes, disloyal king, you shall see Belle-Isle, but it shall be when I am no longer there."

He disappeared, leaving D'Artagnan with the king.

"Captain," said the king, "you will follow M. Fouquet at the distance of a hundred paces."

"Yes, sire."

"He is going to his lodgings again. You will go with him."

"Yes, sire."

"You will arrest him in my name, and will shut him up in a carriage."

"In a carriage. Well, sire?"

"In such a fashion that he may not, on the road, either converse with any one or throw notes to people he may meet."

"That will be rather difficult, sire."

"Not at all."

"Pardon me, sire, I cannot stifle M. Fouquet, and if he

asks for liberty to breathe, I cannot prevent him by closing both the windows and the blinds. He will throw out at the doors all the cries and notes possible."

"The case is provided for, Monsieur d'Artagnan; a carriage with a trellis will obviate both the difficulties you point out."

"A carriage with an iron trellis!" cried D'Artagnan; "but a carriage with an iron trellis is not made in half an hour, and your majesty commands me to go immediately to M. Fouquet's lodgings."

"The carriage in question is already made."

"Ah! that is quite a different thing," said the captain; "if the carriage is ready made, very well, then, we have only to set it in motion."

"It is ready—and the horses harnessed."

"Ah!"

"And the coachman, with the outriders, is waiting in the lower court of the castle."

D'Artagnan bowed. "There only remains for me to ask your majesty whither I shall conduct M. Fouquet."

"To the castle of Angers, at first."

"Very well, sire."

"Afterwards we will see."

"Yes, sire."

"Monsieur d'Artagnan, one last word: you have remarked that, for making this capture of M. Fouquet, I have not employed my guards, on which account M. de Gesvres will be furious."

"Your majesty does not employ your guards," said the captain, a little humiliated, "because you mistrust M. de Gesvres, that is all."

"That is to say, monsieur, that I have more confidence in you."

"I know that very well, sire! and it is of no use to make so much of it."

"It is only for the sake of arriving at this, monsieur, that if, from this moment, it should happen that by any chance whatever M. Fouquet should escape—such chances have been, monsieur—"

"Oh! very often, sire; but for others, not for me."

"And why not with you?"

"Because I, sire, have, for an instant, wished to save M. Fouquet."

The king started. "Because," continued the captain, "I had then a right to do so, having guessed your majesty's plan, without you having spoken to me of it, and that I took an interest in M. Fouquet. Now, was I not at liberty to show my interest in this man?"

"In truth, monsieur, you do not reassure me with regard to your services."

"If I had saved him then, I should have been perfectly innocent; I will say more, I should have done well, for M. Fouquet is not a bad man. But he was not willing; his destiny prevailed; he let the hour of liberty slip by. So much the worse! Now I have orders, I will obey those orders, and M. Fouquet you may consider as a man arrested. He is at the castle of Angers, this very M. Fouquet."

"Oh! you have not got him yet, captain."

"That concerns me; every one to his trade, sire; only, once more, reflect! Do you seriously give me orders to arrest M. Fouquet, sire?"

"Yes, a thousand times, yes!"

"In writing, sire, then."

"Here is the order."

D'Artagnan read it, bowed to the king, and left the room. From the height of the terrace he perceived Gourville, who went by with a joyous air towards the lodgings of M. Fouquet.

CHAPTER 40

The White Horse and the Black.

"That is rather surprising," said D'Artagnan; "Gourville running about the streets so gayly, when he is almost certain that M. Fouquet is in danger; when it is almost equally certain that it was Gourville who warned M. Fouquet just now by the note which was torn into a thousand pieces upon the terrace, and given to the winds by monsieur le surintendant. Gourville is rubbing his hands; that is because he has done something clever. Whence comes M. Gourville? Gourville is coming from the Rue aux Herbes. Whither does the Rue aux Herbes lead?" And D'Artagnan followed, along the tops of the houses of Nantes, dominated by the castle, the line traced by the streets, as he would have done upon a topographical plan; only, instead of the dead, flat paper, the living chart rose in relief with the cries, the movements, and the shadows of men and things. Beyond the inclosure of the city, the great verdant plains stretched out, bordering the Loire, and appeared to run towards the pink horizon, which was cut by the azure of the waters and the dark green of the marshes. Immediately outside the gates of Nantes two white roads were seen diverging like separate fingers of a gigantic hand. D'Artagnan, who had taken in all the panorama at a glance by crossing the terrace, was led by the line of the Rue aux Herbes to the mouth of one of those roads which took its rise under the gates of Nantes. One step more, and he was about to descend the stairs, take his trellised carriage, and go towards the lodgings of M. Fouquet. But chance decreed, at the moment of plunging into the staircase, that he was attracted by a moving point then gaining ground upon that road.

"What is that?" said the musketeer to himself; "a horse galloping,—a runaway horse, no doubt. What a rate he is going at!" The moving point became detached from the road, and entered into the fields. "A white horse," continued the captain, who had just observed the color thrown luminously against the dark ground, "and he is mounted; it must be some boy whose horse is thirsty and has run away with him."

These reflections, rapid as lightning, simultaneous with visual perception, D'Artagnan had already forgotten when he descended the first steps of the staircase. Some morsels of paper were spread over the stairs, and shone out white against the dirty stones. "Eh! eh!" said the captain to himself, "here are some of the fragments of the note torn by M. Fouquet. Poor man! he has given his secret to the wind; the wind will have no more to do with it, and brings it back to the king. Decidedly, Fouquet, you play with misfortune! the game is not a fair one,—fortune is against you. The star of Louis XIV. obscures yours; the adder is stronger and more cunning than the squirrel." D'Artagnan picked up one of these morsels of paper as he descended. "Gourville's pretty little hand!" cried he, whilst examining one of the fragments of the note; "I was not mistaken." And he read the word "horse." "Stop!" said he; and he examined another, upon which there was not a letter traced. Upon a third he read the word "white;" "white horse," repeated he, like a child that is spelling. "Ah, *mordioux!*" cried the suspicious spirit, "a white horse!" And, like that grain of powder which, burning, dilates into ten thousand times its volume, D'Artagnan, enlightened by ideas and suspicions, rapidly reascended the stairs towards the terrace. The white horse was still galloping in the direction of the Loire, at the extremity of which, melting into the vapors of the water, a little sail appeared, wave-balanced like a water-butterfly. "Oh!" cried the musketeer, "only a man who wants to fly would go at that pace across plowed lands; there is but one Fouquet, a financier, to ride thus in open day upon a white horse; there is no one but the lord of Belle-Isle who would make his escape towards the sea, while there are such thick forests on land, and there is but one D'Artagnan in the world to catch M. Fouquet, who has half an hour's start, and who will have gained his boat within an hour." This being said, the musketeer gave orders that the carriage with the iron trellis should be taken immediately to a thicket situated just outside the city. He selected his best horse, jumped upon his back, galloped along the Rue aux Herbes, taking, not the road Fouquet had taken, but the bank itself of the Loire, certain that he should gain ten minutes upon the total distance, and, at the intersection of the two lines, come up with the fugitive, who could have no suspicion of being pursued in that direction. In the rapidity of the pursuit, and with the impatience of the avenger, animating himself as in war, D'Artagnan, so mild, so kind towards Fouquet, was surprised to find himself become ferocious—almost sanguinary. For a long time he galloped without catching sight of the white horse. His rage assumed fury, he doubted himself,—he suspected that Fouquet had buried himself in some subterranean road, or that he had changed the white horse for one of those famous black ones, as swift as the wind, which D'Artagnan, at Saint-Mande, had so frequently admired and envied for their vigor and their fleetness.

At such moments, when the wind cut his eyes so as to make the tears spring from them, when the saddle had become burning hot, when the galled and spurred horse reared with pain, and threw behind him a shower of dust and stones, D'Artagnan, raising himself in his stirrups, and seeing nothing on the waters, nothing beneath the trees, looked up into the air like a madman. He was losing his senses. In the paroxysms of eagerness he dreamt of aerial ways,—the discovery of following century; he called to his mind Daedalus and the vast wings that had saved him from the prisons of Crete. A hoarse sigh broke from his lips, as he repeated, devoured by the fear of ridicule, "I! I! duped by a Gourville! I! They will say that I am growing old,—they will say I have received a million to allow Fouquet to escape!" And he again dug his spurs into the sides of his horse: he had ridden astonishingly fast. Suddenly, at the extremity of some open pasture-ground, behind the hedges, he saw a white form which showed itself, disappeared, and at last remained distinctly visible against the rising ground. D'Artagnan's heart leaped with joy. He wiped the streaming sweat from his brow, relaxed the tension of his knees,—by which the horse breathed more freely,—and, gathering up his reins, moderated the speed of the vigorous animal, his active accomplice on this man-hunt. He had then time to study the direction of the road, and his position with regard to Fouquet. The superintendent had completely winded his horse by crossing the soft ground. He felt the necessity of gaining a firmer footing, and turned towards the road by the shortest secant line. D'Artagnan, on his part, had nothing to do but to ride straight on, concealed by the sloping shore; so that he would cut his quarry off the road when he came up with him. Then the real race would begin,— then the struggle would be in earnest.

D'Artagnan gave his horse good breathing-time. He observed that the superintendent had relaxed into a trot, which was to say, he, too, was favoring his horse. But both of them were too much pressed for time to allow them to continue long at that pace. The white horse sprang off like an arrow the moment his feet touched firm ground. D'Artagnan dropped his head, and his black horse broke into a gallop. Both followed the same route; the quadruple echoes of this new race-course were confounded. Fouquet had not yet perceived D'Artagnan. But on issuing from the slope, a single echo struck the air; it was that of the steps of D'Artagnan's horse, which rolled along like thunder. Fouquet turned round, and saw behind him, within a hundred paces, his enemy bent over the neck of his horse. There could be no doubt—the shining baldrick, the red cassock—it was a musketeer. Fouquet slackened his hand likewise, and the white horse placed twenty feet more between his adversary and himself.

"Oh, but," thought D'Artagnan, becoming very anxious, "that is not a common horse M. Fouquet is upon—let us see!" And he attentively examined with his infallible eye the shape and capabilities of the courser. Round full quarters—a thin long tail—large hocks—thin legs, as dry as bars of steel—hoofs hard as marble. He spurred his own, but the distance between the two remained the same. D'Artagnan listened attentively; not a breath of the horse reached him, and yet he seemed to cut the air. The black horse, on the contrary, began to puff like any blacksmith's bellows.

"I must overtake him, if I kill my horse," thought the musketeer; and he began to saw the mouth of the poor animal, whilst he buried the rowels of his merciless spurs into his sides. The maddened horse gained twenty toises, and came up within pistol-shot of Fouquet.

"Courage!" said the musketeer to himself, "courage! the white horse will perhaps grow weaker, and if the horse does not fall, the master must pull up at last." But horse and rider remained upright together, gaining ground by difficult degrees. D'Artagnan uttered a wild cry, which made Fouquet turn round, and added speed to the white horse.

"A famous horse! a mad rider!" growled the captain. "Hola! *mordioux!* Monsieur Fouquet! stop! in the king's name!" Fouquet made no reply.

"Do you hear me?" shouted D'Artagnan, whose horse had just stumbled.

"*Pardieu!*" replied Fouquet, laconically; and rode on faster.

D'Artagnan was nearly mad; the blood rushed boiling to his temples and his eyes. "In the king's name!" cried he again, "stop, or I will bring you down with a pistol-shot!"

"Do!" replied Fouquet, without relaxing his speed.

D'Artagnan seized a pistol and cocked it, hoping that the double click of the spring would stop his enemy. "You have pistols likewise," said he, "turn and defend yourself."

Fouquet did turn round at the noise, and looking D'Artagnan full in the face, opened, with his right hand, the part of his dress which concealed his body, but he did not even touch his holsters. There were not more than twenty paces between the two.

"*Mordioux!*" said D'Artagnan, "I will not assassinate you; if you will not fire upon me, surrender! what is a prison?"

"I would rather die!" replied Fouquet; "I shall suffer less."

D'Artagnan, drunk with despair, hurled his pistol to the ground. "I will take you alive!" said he; and by a prodigy of skill which this incomparable horseman alone was capable, he threw his horse forward to within ten paces of the white horse; already his hand was stretched out to seize his prey.

"Kill me! kill me!" cried Fouquet, "'twould be more humane!"

"No! alive—alive!" murmured the captain.

At this moment his horse made a false step for the second time, and Fouquet's again took the lead. It was an unheard-of spectacle, this race between two horses which now only kept alive by the will of their riders. It might be said that D'Artagnan rode, carrying his horse along between his knees. To the furious gallop had succeeded the fast trot, and that had sunk to what might be scarcely called a trot at all. But the chase appeared equally warm in the two fatigued *athletoe.* D'Artagnan, quite in despair, seized his second pistol, and cocked it.

"At your horse! not at you!" cried he to Fouquet. And he fired. The animal was hit in the quarters—he made a furious bound, and plunged forward. At that moment D'Artagnan's horse fell dead.

"I am dishonored!" thought the musketeer; "I am a miserable wretch! for pity's sake, M. Fouquet, throw me one of your pistols, that I may blow out my brains!" But Fouquet rode away.

"For mercy's sake! for mercy's sake!" cried D'Artagnan; "that which you will not do at this moment, I myself will do within an hour, but here, upon this road, I should die bravely; I should die esteemed; do me that service, M. Fouquet!"

M. Fouquet made no reply, but continued to trot on. D'Artagnan began to run after his enemy. Successively he threw away his hat, his coat, which embarrassed him, and then the sheath of his sword, which got between his legs as he was running. The sword in his hand itself became too heavy, and he threw it after the sheath. The white horse began to rattle in its throat; D'Artagnan gained upon him. From a trot the exhausted animal sunk to a staggering walk—the foam from his mouth was mixed with blood. D'Artagnan made a desperate effort, sprang towards Fouquet, and seized him by the leg, saying in a broken, breathless voice, "I arrest you in the king's name! blow my brains out, if you like; we have both done our duty."

Fouquet hurled far from him, into the river, the two pistols D'Artagnan might have seized, and dismounting from his horse—"I am your prisoner, monsieur," said he; "will you take my arm, for I see you are ready to faint?"

"Thanks!" murmured D'Artagnan, who, in fact, felt the earth sliding from under his feet, and the light of day turning to blackness around him; then he rolled upon the sand, without breath or strength. Fouquet hastened to the brink of the river, dipped some water in his hat, with which he bathed the temples of the musketeer, and introduced a few drop between his lips. D'Artagnan raised himself with difficulty, and looked about him with a wandering eye. He beheld Fouquet on his knees, with his wet hat in his hand, smiling upon him with ineffable sweetness. "You are not off, then?" cried he. "Oh, monsieur! the true king of royalty, in heart, in soul, is not Louis of the Louvre, or Philippe of Sainte-Marguerite; it is you, proscribed, condemned!"

"I, who this day am ruined by a single error, M. d'Artagnan."

"What, in the name of Heaven, is that?"

"I should have had you for a friend! But how shall we return to Nantes? We are a great way from it."

"That is true," said D'Artagnan, gloomily.

"The white horse will recover, perhaps; he is a good horse! Mount, Monsieur d'Artagnan; I will walk till you have rested a little."

"Poor beast! and wounded, too?" said the musketeer.

"He will go, I tell you; I know him; but we can do better still, let us both get up, and ride slowly."

"We can try," said the captain. But they had scarcely charged the animal with this double load, when he began to stagger, and then with a great effort walked a few minutes, then staggered again, and sank down dead by the side of the black horse, which he had just managed to come up to.

"We will go on foot—destiny wills it so—the walk will be pleasant," said Fouquet, passing his arm through that of D'Artagnan.

"*Mordioux!*" cried the latter, with a fixed eye, a contracted brow, and a swelling heart—"What a disgraceful day!"

They walked slowly the four leagues which separated them from the little wood behind which the carriage and escort were in waiting. When Fouquet perceived that sinister machine, he said to D'Artagnan, who cast down his eyes, ashamed of Louis XIV., "There is an idea that did not emanate from a brave man, Captain d'Artagnan; it is not yours. What are these gratings for?" said he.

"To prevent your throwing letters out."

"Ingenious!"

"But you can speak, if you cannot write," said D'Artagnan.

"Can I speak to you?"

"Why, certainly, if you wish to do so."

Fouquet reflected for a moment, then looking the captain full in the face, "One single word," said he; "will you remember it?"

"I will not forget it."

"Will you speak it to whom I wish?"

"I will."

"Saint-Mande," articulated Fouquet, in a low voice.

"Well! and for whom?"

"For Madame de Belliere or Pelisson."

"It shall be done."

The carriage rolled through Nantes, and took the route to Angers.

CHAPTER 41

In Which the Squirrel Falls,—the Adder Flies.

It was two o'clock in the afternoon. The king, full of impatience, went to his cabinet on the terrace, and kept opening the door of the corridor, to see what his secretaries were doing. M. Colbert, seated in the same place M. de Saint-Aignan had so long occupied in the morning, was chatting in a low voice with M. de Brienne. The king opened the door suddenly, and addressed them. "What is it you are saying?"

"We were speaking of the first sitting of the States," said M. de Brienne, rising.

"Very well," replied the king, and returned to his room.

Five minutes after, the summons of the bell recalled Rose, whose hour it was.

"Have you finished your copies?" asked the king.

"Not yet, sire."

"See if M. d'Artagnan has returned."

"Not yet, sire."

"It is very strange," murmured the king. "Call M. Colbert."

Colbert entered; he had been expecting this all the morning.

"Monsieur Colbert," said the king, very sharply; "you must ascertain what has become of M. d'Artagnan."

Colbert in his calm voice replied, "Where does your majesty desire him to be sought for?"

"Eh! monsieur! do you not know on what I have sent him?" replied Louis, acrimoniously.

"Your majesty did not inform me."

"Monsieur, there are things that must be guessed; and you, above all, are apt to guess them."

"I might have been able to imagine, sire; but I do not presume to be positive."

Colbert had not finished these words when a rougher voice than that of the king interrupted the interesting conversation thus begun between the monarch and his clerk.

"D'Artagnan!" cried the king, with evident joy.

D'Artagnan, pale and in evidently bad humor, cried to the king, as he entered, "Sire, is it your majesty who has given orders to my musketeers?"

"What orders?" said the king.

"About M. Fouquet's house?"

"None!" replied Louis.

"Ha!" said D'Artagnan, biting his mustache; "I was not mistaken, then; it was monsieur here;" and he pointed to Colbert.

"What orders? Let me know," said the king.

"Orders to turn the house topsy-turvy, to beat M. Fouquet's servants, to force the drawers, to give over a peaceful house to pillage! *Mordioux!* these are savage orders!"

"Monsieur!" said Colbert, turning pale.

"Monsieur," interrupted D'Artagnan, "the king alone, understand,—the king alone has a right to command my musketeers; but, as to you, I forbid you to do it, and I tell you so before his majesty; gentlemen who carry swords do not sling pens behind their ears."

"D'Artagnan! D'Artagnan!" murmured the king.

"It is humiliating," continued the musketeer; "my soldiers are disgraced. I do not command *reitres*, thank you, nor clerks of the intendant, *mordioux!*"

"Well! but what is all this about?" said the king with authority.

"About this, sire; monsieur—monsieur, who could not guess your majesty's orders, and consequently could not know I was gone to arrest M. Fouquet; monsieur, who has caused the iron cage to be constructed for his patron of yesterday—has sent M. de Roncherolles to the lodgings of M. Fouquet, and, under the pretense of securing the surintendant's papers, they have taken away the furniture. My musketeers have been posted round the house all the morning; such were my orders. Why did any one presume to order them to enter? Why, by forcing them to assist in this pillage, have they been made accomplices in it? *Mordioux!* we serve the king, we do; but we do not serve M. Colbert!"[5]

"Monsieur d'Artagnan," said the king, sternly, "take care; it is not in my presence that such explanations, and made in such a tone, should take place."

"I have acted for the good of the king," said Colbert, in a faltering voice. "It is hard to be so treated by one of your majesty's officers, and that without redress, on account of the respect I owe the king."

"The respect you owe the king," cried D'Artagnan, his eyes flashing fire, "consists, in the first place, in making his authority respected, and his person beloved. Every agent of a power without control represents that power, and when people curse the hand which strikes them, it is the royal hand that God reproaches, do you hear? Must a soldier, hardened by forty years of wounds and blood, give you this lesson, monsieur? Must mercy be on my side, and ferocity on yours?

[5] Dumas here, and later in the chapter, uses the name Roncherat. Roncherolles is the actual name of the man.

You have caused the innocent to be arrested, bound, and imprisoned!"

"Accomplices, perhaps, of M. Fouquet," said Colbert.

"Who told you M. Fouquet had accomplices, or even that he was guilty? The king alone knows that; his justice is not blind! When he says, 'Arrest and imprison' such and such a man, he is obeyed. Do not talk to me, then, any more of the respect you owe the king, and be careful of your words, that they may not chance to convey the slightest menace; for the king will not allow those to be threatened who do him service by others who do him disservice; and if in case I should have, which God forbid! a master so ungrateful, I would make myself respected."

Thus saying, D'Artagnan took his station haughtily in the king's cabinet, his eyes flashing, his hand on his sword, his lips trembling, affecting much more anger than he really felt. Colbert, humiliated and devoured with rage, bowed to the king as if to ask his permission to leave the room. The king, thwarted alike in pride and in curiosity, knew not which part to take. D'Artagnan saw him hesitate. To remain longer would have been a mistake: it was necessary to score a triumph over Colbert, and the only method was to touch the king so near the quick, that his majesty would have no other means of extrication but choosing between the two antagonists. D'Artagnan bowed as Colbert had done; but the king, who, in preference to everything else, was anxious to have all the exact details of the arrest of the surintendant of the finances from him who had made him tremble for a moment,—the king, perceiving that the ill-humor of D'Artagnan would put off for half an hour at least the details he was burning to be acquainted with,—Louis, we say, forgot Colbert, who had nothing new to tell him, and recalled his captain of the musketeers.

"In the first place," said he, "let me see the result of your commission, monsieur; you may rest yourself hereafter."

D'Artagnan, who was just passing through the doorway, stopped at the voice of the king, retraced his steps, and Colbert was forced to leave the closet. His countenance assumed almost a purple hue, his black and threatening eyes shone with a dark fire beneath their thick brows; he stepped out, bowed before the king, half drew himself up in passing D'Artagnan, and went away with death in his heart. D'Artagnan, on being left alone with the king, softened immediately, and composing his countenance: "Sire," said he, "you are a young king. It is by the dawn that people judge whether the day will be fine or dull. How, sire, will the people, whom the hand of God has placed under your law, argue of your reign, if between them and you, you allow angry and violent ministers to interpose their mischief? But let us speak of myself, sire, let us leave a discussion that may appear idle, and perhaps inconvenient to you. Let us speak of myself. I have arrested M. Fouquet."

"You took plenty of time about it," said the king, sharply.

D'Artagnan looked at the king. "I perceive that I have expressed myself badly. I announced to your majesty that I had arrested Monsieur Fouquet."

"You did; and what then?"

"Well! I ought to have told your majesty that M. Fouquet had arrested me; that would have been more just. I re-establish the truth, then; I have been arrested by M. Fouquet."

It was now the turn of Louis XIV. to be surprised. His majesty was astonished in his turn.

D'Artagnan, with his quick glance, appreciated what was passing in the heart of his master. He did not allow him time to put any questions. He related, with that poetry, that picturesqueness, which perhaps he alone possessed at that period, the escape of Fouquet, the pursuit, the furious race, and, lastly, the inimitable generosity of the surintendant, who might have fled ten times over, who might have killed the adversary in the pursuit, but who had preferred imprisonment, perhaps worse, to the humiliation of one who wished to rob him of his liberty. In proportion as the tale advanced, the king became agitated, devouring the narrator's words, and drumming with his finger-nails upon the table.

"It results from all this, sire, in my eyes, at least, that the man who conducts himself thus is a gallant man, and cannot be an enemy to the king. That is my opinion, and I repeat it to your majesty. I know what the king will say to me, and I bow to it,—reasons of state. So be it! To my ears that sounds highly respectable. But I am a soldier, and I have received my orders, my orders are executed—very unwillingly on my part, it is true, but they are executed. I say no more."

"Where is M. Fouquet at this moment?" asked Louis, after a short silence.

"M. Fouquet, sire," replied D'Artagnan, "is in the iron cage that M. Colbert had prepared for him, and is galloping as fast as four strong horses can drag him, towards Angers."

"Why did you leave him on the road?"

"Because your majesty did not tell me to go to Angers. The proof, the best proof of what I advance, is that the king desired me to be sought for but this minute. And then I had another reason."

"What is that?"

"Whilst I was with him, poor M. Fouquet would never attempt to escape."

"Well!" cried the king, astonished.

"Your majesty ought to understand, and does understand, certainly, that my warmest wish is to know that M. Fouquet is at liberty. I have given him one of my brigadiers, the most stupid I could find among my musketeers, in order that the prisoner might have a chance of escaping."

"Are you mad, Monsieur d'Artagnan?" cried the king, crossing his arms on his breast. "Do people utter such enormities, even when they have the misfortune to think them?"

"Ah! sire, you cannot expect that I should be an enemy

to M. Fouquet, after what he has just done for you and me. No, no; if you desire that he should remain under your lock and bolt, never give him in charge to me; however closely wired might be the cage, the bird would, in the end, take wing."

"I am surprised," said the king, in his sternest tone, "you did not follow the fortunes of the man M. Fouquet wished to place upon my throne. You had in him all you want—affection, gratitude. In my service, monsieur, you will only find a master."

"If M. Fouquet had not gone to seek you in the Bastille, sire," replied D'Artagnan, with a deeply impressive manner, "one single man would have gone there, and I should have been that man—you know that right well, sire."

The king was brought to a pause. Before that speech of his captain of the musketeers, so frankly spoken and so true, the king had nothing to offer. On hearing D'Artagnan, Louis remembered the D'Artagnan of former times; him who, at the Palais Royal, held himself concealed behind the curtains of his bed, when the people of Paris, led by Cardinal de Retz, came to assure themselves of the presence of the king; the D'Artagnan whom he saluted with his hand at the door of his carriage, when repairing to Notre Dame on his return to Paris; the soldier who had quitted his service at Blois; the lieutenant he had recalled to be beside his person when the death of Mazarin restored his power; the man he had always found loyal, courageous, devoted. Louis advanced towards the door and called Colbert. Colbert had not left the corridor where the secretaries were at work. He reappeared.

"Colbert, did you make a perquisition on the house of M. Fouquet?"

"Yes, sire."

"What has it produced?"

"M. de Roncherolles, who was sent with your majesty's musketeers, has remitted me some papers," replied Colbert.

"I will look at them. Give me your hand."

"My hand, sire!"

"Yes, that I may place it in that of M. d'Artagnan. In fact, M. d'Artagnan," added he, with a smile, turning towards the soldier, who, at sight of the clerk, had resumed his haughty attitude, "you do not know this man; make his acquaintance." And he pointed to Colbert. "He has been made but a moderately valuable servant in subaltern positions, but he will be a great man if I raise him to the foremost rank."

"Sire!" stammered Colbert, confused with pleasure and fear.

"I always understood why," murmured D'Artagnan in the king's ear; "he was jealous."

"Precisely, and his jealousy confined his wings."

"He will henceforward be a winged-serpent," grumbled the musketeer, with a remnant of hatred against his recent adversary.

But Colbert, approaching him, offered to his eyes a physiognomy so different from that which he had been accustomed to see him wear; he appeared so good, so mild, so easy; his eyes took the expression of an intelligence so noble, that D'Artagnan, a connoisseur in physiognomies, was moved, and almost changed in his convictions. Colbert pressed his hand.

"That which the king has just told you, monsieur, proves how well his majesty is acquainted with men. The inveterate opposition I have displayed, up to this day, against abuses and not against men, proves that I had it in view to prepare for my king a glorious reign, for my country a great blessing. I have many ideas, M. d'Artagnan. You will see them expand in the sun of public peace; and if I have not the good fortune to conquer the friendship of honest men, I am at least certain, monsieur, that I shall obtain their esteem. For their admiration, monsieur, I would give my life."

This change, this sudden elevation, this mute approbation of the king, gave the musketeer matter for profound reflection. He bowed civilly to Colbert, who did not take his eyes off him. The king, when he saw they were reconciled, dismissed them. They left the room together. As soon as they were out of the cabinet, the new minister, stopping the captain, said:

"Is it possible, M. d'Artagnan, that with such an eye as yours, you did not, at the first glance, at the first impression, discover what sort of man I am?"

"Monsieur Colbert," replied the musketeer, "a ray of the sun in our eyes prevents us from seeing the most vivid flame. The man in power radiates, you know; and since you are there, why should you continue to persecute him who had just fallen into disgrace, and fallen from such a height?"

"I, monsieur!" said Colbert; "oh, monsieur! I would never persecute him. I wished to administer the finances and to administer them alone, because I am ambitious, and, above all, because I have the most entire confidence in my own merit; because I know that all the gold of this country will ebb and flow beneath my eyes, and I love to look at the king's gold; because, if I live thirty years, in thirty years not a *denir* of it will remain in my hands; because, with that gold, I will build granaries, castles, cities, and harbors; because I will create a marine, I will equip navies that shall waft the name of France to the most distant people; because I will create libraries and academies; because I will make France the first country in the world, and the wealthiest. These are the motives for my animosity against M. Fouquet, who prevented my acting. And then, when I shall be great and strong, when France is great and strong, in my turn, then, will I cry, 'Mercy'!"

"Mercy, did you say? then ask his liberty of the king. The king is only crushing him on *your* account."

Colbert again raised his head. "Monsieur," said he, "you know that is not so, and that the king has his own personal animosity against M. Fouquet; it is not for me to teach you that."

"But the king will grow tired; he will forget."

"The king never forgets, M. d'Artagnan. Hark! the king calls. He is going to issue an order. I have not influenced him, have I? Listen."

The king, in fact, was calling his secretaries. "Monsieur d'Artagnan," said he.

"I am here, sire."

"Give twenty of your musketeers to M. de Saint-Aignan, to form a guard for M. Fouquet."

D'Artagnan and Colbert exchanged looks. "And from Angers," continued the king, "they will conduct the prisoner to the Bastille, in Paris."

"You were right," said the captain to the minister.

"Saint-Aignan," continued the king, "you will have any one shot who shall attempt to speak privately with M. Fouquet, during the journey."

"But myself, sire," said the duke.

"You, monsieur, you will only speak to him in the presence of the musketeers." The duke bowed and departed to execute his commission.

D'Artagnan was about to retire likewise; but the king stopped him.

"Monsieur," said he, "you will go immediately, and take possession of the isle and fief of Belle-Ile-en-Mer."

"Yes, sire. Alone?"

"You will take a sufficient number of troops to prevent delay, in case the place should be contumacious."

A murmur of courtly incredulity rose from the group of courtiers. "That shall be done," said D'Artagnan.

"I saw the place in my infancy," resumed the king, "and I do not wish to see it again. You have heard me? Go, monsieur, and do not return without the keys."

Colbert went up to D'Artagnan. "A commission which, if you carry it out well," said he, "will be worth a marechal's baton to you."

"Why do you employ the words, 'if you carry it out well'?"

"Because it is difficult."

"Ah! in what respect?"

"You have friends in Belle-Isle, Monsieur d'Artagnan; and it is not an easy thing for men like you to march over the bodies of their friends to obtain success."

D'Artagnan hung his head in deepest thought, whilst Colbert returned to the king. A quarter of an hour after, the captain received the written order from the king, to blow up the fortress of Belle-Isle, in case of resistance, with power of life and death over all the inhabitants or refugees, and an injunction not to allow one to escape.

"Colbert was right," thought D'Artagnan; "for me the baton of a marechal of France will cost the lives of my two friends. Only they seem to forget that my friends are not more stupid than the birds, and that they will not wait for the hand of the fowler to extend over their wings. I will show them that hand so plainly, that they will have quite time enough to see it. Poor Porthos! Poor Aramis! No; my fortune should shall not cost your wings a feather."

Having thus determined, D'Artagnan assembled the royal army, embarked it at Paimboeuf, and set sail, without the loss of an unnecessary minute.

CHAPTER 42

Belle-Ile-en-Mer.

At the extremity of the mole, against which the furious sea beats at the evening tide, two men, holding each other by the arm, were conversing in an animated and expansive tone, without the possibility of any other human being hearing their words, borne away, as they were, one by one, by the gusts of wind, with the white foam swept from the crests of the waves. The sun had just gone down in the vast sheet of the crimsoned ocean, like a gigantic crucible. From time to time, one of these men, turning towards the east, cast an anxious, inquiring look over the sea. The other, interrogating the features of his companion, seemed to seek for information in his looks. Then, both silent, busied with dismal thoughts, they resumed their walk. Every one has already perceived that these two men were our proscribed heroes, Porthos and Aramis, who had taken refuge in Belle-Isle, since the ruin of their hopes, since the discomfiture of the colossal schemes of M. d'Herblay.

"If is of no use your saying anything to the contrary, my dear Aramis," repeated Porthos, inhaling vigorously the salt breeze with which he charged his massive chest, "It is of no use, Aramis. The disappearance of all the fishing-boats that went out two days ago is not an ordinary circumstance. There has been no storm at sea; the weather has been constantly calm, not even the lightest gale; and even if we had had a tempest, all our boats would not have foundered. I repeat, it is strange. This complete disappearance astonishes me, I tell you."

"True," murmured Aramis. "You are right, friend Porthos; it is true, there is something strange in it."

"And further," added Porthos, whose ideas the assent of the bishop of Vannes seemed to enlarge; "and, further, do you not observe that if the boats have perished, not a single plank has washed ashore?"

"I have remarked it as well as yourself."

"And do you not think it strange that the two only boats we had left in the whole island, and which I sent in search of the others—"

Aramis here interrupted his companion by a cry, and by so sudden a movement, that Porthos stopped as if he were stupefied. "What do you say, Porthos? What!—You have sent the two boats—"

"In search of the others! Yes, to be sure I have," replied Porthos, calmly.

"Unhappy man! What have you done? Then we are indeed lost," cried the bishop.

"Lost!—what did you say?" exclaimed the terrified Porthos. "How lost, Aramis? How are we lost?"

Aramis bit his lips. "Nothing! nothing! Your pardon, I meant to say—"

"What?"

"That if we were inclined—if we took a fancy to make an excursion by sea, we could not."

"Very good! and why should that vex you? A precious pleasure, *ma foi!* For my part, I don't regret it at all. What I regret is certainly not the more or less amusement we can find at Belle-Isle: what I regret, Aramis, is Pierrefonds; Bracieux; le Vallon; beautiful France! Here, we are not in France, my dear friend; we are—I know not where. Oh! I tell you, in full sincerity of soul, and your affection will excuse my frankness, but I declare to you I am not happy at Belle-Isle. No; in good truth, I am not happy!"

Aramis breathed a long, but stifled sigh. "Dear friend," replied he: "that is why it is so sad a thing you have sent the two boats we had left in search of the boats which disappeared two days ago. If you had not sent them away, we would have departed."

"'Departed!' And the orders, Aramis?"

"What orders?"

"*Parbleu!* Why, the orders you have been constantly, in and out of season, repeating to me—that we were to hold Belle-Isle against the usurper. You know very well!"

"That is true!" murmured Aramis again.

"You see, then, plainly, my friend, that we could not depart; and that the sending away of the boats in search of the others cannot prove prejudicial to us in the very least."

Aramis was silent; and his vague glances, luminous as that of an albatross, hovered for a long time over the sea, interrogating space, seeking to pierce the very horizon.

"With all that, Aramis," continued Porthos, who adhered to his idea, and that the more closely from the bishop having apparently endorsed it,—"with all that, you give me no explanation about what can have happened to these unfortunate boats. I am assailed by cries and complaints whichever way I go. The children cry to see the desolation of the women, as if I could restore the absent husbands and fathers. What do you suppose, my friend, and how ought I to answer them?"

"Think all you like, my good Porthos, and say nothing."

This reply did not satisfy Porthos at all. He turned away grumbling something in ill-humor. Aramis stopped the valiant musketeer. "Do you remember," said he, in a melancholy tone, kneading the two hands of the giant between his own with affectionate cordiality, "do you remember, my friend, that in the glorious days of youth—do you remember, Porthos, when we were all strong and valiant—we, and the other two—if we had then had an inclination to return to France, do you think this sheet of salt water would have stopped us?"

"Oh!" said Porthos; "but six leagues."

"If you had seen me get astride of a plank, would you have remained on land, Porthos?"

"No, *pardieu!* No, Aramis. But, nowadays, what sort of a plank should we want, my friend! I, in particular." And the Seigneur de Bracieux cast a profound glance over his colossal rotundity with a loud laugh. "And do you mean seriously to say you are not tired of Belle-Isle a little, and that you would not prefer the comforts of your dwelling—of your episcopal palace, at Vannes? Come, confess."

"No," replied Aramis, without daring to look at Porthos.

"Let us stay where we are, then," said his friend, with a sigh, which, in spite of the efforts he made to restrain it, escaped his echoing breast. "Let us remain!—let us remain! And yet," added he, "and yet, if we seriously wished, but that decidedly—if we had a fixed idea, one firmly taken, to return to France, and there were not boats—"

"Have you remarked another thing, my friend—that is, since the disappearance of our barks, during the last two days' absence of fishermen, not a single small boat has landed on the shores of the isle?"

"Yes, certainly! you are right. I, too, have remarked it, and the observation was the more naturally made, for, before the last two fatal days, barks and shallops were as plentiful as shrimps."

"I must inquire," said Aramis, suddenly, and with great agitation. "And then, if we had a raft constructed—"

"But there are some canoes, my friend; shall I board one?"

"A canoe!—a canoe! Can you think of such a thing, Porthos? A canoe to be upset in. No, no," said the bishop of Vannes; "it is not our trade to ride upon the waves. We will wait, we will wait."

And Aramis continued walking about with increased agitation. Porthos, who grew tired of following all the feverish movements of his friend—Porthos, who in his faith and calmness understood nothing of the sort of exasperation which was betrayed by his companion's continual convulsive starts—Porthos stopped him. "Let us sit down upon this rock," said he. "Place yourself there, close to me, Aramis, and I conjure you, for the last time, to explain to me in a manner I can comprehend—explain to me what we are doing here."

"Porthos," said Aramis, much embarrassed.

"I know that the false king wished to dethrone the true king. That is a fact, that I understand. Well—"

"Yes?" said Aramis.

"I know that the false king formed the project of selling Belle-Isle to the English. I understand that, too."

"Yes?"

"I know that we engineers and captains came and threw ourselves into Belle-Isle to take direction of the works, and the command of ten companies levied and paid by M. Fouquet, or rather the ten companies of his son-in-law. All that is plain."

Aramis rose in a state of great impatience. He might be said to be a lion importuned by a gnat. Porthos held him by the arm. "But what I cannot understand, what, in spite of all the efforts of my mind, and all my reflections, I cannot comprehend, and never shall comprehend, is, that instead of sending us troops, instead of sending us reinforcements of men, munitions, provisions, they leave us without boats, they leave Belle-Isle without arrivals, without help; it is that instead of establishing with us a correspondence, whether by signals, or written or verbal communications, all relations with the shore are intercepted. Tell me, Aramis, answer me, or rather, before answering me, will you allow me to tell you what I have thought? Will you hear what my idea is, the plan I have conceived?"

The bishop raised his head. "Well! Aramis," continued

Porthos, "I have dreamed, I have imagined that an event has taken place in France. I dreamt of M. Fouquet all the night, of lifeless fish, of broken eggs, of chambers badly furnished, meanly kept. Villainous dreams, my dear D'Herblay; very unlucky, such dreams!"

"Porthos, what is that yonder?" interrupted Aramis, rising suddenly, and pointing out to his friend a black spot upon the empurpled line of the water.

"A bark!" said Porthos; "yes, it is a bark! Ah! we shall have some news at last."

"There are two!" cried the bishop, on discovering another mast; "two! three! four!"

"Five!" said Porthos, in his turn. "Six! seven! Ah! *mon Dieu! mon Dieu!* it is a fleet!"

"Our boats returning, probably," said Aramis, very uneasily, in spite of the assurance he affected.

"They are very large for fishing-boats," observed Porthos, "and do you not remark, my friend, that they come from the Loire?"

"They come from the Loire—yes—"

"And look! everybody here sees them as well as ourselves; look, women and children are beginning to crowd the jetty."

An old fisherman passed. "Are those our barks, yonder?" asked Aramis.

The old man looked steadily into the eye of the horizon.

"No, monseigneur," replied he, "they are lighter boars, boats in the king's service."

"Boats in the royal service?" replied Aramis, starting. "How do you know that?" said he.

"By the flag."

"But," said Porthos, "the boat is scarcely visible; how the devil, my friend, can you distinguish the flag?"

"I see there is one," replied the old man; "our boats, trade lighters, do not carry any. That sort of craft is generally used for transport of troops."

"Ah!" groaned Aramis.

"*Vivat!*" cried Porthos, "they are sending us reinforcements, don't you think they are, Aramis?"

"Probably."

"Unless it is the English coming."

"By the Loire? That would have an evil look, Porthos; for they must have come through Paris!"

"You are right; they are reinforcements, decidedly, or provisions."

Aramis leaned his head upon his hands, and made no reply. Then, all at once,—"Porthos," said he, "have the alarm sounded."

"The alarm! do you imagine such a thing?"

"Yes, and let the cannoniers mount their batteries, the artillerymen be at their pieces, and be particularly watchful of the coast batteries."

Porthos opened his eyes to their widest extent. He looked attentively at his friend, to convince himself he was in his proper senses.

"*I* will do it, my dear Porthos," continued Aramis, in his blandest tone; "I will go and have these orders executed myself, if you do not go, my friend."

"Well! I will—instantly!" said Porthos, who went to execute the orders, casting all the while looks behind him, to see if the bishop of Vannes were not deceived; and if, on recovering more rational ideas, he would not recall him. The alarm was sounded, trumpets brayed, drums rolled; the great bronze bell swung in horror from its lofty belfry. The dikes and moles were quickly filled with the curious and soldiers; matches sparkled in the hands of the artillerymen, placed behind the large cannon bedded in their stone carriages. When every man was at his post, when all the preparations for defense were made: "Permit me, Aramis, to try to comprehend," whispered Porthos, timidly, in Aramis's ear.

"My dear friend, you will comprehend but too soon,"

murmured M. d'Herblay, in reply to this question of his lieutenant.

"The fleet which is coming yonder, with sails unfurled, straight towards the port of Belle-Isle, is a royal fleet, is it not?"

"But as there are two kings in France, Porthos, to which of these two kings does this fleet belong?"

"Oh! you open my eyes," replied the giant, stunned by the insinuation.

And Porthos, whose eyes this reply of his friend's had at last opened, or rather thickened the bandage which covered his sight, went with his best speed to the batteries to overlook his people, and exhort every one to do his duty. In the meantime, Aramis, with his eye fixed on the horizon, saw the ships continually drawing nearer. The people and the soldiers, perched on the summits of the rocks, could distinguish the masts, then the lower sails, and at last the hulls of the lighters, bearing at the masthead the royal flag of France. It was night when one of these vessels, which had created such a sensation among the inhabitants of Belle-Isle, dropped anchor within cannon shot of the place. It was soon seen, notwithstanding the darkness, that some sort of agitation reigned on board the vessel, from the side of which a skiff was lowered, of which the three rowers, bending to their oars, took the direction of the port, and in a few instants struck land at the foot of the fort. The commander jumped ashore. He had a letter in his hand, which he waved in the air, and seemed to wish to communicate with somebody. This man was soon recognized by several soldiers as one of the pilots of the island. He was the captain of one of the two barks retained by Aramis, but which Porthos, in his anxiety with regard to the fate of the fishermen who had disappeared, had sent in search of the missing boats. He asked to be conducted to M. d'Herblay. Two soldiers, at a signal from a sergeant, marched him between them, and escorted him.

Aramis was upon the quay. The envoy presented himself before the bishop of Vannes. The darkness was almost absolute, notwithstanding the flambeaux borne at a small distance by the soldiers who were following Aramis in his rounds.

"Well, Jonathan, from whom do you come?"

"Monseigneur, from those who captured me."

"Who captured you?"

"You know, monseigneur, we set out in search of our comrades?"

"Yes; and afterwards?"

"Well! monseigneur, within a short league we were captured by a *chasse maree* belonging to the king."

"Ah!" said Aramis.

"Of which king?" cried Porthos.

Jonathan started.

"Speak!" continued the bishop.

"We were captured, monseigneur, and joined to those who had been taken yesterday morning."

"What was the cause of the mania for capturing you all?" said Porthos.

"Monsieur, to prevent us from telling you," replied Jonathan.

Porthos was again at a loss to comprehend. "And they have released you to-day?" asked he.

"That I might tell you they have captured us, monsieur."

"Trouble upon trouble," thought honest Porthos.

During this time Aramis was reflecting.

"Humph!" said he, "then I suppose it is a royal fleet blockading the coasts?"

"Yes, monseigneur."

"Who commands it?"

"The captain of the king's musketeers."

"D'Artagnan?"

"D'Artagnan!" exclaimed Porthos.

"I believe that is the name."

"And did he give you this letter?"

"Yes, monseigneur."

"Bring the torches nearer."

"It is his writing," said Porthos.

Aramis eagerly read the following lines:

"Order of the king to take Belle-Isle; or to put the garrison to the sword, if they resist; order to make prisoners of all the men of the garrison; signed, D'ARTAGNAN, who, the day before yesterday, arrested M. Fouquet, for the purpose of his being sent to the Bastille."

Aramis turned pale, and crushed the paper in his hands.

"What is it?" asked Porthos.

"Nothing, my friend, nothing."

"Tell me, Jonathan?"

"Monseigneur?"

"Did you speak to M. d'Artagnan?"

"Yes, monseigneur."

"What did he say to you?"

"That for ampler information, he would speak with monseigneur."

"Where?"

"On board his own vessel."

"On board his vessel!" and Porthos repeated, "On board his vessel!"

"M. le mousquetaire," continued Jonathan, "told me to take you both on board my canoe, and bring you to him."

"Let us go at once," exclaimed Porthos. "Dear D'Artagnan!"

But Aramis stopped him. "Are you mad?" cried he. "Who knows that it is not a snare?"

"Of the other king's?" said Porthos, mysteriously.

"A snare, in fact! That's what it is, my friend."

"Very possibly; what is to be done, then? If D'Artagnan sends for us—"

"Who assures you that D'Artagnan sends for us?"

"Well, but—but his writing—"

"Writing is easily counterfeited. This looks counterfeited—unsteady—"

"You are always right; but, in the meantime, we know nothing."

Aramis was silent.

"It is true," said the good Porthos, "we do not want to know anything."

"What shall I do?" asked Jonathan.

"You will return on board this captain's vessel."

"Yes, monseigneur."

"And will tell him that we beg he will himself come into the island."

"Ah! I comprehend!" said Porthos.

"Yes, monseigneur," replied Jonathan; "but if the captain should refuse to come to Belle-Isle?"

"If he refuses, as we have cannon, we will make use of them."

"What! against D'Artagnan?"

"If it is D'Artagnan, Porthos, he will come. Go, Jonathan, go!"

"*Ma foi!* I no longer comprehend anything," murmured Porthos.

"I will make you comprehend it all, my dear friend; the time for it has come; sit down upon this gun-carriage, open your ears, and listen well to me."

"Oh! *pardieu!* I will listen, no fear of that."

"May I depart, monseigneur?" cried Jonathan.

"Yes, begone, and bring back an answer. Allow the canoe to pass, you men there!" And the canoe pushed off to regain the fleet.

Aramis took Porthos by the hand, and commenced his explanations.

CHAPTER 43

Explanations by Aramis.

"What I have to say to you, friend Porthos, will probably surprise you, but it may prove instructive."

"I like to be surprised," said Porthos, in a kindly tone; "do not spare me, therefore, I beg. I am hardened against emotions; don't fear, speak out."

"It is difficult, Porthos—difficult; for, in truth, I warn you a second time, I have very strange things, very extraordinary things, to tell you."

"Oh! you speak so well, my friend, that I could listen to you for days together. Speak, then, I beg—and—stop, I have an idea: I will, to make your task more easy, I will, to assist you in telling me such things, question you."

"I shall be pleased at your doing so."

"What are we going to fight for, Aramis?"

"If you ask me many such questions as that—if you would render my task the easier by interrupting my revelations thus, Porthos, you will not help me at all. So far, on the contrary, that is the very Gordian knot. But, my friend, with a man like you, good, generous, and devoted, the confession must be bravely made. I have deceived you, my worthy friend."

"You have deceived me!"

"Good Heavens! yes."

"Was it for my good, Aramis?"

"I thought so, Porthos; I thought so sincerely, my friend."

"Then," said the honest seigneur of Bracieux, "you have rendered me a service, and I thank you for it; for if you had not deceived me, I might have deceived myself. In what, then, have you deceived me, tell me?"

"In that I was serving the usurper against whom Louis XIV., at this moment, is directing his efforts."

"The usurper!" said Porthos, scratching his head. "That is—well, I do not quite clearly comprehend!"

"He is one of the two kings who are contending fro the crown of France."

"Very well! Then you were serving him who is not Louis XIV.?"

"You have hit the matter in one word."

"It follows that—"

"It follows that we are rebels, my poor friend."

"The devil! the devil!" cried Porthos, much disappointed.

"Oh! but, dear Porthos, be calm, we shall still find means of getting out of the affair, trust me."

"It is not that which makes me uneasy," replied Porthos; "that which alone touches me is that ugly word *rebels*."

"Ah! but—"

"And so, according to this, the duchy that was promised me—"

"It was the usurper that was to give it to you."

"And that is not the same thing, Aramis," said Porthos, majestically.

"My friend, if it had only depended upon me, you should have become a prince."

Porthos began to bite his nails in a melancholy way.

"That is where you have been wrong," continued he, "in deceiving me; for that promised duchy I reckoned upon. Oh!

I reckoned upon it seriously, knowing you to be a man of your word, Aramis."

"Poor Porthos! pardon me, I implore you!"

"So, then," continued Porthos, without replying to the bishop's prayer, "so then, it seems, I have quite fallen out with Louis XIV.?"

"Oh! I will settle all that, my good friend, I will settle all that. I will take it on myself alone!"

"Aramis!"

"No, no, Porthos, I conjure you, let me act. No false generosity! No inopportune devotedness! You knew nothing of my projects. You have done nothing of yourself. With me it is different. I alone am the author of this plot. I stood in need of my inseparable companion; I called upon you, and you came to me in remembrance of our ancient device, 'All for one, one for all.' My crime is that I was an egotist."

"Now, that is a word I like," said Porthos; "and seeing that you have acted entirely for yourself, it is impossible for me to blame you. It is natural."

And upon this sublime reflection, Porthos pressed his friend's hand cordially.

In presence of this ingenuous greatness of soul, Aramis felt his own littleness. It was the second time he had been compelled to bend before real superiority of heart, which is more imposing than brilliancy of mind. He replied by a mute and energetic pressure to the endearment of his friend.

"Now," said Porthos, "that we have come to an explanation, now that I am perfectly aware of our situation with respect to Louis XIV., I think, my friend, it is time to make me comprehend the political intrigue of which we are the victims—for I plainly see there is a political intrigue at the bottom of all this."

"D'Artagnan, my good Porthos, D'Artagnan is coming, and will detail it to you in all its circumstances; but, excuse me, I am deeply grieved, I am bowed down with mental anguish, and I have need of all my presence of mind, all my powers of reflection, to extricate you from the false position in which I have so imprudently involved you; but nothing can be more clear, nothing more plain, than your position, henceforth. The king Louis XIV. has no longer now but one enemy: that enemy is myself, myself alone. I have made you a prisoner, you have followed me, to-day I liberate you, you fly back to your prince. You can perceive, Porthos, there is not one difficulty in all this."

"Do you think so?" said Porthos.

"I am quite sure of it."

"Then why," said the admirable good sense of Porthos, "then why, if we are in such an easy position, why, my friend, do we prepare cannon, muskets, and engines of all sorts? It seems to me it would be much more simple to say to Captain d'Artagnan: 'My dear friend, we have been mistaken; that error is to be repaired; open the door to us, let us pass through, and we will say good-bye.'"

"Ah! that!" said Aramis, shaking his head.

"Why do you say 'that'? Do you not approve of my plan, my friend?"

"I see a difficulty in it."

"What is it?"

"The hypothesis that D'Artagnan may come with orders which will oblige us to defend ourselves."

"What! defend ourselves against D'Artagnan? Folly! Against the good D'Artagnan!"

Aramis once more replied by shaking his head.

"Porthos," at length said he, "if I have had the matches lighted and the guns pointed, if I have had the signal of alarm sounded, if I have called every man to his post upon the ramparts, those good ramparts of Belle-Isle which you have so well fortified, it was not for nothing. Wait to judge; or rather, no, do not wait—"

"What can I do?"

"If I knew, my friend, I would have told you."

"But there is one thing much more simple than defending ourselves:—a boat, and away for France—where—"

"My dear friend," said Aramis, smiling with a strong shade of sadness, "do not let us reason like children; let us be men in council and in execution.—But, hark! I hear a hail for landing at the port. Attention, Porthos, serious attention!"

"It is D'Artagnan, no doubt," said Porthos, in a voice of thunder, approaching the parapet.

"Yes, it is I," replied the captain of the musketeers, running lightly up the steps of the mole, and gaining rapidly the little esplanade on which his two friends waited for him. As soon as he came towards them, Porthos and Aramis observed an officer who followed D'Artagnan, treading apparently in his very steps. The captain stopped upon the stairs of the mole, when half-way up. His companions imitated him.

"Make your men draw back," cried D'Artagnan to Porthos and Aramis; "let them retire out of hearing." This order, given by Porthos, was executed immediately. Then D'Artagnan, turning towards him who followed him:

"Monsieur," said he, "we are no longer on board the king's fleet, where, in virtue of your order, you spoke so arrogantly to me, just now."

"Monsieur," replied the officer, "I did not speak arrogantly to you; I simply, but rigorously, obeyed instructions. I was commanded to follow you. I follow you. I am directed not to allow you to communicate with any one without taking cognizance of what you do; I am in duty bound, accordingly, to overhear your conversations."

D'Artagnan trembled with rage, and Porthos and Aramis, who heard this dialogue, trembled likewise, but with uneasiness and fear. D'Artagnan, biting his mustache with that vivacity which denoted in him exasperation, closely to be followed by an explosion, approached the officer.

"Monsieur," said he, in a low voice, so much the more

impressive, that, affecting calm, it threatened tempest—
"monsieur, when I sent a canoe hither, you wished to know
what I wrote to the defenders of Belle-Isle. You produced an
order to that effect; and, in my turn, I instantly showed you
the note I had written. When the skipper of the boat sent by
me returned, when I received the reply of these two
gentlemen" (and he pointed to Aramis and Porthos), "you
heard every word of what the messenger said. All that was
plainly in your orders, all that was well executed, very punc-
tually, was it not?"

"Yes, monsieur," stammered the officer; "yes, without
doubt, but—"

"Monsieur," continued D'Artagnan, growing warm—
"monsieur, when I manifested the intention of quitting my
vessel to cross to Belle-Isle, you demanded to accompany me;
I did not hesitate; I brought you with me. You are now at
Belle-Isle, are you not?"

"Yes, monsieur; but—"

"But—the question no longer is of M. Colbert, who has
given you that order, or of whomsoever in the world you are
following the instructions; the question now is of a man who
is a clog upon M. d'Artagnan, and who is alone with M.
d'Artagnan upon steps whose feet are bathed by thirty feet
of salt water; a bad position for that man, a bad position,
monsieur! I warn you."

"But, monsieur, if I am a restraint upon you," said the
officer, timidly, and almost faintly, "it is my duty which—"

"Monsieur, you have had the misfortune, either you or
those that sent you, to insult me. It is done. I cannot seek
redress from those who employ you,—they are unknown to
me, or are at too great a distance. But you are under my hand,
and I swear that if you make one step behind me when I raise
my feet to go up to those gentlemen, I swear to you by my
name, I will cleave your head in two with my sword, and
pitch you into the water. Oh! it will happen! it will happen!

I have only been six times angry in my life, monsieur, and all five preceding times *I killed my man*."

The officer did not stir; he became pale under this terrible threat, but replied with simplicity, "Monsieur, you are wrong in acting against my orders."

Porthos and Aramis, mute and trembling at the top of the parapet, cried to the musketeer, "Good D'Artagnan, take care!"

D'Artagnan made them a sign to keep silence, raised his foot with ominous calmness to mount the stair, and turned round, sword in hand, to see if the officer followed him. The officer made a sign of the cross and stepped up. Porthos and Aramis, who knew their D'Artagnan, uttered a cry, and rushed down to prevent the blow they thought they already heard. But D'Artagnan passed his sword into his left hand,—

"Monsieur," said he to the officer, in an agitated voice, "you are a brave man. You will all the better comprehend what I am going to say to you now."

"Speak, Monsieur d'Artagnan, speak," replied the officer.

"These gentlemen we have just seen, and against whom you have orders, are my friends."

"I know they are, monsieur."

"You can understand whether or not I ought to act towards them as your instructions prescribe."

"I understand your reserve."

"Very well; permit me, then, to converse with them without a witness."

"Monsieur d'Artagnan, if I yield to your request, if I do that which you beg me, I break my word; but if I do not do it, I disoblige you. I prefer the one dilemma to the other. Converse with your friends, and do not despise me, monsieur, for doing this for *your* sake, whom I esteem and honor; do not despise me for committing for you, and you alone, an unworthy act." D'Artagnan, much agitated, threw his arm round the neck of the young man, and then went up to his friends. The officer, enveloped in his cloak, sat down on the damp, weed-covered steps.

"Well!" said D'Artagnan to his friends, "such is my position, judge for yourselves." All three embraced as in the glorious days of their youth.

"What is the meaning of all these preparations?" said Porthos.

"You ought to have a suspicion of what they signify," said D'Artagnan.

"Not any, I assure you, my dear captain; for, in fact, I have done nothing, no more has Aramis," the worthy baron hastened to say.

D'Artagnan darted a reproachful look at the prelate, which penetrated that hardened heart.

"Dear Porthos!" cried the bishop of Vannes.

"You see what is being done against you," said D'Artagnan; "interception of all boats coming to or going from Belle-Isle. Your means of transport seized. If you had endeavored to fly, you would have fallen into the hands of the cruisers that plow the sea in all directions, on the watch for you. The king wants you to be taken, and he will take you." D'Artagnan tore at his gray mustache. Aramis grew somber, Porthos angry.

"My idea was this," continued D'Artagnan: "to make you both come on board, to keep you near me, and restore you your liberty. But now, who can say, when I return to my ship, I may not find a superior; that I may not find secret orders which will take from me my command, and give it to another, who will dispose of me and you without hope of help?"

"We must remain at Belle-Isle," said Aramis, resolutely; "and I assure you, for my part, I will not surrender easily." Porthos said nothing. D'Artagnan remarked the silence of his friend.

"I have another trial to make of this officer, of this brave fellow who accompanies me, and whose courageous resistance makes me very happy; for it denotes an honest man, who, though an enemy, is a thousand times better than a complaisant coward. Let us try to learn from him what his instructions are, and what his orders permit or forbid."

"Let us try," said Aramis.

D'Artagnan went to the parapet, leaned over towards the steps of the mole, and called the officer, who immediately came up. "Monsieur," said D'Artagnan, after having exchanged the cordial courtesies natural between gentlemen who know and appreciate each other, "monsieur, if I wished to take away these gentlemen from here, what would you do?"

"I should not oppose it, monsieur; but having direct explicit orders to put them under guard, I should detain them."

"Ah!" said D'Artagnan.

"That's all over," said Aramis, gloomily. Porthos did not stir.

"But still take Porthos," said the bishop of Vannes. "He can prove to the king, and I will help him do so, and you too, Monsieur d'Artagnan, that he had nothing to do with this affair."

"Hum!" said D'Artagnan. "Will you come? Will you follow me, Porthos? The king is merciful."

"I want time for reflection," said Porthos.

"You will remain here, then?"

"Until fresh orders," said Aramis, with vivacity.

"Until we have an idea," resumed D'Artagnan; "and I now believe that will not be long, for I have one already."

"Let us say adieu, then," said Aramis; "but in truth, my good Porthos, you ought to go."

"No," said the latter, laconically.

"As you please," replied Aramis, a little wounded in his susceptibilities at the morose tone of his companion. "Only I am reassured by the promise of an idea from D'Artagnan, an idea I fancy I have divined."

"Let us see," said the musketeer, placing his ear near Aramis's mouth. The latter spoke several words rapidly, to which D'Artagnan replied, "That is it, precisely."

"Infallible!" cried Aramis.

"During the first emotion this resolution will cause, take care of yourself, Aramis."

"Oh! don't be afraid."

"Now, monsieur," said D'Artagnan to the officer, "thanks, a thousand thanks! You have made yourself three friends for life."

"Yes," added Aramis. Porthos alone said nothing, but merely bowed.

D'Artagnan, having tenderly embraced his two old friends, left Belle-Isle with the inseparable companion with whom M. Colbert had saddled him. Thus, with the exception of the explanation with which the worthy Porthos had been willing to be satisfied, nothing had changed in appearance in the fate of one or the other, "Only," said Aramis, "there is D'Artagnan's idea."

D'Artagnan did not return on board without profoundly analyzing the idea he had discovered. Now, we know that whatever D'Artagnan did examine, according to custom, daylight was certain to illuminate. As to the officer, now grown mute again, he had full time for meditation. Therefore, on putting his foot on board his vessel, moored within cannon-shot of the island, the captain of the musketeers had already got together all his means, offensive and defensive.

He immediately assembled his council, which consisted of the officers serving under his orders. These were eight in number; a chief of the maritime forces; a major directing the artillery; an engineer, the officer we are acquainted with, and four lieutenants. Having assembled them, D'Artagnan arose, took of his hat, and addressed them thus:

"Gentlemen, I have been to reconnoiter Belle-Ile-en-Mer, and I have found in it a good and solid garrison; moreover, preparations are made for a defense that may prove trouble-some. I therefore intend to send for two of the principal officers of the place, that we may converse with them. Having separated them from their troops and cannon, we shall be better able to deal with them; particularly by reasoning with them. Is not this your opinion, gentlemen?"

The major of artillery rose.

"Monsieur," said he, with respect, but firmness, "I have heard you say that the place is preparing to make a trouble-some defense. The place is then, as you know, determined on rebellion?"

D'Artagnan was visibly put out by this reply; but he was not the man to allow himself to be subdued by a trifle, and resumed:

"Monsieur," said he, "your reply is just. But you are ignorant that Belle-Isle is a fief of M. Fouquet's, and that former monarchs gave the right to the seigneurs of Belle-Isle to arm their people." The major made a movement. "Oh! do not interrupt me," continued D'Artagnan. "You are going to tell me that that right to arm themselves against the English was not a right to arm themselves against their king. But it is not M. Fouquet, I suppose, who holds Belle-Isle at this moment, since I arrested M. Fouquet the day before yesterday. Now the inhabitants and defenders of Belle-Isle know nothing of this arrest. You would announce it to them in vain. It is a thing so unheard-of and extraordinary, so unexpected, that they would not believe you. A Breton serves his master, and not his masters; he serves his master till he has seen him dead. Now the Bretons, as far as I know, have not seen the body of M. Fouquet. It is not, then, surprising they hold out against that which is neither M. Fouquet nor his signature."

The major bowed in token of assent.

"That is why," continued D'Artagnan, "I propose to cause two of the principal officers of the garrison to come on board my vessel. They will see you, gentlemen; they will see the forces we have at our disposal; they will consequently know to what they have to trust, and the fate that attends them, in case of rebellion. We will affirm to them, upon our honor, that M. Fouquet is a prisoner, and that all resistance can only be prejudicial to them. We will tell them that at the first cannon fired, there will be no further hope of mercy from the king. Then, or so at least I trust, they will resist no longer. They will yield up without fighting, and we shall have a place given up to us in a friendly way which it might cost prodigious efforts to subdue."

The officer who had followed D'Artagnan to Belle-Isle was preparing to speak, but D'Artagnan interrupted him.

"Yes, I know what you are going to tell me, monsieur; I know that there is an order of the king's to prevent all secret communications with the defenders of Belle-Isle, and that is exactly why I do not offer to communicate except in presence of my staff."

And D'Artagnan made an inclination of the head to his officers, who knew him well enough to attach a certain value to the condescension.

The officers looked at each other as if to read each other's opinions in their eyes, with the intention of evidently acting, should they agree, according to the desire of D'Artagnan. And already the latter saw with joy that the result of their consent would be sending a bark to Porthos and Aramis, when the king's officer drew from a pocket a folded paper, which he placed in the hands of D'Artagnan.

This paper bore upon its superscription the number 1.

"What, more!" murmured the surprised captain.

"Read, monsieur," said the officer, with a courtesy that was not free from sadness.

D'Artagnan, full of mistrust, unfolded the paper, and read these words: "Prohibition to M. d'Artagnan to assemble any council whatever, or to deliberate in any way before Belle-Isle be surrendered and the prisoners shot. Signed—LOUIS."

D'Artagnan repressed the quiver of impatience that ran through his whole body, and with a gracious smile:

"That is well, monsieur," said he; "the king's orders shall be complied with."

CHAPTER 44

Result of the Ideas of the King, and the
Ideas of D'Artagnan.

The blow was direct. It was severe, mortal. D'Artagnan,
furious at having been anticipated by an idea of the king's,
did not despair, however, even yet; and reflecting upon the
idea he had brought back from Belle-Isle, he elicited therefrom
novel means of safety for his friends.

"Gentlemen," said he, suddenly, "since the king has
charged some other than myself with his secret orders, it
must be because I no longer possess his confidence, and I
should really be unworthy of it if I had the courage to hold
a command subject to so many injurious suspicions.
Therefore I will go immediately and carry my resignation
to the king. I tender it before you all, enjoining you all to
fall back with me upon the coast of France, in such a way
as not to compromise the safety of the forces his majesty
has confided to me. For this purpose, return all to your
posts; within an hour, we shall have the ebb of the tide. To
your posts, gentlemen! I suppose," added he, on seeing that
all prepared to obey him, except the surveillant officer, "you
have no orders to object, this time?"

And D'Artagnan almost triumphed while speaking
these words. This plan would prove the safety of his friends.

The blockade once raised, they might embark immediately, and set sail for England or Spain, without fear of being molested. Whilst they were making their escape, D'Artagnan would return to the king; would justify his return by the indignation which the mistrust of Colbert had raised in him; he would be sent back with full powers, and he would take Belle-Isle; that is to say, the cage, after the birds had flown. But to this plan the officer opposed a further order of the king's. It was thus conceived:

"From the moment M. d'Artagnan shall have manifested the desire of giving in his resignation, he shall no longer be reckoned leader of the expedition, and every officer placed under his orders shall be held to no longer obey him. Moreover, the said Monsieur d'Artagnan, having lost that quality of leader of the army sent against Belle-Isle, shall set out immediately for France, accompanied by the officer who will have remitted the message to him, and who will consider him a prisoner for whom he is answerable."

Brave and careless as he was, D'Artagnan turned pale. Everything had been calculated with a depth of precognition which, for the first time in thirty years, recalled to him the solid foresight and inflexible logic of the great cardinal. He leaned his head on his hand, thoughtful, scarcely breathing. "If I were to put this order in my pocket," thought he, "who would know it, what would prevent my doing it? Before the king had had time to be informed, I should have saved those poor fellows yonder. Let us exercise some small audacity! My head is not one of those the executioner strikes off for disobedience. We will disobey!" But at the moment he was about to adopt this plan, he saw the officers around him reading similar orders, which the passive agent of the thoughts of that infernal Colbert had distributed to them. This contingency of his disobedience had been foreseen—as all the rest had been.

"Monsieur," said the officer, coming up to him, "I await your good pleasure to depart."

"I am ready, monsieur," replied D'Artagnan, grinding his teeth.

The officer immediately ordered a canoe to receive M. d'Artagnan and himself. At sight of this he became almost distraught with rage.

"How," stammered he, "will you carry on the directions of the different corps?"

"When you are gone, monsieur," replied the commander of the fleet, "it is to me the command of the whole is committed."

"Then, monsieur," rejoined Colbert's man, addressing the new leader, "it is for you that this last order remitted to me is intended. Let us see your powers."

"Here they are," said the officer, exhibiting the royal signature.

"Here are your instructions," replied the officer, placing the folded paper in his hands; and turning round towards D'Artagnan, "Come, monsieur," said he, in an agitated voice (such despair did he behold in that man of iron), "do me the favor to depart at once."

"Immediately!" articulated D'Artagnan, feebly, subdued, crushed by implacable impossibility.

And he painfully subsided into the little boat, which started, favored by wind and tide, for the coast of France. The king's guards embarked with him. The musketeer still preserved the hope of reaching Nantes quickly, and of pleading the cause of his friends eloquently enough to incline the king to mercy. The bark flew like a swallow. D'Artagnan distinctly saw the land of France profiled in black against the white clouds of night.

"Ah! monsieur," said he, in a low voice, to the officer to whom, for an hour, he had ceased speaking, "what would I give to know the instructions for the new commander! They are all pacific, are they not? and—"

He did not finish; the thunder of a distant cannon rolled athwart the waves, another, and two or three still louder. D'Artagnan shuddered.

"They have commenced the siege of Belle-Isle," replied the officer. The canoe had just touched the soil of France.

CHAPTER 45

The Ancestors of Porthos.

When D'Artagnan left Aramis and Porthos, the latter returned to the principal fort, in order to converse with greater liberty. Porthos, still thoughtful, was a restraint on Aramis, whose mind had never felt itself more free.

"Dear Porthos," said he, suddenly, "I will explain D'Artagnan's idea to you."

"What idea, Aramis?"

"An idea to which we shall owe our liberty within twelve hours."

"Ah! indeed!" said Porthos, much astonished. "Let us hear it."

"Did you remark, in the scene our friend had with the officer, that certain orders constrained him with regard to us?"

"Yes, I did notice that."

"Well! D'Artagnan is going to give in his resignation to the king, and during the confusion that will result from his absence, we will get away, or rather you will get away, Porthos, if there is possibility of flight for only one."

Here Porthos shook his head and replied: "We will escape together, Aramis, or we will stay together."

"Thine is a right, a generous heart," said Aramis, "only your melancholy uneasiness affects me."

"I am not uneasy," said Porthos.

"Then you are angry with me."

"I am not angry with you."

"Then why, my friend, do you put on such a dismal countenance?"

"I will tell you; I am making my will." And while saying these words, the good Porthos looked sadly in the face of Aramis.

"Your will!" cried the bishop. "What, then! do you think yourself lost?"

"I feel fatigued. It is the first time, and there is a custom in our family."

"What is it, my friend?"

"My grandfather was a man twice as strong as I am."

"Indeed!" said Aramis; "then your grandfather must have been Samson himself."

"No; his name was Antoine. Well! he was about my age, when, setting out one day for the chase, he felt his legs weak, the man who had never known what weakness was before."

"What was the meaning of that fatigue, my friend?"

"Nothing good, as you will see; for having set out, complaining still of weakness of the legs, he met a wild boar, which made head against him; he missed him with his arquebuse, and was ripped up by the beast and died immediately."

"There is no reason in that why you should alarm yourself, dear Porthos."

"Oh! you will see. My father was as strong again as I am. He was a rough soldier, under Henry III. and Henry IV.; his name was not Antoine, but Gaspard, the same as M. de Coligny. Always on horseback, he had never known what lassitude was. One evening, as he rose from table, his legs failed him."

"He had supped heartily, perhaps," said Aramis, "and that was why he staggered."

"Bah! A friend of M. de Bassompierre, nonsense! No, no, he was astonished at this lassitude, and said to my mother, who laughed at him, 'Would not one believe I was going to meet with a wild boar, as the late M. du Vallon, my father did?'"

"Well?" said Aramis.

"Well, having this weakness, my father insisted upon going down into the garden, instead of going to bed; his foot slipped on the first stair, the staircase was steep; my father fell against a stone in which an iron hinge was fixed. The hinge gashed his temple; and he was stretched out dead upon the spot."

Aramis raised his eyes to his friend: "These are two extraordinary circumstances," said he; "let us not infer that there may succeed a third. It is not becoming in a man of your strength to be superstitious, my brave Porthos. Besides, when were your legs known to fail? Never have you stood so firm, so haughtily; why, you could carry a house on your shoulders."

"At this moment," said Porthos, "I feel myself pretty active; but at times I vacillate; I sink; and lately this phenomenon, as you say, has occurred four times. I will not say this frightens me, but it annoys me. Life is an agreeable thing. I have money; I have fine estates; I have horses that I love; I have also friends that I love: D'Artagnan, Athos, Raoul, and you."

The admirable Porthos did not even take the trouble to dissimulate in the very presence of Aramis the rank he gave him in his friendship. Aramis pressed his hand: "We will still live many years," said he, "to preserve to the world such specimens of its rarest men. Trust yourself to me, my friend; we have no reply from D'Artagnan, that is a good sign. He must have given orders to get the vessels together and clear the seas. On my part I have just issued directions that a bark should be rolled on rollers to the mouth of the great cavern of Locmaria, which you know, where we have so often lain in wait for the foxes."

"Yes, and which terminates at the little creek by a trench where we discovered the day that splendid fox escaped that way."

"Precisely. In case of misfortunes, a bark is to be concealed for us in that cavern; indeed, it must be there by this time. We will wait for a favorable moment, and during the night we will go to sea!"

"That is a grand idea. What shall we gain by it?"

"We shall gain this—nobody knows that grotto, or rather its issue, except ourselves and two or three hunters of the island; we shall gain this—that if the island is occupied, the scouts, seeing no bark upon the shore, will never imagine we can escape, and will cease to watch."

"I understand."

"Well! that weakness in the legs?"

"Oh! better, much, just now."

"You see, then, plainly, that everything conspires to give us quietude and hope. D'Artagnan will sweep the sea and leave us free. No royal fleet or descent to be dreaded. *Vive Dieu!* Porthos, we have still half a century of magnificent adventure before us, and if I once touch Spanish ground, I swear to you," added the bishop with terrible energy, "that your brevet of duke is not such a chance as it is said to be."

"We live by hope," said Porthos, enlivened by the warmth of his companion.

All at once a cry resounded in their ears: "To arms! to arms!"

This cry, repeated by a hundred throats, piercing the chamber where the two friends were conversing, carried surprise to one, and uneasiness to the other. Aramis opened the window; he saw a crowd of people running with flambeaux. Women were seeking places of safety, the armed population were hastening to their posts.

"The fleet! the fleet!" cried a soldier, who recognized Aramis.

"The fleet?" repeated the latter.

"Within half cannon-shot," continued the soldier.

"To arms!" cried Aramis.

"To arms!" repeated Porthos, formidably. And both rushed forth towards the mole to place themselves within the shelter of the batteries. Boats, laden with soldiers, were seen approaching; and in three directions, for the purpose of landing at three points at once.

"What must be done?" said an officer of the guard.

"Stop them; and if they persist, fire!" said Aramis.

Five minutes later, the cannonade commenced. These were the shots that D'Artagnan had heard as he landed in France. But the boats were too near the mole to allow the cannon to aim correctly. They landed, and the combat commenced hand to hand.

"What's the matter, Porthos?" said Aramis to his friend.

"Nothing! nothing!—only my legs; it is really incomprehensible!—they will be better when we charge." In fact, Porthos and Aramis did charge with such vigor, and so thoroughly animated their men, that the royalists re-embarked precipitately, without gaining anything but the wounds they carried away.

"Eh! but Porthos," cried Aramis, "we must have a prisoner, quick! quick!" Porthos bent over the stair of the mole, and seized by the nape of the neck one of the officers of the royal army who was waiting to embark till all his people should be in the boat. The arm of the giant lifted up his prey, which served him as a buckler, and he recovered himself without a shot being fired at him.

"Here is a prisoner for you," said Porthos coolly to Aramis.

"Well!" cried the latter, laughing, "did you not calumniate your legs?"

"It was not with my legs I captured him," said Porthos, "it was with my arms!"

CHAPTER 46

The Son of Biscarrat.

The Bretons of the Isle were very proud of this victory; Aramis did not encourage them in the feeling.

"What will happen," said he to Porthos, when everybody was gone home, "will be that the anger of the king will be roused by the account of the resistance; and that these brave people will be decimated or shot when they are taken, which cannot fail to take place."

"From which it results, then," said Porthos, "that what we have done is of not the slightest use."

"For the moment it may be," replied the bishop, "for we have a prisoner from whom we shall learn what our enemies are preparing to do."

"Yes, let us interrogate the prisoner," said Porthos, "and the means of making him speak are very simple. We are going to supper; we will invite him to join us; as he drinks he will talk."

This was done. The officer was at first rather uneasy, but became reassured on seeing what sort of men he had to deal with. He gave, without having any fear of compromising himself, all the details imaginable of the resignation and departure of D'Artagnan. He explained how, after that departure, the new leader of the expedition had ordered a surprise upon Belle-Isle. There his explanations stopped. Aramis and Porthos exchanged a glance that evinced their despair. No more dependence to be placed now on D'Artagnan's fertile imagination—no further resource in the event of defeat. Aramis, continuing his interrogations, asked the prisoner what the leaders of the expedition contemplated doing with the leaders of Belle-Isle.

"The orders are," replied he, "to kill *during* combat, or hang *afterwards.*"

Porthos and Aramis looked at each other again, and the color mounted to their faces.

"I am too light for the gallows," replied Aramis; "people like me are not hung."

"And I am too heavy," said Porthos; "people like me break the cord."

"I am sure," said the prisoner, gallantly, "that we could have guaranteed you the exact kind of death you preferred."

"A thousand thanks!" said Aramis, seriously. Porthos bowed.

"One more cup of wine to your health," said he, drinking himself. From one subject to another the chat with the officer was prolonged. He was an intelligent gentleman, and suffered himself to be led on by the charm of Aramis's wit and Porthos's cordial *bonhomie.*

"Pardon me," said he, "if I address a question to you; but men who are in their sixth bottle have a clear right to forget themselves a little."

"Address it!" cried Porthos; "address it!"

"Speak," said Aramis.

"Were you not, gentlemen, both in the musketeers of the late king?"

"Yes, monsieur, and amongst the best of them, if you please," said Porthos.

"That is true; I should say even the best of all soldiers, messieurs, if I did not fear to offend the memory of my father."

"Of your father?" cried Aramis.

"Do you know what my name is?"

"*Ma foi!* no, monsieur; but you can tell us, and—"

"I am called Georges de Biscarrat."

"Oh!" cried Porthos, in his turn. "Biscarrat! Do you remember that name, Aramis?"

"Biscarrat!" reflected the bishop. "It seems to me—"

"Try to recollect, monsieur," said the officer.

"*Pardieu!* that won't take me long," said Porthos. "Biscarrat—called Cardinal—one of the four who interrupted us on the day on which we formed our friendship with D'Artagnan, sword in hand."

"Precisely, gentlemen."

"The only one," cried Aramis, eagerly, "we could not scratch."

"Consequently, a capital blade?" said the prisoner.

"That's true! most true!" exclaimed both friends together. "*Ma foi!* Monsieur Biscarrat, we are delighted to make the acquaintance of such a brave man's son."

Biscarrat pressed the hands held out by the two musketeers. Aramis looked at Porthos as much as to say, "Here is a man who will help us," and without delay,—"Confess, monsieur," said he, "that it is good to have once been a good man."

"My father always said so, monsieur."

"Confess, likewise, that it is a sad circumstance in which you find yourself, of falling in with men destined to be shot or hung, and to learn that these men are old acquaintances, in fact, hereditary friends."

"Oh! you are not reserved for such a frightful fate as that, messieurs and friends!" said the young man, warmly.

"Bah! you said so yourself."

"I said so just now, when I did not know you; but now that I know you, I say—you will evade this dismal fate, if you wish!"

"How—if we wish?" echoed Aramis, whose eyes beamed with intelligence as he looked alternately at the prisoner and Porthos.

"Provided," continued Porthos, looking, in his turn, with noble intrepidity, at M. Biscarrat and the bishop—"provided nothing disgraceful be required of us."

"Nothing at all will be required of you, gentlemen," replied the officer—"what should they ask of you? If they find you they will kill you, that is a predetermined thing; try, then, gentlemen, to prevent their finding you."

"I don't think I am mistaken," said Porthos, with dignity; "but it appears evident to me that if they want to find us, they must come and seek us here."

"In that you are perfectly right, my worthy friend," replied Aramis, constantly consulting with his looks the countenance of Biscarrat, who had grown silent and constrained. "You wish, Monsieur de Biscarrat, to say something to us, to make us some overture, and you dare not—is that true?"

"Ah! gentlemen and friends! it is because by speaking I betray the watchword. But, hark! I hear a voice that frees mine by dominating it."

"Cannon!" said Porthos.

"Cannon and musketry, too!" cried the bishop.

On hearing at a distance, among the rocks, these sinister reports of a combat which they thought had ceased:

"What can that be?" asked Porthos.

"Eh! *Pardieu!*" cried Aramis; "that is just what I expected."

"What is that?"

"That the attack made by you was nothing but a feint; is not that true, monsieur? And whilst your companions allowed themselves to be repulsed, you were certain of effecting a landing on the other side of the island."

"Oh! several, monsieur."

"We are lost, then," said the bishop of Vannes, quietly.

"Lost! that is possible," replied the Seigneur de

Pierrefonds, "but we are not taken or hung." And so saying, he rose from the table, went to the wall, and coolly took down his sword and pistols, which he examined with the care of an old soldier who is preparing for battle, and who feels that life, in a great measure, depends upon the excellence and right conditions of his arms.

At the report of the cannon, at the news of the surprise which might deliver up the island to the royal troops, the terrified crowd rushed precipitately to the fort to demand assistance and advice from their leaders. Aramis, pale and downcast, between two flambeaux, showed himself at the window which looked into the principal court, full of soldiers waiting for orders and bewildered inhabitants imploring succor.

"My friends," said D'Herblay, in a grave and sonorous voice, "M. Fouquet, your protector, your friend, you father, has been arrested by an order of the king, and thrown into the Bastille." A sustained yell of vengeful fury came floating up to the window at which the bishop stood, and enveloped him in a magnetic field.

"Avenge Monsieur Fouquet!" cried the most excited of his hearers, "death to the royalists!"

"No, my friends," replied Aramis, solemnly; "no, my friends; no resistance. The king is master in his kingdom. The king is the mandatory of God. The king and God have struck M. Fouquet. Humble yourselves before the hand of God. Love God and the king, who have struck M. Fouquet. But do not avenge your seigneur, do not think of avenging him. You would sacrifice yourselves in vain—you, your wives and children, your property, your liberty. Lay down your arms, my friends—lay down your arms! since the king commands you so to do—and retire peaceably to your dwellings. It is I who ask you to do so; it is I who beg you to do so; it is I who now, in the hour of need, command you to do so, in the name of M. Fouquet."

The crowd collected under the window uttered a prolonged roar of anger and terror. "The soldiers of Louis XIV. have reached the island," continued Aramis. "From this time it would no longer be a fight betwixt them and you—it would be a massacre. Begone, then, begone, and forget; this time I command you, in the name of the Lord of Hosts!"

The mutineers retired slowly, submissive, silent.

"Ah! what have you just been saying, my friend?" said Porthos.

"Monsieur," said Biscarrat to the bishop, "you may save all these inhabitants, but thus you will neither save yourself nor your friend."

"Monsieur de Biscarrat," said the bishop of Vannes, with a singular accent of nobility and courtesy, "Monsieur de Biscarrat, be kind enough to resume your liberty."

"I am very willing to do so, monsieur; but—"

"That would render us a service, for when announcing to the king's lieutenant the submission of the islanders, you will perhaps obtain some grace for us on informing him of the manner in which that submission has been effected."

"Grace!" replied Porthos with flashing eyes, "what is the meaning of that word?"

Aramis touched the elbow of his friend roughly, as he had been accustomed to do in the days of their youth, when he wanted to warn Porthos that he had committed, or was about to commit, a blunder. Porthos understood him, and was silent immediately.

"I will go, messieurs," replied Biscarrat, a little surprised likewise at the word "grace" pronounced by the haughty musketeer, of and to whom, but a few minutes before, he had related with so much enthusiasm the heroic exploits with which his father had delighted him.

"Go, then, Monsieur Biscarrat," said Aramis, bowing to him, "and at parting receive the expression of our entire gratitude."

"But you, messieurs, you whom I think it an honor to call my friends, since you have been willing to accept that title, what will become of you in the meantime?" replied the officer, very much agitated at taking leave of the two ancient adversaries of his father.

"We will wait here."

"But, *mon Dieu!*—the order is precise and formal."

"I am bishop of Vannes, Monsieur de Biscarrat; and they no more shoot a bishop than they hang a gentleman."

"Ah! yes, monsieur—yes, monseigneur," replied Biscarrat; "it is true, you are right, there is still that chance for you. Then, I will depart, I will repair to the commander of the expedition, the king's lieutenant. Adieu! then, messieurs, or rather, to meet again, I hope."

The worthy officer, jumping upon a horse given him by Aramis, departed in the direction of the sound of cannon, which, by surging the crowd into the fort, had interrupted the conversation of the two friends with their prisoner. Aramis watched the departure, and when left alone with Porthos:

"Well, do you comprehend?" said he.

"*Ma foi!* no."

"Did not Biscarrat inconvenience you here?"

"No; he is a brave fellow."

"Yes; but the grotto of Locmaria—is it necessary all the world should know it?"

"Ah! that is true, that is true; I comprehend. We are going to escape by the cavern."

"If you please," cried Aramis, gayly. "Forward, friend Porthos; our boat awaits us. King Louis has not caught us—*yet*."

CHAPTER 47

The Grotto of Locmaria.

The cavern of Locmaria was sufficiently distant from the mole to render it necessary for our friends to husband their strength in order to reach it. Besides, night was advancing; midnight had struck at the fort. Porthos and Aramis were loaded with money and arms. They walked, then, across the heath, which stretched between the mole and the cavern, listening to every noise, in order better to avoid an ambush. From time to time, on the road which they had carefully left on their left, passed fugitives coming from the interior, at the news of the landing of the royal troops. Aramis and Porthos, concealed behind some projecting mass of rock, collected the words that escaped from the poor people, who fled, trembling, carrying with them their most valuable effects, and tried, whilst listening to their complaints, to gather something from them for their own interest. At length, after a rapid race, frequently interrupted by prudent stoppages, they reached the deep grottoes, in which the prophetic bishop of Vannes had taken care to have secreted a bark capable of keeping the sea at this fine season.

"My good friend," said Porthos, panting vigorously, "we have arrived, it seems. But I thought you spoke of three men, three servants, who were to accompany us. I don't see them—where are they?"

"Why should you see them, Porthos?" replied Aramis. "They are certainly waiting for us in the cavern, and, no doubt, are resting, having accomplished their rough and difficult task."

Aramis stopped Porthos, who was preparing to enter the cavern. "Will you allow me, my friend," said he to the giant, "to pass in first? I know the signal I have given to these men; who, not hearing it, would be very likely to fire upon you or slash away with their knives in the dark."

"Go on, then, Aramis; go on—go first; you impersonate wisdom and foresight; go. Ah! there is that fatigue again, of which I spoke to you. It has just seized me afresh."

Aramis left Porthos sitting at the entrance of the grotto, and bowing his head, he penetrated into the interior of the cavern, imitating the cry of the owl. A little plaintive cooing, a scarcely distinct echo, replied from the depths of the cave. Aramis pursued his way cautiously, and soon was stopped by the same kind of cry as he had first uttered, within ten paces of him.

"Are you there, Yves?" said the bishop.

"Yes, monseigneur; Goenne is here likewise. His son accompanies us."

"That is well. Are all things ready?"

"Yes, monseigneur."

"Go to the entrance of the grottoes, my good Yves, and you will there find the Seigneur de Pierrefonds, who is resting after the fatigue of our journey. And if he should happen not to be able to walk, lift him up, and bring him hither to me."

The three men obeyed. But the recommendation given to his servants was superfluous. Porthos, refreshed, had already commenced the descent, and his heavy step resounded amongst the cavities, formed and supported by columns of porphyry and granite. As soon as the Seigneur de Bracieux had rejoined the bishop, the Bretons lighted a lantern with which they were furnished, and Porthos assured his friend that he felt as strong again as ever.

"Let us inspect the boat," said Aramis, "and satisfy ourselves at once what it will hold."

"Do not go too near with the light," said the patron Yves; "for as you desired me, monseigneur, I have placed under the bench of the poop, in the coffer you know of, the barrel of powder, and the musket-charges that you sent me from the fort."

"Very well," said Aramis; and, taking the lantern himself, he examined minutely all parts of the canoe, with the precautions of a man who is neither timid nor ignorant in the face of danger. The canoe was long, light, drawing little water, thin of keel; in short, one of those that have always been so aptly built at Belle-Isle; a little high in its sides, solid upon the water, very manageable, furnished with planks which, in uncertain weather, formed a sort of deck over which the waves might glide, so as to protect the rowers. In two well-closed coffers, placed beneath the benches of the prow and the poop, Aramis found bread, biscuit, dried fruits, a quarter of bacon, a good provision of water in leathern bottles; the whole forming rations sufficient for people who did not mean to quit the coast, and would be able to revictual, if necessity commanded. The arms, eight muskets, and as many horse-pistols, were in good condition, and all loaded. There were additional oars, in case of accident, and that little sail called *trinquet*, which assists the speed of the canoe at the same time the boatmen row, and is so useful when the breeze is slack. When Aramis had seen to all these things, and appeared satisfied with the result of his inspection, "Let us consult Porthos," said he, "to know if we must endeavor to get the boat out by the unknown extremity of the grotto, following the descent and the shade of the cavern, or whether it be better, in the open air, to make it slide upon its rollers through the bushes, leveling the road of the little beach, which is but twenty feet high, and gives, at high tide, three or four fathoms of good water upon a sound bottom."

"It must be as you please, monseigneur," replied the skipper Yves, respectfully; "but I don't believe that by the slope of the cavern, and in the dark in which we shall be obliged to maneuver our boat, the road will be so convenient as the open air. I know the beach well, and can certify that it is as smooth as a grass-plot in a garden; the interior of the grotto, on the contrary, is rough; without reckoning, monseigneur, that at its extremity we shall come to the trench which leads into the sea, and perhaps the canoe will not pass down it."

"I have made my calculation," said the bishop, "and I am certain it will pass."

"So be it; I wish it may, monseigneur," continued Yves; "but your highness knows very well that to make it reach the extremity of the trench, there is an enormous stone to be lifted—that under which the fox always passes, and which closes the trench like a door."

"It can be raised," said Porthos; "that is nothing."

"Oh! I know that monseigneur has the strength of ten men," replied Yves; "but that is giving him a great deal of trouble."

"I think the skipper may be right," said Aramis; "let us try the open-air passage."

"The more so, monseigneur," continued the fisherman, "that we should not be able to embark before day, it will require so much labor, and that as soon as daylight appears, a good *vedette* placed outside the grotto would be necessary, indispensable even, to watch the maneuvers of the lighters or cruisers that are on the look-out for us."

"Yes, yes, Yves, your reasons are good; we will go by the beach."

And the three robust Bretons went to the boat, and were beginning to place their rollers underneath it to put it in motion, when the distant barking of dogs was heard, proceeding from the interior of the island.

Aramis darted out of the grotto, followed by Porthos. Dawn just tinted with purple and white the waves and plain; through the dim light, melancholy fir-trees waved their tender branches over the pebbles, and long flights of crows were skimming with their black wings the shimmering fields of buckwheat. In a quarter of an hour it would be clear daylight; the wakened birds announced it to all nature. The barkings which had been heard, which had stopped the three fishermen engaged in moving the boat, and had brought Aramis and Porthos out of the cavern, now seemed to come from a deep gorge within about a league of the grotto.

"It is a pack of hounds," said Porthos; "the dogs are on a scent."

"Who can be hunting at such a moment as this?" said Aramis.

"And this way, particularly," continued Porthos, "where they might expect the army of the royalists."

"The noise comes nearer. Yes, you are right, Porthos, the dogs are on a scent. But, Yves!" cried Aramis, "come here! come here!"

Yves ran towards him, letting fall the cylinder which he was about to place under the boat when the bishop's call interrupted him.

"What is the meaning of this hunt, skipper?" said Porthos.

"Eh! monseigneur, I cannot understand it," replied the Breton. "It is not at such a moment that the Seigneur de Locmaria would hunt. No, and yet the dogs—"

"Unless they have escaped from the kennel."

"No," said Goenne, "they are not the Seigneur de Locmaria's hounds."

"In common prudence," said Aramis, "let us go back

into the grotto; the voices evidently draw nearer, we shall soon know what we have to trust to."

They re-entered, but had scarcely proceeded a hundred steps in the darkness, when a noise like the hoarse sigh of a creature in distress resounded through the cavern, and breathless, rapid, terrified, a fox passed like a flash of lightning before the fugitives, leaped over the boat and disappeared, leaving behind its sour scent, which was perceptible for several seconds under the low vaults of the cave.

"The fox!" cried the Bretons, with the glad surprise of born hunters.

"Accursed mischance!" cried the bishop, "our retreat is discovered."

"How so?" said Porthos; "are you afraid of a fox?"

"Eh! my friend, what do you mean by that? why do you specify the fox? It is not the fox alone. *Pardieu!* But don't you know, Porthos, that after the foxes come hounds, and after hounds men?"

Porthos hung his head. As though to confirm the words of Aramis, they heard the yelping pack approach with frightful swiftness upon the trail. Six foxhounds burst at once upon the little heath, with mingling yelps of triumph.

"There are the dogs, plain enough!" said Aramis, posted on the look-out behind a chink in the rocks; "now, who are the huntsmen?"

"If it is the Seigneur de Locmaria's," replied the sailor, "he will leave the dogs to hunt the grotto, for he knows them, and will not enter in himself, being quite sure that the fox will come out the other side; it is there he will wait for him."

"It is not the Seigneur de Locmaria who is hunting," replied Aramis, turning pale in spite of his efforts to maintain a placid countenance.

"Who is it, then?" said Porthos.

"Look!"

Porthos applied his eye to the slit, and saw at the summit

of a hillock a dozen horsemen urging on their horses in the track of the dogs, shouting, "*Taiaut! taiaut!*"

"The guards!" said he.

"Yes, my friend, the king's guards."

"The king's guards! do you say, monseigneur?" cried the Bretons, growing pale in turn.

"With Biscarrat at their head, mounted upon my gray horse," continued Aramis.

The hounds at the same moment rushed into the grotto like an avalanche, and the depths of the cavern were filled with their deafening cries.

"Ah! the devil!" said Aramis, resuming all his coolness at the sight of this certain, inevitable danger. "I am perfectly satisfied we are lost, but we have, at least, one chance left. If the guards who follow their hounds happen to discover there is an issue to the grotto, there is no help for us, for on entering they must see both ourselves and our boat. The dogs must not go out of the cavern. Their masters must not enter."

"That is clear," said Porthos.

"You understand," added Aramis, with the rapid precision of command; "there are six dogs that will be forced to stop at the great stone under which the fox has glided—but at the too narrow opening of which they must be themselves stopped and killed."

The Bretons sprang forward, knife in hand. In a few minutes there was a lamentable concert of angry barks and mortal howls—and then, silence.

"That's well!" said Aramis, coolly, "now for the masters!"

"What is to be done with them?" said Porthos.

"Wait their arrival, conceal ourselves, and kill them."

"*Kill them!*" replied Porthos.

"There are sixteen," said Aramis, "at least, at present."

"And well armed," added Porthos, with a smile of consolation.

"It will last about ten minutes," said Aramis. "To work!"

And with a resolute air he took up a musket, and placed a hunting-knife between his teeth.

"Yves, Goenne, and his son," continued Aramis, "will pass the muskets to us. You, Porthos, will fire when they are close. We shall have brought down, at the lowest computation, eight, before the others are aware of anything—that is certain; then all, there are five of us, will dispatch the other eight, knife in hand."

"And poor Biscarrat?" said Porthos.

Aramis reflected a moment—"Biscarrat first," replied he, coolly. "He knows us."

CHAPTER 48

The Grotto.

In spite of the sort of divination which was the remarkable side of the character of Aramis, the event, subject to the risks of things over which uncertainty presides, did not fall out exactly as the bishop of Vannes had foreseen. Biscarrat, better mounted than his companions, arrived first at the opening of the grotto, and comprehended that fox and hounds were one and all engulfed in it. Only, struck by that superstitious terror which every dark and subterraneous way naturally impresses upon the mind of man, he stopped at the outside of the grotto, and waited till his companions should have assembled round him.

"Well!" asked the young men, coming up, out of breath, and unable to understand the meaning of this inaction.

"Well! I cannot hear the dogs; they and the fox must all be lost in this infernal cavern."

"They were too close up," said one of the guards, "to have lost scent all at once. Besides, we should hear them from one side or another. They must, as Biscarrat says, be in this grotto."

"But then," said one of the young men, "why don't they give tongue?"

"It is strange!" muttered another.

"Well, but," said a fourth, "let us go into this grotto. Does it happen to be forbidden we should enter it?"

"No," replied Biscarrat. "Only, as it looks as dark as a wolf's mouth, we might break our necks in it."

"Witness the dogs," said a guard, "who seem to have broken theirs."

"What the devil can have become of them?" asked the young men in chorus. And every master called his dog by his name, whistled to him in his favorite mode, without a single one replying to either call or whistle.

"It is perhaps an enchanted grotto," said Biscarrat; "let us see." And, jumping from his horse, he made a step into the grotto.

"Stop! stop! I will accompany you," said one of the guards, on seeing Biscarrat disappear in the shades of the cavern's mouth.

"No," replied Biscarrat, "there must be something extraordinary in the place—don't let us risk ourselves all at once. If in ten minutes you do not hear of me, you can come in, but not all at once."

"Be it so," said the young man, who, besides, did not imagine that Biscarrat ran much risk in the enterprise, "we will wait for you." And without dismounting from their horses, they formed a circle round the grotto.

Biscarrat entered then alone, and advanced through the darkness till he came in contact with the muzzle of Porthos's musket. The resistance which his chest met with astonished him; he naturally raised his hand and laid hold of the icy barrel. At the same instant, Yves lifted a knife against the young man, which was about to fall upon him with all force of a Breton's arm, when the iron wrist of Porthos stopped it half-way. Then, like low muttering thunder, his voice growled in the darkness, "I will not have him killed!"

Biscarrat found himself between a protection and a threat, the one almost as terrible as the other. However brave the young man might be, he could not prevent a cry escaping him, which Aramis immediately suppressed by placing a handkerchief over his mouth. "Monsieur de Biscarrat," said he, in a low voice, "we mean you no harm, and you must know that if you have recognized us; but, at the first word, the first groan, the first whisper, we shall be forced to kill you as we have killed your dogs."

"Yes, I recognize you, gentlemen," said the officer, in a low voice. "But why are you here—what are you doing, here? Unfortunate men! I thought you were in the fort."

"And you, monsieur, you were to obtain conditions for us, I think?"

"I did all I was able, messieurs, but—"

"But what?"

"But there are positive orders."

"To kill us?"

Biscarrat made no reply. It would have cost him too much to speak of the cord to gentlemen. Aramis understood the silence of the prisoner.

"Monsieur Biscarrat," said he, "you would be already dead if we had not regard for your youth and our ancient association with your father; but you may yet escape from the place by swearing that you will not tell your companions what you have seen."

"I will not only swear that I will not speak of it," said Biscarrat, "but I still further swear that I will do everything in the world to prevent my companions from setting foot in the grotto."

"Biscarrat! Biscarrat!" cried several voices from the outside, coming like a whirlwind into the cave.

"Reply," said Aramis.

"Here I am!" cried Biscarrat.

"Now, begone; we depend on your loyalty." And he left his hold of the young man, who hastily returned towards the light.

"Biscarrat! Biscarrat!" cried the voices, still nearer. And the shadows of several human forms projected into the interior of the grotto. Biscarrat rushed to meet his friends in order to stop them, and met them just as they were adventuring into the cave. Aramis and Porthos listened with the intense attention of men whose life depends upon a breath of air.

"Oh! oh!" exclaimed one of the guards, as he came to the light, "how pale you are!"

"Pale!" cried another; "you ought to say corpse-color."

"I!" said the young man, endeavoring to collect his faculties.

"In the name of Heaven! what has happened?" exclaimed all the voices.

"You have not a drop of blood in your veins, my poor friend," said one of them, laughing.

"Messieurs, it is serious," said another, "he is going to faint; does any one of you happen to have any salts?" And they all laughed.

This hail of jests fell round Biscarrat's ears like musketballs in a *melee*. He recovered himself amidst a deluge of interrogations.

"What do you suppose I have seen?" asked he. "I was too hot when I entered the grotto, and I have been struck with a chill. That is all."

"But the dogs, the dogs; have you seen them again—did you see anything of them—do you know anything about them?"

"I suppose they have got out some other way."

"Messieurs," said one of the young men, "there is in that which is going on, in the paleness and silence of our friend, a mystery which Biscarrat will not, or cannot reveal. Only, and this is certain, Biscarrat has seen something in the grotto. Well, for my part, I am very curious to see what it is, even if it is the devil! To the grotto! messieurs, to the grotto!"

"To the grotto!" repeated all the voices. And the echo

of the cavern carried like a menace to Porthos and Aramis, "To the grotto! to the grotto!"

Biscarrat threw himself before his companions. "Messieurs! messieurs!" cried he, "in the name of Heaven! do not go in!"

"Why, what is there so terrific in the cavern?" asked several at once. "Come, speak, Biscarrat."

"Decidedly, it is the devil he has seen," repeated he who had before advanced that hypothesis.

"Well," said another, "if he has seen him, he need not be selfish; he may as well let us have a look at him in turn."

"Messieurs! messieurs! I beseech you," urged Biscarrat.

"Nonsense! Let us pass!"

"Messieurs, I implore you not to enter!"

"Why, you went in yourself."

Then one of the officers, who—of a riper age than the others—had till this time remained behind, and had said nothing, advanced. "Messieurs," said he, with a calmness which contrasted with the animation of the young men, "there is in there some person, or something, that is not the devil; but which, whatever it may be, has had sufficient power to silence our dogs. We must discover who this some one is, or what this something is."

Biscarrat made a last effort to stop his friends, but it was useless. In vain he threw himself before the rashest; in vain he clung to the rocks to bar the passage; the crowd of young men rushed into the cave, in the steps of the officer who had spoken last, but who had sprung in first, sword in hand, to face the unknown danger. Biscarrat, repulsed by his friends, unable to accompany them, without passing in the eyes of Porthos and Aramis for a traitor and a perjurer, with painfully attentive ear and unconsciously supplicating hands leaned against the rough side of a rock which he thought must be exposed to the fire of the musketeers. As to the guards, they penetrated further and further, with exclamations that grew fainter as they advanced. All at once, a discharge of musketry, growling like thunder, exploded in the entrails of the vault. Two or three balls were flattened against the rock on which Biscarrat was leaning. At the same instant, cries, shrieks, imprecations burst forth, and the little troop of gentlemen reappeared—some pale, some bleeding—all enveloped in a cloud of smoke, which the outer air seemed to suck from the depths of the cavern. "Biscarrat! Biscarrat!" cried the fugitives, "you knew there was an ambuscade in that cavern, and you did not warn us! Biscarrat, you are the cause that four of us are murdered men! Woe be to you, Biscarrat!"

"You are the cause of my being wounded unto death," said one of the young men, letting a gush of scarlet life-blood vomit in his palm, and spattering it into Biscarrat's livid face. "My blood be on your head!" And he rolled in agony at the feet of the young man.

"But, at least, tell us who is there?" cried several furious voices.

Biscarrat remained silent. "Tell us, or die!" cried the wounded man, raising himself upon one knee, and lifting towards his companion an arm bearing a useless sword. Biscarrat rushed towards him, opening his breast for the blow, but the wounded man fell back not to rise again, uttering a groan which was his last. Biscarrat, with hair on end, haggard eyes, and bewildered head, advanced towards the interior of the cavern, saying, "You are right. Death to me, who have allowed my comrades to be assassinated. I am a worthless wretch!" And throwing away his sword, for he wished to die without defending himself, he rushed head foremost into the cavern. The others followed him. The eleven who remained out of sixteen imitated his example; but they did not go further than the first. A second discharge laid five upon the icy sand; and as it was impossible to see whence this murderous thunder issued, the others fell back with a terror that can be better imagined than described. But, far from flying, as the others had done, Biscarrat remained safe and sound, seated on a fragment of rock, and waited. There were only six gentlemen left.

"Seriously," said one of the survivors, "is it the devil?"

"*Ma foi!* it is much worse," said another.

"Ask Biscarrat, he knows."

"Where is Biscarrat?" The young men looked round them, and saw that Biscarrat did not answer.

"He is dead!" said two or three voices.

"Oh! no!" replied another, "I saw him through the smoke, sitting quietly on a rock. He is in the cavern; he is waiting for us."

"He must know who are there."

"And how should he know them?"

"He was taken prisoner by the rebels."

"That is true. Well! let us call him, and learn from him whom we have to deal with." And all voices shouted, "Biscarrat! Biscarrat!" But Biscarrat did not answer.

"Good!" said the officer who had shown so much coolness in the affair. "We have no longer any need of him; here are reinforcements coming."

In fact, a company of guards, left in the rear by their officers, whom the ardor of the chase had carried away—from seventy-five to eighty men—arrived in good order, led by their captain and the first lieutenant. The five officers hastened to meet their soldiers; and, in language the eloquence of which may be easily imagined, they related the adventure, and asked for aid. The captain interrupted them. "Where are your companions?" demanded he.

"Dead!"

"But there were sixteen of you!"

"Ten are dead. Biscarrat is in the cavern, and we are five."

"Biscarrat is a prisoner?"

"Probably."

"No, for here he is—look." In fact, Biscarrat appeared at the opening of the grotto.

"He is making a sign to come on," said the officer. "Come on!"

"Come on!" cried all the troop. And they advanced to meet Biscarrat.

"Monsieur," said the captain, addressing Biscarrat, "I am assured that you know who the men are in that grotto, and who make such a desperate defense. In the king's name I command you to declare what you know."

"Captain," said Biscarrat, "you have no need to command me. My word has been restored to me this very instant; and I came in the name of these men."

"To tell me who they are?"

"To tell you they are determined to defend themselves to the death, unless you grant them satisfactory terms."

"How many are there of them, then?"

"There are two," said Biscarrat.

"There are two—and want to impose conditions upon us?"

"There are two, and they have already killed ten of our men."

"What sort of people are they—giants?"

"Worse than that. Do you remember the history of the Bastion Saint-Gervais, captain?"

"Yes; where four musketeers held out against an army."

"Well, these are two of those same musketeers."

"And their names?"

"At that period they were called Porthos and Aramis. Now they are styled M. d'Herblay and M. du Vallon."

"And what interest have they in all this?"

"It is they who were holding Bell-Isle for M. Fouquet."

A murmur ran through the ranks of the soldiers on hearing the two words "Porthos and Aramis." "The musketeers! the musketeers!" repeated they. And among all these brave men, the idea that they were going to have a struggle against two of the oldest glories of the French army, made a shiver, half enthusiasm, two-thirds terror, run through them. In fact, those four names—D'Artagnan, Athos, Porthos, and Aramis—were venerated among all who wore a sword; as, in antiquity, the names of Hercules, Theseus, Castor, and Pollux were venerated.

"Two men—and they have killed ten in two discharges! It is impossible, Monsieur Biscarrat!"

"Eh! captain," replied the latter, "I do not tell you that they have not with them two or three men, as the musketeers of the Bastion Saint-Gervais had two or three lackeys; but, believe me, captain, I have seen these men, I have been taken prisoner by them—I know they themselves alone are all-sufficient to destroy an army."

"That we shall see," said the captain, "and that in a moment, too. Gentlemen, attention!"

At this reply, no one stirred, and all prepared to obey. Biscarrat alone risked a last attempt.

"Monsieur," said he, in a low voice, "be persuaded by me; let us pass on our way. Those two men, those two lions you are going to attack, will defend themselves to the death. They have already killed ten of our men; they will kill double the number, and end by killing themselves rather than surrender. What shall we gain by fighting them?"

"We shall gain the consciousness, monsieur, of not having allowed eighty of the king's guards to retire before two rebels. If I listened to your advice, monsieur, I should be a dishonored man; and by dishonoring myself I should dishonor the army. Forward, my men!"

And he marched first as far as the opening of the grotto. There he halted. The object of this halt was to give Biscarrat and his companions time to describe to him the interior of the grotto. Then, when he believed he had a sufficient acquaintance with the place, he divided his company into three bodies, which were to enter successively, keeping up a sustained fire in all directions. No doubt, in this attack they would lose five more, perhaps ten; but, certainly, they must end by taking the rebels, since there was no issue; and, at any rate, two men could not kill eighty.

"Captain," said Biscarrat, "I beg to be allowed to march at the head of the first platoon."

"So be it," replied the captain; "you have all the honor. I make you a present of it."

"Thanks!" replied the young man, with all the firmness of his race.

"Take your sword, then."

"I shall go as I am, captain," said Biscarrat, "for I do not go to kill, I go to be killed."

And placing himself at the head of the first platoon, with head uncovered and arms crossed,—"March, gentlemen," said he.

CHAPTER 49

An Homeric Song.

It is time to pass to the other camp, and to describe at once the combatants and the field of battle. Aramis and Porthos had gone to the grotto of Locmaria with the expectation of finding there their canoe ready armed, as well as the three Bretons, their assistants; and they at first hoped to make the bark pass through the little issue of the cavern, concealing in that fashion both their labors and their flight. The arrival of the fox and dogs obliged them to remain concealed. The grotto extended the space of about a hundred *toises*, to that little slope dominating a creek. Formerly a temple of the Celtic divinities, when Belle-Isle was still called Kalonese, this grotto had beheld more than one human sacrifice accomplished in its mystic depths. The first entrance to the cavern was by a moderate descent, above which distorted rocks formed a weird arcade; the interior, very uneven and dangerous from the inequalities of the vault, was subdivided into several compartments, which communicated with each other by means of rough and jagged steps, fixed right and left, in uncouth natural pillars. At the third compartment the vault was so low, the passage so narrow, that the bark would scarcely have passed without touching the side; nevertheless, in moments of despair, wood softens and stone grows flexible beneath the human will. Such was the thought of Aramis, when, after having fought the fight, he decided upon flight—a flight most dangerous, since all the assailants were not dead; and that, admitting the possibility of putting the bark to sea, they would have to fly in open day, before the conquered, so interested on recognizing their small number, in pursuing their conquerors. When the two discharges had killed ten men, Aramis, familiar with the windings of the cavern, went to reconnoiter them one by one, and counted them, for the smoke prevented seeing outside; and he immediately commanded that the canoe should be rolled as far as the great stone, the closure of the liberating issue. Porthos collected all his strength, took the canoe in his arms, and raised it up, whilst the Bretons made it run rapidly along the rollers. They had descended into the third compartment; they had arrived at the stone which walled the outlet. Porthos seized this gigantic stone at its base, applied his robust shoulder, and gave a heave which made the wall crack. A cloud of dust fell from the vault, with the ashes of ten thousand generations of sea birds, whose nests stuck like cement to the rock. At the third shock the stone gave way, and oscillated for a minute. Porthos, placing his back against the neighboring rock, made an arch with his foot, which drove the block out of the calcareous masses which served for hinges and cramps. The stone fell, and daylight was visible, brilliant, radiant, flooding the cavern through the opening, and the blue sea appeared to the delighted Bretons. They began to lift the bark over the barricade. Twenty more *toises*, and it would glide into the ocean. It was during this time that the company arrived, was drawn up by the captain, and disposed for either an escalade or an assault. Aramis watched over everything, to favor the labors of his friends. He saw the reinforcements, counted the men, and convinced himself at a single glance of the insurmountable peril to which fresh combat would expose them. To escape by sea, at the moment the cavern was about to be invaded, was impossible. In fact, the daylight which had just been admitted to the last compartments had exposed to the soldiers the bark being rolled towards the sea, the two rebels within musket-shot; and one of their discharges would riddle the boat if it did not kill the navigators. Besides, allowing everything,—if the bark escaped with the men on board of it, how could the alarm be suppressed—how could notice to the royal lighters be prevented? What could hinder the poor canoe, followed by sea and watched from the shore, from succumbing before the end of the day? Aramis, digging his hands into his gray hair with rage, invoked the assistance of God and the assistance of the demons. Calling to Porthos, who was doing more work than all the rollers—whether of flesh or wood— "My friend," said he, "our adversaries have just received a reinforcement."

"Ah, ah!" said Porthos, quietly, "what is to be done, then?"

"To recommence the combat," said Aramis, "is hazardous."

"Yes," said Porthos, "for it is difficult to suppose that out of two, one should not be killed; and certainly, if one of us was killed, the other would get himself killed also." Porthos spoke these words with that heroic nature which, with him, grew grander with necessity.

Aramis felt it like a spur to his heart. "We shall neither of us be killed if you do what I tell you, friend Porthos."

"Tell me what?"

"These people are coming down into the grotto."

"Yes."

"We could kill about fifteen of them, but no more."

"How many are there in all?" asked Porthos.

"They have received a reinforcement of seventy-five men."

"Seventy-five and five, eighty. Ah!" sighed Porthos.

"If they fire all at once they will riddle us with balls."

"Certainly they will."

"Without reckoning," added Aramis, "that the detonation might occasion a collapse of the cavern."

"Ay," said Porthos, "a piece of falling rock just now grazed my shoulder."

"You see, then?"

"Oh! it is nothing."

"We must determine upon something quickly. Our Bretons are going to continue to roll the canoe towards the sea."

"Very well."

"We two will keep the powder, the balls, and the muskets here."

"But only two, my dear Aramis—we shall never fire three shots together," said Porthos, innocently, "the defense by musketry is a bad one."

"Find a better, then."

"I have found one," said the giant, eagerly; "I will place myself in ambuscade behind the pillar with this iron bar, and invisible, unattackable, if they come in floods, I can let my bar fall upon their skulls, thirty times in a minute. *Hein!* what do you think of the project? You smile!"

"Excellent, dear friend, perfect! I approve it greatly; only you will frighten them, and half of them will remain outside to take us by famine. What we want, my good friend, is the entire destruction of the troop. A single survivor encompasses our ruin."

"You are right, my friend, but how can we attract them, pray?"

"By not stirring, my good Porthos."

"Well! we won't stir, then; but when they are all together—"

"Then leave it to me, I have an idea."

"If it is so, and your idea proves a good one—and your idea is most likely to be good—I am satisfied."

"To your ambuscade, Porthos, and count how many enter."

"But you, what will you do?"

"Don't trouble yourself about me; I have a task to perform."

"I think I hear shouts."

"It is they! To your post. Keep within reach of my voice and hand."

Porthos took refuge in the second compartment, which was in darkness, absolutely black. Aramis glided into the third; the giant held in his hand an iron bar of about fifty pounds weight. Porthos handled this lever, which had been used in rolling the bark, with marvelous facility. During this time, the Bretons had pushed the bark to the beach. In the further and lighter compartment, Aramis, stooping and concealed, was busy with some mysterious maneuver. A command was given in a loud voice. It was the last order of the captain commandant. Twenty-five men jumped from the upper rocks into the first compartment of the grotto, and having taken their ground, began to fire. The echoes shrieked and barked, the hissing balls seemed actually to rarefy the air, and then opaque smoke filled the vault.

"To the left! to the left!" cried Biscarrat, who, in his first assault, had seen the passage to the second chamber, and who, animated by the smell of powder, wished to guide his soldiers in that direction. The troop, accordingly, precipitated themselves to the left—the passage gradually growing narrower. Biscarrat, with his hands stretched forward, devoted to death, marched in advance of the muskets. "Come on! come on!" exclaimed he, "I see daylight!"

"Strike, Porthos!" cried the sepulchral voice of Aramis.

Porthos breathed a heavy sigh—but he obeyed. The iron

bar fell full and direct upon the head of Biscarrat, who was dead before he had ended his cry. Then the formidable lever rose ten times in ten seconds, and made ten corpses. The soldiers could see nothing; they heard sighs and groans; they stumbled over dead bodies, but as they had no conception of the cause of all this, they came forward jostling each other. The implacable bar, still falling, annihilated the first platoon, without a single sound to warn the second, which was quietly advancing; only, commanded by the captain, the men had stripped a fir, growing on the shore, and, with its resinous branches twisted together, the captain had made a flambeau. On arriving at the compartment where Porthos, like the exterminating angel, had destroyed all he touched, the first rank drew back in terror. No firing had replied to that of the guards, and yet their way was stopped by a heap of dead bodies—they literally walked in blood. Porthos was still behind his pillar. The captain, illumining with trembling pine-torch this frightful carnage, of which he in vain sought the cause, drew back towards the pillar behind which Porthos was concealed. Then a gigantic hand issued from the shade, and fastened on the throat of the captain, who uttered a stifle rattle; his stretched-out arms beating the air, the torch fell and was extinguished in blood. A second after, the corpse of the captain dropped close to the extinguished torch, and added another body to the heap of dead which blocked up the passage. All this was effected as mysteriously as though by magic. At hearing the rattling in the throat of the captain, the soldiers who accompanied him had turned round, caught a glimpse of his extended arms, his eyes starting from their sockets, and then the torch fell and they were left in darkness. From an unreflective, instinctive, mechanical feeling, the lieutenant cried:

"Fire!"

Immediately a volley of musketry flamed, thundered, roared in the cavern, bringing down enormous fragments from the vaults. The cavern was lighted for an instant by this discharge, and then immediately returned to pitchy darkness rendered thicker by the smoke. To this succeeded a profound silence, broken only by the steps of the third brigade, now entering the cavern.

CHAPTER 50

The Death of a Titan.

At the moment when Porthos, more accustomed to the darkness than these men, coming from open daylight, was looking round him to see if through this artificial midnight Aramis were not making him some signal, he felt his arm gently touched, and a voice low as a breath murmured in his ear, "Come."

"Oh!" said Porthos.

"Hush!" said Aramis, if possible, yet more softly.

And amidst the noise of the third brigade, which continued to advance, the imprecations of the guards still left alive, the muffled groans of the dying, Aramis and Porthos glided unseen along the granite walls of the cavern. Aramis led Porthos into the last but one compartment, and showed him, in a hollow of the rocky wall, a barrel of powder weighing from seventy to eighty pounds, to which he had just attached a fuse. "My friend," said he to Porthos, "you will take this barrel, the match of which I am going to set fire to, and throw it amidst our enemies; can you do so?"

"*Parbleu!*" replied Porthos; and he lifted the barrel with one hand. "Light it!"

"Stop," said Aramis, "till they are all massed together, and then, my Jupiter, hurl your thunderbolt among them."

"Light it," repeated Porthos.

"On my part," continued Aramis, "I will join our Bretons, and help them to get the canoe to the sea. I will wait for you on the shore; launch it strongly, and hasten to us."

"Light it," said Porthos, a third time.

"But do you understand me?"

"*Parbleu!*" said Porthos again, with laughter that he did not even attempt to restrain, "when a thing is explained to me I understand it; begone, and give me the light."

Aramis gave the burning match to Porthos, who held out his arm to him, his hands being engaged. Aramis pressed the arm of Porthos with both his hands, and fell back to the outlet of the cavern where the three rowers awaited him.

Porthos, left alone, applied the spark bravely to the match. The spark—a feeble spark, first principle of conflagration—shone in the darkness like a glow-worm, then was deadened against the match which it set fire to, Porthos enlivening the flame with his breath. The smoke was a little dispersed, and by the light of the sparkling match objects might, for two seconds, be distinguished. It was a brief but splendid spectacle, that of this giant, pale, bloody, his countenance lighted by the fire of the match burning in surrounding darkness! The soldiers saw him, they saw the barrel he held in his hand—they at once understood what was going to happen. Then, these men, already choked with horror at the sight of what had been accomplished, filled with terror at thought of what was about to be accomplished, gave out a simultaneous shriek of agony. Some endeavored to fly, but they encountered the third brigade, which barred their passage; others mechanically took aim and attempted to fire their discharged muskets; others fell instinctively upon their knees. Two or three officers cried out to Porthos to promise him his liberty if he would spare their lives. The lieutenant of the third brigade commanded his men to fire; but the guards had before them their terrified companions, who served as a living rampart for Porthos. We have said that the light produced by the spark and the match did not last more than two seconds; but during these two seconds this is what it illumined: in the first place, the giant, enlarged in the darkness; then, at ten paces off, a heap of bleeding bodies, crushed, mutilated, in the midst of which some still heaved in the last agony, lifting the mass as a last respiration inflating the sides of some old monster dying in the night. Every breath of Porthos, thus vivifying the match, sent towards this heap of bodies a phosphorescent aura, mingled with streaks of purple. In addition to this principal group scattered about the grotto, as the chances of death or surprise had stretched them, isolated bodies seemed to be making ghastly exhibitions of their gaping wounds. Above ground, bedded in pools of blood, rose, heavy and sparkling, the short, thick pillars of the cavern, of which the strongly marked shades threw out the luminous particles. And all this was seen by the tremulous light of a match attached to a barrel of powder, that is to say, a torch which, whilst throwing a light on the dead past, showed death to come.

As I have said, this spectacle did not last above two seconds. During this short space of time an officer of the third brigade got together eight men armed with muskets, and, through an opening, ordered them to fire upon Porthos. But they who received the order to fire trembled so that three guards fell by the discharge, and the five remaining balls hissed on to splinter the vault, plow the ground, or indent the pillars of the cavern.

A burst of laughter replied to this volley; then the arm of the giant swung round; then was seen whirling through the air, like a falling star, the train of fire. The barrel, hurled a distance of thirty feet, cleared the barricade of dead bodies, and fell amidst a group of shrieking soldiers, who threw themselves on their faces. The officer had followed the brilliant train in the air; he endeavored to precipitate himself upon the barrel and tear out the match before it reached the powder it contained. Useless! The air had made the flame attached to the conductor more active; the match, which at rest might have burnt five minutes, was consumed in thirty seconds, and the infernal work exploded. Furious vortices of sulphur and nitre, devouring shoals of fire which caught every object, the terrible thunder of the explosion, this is what the second which followed disclosed in that cavern of horrors. The rocks split like planks of deal beneath the axe. A jet of fire, smoke, and *debris* sprang from the middle of the grotto, enlarging as it mounted. The large walls of silex tottered and fell upon the sand, and the sand itself, an instrument of pain when launched from its hard bed, riddled the faces with its myriad cutting atoms. Shrieks, imprecations, human life, dead bodies—all were engulfed in one terrific crash.

The three first compartments became one sepulchral sink into which fell grimly back, in the order of their weight, every vegetable, mineral, or human fragment. Then the lighter sand and ash came down in turn, stretching like a winding sheet and smoking over the dismal scene. And now, in this burning tomb, this subterranean volcano, seek the king's guards with their blue coats laced with silver. Seek the officers, brilliant in gold, seek for the arms upon which they depended for their defense. One single man has made of all of those things a chaos more confused, more shapeless, more terrible than the chaos which existed before the creation of the world. There remained nothing of the three compartments—nothing by which God could have recognized His handiwork. As for Porthos, after having hurled the barrel of powder amidst his enemies, he had fled, as Aramis had directed him to do, and had gained the last compartment, into which air, light, and sunshine penetrated through the opening. Scarcely had he turned the angle which separated the third compartment from the fourth when he perceived at a hundred paces from him the bark dancing on the waves. There were his friends, there liberty, there life and victory. Six more of his formidable strides, and he would be out of the vault; out of the vault! a dozen of his vigorous leaps and he would reach the canoe. Suddenly he felt his knees give way; his knees seemed powerless, his legs to yield beneath him.

"Oh! oh!" murmured he, "there is my weakness seizing me again! I can walk no further! What is this?"

Aramis perceived him through the opening, and unable to conceive what could induce him to stop thus—"Come on, Porthos! come on," he cried; "come quickly!"

"Oh!" replied the giant, making an effort that contorted every muscle of his body—"oh! but I cannot." While saying these words, he fell upon his knees, but with his mighty hands he clung to the rocks, and raised himself up again.

"Quick! quick!" repeated Aramis, bending forward towards the shore, as if to draw Porthos towards him with his arms.

"Here I am," stammered Porthos, collecting all his strength to make one step more.

"In the name of Heaven! Porthos, make haste! the barrel will blow up!"

"Make haste, monseigneur!" shouted the Bretons to Porthos, who was floundering as in a dream.

But there was no time; the explosion thundered, earth gaped, the smoke which hurled through the clefts obscured the sky; the sea flowed back as though driven by the blast of flame which darted from the grotto as if from the jaws of some gigantic fiery chimera; the reflux took the bark out twenty *toises*; the solid rocks cracked to their base, and separated like blocks beneath the operation of the wedge; a portion of the vault was carried up towards heaven, as if it had been built of cardboard; the green and blue and topaz conflagration and black lava of liquefactions clashed and combated an instant beneath a majestic dome of smoke; then oscillated, declined, and fell successively the mighty monoliths of rock which the violence of the explosion had not been able to uproot from the bed of ages; they bowed to each other like grave and stiff old men, then prostrating themselves, lay down forever in their dusty tomb.

This frightful shock seemed to restore Porthos the strength that he had lost; he arose, a giant among granite giants. But at the moment he was flying between the double hedge of granite phantoms, these latter, which were no longer supported by the corresponding links, began to roll and totter round our Titan, who looked as if precipitated from heaven amidst rocks which he had just been launching. Porthos felt the very earth beneath his feet becoming jelly-tremulous. He stretched both hands to repulse the falling rocks. A gigantic block was held back by each of his extended arms. He bent his head, and a third granite mass sank between his shoulders. For an instant the power of Porthos seemed about to fail him, but this new Hercules united all his force, and the two walls of the prison in which he was buried fell back slowly and gave him place. For an instant he appeared, in this frame of granite, like the angel of chaos, but in pushing back the lateral rocks, he lost his point of support, for the monolith which weighed upon his shoulders, and the boulder, pressing upon him with all its weight, brought the giant down upon his knees. The lateral rocks, for an instant pushed back, drew together again, and added their weight to the ponderous mass which would have been sufficient to crush ten men. The hero fell without a groan—he fell while answering Aramis with words of encouragement and hope, for, thanks to the powerful arch of his hands, for an instant he believed that, like Enceladus, he would succeed in shaking off the triple load. But by degrees Aramis beheld the block sink; the hands, strung for an instant, the arms stiffened for a last effort, gave way, the extended shoulders sank, wounded and torn, and the rocks continued to gradually collapse.

"Porthos! Porthos!" cried Aramis, tearing his hair. "Porthos! where are you? Speak!"

"Here, here," murmured Porthos, with a voice growing evidently weaker, "patience! patience!"

Scarcely had he pronounced these words, when the impulse of the fall augmented the weight; the enormous rock sank down, pressed by those others which sank in from the sides, and, as it were, swallowed up Porthos in a sepulcher of badly jointed stones. On hearing the dying voice of his friend, Aramis had sprung to land. Two of the Bretons followed him, with each a lever in his hand—one being sufficient to take care of the bark. The dying rattle of the valiant gladiator guided them amidst the ruins. Aramis, animated, active and young as at twenty, sprang towards the triple mass, and with his hands, delicate as those of a woman, raised by a miracle of strength the corner-stone of this great granite grave. Then he caught a glimpse, through the darkness of that charnel-house, of the still brilliant eye of his friend, to whom the momentary lifting of the mass restored a momentary respiration. The two men came rushing up, grasped their iron levers, united their triple strength, not merely to raise it, but sustain it. All was useless. They gave way with cries of grief, and the rough voice of Porthos, seeing them exhaust themselves in a useless struggle, murmured in an almost cheerful tone those supreme words which came to his lips with the last respiration, "Too heavy!"

After which his eyes darkened and closed, his face grew ashy pale, the hands whitened, and the colossus sank quite down, breathing his last sigh. With him sank the rock, which, even in his dying agony he had still held up. The three men dropped the levers, which rolled upon the tumulary stone. Then, breathless, pale, his brow covered with sweat, Aramis listened, his breast oppressed, his heart ready to break.

Nothing more. The giant slept the eternal sleep, in the sepulcher which God had built about him to his measure.

CHAPTER 51

Porthos's Epitaph.

Aramis, silent and sad as ice, trembling like a timid child, arose shivering from the stone. A Christian does not walk on tombs. But, though capable of standing, he was not capable of walking. It might be said that something of dead Porthos had just died within him. His Bretons surrounded him; Aramis yielded to their kind exertions, and the three sailors, lifting him up, carried him to the canoe. Then, having laid him down upon the bench near the rudder, they took to their oars, preferring this to hoisting sail, which might betray them.

On all that leveled surface of the ancient grotto of Locmaria, one single hillock attracted their eyes. Aramis never removed his from it; and, at a distance out in the sea, in proportion as the shore receded, that menacing proud mass of rock seemed to draw itself up, as formerly Porthos used to draw himself up, raising a smiling, yet invincible head towards heaven, like that of his dear old honest valiant friend, the strongest of the four, yet the first dead. Strange destiny of these men of brass! The most simple of heart allied to the most crafty; strength of body guided by subtlety of mind; and in the decisive moment, when vigor alone could save mind and body, a stone, a rock, a vile material weight, triumphed over manly strength, and falling upon the body, drove out the mind.

Worthy Porthos! born to help other men, always ready to sacrifice himself for the safety of the weak, as if God had only given him strength for that purpose; when dying he only thought he was carrying out the conditions of his compact with Aramis, a compact, however, which Aramis alone had drawn up, and which Porthos had only known to suffer by its terrible solidarity. Noble Porthos! of what good now are thy chateaux overflowing with sumptuous furniture, forests overflowing with game, lakes overflowing with fish, cellars overflowing with wealth! Of what service to thee now thy lackeys in brilliant liveries, and in the midst of them Mousqueton, proud of the power delegated by thee! Oh, noble Porthos! careful heaper-up of treasure, was it worth while to labor to sweeten and gild life, to come upon a desert shore, surrounded by the cries of seagulls, and lay thyself, with broken bones, beneath a torpid stone? Was it worth while, in short, noble Porthos, to heap so much gold, and not have even the distich of a poor poet engraven upon thy monument? Valiant Porthos! he still, without doubt, sleeps, lost, forgotten, beneath the rock the shepherds of the heath take for the gigantic abode of a *dolmen*. And so many twining branches, so many mosses, bent by the bitter wind of ocean, so many lichens solder thy sepulcher to earth, that no passers-by will imagine such a block of granite could ever have been supported by the shoulders of one man.

Aramis, still pale, still icy-cold, his heart upon his lips, looked, even till, with the last ray of daylight, the shore faded on the horizon. Not a word escaped him, not a sigh rose from his deep breast. The superstitious Bretons looked upon him, trembling. Such silence was not that of a man, it was the silence of a statue. In the meantime, with the first gray lines that lighted up the heavens, the canoe hoisted its little sail, which, swelling with the kisses of the breeze, and carrying them rapidly from the coast, made bravest way towards Spain, across the dreaded Gulf of Gascony, so rife with storms. But scarcely half an hour after the sail had been hoisted, the rowers became inactive, reclining on their benches, and, making an eye-shade with their hands, pointed out to each other a white spot which appeared on the horizon as motion-less as a gull rocked by the viewless respiration of the waves. But that which might have appeared motionless to ordinary eyes was moving at a quick rate to the experienced eye of the sailor; that which appeared stationary upon the ocean was cutting a rapid way through it. For some time, seeing the profound torpor in which their master was plunged, they did not dare to rouse him, and satisfied themselves with exchanging their conjectures in whispers. Aramis, in fact, so vigilant, so active—Aramis, whose eye, like that of the lynx, watched without ceasing, and saw better by night than by day—Aramis seemed to sleep in this despair of soul. An hour passed thus, during which daylight gradually disappeared, but during which also the sail in view gained so swiftly on the bark, that Goenne, one of the three sailors, ventured to say aloud:

"Monseigneur, we are being chased!"

Aramis made no reply; the ship still gained upon them. Then, of their own accord, two of the sailors, by the direc-tion of the patron Yves, lowered the sail, in order that that single point upon the surface of the waters should cease to be a guide to the eye of the enemy pursuing them. On the part of the ship in sight, on the contrary, two more small sails were run up at the extremities of the masts. Unfortunately, it was the time of the finest and longest days of the year, and the moon, in all her brilliancy, succeeded inauspicious daylight. The *balancelle*, which was pursuing the little bark before the wind, had then still half an hour of twilight, and a whole night almost as light as day.

"Monseigneur! monseigneur! we are lost!" said the

captain. "Look! they see us plainly, though we have lowered sail."

"That is not to be wondered at," murmured one of the sailors, "since they say that, by the aid of the devil, the Paris-folk have fabricated instruments with which they see as well at a distance as near, by night as well as by day."

Aramis took a telescope from the bottom of the boat, focussed it silently, and passing it to the sailor, "Here," said he, "look!" The sailor hesitated.

"Don't be alarmed," said the bishop, "there is no sin in it; and if there is any sin, I will take it on myself."

The sailor lifted the glass to his eye, and uttered a cry. He believed that the vessel, which appeared to be distant about cannon-shot, had at a single bound cleared the whole distance. But, on withdrawing the instrument from his eye, he saw that, except the way which the *balancelle* had been able to make during that brief instant, it was still at the same distance.

"So," murmured the sailor, "they can see us as we see them."

"They see us," said Aramis, and sank again into impassibility.

"What!—they see us!" said Yves. "Impossible!"

"Well, captain, look yourself," said the sailor. And he passed him the glass.

"Monseigneur assures me that the devil has nothing to do with this?" asked Yves.

Aramis shrugged his shoulders.

The skipper lifted the glass to his eye. "Oh! monseigneur," said he, "it is a miracle—there they are; it seems as if I were going to touch them. Twenty-five men at least! Ah! I see the captain forward. He holds a glass like this, and is looking at us. Ah! he turns round, and gives an order; they are rolling a piece of cannon forward—they are loading it—pointing it. *Misericorde!* they are firing at us!"

And by a mechanical movement, the skipper put aside the telescope, and the pursuing ship, relegated to the horizon, appeared again in its true aspect. The vessel was still at the distance of nearly a league, but the maneuver sighted thus was not less real. A light cloud of smoke appeared beneath the sails, more blue than they, and spreading like a flower opening; then, at about a mile from the little canoe, they saw the ball take the crown off two or three waves, dig a white furrow in the sea, and disappear at the end of it, as inoffensive as the stone with which, in play, a boy makes ducks and drakes. It was at once a menace and a warning.

"What is to be done?" asked the patron.

"They will sink us!" said Goenne, "give us absolution, monseigneur!" And the sailors fell on their knees before him.

"You forget that they can see you," said he.

"That is true!" said the sailors, ashamed of their weakness. "Give us your orders, monseigneur, we are prepared to die for you."

"Let us wait," said Aramis.

"How—let us wait?"

"Yes; do you not see, as you just now said, that if we endeavor to fly, they will sink us?"

"But, perhaps," the patron ventured to say, "perhaps under cover of night, we could escape them."

"Oh!" said Aramis, "they have, no doubt, Greek fire with which to lighten their own course and ours likewise."

At the same moment, as if the vessel was responsive to the appeal of Aramis, a second cloud of smoke mounted slowly to the heavens, and from the bosom of that cloud sparkled an arrow of flame, which described a parabola like a rainbow, and fell into the sea, where it continued to burn, illuminating a space of a quarter of a league in diameter.

The Bretons looked at each other in terror. "You see plainly," said Aramis, "it will be better to wait for them."

The oars dropped from the hands of the sailors, and

the bark, ceasing to make way, rocked motionless upon the summits of the waves. Night came on, but still the ship drew nearer. It might be imagined it redoubled its speed with darkness. From time to time, as a vulture rears its head out of its nest, the formidable Greek fire darted from its sides, and cast its flame upon the ocean like an incandescent snowfall. At last it came within musket-shot. All the men were on deck, arms in hand; the cannoniers were at their guns, the matches burning. It might be thought they were about to board a frigate and to fight a crew superior in number to their own, not to attempt the capture of a canoe manned by four people.

"Surrender!" cried the commander of the *balancelle*, with the aid of his speaking-trumpet.

The sailors looked at Aramis. Aramis made a sign with his head. Yves waved a white cloth at the end of a gaff. This was like striking their flag. The pursuer came on like a race-horse. It launched a fresh Greek fire, which fell within twenty paces of the little canoe, and threw a light upon them as white as sunshine.

"At the first sign of resistance," cried the commander of the *balancelle*, "fire!" The soldiers brought their muskets to the present.

"Did we not say we surrendered?" said Yves.

"Alive, alive, captain!" cried one excited soldier, "they must be taken alive."

"Well, yes—living," said the captain. Then turning towards the Bretons, "Your lives are safe, my friends!" cried he, "all but the Chevalier d'Herblay."

Aramis stared imperceptibly. For an instant his eye was fixed upon the depths of the ocean, illumined by the last flashes of the Greek fire, which ran along the sides of the waves, played on the crests like plumes, and rendered still darker and more terrible the gulfs they covered.

"Do you hear, monseigneur?" said the sailors.

"Yes."

"What are your orders?"

"Accept!"

"But you, monseigneur?"

Aramis leaned still more forward, and dipped the ends of his long white fingers in the green limpid waters of the sea, to which he turned with smiles as to a friend.

"Accept!" repeated he.

"We accept," repeated the sailors; "but what security have we?"

"The word of a gentleman," said the officer. "By my rank and by my name I swear that all except M. le Chevalier d'Herblay shall have their lives spared. I am lieutenant of the king's frigate the 'Pomona,' and my name is Louis Constant de Pressigny."

With a rapid gesture, Aramis—already bent over the side of the bark towards the sea—drew himself up, and with a flashing eye, and a smile upon his lips, "Throw out the ladder, messieurs," said he, as if the command had belonged to him. He was obeyed. When Aramis, seizing the rope ladder, walked straight up to the commander, with a firm step, looked at him earnestly, made a sign to him with his hand, a mysterious and unknown sign at sight of which the officer turned pale, trembled, and bowed his head, the sailors were profoundly astonished. Without a word Aramis then raised his hand to the eyes of the commander and showed him the collet of a ring he wore on the ring-finger of his left hand. And while making this sign Aramis, draped in cold and haughty majesty, had the air of an emperor giving his hand to be kissed. The commandant, who for a moment had raised his head, bowed a second time with marks of the most profound respect. Then stretching his hand out, in his turn, towards the poop, that is to say, towards his own cabin, he drew back to allow Aramis to go first. The three Bretons, who had come on board after their bishop, looked at each other, stupefied. The crew were awed to silence. Five minutes after, the commander called the second lieutenant, who returned immediately, ordering the head to be put towards Corunna. Whilst this order was being executed, Aramis reappeared upon the deck, and took a seat near the *bastingage*. Night had fallen; the moon had not yet risen, yet Aramis looked incessantly towards Belle-Isle. Yves then approached the captain, who had returned to take his post in the stern, and said, in a low and humble voice, "What course are we to follow, captain?"

"We take what course monseigneur pleases," replied the officer.

Aramis passed the night leaning upon the *bastingage*. Yves, on approaching him next morning, remarked that "the night must have been a very damp one, for the wood on which the bishop's head had rested was soaked with dew." Who knows?—that dew was, it may be, the first tears that had ever fallen from the eyes of Aramis!

What epitaph would have been worth that, good Porthos?

CHAPTER 52

M. de Gesvres's Round.

D'Artagnan was little used to resistance like that he had just
experienced. He returned, profoundly irritated, to Nantes.
Irritation, with this vigorous man, usually vented itself in
impetuous attack, which few people, hitherto, were they king,
were they giants, had been able to resist. Trembling with rage,
he went straight to the castle, and asked an audience with
the king. It might be about seven o'clock in the morning, and,
since his arrival at Nantes, the king had been an early riser.
But on arriving at the corridor with which we are acquainted,
D'Artagnan found M. de Gesvres, who stopped him politely,
telling him not to speak too loud and disturb the king. "Is
the king asleep?" said D'Artagnan. "Well, I will let him sleep.
But about what o'clock do you suppose he will rise?"

"Oh! in about two hours; his majesty has been up all
night."

D'Artagnan took his hat again, bowed to M. de Gesvres,
and returned to his own apartments. He came back at half-
past nine, and was told that the king was at breakfast. "That
will just suit me," said D'Artagnan. "I will talk to the king
while he is eating."

M. de Brienne reminded D'Artagnan that the king would
not see any one at meal-time.

"But," said D'Artagnan, looking askant at Brienne, "you do not know, perhaps, monsieur, that I have the privilege of *entree* anywhere—and at any hour."

Brienne took the captain's hand kindly, and said, "Not at Nantes, dear Monsieur d'Artagnan. The king, in this journey, has changed everything."

D'Artagnan, a little softened, asked about what o'clock the king would have finished his breakfast.

"We don't know."

"Eh?—don't know! What does that mean? You don't know how much time the king devotes to eating? It is generally an hour; and, if we admit that the air of the Loire gives an additional appetite, we will extend it to an hour and a half; that is enough, I think. I will wait where I am."

"Oh! dear Monsieur d'Artagnan, the order of the day is not to allow any person to remain in this corridor; I am on guard for that particular purpose."

D'Artagnan felt his anger mounting to his brain a second time. He went out quickly, for fear of complicating the affair by a display of premature ill-humor. As soon as he was out he began to reflect. "The king," said he, "will not receive me, that is evident. The young man is angry; he is afraid, beforehand, of the words that I may speak to him. Yes; but in the meantime Belle-Isle is besieged, and my two friends by now probably taken or killed. Poor Porthos! As to Master Aramis, he is always full of resources, and I am easy on his account. But, no, no; Porthos is not yet an invalid, nor is Aramis in his dotage. The one with his arm, the other with his imagination, will find work for his majesty's soldiers. Who knows if these brave men may not get up for the edification of his most Christian majesty a little bastion of Saint-Gervais! I don't despair of it. They have cannon and a garrison. And yet," continued D'Artagnan, "I don't know whether it would not be better to stop the combat. For myself alone I will not put up with either surly looks or insults from the king; but for my friends I must put up with everything. Shall I go to M. Colbert? Now, there is a man I must acquire the habit of terrifying. I will go to M. Colbert." And D'Artagnan set forward bravely to find M. Colbert, but was informed that he was working with the king, at the castle of Nantes. "Good!" cried he, "the times have come again in which I measured my steps from De Treville to the cardinal, from the cardinal to the queen, from the queen to Louis XIII. Truly is it said that men, in growing old, become children again!—To the castle, then!" He returned thither. M. de Lyonne was coming out. He gave D'Artagnan both hands, but told him that the king had been busy all the preceding evening and all night, and that orders had been given that no one should be admitted. "Not even the captain who takes the order?" cried D'Artagnan. "I think that is rather too strong."

"Not even he," said M. de Lyonne.

"Since that is the case," replied D'Artagnan, wounded to the heart; "since the captain of the musketeers, who has always entered the king's chamber, is no longer allowed to enter it, his cabinet, or his *salle-a-manger*, either the king is dead, or his captain is in disgrace. Do me the favor, then, M. de Lyonne, who are in favor, to return and tell the king, plainly, I send him my resignation."

"D'Artagnan, beware of what you are doing!"

"For friendship's sake, go!" and he pushed him gently towards the cabinet.

"Well, I will go," said Lyonne.

D'Artagnan waited, walking about the corridor in no enviable mood. Lyonne returned.

"Well, what did the king say?" exclaimed D'Artagnan.

"He simply answered, ''Tis well,'" replied Lyonne.

"That it was well!" said the captain, with an explosion. "That is to say, that he accepts it? Good! Now, then, I am free! I am only a plain citizen, M. de Lyonne. I have the pleasure of bidding you good-bye! Farewell, castle, corridor, ante-chamber! a *bourgeois*, about to breathe at liberty, takes his farewell of you."

And without waiting longer, the captain sprang from the terrace down the staircase, where he had picked up the fragments of Gourville's letter. Five minutes after, he was at the hostelry, where, according to the custom of all great officers who have lodgings at the castle, he had taken what was called his city-chamber. But when he arrived there, instead of throwing off his sword and cloak, he took his pistols, put his money into a large leather purse, sent for his horses from the castle-stables, and gave orders that would ensure their reaching Vannes during the night. Everything went on according to his wishes. At eight o'clock in the evening, he was putting his foot in the stirrup, when M. de Gesvres appeared, at the head of twelve guards, in front of the hostelry. D'Artagnan saw all from the corner of his eye; he could not fail seeing thirteen men and thirteen horses. But he feigned not to observe anything, and was about to put his horse in motion. Gesvres rode up to him. "Monsieur d'Artagnan!" said he, aloud.

"Ah, Monsieur de Gesvres! good evening!"

"One would say you were getting on horseback."

"More than that,—I am mounted,—as you see."

"It is fortunate I have met with you."

"Were you looking for me, then?"

"*Mon Dieu!* yes."

"On the part of the king, I will wager?"

"Yes."

"As I, three days ago, went in search of M. Fouquet?"

"Oh!"

"Nonsense! It is of no use being over-delicate with me; that is all labor lost. Tell me at once you are come to arrest me."

"To arrest you?—Good heavens! no."

"Why do you come to accost me with twelve horsemen at your heels, then?"

"I am making my round."

"That isn't bad! And so you pick me up in your round, eh?"

"I don't pick you up; I meet with you, and I beg you to come with me."

"Where?"

"To the king."

"Good!" said D'Artagnan, with a bantering air; "the king is disengaged."

"For Heaven's sake, captain," said M. de Gesvres, in a low voice to the musketeer, "do not compromise yourself! these men hear you."

D'Artagnan laughed aloud, and replied:

"March! People who are arrested are placed between the six first guards and the six last."

"But as I am not arresting you," said M. de Gesvres, "you will march behind, with me, if you please."

"Well," said D'Artagnan, "that is very polite, duke, and you are right in being so; for if ever I had had to make my rounds near your *chambre-de-ville*, I should have been courteous to you, I assure you, on the word of a gentleman! Now, one favor more; what does the king want with me?"

"Oh, the king is furious!"

"Very well! the king, who has thought it worth while to be angry, may take the trouble to grow calm again; that is all. I shan't die of that, I will swear."

"No, but—"

"But—I shall be sent to keep company with unfortunate M. Fouquet. *Mordioux!* That is a gallant man, a worthy man! We shall live very sociably together, I will be sworn."

"Here we are at our place of destination," said the duke. "Captain, for Heaven's sake be calm with the king!"

"Ah! ah! you are playing the brave man with me, duke!"

said D'Artagnan, throwing one of his defiant glances over Gesvres. "I have been told that you are ambitious of uniting your guards with my musketeers. This strikes me as a splendid opportunity."

"I will take exceeding good care not to avail myself of it, captain."

"And why not, pray?"

"Oh, for many reasons—in the first place, for this: if I were to succeed you in the musketeers after having arrested you—"

"Ah! then you admit you have arrested me?"

"No, I *don't*."

"Say met me, then. So, you were saying *if* you were to succeed me after having arrested me?"

"Your musketeers, at the first exercise with ball cartridges, would fire *my* way, by mistake."

"Oh, as to that I won't say; for the fellows *do* love me a little."

Gesvres made D'Artagnan pass in first, and took him straight to the cabinet where Louis was waiting for his captain of the musketeers, and placed himself behind his colleague in the ante-chamber. The king could be heard distinctly, speaking aloud to Colbert in the same cabinet where Colbert might have heard, a few days before, the king speaking aloud with M. d'Artagnan. The guards remained as a mounted picket before the principal gate; and the report was quickly spread throughout the city that monsieur le capitaine of the musketeers had been arrested by order of the king. Then these men were seen to be in motion, and as in the good old times of Louis XIII. and M. de Treville, groups were formed, and staircases were filled; vague murmurs, issuing from the court below, came rolling to the upper stories, like the distant moaning of the waves. M. de Gesvres became uneasy. He looked at his guards, who, after being interrogated by the musketeers who had just got among their ranks, began to shun them with a manifestation of innocence. D'Artagnan was certainly less disturbed by all this than M. de Gesvres, the captain of the guards. As soon as he entered, he seated himself on the ledge of a window whence with his eagle glance he saw all that was going on without the least emotion. No step of the progressive fermentation which had shown itself at the report of his arrest escaped him. He foresaw the very moment the explosion would take place; and we know that his previsions were in general correct.

"It would be very whimsical," thought he, "if, this evening, my praetorians should make me king of France. How I should laugh!"

But, at the height, all was stopped. Guards, musketeers, officers, soldiers, murmurs, uneasiness, dispersed, vanished, died away; there was an end of menace and sedition. One word had calmed the waves. The king had desired Brienne to say, "Hush, messieurs! you disturb the king."

D'Artagnan sighed. "All is over!" said he; "the musketeers of the present day are not those of his majesty Louis XIII. All is over!"

"Monsieur d'Artagnan, you are wanted in the antechamber of the king," proclaimed an usher.

CHAPTER 53

King Louis XIV.

The king was seated in his cabinet, with his back turned towards the door of entrance. In front of him was a mirror, in which, while turning over his papers, he could see at a glance those who came in. He did not take any notice of the entrance of D'Artagnan, but spread above his letters and plans the large silk cloth he used to conceal his secrets from the importunate. D'Artagnan understood this by-play, and kept in the background; so that at the end of a minute the king, who heard nothing, and saw nothing save from the corner of his eye, was obliged to cry, "Is not M. d'Artagnan there?"

"I am here, sire," replied the musketeer, advancing.

"Well, monsieur," said the king, fixing his pellucid eyes on D'Artagnan, "what have you to say to me?"

"I, sire!" replied the latter, who watched the first blow of his adversary to make a good retort; "I have nothing to say to your majesty, unless it be that you have caused me to be arrested, and here I am."

The king was going to reply that he had not had D'Artagnan arrested, but any such sentence appeared too much like an excuse, and he was silent. D'Artagnan likewise preserved an obstinate silence.

"Monsieur," at length resumed the king, "what did I charge you to go and do at Belle-Isle? Tell me, if you please."

The king while uttering these words looked intently at his captain. Here D'Artagnan was fortunate; the king seemed to place the game in his hands.

"I believe," replied he, "that your majesty does me the honor to ask what I went to Belle-Isle to accomplish?"

"Yes, monsieur."

"Well! sire, I know nothing about it; it is not of me that question should be asked, but of that infinite number of officers of all kinds, to whom have been given innumerable orders of all kinds, whilst to me, head of the expedition, nothing precise was said or stated in any form whatever."

The king was hurt: he showed it by his reply. "Monsieur," said he, "orders have only been given to such as were judged faithful."

"And, therefore, I have been astonished, sire," retorted the musketeer, "that a captain like myself, who ranks with a marechal of France, should have found himself under the orders of five or six lieutenants or majors, good to make spies of, possibly, but not at all fit to conduct a warlike expedition. It was upon this subject I came to demand an explanation of your majesty, when I found the door closed against me, which, the final insult offered to a brave man, has led me to quit your majesty's service."

"Monsieur," replied the king, "you still believe that you are living in an age when kings were, as you complain of having been, under the orders and at the discretion of their inferiors. You seem to forget that a king owes an account of his actions to none but God."

"I forget nothing, sire," said the musketeer, wounded by this lesson. "Besides, I do not see in what an honest man, when he asks of his king how he has ill-served him, offends him."

"You have ill-served me, monsieur, by siding with my enemies against me."

"Who are your enemies, sire?"

"The men I sent you to fight."

"Two men the enemies of the whole of your majesty's army! That is incredible."

"You have no power to judge of my will."

"But I have to judge of my own friendships, sire."

"He who serves his friends does not serve his master."

"I so well understand this, sire, that I have respectfully offered your majesty my resignation."

"And I have accepted it, monsieur," said the king. "Before being separated from you I was willing to prove to you that I know how to keep my word."

"Your majesty has kept more than your word, for your majesty has had me arrested," said D'Artagnan, with his cold, bantering air; "you did not promise me that, sire."

The king would not condescend to perceive the pleasantry, and continued, seriously, "You see, monsieur, to what grave steps your disobedience forces me."

"My disobedience!" cried D'Artagnan, red with anger.

"It is the mildest term that I can find," pursued the king. "My idea was to take and punish rebels; was I bound to inquire whether these rebels were your friends or not?"

"But I was," replied D'Artagnan. "It was a cruelty on your majesty's part to send me to capture my friends and lead them to your gibbets."

"It was a trial I had to make, monsieur, of pretended servants, who eat my bread and *should* defend my person. The trial has succeeded ill, Monsieur d'Artagnan."

"For one bad servant your majesty loses," said the musketeer, with bitterness, "there are ten who, on that same day, go through a like ordeal. Listen to me, sire; I am not accustomed to that service. Mine is a rebel sword when I am required to do ill. It was ill to send me in pursuit of two men whose lives M. Fouquet, your majesty's preserver, implored you to save. Still further, these men were my friends. They did not attack your majesty, they succumbed to your blind anger. Besides, why were they not allowed to escape? What crime had they committed? I admit you may contest with me the right of judging their conduct. But why suspect me before the action? Why surround me with spies? Why disgrace me before the army? Why me, in whom till now you showed the most entire confidence—who for thirty years have been attached to your person, and have given you a thousand proofs of my devotion—for it must be said, now that I am accused—why reduce me to see three thousand of the king's soldiers march in battle against two men?"

"One would say you have forgotten what these men have done to me!" said the king, in a hollow voice, "and that it was no merit of theirs I was not lost."

"Sire, one would imagine you forget that I was there."

"Enough, Monsieur d'Artagnan, enough of these dominating interests which arise to keep the sun itself from my interests. I am founding a state in which there shall be but one master, as I promised you; the moment is at hand for me to keep my promise. You wish to be, according to your tastes or private friendships, free to destroy my plans and save my enemies? I will thwart you or will drop you—seek a more compliant master. I know full well that another king would not conduct himself as I do, and would allow himself to be dominated by you, at the risk of sending you some day to keep company with M. Fouquet and the rest; but I have an excellent memory, and for me, services are sacred titles to gratitude, to impunity. You shall only have this lesson, Monsieur d'Artagnan, as the punishment of your want of discipline, and I will not imitate my predecessors in anger, not having imitated them in favor. And, then, other reasons make me act mildly towards you; in the first place, because you are a man of sense, a man of excellent sense, a man of heart, and that you will be a capital servant to him who shall have mastered you; secondly, because you will cease to have any motives for insubordination. Your friends are now destroyed or ruined by me. These supports on which your capricious mind instinctively relied I have caused to disappear. At this moment, my soldiers have taken or killed the rebels of Belle-Isle."

D'Artagnan became pale. "Taken or killed!" cried he. "Oh! sire, if you thought what you tell, if you were sure you were telling me the truth, I should forget all that is just, all that is magnanimous in your words, to call you a barbarous king, and an unnatural man. But I pardon you these words," said he, smiling with pride; "I pardon them to a young prince who does not know, who cannot comprehend what such men as M. d'Herblay, M. du Vallon, and myself are. Taken or killed! Ah! Ah! sire! tell me, if the news is true, how much has it cost you in men and money. We will then reckon if the game has been worth the stakes."

As he spoke thus, the king went up to him in great anger, and said, "Monsieur d'Artagnan, your replies are those of a rebel! Tell me, if you please, who is king of France? Do you know any other?"

"Sire," replied the captain of the musketeers, coldly, "I very well remember that one morning at Vaux you addressed that question to many people who did not answer to it, whilst I, on my part, did answer to it. If I recognized my king on that day, when the thing was not easy, I think it would be useless to ask the question of me now, when your majesty and I are alone."

At these words Louis cast down his eyes. It appeared to him that the shade of the unfortunate Philippe passed between D'Artagnan and himself, to evoke the remembrance of that terrible adventure. Almost at the same moment an officer entered and placed a dispatch in the hands of the king, who, in his turn, changed color, while reading it.

"Monsieur," said he, "what I learn here you would know later; it is better I should tell you, and that you should learn it from the mouth of your king. A battle has taken place at Belle-Isle."

"Is it possible?" said D'Artagnan, with a calm air, though his heart was beating fast enough to choke him. "Well, sire?"

"Well, monsieur—and I have lost a hundred and ten men."

A beam of joy and pride shone in the eyes of D'Artagnan. "And the rebels?" said he.

"The rebels have fled," said the king.

D'Artagnan could not restrain a cry of triumph. "Only," added the king, "I have a fleet which closely blockades Belle-Isle, and I am certain not a bark can escape."

"So that," said the musketeer, brought back to his dismal idea, "if these two gentlemen are taken—"

"They will be hanged," said the king, quietly.

"And do they know it?" replied D'Artagnan, repressing his trembling.

"They know it, because you must have told them yourself; and all the country knows it."

"Then, sire, they will never be taken alive, I will answer for that."

"Ah!" said the king, negligently, and taking up his letter again. "Very well, they will be dead, then, Monsieur d'Artagnan, and that will come to the same thing, since I should only take them to have them hanged."

D'Artagnan wiped the sweat which flowed from his brow.

"I have told you," pursued Louis XIV., "that I would one day be an affectionate, generous, and constant master. You are now the only man of former times worthy of my anger or my friendship. I will not spare you either sentiment, according to your conduct. Could you serve a king, Monsieur d'Artagnan, who should have a hundred kings, his equals, in the kingdom? Could I, tell me, do with such weak instruments the great things I meditate? Did you ever see an artist effect great works with an unworthy tool? Far from us, monsieur, the old leaven of feudal abuse! The Fronde, which threatened to ruin monarchy, has emancipated it. I am master at home, Captain d'Artagnan, and I shall have servants who, lacking, perhaps, your genius, will carry devotion and obedience to the verge of heroism. Of what consequence, I ask you, of what consequence is it that God has given no sense to arms and legs? It is to the head he has given genius, and the head, you know, the rest obey. I am the head."

D'Artagnan started. Louis XIV. continued as if he had seen nothing, although this emotion had not by any means escaped him. "Now, let us conclude between us two the bargain I promised to make with you one day when you found me in a very strange predicament at Blois. Do me justice, monsieur, when you admit I do not make any one pay for the tears of shame that I then shed. Look around you; lofty heads have bowed. Bow yours, or choose such exile as will suit you. Perhaps, when reflecting upon it, you will find your king has a generous heart, who reckons sufficiently upon your loyalty to allow you to leave him dissatisfied, when you possess a great state secret. You are a brave man; I know you to be so. Why have you judged me prematurely? Judge me from this day forward, D'Artagnan, and be as severe as you please."

D'Artagnan remained bewildered, mute, undecided for the first time in his life. At last he had found an adversary worthy of him. This was no longer trick, it was calculation; no longer violence, but strength; no longer passion, but will; no longer boasting, but council. This young man who had brought down a Fouquet, and could do without a D'Artagnan, deranged the somewhat headstrong calculations of the musketeer.

"Come, let us see what stops you?" said the king, kindly. "You have given in your resignation; shall I refuse to accept it? I admit that it may be hard for such an old captain to recover lost good-humor."

"Oh!" replied D'Artagnan, in a melancholy tone, "that is not my most serious care. I hesitate to take back my resignation because I am old in comparison with you, and have habits difficult to abandon. Henceforward, you must have courtiers who know how to amuse you—madmen who will get themselves killed to carry out what you call your great works. Great they will be, I feel—but, if by chance I should not think them so? I have seen war, sire, I have seen peace; I have served Richelieu and Mazarin; I have been scorched with your father, at the fire of Rochelle; riddled with sword-thrusts like a sieve, having grown a new skin ten times, as serpents do. After affronts and injustices, I have a command which was formerly something, because it gave the bearer the right of speaking as he liked to his king. But your captain of the musketeers will henceforward be an officer guarding the outer doors. Truly, sire, if that is to be my employment from this time, seize the opportunity of our being on good terms, to take it from me. Do not imagine that I bear malice; no, you have tamed me, as you say; but it must be confessed that in taming me you have lowered me; by bowing me you have convicted me of weakness. If you knew how well it suits me to carry my head high, and what a pitiful mien I shall have while scenting the dust of your carpets! Oh! sire, I regret sincerely, and you will regret as I do, the old days when the king of France saw in every vestibule those insolent gentlemen, lean, always swearing— cross-grained mastiffs, who could bite mortally in the hour of danger or of battle. These men were the best of courtiers to the hand which fed them—they would lick it; but for the hand that struck them, oh! the bite that followed! A little gold on the lace of their cloaks, a slender stomach in their *hauts-de-chausses*, a little sparkling of gray in their dry hair, and you will behold the handsome dukes and peers, the haughty *marechaux* of France. But why should I tell you all this? The king is master; he wills that I should make verses, he wills that I should polish the mosaics of his ante-chambers with satin shoes. *Mordioux!* that is difficult, but I have got over greater difficulties. I will do it. Why should I do it? Because I love money?—I have enough. Because I am ambitious?—my career is almost at an end. Because I love the court? No. I will remain here because I have been accustomed for thirty years to go and take the orderly word of the king, and to have said to me 'Good evening, D'Artagnan,' with a smile I did not beg for. That smile I will beg for! Are you content, sire?" And D'Artagnan bowed his silver head, upon which the smiling king placed his white hand with pride.

"Thanks, my old servant, my faithful friend," said he. "As, reckoning from this day, I have no longer any enemies in France, it remains with me to send you to a foreign field to gather your marshal's baton. Depend upon me for finding you an opportunity. In the meanwhile, eat of my very best bread, and sleep in absolute tranquillity."

"That is all kind and well!" said D'Artagnan, much agitated. "But those poor men at Belle-Isle? One of them, in particular—so good! so brave! so true!"

"Do you ask their pardon of me?"

"Upon my knees, sire!"

"Well! then, go and take it to them, if it be still in time. But do you answer for them?"

"With my life, sire."

"Go, then. To-morrow I set out for Paris. Return by that time, for I do not wish you to leave me in the future."

"Be assured of that, sire," said D'Artagnan, kissing the royal hand.

And with a heart swelling with joy, he rushed out of the castle on his way to Belle-Isle.

CHAPTER 54

M. Fouquet's Friends.

The king had returned to Paris, and with him D'Artagnan, who, in twenty-four hours, having made with greatest care all possible inquiries at Belle-Isle, succeeded in learning nothing of the secret so well kept by the heavy rock of Locmaria, which had fallen on the heroic Porthos. The captain of the musketeers only knew what those two valiant men— these two friends, whose defense he had so nobly taken up, whose lives he had so earnestly endeavored to save—aided by three faithful Bretons, had accomplished against a whole army. He had seen, spread on the neighboring heath, the human remains which had stained with clouted blood the scattered stones among the flowering broom. He learned also that a bark had been seen far out at sea, and that, like a bird of prey, a royal vessel had pursued, overtaken, and devoured the poor little bird that was flying with such palpitating wings. But there D'Artagnan's certainties ended. The field of supposition was thrown open. Now, what could he conjecture? The vessel had not returned. It is true that a brisk wind had prevailed for three days; but the corvette was known to be a good sailer and solid in its timbers; it had no need to fear a gale of wind, and it ought, according to the calculation of D'Artagnan, to have either returned to Brest, or come back to the mouth of the Loire. Such was the news, ambiguous, it is true, but in some degree reassuring to him personally, which D'Artagnan brought to Louis XIV., when the king, followed by all the court, returned to Paris.

Louis, satisfied with his success—Louis, more mild and affable as he felt himself more powerful—had not ceased for an instant to ride beside the carriage door of Mademoiselle de la Valliere. Everybody was anxious to amuse the two queens, so as to make them forget this abandonment by son and husband. Everything breathed the future, the past was nothing to anybody. Only that past was like a painful bleeding wound to the hearts of certain tender and devoted spirits. Scarcely was the king reinstalled in Paris, when he received a touching proof of this. Louis XIV. had just risen and taken his first repast when his captain of the musketeers presented himself before him. D'Artagnan was pale and looked unhappy. The king, at the first glance, perceived the change in a countenance generally so unconcerned. "What is the matter, D'Artagnan?" said he.

"Sire, a great misfortune has happened to me."

"Good heavens! what is that?"

"Sire, I have lost one of my friends, M. du Vallon, in the affair of Belle-Isle."

And, while speaking these words, D'Artagnan fixed his falcon eye upon Louis XIV., to catch the first feeling that would show itself.

"I knew it," replied the king, quietly.

"You knew it, and did not tell me!" cried the musketeer.

"To what good? Your grief, my friend, was so well worthy of respect. It was my duty to treat it gently. To have informed you of this misfortune, which I knew would pain you so greatly, D'Artagnan, would have been, in your eyes, to have triumphed over you. Yes, I knew that M. du Vallon had buried himself beneath the rocks of Locmaria; I knew that M. d'Herblay had taken one of my vessels with its crew, and had compelled it to convey him to Bayonne. But I was willing you should learn these matters in a direct manner, in order that you might be convinced my friends are with me respected and sacred; that always in me the man will sacrifice himself to subjects, whilst the king is so often found to sacrifice men to majesty and power."

"But, sire, how could you know?"

"How do you yourself know, D'Artagnan?"

"By this letter, sire, which M. d'Herblay, free and out of danger, writes me from Bayonne."

"Look here," said the king, drawing from a casket placed upon the table closet to the seat upon which D'Artagnan was leaning, "here is a letter copied exactly from that of M. d'Herblay. Here is the very letter, which Colbert placed in my hands a week before you received yours. I am well served, you may perceive."

"Yes, sire," murmured the musketeer, "you were the only man whose star was equal to the task of dominating the fortune and strength of my two friends. You have used your power, sire, you will not abuse it, will you?"

"D'Artagnan," said the king, with a smile beaming with kindness, "I could have M. d'Herblay carried off from the territories of the king of Spain, and brought here, alive, to inflict justice upon him. But, D'Artagnan, be assured I will not yield to this first and natural impulse. He is free—let him continue free."

"Oh, sire! you will not always remain so clement, so noble, so generous as you have shown yourself with respect to me and M. d'Herblay; you will have about you counselors who will cure you of that weakness."

"No, D'Artagnan, you are mistaken when you accuse my council of urging me to pursue rigorous measures. The advice to spare M. d'Herblay comes from Colbert himself."

"Oh, sire!" said D'Artagnan, extremely surprised.

"As for you," continued the king, with a kindness very

uncommon to him, "I have several pieces of good news to announce to you; but you shall know them, my dear captain, the moment I have made my accounts all straight. I have said that I wish to make, and would make, your fortune; that promise will soon become reality."

"A thousand times thanks, sire! I can wait. But I implore you, whilst I go and practice patience, that your majesty will deign to notice those poor people who have for so long a time besieged your ante-chamber, and come humbly to lay a petition at your feet."

"Who are they?"

"Enemies of your majesty." The king raised his head.

"Friends of M. Fouquet," added D'Artagnan.

"Their names?"

"M. Gourville, M. Pelisson, and a poet, M. Jean de la Fontaine."

The king took a moment to reflect. "What do they want?"

"I do not know."

"How do they appear?"

"In great affliction."

"What do they say?"

"Nothing."

"What do they do?"

"They weep."

"Let them come in," said the king, with a serious brow.

D'Artagnan turned rapidly on his heel, raised the tapestry which closed the entrance to the royal chamber, and directing his voice to the adjoining room, cried, "Enter."

The three men D'Artagnan had named immediately appeared at the door of the cabinet in which were the king and his captain. A profound silence prevailed in their passage. The courtiers, at the approach of the friends of the unfortunate superintendent of finances, drew back, as if fearful of being affected by contagion with disgrace and misfortune. D'Artagnan, with a quick step, came forward to take by the hand the unhappy men who stood trembling at the door of the cabinet; he led them in front of the king's *fauteuil*, who, having placed himself in the embrasure of a window, awaited the moment of presentation, and was preparing himself to give the supplicants a rigorously diplomatic reception.

The first of the friends of Fouquet's to advance was Pelisson. He did not weep, but his tears were only restrained that the king might better hear his voice and prayer. Gourville bit his lips to check his tears, out of respect for the king. La Fontaine buried his face in his handkerchief, and the only signs of life he gave were the convulsive motions of his shoulders, raised by his sobs.

The king preserved his dignity. His countenance was impassible. He even maintained the frown which appeared when D'Artagnan announced his enemies. He made a gesture which signified, "Speak;" and he remained standing, with his eyes fixed searchingly on these desponding men. Pelisson bowed to the ground, and La Fontaine knelt as people do in churches. This dismal silence, disturbed only by sighs and groans, began to excite in the king, not compassion, but impatience.

"Monsieur Pelisson," said he, in a sharp, dry tone. "Monsieur Gourville, and you, Monsieur—" and he did not name La Fontaine, "I cannot, without sensible displeasure, see you come to plead for one of the greatest criminals it is the duty of justice to punish. A king does not allow himself to soften save at the tears of the innocent, the remorse of the guilty. I have no faith either in the remorse of M. Fouquet or the tears of his friends, because the one is tainted to the very heart, and the others ought to dread offending me in my own palace. For these reasons, I beg you, Monsieur Pelisson, Monsieur Gourville, and you, Monsieur—, to say nothing that will not plainly proclaim the respect you have for my will."

"Sire," replied Pelisson, trembling at these words, "we are come to say nothing to your majesty that is not the most profound expression of the most sincere respect and love that are due to a king from all his subjects. Your majesty's justice is redoubtable; every one must yield to the sentences it pronounces. We respectfully bow before it. Far from us the idea of coming to defend him who has had the misfortune to offend your majesty. He who has incurred your displeasure may be a friend of ours, but he is an enemy to the state. We abandon him, but with tears, to the severity of the king."

"Besides," interrupted the king, calmed by that supplicating voice, and those persuasive words, "my parliament will decide. I do not strike without first having weighed the crime; my justice does not wield the sword without employing first a pair of scales."

"Therefore we have every confidence in that impartiality of the king, and hope to make our feeble voices heard, with the consent of your majesty, when the hour for defending an accused friend strikes."

"In that case, messieurs, what do you ask of me?" said the king, with his most imposing air.

"Sire," continued Pelisson, "the accused has a wife and family. The little property he had was scarcely sufficient to pay his debts, and Madame Fouquet, since her husband's captivity, is abandoned by everybody. The hand of your majesty strikes like the hand of God. When the Lord sends the curse of leprosy or pestilence into a family, every one flies and shuns the abode of the leprous or plague-stricken. Sometimes, but very rarely, a generous physician alone ventures to approach the ill-reputed threshold, passes it with courage, and risks his life to combat death. He is the last resource of the dying, the chosen instrument of heavenly mercy. Sire, we supplicate you, with clasped hands and bended knees, as a divinity is supplicated! Madame Fouquet has no longer any friends, no longer any means of support; she weeps in her deserted home, abandoned by all those who besieged its doors in the hour of prosperity; she has neither credit nor hope left. At least, the unhappy wretch upon whom your anger falls receives from you, however culpable he may be, his daily bread though moistened by his tears. As much afflicted, more destitute than her husband, Madame Fouquet—the lady who had the honor to receive your majesty at her table—Madame Fouquet, the wife of the ancient superintendent of your majesty's finances, Madame Fouquet has no longer bread."

Here the mortal silence which had chained the breath of Pelisson's two friends was broken by an outburst of sobs; and D'Artagnan, whose chest heaved at hearing this humble prayer, turned round towards the angle of the cabinet to bite his mustache and conceal a groan.

The king had preserved his eye dry and his countenance severe; but the blood had mounted to his cheeks, and the firmness of his look was visibly diminished.

"What do you wish?" said he, in an agitated voice.

"We come humbly to ask your majesty," replied Pelisson, upon whom emotion was fast gaining, "to permit us, without incurring the displeasure of your majesty, to lend to Madame Fouquet two thousand pistoles collected among the old friends of her husband, in order that the widow may not stand in need of the necessaries of life."

At the word *widow*, pronounced by Pelisson whilst Fouquet was still alive, the king turned very pale;—his pride disappeared; pity rose from his heart to his lips; he cast a softened look upon the men who knelt sobbing at his feet.

"God forbid," said he, "that I should confound the innocent with the guilty. They know me but ill who doubt my mercy towards the weak. I strike none but the arrogant. Do, messieurs, do all that your hearts counsel you to assuage the grief of Madame Fouquet. Go, messieurs—go!"

The three now rose in silence with dry eyes. The tears had been scorched away by contact with their burning cheeks and eyelids. They had not the strength to address their thanks to the king, who himself cut short their solemn reverences by entrenching himself suddenly behind the *fauteuil*.

D'Artagnan remained alone with the king.

"Well," said he, approaching the young prince, who interrogated him with his look. "Well, my master! If you had not the device which belongs to your sun, I would recommend you one which M. Conrart might translate into eclectic Latin, 'Calm with the lowly; stormy with the strong.'"

The king smiled, and passed into the next apartment, after having said to D'Artagnan, "I give you the leave of absence you must want to put the affairs of your friend, the late M. du Vallon, in order."

CHAPTER 55

Porthos's Will.

At Pierrefonds everything was in mourning. The courts were deserted—the stables closed—the parterres neglected. In the basins, the fountains, formerly so jubilantly fresh and noisy, had stopped of themselves. Along the roads around the chateau came a few grave personages mounted on mules or country nags. These were rural neighbors, cures and bailiffs of adjacent estates. All these people entered the chateau silently, handed their horses to a melancholy-looking groom, and directed their steps, conducted by a huntsman in black, to the great dining-room, where Mousqueton received them at the door. Mousqueton had become so thin in two days that his clothes moved upon him like an ill-fitting scabbard in which the sword-blade dances at each motion. His face, composed of red and white, like that of the Madonna of Vandyke, was furrowed by two silver rivulets which had dug their beds in his cheeks, as full formerly as they had become flabby since his grief began. At each fresh arrival, Mousqueton found fresh tears, and it was pitiful to see him press his throat with his fat hand to keep from bursting into sobs and lamentations. All these visits were for the purpose of hearing the reading of Porthos's will, announced for that day, and at which all the covetous friends of the dead man were anxious to be present, as he had left no relations behind him.

The visitors took their places as they arrived, and the great room had just been closed when the clock struck twelve, the hour fixed for the reading of the important document. Porthos's procureur—and that was naturally the successor of Master Coquenard—commenced by slowly unfolding the vast parchment upon which the powerful hand of Porthos had traced his sovereign will. The seal broken—the spectacles put on—the preliminary cough having sounded—every one pricked up his ears. Mousqueton had squatted himself in a corner, the better to weep and the better to hear. All at once the folding-doors of the great room, which had been shut, were thrown open as if by magic, and a warlike figure appeared upon the threshold, resplendent in the full light of the sun. This was D'Artagnan, who had come alone to the gate, and finding nobody to hold his stirrup, had tied his horse to the knocker and announced himself. The splendor of daylight invading the room, the murmur of all present, and, more than all, the instinct of the faithful dog, drew Mousqueton from his reverie; he raised his head, recognized the old friend of his master, and, screaming with grief, he embraced his knees, watering the floor with his tears. D'Artagnan raised the poor intendant, embraced him as if he had been a brother, and, having nobly saluted the assembly, who all bowed as they whispered to each other his name, he went and took his seat at the extremity of the great carved oak hall, still holding by the hand poor Mousqueton, who was suffocating with excess of woe, and sank upon the steps. Then the procureur, who, like the rest, was considerably agitated, commenced.

Porthos, after a profession of faith of the most Christian character, asked pardon of his enemies for all the injuries he might have done them. At this paragraph, a ray of inexpressible pride beamed from the eyes of D'Artagnan.

He recalled to his mind the old soldier; all those enemies of Porthos brought to earth by his valiant hand; he reckoned up the numbers of them, and said to himself that Porthos had acted wisely, not to enumerate his enemies or the injuries done to them, or the task would have been too much for the reader. Then came the following schedule of his extensive lands:

"I possess at this present time, by the grace of God—

1. The domain of Pierrefonds, lands, woods, meadows, waters, and forests, surrounded by good walls.
2. The domain of Bracieux, chateaux, forests, plowed lands, forming three farms.
3. The little estate Du Vallon, so named because it is in the valley. (Brave Porthos!)
4. Fifty farms in Touraine, amounting to five hundred acres.
5. Three mills upon the Cher, bringing in six hundred livres each.
6. Three fish-pools in Berry, producing two hundred livres a year.

"As to my personal or movable property, so called because it can be moved, as is so well explained by my learned friend the bishop of Vannes—" (D'Artagnan shuddered at the dismal remembrance attached to that name)—the procureur continued imperturbably—"they consist—

1. In goods which I cannot detail here for want of room, and which furnish all my chateaux or houses, but of which the list is drawn up by my intendant."

Every one turned his eyes towards Mousqueton, who was still lost in grief.

2. "In twenty horses for saddle and draught, which I have particularly at my chateau of Pierrefonds, and which are called—Bayard, Roland, Charlemagne, Pepin, Dunois, La Hire, Ogier, Samson, Milo, Nimrod, Urganda, Armida, Flastrade, Dalilah, Rebecca, Yolande, Finette, Grisette, Lisette, and Musette.

3. In sixty dogs, forming six packs, divided as follows: the first, for the stag; the second, for the wolf; the third, for the wild boar; the fourth, for the hare; and the two others, for setters and protection.

4. In arms for war and the chase contained in my gallery of arms.

5. My wines of Anjou, selected for Athos, who liked them formerly; my wines of Burgundy, Champagne, Bordeaux, and Spain, stocking eight cellars and twelve vaults, in my various houses.

6. My pictures and statues, which are said to be of great value, and which are sufficiently numerous to fatigue the sight.

7. My library, consisting of six thousand volumes, quite new, and have never been opened.

8. My silver plate, which is perhaps a little worn, but which ought to weigh from a thousand to twelve hundred pounds, for I had great trouble in lifting the coffer that contained it and could not carry it more than six times round my chamber.

9. All these objects, in addition to the table and house linen, are divided in the residences I liked the best."

Here the reader stopped to take breath. Every one sighed, coughed, and redoubled his attention. The procureur resumed:

"I have lived without having any children, and it is probable I never shall have any, which to me is a cutting grief. And yet I am mistaken, for I have a son, in common with my other friends; that is, M. Raoul Auguste Jules de Bragelonne, the true son of M. le Comte de la Fere.

"This young nobleman appears to me extremely worthy to succeed the valiant gentleman of whom I am the friend and very humble servant."

Here a sharp sound interrupted the reader. It was D'Artagnan's sword, which, slipping from his baldric, had fallen on the sonorous flooring. Every one turned his eyes that way, and saw that a large tear had rolled from the thick lid of D'Artagnan, half-way down to his aquiline nose, the luminous edge of which shone like a little crescent moon.

"This is why," continued the procureur, "I have left all my property, movable, or immovable, comprised in the above enumerations, to M. le Vicomte Raoul Auguste Jules de Bragelonne, son of M. le Comte de la Fere, to console him for the grief he seems to suffer, and enable him to add more luster to his already glorious name."

A vague murmur ran through the auditory. The procureur continued, seconded by the flashing eye of D'Artagnan, which, glancing over the assembly, quickly restored the interrupted silence:

"On condition that M. le Vicomte de Bragelonne do give to M. le Chevalier d'Artagnan, captain of the king's musketeers, whatever the said Chevalier d'Artagnan may demand of my property. On condition that M. le Vicomte de Bragelonne do pay a good pension to M. le Chevalier d'Herblay, my friend, if he should need it in exile. I leave to my intendant Mousqueton all of my clothes, of city, war, or chase, to the number of forty-seven suits, in the assurance that he will wear them till they are worn out, for the love of and in remembrance of his master. Moreover, I bequeath to M. le Vicomte de Bragelonne my old servant and faithful friend Mousqueton, already named, providing that the said vicomte shall so act that Mousqueton shall declare, when dying, he has never ceased to be happy."

On hearing these words, Mousqueton bowed, pale and trembling; his shoulders shook convulsively; his countenance, compressed by a frightful grief, appeared from between his icy hands, and the spectators saw him stagger and hesitate, as if, though wishing to leave the hall, he did not know the way.

"Mousqueton, my good friend," said D'Artagnan, "go and make your preparations. I will take you with me to Athos's house, whither I shall go on leaving Pierrefonds."

Mousqueton made no reply. He scarcely breathed, as if everything in that hall would from that time be foreign. He opened the door, and slowly disappeared.

The procureur finished his reading, after which the greater part of those who had come to hear the last will of Porthos dispersed by degrees, many disappointed, but all penetrated with respect. As for D'Artagnan, thus left alone, after having received the formal compliments of the procureur, he was lost in admiration of the wisdom of the testator, who had so judiciously bestowed his wealth upon the most necessitous and the most worthy, with a delicacy that neither nobleman nor courtier could have displayed more kindly. When Porthos enjoined Raoul de Bragelonne to give D'Artagnan all that he would ask, he knew well, our worthy Porthos, that D'Artagnan would ask or take nothing; and in case he did demand anything, none but himself could say what. Porthos left a pension to Aramis, who, if he should be inclined to ask too much, was checked by the example of D'Artagnan; and that word *exile*, thrown out by the testator, without apparent intention, was it not the mildest, most exquisite criticism upon that conduct of Aramis which had brought about the death of Porthos? But there was no mention of Athos in the testament of the dead. Could the latter for a moment suppose that the son would not offer the best part to the father? The rough mind of Porthos had fathomed all these causes, seized all these shades more clearly than law, better than custom, with more propriety than taste.

"Porthos had indeed a heart," said D'Artagnan to himself with a sigh. As he made this reflection, he fancied he hard a groan in the room above him; and he thought immediately of poor Mousqueton, whom he felt it was a pleasing duty to divert from his grief. For this purpose he left the hall hastily to seek the worthy intendant, as he had not returned. He ascended the staircase leading to the first story, and perceived, in Porthos's own chamber, a heap of clothes of all colors and materials, upon which Mousqueton had laid himself down after heaping them all on the floor together. It was the legacy of the faithful friend. Those clothes were truly his own; they had been given to him; the hand of Mousqueton was stretched over these relics, which he was kissing with his lips, with all his face, and covered with his body. D'Artagnan approached to console the poor fellow.

"My God!" said he, "he does not stir—he has fainted!"

But D'Artagnan was mistaken. Mousqueton was dead! Dead, like the dog who, having lost his master, crawls back to die upon his cloak.

CHAPTER 56

The Old Age of Athos.

While these affairs were separating forever the four musketeers, formerly bound together in a manner that seemed indissoluble, Athos, left alone after the departure of Raoul, began to pay his tribute to that foretaste of death which is called the absence of those we love. Back in his house at Blois, no longer having even Grimaud to receive a poor smile as he passed through the parterre, Athos daily felt the decline of vigor of a nature which for so long a time had seemed impregnable. Age, which had been kept back by the presence of the beloved object, arrived with that *cortege* of pains and inconveniences, which grows by geometrical accretion. Athos had no longer his son to induce him to walk firmly, with head erect, as a good example; he had no longer, in those brilliant eyes of the young man, an ever-ardent focus at which to kindle anew the fire of his looks. And then, must it be said, that nature, exquisite in tenderness and reserve, no longer finding anything to understand its feelings, gave itself up to grief with all the warmth of common natures when they yield to joy. The Comte de la Fere, who had remained a young man to his sixty-second year; the warrior who had preserved his strength in spite of fatigue; his freshness of mind in spite of misfortune, his mild serenity of soul and body in spite of Milady, in spite of Mazarin, in spite of La Valliere; Athos had become an old man in a week, from the moment at which he lost the comfort of his later youth. Still handsome, though bent, noble, but sad, he sought, since his solitude, the deeper glades where sunshine scarcely penetrated. He discontinued all the mighty exercises he had enjoyed through life, when Raoul was no longer with him. The servants, accustomed to see him stirring with the dawn at all seasons, were astonished to hear seven o'clock strike before their master quitted his bed. Athos remained in bed with a book under his pillow—but he did not sleep, neither did he read. Remaining in bed that he might no longer have to carry his body, he allowed his soul and spirit to wander from their envelope and return to his son, or to God.[6]

His people were sometimes terrified to see him, for hours together, absorbed in silent reverie, mute and insensible; he no longer heard the timid step of the servant who came to the door of his chamber to watch the sleeping or waking of his master. It often occurred that he forgot the day had half passed away, that the hours for the two first meals were gone by. Then he was awakened. He rose, descended to his shady walk, then came out a little into the sun, as though to partake of its warmth for a minute in memory of his absent child. And then the dismal monotonous walk recommenced, until, exhausted, he regained the chamber and his bed, his domicile by choice. For several days the comte did not speak a single word. He refused to receive the visits that were paid him, and during the night he was seen to relight his lamp and pass long hours in writing, or examining parchments.

Athos wrote one of these letters to Vannes, another to Fontainebleau; they remained without answers. We know why: Aramis had quitted France, and D'Artagnan was traveling from Nantes to Paris, from Paris to Pierrefonds. His *valet*

[6] In some editions, "in spite of Milady" reads "in spite of malady".

de chambre observed that he shortened his walk every day by several turns. The great alley of limes soon became too long for feet that used to traverse it formerly a hundred times a day. The comte walked feebly as far as the middle trees, seated himself upon a mossy bank that sloped towards a sidewalk, and there waited the return of his strength, or rather the return of night. Very shortly a hundred steps exhausted him. At length Athos refused to rise at all; he declined all nourishment, and his terrified people, although he did not complain, although he wore a smile upon his lips, although he continued to speak with his sweet voice—his people went to Blois in search of the ancient physician of the late Monsieur, and brought him to the Comte de la Fere in such a fashion that he could see the comte without being himself seen. For this purpose, they placed him in a closet adjoining the chamber of the patient, and implored him not to show himself, for fear of displeasing their master, who had not asked for a physician. The doctor obeyed. Athos was a sort of model for the gentlemen of the country; the Blaisois boasted of possessing this sacred relic of French glory. Athos was a great seigneur compared with such nobles as the king improvised by touching with his artificial scepter the parched-up trunks of the heraldic trees of the province.

People respected Athos, we say, and they loved him. The physician could not bear to see his people weep, to see flock round him the poor of the canton, to whom Athos had so often given life and consolation by his kind words and his charities. He examined, therefore, from the depths of his hiding-place, the nature of that mysterious malady which bent and aged more mortally every day a man but lately so full of life and a desire to live. He remarked upon the cheeks of Athos the hectic hue of fever, which feeds upon itself; slow fever, pitiless, born in a fold of the heart, sheltering itself behind that rampart, growing from the suffering it engenders, at once cause and effect of a perilous situation. The comte spoke to nobody; he did not even talk to himself. His thought feared noise; it approached to that degree of over-excitement which borders upon ecstasy. Man thus absorbed, though he does not yet belong to God, already appertains no longer to the earth. The doctor remained for several hours studying this painful struggle of the will against superior power; he was terrified at seeing those eyes always fixed, ever directed on some invisible object; was terrified at the monotonous beating of that heart from which never a sigh arose to vary the melancholy state; for often pain becomes the hope of the physician. Half a day passed away thus. The doctor formed his resolution like a brave man; he issued suddenly from his place of retreat, and went straight up to Athos, who beheld him without evincing more surprise than if he had understood nothing of the apparition.

"Monsieur le comte, I crave your pardon," said the doctor, coming up to the patient with open arms; "but I have a reproach to make you—you shall hear me." And he seated himself by the pillow of Athos, who had great trouble in rousing himself from his preoccupation.

"What is the matter, doctor?" asked the comte, after a silence.

"The matter is, you are ill, monsieur, and have had no advice."

"I! ill!" said Athos, smiling.

"Fever, consumption, weakness, decay, monsieur le comte!"

"Weakness!" replied Athos; "is it possible? I do not get up."

"Come, come! monsieur le comte, no subterfuges; you are a good Christian?"

"I hope so," said Athos.

"Is it your wish to kill yourself?"

"Never, doctor."

"Well! monsieur, you are in a fair way of doing so. Thus to remain is suicide. Get well! monsieur le comte, get well!"

"Of what? Find the disease first. For my part, I never knew myself better; never did the sky appear more blue to me; never did I take more care of my flowers."

"You have a hidden grief."

"Concealed!—not at all; the absence of my son, doctor, that is my malady, and I do not conceal it."

"Monsieur le comte, your son lives, he is strong, he has all the future before him—the future of men of merit, of his race; live for him—"

"But I do live, doctor; oh! be satisfied of that," added he, with a melancholy smile; "for as long as Raoul lives, it will be plainly known, for as long as he lives, I shall live."

"What do you say?"

"A very simple thing. At this moment, doctor, I leave life suspended within me. A forgetful, dissipated, indifferent life would be beyond my strength, now I have no longer Raoul with me. You do not ask the lamp to burn when the match has not illumed the flame; do not ask me to live amidst noise and merriment. I vegetate, I prepare myself, I wait. Look, doctor; remember those soldiers we have so often seen together at the ports, where they were waiting to embark; lying down, indifferent, half on one element, half on the other; they were neither at the place where the sea was going to carry them, nor at the place the earth was going to lose them; baggage prepared, minds on the stretch, arms stacked—they waited. I repeat it, the word is the one which paints my present life. Lying down like the soldiers, my ear on the stretch for the report that may reach me, I wish to be ready to set out at the first summons. Who will make me that summons? life or death? God or Raoul? My baggage is packed, my soul is prepared, I await the signal—I wait, doctor, I wait!"

The doctor knew the temper of that mind; he appreciated the strength of that body; he reflected for the moment, told himself that words were useless, remedies absurd, and left the chateau, exhorting Athos's servants not to quit him for a moment.

The doctor being gone, Athos evinced neither anger nor vexation at having been disturbed. He did not even desire that all letters that came should be brought to him directly. He knew very well that every distraction which should arise would be a joy, a hope, which his servants would have paid with their blood to procure him. Sleep had become rare. By intense thinking, Athos forgot himself, for a few hours at most, in a reverie most profound, more obscure than other people would have called a dream. The momentary repose which this forget-fulness thus gave the body, still further fatigued the soul, for Athos lived a double life during these wanderings of his under-standing. One night, he dreamt that Raoul was dressing himself in a tent, to go upon an expedition commanded by M. de Beaufort in person. The young man was sad; he clasped his cuirass slowly, and slowly he girded on his sword.

"What is the matter?" asked his father, tenderly.

"What afflicts me is the death of Porthos, ever so dear a friend," replied Raoul. "I suffer here the grief you soon will feel at home."

And the vision disappeared with the slumber of Athos. At daybreak one of his servants entered his master's apart-ment, and gave him a letter which came from Spain.

"The writing of Aramis," thought the comte; and he read.

"Porthos is dead!" cried he, after the first lines. "Oh! Raoul, Raoul! thanks! thou keepest thy promise, thou warnest me!"

And Athos, seized with a mortal sweat, fainted in his bed, without any other cause than weakness.

CHAPTER 57

Athos's Vision.

When this fainting of Athos had ceased, the comte, almost ashamed of having given way before this superior natural event, dressed himself and ordered his horse, determined to ride to Blois, to open more certain correspondences with either Africa, D'Artagnan, or Aramis. In fact, this letter from Aramis informed the Comte de la Fere of the bad success of the expedition of Belle-Isle. It gave him sufficient details of the death of Porthos to move the tender and devoted heart of Athos to its innermost fibers. Athos wished to go and pay his friend Porthos a last visit. To render this honor to his companion in arms, he meant to send to D'Artagnan, to prevail upon him to recommence the painful voyage to Belle-Isle, to accomplish in his company that sad pilgrimage to the tomb of the giant he had so much loved, then to return to his dwelling to obey that secret influence which was conducting him to eternity by a mysterious road. But scarcely had his joyous servants dressed their master, whom they saw with pleasure preparing for a journey which might dissipate his melancholy; scarcely had the comte's gentlest horse been saddled and brought to the door, when the father of Raoul felt his head become confused, his legs give way, and he clearly perceived the impossibility of going one step further. He ordered himself to be carried into the sun; they laid him upon his bed of moss where he passed a full hour before he could recover his spirits. Nothing could be more natural than this weakness after then inert repose of the latter days. Athos took a *bouillon*, to give him strength, and bathed his dried lips in a glassful of the wine he loved the best—that old Anjou wine mentioned by Porthos in his admirable will. Then, refreshed, free in mind, he had his horse brought again; but only with the aid of his servants was he able painfully to climb into the saddle. He did not go a hundred paces; a shivering seized him again at the turning of the road.

"This is very strange!" said he to his *valet de chambre*, who accompanied him.

"Let us stop, monsieur—I conjure you!" replied the faithful servant; "how pale you are getting!"

"That will not prevent my pursuing my route, now I have once started," replied the comte. And he gave his horse his head again. But suddenly, the animal, instead of obeying the thought of his master, stopped. A movement, of which Athos was unconscious, had checked the bit.

"Something," said Athos, "wills that I should go no further. Support me," added he, stretching out his arms; "quick! come closer! I feel my muscles relax—I shall fall from my horse."

The valet had seen the movement made by his master at the moment he received the order. He went up to him quickly, received the comte in his arms, and as they were not yet sufficiently distant from the house for the servants, who had remained at the door to watch their master's departure, not to perceive the disorder in the usually regular proceeding of the comte, the valet called his comrades by gestures and voice, and all hastened to his assistance. Athos had gone but a few steps on his return, when he felt himself better again. His strength seemed to revive and with it the desire to go to Blois. He made his horse turn round: but, at the animal's first steps, he sunk again into a state of torpor and anguish.

"Well! decidedly," said he, "it is *willed* that I should stay at home." His people flocked around him; they lifted him from his horse, and carried him as quickly as possible into the house. Everything was prepared in his chamber, and they put him to bed.

"You will be sure to remember," said he, disposing himself to sleep, "that I expect letters from Africa this very day."

"Monsieur will no doubt hear with pleasure that Blaisois's son is gone on horseback, to gain an hour over the courier of Blois," replied his *valet de chambre*.

"Thank you," replied Athos, with his placid smile.

The comte fell asleep, but his disturbed slumber resembled torture rather than repose. The servant who watched him saw several times the expression of internal suffering shadowed on his features. Perhaps Athos was dreaming.

The day passed away. Blaisois's son returned; the courier had brought no news. The comte reckoned the minutes with despair; he shuddered when those minutes made an hour. The idea that he was forgotten seized him once, and brought on a fearful pang of the heart. Everybody in the house had given up all hopes of the courier—his hour had long passed. Four times the express sent to Blois had repeated his journey, and there was nothing to the address of the comte. Athos knew that the courier only arrived once a week. Here, then, was a delay of eight mortal days to be endured. He commenced the night in this painful persuasion. All that a sick man, irritated by suffering, can add of melancholy suppositions to probabilities already gloomy, Athos heaped up during the early hours of this dismal night. The fever rose: it invaded the chest, where the fire soon caught, according to the expression of the physician, who had been brought back from Blois by Blaisois at his last journey. Soon it gained the head. The physician made two successive bleedings, which dislodged it for the time, but left the patient very weak, and without power of action in anything but his brain. And yet this redoubtable fever had ceased. It besieged with its last palpitations the tense extremities; it ended by yielding as midnight struck.

The physician, seeing the incontestable improvement, returned to Blois, after having ordered some prescriptions, and declared that the comte was saved. Then commenced for Athos a strange, indefinable state. Free to think, his mind turned towards Raoul, that beloved son. His imagination penetrated the fields of Africa in the environs of Gigelli, where M. de Beaufort must have landed with his army. A waste of gray rocks, rendered green in certain parts by the waters of the sea, when it lashed the shore in storms and tempest. Beyond, the shore, strewed over with these rocks like gravestones, ascended, in form of an amphitheater among mastic-trees and cactus, a sort of small town, full of smoke, confused noises, and terrified movements. All of a sudden, from the bosom of this smoke arose a flame, which succeeded, creeping along the houses, in covering the entire surface of the town, and increased by degrees, uniting in its red and angry vortices tears, screams, and supplicating arms outstretched to Heaven.

There was, for a moment, a frightful *pele-mele* of timbers falling to pieces, of swords broken, of stones calcined, trees burnt and disappearing. It was a strange thing that in this chaos, in which Athos distinguished raised arms, in which he heard cries, sobs, and groans, he did not see one human figure. The cannon thundered at a distance, musketry madly barked, the sea moaned, flocks made their escape, bounding over the verdant slope. But not a soldier to apply the match to the batteries of cannon, not a sailor to assist in maneuvering the fleet, not a shepherd in charge of the flocks. After the ruin of the village, the destruction of the forts which dominated it, a ruin and destruction magically wrought without the co-operation of a single human being, the flames were extinguished, the smoke began to subside, then diminished in intensity, paled and disappeared entirely. Night then came over the scene; night dark upon the earth, brilliant in the firmament. The large blazing stars which spangled the African sky glittered and gleamed without illuminating anything.

A long silence ensued, which gave, for a moment, repose to the troubled imagination of Athos; and as he felt that that which he saw was not terminated, he applied more attentively the eyes of his understanding on the strange spectacle which his imagination had presented. This spectacle was soon continued for him. A mild pale moon rose behind the declivities of the coast, streaking at first the undulating ripples of the sea, which appeared to have calmed after the roaring it had sent forth during the vision of Athos—the moon, we say, shed its diamonds and opals upon the briers and bushes of the hills. The gray rocks, so many silent and attentive phantoms, appeared to raise their heads to examine likewise the field of battle by the light of the moon, and Athos perceived that the field, empty during the combat, was now strewn with fallen bodies.

An inexpressible shudder of fear and horror seized his soul as he recognized the white and blue uniforms of the soldiers of Picardy, with their long pikes and blue handles, and muskets marked with the *fleur-de-lis* on the butts. When he saw all the gaping wounds, looking up to the bright heavens as if to demand back of them the souls to which they had opened a passage,—when he saw the slaughtered horses, stiff, their tongues hanging out at one side of their mouths, sleeping in the shiny blood congealed around them, staining their furniture and their manes,—when he saw the white horse of M. de Beaufort, with his head beaten to pieces, in the first ranks of the dead, Athos passed a cold hand over his brow, which he was astonished not to find burning. He was convinced by this touch that he was present, as a spectator, without delirium's dreadful aid, the day after the battle fought upon the shores of Gigelli by the army of the expedition, which he had seen leave the coast of France and disappear upon the dim horizon, and of which he had saluted with thought and gesture the last cannon-shot fired by the duke as a signal of farewell to his country.

Who can paint the mortal agony with which his soul followed, like a vigilant eye, these effigies of clay-cold soldiers, and examined them, one after the other, to see if Raoul slept among them? Who can express the intoxication of joy with which Athos bowed before God, and thanked Him for not having seen him he sought with so much fear among the dead? In fact, fallen in their ranks, stiff, icy, the dead, still recognizable with ease, seemed to turn with complacency towards the Comte de la Fere, to be the better seen by him, during his sad review. But yet, he was astonished, while viewing all these bodies, not to perceive the survivors. To such a point did the illusion extend, that this vision was for him a real voyage made by the father into Africa, to obtain more exact information respecting his son.

Fatigued, therefore, with having traversed seas and continents, he sought repose under one of the tents sheltered behind a rock, on the top of which floated the white *fleur-de-lised* pennon. He looked for a soldier to conduct him to the tent of M. de Beaufort. Then, while his eye was wandering over the plain, turning on all sides, he saw a white form appear behind the scented myrtles. This figure was clothed in the costume of an officer; it held in its hand a broken sword; it advanced slowly towards Athos, who, stopping short and fixing his eyes upon it, neither spoke nor moved, but wished to open his arms, because in this silent officer he had already recognized Raoul. The comte attempted to utter a cry, but it was stifled in his throat. Raoul, with a gesture, directed him to be silent, placing his finger on his lips and drawing back by degrees, without Athos being able to see his legs move. The comte, still paler than Raoul, followed his son, painfully traversing briers and bushes, stones and ditches, Raoul not appearing to touch the earth, no obstacle seeming to impede the lightness of his march. The comte, whom the inequalities of the path fatigued, soon stopped, exhausted. Raoul still continued to beckon him to follow him. The tender father, to whom love restored strength, made a last effort, and climbed the mountain after the young man, who attracted him by gesture and by smile.

At length he gained the crest of the hill, and saw, thrown out in black, upon the horizon whitened by the moon, the aerial form of Raoul. Athos reached forth his hand to get closer to his beloved son upon the plateau, and the latter also stretched out his; but suddenly, as if the young man had been drawn away in his own despite, still retreating, he left the earth, and Athos saw the clear blue sky shine between the feet of his child and the ground of the hill. Raoul rose insensibly into the void, smiling, still calling with gesture:—he departed towards heaven. Athos uttered a cry of tenderness and terror. He looked below again. He saw a camp destroyed, and all those white bodies of the royal army, like so many motionless atoms. And, then, raising his head, he saw the figure of his son still beckoning him to climb the mystic void.

CHAPTER 58

The Angel of Death.

Athos was at this part of his marvelous vision, when the charm was suddenly broken by a great noise rising from the outer gates. A horse was heard galloping over the hard gravel of the great alley, and the sound of noisy and animated conversations ascended to the chamber in which the comte was dreaming. Athos did not stir from the place he occupied; he scarcely turned his head towards the door to ascertain the sooner what these noises could be. A heavy step ascended the stairs; the horse, which had recently galloped, departed slowly towards the stables. Great hesitation appeared in the steps, which by degrees approached the chamber. A door was opened, and Athos, turning a little towards the part of the room the noise came from, cried, in a weak voice:

"It is a courier from Africa, is it not?"

"No, monsieur le comte," replied a voice which made the father of Raoul start upright in his bed.

"Grimaud!" murmured he. And the sweat began to pour down his face. Grimaud appeared in the doorway. It was no longer the Grimaud we have seen, still young with courage and devotion, when he jumped the first into the boat destined to convey Raoul de Bragelonne to the vessels of the royal fleet. 'Twas now a stern and pale old man, his clothes covered with dust, and hair whitened by old age. He trembled whilst leaning against the door-frame, and was near falling on seeing, by the light of the lamps, the countenance of his master. These two men who had lived so long together in a community of intelligence, and whose eyes, accustomed to economize expressions, knew how to say so many things silently—these two old friends, one as noble as the other in heart, if they were unequal in fortune and birth, remained tongue-tied whilst looking at each other. By the exchange of a single glance they had just read to the bottom of each other's hearts. The old servitor bore upon his countenance the impression of a grief already old, the outward token of a grim familiarity with woe. He appeared to have no longer in use more than a single version of his thoughts. As formerly he was accustomed not to speak much, he was now accustomed not to smile at all. Athos read at a glance all these shades upon the visage of his faithful servant, and in the same tone he would have employed to speak to Raoul in his dream:

"Grimaud," said he, "Raoul is dead. *Is it not so?*"

Behind Grimaud the other servants listened breathlessly, with their eyes fixed upon the bed of their sick master. They heard the terrible question, and a heart-breaking silence followed.

"Yes," replied the old man, heaving the monosyllable from his chest with a hoarse, broken sigh.

Then arose voices of lamentation, which groaned without measure, and filled with regrets and prayers the chamber where the agonized father sought with his eyes the portrait of his son. This was for Athos like the transition which led to his dream. Without uttering a cry, without shedding a tear, patient, mild, resigned as a martyr, he raised his eyes towards Heaven, in order there to see again, rising above the mountain of Gigelli, the beloved shade that was leaving him at the moment of Grimaud's arrival. Without doubt, while looking towards the heavens, resuming his marvelous dream, he repassed by the same road by which the vision, at once so terrible and sweet, had led him before; for after having gently closed his eyes, he reopened them and began to smile: he had just seen Raoul, who had smiled upon him. With his hands joined upon his breast, his face turned towards the window, bathed by the fresh air of night, which brought upon its wings the aroma of the flowers and the woods, Athos entered, never again to come out of it, into the contemplation of that paradise which the living never see. God willed, no doubt, to open to this elect the treasures of eternal beatitude, at this hour when other men tremble with the idea of being severely received by the Lord, and cling to this life they know, in the dread of the other life of which they get but merest glimpses by the dismal murky torch of death. Athos was spirit-guided by the pure serene soul of his son, which aspired to be like the paternal soul. Everything for this just man was melody and perfume in the rough road souls take to return to the celestial country. After an hour of this ecstasy, Athos softly raised his hands as white as wax; the smile did not quit his lips, and he murmured low, so low as scarcely to be audible, these three words addressed to God or to Raoul:

"HERE I AM!"

And his hands fell slowly, as though he himself had laid them on the bed.

Death had been kind and mild to this noble creature. It had spared him the tortures of the agony, convulsions of the last departure; had opened with an indulgent finger the gates of eternity to that noble soul. God had no doubt ordered it thus that the pious remembrance of this death should remain in the hearts of those present, and in the memory of other men—a death which caused to be loved the passage from this life to the other by those whose existence upon this earth leads them not to dread the last judgment. Athos preserved, even in the eternal sleep, that placid and sincere smile—an ornament which was to accompany him to the tomb. The quietude and calm of his fine features made his servants for a long time doubt whether he had really quitted life. The comte's people wished to remove Grimaud, who, from a distance, devoured the face now quickly growing marble-pale, and did not approach, from pious fear of bringing to him the breath of death. But Grimaud, fatigued as he was, refused to leave the room. He sat himself down upon the threshold, watching his master with the vigilance of a sentinel, jealous to receive either his first waking look or his last dying sigh. The noises all were quiet in the house—every one respected the slumber of their lord. But Grimaud, by anxiously listening, perceived that the comte no longer breathed. He raised himself with his hands leaning on the ground, looked to see if there did not appear some motion in the body of his master. Nothing! Fear seized him; he rose completely up, and, at the very moment, heard some one coming up the stairs. A noise of spurs knocking against a sword—a warlike sound familiar to his ears—stopped him as he was going towards the bed of Athos. A voice more sonorous than brass or steel resounded within three paces of him.

"Athos! Athos! my friend!" cried this voice, agitated even to tears.

"Monsieur le Chevalier d'Artagnan," faltered out Grimaud.

"Where is he? Where is he?" continued the musketeer. Grimaud seized his arm in his bony fingers, and pointed to the bed, upon the sheets of which the livid tints of death already showed.

A choked respiration, the opposite to a sharp cry, swelled the throat of D'Artagnan. He advanced on tip-toe, trembling, frightened at the noise his feet made on the floor, his heart rent by a nameless agony. He placed his ear to the breast of Athos, his face to the comte's mouth. Neither noise, nor breath! D'Artagnan drew back. Grimaud, who had followed him with his eyes, and for whom each of his movements had been a revelation, came timidly; seated himself at the foot of the bed, and glued his lips to the sheet which was raised by the stiffened feet of his master. Then large drops began to flow from his red eyes. This old man in invincible despair, who wept, bent doubled without uttering a word, presented the most touching spectacle that D'Artagnan, in a life so filled with emotion, had ever met with.

The captain resumed standing in contemplation before that smiling dead man, who seemed to have burnished his last thought, to give his best friend, the man he had loved next to Raoul, a gracious welcome even beyond life. And for reply to that exalted flattery of hospitality, D'Artagnan went and kissed Athos fervently on the brow, and with his trembling fingers closed his eyes. Then he seated himself by the pillow without dread of that dead man, who had been so kind and affectionate to him for five and thirty years. He was feeding his soul with the remembrances the noble visage of the comte brought to his mind in crowds—some blooming and charming as that smile—some dark, dismal, and icy as that visage with its eyes now closed to all eternity.

All at once the bitter flood which mounted from minute to minute invaded his heart, and swelled his breast almost to bursting. Incapable of mastering his emotion, he arose, and tearing himself violently from the chamber where he had just found dead him to whom he came to report the news of the death of Porthos, he uttered sobs so heart-rending that the servants, who seemed only to wait for an explosion of grief, answered to it by their lugubrious clamors, and the dogs of the late comte by their lamentable howlings. Grimaud was the only one who did not lift up his voice. Even in the paroxysm of his grief he would not have dared to profane the dead, or for the first time disturb the slumber of his master. Had not Athos always bidden him be dumb?

At daybreak D'Artagnan, who had wandered about the

lower hall, biting his fingers to stifle his sighs—D'Artagnan went up once more; and watching the moments when Grimaud turned his head towards him, he made him a sign to come to him, which the faithful servant obeyed without making more noise than a shadow. D'Artagnan went down again, followed by Grimaud; and when he had gained the vestibule, taking the old man's hands, "Grimaud," said he, "I have seen how the father died; now let me know about the son."

Grimaud drew from his breast a large letter, upon the envelope of which was traced the address of Athos. He recognized the writing of M. de Beaufort, broke the seal, and began to read, while walking about in the first steel-chill rays of dawn, in the dark alley of old limes, marked by the still visible footsteps of the comte who had just died.

CHAPTER 59

The Bulletin.

The Duc de Beaufort wrote to Athos. The letter destined for the living only reached the dead. God had changed the address.

> "MY DEAR COMTE," wrote the prince, in his large, school-boy's hand,—"a great misfortune has struck us amidst a great triumph. The king loses one of the bravest of soldiers. I lose a friend. You lose M. de Bragelonne. He has died gloriously, so gloriously that I have not the strength to weep as I could wish. Receive my sad compliments, my dear comte. Heaven distributes trials according to the greatness of our hearts. This is an immense one, but not above your courage.
>
> Your good friend,
> "LE DUC DE BEAUFORT."

The letter contained a relation written by one of the prince's secretaries. It was the most touching recital, and the most true, of that dismal episode which unraveled two existences. D'Artagnan, accustomed to battle emotions, and with a heart armed against tenderness, could not help starting on reading the name of Raoul, the name of that beloved boy who had become a shade now—like his father.

"In the morning," said the prince's secretary, "monseigneur commanded the attack. Normandy and Picardy had taken positions in the rocks dominated by the heights of the mountain, upon the declivity of which were raised the bastions of Gigelli.

"The cannon opened the action; the regiments marched full of resolution; the pikemen with pikes elevated, the musket-bearers with their weapons ready. The prince followed attentively the march and movements of the troops, so as to be able to sustain them with a strong reserve. With monseigneur were the oldest captains and his aides-de-camp. M. le Vicomte de Bragelonne had received orders not to leave his highness. In the meantime the enemy's cannon, which at first thundered with little success against the masses, began to regulate their fire, and the balls, better directed, killed several men near the prince. The regiments formed in column, and, advancing against the ramparts, were rather roughly handled. There was a sort of hesitation in our troops, who found themselves ill-seconded by the artillery. In fact, the batteries which had been established the evening before had but a weak and uncertain aim, on account of their position. The upward direction of the aim lessened the justness of the shots as well as their range.

"Monseigneur, comprehending the bad effect of this position on the siege artillery, commanded the frigates moored in the little road to commence a regular fire against the place. M. de Bragelonne offered himself at once to carry this order. But monseigneur refused to acquiesce in the vicomte's request. Monseigneur was right, for he loved and wished to spare the young nobleman. He was quite right, and the event took upon itself to justify his foresight and refusal; for scarcely had the sergeant charged with the message solicited by M. de Bragelonne gained the seashore, when two shots from long carbines issued from the enemy's ranks and laid him low. The sergeant fell, dyeing the sand with his blood; observing which, M. de Bragelonne smiled at monseigneur, who said to him, 'You see, vicomte, I have saved your life. Report that, some day, to M. le Comte de la Fere, in order that, learning it from you, he may thank me.' The young nobleman smiled sadly, and replied to the duke, 'It is true, monseigneur, that but for your kindness I should have been killed, where the poor sergeant has fallen, and should be at rest.' M. de Bragelonne made this reply in such a tone that monseigneur answered him warmly, '*Vrai Dieu!* Young man, one would say that your mouth waters for death; but, by the soul of Henry IV., I have promised your father to bring you back alive; and, please the Lord, I mean to keep my word.'

"Monseigneur de Bragelonne colored, and replied, in a lower voice, 'Monseigneur, pardon me, I beseech you. I have always had a desire to meet good opportunities; and it is so delightful to distinguish ourselves before our general, particularly when that general is M. le Duc de Beaufort.'

"Monseigneur was a little softened by this; and, turning to the officers who surrounded him, gave different orders. The grenadiers of the two regiments got near enough to the ditches and intrenchments to launch their grenades, which had but small effect. In the meanwhile, M. d'Estrees, who commanded the fleet, having seen the attempt of the sergeant to approach the vessels, understood that he must act without orders, and opened fire. Then the Arabs, finding themselves seriously injured by the balls from the fleet, and beholding the destruction and the ruin of their walls, uttered the most fearful cries. Their horsemen descended the mountain at a gallop, bent over their saddles, and rushed full tilt upon the columns of infantry, which, crossing their pikes, stopped this mad assault. Repulsed by the firm attitude of the battalion, the Arabs threw themselves with fury towards the *etat-major*, which was not on its guard at that moment.

"The danger was great; monseigneur drew his sword; his secretaries and people imitated him; the officers of the suite engaged in combat with the furious Arabs. It was then M. de Bragelonne was able to satisfy the inclination he had so clearly shown from the commencement of the action. He fought near the prince with the valor of a Roman, and killed three Arabs with his small sword. But it was evident that his bravery did not arise from that sentiment of pride so natural to all who fight. It was impetuous, affected, even forced; he sought to glut, intoxicate himself with strife and carnage. He excited himself to such a degree that monseigneur called to him to stop. He must have heard the voice of monseigneur, because we who were close to him heard it. He did not, however, stop, but continued his course to the intrenchments. As M. de Bragelonne was a well-disciplined officer, this disobedience to the orders of monseigneur very much surprised everybody, and M. de Beaufort redoubled his earnestness, crying, 'Stop, Bragelonne! Where are you going? Stop,' repeated monseigneur, 'I command you!'

"We all, imitating the gesture of M. le duc, we all raised our hands. We expected that the cavalier would turn bridle; but M. de Bragelonne continued to ride towards the palisades.

"'Stop, Bragelonne!' repeated the prince, in a very loud voice, 'stop! in the name of your father!'

"At these words M. de Bragelonne turned round; his countenance expressed a lively grief, but he did not stop; we then concluded that his horse must have run away with him. When M. le duc saw cause to conclude that the vicomte was no longer master of his horse, and had watched him precede the first grenadiers, his highness cried, 'Musketeers, kill his horse! A hundred pistoles for the man who kills his horse!' But who could expect to hit the beast without at least wounding his rider? No one dared the attempt. At length one presented himself; he was a sharp-shooter of the regiment of Picardy, named Luzerne, who took aim at the animal, fired, and hit him in the quarters, for we saw the blood redden the hair of the horse. Instead of falling, the cursed jennet was irritated, and carried him on more furiously than ever. Every Picard who saw this unfortunate young man rushing on to meet certain death, shouted in the loudest manner, 'Throw yourself off, monsieur le vicomte!—off!—off! throw yourself off!' M. de Bragelonne was an officer much beloved in the army. Already had the vicomte arrived within pistol-shot of the ramparts, when a discharge was poured upon him that enshrouded him in fire and smoke. We lost sight of him; the smoke dispersed; he was on foot, upright; his horse was killed.

"The vicomte was summoned to surrender by the Arabs, but he made them a negative sign with his head, and continued to march towards the palisades. This was a mortal imprudence. Nevertheless the entire army was pleased that he would not retreat, since ill-chance had led him so near. He marched a few paces further, and the two regiments clapped their hands. It was at this moment the second discharge shook the walls, and the Vicomte de Bragelonne again disappeared in the smoke; but this time the smoke dispersed in vain; we no longer saw him standing. He was down, with his head lower than his legs, among the bushes, and the Arabs began to think of leaving their intrenchments to come and cut off his head or take his body—as is the custom with the infidels. But Monseigneur le Duc de Beaufort had followed all this with his eyes, and the sad spectacle drew from him many painful sighs. He then cried aloud, seeing the Arabs running like white phantoms among the mastic-trees, 'Grenadiers! lancers! will you let them take that noble body?'

"Saying these words and waving his sword, he himself rode towards the enemy. The regiments, rushing in his steps, ran in their turn, uttering cries as terrible as those of the Arabs were wild.

"The combat commenced over the body of M. de Bragelonne, and with such inveteracy was it fought that a hundred and sixty Arabs were left upon the field, by the side of at least fifty of our troops. It was a lieutenant from Normandy who took the body of the vicomte on his shoulders and carried it back to the lines. The advantage was, however, pursued, the regiments took the reserve with them, and the enemy's palisades were utterly destroyed. At three o'clock the fire of the Arabs ceased; the hand-to-hand fight lasted two hours; it was a massacre. At five o'clock we were victorious at all points; the enemy had abandoned his positions, and M. le duc ordered the white flag to be planted on the summit of the little mountain. It was then we had time to think of M. de Bragelonne, who had eight large wounds in his body, through which almost all his blood had welled away. Still, however, he had breathed, which afforded inexpressible joy to monseigneur, who insisted on being present at the first dressing of the wounds and the consultation of the surgeons. There were two among them who declared M. de Bragelonne would live. Monseigneur threw his arms around their necks, and promised them a thousand louis each if they could save him.

"The vicomte heard these transports of joy, and whether he was in despair, or whether he suffered much from his wounds, he expressed by his countenance a contradiction, which gave rise to reflection, particularly in one of the secretaries when he had heard what follows. The third surgeon was the brother of Sylvain de Saint-Cosme, the most learned of them all. He probed the wounds in his turn, and said nothing. M. de Bragelonne fixed his eyes steadily upon the skillful surgeon, and seemed to interrogate his every movement. The latter, upon being questioned by monseigneur, replied that he saw plainly three mortal wounds out of eight, but so strong was the constitution of the wounded, so rich was he in youth, and so merciful was the goodness of God, that perhaps M. de Bragelonne might recover, particularly if he did not move in the slightest manner. Frere Sylvain added, turning towards his assistants, 'Above everything, do not allow him to move, even a finger, or you will kill him;' and we all left the tent in very low spirits. That secretary I have mentioned, on leaving the tent, thought he perceived a faint and sad smile glide over the lips of M. de Bragelonne when the duke said to him, in a cheerful, kind voice, 'We will save you, vicomte, we will save you yet.'

"In the evening, when it was believed the wounded youth had taken some repose, one of the assistants entered his tent, but rushed out again immediately, uttering loud cries. We all ran up in disorder, M. le duc with us, and the assistant pointed to the body of M. de Bragelonne upon the ground, at the foot of his bed, bathed in the remainder of his blood. It appeared that he had suffered some convulsion, some delirium, and that he had fallen; that the fall had accelerated his end, according to the prognosis of Frere Sylvain. We raised the vicomte; he was cold and dead. He held a lock of fair hair in his right hand, and that hand was tightly pressed upon his heart."

Then followed the details of the expedition, and of the victory obtained over the Arabs. D'Artagnan stopped at the account of the death of poor Raoul. "Oh!" murmured he, "unhappy boy! a suicide!" And turning his eyes towards the chamber of the chateau, in which Athos slept in eternal sleep, "They kept their words with each other," said he, in a low voice; "now I believe them to be happy; they must be reunited." And he returned through the parterre with slow and melancholy steps. All the village—all the neighborhood— were filled with grieving neighbors relating to each other the double catastrophe, and making preparations for the funeral.

CHAPTER 60

The Last Canto of the Poem.

On the morrow, all the *noblesse* of the provinces, of the environs, and wherever messengers had carried the news, might have been seen arriving in detachments. D'Artagnan had shut himself up, without being willing to speak to anybody. Two such heavy deaths falling upon the captain, so closely after the death of Porthos, for a long time oppressed that spirit which had hitherto been so indefatigable and invulnerable. Except Grimaud, who entered his chamber once, the musketeer saw neither servants nor guests. He supposed, from the noises in the house, and the continual coming and going, that preparations were being made for the funeral of the comte. He wrote to the king to ask for an extension of his leave of absence. Grimaud, as we have said, had entered D'Artagnan's apartment, had seated himself upon a joint-stool near the door, like a man who meditates profoundly; then, rising, he made a sign to D'Artagnan to follow him. The latter obeyed in silence. Grimaud descended to the comte's bed-chamber, showed the captain with his finger the place of the empty bed, and raised his eyes eloquently towards Heaven.

"Yes," replied D'Artagnan, "yes, good Grimaud—now with the son he loved so much!"

Grimaud left the chamber, and led the way to the hall, where, according to the custom of the province, the body was laid out, previously to being put away forever. D'Artagnan was struck at seeing two open coffins in the hall. In reply to the mute invitation of Grimaud, he approached, and saw in one of them Athos, still handsome in death, and, in the other, Raoul with his eyes closed, his cheeks pearly as those of the Palls of Virgil, with a smile on his violet lips. He shuddered at seeing the father and son, those two departed souls, represented on earth by two silent, melancholy bodies, incapable of touching each other, however close they might be.

"Raoul here!" murmured he. "Oh! Grimaud, why did you not tell me this?"

Grimaud shook his head, and made no reply; but taking D'Artagnan by the hand, he led him to the coffin, and showed him, under the thin winding-sheet, the black wounds by which life had escaped. The captain turned away his eyes, and, judging it was useless to question Grimaud, who would not answer, he recollected that M. de Beaufort's secretary had written more than he, D'Artagnan, had had the courage to read. Taking up the recital of the affair which had cost Raoul his life, he found these words, which ended the concluding paragraph of the letter:

"Monseigneur le duc has ordered that the body of monsieur le vicomte should be embalmed, after the manner practiced by the Arabs when they wish their dead to be carried to their native land; and monsieur le duc has appointed relays, so that the same confidential servant who brought up the young man might take back his remains to M. le Comte de la Fere."

"And so," thought D'Artagnan, "I shall follow thy funeral, my dear boy—I, already old—I, who am of no value on earth—and I shall scatter dust upon that brow I kissed but two months since. God has willed it to be so. Thou hast willed it to be so, thyself. I have no longer the right even to weep.

Thou hast chosen death; it seemed to thee a preferable gift to life."

At length arrived the moment when the chill remains of these two gentlemen were to be given back to mother earth. There was such an affluence of military and other people that up to the place of the sepulture, which was a little chapel on the plain, the road from the city was filled with horsemen and pedestrians in mourning. Athos had chosen for his resting-place the little inclosure of a chapel erected by himself near the boundary of his estates. He had had the stones, cut in 1550, brought from an old Gothic manor-house in Berry, which had sheltered his early youth. The chapel, thus rebuilt, transported, was pleasing to the eye beneath its leafy curtains of poplars and sycamores. It was ministered in every Sunday, by the cure of the neighboring bourg, to whom Athos paid an allowance of two hundred francs for this service; and all the vassals of his domain, with their families, came thither to hear mass, without having any occasion to go to the city.

Behind the chapel extended, surrounded by two high hedges of hazel, elder and white thorn, and a deep ditch, the little inclosure—uncultivated, though gay in its sterility; because the mosses there grew thick, wild heliotrope and ravenelles there mingled perfumes, while from beneath an ancient chestnut issued a crystal spring, a prisoner in its marble cistern, and on the thyme all around alighted thousands of bees from the neighboring plants, whilst chaffinches and redthroats sang cheerfully among the flower-spangled hedges. It was to this place the somber coffins were carried, attended by a silent and respectful crowd. The office of the dead being celebrated, the last adieux paid to the noble departed, the assembly dispersed, talking, along the roads, of the virtues and mild death of the father, of the hopes the son had given, and of his melancholy end upon the arid coast of Africa.

Little by little, all noises were extinguished, like the

lamps illuminating the humble nave. The minister bowed for the last time to the altar and the still fresh graves; then, followed by his assistant, he slowly took the road back to the presbytery. D'Artagnan, left alone, perceived that night was coming on. He had forgotten the hour, thinking only of the dead. He arose from the oaken bench on which he was seated in the chapel, and wished, as the priest had done, to go and bid a last adieu to the double grave which contained his two lost friends.

A woman was praying, kneeling on the moist earth. D'Artagnan stopped at the door of the chapel, to avoid disturbing her, and also to endeavor to find out who was the pious friend who performed this sacred duty with so much zeal and perseverance. The unknown had hidden her face in her hands, which were white as alabaster. From the noble simplicity of her costume, she must be a woman of distinction. Outside the inclosure were several horses mounted by servants; a travelling carriage was in waiting for this lady. D'Artagnan in vain sought to make out what caused her delay. She continued praying, and frequently pressed her handkerchief to her face, by which D'Artagnan perceived she was weeping. He beheld her strike her breast with the compunction of a Christian woman. He heard her several times exclaim as from a wounded heart: "Pardon! pardon!" And as she appeared to abandon herself entirely to her grief, as she threw herself down, almost fainting, exhausted by complaints and prayers, D'Artagnan, touched by this love for his so much regretted friends, made a few steps towards the grave, in order to interrupt the melancholy colloquy of the penitent with the dead. But as soon as his step sounded on the gravel, the unknown raised her head, revealing to D'Artagnan a face aflood with tears, a well-known face. It was Mademoiselle de la Valliere! "Monsieur d'Artagnan!" murmured she.

"You!" replied the captain, in a stern voice, "you here!— oh! madame, I should better have liked to see you decked with flowers in the mansion of the Comte de la Fère. You would have wept less—and they too—and I!"

"Monsieur!" said she, sobbing.

"For it was you," added this pitiless friend of the dead,— "it was you who sped these two men to the grave."

"Oh! spare me!"

"God forbid, madame, that I should offend a woman, or that I should make her weep in vain; but I must say that the place of the murderer is not upon the grave of her victims." She wished to reply.

"What I now tell you," added he, coldly, "I have already told the king."

She clasped her hands. "I know," said she, "I have caused the death of the Vicomte de Bragelonne."

"Ah! you know it?"

"The news arrived at court yesterday. I have traveled during the night forty leagues to come and ask pardon of the comte, whom I supposed to be still living, and to pray God, on the tomb of Raoul, that he would send me all the misfortunes I have merited, except a single one. Now, monsieur, I know that the death of the son has killed the father; I have two crimes to reproach myself with; I have two punishments to expect from Heaven."

"I will repeat to you, mademoiselle," said D'Artagnan, "what M. de Bragelonne said of you, at Antibes, when he already meditated death: 'If pride and coquetry have misled her, I pardon her while despising her. If love has produced her error, I pardon her, but I swear that no one could have loved her as I have done.'"

"You know," interrupted Louise, "that of my love I was about to sacrifice myself; you know whether I suffered when you met me lost, dying, abandoned. Well! never have I suffered so much as now; because then I hoped, desired,—now I have no longer anything to wish for; because this death drags all my joy into the tomb; because I can no longer dare to love without remorse, and I feel that he whom I love—oh! it is but just!—will repay me with the tortures I have made others undergo."

D'Artagnan made no reply; he was too well convinced that she was not mistaken.

"Well, then," added she, "dear Monsieur d'Artagnan, do not overwhelm me to-day, I again implore you! I am like the branch torn from the trunk, I no longer hold to anything in this world—a current drags me on, I know not whither. I love madly, even to the point of coming to tell it, wretch that I am, over the ashes of the dead, and I do not blush for it—I have no remorse on this account. Such love is a religion. Only, as hereafter you will see me alone, forgotten, disdained; as you will see me punished, as I am destined to be punished, spare me in my ephemeral happiness, leave it to me for a few days, for a few minutes. Now, even at the moment I am speaking to you, perhaps it no longer exists. My God! this double murder is perhaps already expiated!"

While she was speaking thus, the sound of voices and of horses drew the attention of the captain. M. de Saint-Aignan came to seek La Valliere. "The king," he said, "is a prey to jealousy and uneasiness." Saint-Aignan did not perceive D'Artagnan, half concealed by the trunk of a chestnut-tree which shaded the double grave. Louise thanked Saint-Aignan, and dismissed him with a gesture. He rejoined the party outside the inclosure.

"You see, madame," said the captain bitterly to the young woman,—"you see your happiness still lasts."

The young woman raised her head with a solemn air. "A day will come," said she, "when you will repent of having so misjudged me. On that day, it is I who will pray God to forgive you for having been unjust towards me. Besides, I shall suffer so much that you yourself will be the first to pity my sufferings. Do not reproach me with my fleeting happiness, Monsieur d'Artagnan; it costs me dear, and I have not paid all my debt." Saying these words, she again knelt down, softly and affectionately.

"Pardon me the last time, my affianced Raoul!" said she. "I have broken our chain; we are both destined to die of grief. It is thou who departest first; fear nothing, I shall follow thee. See, only, that I have not been base, and that I have come to bid thee this last adieu. The Lord is my witness, Raoul, that if with my life I could have redeemed thine, I would have given that life without hesitation. I could not give my love. Once more, forgive me, dearest, kindest friend."

She strewed a few sweet flowers on the freshly sodded earth; then, wiping the tears from her eyes, the heavily stricken lady bowed to D'Artagnan, and disappeared.

The captain watched the departure of the horses, horsemen, and carriage, then crossing his arms upon his swelling chest, "When will it be my turn to depart?" said he, in an agitated voice. "What is there left for man after youth, love, glory, friendship, strength, and wealth have disappeared? That rock, under which sleeps Porthos, who possessed all I have named; this moss, under which repose Athos and Raoul, who possessed much more!"

He hesitated for a moment, with a dull eye; then, drawing himself up, "Forward! still forward!" said he. "When it is time, God will tell me, as he foretold the others."

He touched the earth, moistened with the evening dew, with the ends of his fingers, signed himself as if he had been at the *benitier* in church, and retook alone—ever alone—the road to Paris.

EPILOGUE

Four years after the scene we have just described, two horsemen, well mounted, traversed Blois early in the morning, for the purpose of arranging a hawking party the king had arranged to make in that uneven plain the Loire divides in two, which borders on the one side Meung, on the other Amboise. These were the keeper of the king's harriers and the master of the falcons, personages greatly respected in the time of Louis XIII., but rather neglected by his successor. The horsemen, having reconnoitered the ground, were returning, their observations made, when they perceived certain little groups of soldiers, here and there, whom the sergeants were placing at distances at the openings of the inclosures. These were the king's musketeers. Behind them came, upon a splendid horse, the captain, known by his richly embroidered uniform. His hair was gray, his beard turning so. He seemed a little bent, although sitting and handling his horse gracefully. He was looking about him watchfully.

"M. d'Artagnan does not get any older," said the keeper of the harriers to his colleague the falconer; "with ten years more to carry than either of us, he has the seat of a young man on horseback."

"That is true," replied the falconer. "I don't see any change in him for the last twenty years."

But this officer was mistaken; D'Artagnan in the last four years had lived a dozen. Age had printed its pitiless claws at each angle of his eyes; his brow was bald; his hands, formerly brown and nervous, were getting white, as if the blood had half forgotten them.

D'Artagnan accosted the officers with the shade of affability which distinguishes superiors, and received in turn for his courtesy two most respectful bows.

"Ah! what a lucky chance to see you here, Monsieur d'Artagnan!" cried the falconer.

"It is rather I who should say that, messieurs," replied the captain, "for nowadays, the king makes more frequent use of his musketeers than of his falcons."

"Ah! it is not as it was in the good old times," sighed the falconer. "Do you remember, Monsieur d'Artagnan, when the late king flew the pie in the vineyards beyond Beaugence? Ah! *dame!* you were not the captain of the musketeers at that time, Monsieur d'Artagnan."[7]

"And you were nothing but under-corporal of the tiercelets," replied D'Artagnan, laughing. "Never mind that, it was a good time, seeing that it is always a good time when we are young. Good day, monsieur the keeper of the harriers."

"You do me honor, monsieur le comte," said the latter. D'Artagnan made no reply. The title of comte had hardly struck him; D'Artagnan had been a comte four years.

"Are you not very much fatigued with the long journey you have taken, monsieur le capitaine?" continued the falconer. "It must be full two hundred leagues from hence to Pignerol."

"Two hundred and sixty to go, and as many to return," said D'Artagnan, quietly.

---

[7] "Pie" in this case refers to magpies, the prey for the falcons.

"And," said the falconer, "is *he* well?"

"Who?" asked D'Artagnan.

"Why, poor M. Fouquet," continued the falconer, in a low voice. The keeper of the harriers had prudently withdrawn.

"No," replied D'Artagnan, "the poor man frets terribly; he cannot comprehend how imprisonment can be a favor; he says that parliament absolved him by banishing him, and banishment is, or should be, liberty. He cannot imagine that they had sworn his death, and that to save his life from the claws of parliament was to be under too much obligation to Heaven."

"Ah! yes; the poor man had a close chance of the scaffold," replied the falconer; "it is said that M. Colbert had given orders to the governor of the Bastille, and that the execution was ordered."

"Enough!" said D'Artagnan, pensively, and with a view of cutting short the conversation.

"Yes," said the keeper of the harriers, drawing towards them, "M. Fouquet is now at Pignerol; he has richly deserved it. He had the good fortune to be conducted there by you; he robbed the king sufficiently."

D'Artagnan launched at the master of the dogs one of his crossest looks, and said to him, "Monsieur, if any one told me you had eaten your dogs' meat, not only would I refuse to believe it; but still more, if you were condemned to the lash or to jail for it, I should pity you and would not allow people to speak ill of you. And yet, monsieur, honest man as you may be, I assure you that you are not more so than poor M. Fouquet was."

After having undergone this sharp rebuke, the keeper of the harriers hung his head, and allowed the falconer to get two steps in advance of him nearer to D'Artagnan.

"He is content," said the falconer, in a low voice, to the musketeer; "we all know that harriers are in fashion nowadays; if he were a falconer he would not talk in that way."

D'Artagnan smiled in a melancholy manner at seeing this great political question resolved by the discontent of such humble interest. He for a moment ran over in his mind the glorious existence of the surintendant, the crumbling of his fortunes, and the melancholy death that awaited him; and to conclude, "Did M. Fouquet love falconry?" said he.

"Oh, passionately, monsieur!" repeated the falconer, with an accent of bitter regret and a sigh that was the funeral oration of Fouquet.

D'Artagnan allowed the ill-humor of the one and the regret of the other to pass, and continued to advance. They could already catch glimpses of the huntsmen at the issue of the wood, the feathers of the outriders passing like shooting stars across the clearings, and the white horses skirting the bosky thickets looking like illuminated apparitions.

"But," resumed D'Artagnan, "will the sport last long? Pray, give us a good swift bird, for I am very tired. Is it a heron or a swan?"

"Both, Monsieur d'Artagnan," said the falconer; "but you need not be alarmed; the king is not much of a sportsman; he does not take the field on his own account, he only wishes to amuse the ladies."

The words "to amuse the ladies" were so strongly accented they set D'Artagnan thinking.

"Ah!" said he, looking keenly at the falconer.

The keeper of the harriers smiled, no doubt with a view of making it up with the musketeer.

"Oh! you may safely laugh," said D'Artagnan; "I know nothing of current news; I only arrived yesterday, after a month's absence. I left the court mourning the death of the queen-mother. The king was not willing to take any amusement after receiving the last sigh of Anne of Austria; but everything comes to an end in this world. Well! then he is no longer sad? So much the better."[8]

"And everything begins as well as ends," said the keeper with a coarse laugh.

"Ah!" said D'Artagnan, a second time,—he burned to know, but dignity would not allow him to interrogate people below him,—"there is something beginning, then, it seems?"

The keeper gave him a significant wink; but D'Artagnan was unwilling to learn anything from this man.

"Shall we see the king early?" asked he of the falconer.

"At seven o'clock, monsieur, I shall fly the birds."

"Who comes with the king? How is Madame? How is the queen?"

"Better, monsieur."

"Has she been ill, then?"

"Monsieur, since the last chagrin she suffered, her majesty has been unwell."

"What chagrin? You need not fancy your news is old. I have but just returned."

"It appears that the queen, a little neglected since the death of her mother-in-law, complained to the king, who answered her,—'Do I not sleep at home every night, madame? What more do you expect?'"

"Ah!" said D'Artagnan,—"poor woman! She must heartily hate Mademoiselle de la Valliere."

"Oh, no! not Mademoiselle de la Valliere," replied the falconer.

"Who then—" The blast of a hunting-horn interrupted this conversation. It summoned the dogs and the hawks. The falconer and his companions set off immediately, leaving D'Artagnan alone in the midst of the suspended sentence. The king appeared at a distance, surrounded by ladies and

---

[8] Anne of Austria did not die until 1666, and Dumas sets the current year as 1665.

horsemen. All the troop advanced in beautiful order, at a foot's pace, the horns of various sorts animating the dogs and horses. There was an animation in the scene, a mirage of light, of which nothing now can give an idea, unless it be the ficti-tious splendor of a theatric spectacle. D'Artagnan, with an eye a little, just a little, dimmed by age, distinguished behind the group three carriages. The first was intended for the queen; it was empty. D'Artagnan, who did not see Mademoiselle de la Valliere by the king's side, on looking about for her, saw her in the second carriage. She was alone with two of her women, who seemed as dull as their mistress. On the left hand of the king, upon a high-spirited horse, restrained by a bold and skillful hand, shone a lady of most dazzling beauty. The king smiled upon her, and she smiled upon the king. Loud laughter followed every word she uttered.

"I must know that woman," thought the musketeer; "who can she be?" And he stooped towards his friend, the falconer, to whom he addressed the question he had put to himself.

The falconer was about to reply, when the king, perceiving D'Artagnan, "Ah, comte!" said he, "you are amongst us once more then! Why have I not seen you?"

"Sire," replied the captain, "because your majesty was asleep when I arrived, and not awake when I resumed my duties this morning."

"Still the same," said Louis, in a loud voice, denoting satisfaction. "Take some rest, comte; I command you to do so. You will dine with me to-day."

A murmur of admiration surrounded D'Artagnan like a caress. Every one was eager to salute him. Dining with the king was an honor his majesty was not so prodigal of as Henry IV. had been. The king passed a few steps in advance, and D'Artagnan found himself in the midst of a fresh group, among whom shone Colbert.

"Good-day, Monsieur d'Artagnan," said the minister, with marked affability, "have you had a pleasant journey?"

"Yes, monsieur," said D'Artagnan, bowing to the neck of his horse.

"I heard the king invite you to his table for this evening," continued the minister; "you will meet an old friend there."

"An old friend of mine?" asked D'Artagnan, plunging painfully into the dark waves of the past, which had swallowed up for him so many friendships and so many hatreds.

"M. le Duc d'Almeda, who is arrived this morning from Spain."

"The Duc d'Almeda?" said D'Artagnan, reflecting in vain.

"Here!" cried an old man, white as snow, sitting bent in his carriage, which he caused to be thrown open to make room for the musketeer.

"*Aramis!*" cried D'Artagnan, struck with profound amazement. And he felt, inert as it was, the thin arm of the old nobleman hanging round his neck.

Colbert, after having observed them in silence for a few moments, urged his horse forward, and left the two old friends together.

"And so," said the musketeer, taking Aramis's arm, "you, the exile, the rebel, are again in France?"

"Ah! and I shall dine with you at the king's table," said Aramis, smiling. "Yes, will you not ask yourself what is the use of fidelity in this world? Stop! let us allow poor La Valliere's carriage to pass. Look, how uneasy she is! How her eyes, dim with tears, follow the king, who is riding on horseback yonder!"

"With whom?"

"With Mademoiselle de Tonnay-Charente, now Madame de Montespan," replied Aramis.

"She is jealous. Is she then deserted?"

"Not quite yet, but it will not be long before she *is*." [9]

---

[9] Madame de Montespan would oust Louise from the king's affections by 1667.

They chatted together, while following the sport, and Aramis's coachman drove them so cleverly that they arrived at the instant when the falcon, attacking the bird, beat him down, and fell upon him. The king alighted; Madame de Montespan followed his example. They were in front of an isolated chapel, concealed by huge trees, already despoiled of their leaves by the first cutting winds of autumn. Behind this chapel was an inclosure, closed by a latticed gate. The falcon had beaten down his prey in the inclosure belonging to this little chapel, and the king was desirous of going in to take the first feather, according to custom. The *cortege* formed a circle round the building and the hedges, too small to receive so many. D'Artagnan held back Aramis by the arm, as he was about, like the rest, to alight from his carriage, and in a hoarse, broken voice, "Do you know, Aramis," said he, "whither chance has conducted us?"

"No," replied the duke.

"Here repose men that we knew well," said D'Artagnan, greatly agitated.

Aramis, without divining anything, and with a trembling step, penetrated into the chapel by a little door which D'Artagnan opened for him. "Where are they buried?" said he.

"There, in the inclosure. There is a cross, you see, beneath yon little cypress. The tree of grief is planted over their tomb; don't go to it; the king is going that way; the heron has fallen just there."

Aramis stopped, and concealed himself in the shade. They then saw, without being seen, the pale face of La Valliere, who, neglected in her carriage, at first looked on, with a melancholy heart, from the door, and then, carried away by jealousy, advanced into the chapel, whence, leaning against a pillar, she contemplated the king smiling and making signs to Madame de Montespan to approach, as there was nothing to be afraid of. Madame de Montespan complied; she took the hand the king held out to her, and he, plucking out the first feather from the heron, which the falconer had strangled, placed it in his beautiful companion's hat. She, smiling in her turn, kissed the hand tenderly which made her this present. The king grew scarlet with vanity and pleasure; he looked at Madame de Montespan with all the fire of new love.

"What will you give me in exchange?" said he.

She broke off a little branch of cypress and offered it to the king, who looked intoxicated with hope.

"Humph!" said Aramis to D'Artagnan; "the present is but a sad one, for that cypress shades a tomb."

"Yes, and the tomb is that of Raoul de Bragelonne," said D'Artagnan aloud; "of Raoul, who sleeps under that cross with his father."

A groan resounded—they saw a woman fall fainting to the ground. Mademoiselle de la Valliere had seen all, heard all.

"Poor woman!" muttered D'Artagnan, as he helped the attendants to carry back to her carriage the lonely lady whose lot henceforth in life was suffering.

That evening D'Artagnan was seated at the king's table, near M. Colbert and M. le Duc d'Almeda. The king was very gay. He paid a thousand little attentions to the queen, a thousand kindnesses to Madame, seated at his left hand, and very sad. It might have been supposed that time of calm when the king was wont to watch his mother's eyes for the approval or disapproval of what he had just done.

Of mistresses there was no question at this dinner. The king addressed Aramis two or three times, calling him M. l'ambassadeur, which increased the surprise already felt by D'Artagnan at seeing his friend the rebel so marvelously well received at court.

The king, on rising from table, gave his hand to the queen, and made a sign to Colbert, whose eye was on his master's face. Colbert took D'Artagnan and Aramis on one side. The king began to chat with his sister, whilst Monsieur, very uneasy, entertained the queen with a preoccupied air, without ceasing to watch his wife and brother from the corner of his eye. The conversation between Aramis, D'Artagnan, and Colbert turned upon indifferent subjects. They spoke of preceding ministers; Colbert related the successful tricks of Mazarin, and desired those of Richelieu to be related to him. D'Artagnan could not overcome his surprise at finding this man, with his heavy eyebrows and low forehead, display so much sound knowledge and cheerful spirits. Aramis was astonished at that lightness of character which permitted this serious man to retard with advantage the moment for more important conversation, to which nobody made any allusion, although all three interlocutors felt its imminence. It was very plain, from the embarrassed appearance of Monsieur, how much the conversation of the king and Madame annoyed him. Madame's eyes were almost red: was she going to complain? Was she going to expose a little scandal in open court? The king took her on one side, and in a tone so tender that it must have reminded the princess of the time when she was loved for herself:

"Sister," said he, "why do I see tears in those lovely eyes?"

"Why—sire—" said she.

"Monsieur is jealous, is he not, sister?"

She looked towards Monsieur, an infallible sign that they were talking about him.

"Yes," said she.

"Listen to me," said the king; "if your friends compromise you, it is not Monsieur's fault."

He spoke these words with so much kindness that Madame, encouraged, having borne so many solitary griefs so long, was nearly bursting into tears, so full was her heart.

"Come, come, dear little sister," said the king, "tell me

your griefs; on the word of a brother, I pity them; on the word of a king, I will put an end to them."

She raised her glorious eyes and, in a melancholy tone:

"It is not my friends who compromise me," said she; "they are either absent or concealed; they have been brought into disgrace with your majesty; they, so devoted, so good, so loyal!"

"You say this on account of De Guiche, whom I have exiled, at Monsieur's desire?"

"And who, since that unjust exile, has endeavored to get himself killed once every day."

"Unjust, say you, sister?"

"So unjust, that if I had not had the respect mixed with friendship that I have always entertained for your majesty—"

"Well!"

"Well! I would have asked my brother Charles, upon whom I can always—"

The king started. "What, then?"

"I would have asked him to have had it represented to you that Monsieur and his favorite M. le Chevalier de Lorraine ought not with impunity to constitute themselves the executioners of my honor and my happiness."

"The Chevalier de Lorraine," said the king; "that dismal fellow?"

"Is my mortal enemy. Whilst that man lives in my household, where Monsieur retains him and delegates his power to him, I shall be the most miserable woman in the kingdom."

"So," said the king, slowly, "you call your brother of England a better friend than I am?"

"Actions speak for themselves, sire."

"And you would prefer going to ask assistance there—"

"To my own country!" said she with pride; "yes, sire."

"You are the grandchild of Henry IV. as well as myself, lady. Cousin and brother-in-law, does not that amount pretty well to the title of brother-germain?"

"Then," said Henrietta, "act!"

"Let us form an alliance."

"Begin."

"I have, you say, unjustly exiled De Guiche."

"Oh! yes," said she, blushing.

"De Guiche shall return."[10]

"So far, well."

"And now you say that I do wrong in having in your household the Chevalier de Lorraine, who gives Monsieur ill advice respecting you?"

"Remember well what I tell you, sire; the Chevalier de Lorraine some day—Observe, if ever I come to a dreadful end, I beforehand accuse the Chevalier de Lorraine; he has a spirit that is capable of any crime!"

"The Chevalier de Lorraine shall no longer annoy you—I promise you that."[11]

"Then that will be a true preliminary of alliance, sire,—I sign; but since you have done your part, tell me what shall be mine."

"Instead of embroiling me with your brother Charles, you must make him a more intimate friend than ever."

"That is very easy."

"Oh! not quite so easy as you may suppose, for in ordinary friendship people embrace or exercise hospitality, and that only costs a kiss or a return, profitable expenses; but in political friendship—"

"Ah! it's a political friendship, is it?"

"Yes, my sister; and then, instead of embraces and feasts, it is soldiers—it is soldiers all alive and well equipped—that we must serve up to our friends; vessels we must offer, all armed with cannons and stored with provisions. It hence

[10] De Guiche would not return to court until 1671.

[11] Madame did die of poison in 1670, shortly after returning from the mission described later. The Chevalier de Lorraine had actually been ordered out of France in 1662.

results that we have not always coffers in a fit condition for such friendships."

"Ah! you are quite right," said Madame; "the coffers of the king of England have been sonorous for some time."

"But you, my sister, who have so much influence over your brother, you can secure more than an ambassador could ever get the promise of."

"To effect that I must go to London, my dear brother."

"I have thought so," replied the king, eagerly; "and I have said to myself that such a voyage would do your health and spirits good."

"Only," interrupted Madame, "it is possible I should fail. The king of England has dangerous counselors."

"Counselors, do you say?"

"Precisely. If, by chance, your majesty had any intention—I am only supposing so—of asking Charles II. his alliance in a war—"

"A war?"

"Yes; well! then the king's counselors, who are in number seven—Mademoiselle Stewart, Mademoiselle Wells, Mademoiselle Gwyn, Miss Orchay, Mademoiselle Zunga, Miss Davies, and the proud Countess of Castlemaine—will represent to the king that war costs a great deal of money; that it is better to give balls and suppers at Hampton Court than to equip ships of the line at Portsmouth and Greenwich."

"And then your negotiations will fail?"

"Oh! those ladies cause all negotiations to fall through which they don't make themselves."

"Do you know the idea that has struck me, sister?"

"No; inform me what it is."

"It is that, searching well around you, you might perhaps find a female counselor to take with you to your brother, whose eloquence might paralyze the ill-will of the seven others."

"That is really an idea, sire, and I will search."

"You will find what you want."

"I hope so."

"A pretty ambassadress is necessary; an agreeable face is better than an ugly one, is it not?"

"Most assuredly."

"An animated, lively, audacious character."

"Certainly."

"Nobility; that is, enough to enable her to approach the king without awkwardness—not too lofty, so as not to trouble herself about the dignity of her race."

"Very true."

"And who knows a little English."

"*Mon Dieu!* why, some one," cried Madame, "like Mademoiselle de Keroualle, for instance!"

"Oh! why, yes!" said Louis XIV.; "you have hit the mark,—it is you who have found, my sister."

"I will take her; she will have no cause to complain, I suppose."

"Oh! no, I will name her *seductrice plenipotentiaire* at once, and will add a dowry to the title."

"That is well."

"I fancy you already on your road, my dear little sister, consoled for all your griefs."

"I will go, on two conditions. The first is, that I shall know what I am negotiating about."

"That is it. The Dutch, you know, insult me daily in their gazettes, and by their republican attitude. I do not like republics."

"That may easily be imagined, sire."

"I see with pain that these kings of the sea—they call themselves so—keep trade from France in the Indies, and that their vessels will soon occupy all the ports of Europe. Such a power is too near me, sister."

"They are your allies, nevertheless."

"That is why they were wrong in having the medal you

have heard of struck; a medal which represents Holland stopping the sun, as Joshua did, with this legend: *The sun had stopped before me.* There is not much fraternity in that, *is* there?"

"I thought you had forgotten that miserable episode?"

"I never forget anything, sister. And if my true friends, such as your brother Charles, are willing to second me—" The princess remained pensively silent.

"Listen to me; there is the empire of the seas to be shared," said Louis XIV. "For this partition, which England submits to, could I not represent the second party as well as the Dutch?"

"We have Mademoiselle de Keroualle to treat that question," replied Madame.

"Your second condition for going, if you please, sister?"

"The consent of Monsieur, my husband."

"You shall have it."

"Then consider me already gone, brother."

On hearing these words, Louis XIV. turned round towards the corner of the room in which D'Artagnan, Colbert, and Aramis stood, and made an affirmative sign to his minister. Colbert then broke in on the conversation suddenly, and said to Aramis:

"Monsieur l'ambassadeur, shall we talk about business?"

D'Artagnan immediately withdrew, from politeness. He directed his steps towards the fireplace, within hearing of what the king was about to say to Monsieur, who, evidently uneasy, had gone to him. The face of the king was animated. Upon his brow was stamped a strength of will, the expression of which already met no further contradiction in France, and was soon to meet no more in Europe.

"Monsieur," said the king to his brother, "I am not pleased with M. le Chevalier de Lorraine. You, who do him the honor to protect him, must advise him to travel for a few months."

These words fell with the crush of an avalanche upon Monsieur, who adored his favorite, and concentrated all his affections in him.

"In what has the chevalier been inconsiderate enough to displease your majesty?" cried he, darting a furious look at Madame.

"I will tell you that when he is gone," said the king, suavely. "And also when Madame, here, shall have crossed over into England."

"Madame! in England!" murmured Monsieur, in amazement.

"In a week, brother," continued the king, "whilst we will go whither I will shortly tell you." And the king turned on his heel, smiling in his brother's face, to sweeten, as it were, the bitter draught he had given him.

During this time Colbert was talking with the Duc d'Almeda.

"Monsieur," said Colbert to Aramis, "this is the moment for us to come to an understanding. I have made your peace with the king, and I owed that clearly to a man of so much merit; but you have often expressed friendship for me, an opportunity presents itself for giving me a proof of it. You are, besides, more a Frenchman than a Spaniard. Shall we secure— answer me frankly—the neutrality of Spain, if we undertake anything against the United Provinces?"

"Monsieur," replied Aramis, "the interest of Spain is clear. To embroil Europe with the Provinces would doubtless be our policy, but the king of France is an ally of the United Provinces. You are not ignorant, besides, that it would infer a maritime war, and that France is in no state to undertake this with advantage."

Colbert, turning round at this moment, saw D'Artagnan who was seeking some interlocutor, during this "aside" of the king and Monsieur. He called him, at the same time saying in a low voice to Aramis, "We may talk openly with D'Artagnan, I suppose?"

"Oh! certainly," replied the ambassador.

"We were saying, M. d'Almeda and I," said Colbert, "that a conflict with the United Provinces would mean a maritime war."

"That's evident enough," replied the musketeer.

"And what do you think of it, Monsieur d'Artagnan?"

"I think that to carry on such a war successfully, you must have very large land forces."

"What did you say?" said Colbert, thinking he had ill understood him.

"Why such a large land army?" said Aramis.

"Because the king will be beaten by sea if he has not the English with him, and that when beaten by sea, he will soon be invaded, either by the Dutch in his ports, or by the Spaniards by land."

"And Spain neutral?" asked Aramis.

"Neutral as long as the king shall prove stronger," rejoined D'Artagnan.

Colbert admired that sagacity which never touched a question without enlightening it thoroughly. Aramis smiled, as he had long known that in diplomacy D'Artagnan acknowledged no superior. Colbert, who, like all proud men, dwelt upon his fantasy with a certainty of success, resumed the subject, "Who told you, M. d'Artagnan, that the king had no navy?"

"Oh! I take no heed of these details," replied the captain. "I am but an indifferent sailor. Like all nervous people, I hate the sea; and yet I have an idea that, with ships, France being a seaport with two hundred exits, we might have sailors."

Colbert drew from his pocket a little oblong book divided into two columns. On the first were the names of vessels, on the other the figures recapitulating the number of cannon and men requisite to equip these ships. "I have had the same idea as you," said he to D'Artagnan, "and I have had an account drawn up of the vessels we have alto-gether—thirty-five ships."

"Thirty-five ships! impossible!" cried D'Artagnan.

"Something like two thousand pieces of cannon," said Colbert. "That is what the king possesses at this moment. Of five and thirty vessels we can make three squadrons, but I must have five."

"Five!" cried Aramis.

"They will be afloat before the end of the year, gentlemen; the king will have fifty ship of the line. We may venture on a contest with them, may we not?"

"To build vessels," said D'Artagnan, "is difficult, but possible. As to arming them, how is that to be done? In France there are neither foundries nor military docks."

"Bah!" replied Colbert, in a bantering tone, "I have planned all that this year and a half past, did you not know it? Do you know M. d'Imfreville?"

"D'Imfreville?" replied D'Artagnan; "no."

"He is a man I have discovered; he has a specialty; he is a man of genius—he knows how to set men to work. It is he who has cast cannon and cut the woods of Bourgogne. And then, monsieur l'ambassadeur, you may not believe what I am going to tell you, but I have a still further idea."

"Oh, monsieur!" said Aramis, civilly, "I always believe you."

"Calculating upon the character of the Dutch, our allies, I said to myself, 'They are merchants, they are friendly with the king; they will be happy to sell to the king what they fabricate for themselves; then the more we buy'—Ah! I must add this: I have Forant—do you know Forant, D'Artagnan?"

Colbert, in his warmth, forgot himself; he called the

captain simply *D'Artagnan*, as the king did. But the captain only smiled at it.

"No," replied he, "I do not know him."

"That is another man I have discovered, with a genius for buying. This Forant has purchased for me 350,000 pounds of iron in balls, 200,000 pounds of powder, twelve cargoes of Northern timber, matches, grenades, pitch, tar—I know not what! with a saving of seven per cent upon what all those articles would cost me fabricated in France."

"That is a capital and quaint idea," replied D'Artagnan, "to have Dutch cannon-balls cast which will return to the Dutch."

"Is it not, with loss, too?" And Colbert laughed aloud. He was delighted with his own joke.

"Still further," added he, "these same Dutch are building for the king, at this moment, six vessels after the model of the best of their name. Destouches—Ah! perhaps you don't know Destouches?"

"No, monsieur."

"He is a man who has a sure glance to discern, when a ship is launched, what are the defects and qualities of that ship—that is valuable, observe! Nature is truly whimsical. Well, this Destouches appeared to me to be a man likely to prove useful in marine affairs, and he is superintending the construction of six vessels of seventy-eight guns, which the Provinces are building for his majesty. It results from this, my dear Monsieur d'Artagnan, that the king, if he wished to quarrel with the Provinces, would have a very pretty fleet. Now, you know better than anybody else if the land army is efficient."

D'Artagnan and Aramis looked at each other, wondering at the mysterious labors this man had undertaken in so short a time. Colbert understood them, and was touched by this best of flatteries.

"If we, in France, were ignorant of what was going

on," said D'Artagnan, "out of France still less must be known."

"That is why I told monsieur l'ambassadeur," said Colbert, "that, Spain promising its neutrality, England helping us—"

"If England assists you," said Aramis, "I promise the neutrality of Spain."

"I take you at your word," Colbert hastened to reply with his blunt *bonhomie*. "And, *a propos* of Spain, you have not the 'Golden Fleece,' Monsieur d'Almeda. I heard the king say the other day that he should like to see you wear the *grand cordon* of St. Michael."

Aramis bowed. "Oh!" thought D'Artagnan, "and Porthos is no longer here! What ells of ribbons would there be for him in these *largesses!* Dear Porthos!"

"Monsieur d'Artagnan," resumed Colbert, "between us two, you will have, I wager, an inclination to lead your musketeers into Holland. Can you swim?" And he laughed like a man in high good humor.

"Like an eel," replied D'Artagnan.

"Ah! but there are some bitter passages of canals and marshes yonder, Monsieur d'Artagnan, and the best swimmers are sometimes drowned there."

"It is my profession to die for his majesty," said the musketeer. "Only, as it is seldom in war that much water is met with without a little fire, I declare to you beforehand, that I will do my best to choose fire. I am getting old; water freezes me—but fire warms, Monsieur Colbert."

And D'Artagnan looked so handsome still in quasi-juvenile strength as he pronounced these words, that Colbert, in his turn, could not help admiring him. D'Artagnan perceived the effect he had produced. He remembered that the best tradesman is he who fixes a high price upon his goods, when they are valuable. He prepared his price in advance.

"So, then," said Colbert, "we go into Holland?"

"Yes," replied D'Artagnan; "only—"

"Only?" said M. Colbert.

"Only," repeated D'Artagnan, "there lurks in everything the question of interest, the question of self-love. It is a very fine title, that of captain of the musketeers; but observe this: we have now the king's guards and the military household of the king. A captain of musketeers ought to command all that, and then he would absorb a hundred thousand livres a year for expenses."

"Well! but do you suppose the king would haggle with you?" said Colbert.

"Eh! monsieur, you have not understood me," replied D'Artagnan, sure of carrying his point. "I was telling you that I, an old captain, formerly chief of the king's guard, having precedence of the *marechaux* of France—I saw myself one day in the trenches with two other equals, the captain of the guards and the colonel commanding the Swiss. Now, at no price will I suffer that. I have old habits, and I will stand or fall by them."

Colbert felt this blow, but he was prepared for it.

"I have been thinking of what you said just now," replied he.

"About what, monsieur?"

"We were speaking of canals and marshes in which people are drowned."

"Well!"

"Well! if they are drowned, it is for want of a boat, a plank, or a stick."

"Of a stick, however short it may be," said D'Artagnan.

"Exactly," said Colbert. "And, therefore, I never heard of an instance of a *marechal* of France being drowned."

D'Artagnan became very pale with joy, and in a not very firm voice, "People would be very proud of me in my country," said he, "if I were a *marechal* of France; but a man must have commanded an expedition in chief to obtain the *baton*."

"Monsieur!" said Colbert, "here is in this pocket-book which you will study, a plan of campaign you will have to lead a body of troops to carry out in the next spring."[12]

D'Artagnan took the book, tremblingly, and his fingers meeting those of Colbert, the minister pressed the hand of the musketeer loyally.

"Monsieur," said he, "we had both a revenge to take, one over the other. I have begun; it is now your turn!"

"I will do you justice, monsieur," replied D'Artagnan, "and implore you to tell the king that the first opportunity that shall offer, he may depend upon a victory, or to behold me dead—*or both*."

"Then I will have the *fleurs-de-lis* for your *marechal's baton* prepared immediately," said Colbert.

On the morrow, Aramis, who was setting out for Madrid, to negotiate the neutrality of Spain, came to embrace D'Artagnan at his hotel.

"Let us love each other for four," said D'Artagnan. "We are now but two."

"And you will, perhaps, never see me again, dear D'Artagnan," said Aramis; "if you knew how I have loved you! I am old, I am extinct—ah, I am almost dead."

"My friend," said D'Artagnan, "you will live longer than I shall: diplomacy commands you to live; but, for my part, honor condemns me to die."

"Bah! such men as we are, monsieur le marechal," said Aramis, "only die satisfied with joy in glory."

"Ah!" replied D'Artagnan, with a melancholy smile, "I assure you, monsieur le duc, I feel very little appetite for either."

They once more embraced, and, two hours after, separated—forever.

---

[12] This particular campaign did not actually occur until 1673.

The Death of D'Artagnan.

Contrary to that which generally happens, whether in politics or morals, each kept his promises, and did honor to his engagements.

The king recalled M. de Guiche, and banished M. le Chevalier de Lorraine; so that Monsieur became ill in consequence. Madame set out for London, where she applied herself so earnestly to make her brother, Charles II., acquire a taste for the political counsels of Mademoiselle de Keroualle, that the alliance between England and France was signed, and the English vessels, ballasted by a few millions of French gold, made a terrible campaign against the fleets of the United Provinces. Charles II. had promised Mademoiselle de Keroualle a little gratitude for her good counsels; he made her Duchess of Portsmouth. Colbert had promised the king vessels, munitions, victories. He kept his word, as is well known. At length Aramis, upon whose promises there was least dependence to be placed, wrote Colbert the following letter, on the subject of the negotiations which he had undertaken at Madrid:

"MONSIEUR COLBERT, —I have the honor to expedite to you the R. P. Oliva, general *ad interim* of the Society of Jesus, my provisional successor. The reverend father will explain to you, Monsieur Colbert, that I preserve to myself the direction of all the affairs of the order which concern France and Spain; but that I am not willing to retain the title of general, which would throw too high a side-light on the progress of the negotiations with which His Catholic Majesty wishes to intrust me. I shall resume that title by the command of his majesty, when the labors I have undertaken in concert with you, for the great glory of God and

His Church, shall be brought to a good end.
The R. P. Oliva will inform you likewise,
monsieur, of the consent His Catholic Majesty
gives to the signature of a treaty which assures
the neutrality of Spain in the event of a war
between France and the United Provinces. This
consent will be valid even if England, instead of
being active, should satisfy herself with
remaining neutral. As for Portugal, of which you
and I have spoken, monsieur, I can assure you it
will contribute with all its resources to assist
the Most Christian King in his war. I beg you,
Monsieur Colbert, to preserve your friendship
and also to believe in my profound attachment,
and to lay my respect at the feet of His Most
Christian Majesty.

Signed,
"LE DUC D'ALMEDA."[13]

Aramis had performed more than he had promised; it
remained to be seen how the king, M. Colbert, and D'Artagnan
would be faithful to each other. In the spring, as Colbert had
predicted, the land army entered on its campaign. It preceded,
in magnificent order, the court of Louis XIV., who, setting
out on horseback, surrounded by carriages filled with ladies
and courtiers, conducted the *elite* of his kingdom to this
sanguinary *fete*. The officers of the army, it is true, had no
other music save the artillery of the Dutch forts; but it was
enough for a great number, who found in this war honor,
advancement, fortune—or death.

M. d'Artagnan set out commanding a body of twelve
thousand men, cavalry, and infantry, with which he was
ordered to take the different places which form knots of

---

[13] Jean-Paul Oliva was the actual general of the Jesuits from 1664-1681.

that strategic network called La Frise. Never was an army conducted more gallantly to an expedition. The officers knew that their leader, prudent and skillful as he was brave, would not sacrifice a single man, nor yield an inch of ground without necessity. He had the old habits of war, to live upon the country, keeping his soldiers singing and the enemy weeping. The captain of the king's musketeers well knew his business. Never were opportunities better chosen, *coups-de-main* better supported, errors of the besieged more quickly taken advantage of.

The army commanded by D'Artagnan took twelve small places within a month. He was engaged in besieging the thirteenth, which had held out five days. D'Artagnan caused the trenches to be opened without appearing to suppose that these people would ever allow themselves to be taken. The pioneers and laborers were, in the army of this man, a body full of ideas and zeal, because their commander treated them like soldiers, knew how to render their work glorious, and never allowed them to be killed if he could help it. It should have been seen with what eagerness the marshy glebes of Holland were turned over. Those turf-heaps, mounds of potter's clay, melted at the word of the soldiers like butter in the frying-pans of Friesland housewives.

M. d'Artagnan dispatched a courier to the king to give him an account of the last success, which redoubled the good humor of his majesty and his inclination to amuse the ladies. These victories of M. d'Artagnan gave so much majesty to the prince, that Madame de Montespan no longer called him anything but Louis the Invincible. So that Mademoiselle de la Valliere, who only called the king Louis the Victorious, lost much of his majesty's favor. Besides, her eyes were frequently red, and to an Invincible nothing is more disagreeable than a mistress who weeps while everything is smiling round her. The star of Mademoiselle de la Valliere was being drowned in clouds and tears. But

the gayety of Madame de Montespan redoubled with the
successes of the king, and consoled him for every other
unpleasant circumstance. It was to D'Artagnan the king
owed this; and his majesty was anxious to acknowledge these
services; he wrote to M. Colbert:

> "MONSIEUR COLBERT,—We have a promise to
> fulfil with M. d'Artagnan, who so well keeps his.
> This is to inform you that the time is come for
> performing it. All provisions for this purpose you
> shall be furnished with in due time.
>
> LOUIS."

In consequence of this, Colbert, detaining D'Artagnan's
envoy, placed in the hands of that messenger a letter from
himself, and a small coffer of ebony inlaid with gold, not very
important in appearance, but which, without doubt, was very
heavy, as a guard of five men was given to the messenger, to
assist him in carrying it. These people arrived before the place
which D'Artagnan was besieging towards daybreak, and
presented themselves at the lodgings of the general. They
were told that M. d'Artagnan, annoyed by a sortie which the
governor, an artful man, had made the evening before, and
in which the works had been destroyed and seventy-seven
men killed, and the reparation of the breaches commenced,
had just gone with twenty companies of grenadiers to reconstruct the works.

M. Colbert's envoy had orders to go and seek
M. d'Artagnan, wherever he might be, or at whatever hour
of the day or night. He directed his course, therefore,
towards the trenches, followed by his escort, all on horseback. They perceived M. d'Artagnan in the open plain, with
his gold-laced hat, his long cane, and gilt cuffs. He was
biting his white mustache, and wiping off, with his left
hand, the dust which the passing balls threw up from the

ground they plowed so near him. They also saw, amidst this terrible fire, which filled the air with whistling hisses, officers handling the shovel, soldiers rolling barrows, and vast fascines, rising by being either carried or dragged by from ten to twenty men, cover the front of the trench reopened to the center by this extraordinary effort of the general. In three hours, all was reinstated. D'Artagnan began to speak more mildly; and he became quite calm when the captain of the pioneers approached him, hat in hand, to tell him that the trench was again in proper order. This man had scarcely finished speaking, when a ball took off one of his legs, and he fell into the arms of D'Artagnan. The latter lifted up his soldier, and quietly, with soothing words, carried him into the trench, amidst the enthusiastic applause of the regiments. From that time it was no longer a question of valor—the army was delirious; two companies stole away to the advanced posts, which they instantly destroyed.

When their comrades, restrained with great difficulty by D'Artagnan, saw them lodged upon the bastions, they rushed forward likewise; and soon a furious assault was made upon the counterscarp, upon which depended the safety of the place. D'Artagnan perceived there was only one means left of checking his army—to take the place. He directed all his force to the two breaches, where the besieged were busy in repairing. The shock was terrible; eighteen companies took part in it, and D'Artagnan went with the rest, within half cannon-shot of the place, to support the attack by *echelons*. The cries of the Dutch, who were being poniarded upon their guns by D'Artagnan's grenadiers, were distinctly audible. The struggle grew fiercer with the despair of the governor, who disputed his position foot by foot. D'Artagnan, to put an end to the affair, and to silence the fire, which was unceasing, sent a fresh column, which penetrated like a very wedge; and he soon perceived upon the ramparts, through the fire, the terrified flight of the besieged, pursued by the besiegers.

At this moment the general, breathing feely and full of joy, heard a voice behind him, saying, "Monsieur, if you please, from M. Colbert."

He broke the seal of the letter, which contained these words:

> "MONSIEUR D'ARTAGNAN:— The king commands me to inform you that he has nominated you marechal of France, as a reward for your magnificent services, and the honor you do to his arms. The king is highly pleased, monsieur, with the captures you have made; he commands you, in particular, to finish the siege you have commenced, with good fortune to you, and success for him."

D'Artagnan was standing with a radiant countenance and sparkling eye. He looked up to watch the progress of his troops upon the walls, still enveloped in red and black volumes of smoke. "I have finished," replied he to the messenger; "the city will have surrendered in a quarter of an hour." He then resumed his reading:

> "The *coffret*, Monsieur d'Artagnan, is my own present. You will not be sorry to see that, whilst you warriors are drawing the sword to defend the king, I am moving the pacific arts to ornament a present worthy of you. I commend myself to your friendship, monsieur le marechal, and beg you to believe in mine.
>
> COLBERT"

D'Artagnan, intoxicated with joy, made a sign to the messenger, who approached, with his *coffret* in his hands. But at the moment the *marechal* was going to look at it, a loud explosion resounded from the ramparts, and called his attention towards the city. "It is strange," said D'Artagnan, "that I don't yet see the king's flag on the walls, or hear the drums beat the *chamade*." He launched three hundred fresh men, under a high-spirited officer, and ordered another breach to be made. Then, more tranquilly, he turned towards the *coffret*, which Colbert's envoy held out to him.—It was his treasure—he had won it.

D'Artagnan was holding out his hand to open the *coffret*, when a ball from the city crushed the *coffret* in the arms of the officer, struck D'Artagnan full in the chest, and knocked him down upon a sloping heap of earth, whilst the *fleur-de-lised baton*, escaping from the broken box, came rolling under the powerless hand of the *marechal*. D'Artagnan endeavored to raise himself. It was thought he had been knocked down without being wounded. A terrible cry broke from the group of terrified officers; the *marechal* was covered with blood; the pallor of death ascended slowly to his noble countenance. Leaning upon the arms held out on all sides to receive him, he was able once more to turn his eyes towards the place, and to distinguish the white flag at the crest of the principal bastion; his ears, already deaf to the sounds of life, caught feebly the rolling of the drum which announced the victory. Then, clasping in his nerveless hand the *baton*, ornamented with its *fleurs-de-lis*, he cast on it his eyes, which had no longer the power of looking upwards towards Heaven, and fell back, murmuring strange words, which appeared to the soldiers cabalistic—words which had formerly represented so many things on earth, and which none but the dying man any longer comprehended:

"Athos—Porthos, farewell till we meet again! Aramis, adieu forever!"

Of the four valiant men whose history we have related, there now remained but one. Heaven had taken to itself three noble souls.[14]

[14] In earlier editions, the last line reads, "Of the four valiant men whose history we have related, there now no longer remained but one single body; God had resumed the souls." Dumas made the revision in later editions.

CLASSIC LITERATURE: WORDS AND PHRASES
adapted from the Collins English Dictionary

Accoucheur NOUN a male midwife or doctor ❏ *I think my sister must have had some general idea that I was a young offender whom an Accoucheur Policemen had taken up (on my birthday) and delivered over to her* (*Great Expectations* by Charles Dickens)

addled ADJ confused and unable to think properly ❏ *But she counted and counted till she got that addled* (*The Adventures of Huckleberry Finn* by Mark Twain)

admiration NOUN amazement or wonder ❏ *lifting up his hands and eyes by way of admiration* (*Gulliver's Travels* by Jonathan Swift)

afeard ADJ afeard means afraid ❏ *shake it – and don't be afeard* (*The Adventures of Huckleberry Finn* by Mark Twain)

affected VERB affected means followed ❏ *Hadst thou affected sweet divinity* (*Doctor Faustus 5.2* by Christopher Marlowe)

aground ADV when a boat runs aground, it touches the ground in a shallow part of the water and gets stuck ❏ *what kep' you? – boat get aground?* (*The Adventures of Huckleberry Finn* by Mark Twain)

ague NOUN a fever in which the patient has alternate hot and cold shivering fits ❏ *his exposure to the wet and cold had brought on fever and ague* (*Oliver Twist* by Charles Dickens)

alchemy ADJ false or worthless ❏ *all wealth alchemy* (*The Sun Rising* by John Donne)

all alike PHRASE the same all the time ❏ *Love, all alike* (*The Sun Rising* by John Donne)

alow and aloft PHRASE alow means in the lower part or bottom, and aloft means on the top, so alow and aloft means on the top and in the bottom or throughout ❏ *Someone's turned the chest out alow and aloft* (*Treasure Island* by Robert Louis Stevenson)

ambuscade NOUN ambuscade is not a proper word. Tom means an ambush, which is when a group of people attack their enemies, after hiding and waiting for them ❏ *and so we would lie in ambuscade, as he called it* (*The Adventures of Huckleberry Finn* by Mark Twain)

amiable ADJ likeable or pleasant ❏ *Such amiable qualities must speak for themselves* (*Pride and Prejudice* by Jane Austen)

amulet NOUN an amulet is a charm thought to drive away evil spirits. ❏ *uttered phrases at once occult and familiar, like the amulet worn on the heart* (*Silas Marner* by George Eliot)

amusement NOUN here amusement means a strange and disturbing puzzle ❏ *this was an amusement the other way* (*Robinson Crusoe* by Daniel Defoe)

ancient NOUN an ancient was the flag displayed on a ship to show which country it belongs to. It is also called the ensign ❏ *her ancient and pendants out* (*Robinson Crusoe* by Daniel Defoe)

antic ADJ here antic means horrible or grotesque ❏ *armed and dressed after a very antic manner* (*Gulliver's Travels* by Jonathan Swift)

antics NOUN antics is an old word meaning clowns, or people who do silly things to make other people laugh ❏ *And point like antics at his triple crown* (*Doctor Faustus 3.2* by Christopher Marlowe)

appanage NOUN an appanage is a living allowance ❏ *As if loveliness were* *not the special prerogative of woman – her legitimate appanage and heritage!* (*Jane Eyre* by Charlotte Brontë)

appended VERB appended means attached or added to ❏ *and these words appended* (*Treasure Island* by Robert Louis Stevenson)

approver NOUN an approver is someone who gives evidence against someone he used to work with ❏ *Mr. Noah Claypole: receiving a free pardon from the Crown in consequence of being admitted approver against Fagin* (*Oliver Twist* by Charles Dickens)

areas NOUN the areas is the space, below street level, in front of the basement of a house ❏ *The Dodger had a vicious propensity, too, of pulling the caps from the heads of small boys and tossing them down areas* (*Oliver Twist* by Charles Dickens)

argument NOUN theme or important idea or subject which runs through a piece of writing ❏ *Thrice needful to the argument which now* (*The Prelude* by William Wordsworth)

artificially ADJ artfully or cleverly ❏ *and he with a sharp flint sharpened very artificially* (*Gulliver's Travels* by Jonathan Swift)

artist NOUN here artist means a skilled workman ❏ *This man was a most ingenious artist* (*Gulliver's Travels* by Jonathan Swift)

assizes NOUN assizes were regular court sessions which a visiting judge was in charge of ❏ *you shall hang at the next assizes* (*Treasure Island* by Robert Louis Stevenson)

attraction NOUN gravitation, or Newton's theory of gravitation ❏ *he predicted the same fate to attraction* (*Gulliver's Travels* by Jonathan Swift)

aver VERB to aver is to claim something strongly ❏ *for Jem Rodney, the mole catcher, averred that one evening as*

he was returning homeward (*Silas Marner* by George Eliot)

baby NOUN here baby means doll, which is a child's toy that looks like a small person ❏ *and skilful dressing her baby* (*Gulliver's Travels* by Jonathan Swift)

bagatelle NOUN bagatelle is a game rather like billiards and pool ❏ *Breakfast had been ordered at a pleasant little tavern, a mile or so away upon the rising ground beyond the green; and there was a bagatelle board in the room, in case we should desire to unbend our minds after the solemnity.* (*Great Expectations* by Charles Dickens)

bah EXCLAM Bah is an exclamation of frustration or anger ❏ *"Bah," said Scrooge.* (*A Christmas Carol* by Charles Dickens)

bairn NOUN a northern word for child ❏ *Who has taught you those fine words, my bairn?* (*Wuthering Heights* by Emily Brontë)

bait VERB to bait means to stop on a journey to take refreshment ❏ *So, when they stopped to bait the horse, and ate and drank and enjoyed themselves, I could touch nothing that they touched, but kept my fast unbroken.* (*David Copperfield* by Charles Dickens)

balustrade NOUN a balustrade is a row of vertical columns that form railings ❏ *but I mean to say you might have got a hearse up that staircase, and taken it broadwise, with the splinter-bar towards the wall, and the door towards the balustrades: and done it easy* (*A Christmas Carol* by Charles Dickens)

bandbox NOUN a large lightweight box for carrying bonnets or hats ❏ *I am glad I bought my bonnet, if it is only for the fun of having another bandbox* (*Pride and Prejudice* by Jane Austen)

barren NOUN a barren here is a stretch or expanse of barren land ❏ *a line of upright stones, continued the* length of the barren (*Wuthering Heights* by Emily Brontë)

basin NOUN a basin was a cup without a handle ❑ *who is drinking his tea out of a basin* (*Wuthering Heights* by Emily Brontë)

battalia NOUN the order of battle ❑ *till I saw part of his army in battalia* (*Gulliver's Travels* by Jonathan Swift)

battery NOUN a Battery is a fort or a place where guns are positioned ❑ *You bring the lot to me, at that old Battery over yonder* (*Great Expectations* by Charles Dickens)

battledore and shuttlecock NOUN The game battledore and shuttlecock was an early version of the game now known as badminton. The aim of the early game was simply to keep the shuttlecock from hitting the ground. ❑ *Battledore and shuttlecock's a wery good game vhen you an't the shuttlecock and two lawyers the battledores, in which case it gets too excitin' to be pleasant* (*Pickwick Papers* by Charles Dickens)

beadle NOUN a beadle was a local official who had power over the poor ❑ *But these impertinences were speedily checked by the evidence of the surgeon, and the testimony of the beadle* (*Oliver Twist* by Charles Dickens)

bearings NOUN the bearings of a place are the measurements or directions that are used to find or locate it ❑ *the bearings of the island* (*Treasure Island* by Robert Louis Stevenson)

beaufet NOUN a beaufet was a sideboard ❑ *and sweet-cake from the beaufet* (*Emma* by Jane Austen)

beck NOUN a beck is a small stream ❑ *a beck which follows the bend of the glen* (*Wuthering Heights* by Emily Brontë)

bedight VERB decorated ❑ *and bedight with Christmas holly stuck into the top.* (*A Christmas Carol* by Charles Dickens)

Bedlam NOUN Bedlam was a lunatic asylum in London which had statues carved by Caius Gabriel Cibber at its entrance ❑ *Bedlam, and those carved maniacs at the gates* (*The Prelude* by William Wordsworth)

beeves NOUN oxen or castrated bulls which are animals used for pulling vehicles or carrying things ❑ *to deliver in every morning six beeves* (*Gulliver's Travels* by Jonathan Swift)

begot VERB created or caused ❑ *Begot in thee* (*On His Mistress* by John Donne)

behoof NOUN behoof means benefit ❑ *"Yes, young man," said he, releasing the handle of the article in question, retiring a step or two from my table, and speaking for the behoof of the landlord and waiter at the door* (*Great Expectations* by Charles Dickens)

berth NOUN a berth is a bed on a boat ❑ *this is the berth for me* (*Treasure Island* by Robert Louis Stevenson)

bevers NOUN a bever was a snack, or small portion of food, eaten between main meals ❑ *that buys me thirty meals a day and ten bevers* (*Doctor Faustus 2.1* by Christopher Marlowe)

bilge water NOUN the bilge is the widest part of a ship's bottom, and the bilge water is the dirty water that collects there ❑ *no gush of bilge-water had turned it to fetid puddle* (*Jane Eyre* by Charlotte Brontë)

bills NOUN bills is an old term meaning prescription. A prescription is the piece of paper on which your doctor writes an order for medicine and which you give to a chemist to get the medicine ❑ *Are not thy bills hung up as monuments* (*Doctor Faustus 1.1* by Christopher Marlowe)

black cap NOUN a judge wore a black cap when he was about to sentence a prisoner to death ❑ *The judge assumed the black cap, and the prisoner still stood with the same air*

*and gesture. (Oliver Twist by
Charles Dickens)*

black gentleman NOUN this was
another word for the devil ❑ *for
she is as impatient as the black
gentleman (Emma by Jane Austen)*

boot-jack NOUN a wooden device to
help take boots off ❑ *The speaker
appeared to throw a boot-jack, or
some such article, at the person he
addressed (Oliver Twist by Charles
Dickens)*

booty NOUN booty means treasure or
prizes ❑ *would be inclined to give
up their booty in payment of the
dead man's debts (Treasure Island
by Robert Louis Stevenson)*

Bow Street runner PHRASE Bow
Street runners were the first British
police force, set up by the author
Henry Fielding in the eighteenth
century ❑ *as would have convinced
a judge or a Bow Street runner
(Treasure Island by Robert Louis
Stevenson)*

brawn NOUN brawn is a dish of meat
which is set in jelly ❑ *Heaped up
upon the floor, to form a kind of
throne, were turkeys, geese, game,
poultry, brawn, great joints of meat,
sucking-pigs (A Christmas Carol by
Charles Dickens)*

bray VERB when a donkey brays, it
makes a loud, harsh sound ❑ *and
she doesn't bray like a jackass (The
Adventures of Huckleberry Finn by
Mark Twain)*

break VERB in order to train a horse
you first have to break it ❑"*If a
high-mettled creature like this," said
he, "can't be broken by fair means,
she will never be good for anything"
(Black Beauty by Anna Sewell)*

bullyragging VERB bullyragging is an
old word which means bullying. To
bullyrag someone is to threaten or
force someone to do something
they don't want to do ❑ *and a lot
of loafers bullyragging him for sport
(The Adventures of Huckleberry
Finn by Mark Twain)*

but PREP except for (this) ❑ *but this,
all pleasures fancies be (The
Good-Morrow by John Donne)*

by hand PHRASE by hand was a
common expression of the time
meaning that baby had been fed
either using a spoon or a bottle
rather than by breast-feeding ❑ *My
sister, Mrs. Joe Gargery, was more
than twenty years older than I, and
had established a great reputation
with herself . . . because she had
bought me up 'by hand' (Great
Expectations by Charles Dickens)*

bye-spots NOUN bye-spots are lonely
places ❑ *and bye-spots of tales rich
with indigenous produce (The
Prelude by William Wordsworth)*

calico NOUN calico is plain white fabric
made from cotton ❑ *There was two
old dirty calico dresses (The
Adventures of Huckleberry Finn by
Mark Twain)*

camp-fever NOUN camp-fever was
another word for the disease typhus
❑ *during a severe camp-fever
(Emma by Jane Austen)*

cant NOUN cant is insincere or empty
talk ❑ *"Man," said the Ghost, "if
man you be in heart, not adamant,
forbear that wicked cant until you
have discovered What the surplus is,
and Where it is." (A Christmas
Carol by Charles Dickens)*

canty ADJ canty means lively, full of
life ❑ *My mother lived til eighty, a
canty dame to the last (Wuthering
Heights by Emily Brontë)*

canvas VERB to canvas is to discuss ❑
*We think so very differently on this
point Mr Knightley, that there can
be no use in canvassing it (Emma
by Jane Austen)*

capital ADJ capital means excellent or
extremely good ❑ *for it's capital, so
shady, light, and big (Little Women
by Louisa May Alcott)*

capstan NOUN a capstan is a device used
on a ship to lift sails and anchors ❑
*capstans going, ships going out to sea,
and unintelligible sea creatures*

roaring curses over the bulwarks at respondent lightermen (*Great Expectations* by Charles Dickens)

case-bottle NOUN a square bottle designed to fit with others into a case ❑ *The spirit being set before him in a huge case-bottle, which had originally come out of some ship's locker* (*The Old Curiosity Shop* by Charles Dickens)

casement NOUN casement is a word meaning window. The teacher in Nicholas Nickleby misspells window showing what a bad teacher he is ❑ *W-i-n, win, d-e-r, der, winder, a casement.'* (*Nicholas Nickleby* by Charles Dickens)

cataleptic ADJ a cataleptic fit is one in which the victim goes into a trancelike state and remains still for a long time ❑ *It was at this point in their history that Silas's cataleptic fit occurred during the prayer-meeting* (*Silas Marner* by George Eliot)

cauldron NOUN a cauldron is a large cooking pot made of metal ❑ *stirring a large cauldron which seemed to be full of soup* (*Alice's Adventures in Wonderland* by Lewis Carroll)

cephalic ADJ cephalic means to do with the head ❑ *with ink composed of a cephalic tincture* (*Gulliver's Travels* by Jonathan Swift)

chaise and four NOUN a closed four-wheel carriage pulled by four horses ❑ *he came down on Monday in a chaise and four to see the place* (*Pride and Prejudice* by Jane Austen)

chamberlain NOUN the main servant in a household ❑ *In those times a bed was always to be got there at any hour of the night, and the chamberlain, letting me in at his ready wicket, lighted the candle next in order on his shelf* (*Great Expectations* by Charles Dickens)

characters NOUN distinguishing marks ❑ *Impressed upon all forms the characters* (*The Prelude* by William Wordsworth)

chary ADJ cautious ❑ *I should have been chary of discussing my guardian too freely even with her* (*Great Expectations* by Charles Dickens)

cherishes VERB here cherishes means cheers or brightens ❑ *some philosophical song of Truth that cherishes our daily life* (*The Prelude* by William Wordsworth)

chickens' meat PHRASE chickens' meat is an old term which means chickens' feed or food ❑ *I had shook a bag of chickens' meat out in that place* (*Robinson Crusoe* by Daniel Defoe)

chimeras NOUN a chimera is an unrealistic idea or a wish which is unlikely to be fulfilled ❑ *with many other wild impossible chimeras* (*Gulliver's Travels* by Jonathan Swift)

chines NOUN chine is a cut of meat that includes part or all of the backbone of the animal ❑ *and they found hams and chines uncut* (*Silas Marner* by George Eliot)

chits NOUN chits is a slang word which means girls ❑ *I hate affected, niminy-piminy chits!* (*Little Women* by Louisa May Alcott)

chopped VERB chopped means come suddenly or accidentally ❑ *if I had chopped upon them* (*Robinson Crusoe* by Daniel Defoe)

chute NOUN a narrow channel ❑ *One morning about day-break, I found a canoe and crossed over a chute to the main shore* (*The Adventures of Huckleberry Finn* by Mark Twain)

circumspection NOUN careful observation of events and circumstances; caution ❑ *I honour your circumspection* (*Pride and Prejudice* by Jane Austen)

clambered VERB clambered means to climb somewhere with difficulty, usually using your hands and your feet ❑ *he clambered up and down stairs* (*Treasure Island* by Robert Louis Stevenson)

clime NOUN climate ❏ *no season knows nor clime* (*The Sun Rising* by John Donne)

clinched VERB clenched ❏ *the tops whereof I could but just reach with my fist clinched* (*Gulliver's Travels* by Jonathan Swift)

close chair NOUN a close chair is a sedan chair, which is a covered chair which has room for one person. The sedan chair is carried on two poles by two men, one in front and one behind ❏ *persuaded even the Empress herself to let me hold her in her close chair* (*Gulliver's Travels* by Jonathan Swift)

clown NOUN clown here means peasant or person who lives off the land ❏ *In ancient days by emperor and clown* (*Ode on a Nightingale* by John Keats)

coalheaver NOUN a coalheaver loaded coal onto ships using a spade ❏ *Good, strong, wholesome medicine, as was given with great success to two Irish labourers and a coalheaver* (*Oliver Twist* by Charles Dickens)

coal-whippers NOUN men who worked at docks using machines to load coal onto ships ❏ *here, were colliers by the score and score, with the coal-whippers plunging off stages on deck* (*Great Expectations* by Charles Dickens)

cobweb NOUN a cobweb is the net which a spider makes for catching insects ❏ *the walls and ceilings were all hung round with cobwebs* (*Gulliver's Travels* by Jonathan Swift)

coddling VERB coddling means to treat someone too kindly or protect them too much ❏ *and I've been coddling the fellow as if I'd been his grandmother* (*Little Women* by Louisa May Alcott)

coil NOUN coil means noise or fuss or disturbance ❏ *What a coil is there?* (*Doctor Faustus 4.7* by Christopher Marlowe)

collared VERB to collar something is a slang term which means to capture.

In this sentence, it means he stole it [the money] ❏ *he collared it* (*The Adventures of Huckleberry Finn* by Mark Twain)

colling VERB colling is an old word which means to embrace and kiss ❏ *and no clasping and colling at all* (*Tess of the D'Urbervilles* by Thomas Hardy)

colloquies NOUN colloquy is a formal conversation or dialogue ❏ *Such colloquies have occupied many a pair of pale-faced weavers* (*Silas Marner* by George Eliot)

comfit NOUN sugar-covered pieces of fruit or nut eaten as sweets ❏ *and pulled out a box of comfits* (*Alice's Adventures in Wonderland* by Lewis Carroll)

coming out VERB when a girl came out in society it meant she was of marriageable age. In order to 'come out' girls were expecting to attend balls and other parties during a season ❏ *The younger girls formed hopes of coming out a year or two sooner than they might otherwise have done* (*Pride and Prejudice* by Jane Austen)

commit VERB commit means arrest or stop ❏ *Commit the rascals* (*Doctor Faustus 4.7* by Christopher Marlowe)

commodious ADJ commodious means convenient ❏ *the most commodious and effectual ways* (*Gulliver's Travels* by Jonathan Swift)

commons NOUN commons is an old term meaning food shared with others ❏ *his pauper assistants ranged themselves behind him; the gruel was served out; and a long grace was said over the short commons.* (*Oliver Twist* by Charles Dickens)

complacency NOUN here complacency means a desire to please others. To-day complacency means feeling pleased with oneself without good reason. ❏ *Twas thy power that raised the first complacency in me* (*The Prelude* by William Wordsworth)

complaisance NOUN complaisance was eagerness to please ❑ *we cannot wonder at his complaisance* (*Pride and Prejudice* by Jane Austen)

complaisant ADJ complaisant means polite ❑ *extremely cheerful and complaisant to their guest* (*Gulliver's Travels* by Jonathan Swift)

conning VERB conning means learning by heart ❑ *Or conning more* (*The Prelude* by William Wordsworth)

consequent NOUN consequence ❑ *as avarice is the necessary consequent of old age* (*Gulliver's Travels* by Jonathan Swift)

consorts NOUN concerts ❑ *The King, who delighted in music, had frequent consorts at Court* (*Gulliver's Travels* by Jonathan Swift)

conversible ADJ conversible meant easy to talk to, companionable ❑ *He can be a conversible companion* (*Pride and Prejudice* by Jane Austen)

copper NOUN a copper is a large pot that can be heated directly over a fire ❑ *He gazed in stupefied astonishment on the small rebel for some seconds, and then clung for support to the copper* (*Oliver Twist* by Charles Dickens)

copper-stick NOUN a copper-stick is the long piece of wood used to stir washing in the copper (or boiler) which was usually the biggest cooking pot in the house ❑ *It was Christmas Eve, and I had to stir the pudding for next day, with a copper-stick, from seven to eight by the Dutch clock* (*Great Expectations* by Charles Dickens)

counting-house NOUN a counting house is a place where accountants work ❑ *Once upon a time – of all the good days in the year, on Christmas Eve – old Scrooge sat busy in his countinghouse* (*A Christmas Carol* by Charles Dickens)

courtier NOUN a courtier is someone who attends the king or queen – a member of the court ❑ *next the ten courtiers;* (*Alice's Adventures in Wonderland* by Lewis Carroll)

covies NOUN covies were flocks of partridges ❑ *and will save all of the best covies for you* (*Pride and Prejudice* by Jane Austen)

cowed VERB cowed means frightened or intimidated ❑ *it cowed me more than the pain* (*Treasure Island* by Robert Louis Stevenson)

cozened VERB cozened means tricked or deceived ❑ *Do you remember, sir, how you cozened me* (*Doctor Faustus 4.7* by Christopher Marlowe)

cravats NOUN a cravat is a folded cloth that a man wears wrapped around his neck as a decorative item of clothing ❑ *we'd a' slept in our cravats to-night* (*The Adventures of Huckleberry Finn* by Mark Twain)

crock and dirt PHRASE crock and dirt is an old expression meaning soot and dirt ❑ *and the mare catching cold at the door, and the boy grimed with crock and dirt* (*Great Expectations* by Charles Dickens)

crockery NOUN here crockery means pottery ❑ *By one of the parrots was a cat made of crockery* (*The Adventures of Huckleberry Finn* by Mark Twain)

crooked sixpence PHRASE it was considered unlucky to have a bent sixpence ❑ *You've got the beauty, you see, and I've got the luck, so you must keep me by you for your crooked sixpence* (*Silas Marner* by George Eliot)

croquet NOUN croquet is a traditional English summer game in which players try to hit wooden balls through hoops ❑ *and once she remembered trying to box her own ears for having cheated herself in a game of croquet* (*Alice's Adventures in Wonderland* by Lewis Carroll)

cross PREP across ❑ *The two great streets, which run cross and divide it into four quarters* (*Gulliver's Travels* by Jonathan Swift)

culpable ADJ if you are culpable for something it means you are to blame ❑ *deep are the sorrows that spring from false ideas for which no man is culpable.* (*Silas Marner* by George Eliot)

cultured ADJ cultivated ❑ *Nor less when spring had warmed the cultured Vale* (*The Prelude* by William Wordsworth)

cupidity NOUN cupidity is greed ❑ *These people hated me with the hatred of cupidity and disappointment.* (*Great Expectations* by Charles Dickens)

curricle NOUN an open two-wheeled carriage with one seat for the driver and space for a single passenger ❑ *and they saw a lady and a gentleman in a curricle* (*Pride and Prejudice* by Jane Austen)

cynosure NOUN a cynosure is something that strongly attracts attention or admiration ❑ *Then I thought of Eliza and Georgiana; I beheld one the cynosure of a ballroom, the other the inmate of a convent cell* (*Jane Eyre* by Charlotte Brontë)

dalliance NOUN someone's dalliance with something is a brief involvement with it ❑ *nor sporting in the dalliance of love* (*Doctor Faustus Chorus* by Christopher Marlowe)

darkling ADV darkling is an archaic way of saying in the dark ❑ *Darkling I listen* (*Ode on a Nightingale* by John Keats)

delf-case NOUN a sideboard for holding dishes and crockery ❑ *at the pewter dishes and delf-case* (*Wuthering Heights* by Emily Brontë)

determined ■ VERB here determined means ended ❑ *and be out of vogue when that was determined* (*Gulliver's Travels* by Jonathan Swift) ■ VERB determined can mean to have been learned or found especially by investigation or experience ❑ *All the sensitive feelings it wounded so cruelly, all the shame and misery it kept alive within my breast, became more*

poignant as I thought of this; and I determined that the life was unendurable (*David Copperfield* by Charles Dickens)

Deuce NOUN a slang term for the Devil ❑ *Ah, I dare say I did. Deuce take me, he added suddenly, I know I did. I find I am not quite unscrewed yet.* (*Great Expectations* by Charles Dickens)

diabolical ADJ diabolical means devilish or evil ❑ *and with a thousand diabolical expressions* (*Treasure Island* by Robert Louis Stevenson)

direction NOUN here direction means address ❑ *Elizabeth was not surprised at it, as Jane had written the direction remarkably ill* (*Pride and Prejudice* by Jane Austen)

discover VERB to make known or announce ❑ *the Emperor would discover the secret while I was out of his power* (*Gulliver's Travels* by Jonathan Swift)

dissemble VERB hide or conceal ❑ *Dissemble nothing* (*On His Mistress* by John Donne)

dissolve VERB dissolve here means to release from life, to die ❑ *Fade far away, dissolve, and quite forget* (*Ode on a Nightingale* by John Keats)

distrain VERB to distrain is to seize the property of someone who is in debt in compensation for the money owed ❑ *for he's threatening to distrain for it* (*Silas Marner* by George Eliot)

Divan NOUN a Divan was originally a Turkish council of state – the name was transferred to the couches they sat on and is used to mean this in English ❑ *Mr Brass applauded this picture very much, and the bed being soft and comfortable, Mr Quilp determined to use it, both as a sleeping place by night and as a kind of Divan by day.* (*The Old Curiosity Shop* by Charles Dickens)

divorcement NOUN separation ❑ *By all pains which want and* *divorcement hath* (*On His Mistress* by John Donne)

dog in the manger, PHRASE this phrase describes someone who prevents you from enjoying something that they themselves have no need for ❏ *You are a dog in the manger, Cathy, and desire no one to be loved but yourself* (*Wuthering Heights* by Emily Brontë)

dolorifuge NOUN dolorifuge is a word which Thomas Hardy invented. It means pain-killer or comfort ❏ *as a species of dolorifuge* (*Tess of the D'Urbervilles* by Thomas Hardy)

dome NOUN building ❏ *that river and that mouldering dome* (*The Prelude* by William Wordsworth)

domestic PHRASE here domestic means a person's management of the house ❏ *to give some account of my domestic* (*Gulliver's Travels* by Jonathan Swift)

dunce NOUN a dunce is another word for idiot ❏ *Do you take me for a dunce? Go on?* (*Alice's Adventures in Wonderland* by Lewis Carroll)

Ecod EXCLAM a slang exclamation meaning 'oh God!' ❏ *"Ecod," replied Wemmick, shaking his head, "that's not my trade."* (*Great Expectations* by Charles Dickens)

egg-hot NOUN an egg-hot (see also 'flip' and 'negus') was a hot drink made from beer and eggs, sweetened with nutmeg ❏ *She fainted when she saw me return, and made a little jug of egg-hot afterwards to console us while we talked it over.* (*David Copperfield* by Charles Dickens)

encores NOUN an encore is a short extra performance at the end of a longer one, which the entertainer gives because the audience has enthusiastically asked for it ❏ *we want a little something to answer encores with, anyway* (*The Adventures of Huckleberry Finn* by Mark Twain)

equipage NOUN an elegant and impressive carriage ❏ *and besides, the equipage did not answer to any*

of their neighbours (*Pride and Prejudice* by Jane Austen)

exordium NOUN an exordium is the opening part of a speech ❏ *"Now, Handel," as if it were the grave beginning of a portentous business exordium, he had suddenly given up that tone* (*Great Expectations* by Charles Dickens)

expect VERB here expect means to wait for ❏ *to expect his farther commands* (*Gulliver's Travels* by Jonathan Swift)

familiars NOUN familiars means spirits or devils who come to someone when they are called ❏ *I'll turn all the lice about thee into familiars* (*Doctor Faustus 1.4* by Christopher Marlowe)

fantods NOUN a fantod is a person who fidgets or can't stop moving nervously ❏ *It most give me the fantods* (*The Adventures of Huckleberry Finn* by Mark Twain)

farthing NOUN a farthing is an old unit of British currency which was worth a quarter of a penny ❏ *Not a farthing less. A great many back-payments are included in it, I assure you.* (*A Christmas Carol* by Charles Dickens)

farthingale NOUN a hoop worn under a skirt to extend it ❏ *A bell with an old voice – which I dare say in its time had often said to the house, Here is the green farthingale* (*Great Expectations* by Charles Dickens)

favours NOUN here favours is an old word which means ribbons ❏ *A group of humble mourners entered the gate: wearing white favours* (*Oliver Twist* by Charles Dickens)

feigned VERB pretend or pretending ❏ *not my feigned page* (*On His Mistress* by John Donne)

fence ■ NOUN a fence is someone who receives and sells stolen goods ❏ *What are you up to? Ill-treating the boys, you covetous, avaricious, in-sa-ti-a-ble old fence?* (*Oliver Twist* by

Charles Dickens) ■ NOUN defence or protection ❑ *but honesty hath no fence against superior cunning* (*Gulliver's Travels* by Jonathan Swift)

fess ADJ fess is an old word which means pleased or proud ❑ *You'll be fess enough, my poppet* (*Tess of the D'Urbervilles* by Thomas Hardy)

fettered ADJ fettered means bound in chains or chained ❑ *"You are fettered," said Scrooge, trembling. "Tell me why?"* (*A Christmas Carol* by Charles Dickens)

fidges VERB fidges means fidgets, which is to keep moving your hands slightly because you are nervous or excited ❑ *Look, Jim, how my fingers fidges* (*Treasure Island* by Robert Louis Stevenson)

finger-post NOUN a finger-post is a sign-post showing the direction to different places ❑ *"The gallows," continued Fagin, "the gallows, my dear, is an ugly finger-post, which points out a very short and sharp turning that has stopped many a bold fellow's career on the broad highway."* (*Oliver Twist* by Charles Dickens)

fire-irons NOUN fire-irons are tools kept by the side of the fire to either cook with or look after the fire ❑ *the fire-irons came first* (*Alice's Adventures in Wonderland* by Lewis Carroll)

fire-plug NOUN a fire-plug is another word for a fire hydrant ❑ *The pony looked with great attention into a fire-plug, which was near him, and appeared to be quite absorbed in contemplating it* (*The Old Curiosity Shop* by Charles Dickens)

flank NOUN flank is the side of an animal ❑ *And all her silken flanks with garlands dressed* (*Ode on a Grecian Urn* by John Keats)

flip NOUN a flip is a drink made from warmed ale, sugar, spice and beaten egg ❑ *The events of the day, in combination with the twins, if not with the flip, had made Mrs. Micawber hysterical, and she shed tears as she replied* (*David Copperfield* by Charles Dickens)

flit VERB flit means to move quickly ❑ *and if he had meant to flit to Thrushcross Grange* (*Wuthering Heights* by Emily Brontë)

floorcloth NOUN a floorcloth was a hard-wearing piece of canvas used instead of carpet ❑ *This avenging phantom was ordered to be on duty at eight on Tuesday morning in the hall (it was two feet square, as charged for floorcloth)* (*Great Expectations* by Charles Dickens)

fly-driver NOUN a fly-driver is a carriage drawn by a single horse ❑ *The fly-drivers, among whom I inquired next, were equally jocose and equally disrespectful* (*David Copperfield* by Charles Dickens)

fob NOUN a small pocket in which a watch is kept ❑ *"Certain," replied the man, drawing a gold watch from his fob* (*Oliver Twist* by Charles Dickens)

folly NOUN folly means foolishness or stupidity ❑ *the folly of beginning a work* (*Robinson Crusoe* by Daniel Defoe)

fond ADJ fond means foolish ❑ *Fond worldling* (*Doctor Faustus 5.2* by Christopher Marlowe)

fondness NOUN silly or foolish affection ❑ *They have no fondness for their colts or foals* (*Gulliver's Travels* by Jonathan Swift)

for his fancy PHRASE for his fancy means for his liking or as he wanted ❑ *and as I did not obey quick enough for his fancy* (*Treasure Island* by Robert Louis Stevenson)

forlorn ADJ lost or very upset ❑ *you are from that day forlorn* (*Gulliver's Travels* by Jonathan Swift)

foster-sister NOUN a foster-sister was someone brought up by the same nurse or in the same household ❑ *I had been his foster-sister* (*Wuthering Heights* by Emily Brontë)

fox-fire NOUN fox-fire is a weak glow that is given off by decaying, rotten wood ❏ *what we must have was a lot of them rotten chunks that's called fox-fire* (*The Adventures of Huckleberry Finn* by Mark Twain)

frozen sea PHRASE the Arctic Ocean ❏ *into the frozen sea* (*Gulliver's Travels* by Jonathan Swift)

gainsay VERB to gainsay something is to say it isn't true or to deny it ❏ *"So she had," cried Scrooge. "You're right. I'll not gainsay it, Spirit. God forbid!"* (*A Christmas Carol* by Charles Dickens)

gaiters NOUN gaiters were leggings made of a cloth or piece of leather which covered the leg from the knee to the ankle ❏ *Mr Knightley was hard at work upon the lower buttons of his thick leather gaiters* (*Emma* by Jane Austen)

galluses NOUN galluses is an old spelling of gallows, and here means suspenders. Suspenders are straps worn over someone's shoulders and fastened to their trousers to prevent the trousers falling down ❏ *and home-knit galluses* (*The Adventures of Huckleberry Finn* by Mark Twain)

galoot NOUN a sailor but also a clumsy person ❏ *and maybe a galoot on it chopping* (*The Adventures of Huckleberry Finn* by Mark Twain)

gayest ADJ gayest means the most lively and bright or merry ❏ *Beth played her gayest march* (*Little Women* by Louisa May Alcott)

gem NOUN here gem means jewellery ❏ *the mountain shook off turf and flower, had only heath for raiment and crag for gem* (*Jane Eyre* by Charlotte Brontë)

giddy ADJ giddy means dizzy ❏ *and I wish you wouldn't keep appearing and vanishing so suddenly; you make one quite giddy.* (*Alice's Adventures in Wonderland* by Lewis Carroll)

gig NOUN a light two-wheeled carriage ❏ *when a gig drove up to the garden gate: out of which there jumped a fat gentleman* (*Oliver Twist* by Charles Dickens)

gladsome ADJ gladsome is an old word meaning glad or happy ❏ *Nobody ever stopped him in the street to say, with gladsome looks* (*A Christmas Carol* by Charles Dickens)

glen NOUN a glen is a small valley; the word is used commonly in Scotland ❏ *a beck which follows the bend of the glen* (*Wuthering Heights* by Emily Brontë)

gravelled VERB gravelled is an old term which means to baffle or defeat someone ❏ *Gravelled the pastors of the German Church* (*Doctor Faustus* 1.1 by Christopher Marlowe)

grinder NOUN a grinder was a private tutor ❏ *but that when he had had the happiness of marrying Mrs Pocket very early in his life, he had impaired his prospects and taken up the calling of a Grinder* (*Great Expectations* by Charles Dickens)

gruel NOUN gruel is a thin, watery cornmeal or oatmeal soup ❏ *and the little saucepan of gruel (Scrooge had a cold in his head) upon the hob.* (*A Christmas Carol* by Charles Dickens)

guinea, half NOUN a half guinea was ten shillings and sixpence ❏ *but lay out half a guinea at Ford's* (*Emma* by Jane Austen)

gull VERB gull is an old term which means to fool or deceive someone ❏ *Hush, I'll gull him supernaturally* (*Doctor Faustus* 3.4 by Christopher Marlowe)

gunnel NOUN the gunnel, or gunwhale, is the upper edge of a boat's side ❏ *But he put his foot on the gunnel and rocked her* (*The Adventures of Huckleberry Finn* by Mark Twain)

gunwale NOUN the side of a ship ❏ *He dipped his hand in the water over the boat's gunwale* (*Great Expectations* by Charles Dickens)

Gytrash NOUN a Gytrash is an omen of misfortune to the superstitious, usually taking the form of a hound ❑ *I remembered certain of Bessie's tales, wherein figured a North-of-England spirit, called a 'Gytrash'* (*Jane Eyre* by Charlotte Brontë)

hackney-cabriolet NOUN a two-wheeled carriage with four seats for hire and pulled by a horse ❑ *A hackney-cabriolet was in waiting; with the same vehemence which she had exhibited in addressing Oliver, the girl pulled him in with her, and drew the curtains close.* (*Oliver Twist* by Charles Dickens)

hackney-coach NOUN a four-wheeled horse-drawn vehicle for hire ❑ *The twilight was beginning to close in, when Mr. Brownlow alighted from a hackney-coach at his own door, and knocked softly.* (*Oliver Twist* by Charles Dickens)

haggler NOUN a haggler is someone who travels from place to place selling small goods and items ❑ *when I be plain Jack Durbeyfield, the haggler* (*Tess of the D'Urbervilles* by Thomas Hardy)

halter NOUN a halter is a rope or strap used to lead an animal or to tie it up ❑ *I had of course long been used to a halter and a headstall* (*Black Beauty* by Anna Sewell)

hamlet NOUN a hamlet is a small village or a group of houses in the countryside ❑ *down from the hamlet* (*Treasure Island* by Robert Louis Stevenson)

hand-barrow NOUN a hand-barrow is a device for carrying heavy objects. It is like a wheelbarrow except that it has handles, rather than wheels, for moving the barrow ❑ *his sea chest following behind him in a hand-barrow* (*Treasure Island* by Robert Louis Stevenson)

handspike NOUN a handspike was a stick which was used as a lever ❑ *a bit of stick like a handspike* (*Treasure Island* by Robert Louis Stevenson)

haply ADV haply means by chance or perhaps ❑ *And haply the Queen-Moon is on her throne* (*Ode on a Nightingale* by John Keats)

harem NOUN the harem was the part of the house where the women lived ❑ *mostly they hang round the harem* (*The Adventures of Huckleberry Finn* by Mark Twain)

hautboys NOUN hautboys are oboes ❑ *sausages and puddings resembling flutes and hautboys* (*Gulliver's Travels* by Jonathan Swift)

hawker NOUN a hawker is someone who sells goods to people as he travels rather than from a fixed place like a shop ❑ *to buy some stockings from a hawker* (*Treasure Island* by Robert Louis Stevenson)

hawser NOUN a hawser is a rope used to tie up or tow a ship or boat ❑ *Again among the tiers of shipping, in and out, avoiding rusty chain-cables, frayed hempen hawsers* (*Great Expectations* by Charles Dickens)

headstall NOUN the headstall is the part of the bridle or halter that goes around a horse's head ❑ *I had of course long been used to a halter and a headstall* (*Black Beauty* by Anna Sewell)

hearken VERB hearken means to listen ❑ *though we sometimes stopped to lay hold of each other and hearken* (*Treasure Island* by Robert Louis Stevenson)

heartless ADJ here heartless means without heart or dejected ❑ *I am not heartless* (*The Prelude* by William Wordsworth)

hebdomadal ADJ hebdomadal means weekly ❑ *It was the hebdomadal treat to which we all looked forward from Sabbath to Sabbath* (*Jane Eyre* by Charlotte Brontë)

highwaymen NOUN highwaymen were people who stopped travellers and robbed them ❑ *We are highwaymen* (*The Adventures of Huckleberry Finn* by Mark Twain)

hinds NOUN hinds means farm hands, or people who work on a farm ❑ *He called his hinds about him* (*Gulliver's Travels* by Jonathan Swift)

histrionic ADJ if you refer to someone's behaviour as histrionic, you are being critical of it because it is dramatic and exaggerated ❑ *But the histrionic muse is the darling* (*The Adventures of Huckleberry Finn* by Mark Twain)

hogs NOUN hogs is another word for pigs ❑ *Tom called the hogs 'ingots'* (*The Adventures of Huckleberry Finn* by Mark Twain)

horrors NOUN the horrors are a fit, called delirium tremens, which is caused by drinking too much alcohol ❑ *I'll have the horrors* (*Treasure Island* by Robert Louis Stevenson)

huffy ADJ huffy means to be obviously annoyed or offended about something ❑ *They will feel that more than angry speeches or huffy actions* (*Little Women* by Louisa May Alcott)

hulks NOUN hulks were prison-ships ❑ *The miserable companion of thieves and ruffians, the fallen outcast of low haunts, the associate of the scourings of the jails and hulks* (*Oliver Twist* by Charles Dickens)

humbug NOUN humbug means nonsense or rubbish ❑ *"Bah," said Scrooge. "Humbug!"* (*A Christmas Carol* by Charles Dickens)

humours NOUN it was believed that there were four fluids in the body called humours which decided the temperament of a person depending on how much of each fluid was present ❑ *other peccant humours* (*Gulliver's Travels* by Jonathan Swift)

husbandry NOUN husbandry is farming animals ❑ *bad husbandry were plentifully anointing their wheels* (*Silas Marner* by George Eliot)

huswife NOUN a huswife was a small sewing kit ❑ *but I had put my huswife on it* (*Emma* by Jane Austen)

ideal ADJ ideal in this context means imaginary ❑ *I discovered the yell was not ideal* (*Wuthering Heights* by Emily Brontë)

If our two PHRASE if both our ❑ *If our two loves be one* (*The Good-Morrow* by John Donne)

ignis-fatuus NOUN ignis-fatuus is the light given out by burning marsh gases, which lead careless travellers into danger ❑ *it is madness in all women to let a secret love kindle within them, which, if unreturned and unknown, must devour the life that feeds it; and, if discovered and responded to, must lead ignis-fatuus-like, into miry wilds whence there is no extrication.* (*Jane Eyre* by Charlotte Brontë)

imaginations NOUN here imaginations means schemes or plans ❑ *soon drove out those imaginations* (*Gulliver's Travels* by Jonathan Swift)

impressible ADJ impressible means open or impressionable ❑ *for Marner had one of those impressible, self-doubting natures* (*Silas Marner* by George Eliot)

in good intelligence PHRASE friendly with each other ❑ *that these two persons were in good intelligence with each other* (*Gulliver's Travels* by Jonathan Swift)

inanity NOUN inanity is silliness or dull stupidity ❑ *Do we not wile away moments of inanity* (*Silas Marner* by George Eliot)

incivility NOUN incivility means rudeness or impoliteness ❑ *if it's only for a piece of incivility like to-night's* (*Treasure Island* by Robert Louis Stevenson)

indigenae NOUN indigenae means natives or people from that area ❑ *an exotic that the surly indigenae will not recognise for kin* (*Wuthering Heights* by Emily Brontë)

indocible ADJ unteachable ❑ *so they were the most restive and indocible* (*Gulliver's Travels* by Jonathan Swift)

ingenuity NOUN inventiveness ❏ *entreated me to give him something as an encouragement to ingenuity* (*Gulliver's Travels* by Jonathan Swift)

ingots NOUN an ingot is a lump of a valuable metal like gold, usually shaped like a brick ❏ *Tom called the hogs 'ingots'* (*The Adventures of Huckleberry Finn* by Mark Twain)

inkstand NOUN an inkstand is a pot which was put on a desk to contain either ink or pencils and pens ❏ *throwing an inkstand at the Lizard as she spoke* (*Alice's Adventures in Wonderland* by Lewis Carroll)

inordinate ADJ without order. To-day inordinate means 'excessive'. ❏ *Though yet untutored and inordinate* (*The Prelude* by William Wordsworth)

intellectuals NOUN here intellectuals means the minds (of the workmen) ❏ *those instructions they give being too refined for the intellectuals of their workmen* (*Gulliver's Travels* by Jonathan Swift)

interview NOUN meeting ❏ *By our first strange and fatal interview* (*On His Mistress* by John Donne)

jacks NOUN jacks are rods for turning a spit over a fire ❏ *It was a small bit of pork suspended from the kettle hanger by a string passed through a large door key, in a way known to primitive housekeepers unpossessed of jacks* (*Silas Marner* by George Eliot)

jews-harp NOUN a jews-harp is a small, metal, musical instrument that is played by the mouth ❏ *A jews-harp's plenty good enough for a rat* (*The Adventures of Huckleberry Finn* by Mark Twain)

jorum NOUN a large bowl ❏ *while Miss Skiffins brewed such a jorum of tea, that the pig in the back premises became strongly excited* (*Great Expectations* by Charles Dickens)

jostled VERB jostled means bumped or pushed by someone or some people

❏ *being jostled himself into the kennel* (*Gulliver's Travels* by Jonathan Swift)

keepsake NOUN a keepsake is a gift which reminds someone of an event or of the person who gave it to them. ❏ *books and ornaments they had in their boudoirs at home: keepsakes that different relations had presented to them* (*Jane Eyre* by Charlotte Brontë)

kenned VERB kenned means knew ❏ *though little kenned the lamplighter that he had any company but Christmas!* (*A Christmas Carol* by Charles Dickens)

kennel NOUN kennel means gutter, which is the edge of a road next to the pavement, where rain water collects and flows away ❏ *being jostled himself into the kennel* (*Gulliver's Travels* by Jonathan Swift)

knock-knee ADJ knock-knee means slanted, at an angle. ❏ *LOT 1 was marked in whitewashed knock-knee letters on the brewhouse* (*Great Expectations* by Charles Dickens)

ladylike ADJ to be ladylike is to behave in a polite, dignified and graceful way ❏ *No, winking isn't ladylike* (*Little Women* by Louisa May Alcott)

lapse NOUN flow ❏ *Stealing with silent lapse to join the brook* (*The Prelude* by William Wordsworth)

larry NOUN larry is an old word which means commotion or noisy celebration ❏ *That was all a part of the larry!* (*Tess of the D'Urbervilles* by Thomas Hardy)

laths NOUN laths are strips of wood ❏ *The panels shrunk, the windows cracked; fragments of plaster fell out of the ceiling, and the naked laths were shown instead* (*A Christmas Carol* by Charles Dickens)

leer NOUN a leer is an unpleasant smile ❏ *with a kind of leer* (*Treasure Island* by Robert Louis Stevenson)

lenitives NOUN these are different kinds of drugs or medicines:

lenitives and palliatives were pain relievers; aperitives were laxatives; abstersives caused vomiting; corrosives destroyed human tissue; restringents caused constipation; cephalalgics stopped headaches; icterics were used as medicine for jaundice; apophlegmatics were cough medicine, and acoustics were cures for the loss of hearing ❑ *lenitives, aperitives, abstersives, corrosives, restringents, palliatives, laxatives, cephalalgics, icterics, apophlegmatics, acoustics* (*Gulliver's Travels* by Jonathan Swift)

lest CONJ in case. If you do something lest something (usually) unpleasant happens you do it to try to prevent it happening ❑ *She went in without knocking, and hurried upstairs, in great fear lest she should meet the real Mary Ann* (*Alice's Adventures in Wonderland* by Lewis Carroll)

levee NOUN a levee is an old term for a meeting held in the morning, shortly after the person holding the meeting has got out of bed ❑ *I used to attend the King's levee once or twice a week* (*Gulliver's Travels* by Jonathan Swift)

life-preserver NOUN a club which had lead inside it to make it heavier and therefore more dangerous ❑ *and with no more suspicious articles displayed to view than two or three heavy bludgeons which stood in a corner, and a 'life-preserver' that hung over the chimney-piece.* (*Oliver Twist* by Charles Dickens)

lighterman NOUN a lighterman is another word for sailor ❑ *in and out, hammers going in ship-builders' yards, saws going at timber, clashing engines going at things unknown, pumps going in leaky ships, capstans going, ships going out to sea, and unintelligible sea creatures roaring curses over the bulwarks at respondent lightermen* (*Great Expectations* by Charles Dickens)

livery NOUN servants often wore a uniform known as a livery ❑ *suddenly a footman in livery came running out of the wood* (*Alice's Adventures in Wonderland* by Lewis Carroll)

livid ADJ livid means pale or ash coloured. Livid also means very angry ❑ *a dirty, livid white* (*Treasure Island* by Robert Louis Stevenson)

lottery-tickets NOUN a popular card game ❑ *and Mrs. Philips protested that they would have a nice comfortable noisy game of lottery tickets* (*Pride and Prejudice* by Jane Austen)

lower and upper world PHRASE the earth and the heavens are the lower and upper worlds ❑ *the changes in the lower and upper world* (*Gulliver's Travels* by Jonathan Swift)

lustres NOUN lustres are chandeliers. A chandelier is a large, decorative frame which holds light bulbs or candles and hangs from the ceiling ❑ *the lustres, lights, the carving and the guilding* (*The Prelude* by William Wordsworth)

lynched VERB killed without a criminal trial by a crowd of people ❑ *He'll never know how nigh he come to getting lynched* (*The Adventures of Huckleberry Finn* by Mark Twain)

malingering VERB if someone is malingering they are pretending to be ill to avoid working ❑ *And you stand there malingering* (*Treasure Island* by Robert Louis Stevenson)

managing PHRASE treating with consideration ❑ *to think the honour of my own kind not worth managing* (*Gulliver's Travels* by Jonathan Swift)

manhood PHRASE manhood means human nature ❑ *concerning the nature of manhood* (*Gulliver's Travels* by Jonathan Swift)

man-trap NOUN a man-trap is a set of steel jaws that snap shut when trodden on and trap a person's leg

❑ *"Don't go to him," I called out of the window, "he's an assassin! A man-trap!" (Oliver Twist* by Charles Dickens)

maps NOUN charts of the night sky ❑ *Let maps to others, worlds on worlds have shown (The Good-Morrow* by John Donne)

mark VERB look at or notice ❑ *Mark but this flea, and mark in this (The Flea* by John Donne)

maroons NOUN A maroon is someone who has been left in a place which it is difficult for them to escape from, like a small island ❑ *if schooners, islands, and maroons (Treasure Island* by Robert Louis Stevenson)

mast NOUN here mast means the fruit of forest trees ❑ *a quantity of acorns, dates, chestnuts, and other mast (Gulliver's Travels* by Jonathan Swift)

mate VERB defeat ❑ *Where Mars did mate the warlike Carthigens (Doctor Faustus Chorus* by Christopher Marlowe)

mealy ADJ Mealy when used to describe a face meant pallid, pale or colourless ❑ *I only know two sorts of boys. Mealy boys, and beef-faced boys (Oliver Twist* by Charles Dickens)

middling ADJ fairly or moderately ❑ *she worked me middling hard for about an hour (The Adventures of Huckleberry Finn* by Mark Twain)

mill NOUN a mill, or treadmill, was a device for hard labour or punishment in prison ❑ *Was you never on the mill? (Oliver Twist* by Charles Dickens)

milliner's shop NOUN a milliner's sold fabrics, clothing, lace and accessories; as time went on they specialized more and more in hats ❑ *to pay their duty to their aunt and to a milliner's shop just over the way (Pride and Prejudice* by Jane Austen)

minching un' munching PHRASE how people in the north of England

used to describe the way people from the south speak ❑ *Minching un' munching! (Wuthering Heights* by Emily Brontë)

mine NOUN gold ❑ *Whether both th'Indias of spice and mine (The Sun Rising* by John Donne)

mire NOUN mud ❑ *Tis my fate to be always ground into the mire under the iron heel of oppression (The Adventures of Huckleberry Finn* by Mark Twain)

miscellany NOUN a miscellany is a collection of many different kinds of things ❑ *under that, the miscellany began (Treasure Island* by Robert Louis Stevenson)

mistarshers NOUN mistarshers means moustache, which is the hair that grows on a man's upper lip ❑ *when he put his hand up to his mistarshers (Tess of the D'Urbervilles* by Thomas Hardy)

morrow NOUN here good-morrow means tomorrow and a new and better life ❑ *And now good-morrow to our waking souls (The Good-Morrow* by John Donne)

mortification NOUN mortification is an old word for gangrene which is when part of the body decays or 'dies' because of disease ❑ *Yes, it was a mortification – that was it (The Adventures of Huckleberry Finn* by Mark Twain)

mought PARTICIPLE mought is an old spelling of might ❑ *what you mought call me? You mought call me captain (Treasure Island* by Robert Louis Stevenson)

move VERB move me not means do not make me angry ❑ *Move me not, Faustus (Doctor Faustus 2.1* by Christopher Marlowe)

muffin-cap NOUN a muffin cap is a flat cap made from wool ❑ *the old one, remained stationary in the muffin-cap and leathers (Oliver Twist* by Charles Dickens)

mulatter NOUN a mulatter was another word for mulatto, which is a person with parents who are from different races ❏ *a mulatter, most as white as a white man* (*The Adventures of Huckleberry Finn* by Mark Twain)

mummery NOUN mummery is an old word that meant meaningless (or pretentious) ceremony ❏ *When they were all gone, and when Trabb and his men – but not his boy: I looked for him – had crammed their mummery into bags, and were gone too, the house felt wholesomer.* (*Great Expectations* by Charles Dickens)

nap NOUN the nap is the woolly surface on a new item of clothing. Here the surface has been worn away so it looks bare ❏ *like an old hat with the nap rubbed off* (*The Adventures of Huckleberry Finn* by Mark Twain)

natural ■ NOUN a natural is a person born with learning difficulties ❏ *though he had been left to his particular care by their deceased father, who thought him almost a natural.* (*David Copperfield* by Charles Dickens) ■ ADJ natural meant illegitimate ❏ *Harriet Smith was the natural daughter of somebody* (*Emma* by Jane Austen)

navigator NOUN a navigator was originally someone employed to dig canals. It is the origin of the word 'navvy' meaning a labourer ❏ *She ascertained from me in a few words what it was all about, comforted Dora, and gradually convinced her that I was not a labourer – from my manner of stating the case I believe Dora concluded that I was a navigator, and went balancing myself up and down a plank all day with a wheelbarrow – and so brought us together in peace.* (*David Copperfield* by Charles Dickens)

necromancy NOUN necromancy means a kind of magic where the magician speaks to spirits or ghosts to find out what will happen in the future ❏ *He surfeits upon cursed necromancy* (*Doctor Faustus chorus* by Christopher Marlowe)

negus NOUN a negus is a hot drink made from sweetened wine and water ❏ *He sat placidly perusing the newspaper, with his little head on one side, and a glass of warm sherry negus at his elbow.* (*David Copperfield* by Charles Dickens)

nice ADJ discriminating. Able to make good judgements or choices ❏ *consequently a claim to be nice* (*Emma* by Jane Austen)

nigh ADV nigh means near ❏ *He'll never know how nigh he come to getting lynched* (*The Adventures of Huckleberry Finn* by Mark Twain)

nimbleness NOUN nimbleness means being able to move very quickly or skillfully ❏ *and with incredible accuracy and nimbleness* (*Treasure Island* by Robert Louis Stevenson)

noggin NOUN a noggin is a small mug or a wooden cup ❏ *you'll bring me one noggin of rum* (*Treasure Island* by Robert Louis Stevenson)

none ADJ neither ❏ *none can die* (*The Good-Morrow* by John Donne)

notices NOUN observations ❏ *Arch are his notices* (*The Prelude* by William Wordsworth)

occiput NOUN occiput means the back of the head ❏ *saw off the occiput of each couple* (*Gulliver's Travels* by Jonathan Swift)

officiously ADJ kindly ❏ *the governess who attended Glumdalclitch very officiously lifted me up* (*Gulliver's Travels* by Jonathan Swift)

old salt PHRASE old salt is a slang term for an experienced sailor ❏ *a 'true sea-dog', and a 'real old salt'* (*Treasure Island* by Robert Louis Stevenson)

or ere PHRASE before ❏ *or ere the Hall was built* (*The Prelude* by William Wordsworth)

ostler NOUN one who looks after horses at an inn ❏ *The bill paid, and the waiter remembered, and the ostler not forgotten, and the chambermaid taken into consideration*

(*Great Expectations* by Charles Dickens)

ostry NOUN an ostry is an old word for a pub or hotel ❑ *lest I send you into the ostry with a vengeance* (*Doctor Faustus 2.2* by Christopher Marlowe)

outrunning the constable PHRASE outrunning the constable meant spending more than you earn ❑ *but I shall by this means be able to check your bills and to pull you up if I find you outrunning the constable.* (*Great Expectations* by Charles Dickens)

over ADJ across ❑ *It is in length six yards, and in the thickest part at least three yards over* (*Gulliver's Travels* by Jonathan Swift)

over the broomstick PHRASE this is a phrase meaning 'getting married without a formal ceremony' ❑ *They both led tramping lives, and this woman in Gerrard-street here, had been married very young, over the broomstick (as we say), to a tramping man, and was a perfect fury in point of jealousy.* (*Great Expectations* by Charles Dickens)

own VERB own means to admit or to acknowledge ❑ *It's my old girl that advises. She has the head. But I never own to it before her. Discipline must be maintained* (*Bleak House* by Charles Dickens)

page NOUN here page means a boy employed to run errands ❑ *not my feigned page* (*On His Mistress* by John Donne)

paid pretty dear PHRASE paid pretty dear means paid a high price or suffered quite a lot ❑ *I paid pretty dear for my monthly fourpenny piece* (*Treasure Island* by Robert Louis Stevenson)

pannikins NOUN pannikins were small tin cups ❑ *of lifting light glasses and cups to his lips, as if they were clumsy pannikins* (*Great Expectations* by Charles Dickens)

pards NOUN pards are leopards ❑ *Not charioted by Bacchus and his pards*

(*Ode on a Nightingale* by John Keats)

parlour boarder NOUN a pupil who lived with the family ❑ *and somebody had lately raised her from the condition of scholar to parlour boarder* (*Emma* by Jane Austen)

particular, a London PHRASE London in Victorian times and up to the 1950s was famous for having very dense fog – which was a combination of real fog and the smog of pollution from factories ❑ *This is a London particular . . . A fog, miss'* (*Bleak House* by Charles Dickens)

patten NOUN pattens were wooden soles which were fixed to shoes by straps to protect the shoes in wet weather ❑ *carrying a basket like the Great Seal of England in plaited straw, a pair of pattens, a spare shawl, and an umbrella, though it was a fine bright day* (*Great Expectations* by Charles Dickens)

paviour NOUN a paviour was a labourer who worked on the street pavement ❑ *the paviour his pickaxe* (*Oliver Twist* by Charles Dickens)

peccant ADJ peccant means unhealthy ❑ *other peccant humours* (*Gulliver's Travels* by Jonathan Swift)

penetralium NOUN penetralium is a word used to describe the inner rooms of the house ❑ *and I had no desire to aggravate his impatience previous to inspecting the penetralium* (*Wuthering Heights* by Emily Brontë)

pensive ADV pensive means deep in thought or thinking seriously about something ❑ *and she was leaning pensive on a tomb-stone on her right elbow* (*The Adventures of Huckleberry Finn* by Mark Twain)

penury NOUN penury is the state of being extremely poor ❑ *Distress, if not penury, loomed in the distance* (*Tess of the D'Urbervilles* by Thomas Hardy)

perspective NOUN telescope ❑ *a pocket perspective* (*Gulliver's Travels* by Jonathan Swift)

phaeton NOUN a phaeton was an open carriage for four people ❏ *often condescends to drive by my humble abode in her little phaeton and ponies* (*Pride and Prejudice* by Jane Austen)

phantasm NOUN a phantasm is an illusion, something that is not real. It is sometimes used to mean ghost ❏ *Experience had bred no fancies in him that could raise the phantasm of appetite* (*Silas Marner* by George Eliot)

physic NOUN here physic means medicine ❏ *there I studied physic two years and seven months* (*Gulliver's Travels* by Jonathan Swift)

pinioned VERB to pinion is to hold both arms so that a person cannot move them ❏ *But the relentless Ghost pinioned him in both his arms, and forced him to observe what happened next.* (*A Christmas Carol* by Charles Dickens)

piquet NOUN piquet was a popular card game in the C18th ❏ *Mr Hurst and Mr Bingley were at piquet* (*Pride and Prejudice* by Jane Austen)

plaister NOUN a plaister is a piece of cloth on which an apothecary (or pharmacist) would spread ointment. The cloth is then applied to wounds or bruises to treat them ❏ *Then, she gave the knife a final smart wipe on the edge of the plaister, and then sawed a very thick round off the loaf: which she finally, before separating from the loaf, hewed into two halves, of which Joe got one, and I the other.* (*Great Expectations* by Charles Dickens)

plantations NOUN here plantations means colonies, which are countries controlled by a more powerful country ❏ *besides our plantations in America* (*Gulliver's Travels* by Jonathan Swift)

plastic ADV here plastic is an old term meaning shaping or a power that was forming ❏ *A plastic power abode with me* (*The Prelude* by William Wordsworth)

players NOUN actors ❏ *of players which upon the world's stage be* (*On His Mistress* by John Donne)

plump ADV all at once, suddenly ❏ *But it took a bit of time to get it well round, the change come so uncommon plump, didn't it?* (*Great Expectations* by Charles Dickens)

plundered VERB to plunder is to rob or steal from ❏ *These crosses stand for the names of ships or towns that they sank or plundered* (*Treasure Island* by Robert Louis Stevenson)

pommel ■ VERB to pommel someone is to hit them repeatedly with your fists ❏ *hug him round the neck, pommel his back, and kick his legs in irrepressible affection!* (*A Christmas Carol* by Charles Dickens) ■ NOUN a pommel is the part of a saddle that rises up at the front ❏ *He had his gun across his pommel* (*The Adventures of Huckleberry Finn* by Mark Twain)

poor's rates NOUN poor's rates were property taxes which were used to support the poor ❏ *"Oh!" replied the undertaker; "why, you know, Mr. Bumble, I pay a good deal towards the poor's rates."* (*Oliver Twist* by Charles Dickens)

popular ADJ popular means ruled by the people, or Republican, rather than ruled by a monarch ❏ *With those of Greece compared and popular Rome* (*The Prelude* by William Wordsworth)

porringer NOUN a porringer is a small bowl ❏ *Of this festive composition each boy had one porringer, and no more* (*Oliver Twist* by Charles Dickens)

postboy NOUN a postboy was the driver of a horse-drawn carriage ❏ *He spoke to a postboy who was dozing under the gateway* (*Oliver Twist* by Charles Dickens)

post-chaise NOUN a fast carriage for two or four passengers ❏ *Looking round, he saw that it was a post-chaise, driven at great speed* (*Oliver Twist* by Charles Dickens)

ALEXANDRE DUMAS

postern NOUN a small gate usually at the back of a building ❑ *The little servant happening to be entering the fortress with two hot rolls, I passed through the postern and crossed the drawbridge, in her company* (*Great Expectations* by Charles Dickens)

pottle NOUN a pottle was a small basket ❑ *He had a paper-bag under each arm and a pottle of strawberries in one hand . . .* (*Great Expectations* by Charles Dickens)

pounce NOUN pounce is a fine powder used to prevent ink spreading on untreated paper ❑ *in that grim atmosphere of pounce and parchment, red-tape, dusty wafers, ink-jars, brief and draft paper, law reports, writs, declarations, and bills of costs* (*David Copperfield* by Charles Dickens)

pox NOUN pox means sexually transmitted diseases like syphilis ❑ *how the pox in all its consequences and denominations* (*Gulliver's Travels* by Jonathan Swift)

prelibation NOUN prelibation means a foretaste of or an example of something to come ❑ *A prelibation to the mower's scythe* (*The Prelude* by William Wordsworth)

prentice NOUN an apprentice ❑ *and Joe, sitting on an old gun, had told me that when I was 'prentice to him regularly bound, we would have such Larks there!* (*Great Expectations* by Charles Dickens)

presently ADV immediately ❑ *I presently knew what they meant* (*Gulliver's Travels* by Jonathan Swift)

pumpion NOUN pumpkin ❑ *for it was almost as large as a small pumpion* (*Gulliver's Travels* by Jonathan Swift)

punctual ADJ kept in one place ❑ *was not a punctual presence, but a spirit* (*The Prelude* by William Wordsworth)

quadrille ◼ NOUN a quadrille is a dance invented in France which is usually performed by four couples ❑ *However, Mr Swiveller had Miss Sophy's hand for the first quadrille (country-dances being low, were utterly proscribed)* (*The Old Curiosity Shop* by Charles Dickens) ◼ NOUN quadrille was a card game for four people ❑ *to make up her pool of quadrille in the evening* (*Pride and Prejudice* by Jane Austen)

quality NOUN gentry or upper-class people ❑ *if you are with the quality* (*The Adventures of Huckleberry Finn* by Mark Twain)

quick parts PHRASE quick-witted ❑ *Mr Bennet was so odd a mixture of quick parts* (*Pride and Prejudice* by Jane Austen)

quid NOUN a quid is something chewed or kept in the mouth, like a piece of tobacco ❑ *rolling his quid* (*Treasure Island* by Robert Louis Stevenson)

quit VERB quit means to avenge or to make even ❑ *But Faustus's death shall quit my infamy* (*Doctor Faustus 4.3* by Christopher Marlowe)

rags NOUN divisions ❑ *Nor hours, days, months, which are the rags of time* (*The Sun Rising* by John Donne)

raiment NOUN raiment means clothing ❑ *the mountain shook off turf and flower, had only heath for raiment and crag for gem* (*Jane Eyre* by Charlotte Brontë)

rain cats and dogs PHRASE an expression meaning rain heavily. The origin of the expression is unclear ❑ *But it'll perhaps rain cats and dogs to-morrow* (*Silas Marner* by George Eliot)

raised Cain PHRASE raised Cain means caused a lot of trouble. Cain is a character in the Bible who killed his brother Abel ❑ *and every time he got drunk he raised Cain around town* (*The Adventures of Huckleberry Finn* by Mark Twain)

rambling ADJ rambling means confused and not very clear ❑ *my* head began to be filled very early with rambling thoughts (*Robinson Crusoe* by Daniel Defoe)

raree-show NOUN a raree-show is an old term for a peep-show or a fairground entertainment ❑ *A raree-show is here, with children gathered round* (*The Prelude* by William Wordsworth)

recusants NOUN people who resisted authority ❑ *hardy recusants* (*The Prelude* by William Wordsworth)

redounding VERB eddying. An eddy is a movement in water or air which goes round and round instead of flowing in one direction ❑ *mists and steam-like fogs redounding everywhere* (*The Prelude* by William Wordsworth)

redundant ADJ here redundant means overflowing but Wordsworth also uses it to mean excessively large or too big ❑ *A tempest, a redundant energy* (*The Prelude* by William Wordsworth)

reflex NOUN reflex is a shortened version of reflexion, which is an alternative spelling of reflection ❑ *To cut across the reflex of a star* (*The Prelude* by William Wordsworth)

Reformatory NOUN a prison for young offenders/criminals ❑ *Even when I was taken to have a new suit of clothes, the tailor had orders to make them like a kind of Reformatory, and on no account to let me have the free use of my limbs.* (*Great Expectations* by Charles Dickens)

remorse NOUN pity or compassion ❑ *by that remorse* (*On His Mistress* by John Donne)

render VERB in this context render means give. ❑ *and Sarah could render no reason that would be sanctioned by the feeling of the community.* (*Silas Marner* by George Eliot)

repeater NOUN a repeater was a watch that chimed the last hour when a button was pressed – as a result it

was useful in the dark ❑ *And his watch is a gold repeater, and worth a hundred pound if it's worth a penny.* (*Great Expectations* by Charles Dickens)

repugnance NOUN repugnance means a strong dislike of something or someone ❑ *overcoming a strong repugnance* (*Treasure Island* by Robert Louis Stevenson)

reverence NOUN reverence means bow. When you bow to someone, you briefly bend your body towards them as a formal way of showing them respect ❑ *made my reverence* (*Gulliver's Travels* by Jonathan Swift)

reverie NOUN a reverie is a day dream ❑ *I can guess the subject of your reverie* (*Pride and Prejudice* by Jane Austen)

revival NOUN a religious meeting held in public ❑ *well I'd ben a-running' a little temperance revival thar' bout a week* (*The Adventures of Huckleberry Finn* by Mark Twain)

revolt VERB revolt means turn back or stop your present course of action and go back to what you were doing before ❑ *Revolt, or I'll in piecemeal tear thy flesh* (*Doctor Faustus 5.1* by Christopher Marlowe)

rheumatics/rheumatism NOUN rheumatics [rheumatism] is an illness that makes your joints or muscles stiff and painful ❑ *a new cure for the rheumatics* (*Treasure Island* by Robert Louis Stevenson)

riddance NOUN riddance is usually used in the form good riddance which you say when you are pleased that something has gone or been left behind ❑ *I'd better go into the house, and die and be a riddance* (*David Copperfield* by Charles Dickens)

rimy ADJ rimy is an ADJECTIVE which means covered in ice or frost ❑ *It was a rimy morning, and very damp* (*Great Expectations* by Charles Dickens)

riper ADJ riper means more mature or older ❑ *At riper years to Wittenberg he went* (*Doctor Faustus chorus* by Christopher Marlowe)

rubber NOUN a set of games in whist or backgammon ❑ *her father was sure of his rubber* (*Emma* by Jane Austen)

ruffian NOUN a ruffian is a person who behaves violently ❑ *and when the ruffian had told him* (*Treasure Island* by Robert Louis Stevenson)

sadness NOUN sadness is an old term meaning seriousness ❑ *But I prithee tell me, in good sadness* (*Doctor Faustus 2.2* by Christopher Marlowe)

sailed before the mast PHRASE this phrase meant someone who did not look like a sailor ❑ *he had none of the appearance of a man that sailed before the mast* (*Treasure Island* by Robert Louis Stevenson)

scabbard NOUN a scabbard is the covering for a sword or dagger ❑ *Girded round its middle was an antique scabbard; but no sword was in it, and the ancient sheath was eaten up with rust* (*A Christmas Carol* by Charles Dickens)

schooners NOUN A schooner is a fast, medium-sized sailing ship ❑ *if schooners, islands, and maroons* (*Treasure Island* by Robert Louis Stevenson)

science NOUN learning or knowledge ❑ *Even Science, too, at hand* (*The Prelude* by William Wordsworth)

scrouge VERB to scrouge means to squeeze or to crowd ❑ *to scrouge in and get a sight* (*The Adventures of Huckleberry Finn* by Mark Twain)

scrutore NOUN a scrutore, or escritoire, was a writing table ❑ *set me gently on my feet upon the scrutore* (*Gulliver's Travels* by Jonathan Swift)

scutcheon/escutcheon NOUN an escutcheon is a shield with a coat of arms, or the symbols of a family name, engraved on it ❑ *On the scutcheon we'll have a bend* (*The Adventures of Huckleberry Finn* by Mark Twain)

sea-dog PHRASE sea-dog is a slang term for an experienced sailor or pirate ❑ *a 'true sea-dog', and a 'real old salt,'* (*Treasure Island* by Robert Louis Stevenson)

see the lions PHRASE to see the lions was to go and see the sights of London. Originally the phrase referred to the menagerie in the Tower of London and later in Regent's Park ❑ *We will go and see the lions for an hour or two – it's something to have a fresh fellow like you to show them to, Copperfield* (*David Copperfield* by Charles Dickens)

self-conceit NOUN self-conceit is an old term which means having too high an opinion of oneself, or deceiving yourself ❑ *Till swollen with cunning, of a self-conceit* (*Doctor Faustus chorus* by Christopher Marlowe)

seneschal NOUN a steward ❑ *where a grey-headed seneschal sings a funny chorus with a funnier body of vassals* (*Oliver Twist* by Charles Dickens)

sensible ADJ if you were sensible of something you are aware or conscious of something ❑ *If my children are silly I must hope to be always sensible of it* (*Pride and Prejudice* by Jane Austen)

sessions NOUN court cases were heard at specific times of the year called sessions ❑ *He lay in prison very ill, during the whole interval between his committal for trial, and the coming round of the Sessions.* (*Great Expectations* by Charles Dickens)

shabby ADJ shabby places look old and in bad condition ❑ *a little bit of a shabby village named Pikesville* (*The Adventures of Huckleberry Finn* by Mark Twain)

shay-cart NOUN a shay-cart was a small cart drawn by one horse ❑ *"I were at the Bargemen t'other night, Pip;"*

whenever he subsided into affection, he called me Pip, and whenever he relapsed into politeness he called me Sir; "when there come up in his shay-cart Pumblechook." (*Great Expectations* by Charles Dickens)

shilling NOUN a shilling is an old unit of currency. There were twenty shillings in every British pound ❑ "*Ten shillings too much,*" *said the gentleman in the white waistcoat.* (*Oliver Twist* by Charles Dickens)

shines NOUN tricks or games ❑ *well, it would make a cow laugh to see the shines that old idiot cut* (*The Adventures of Huckleberry Finn* by Mark Twain)

shirking VERB shirking means not doing what you are meant to be doing, or evading your duties ❑ *some of you shirking lubbers* (*Treasure Island* by Robert Louis Stevenson)

shiver my timbers PHRASE shiver my timbers is an expression which was used by sailors and pirates to express surprise ❑ *why, shiver my timbers, if I hadn't forgotten my score!* (*Treasure Island* by Robert Louis Stevenson)

shoe-roses NOUN shoe-roses were roses made from ribbons which were stuck on to shoes as decoration ❑ *the very shoe-roses for Netherfield were got by proxy* (*Pride and Prejudice* by Jane Austen)

singular ADJ singular means very great and remarkable or strange ❑ "*Singular dream,*" *he says* (*The Adventures of Huckleberry Finn* by Mark Twain)

sire NOUN sire is an old word which means lord or master or elder ❑ *She also defied her sire* (*Little Women* by Louisa May Alcott)

sixpence NOUN a sixpence was half of a shilling ❑ *if she had only a shilling in the world, she would be very lilkely to give away sixpence of it* (*Emma* by Jane Austen)

slavey NOUN the word slavey was used when there was only one servant in

a house or boarding-house – so she had to perform all the duties of a larger staff ❑ *Two distinct knocks, sir, will produce the slavey at any time* (*The Old Curiosity Shop* by Charles Dickens)

slender ADJ weak ❑ *In slender accents of sweet verse* (*The Prelude* by William Wordsworth)

slop-shops NOUN slop-shops were shops where cheap ready-made clothes were sold. They mainly sold clothes to sailors ❑ *Accordingly, I took the jacket off, that I might learn to do without it; and carrying it under my arm, began a tour of inspection of the various slop-shops.* (*David Copperfield* by Charles Dickens)

sluggard NOUN a lazy person ❑ "*Stand up and repeat 'Tis the voice of the sluggard,'*" *said the Gryphon.* (*Alice's Adventures in Wonderland* by Lewis Carroll)

smallpox NOUN smallpox is a serious infectious disease ❑ *by telling the men we had smallpox aboard* (*The Adventures of Huckleberry Finn* by Mark Twain)

smalls NOUN smalls are short trousers ❑ *It is difficult for a large-headed, small-eyed youth, of lumbering make and heavy countenance, to look dignified under any circumstances; but it is more especially so, when superadded to these personal attractions are a red nose and yellow smalls* (*Oliver Twist* by Charles Dickens)

sneeze-box NOUN a box for snuff was called a sneeze-box because sniffing snuff makes the user sneeze ❑ *To think of Jack Dawkins — lummy Jack — the Dodger — the Artful Dodger — going abroad for a common twopenny-halfpenny sneeze-box!* (*Oliver Twist* by Charles Dickens)

snorted VERB slept ❑ *Or snorted we in the Seven Sleepers' den?* (*The Good-Morrow* by John Donne)

snuff NOUN snuff is tobacco in powder form which is taken by sniffing ❑

as he thrust his thumb and fore-finger into the proffered snuff-box of the undertaker: which was an ingenious little model of a patent coffin. (*Oliver Twist* by Charles Dickens)

soliloquized VERB to soliloquize is when an actor in a play speaks to himself or herself rather than to another actor ❑ *"A new servitude! There is something in that," I soliloquized (mentally, be it understood; I did not talk aloud) (Jane Eyre* by Charlotte Brontë)

sough NOUN a sough is a drain or a ditch ❑ *as you may have noticed the sough that runs from the marshes* (*Wuthering Heights* by Emily Brontë)

spirits NOUN a spirit is the nonphysical part of a person which is believed to remain alive after their death ❑ *that I might raise up spirits when I please* (*Doctor Faustus* 1.5 by Christopher Marlowe)

spleen ■ NOUN here spleen means a type of sadness or depression which was thought to only affect the wealthy ❑ *yet here I could plainly discover the true seeds of spleen* (*Gulliver's Travels* by Jonathan Swift) ■ NOUN irritability and low spirits ❑ *Adieu to disappointment and spleen* (*Pride and Prejudice* by Jane Austen)

spondulicks NOUN spondulicks is a slang word which means money ❑ *not for all his spondulicks and as much more on top of it* (*The Adventures of Huckleberry Finn* by Mark Twain)

stalled of VERB to be stalled of something is to be bored with it ❑ *I'm stalled of doing naught* (*Wuthering Heights* by Emily Brontë)

stanchion NOUN a stanchion is a pole or bar that stands upright and is used as a buidling support ❑ *and slid down a stanchion* (*The Adventures of Huckleberry Finn* by Mark Twain)

stang NOUN stang is another word for pole which was an old measurement ❑ *These fields were intermingled with woods of half a stang* (*Gulliver's Travels* by Jonathan Swift)

starlings NOUN a starling is a wall built around the pillars that support a bridge to protect the pillars ❑ *There were states of the tide when, having been down the river, I could not get back through the eddy-chafed arches and starlings of old London Bridge* (*Great Expectations* by Charles Dickens)

startings NOUN twitching or night-time movements of the body ❑ *with midnight's startings* (*On His Mistress* by John Donne)

stomacher NOUN a panel at the front of a dress ❑ *but send her aunt the pattern of a stomacher* (*Emma* by Jane Austen)

stoop VERB swoop ❑ *Once a kite hovering over the garden made a stoop at me* (*Gulliver's Travels* by Jonathan Swift)

succedaneum NOUN a succedaneum is a substitute ❑ *But as a succedaneum* (*The Prelude* by William Wordsworth)

suet NOUN a hard animal fat used in cooking ❑ *and your jaws are too weak For anything tougher than suet* (*Alice's Adventures in Wonderland* by Lewis Carroll)

sultry ADJ sultry weather is hot and damp. Here sultry means unpleasant or risky ❑ *for it was getting pretty sultry for us* (*The Adventures of Huckleberry Finn* by Mark Twain)

summerset NOUN summerset is an old spelling of somersault. If someone does a somersault, they turn over completely in the air ❑ *I have seen him do the summerset* (*Gulliver's Travels* by Jonathan Swift)

supper NOUN supper was a light meal taken late in the evening. The main meal was dinner which was eaten at four or five in the afternoon ❑ *and the supper table was all set out* (*Emma* by Jane Austen)

surfeits VERB to surfeit in something is to have far too much of it, or to overindulge in it to an unhealthy degree ❑ *He surfeits upon cursed necromancy* (*Doctor Faustus chorus* by Christopher Marlowe)

surtout NOUN a surtout is a long close-fitting overcoat ❑ *He wore a long black surtout reaching nearly to his ankles* (*The Old Curiosity Shop* by Charles Dickens)

swath NOUN swath is the width of corn cut by a scythe ❑ *while thy hook Spares the next swath* (*Ode to Autumn* by John Keats)

sylvan ADJ sylvan means belonging to the woods ❑ *Sylvan historian* (*Ode on a Grecian Urn* by John Keats)

taction NOUN taction means touch. This means that the people had to be touched on the mouth or the ears to get their attention ❑ *without being roused by some external taction upon the organs of speech and hearing* (*Gulliver's Travels* by Jonathan Swift)

Tag and Rag and Bobtail PHRASE the riff-raff, or lower classes. Used in an insulting way ❑ *"No," said he; "not till it got about that there was no protection on the premises, and it come to be considered dangerous, with convicts and Tag and Rag and Bobtail going up and down."* (*Great Expectations* by Charles Dickens)

tallow NOUN tallow is hard animal fat that is used to make candles and soap ❑ *and a lot of tallow candles* (*The Adventures of Huckleberry Finn* by Mark Twain)

tan VERB to tan means to beat or whip ❑ *and if I catch you about that school I'll tan you good* (*The Adventures of Huckleberry Finn* by Mark Twain)

tanyard NOUN the tanyard is part of a tannery, which is a place where leather is made from animal skins ❑ *hid in the old tanyard* (*The Adventures of Huckleberry Finn* by Mark Twain)

tarry ADJ tarry means the colour of tar or black ❑ *his tarry pig-tail* (*Treasure Island* by Robert Louis Stevenson)

thereof PHRASE from there ❑ *By all desires which thereof did ensue* (*On His Mistress* by John Donne)

thick with, be PHRASE if you are 'thick with someone' you are very close, sharing secrets – it is often used to describe people who are planning something secret ❑ *Hasn't he been thick with Mr Heathcliff lately?* (*Wuthering Heights* by Emily Brontë)

thimble NOUN a thimble is a small cover used to protect the finger while sewing ❑ *The paper had been sealed in several places by a thimble* (*Treasure Island* by Robert Louis Stevenson)

thirtover ADJ thirtover is an old word which means obstinate or that someone is very determined to do want they want and can not be persuaded to do something in another way ❑ *I have been living on in a thirtover, lackadaisical way* (*Tess of the D'Urbervilles* by Thomas Hardy)

timbrel NOUN timbrel is a tambourine ❑ *What pipes and timbrels?* (*Ode on a Grecian Urn* by John Keats)

tin NOUN tin is slang for money/cash ❑ *Then the plain question is, an't it a pity that this state of things should continue, and how much better would it be for the old gentleman to hand over a reasonable amount of tin, and make it all right and comfortable* (*The Old Curiosity Shop* by Charles Dickens)

tincture NOUN a tincture is a medicine made with alcohol and a small amount of a drug ❑ *with ink composed of a cephalic tincture* (*Gulliver's Travels* by Jonathan Swift)

tithe NOUN a tithe is a tax paid to the church ❑ *and held farms which, speaking from a spiritual point of view, paid highly-desirable tithes* (*Silas Marner* by George Eliot)

towardly ADJ a towardly child is dutiful or obedient ❑ *and a towardly child* (*Gulliver's Travels* by Jonathan Swift)

toys NOUN trifles are things which are considered to have little importance, value, or significance ❑ *purchase my life from them bysome bracelets, glass rings, and other toys* (*Gulliver's Travels* by Jonathan Swift)

tract NOUN a tract is a religious pamphlet or leaflet ❑ *and Joe Harper got a hymn-book and a tract* (*The Adventures of Huckleberry Finn* by Mark Twain)

train-oil NOUN train-oil is oil from whale blubber ❑ *The train-oil and gunpowder were shoved out of sight in a minute* (*Wuthering Heights* by Emily Brontë)

tribulation NOUN tribulation means the suffering or difficulty you experience in a particular situation ❑ *Amy was learning this distinction through much tribulation* (*Little Women* by Louisa May Alcott)

trivet NOUN a trivet is a three-legged stand for resting a pot or kettle ❑ *a pocket-knife in his right; and a pewter pot on the trivet* (*Oliver Twist* by Charles Dickens)

trot line NOUN a trot line is a fishing line to which a row of smaller fishing lines are attached ❑ *when he got along I was hard at it taking up a trot line* (*The Adventures of Huckleberry Finn* by Mark Twain)

troth NOUN oath or pledge ❑ *I wonder, by my troth* (*The Good-Morrow* by John Donne)

truckle NOUN a truckle bedstead is a bed that is on wheels and can be slid under another bed to save space ❑ *It rose under my hand, and the door yielded. Looking in, I saw a lighted candle on a table, a bench, and a mattress on a truckle bedstead.* (*Great Expectations* by Charles Dickens)

trump NOUN a trump is a good, reliable person wo can be trusted ❑ This lad Hawkins is a trump, I perceive (*Treasure Island* by Robert Louis Stevenson)

tucker NOUN a tucker is a frilly lace collar which is worn around the neck ❑ *Whereat Scrooge's niece's sister – the plump one with the lace tucker: not the one with the roses – blushed.* (*A Christmas Carol* by Charles Dickens)

tureen NOUN a large bowl with a lid from which soup or vegetables are served ❑ *Waiting in a hot tureen!* (*Alice's Adventures in Wonderland* by Lewis Carroll)

turnkey NOUN a prison officer; jailer ❑ *As we came out of the prison through the lodge, I found that the great importance of my guardian was appreciated by the turnkeys, no less than by those whom they held in charge.* (*Great Expectations* by Charles Dickens)

turnpike NOUN the upkeep of many roads of the time was paid for by tolls (fees) collected at posts along the road. There was a gate to prevent people travelling further along the road until the toll had been paid. ❑ *Traddles, whom I have taken up by appointment at the turnpike, presents a dazzling combination of cream colour and light blue; and both he and Mr. Dick have a general effect about them of being all gloves.* (*David Copperfield* by Charles Dickens)

twas PHRASE it was ❑ *twas but a dream of thee* (*The Good-Morrow* by John Donne)

tyrannized VERB tyrannized means bullied or forced to do things against their will ❑ *for people would soon cease coming there to be tyrannized over and put down* (*Treasure Island* by Robert Louis Stevenson)

'un NOUN 'un is a slang term for one – usually used to refer to a person ❑ *She's been thinking the old 'un* (*David Copperfield* by Charles Dickens)

undistinguished ADJ undiscriminating or incapable of making a distinction between good and bad things ❏ *their undistinguished appetite to devour everything* (*Gulliver's Travels* by Jonathan Swift)

use NOUN habit ❏ *Though use make you apt to kill me* (*The Flea* by John Donne)

vacant ADJ vacant usually means empty, but here Wordsworth uses it to mean carefree ❏ *To vacant musing, unreproved neglect* (*The Prelude* by William Wordsworth)

valetudinarian NOUN one too concerned with his or her own health. ❏ *for having been a valetudinarian all his life* (*Emma* by Jane Austen)

vamp VERB vamp means to walk or tramp to somewhere ❏ *Well, vamp on to Marlott, will 'ee* (*Tess of the D'Urbervilles* by Thomas Hardy)

vapours NOUN the vapours is an old term which means unpleasant and strange thoughts, which make the person feel nervous and unhappy ❏ *and my head was full of vapours* (*Robinson Crusoe* by Daniel Defoe)

vegetables NOUN here vegetables means plants ❏ *the other vegetables are in the same proportion* (*Gulliver's Travels* by Jonathan Swift)

venturesome ADJ if you are venturesome you are willing to take risks ❏ *he must be either hopelessly stupid or a venturesome fool* (*Wuthering Heights* by Emily Brontë)

verily ADJ verily means really or truly ❏ *though I believe verily* (*Robinson Crusoe* by Daniel Defoe)

vicinage NOUN vicinage is an area or the residents of an area ❏ *and to his thought the whole vicinage was haunted by her.* (*Silas Marner* by George Eliot)

victuals NOUN victuals means food ❏ *grumble a little over the victuals* (*The Adventures of Huckleberry Finn* by Mark Twain)

vintage NOUN vintage in this context means wine ❏ *Oh, for a draught of*

vintage! (*Ode on a Nightingale* by John Keats)

virtual ADJ here virtual means powerful or strong ❏ *had virtual faith* (*The Prelude* by William Wordsworth)

vittles NOUN vittles is a slang word which means food ❏ *There never was such a woman for givin' away vittles and drink* (*Little Women* by Louisa May Alcott)

voided straight PHRASE voided straight is an old expression which means emptied immediately ❏ *see the rooms be voided straight* (*Doctor Faustus* 4.1 by Christopher Marlowe)

wainscot NOUN wainscot is wood panel lining in a room so wainscoted means a room lined with wooden panels ❏ *in the dark wainscoted parlor* (*Silas Marner* by George Eliot)

walking the plank PHRASE walking the plank was a punishment in which a prisoner would be made to walk along a plank on the side of the ship and fall into the sea, where they would be abandoned ❏ *about hanging, and walking the plank* (*Treasure Island* by Robert Louis Stevenson)

want VERB want means to be lacking or short of ❏ *The next thing wanted was to get the picture framed* (*Emma* by Jane Austen)

wanting ADJ wanting means lacking or missing ❏ *wanting two fingers of the left hand* (*Treasure Island* by Robert Louis Stevenson)

wanting, I was not PHRASE I was not wanting means I did not fail ❏ *I was not wanting to lay a foundation of religious knowledge in his mind* (*Robinson Crusoe* by Daniel Defoe)

ward NOUN a ward is, usually, a child who has been put under the protection of the court or a guardian for his or her protection ❏ *I call the Wards in Jarndcye. The* *are caged up with all the others.* (*Bleak House* by Charles Dickens)

waylay VERB to waylay someone is to lie in wait for them or to intercept them ❑ *I must go up the road and waylay him* (*The Adventures of Huckleberry Finn* by Mark Twain)

weazen NOUN weazen is a slang word for throat. It actually means shrivelled ❑ *You with a uncle too! Why, I knowed you at Gargery's when you was so small a wolf that I could have took your weazen betwixt this finger and thumb and chucked you away dead* (*Great Expectations* by Charles Dickens)

wery ■ ADV very ❑ *Be wery careful o' vidders all your life* (*Pickwick Papers* by Charles Dickens) ■ *See* wibrated

wherry NOUN wherry is a small swift rowing boat for one person ❑ *It was flood tide when Daniel Quilp sat himself down in the wherry to cross to the opposite shore.* (*The Old Curiosity Shop* by Charles Dickens)

whether PREP whether means which of the two in this example ❑ *we came in full view of a great island or continent (for we knew not whether)* (*Gulliver's Travels* by Jonathan Swift)

whetstone NOUN a whetstone is a stone used to sharpen knives and other tools ❑ *I dropped pap's whetstone there too* (*The Adventures of Huckleberry Finn* by Mark Twain)

wibrated VERB in Dickens's use of the English language 'w' often replaces 'v' when he is reporting speech. So here 'wibrated' means 'vibrated'. In Pickwick Papers a judge asks Sam Weller (who constantly confuses the two letters) 'Do you spell is with a 'v' or a 'w'?' to which Weller replies 'That depends upon the taste and fancy of the speller, my Lord' ❑ *There are strings . . . in the human heart that had better not be wibrated* (*Barnaby Rudge* by Charles Dickens)

wicket NOUN a wicket is a little door in a larger entrance ❑ *Having rested here, for a minute or so, to collect a good burst of sobs and an imposing show of tears and terror, he knocked loudly at the wicket;* (*Oliver Twist* by Charles Dickens)

without CONJ without means unless ❑ *You don't know about me, without you have read a book by the name of* The Adventures of Tom Sawyer (*The Adventures of Huckleberry Finn* by Mark Twain)

wittles ■ NOUN vittles is a slang word which means food ❑ *I live on broken wittles – and I sleep on the coals* (*David Copperfield* by Charles Dickens) ■ *See* wibrated

woo VERB courts or forms a proper relationship with ❑ *before it woo* (*The Flea* by John Donne)

words, to have PHRASE if you have words with someone you have a disagreement or an argument ❑ *I do not want to have words with a young thing like you.* (*Black Beauty* by Anna Sewell)

workhouse NOUN workhouses were places where the homeless were given food and a place to live in return for doing very hard work ❑ *And the Union workhouses? demanded Scrooge. Are they still in operation?* (*A Christmas Carol* by Charles Dickens)

yawl NOUN a yawl is a small boat kept on a bigger boat for short trips. Yawl is also the name for a small fishing boat ❑ *She sent out her yawl, and we went aboard* (*The Adventures of Huckleberry Finn* by Mark Twain)

yeomanry NOUN the yeomanry was a collective term for the middle classes involved in agriculture ❑ *The yeomanry are precisely the order of people with whom I feel I can have nothing to do* (*Emma* by Jane Austen)

yonder ADV yonder means over there ❑ *all in the same second we seem to hear low voices in yonder!* (*The Adventures of Huckleberry Finn* by Mark Twain)